SOUTH OF BROAD

ALSO BY PAT CONROY

The Boo
The Water Is Wide
The Great Santini
The Lords of Discipline
The Prince of Tides
Beach Music
My Losing Season
The Pat Conroy Cookbook: Recipes of My Life

NAN A. TALESE
Doubleday

NEW YORK
LONDON
TORONTO
SYDNEY
AUCKLAND

PAT CONROY

SOUTH OF BROAD

A NOVEL

All rights reserved. Published in the United States by Nan A. Talese, a division of Random House, Inc., New York, and in Canada by Random House of Canada Limited, Toronto.
www.nanatalese.com

DOUBLEDAY is a registered trademark of Random House, Inc.
Nan A. Talese and the colophon are trademarks of Random House, Inc.

Book design by Elizabeth Rendfleisch
Title page illustration by John Burgoyne

Library of Congress Cataloging-in-Publication Data
Conroy, Pat.
South of Broad : a novel / Pat Conroy. — 1st ed.
p. cm.
(alk. paper)
1. Charleston (S.C.)—Fiction. I. Title.
PS3553.O5198S68 2009
813'.54—dc22
2008045681

ISBN 978-0-385-41305-3

PRINTED IN THE UNITED STATES OF AMERICA

5   7   9   10   8   6

This book is dedicated to my wife and fellow novelist, Cassandra King, who helped more than anyone in bringing South of Broad *to its publication. To me, she is the finest thing ever produced on an Alabama farm.*

SOUTH OF BROAD

The Mansion on the River

I t was my father who called the city the Mansion on the River.

He was talking about Charleston, South Carolina, and he was a native son, peacock proud of a town so pretty it makes your eyes ache with pleasure just to walk down its spellbinding, narrow streets. Charleston was my father's ministry, his hobbyhorse, his quiet obsession, and the great love of his life. His bloodstream lit up my own with a passion for the city that I've never lost nor ever will. I'm Charleston-born, and bred. The city's two rivers, the Ashley and the Cooper, have flooded and shaped all the days of my life on this storied peninsula.

I carry the delicate porcelain beauty of Charleston like the hinged shell of some soft-tissued mollusk. My soul is peninsula-shaped and sun-hardened and river-swollen. The high tides of the city flood my consciousness each day, subject to the whims and harmonies of full moons rising out of the Atlantic. I grow calm when I see the ranks of palmetto trees pulling guard duty on the banks of Colonial Lake or hear the bells of St. Michael's calling cadence in the cicada-filled trees along Meeting Street. Deep in my bones, I knew early that I was one of those incorrigible creatures known as Charlestonians. It comes to me as a surprising form of knowledge that my time in the city is more vocation than gift; it is my destiny, not my choice. I consider it a high privilege to be a native of one of the loveliest American cities, not a high-kicking, glossy, or lipsticked city, not a city with bells on its fingers or brightly painted toenails, but a ruffled, low-slung city, understated and tolerant of nothing mismade or ostentatious. Though Charleston feels a seersuckered, tuxedoed view of itself, it approves of restraint far more than vainglory.

As a boy, in my own backyard I could catch a basket of blue crabs, a string of flounder, a dozen redfish, or a net full of white shrimp. All this I could do in a city enchanting enough to charm cobras out of baskets, one so corniced and filigreed and elaborate that it leaves strangers awed and natives self-satisfied. In its shadows you can find metalwork as delicate as lace and spiral staircases as elaborate as yachts. In the secrecy of its gardens you can discover jasmine and camellias and hundreds of other plants that look embroidered and stolen from the Garden of Eden for the sheer love of richness and the joy of stealing from the gods. In its kitchens, the stoves are lit up in happiness as the lamb is marinating in red wine sauce, vinaigrette is prepared for the salad, crabmeat is anointed with sherry, custards are baked in the oven, and buttermilk biscuits cool on the counter.

Because of its devotional, graceful attraction to food and gardens and architecture, Charleston stands for all the principles that make living well both a civic virtue and a standard. It is a rapturous, defining place to grow up. Everything I reveal to you now will be Charleston-shaped and Charleston-governed, and sometimes even Charleston-ruined. But it is my fault and not the city's that it came close to destroying me. Not everyone responds to beauty in the same way. Though Charleston can do much, it can't always improve on the strangeness of human behavior. But Charleston has a high tolerance for eccentricity and bemusement. There is a tastefulness in its gentility that comes from the knowledge that Charleston is a permanent dimple in the understated skyline, while the rest of us are only visitors.

My father was an immensely gifted science teacher who could make the beach at Sullivan's Island seem like a laboratory created for his own pleasures and devices. He could pick up a starfish, or describe the last excruciating moments of an oyster's life on a flat a hundred yards from where we stood. He made Christmas ornaments out of the braceletlike egg casings of whelks. In my mother's gardens he would show me where the ladybug disguised her eggs beneath the leaves of basil and arugula. In the Congaree Swamp, he discovered a new species of salamander that was named in his honor. There was no butterfly that drifted into our life he could not identify by sight. At night, he would take my brother, Steve, and I out into the boat to the middle of Charleston Harbor and make us memorize the constellations. He treated the stars as though they were love songs written to him by God. With such reverence he would point out Canis Major, the hound of Orion, the Hunter; or Cygnus, the Swan; or Andromeda, the Chained Lady; or Cassiopeia, the Lady in the Chair. My father turned the heavens into a fresh puzzlement of stars: "Ah, look at Jupiter tonight. And red Mars. And isn't Venus fresh on her throne?" A stargazer of the first order, he squealed with pleasure on the moonless nights when the stars winked at him in some mysterious, soul-stirring graffiti of ballet-footed light. He would clap his hands with irresistible joy on a cloudless night when he made every star in the sky a silver dollar in his pocket.

He was more North Star than father. His curiosity about the earth ennobled his every waking moment. His earth was billion-footed, with unseen worlds in every drop of water and every seedling and every blade of grass. The earth was so generous. It was this same earth that he prayed to because it was his synonym for God.

My mother is also a Charlestonian, but her personality strikes far darker harmonies than my father's did. She is God-haunted and pious in a city with enough church spires to have earned the name of the Holy City. She is a scholar of prodigious gifts, who once wrote a critique of Richard Ellman's biography of James Joyce for the *New York Review of Books.* For most of my life she was a high school principal, and her house felt something like the hallway of a well-run school. Among her students, she could run a fine line between fear and respect. There was not much horseplay or lollygagging about in one of Dr. Lindsay King's schools. I knew kids who were afraid of me just because she was my mother. She almost never wears makeup other than lipstick. Besides her wedding band, the only jewelry she owns is the string of pearls my father bought her for their honeymoon.

Singularly, without artifice or guile, my mother's world seemed disconsolate and tragic before she really knew how tragic life could be. Once she learned that no life could avoid the consequences of tragedy, she softened into an ascetic's acknowledgment of the illusory nature of life. She became a true believer in the rude awakening.

My older brother, Steve, was her favorite by far, but that seemed only natural to everyone, including me. Steve was blond and athletic and charismatic, and had a natural way about him that appealed to the higher instincts of adults. He could make my mother howl with laughter by telling her a story of one of his teachers or about something he had read in a book; I could not have made my mother smile if I had exchanged arm farts with the Pope in the Sistine Chapel. Because I hero-worshipped Steve, it never occurred to me to be jealous of him. He was both solicitous and protective of me; my natural shyness brought out an instinctive championing of me. The world of children terrified me, and I found it perilous as soon as I was exposed to it. Steve cleared a path for me until he died.

Now, looking back, I think the family suffered a collective nervous breakdown after we buried Steve. His sudden, inexplicable death sent me reeling into a downward spiral that would take me many years to fight my way out of and then back into the light. My bashfulness turned to morbidity. My alarm systems all froze up inside me. I went directly from a fearful childhood to a hopeless one without skipping a beat. It was not just the wordless awfulness of losing a brother that unmoored me but the realization that I had never bothered to make any other friends, rather had satisfied myself by being absorbed into that wisecracking circle of girls and boys who found my brother so delicious that his tagalong brother was at least acceptable. After Steve's death, that circle abandoned me before the flowers at his graveside had withered. Like Steve, they were bright and flashy children, and I always felt something like a toadstool placed outside the watch fires of their mysteries and attractions.

So I began the Great Drift when Steve left my family forever. I found myself thoroughly unable to fulfill my enhanced duties as an only child. I could not take a step without incurring my mother's helpless wrath over my raw un-Stephenness, her contempt for my not being blond and acrobatic and a Charleston boy to watch. It never occurred to me that my mother could hold against me my unfitness to transfer myself into the child she had relished and lost. For years, I sank into the unclear depths of myself, and learned with some surprise that their haunted explorations would both thrill and alarm me for the rest of my life. A measurable touch of madness was enough to send my fragile boyhood down the river, and it took some hard labor to get things right again. I could always feel a flinty, unconquerable spirit staring out of the mangroves and the impenetrable rain forests inside me, a spirit who waited with a mineral patience for that day I was to claim myself back because of my own fierce need of survival. In the worst of times, there was something that lived in isolation and commitment that would come at my bidding and stand beside me, shoulder-to-shoulder, when I decided to face the world on my own terms.

I turned out to be a late bloomer, which I long regretted. My parents suffered needlessly because it took me so long to find my way to a place at their table. But I sighted the early signs of my recovery long before they did. My mother had given up on me at such an early age that a comeback was something she no longer even prayed for in her wildest dreams. Yet in my anonymous and underachieving high school career, I laid the foundation for a strong finish without my mother noticing that I was, at last, up to some good. I had built an impregnable castle of solitude for myself and then set out to bring that castle down, no matter how serious the collateral damage or who might get hurt.

I was eighteen years old and did not have a friend my own age. There wasn't a boy in Charleston who would think about inviting me to a party or to come out to spend the weekend at his family's beach house.

I planned for all that to change. I had decided to become the most interesting boy to ever grow up in Charleston, and I revealed this secret to my parents.

Outside my house in the languid summer air of my eighteenth year, I climbed the magnolia tree nearest to the Ashley River with the agility that constant practice had granted me. From its highest branches, I surveyed my city as it lay simmering in the hot-blooded saps of June while the sun began to set, reddening the vest of cirrus clouds that had gathered along the western horizon. In the other direction, I saw the city of rooftops and columns and gables that was my native land. What I had just promised my parents, I wanted very much for them and for myself. Yet I also wanted it for Charleston. I desired to turn myself into a worthy townsman of such a many-storied city.

Charleston has its own heartbeat and fingerprint, its own mug shots and photo ops and police lineups. It is a city of contrivance, of blueprints; devotion to pattern that is like a bent knee to the nature of beauty itself. I could feel my destiny forming in the leaves high above the city. Like Charleston, I had my alleyways that were dead ends and led to nowhere, but mansions were forming like jewels in my bloodstream. Looking down, I studied the layout of my city, the one that had taught me all the lures of attractiveness, yet made me suspicious of the showy or the makeshift. I turned to the stars and was about to make a bad throw of the dice and try to predict the future, but stopped myself in time.

A boy stopped in time, in a city of amber-colored life that possessed the glamour forbidden to a lesser angel.

PART ONE

CHAPTER 1

June 16, 1969

Nothing happens by accident. I learned this the hard way, long before I knew that the hard way was the only path to true, certain
knowledge. Early in my life, I came to fear the power of strange
conveyances. Though I thought I always chose the safest path, I found
myself powerless to avoid the small treacheries of fate. Because I was a
timid boy, I grew up fearful and knew deep in my heart the world was out
to get me. Before the summer of my senior year in high school, the real
life I was always meant to lead lay coiled and ready to spring in the hot
Charleston days that followed.

On June 16, 1969, a series of unrelated events occurred: I discovered
that my mother once had been a Roman Catholic nun in the Sacred
Heart order; an Atlas moving van backed into the driveway of a
nineteenth-century Charleston single house across the street from ours;
two orphans arrived at the gates of St. Jude's Orphanage behind the cathedral on Broad Street; and the *News and Courier* recorded that a drug
bust had taken place on East Bay Street at the Rutledge-Bennet house. I
was eighteen, with a reputation as a slow starter, so I could not feel the
tectonic shift in my fate as my history began to launch of its own volition. It would be many years before I learned that your fate could scuttle

up behind you, touch you with its bloody claws, and when you turn to face the worst, you find it disguised in all innocence and camouflaged as a moving van, an orphanage, and a drug bust south of Broad. If I knew then what I have come to learn, I would never have made a batch of cookies for the new family across the street, never uttered a single word to the orphans, and never introduced myself to the two students who were kicked out of Porter-Gaud School and quickly enrolled at my own Peninsula High for their senior year.

But fate comes at you cat-footed, unavoidable, and bloodthirsty. The moment you are born your death is foretold by your newly minted cells as your mother holds you up, then hands you to your father, who gently tickles the stomach where the cancer will one day form, studies the eyes where melanoma's dark signature is already written along the optic nerve, touches the back where the liver will one day house the cirrhosis, feels the bloodstream that will sweeten itself into diabetes, admires the shape of the head where the brain will fall to the ax-handle of stroke, or listens to your heart, which, exhausted by the fearful ways and humiliations and indecencies of life, will explode in your chest like a light going out in the world. Death lives in each one of us and begins its countdown on our birthdays and makes its rough entrance at the last hour and the perfect time.

I awoke at four-thirty that June morning, threw on my clothes, then rode my bike to the northeast corner of Colonial Lake, where a *News and Courier* truck was idling in the darkness waiting for my arrival. I began folding a huge pile of papers and placing them tightly wrapped with rubber bands into one of two capacious bags that hung from my shoulders. It took fifteen minutes for me to get the bike right for the morning run, but I was fast and efficient at what I did. I had been a newspaper boy for three years. In the light of the truck I watched Eugene Haverford writing down the addresses of new customers or complaints from one of my regulars. Already, he was on his second Swisher Sweets cigar of the morning, and I could smell the Four Roses bourbon on his breath. He thought the cigar smoke masked his early-morning drinking.

"Hey, Leo, my distinguished Charleston gentleman friend," Mr. Haverford said, his voice as slow as his movements.

"Hey, Mr. Haverford."

"Got two new subscriptions for you. One on Gibbes Street, one on South Battery." He handed me two notes printed out in large letters. "One complaint—that lunatic on Legare Street claims she has not gotten her newspaper all week."

"I hand-delivered it to her, Mr. Haverford. She's getting forgetful."

"Push her down a flight of stairs for both of us. She's the only customer to ever complain about you."

"She gets afraid, living in that big house," I said. "She's going to need some help soon."

"How in the hell do you know that, Charleston gentleman?"

"I pay attention to my customers," I said. "Part of the job."

"We bring the news of the world to their front doors, don't we, Charleston gentleman?"

"Every day of the year, sir."

"Your parole officer called me again," he said. "I told her what I always tell her—that you're the best newspaper boy I've seen in my thirty years with the company. I tell her the *News and Courier* is lucky to have you."

"Thanks," I said. "I go off probation soon. She won't bother you much longer."

"Your old lady made her weekly pain-in-the-ass call too," he said.

"Mother'll probably call you the rest of her life."

"Not after what I told her yesterday. You're eighteen, Leo, a man as far as I'm concerned. Your mother's a stiff bitch. Not my kind of broad. But she asked me if you were fulfilling your duties properly. Her exact words, by the way. Listen up, Leo. Here's what I told her: If I ever have a kid, which I won't, I'd like him to be exactly like Leo King. I wouldn't change one thing. Not one thing. My exact words, by the way."

"That's so nice of you, Mr. Haverford."

"Quit being so naïve, Leo. I keep telling you that. Quit being so open to the world's shitting all over you."

"Yes, sir. My naïve days are over."

"You goddamn Charleston gentleman."

With a squeaking of wheels, he drove off into the darkness, his cigar glowing like a firefly in his cab, and I pedaled my bicycle forward.

Heading south on Rutledge Avenue, I lobbed a rolled-up newspaper on the first piazza of every house on the street, except for Burbage Eliot, who was famous as a tightwad even in penny-pinching Charleston. He borrowed his paper from Mrs. Wilson. She read it over her breakfast of soft-boiled egg, stone-ground grits, and chamomile tea, then recycled it to her stingy neighbor by tossing it onto his back porch.

I could lob a newspaper with either hand. When I turned left on Tradd Street, I looked like an ambitious acrobat hurling papers to my right and left as I made my way toward the Cooper River and the rising sun that began to finger the morning tides of the harbor, to dance along the spillways of palmetto fronds and water oaks until the street itself burst into the first flame of morning. The lawyer Compson Brailsford awaited me in his yard and got down in a wide receiver's stance as I neared the serene stillness of his family's mansion. As I passed, he sprinted out in his seersucker suit, elegant as a Swiss Army knife, and ran a quick button-hook pattern in the trimmed grass. On the days when I was good, the paper was already in the air when he turned and made his move back toward the imaginary quarterback at The Citadel; he was an All-Southern Conference end. On this morning his movements were letter-perfect and efficient, and my pass arrived at the precise moment. It was a game that had begun between us by accident, but it continued every day unless he was out of town or the weather too inclement for a well-dressed Charleston lawyer.

The gardens of Charleston were mysteries walled away in ivied jewel boxes emitting their special fragrances over high walls. The summer had proven good for the magnolias that had bloomed late. I passed one old forty-foot tree that looked as though a hundred white doves had gathered there in search of mates. My sense of smell lit up as the temperature rose and the dew started to burn off the tea olive and the jasmine. My armpits moistened, and I began to offer my own scent back to the streets where coffee began brewing in hidden kitchens and the noise of the newspapers hitting the soft wood of the verandas sounded like mullets jumping for joy in giant lagoons. Turning right on Legare, I was hitting my stride;

moving fast down the center of the street, I arched my longest throw of
the morning at the mansion behind the Sword Gate House, putting it on
the third step. At the Ravenel house toward the end of the street, I made
my first real misfire on what had been a morning of machinelike precision, and hurled a paper into a mass of oversized camellias. I stopped the
bike, skipped through the gate, retrieved the paper from the top branches,
and sailed it up to the front door. The small dark nose of a King Charles
spaniel named Virginia poked through the bottom of the fence across
from the Ravenels', and I hurled a paper to the far corner of the yard,
where the exquisitely tricolored dog retrieved it in a flash and carried it in
triumph to its master's doormat. I followed that throw by tossing a small
dog biscuit into the same yard, which Virginia would then walk down to
retrieve with great dignity.

When I'd taken the job three years earlier, all the arrayed stars of my
life had been aberrant and off course. So I promised myself I would do
this job well. If I heard of a customer rummaging around in the garden
hunting for their morning paper, I always called to apologize. A good
paperboy was a study in timeliness and steadfastness and accuracy, and
that's what I wanted to bring to my customers. It was what Eugene Haverford had growled at me during my week of orientation.

So there I was, a delivery boy making my rounds in a city where
beauty ambushed you at every turn of the wheel, rewarded every patient
inspection, and entered your pores and bloodstream from every angle;
these images could change the way the whole world felt. It was a city that
shaped the architecture of my memories and dreaming, adding cornices
and parapets and the arched glooms of Palladian windows every time I
rode those streets, full of purpose and duty. I threw missile after missile
of pages chock-full of news as well as art show openings on King Street
and sales taxes making their way through senate committees in Columbia, a total eclipse of the sun due in the fall, and a terrific sale at Berlin's
clothing store entering its last week.

When I started the job, my life was at a standstill, my choices down
to one, and my opportunities barren on the vine. From the day I took
the job, I was watched over by the South Carolina Juvenile Court, a child
psychiatrist connected to Roper Hospital, my worried and overarching

mother, and a gruff hillbilly from a North Charleston trailer park, Eugene Haverford. I looked upon this paper route as a source of redemption, a last chance to salvage a childhood ruined by my own baffling character and one unspeakable tragedy. When my share of the world's cruelty struck, I was nine years old. It would take a great portion of my time as an adult before I realized that tragedy was hurled freely into everyone's life as though it were a cheap newspaper advertising porno shops and strip shows thrown into an overgrown yard. I was an old man by the time I turned ten years old, and I caught the terrible drift of things many years before my number should have been called.

But by age seventeen, I had come through the bad times intact and functioning, leaving friends behind in the impersonal mental wards of my state whose eyes stayed opaque with a milky, nameless rage. I had loved the faces of the hopeless up close and held them trembling through hallucinations that never left them a minute's peace. Living among them, I discovered I was not one of them; yet they hated me when they saw a calmness return to me years after I found my beloved older brother, his arteries severed, dead in the bathtub we both shared, my father's straight razor on the tiles of our bathroom floor. My screaming brought a neighbor running to the house through a first-story window and finding me, in hysterics, trying to pull my brother's lifeless body from the tub. A serene, uneventful childhood ended for me that night. When my parents returned from the Dock Street Theatre, Steve's body lay in an unnatural peace in the downtown morgue. The police were trying to calm me down to question me. A doctor administered a sedative by injection, and my life among drugs and needles and psychological testing and shrinks and therapists and priests began. It was a time that I believe to this day ruined both my parents' lives.

When I turned my bicycle left on Meeting Street, the sun was high enough on the horizon for me to cut off the bike lamp. Meeting was spacious and cocky, with mansions on both sides of the street, a showboat of a street in a city brimful with them. Here, I zigzagged from one side to the other, taking dead aim at front doors heavy and sumptuous enough to be the entrances to the residences of kings. The traffic was still light, and if my rhythm was true, I could service the length of the street all the way

to Broad in five to seven minutes. Taking a right at Broad Street, I hit the
doorways of a dozen lawyers' offices, sometimes three at a doorway, four
at one, and six at the Darcy, Rutledge, and Sinkler law firm, the largest in
the city. At Church and Broad on the southeast corner, there were several
fresh piles of newspapers waiting for me. I stopped to reload, not losing
my rhythm while noticing the increasing traffic of ambulatory lawyers
picking their way to favorite restaurants and cafés. The street began to
smell of coffee and bacon frying on grills, and a slight wind from the
harbor told of buoys and ship hulls brined by the tides and the years; the
awakening of gulls followed the first freighter making the turn toward
the Atlantic, and the bells of St. Michael's answered the puny, half-human
cry of the gulls. Working fast, I loaded up with the last hundred newspapers of my route and blasted down Church Street, my arms whirling
again in the eccentric morning dance of paperboys.

Early on, I could feel the redemptive powers of hard work, and I basked
in the praise of Mr. Haverford and my customers who lived on this island
of the peninsula city. My predecessor had been born to great privilege
and lived in one of the houses I now served, but the hours proved too
early for him and the labor too intrusive on his late-night social life. He
was soon let go, not fired, because of his family connections that traced
back to the actual founding of the colony. When the upper management
of the *News and Courier* decided to take a chance on me, it was a nod of
approval and gratitude to my parents' distinguished life as educators in
the city as well as a way to pull my entire family back from the brink after
the death of my brother. Steve's death had wounded the city in some profound, inchoate way. I was granted the job not because of who I was, but
because of who Steve had been.

And what a boy Steve had been, I thought, as I took a right on South
Battery, bringing the sweet-smelling papers onto the steps of what I considered the prettiest row of mansions in the city. Steve would one day
have lived in one of those houses, after marrying the most comely and
glittering debutante in Charleston, after graduating from Harvard and
coming back to South Carolina for law school. In my mind, Steve would
always remain eighteen months older than I would ever be, a natural
leader known for his great wit and charm. Many people thought he

would ripen into one of the best athletes ever raised in Charleston. In the summer he turned into a new color of gold, his hair a shade of blond that reminded one of the tawniness of Siamese cats. His eyes were bright blue and emotionless and almost textureless when you saw him sizing up a new person or situation. All of Charleston agreed that he was the last boy on earth who would take a razor to his arteries and fill up a bathtub with his own blood. He was so dazzling in both presentation and personality that the city could not come to terms with the violent self-hatred suggested by his death. On the other hand, I was exactly the melancholy, apprehensive kind of child, a Venus-flytrap type of boy overshadowed by his rosy-cheeked, overachieving brother, who could commit such a terrible crime to himself and to the image the city had of itself.

Ahead of me, I saw Miss Ophelia Simms watering her flower boxes in front of her house. Stopping the bicycle, I handed a newspaper to her. "How's that for service, Miss Simms?"

"I should think it approaches perfection, Leo," she said. "And how are we today?"

"We are fine today." I was always thrilled that Miss Simms referred to me in the lordly plural. "And how are our flowers today?"

"A little piqued," she would always say during our rare encounters among her phlox and impatiens. To me, Miss Simms was a knockout, and I knew that she had celebrated her fiftieth birthday that year. I hoped that I would one day marry a girl in her twenties half as lovely as Miss Simms. But that probably was a long shot, and I was reminded of it every time I looked at myself in the mirror. Though I wouldn't call myself ugly, it wouldn't surprise me if I heard that someone else had said it. I blamed it on the black horn-rimmed glasses my mother had bought me, but I was so nearsighted that the lenses looked like they could have served as the portholes of ships. My eyes held a fishlike cast that those lenses managed to overemphasize, and had been the butt of much teasing among my peers, unless my brother was around. Steve was overprotective of his baby brother as he hovered over me, patrolling the cruel airways above the school playground like a red-tailed hawk. Fearless and sharp-tongued, he let no one bully his little brother. Steve's obvious superiority caused me some discomfort and even resentment as a child, but his fierce championing and unwavering love of me made me feel special. My brother was so handsome that I could sense my own mother's disappointment every time she looked at me.

Zigzagging through the smaller streets and alleys south of Broad, I would finally reach the coast guard station and pause to rest for a minute or two. I could make this run blindfolded, and I also prided myself on hitting certain corners at the correct time. I always checked my watch to see how I was doing, panting from exertion and the good pain I felt in my thigh and arm muscles. Putting myself into high gear again, I pushed off with the sparkling Ashley River to my right, a river I could hear beating against a seawall on stormy nights near my house. The Ashley was the playground of my father's childhood, and the river's smell was the smell my mother opened the windows to inhale after her long labors, bearing my brother, and then me. A freshwater river let mankind drink and be refreshed, but a saltwater river let it return to first things, to moonstruck tides, the rush of spawning fish, the love of language felt in the rhythm of the wasp-waisted swells, and a paperboy's hands covered with news-print, thinking the Ashley was as pretty a river as ever a god could make. I would start the last sprint of my route, flinging papers with confidence and verve, serving the newer houses built in the filled-in corpses of salt-water marshes as I headed due east again. Running past White Point Gar-dens, I would turn north when I saw Fort Sumter in the distance, sitting like a leatherback turtle in the middle of Charleston Harbor. I would service the really big mansions on East Bay, then Rainbow Row, take a left at Broad and do both sides of the street, weaving through traffic and still more strolling lawyers, young hotshots and old lions alike; the Riley Real Estate firm; the travel agency; ten for city hall; and the final paper of the morning I sent crashing into the front door of Henry Berlin's Men's Store.

With the last paper nesting against Berlin's doorstep, Charleston ceased to be mine, and I released ownership to the other early risers who had a greater claim on it than I ever would, a boy at ease in darkness.

In my three years of high school, I had become a familiar, even famous, sight on the early-morning streets south of Broad. Later, people told me they could set their watches when I passed their houses before and after first light. All of them knew about the death of my brother, my subsequent breakdown and disappearance, and all would later tell me how they rooted for me during my long penitential season of redemption. When I made my monthly collection runs for their subscriptions, the adults appreciated that I came to their doorsteps in a sports coat, tie, and white shirt, penny loafers impeccably shined. They admired the correctness, if not the stiffness, of my manners, and they appreciated my inarticulate attempts to initiate conversation and that I always brought treats to the families owning cats and dogs; I always remembered the names of these animals. I asked about their kids. They accepted my painful shyness as a kind of initial calling card, but most households remarked that my confidence gradually grew as I grew comfortable approaching their front doors. When it rained, they loved it that I rose an hour earlier to hand-deliver the newspapers to dry porches I was not sure I could reach with my usual toss. They assured me, later, of their certainty that I was well on my way to becoming both a charming and a fascinating young man.

But on June 16, 1969, as I rode my bike the two short blocks between Berlin's and the Cathedral of St. John the Baptist, my portrait of myself was of a natural-born loser who at eighteen had never been on a date or danced with a girl, nor had a best friend, nor had ever received an A on a report card, nor would ever cleanse his mind of that moment when he discovered his carefree, one-of-a-kind brother in a bath of his own blood. In all the days since that unkillable day, neither my mother or my father, nor any shrink or social worker, nor priest or nun, nor relative or friend of the family, could show me the pathway to a normal productive life with that ghoulish entry visa affixed to my passport. During the rosary for my brother's funeral, I had retreated to the men's room and locked myself into a stall where I wept silently and out of control because the inconsolable nature of my grief seemed selfish in the face of my parents' complete devastation.

From that moment I marked the time when the earth opened up to swallow me whole. I left simple grief on the road behind me and held madness at arm's length as it stormed the walls of my boyhood with its tireless regiments coming at the most tender parts of my psyche in wave after unappeasable wave. For three years, I entered the country of the pit viper. Every dream contained poisonous snakes lying in wait for me—the cottonmouth moccasin coiled against the cypress root, the coral snake beneath the hollowed-out log, the copperhead invisible in a bright carpet of autumn leaves, and the eastern diamondback with its deadly warning rattle serving as the lone musician composing the debased libretto of my distress, my fury, and my helpless sadness. The doctors called it a nervous breakdown, terminology I found to be correct. I came apart. Then, with the encouragement of some good people, I put myself together again. The snakes acknowledged my returning health by their silent withdrawal from my dreaming life and I was never afraid of snakes again, acknowledging that even they had played a necessary role in my recovery. Because I had long feared them with my body and soul, their mordant shapes, their curved fangs, and their venom, they kept my brother's face out of my night world and I awoke to his permanent residence in my psyche only at daybreak. When I look back, I see that my tragedy was that I could never summon Steve in all his apple-cheeked, athletic good looks and ornamental charm. Once he had died and I had found him, I could never pull my brother out of that horrible tub.

I parked my bike in the rack beside the elementary school, and skipped into the back entrance of the cathedral as I did every morning, the entrance that all the insiders knew—from bishop and priests to nuns and altar boys like me. When I opened the door, the smell of the Catholic world washed over me. I walked to the room where Monsignor Maxwell Sadler had almost finished decking himself out in the sumptuous finery of a summer morning Mass. Monsignor Max had been a fixture in my family drama since well before I was born: he had taught my parents in their 1938 graduating class at Bishop Ireland High School. He had married my parents, baptized both Steve and me, placed the wafer on my tongue at First Communion. Steve and I were altar boys together when I served my first Mass. When Steve died, the monsignor hovered about our house, as ubiquitous as my mother's reading chair. When the bishop of Charleston refused to bury Steve in holy ground, Monsignor Max (Father Max then) worked through the creaky, impenetrable bureaucracy of the pre-Vatican II Church and had Stephen's body exhumed from a public cemetery west of the Ashley and reburied in the sacred ground of St. Mary's Church among my mother's people.

I was the cause of ceaseless trouble in those days, and had given up the

Catholic faith in a titanic schoolboy's rage, refusing to worship my God or belong to any church. The Catholic Church had rejected the corpse of my brother. Then I entered the realm of child psychiatry and understaffed mental hospitals and yawning tutors as my poor parents tried to mend the broken boy they had on their hands after their favorite son left them. Monsignor Max remained faithful to us in our darkest days, and told me that the Church was patient and would always be waiting for me to return. It was, and so was he.

I watched Monsignor Max comb his hair with flair, making certain that the crease on the left side of his head was as straight as a guy wire. He saw me in his mirror and said, "Leo, my altar boy called in sick. Get in your cassock and surplice. Your mother and father are out there already. And this is your mother's special day, Bloomsday."

Of all the elements of my childhood that rang a false note, I was the only kid in the American South whose mother had received a doctorate by writing a perfectly unreadable dissertation on the religious symbolism in James Joyce's equally unreadable *Ulysses,* which I considered the worst book ever written by anyone. June 16 was the endless day when Leopold Bloom makes his nervous Nellie way, stopping at bars and consorting with whores and then returning home to his horny wife, Molly, who has a final soliloquy that goes on for what seemed like six thousand pages when my mother force-fed me the book in tenth grade. Joyce-nuts like my mother consider June 16 to be a consecrated mythical day in the Gregorian calendar. She bristled with uncontrollable fury when I threw the book out the window after I had finished it following an agonizing six months of unpleasurable reading.

It took me seconds to dress in my surplice and cassock, then I stood before the radiant, comely monsignor as he admired his own image in the mirror. Ever since I had known him I had heard the women of the parish whisper "What a total waste" when their stylish movie star of a priest floated out toward the altar in all his gallant finery.

"Happy Bloomsday, Monsignor Max," I said.

"Don't make fun of your mother, young man. *Ulysses* is her passion, James Joyce the great literary love of her life."

"I still think it's weird," I said.

"One must always forgive another's passion."

"I could forgive her if she hadn't named me Leopold Bloom King. Or my brother Stephen Dedalus King. That's taking it a little far. Have you ever read *Ulysses*?"

"Of course not. He is a flagrant anti-Catholic. I'm a Chesterston man myself."

I felt an old flush of pride as I led the monsignor out to the central altar and spotted my parents in the front row, both of them saying the rosary. My father looked up and smiled when he saw me and gave me an exaggerated wink of his right eye, the one my mother could not see. She tolerated playfulness at church not at all. At every Mass, she wore her game face for a crucifixion as though she were an actual eyewitness to the death of Jesus each time she knelt in her pew.

As he faced the small, mostly octogenarian congregation, Monsignor Max began the Mass in the name of the Father and the Son and the Holy Ghost. The words I heard him utter in his operatic voice washed over me like a clean stream from my boyhood, the delicate latticework of memory and language.

"I will go to the altar of God."

And I went with him and let the ancient, sacrosanct rhythms of the Church seize me. When the priest called for water, I provided him with water. When he needed to cleanse his hands for the coming mystery, I emptied cruets over his fingers. When he called for wine, I supplied him with wine in the gold shine of chalices. At the moment of consecration, when he turned the wine into the blood of Christ and the bread into the body of the same God, I rang the bells that had sounded beneath altars for two thousand years. When I opened my mouth and received the un-leavened bread from the consecrated finger and thumb of the priest, I felt the touch of God on my tongue, His taste in my palate, His bloodstream mingling in my own. I had come back to Him, after a full-pledged embit-tered retreat, after He stole my brother from my bedroom and killed him in my bathtub.

But I had come back to Him, and that is part of my story.

After Mass, we walked down to Cleo's restaurant for breakfast, a rit-ual of summer as ingrained in the texture of our family life as daily Mass. Cleo was a fast-talking Greek girl who ran the cash register as though she were reloading an M16 rifle for snipers. Her patter was endless and profane, until my parents walked in for breakfast and her attitude turned beatific. Both of my parents had taught her when they were at Bishop Ireland High, and she held fast to the respect that high school kids who never go to college continue to feel for the last teachers of their lives. Even the young waitresses displayed new vigor when my parents appeared in the doorway, and Cleo delivered hand signals to the kitchen staff that translated into hot coffee, orange juice, and ice water on the table. Since I was in training for football season, I ordered two eggs over light, grits with redeye gravy, and three slices of bacon. My father would dig into country ham and biscuits with a side order of hash browns. Even though it was the most celebrated day of the year for my mother, she retained the strong-willed discipline that made up every habit of her life: she ordered half a grapefruit and a bowl of oatmeal. My mother admitted to needs such as nourishment, but not of appetites. "Happy Bloomsday, darling," my father said to my mother, leaning to kiss her on the cheek. "This is your day and your every wish is our command. Isn't that right, Leo?"

"That's right," I said. "We're at your beck and call."

"Very good, Leo," Mother said. "Though you fight me on it, your vocabulary shows constant improvement. Here's your list of five words to memorize today." She handed me a piece of folded-over notebook paper.

I made a groaning noise, as I did every morning, and opened the notebook paper to read five words that no one would use in normal conversation: *sedulous, perspicacious, ribald, vivisection, and tumid.*

"Do you know what any of those words mean?" Mother asked.

"Of course not." I sipped my coffee.

"Did you memorize the five I gave you yesterday?"

"Of course."

"Use two of the words in a sentence," she commanded.

"I felt a certain need to regurgitate when I cogitated on the works of James Joyce."

My father laughed, but the laughter was stifled when my mother cut her pale eyes toward him. "You heard your father. This is my special day. Bloomsday, a day celebrated all over the world by aficionados of James Joyce."

"The three of you ought to get together sometime," I said.

"His admirers are legion," she said. "Even if I walk alone in my own household."

"Leo and I are cooking you a special meal tonight," my father told her. "The menu is taken directly from the text of *Ulysses*. It was Leo's idea."

"Thank you, Leo. That's very thoughtful of you."

"I'm not going to eat it. Just cook it," I said. Although I meant it as a joke, my mother took instant offense. She could freeze me with a gaze that made the dead of winter seem like the best time for planting. From the time I could talk, I heard the men and women of Charleston praise my mother's physical attractiveness, her immaculate grooming, her stylish carriage. I could always see what they were talking about, but could never fully partake in their pleasure over her textured beauty. For me, her prettiness was easy to admire, but difficult to love. Since the death of Steve, she had rarely kissed me. Hugged me, yes, again and again. But kissed me like she used to do when I was a small boy, no. She had taken little pleasure in my childhood, and I could read her disapproval like a page of newsprint whenever she looked at me. We played hard at looking the part of a happy family, and as far as I knew we succeeded admirably. Only three people in the world knew of our deep and hopeless despair in the company of one another.

The waitress refilled our coffee cups at the same time.

My father's face was baffled and amused and anxious as he witnessed the chilly interplay between me and my mother. He got dizzy with the goofiest kind of love whenever he was with the two of us, yet his solicitousness and kindness to me always remained a red flag, an arena of sudden warfare between them. My brother's death had almost killed both my parents, but it did not change my father's fundamental good nature and graceful optimism. He turned his full attention to me and tried to love me harder because I was not Steve. Unlike my mother, who handled his death in the only way she knew how, so I feared that she could never love anyone again who was not Steve.

"So," Mother said as she adjusted her lipstick in a compact mirror. That gesture was a signal to the waitress that our breakfast had ended and she was free to clear the dishes. "Your father knows the orders of the day. Leo, I want you to bake two dozen chocolate chip cookies for the new neighbors who are moving in today across the street from us, a set of twins. Your age, exactly, and they'll be your classmates at Peninsula."

"Okay. What else?" I asked.

"I got a call from Sister Mary Polycarp at the orphanage. They received two new orphans from Atlanta. Both runaways. They too are brother and sister. You will welcome them to Charleston. Then you will bird-dog them all year. Watch over them. They've had a terrible life."

"They've had great lives. Wait till they spend a year with Polycarp. What a monster! I thought they threw her out of the convent."

"Wasn't she the nun who hit that Wallace girl across the eye with a ruler?" Father asked.

"An unfortunate accident," said my mother.

"I was there," I said. "She cut her eyeball. Severed the optic nerve. Blinded her."

"She's no longer allowed to teach. The order almost expelled her," Mother explained.

"In the third grade, she hit so many boys in the face and made so many of us bleed that I nicknamed her the Red Cross."

My father chuckled, but was stopped cold by a sudden glitter in Mother's eye.

"Very witty, son," she snapped. "If only some of this wit could translate into solid achievement on your Scholastic Aptitude Test."

"Leo does not test well, darling," my father said.

"But isn't he the life of the party," she said. "This afternoon I want you to report to your principal's office and meet your new football coach."

"You are my principal, Mother," I said. "And Coach Ogburn is my football coach."

"He resigned yesterday."

"Why on earth?" Father asked. "He was so close to retirement."

"He refused to coach when he learned his assistant was going to be a black man," my mother said. "So I hired Coach Jefferson from Brooks High as head coach, and made him athletic director too. They're not pussyfooting with integration this year."

"Why do you want me to meet Coach Jefferson?" I asked.

"Because you're his first-string center."

"I've always played second-string behind Choppy Sargent."

"Choppy and three others are following Coach Ogburn to a new segregated academy west of the Ashley. Coach Jefferson wants you to try to keep any other of the white boys on the team from following suit."

I was making a mental list: chocolate chip cookies, the orphans of Polycarp, Coach Jefferson. "Anything else, Mother?"

"You've got iced tea duty after the hospital workers' march. We'll eat a late dinner." My mother gave her lipstick a final glance in her mirror, and then met my eye evenly. "Your probation hearing is set for June twenty-sixth. You're finally finished with probation."

My father added gratefully, "Your record is clean, son. You have a clean slate again."

"Not with me, young man," Mother inserted quickly. "I don't know how you sleep at night, after what you put your father and me through."

My father's voice lowered as he said, "Darling."

"Leo knows what I mean." Mother did not look up.

"Do you know what she means, Leo?" Father asked.

"He knows," my mother shot back.

"Are you talking about my hatred of James Joyce?" I asked.

"You pretend to hate James Joyce because it's an easier way to say you hate me," she retorted.

"Tell your mother you don't hate her, Leo." Father was a man comfortable with the formulas of scientific law, but lost at sea when it came to engaging the tidal forces of the emotions. "No, tell her you love her. That's an order."

"I love you, Mother," I said, but even I could measure the perfect note of insincerity I sounded.

"Meet me at my office at four this afternoon, Leo," she said. "You have your other tasks for the day."

My parents left the table at the same time, and I watched as my father paid Cleo for the meal. Cleo then came over and sat across from me.

"Here's all the wisdom I got to share, Leo: Being a kid's a pain in the ass. Being an adult is ten times worse. That's Cleo the Greek, who came from the people who brought you Plato and Socrates and all those other assholes."

CHAPTER 2

New Friends

After leaving Cleo's, I rang the ivory-white button of St. Jude's orphanage in the warren of intersecting streets behind the cathedral. Its buzz was irritating and subhuman, insectlike. I associated the orphanage with all things Catholic, from rectories to convents.

A huge black man named Clayton Lafayette answered the door and smiled when he saw me. Mr. Lafayette played out a dozen roles at the orphanage, but one was marching the high school kids each day to Peninsula High, a task he performed with military precision and relish. Though his disposition was sunny and affable, his body was brutish.

"Leo the Lion," he said to me.

"Count Lafayette." We shook hands. "I've got an appointment to see Sister Mary Polycarp."

"The orphans already call her the Pollywog," he whispered. "She told me your mama was sending you over."

"You be careful around the Pollywog, Count," I whispered back. "She's bad news."

I walked the length of a long corridor of a building designed by a man who held an unbelievable grudge against orphans. It was grim to the point of parody, and the woman who sat behind the government-issue steel desk as I entered her office looked congruent with the spectral glooms of the architecture.

Among Roman Catholics of my generation, we play a parlor sport that is mean-spirited and partisan in nature but guaranteed to elicit laughter and to cause blood to pool in our collective memories: we tell nun stories. We have no shame in it, as any religion that flaunts those plaster-of-Paris murdered saints in their sanctuaries and crucifix effigies that seem to compete for the most barbarous slaughter of Jesus, the living God, could certainly produce communicants who could invent atrocities for the women of the veil who whomped our souls into shape in preparation for eternal life. Some of the nuns of our youth in the fifties and sixties ranked among the finest women we would ever encounter. But the nun with the black heart and the most merciless imagination stamped her brand most indelibly. I once had a nun who stood up her class whenever we heard fire sirens pass our school, then led us in the recitation of the Lord's Prayer that it was not a Catholic home on fire. Another nun would put clothespins on our ears if we acted up in school, and our parents would know by the purple bruises, the dead giveaway that we had displeased the good sister. Like eastern diamondbacks, you could always hear the approach of nuns by the rattling of the sinister beads of their rosaries.

In second grade I had passed a surreptitious note between two boys who were best friends, and the three of us were marched to the front of the room to accept our punishments in full view of the class. Sister Veronica never hit any of her students, but her retaliations were fiendish and inventive. Standing us by the blackboard, she ordered us to hold out our arms like the crucified Christ. In ten minutes this punishment seemed benign. But after an hour Joe McBride burst into tears, his triceps quivering in agony. In contempt she said to Joe, "Jesus had to hold his arms out on the cross for three hours."

Joe answered through tears, "But Sister! Jesus had help. He had nails." And the class howled with helpless, forbidden laughter.

That morning at the orphanage, my old fear of nuns formed bile in my throat as I said, "Good morning, Sister Mary Polycarp."

"Hello, Leo. I taught you, didn't I? First or second grade?"

"It was third."

"You were very slow, if I remember correctly."

"That's me, Sister."

"But very polite. You can always tell the ones from good families," she said. "I read the papers when you were kicked out of Bishop Ireland."

"Yes, Sister, I made a bad mistake."

"Didn't you go to jail or something?"

"No. They put me on probation," I said, uncomfortable with this subject, this situation, and this particular nun.

"I didn't think you were very smart," she said. "But I never thought you would be a convict."

"Probation. Not jail, Sister."

"Same difference to me." She studied two files on her desk. "Did your mother tell you about our big problem?"

"No, Sister. She told me to meet two kids who would be rising seniors, and help them make the adjustment to their new high school."

"Did she tell you they are both thieves, liars, criminals, and runaways? Add to my list of complaints, the diocese is sending over five colored orphans this afternoon."

"No, Sister. She didn't tell me any of that."

"Since you've spent time in prison and reformed yourself, I thought you might be good for them. Lead them in the right direction, so to speak. But I warn you, they're very clever and both are natural-born liars. They are from the North Carolina mountains, way up in the hills, and there's no kind of white trash like mountain trash. That's a sociological fact. Do you know I've got a master's degree in sociology, Leo?"

"No, Sister, I didn't."

"They're in the library waiting for you. Mr. Lafayette will be watching from a distance—to make sure there is no trouble," she said.

"What kind of trouble could there be? I'm just going to tell them what to expect from the high school."

"In the world of orphanages, these two are called long riders because they've run away so often," she informed me. "They've been in orphanages from New Orleans to Richmond, Birmingham to Orlando. Long riders are kids looking for something they're never going to find because it doesn't exist in the first place. Their names are Starla and Niles White-head. Both are very bright. He's flunked a grade on purpose, but that's because he wanted to be with his sister."

I walked down to the library, which lay on the opposite side of the orphanage, where every Christmas, my father, dressed as an underweight Santa Claus, handed out gifts to the orphans. It was one of those sad-sack libraries overflowing with books that had never been checked out. There was an eerie relationship between the cast-off children and the unopened books, but I was too young to make those kinds of analogies when I entered the huge room to meet Starla and Niles Whitehead. The two of them sat in the rear and looked about as welcoming as scorpions in a bottle, their hostile gazes unnerving me. It surprised me how attractive they were, both with high cheekbones and the fine chiseled features that hinted at a Cherokee bloodline. As I took a chair in front of them, they studied me, the sister with eyes a deep shade of brown that suggested melted chocolate.

Uncomfortably, I looked around the room and out the windows at the overrun garden of untended grounds. I cleared my throat and realized my mother had given me no clear directions about why I was meeting these two hostile strangers.

"Hey," I said, at last. "Must be great being orphans, ending up in a swell place like this."

Both of them glared at me as though I had not spoken.

"That was sort of meant as a joke," I said. "You know, to break the ice between us."

Again, I was met with those hollowed-out stares. I started over. "Hello, Starla and Niles Whitehead. My name is Leo King. My mother is the principal of your new high school. She wanted me to come over and meet you, to see if I could help you. I know it's hard to change schools."

"Nothing I hate worse than a brownnosing little booger," the girl said. "How about you, brother?"

"They're always the same." Both spoke in bored, lethargic voices as though I were not in the room to hear.

"But I'm still in hysterics over his orphan joke," she said.

"I was trying to be friendly," I explained.

The brother and sister looked at each other and a sneer passed between them.

"Why did you run away from the last orphanage?" I asked.

"For the chance of meeting swell guys like you," Niles said.

"Take the hint, Leo. Isn't that your name? We don't want your help. We'll figure things out on our own," said Starla. As she brushed a wave of black hair away from her eyes, I noticed the strabismus in her left eye. When she saw me notice it, she shook her head and a curtain of her straight hair half-covered the wandering eye again.

"I can help you. I really can," I said.

Niles looked at me with a hard manlike stare, and I took his measure for the first time. Though he was seated, his physical presence was impressive; he looked a couple of inches over six feet tall. His long arms were muscled and veiny, even in repose, but his eyes were bright blue and seemed purloined from a Scandinavian face. The girl was cross-eyed but cute; the stiff face of Niles Whitehead was simply beautiful.

"If you want to know the really good teachers, I can tell you who they are," I said. "If you want to have the easy ones, I know them too."

"We want to know when you're going to leave us alone," Niles said.

"I can see why your parents left you on the orphanage steps, Niles, old boy," I said. He flung himself across the table, his left hand going for my throat. It was only then that I saw that someone had handcuffed the right hands of the orphans to their chairs.

"Count! Count Lafayette!" I shouted, and the large man came running through the library door.

"Get them out of the handcuffs," I said.

He stiffened and said, "Believe me, those two deserved the cuffs. And a lot worse too."

"Go ask Sister Polycarp to uncuff them," I said, "or I'm calling my mother. Remind the sister that my mother assigned these kids to me as a project because I have to complete three hundred hours of community service. She won't like it that they're handcuffed to their chairs." The mention of my mother's name struck the right chord of terror in the hearts of most Charlestonians. "You handcuff criminals. They're going to be my high school classmates," I continued. "Besides, they promised me they wouldn't run away if you took off the cuffs."

"They did?" Mr. Lafayette eyed the boy and girl with suspicion, and it was clear that he liked neither one of them.

"We just made an agreement, and they gave me their word of honor. Tell him," I said to them.

"Yeah, boy," Mr. Lafayette said to Niles. "You made that promise?"

"Sure did," Niles said.

"Wait here. I'll go ask Sister Polycarp," he said while walking toward the main door.

I turned and leaned across the table, talking fast. "I can help you two fruitcakes if you'll let me. You don't want my help, tell me now, and I'm out of here."

The brother turned to the sister, and I watched them pass information back and forth with a wordless intensity. Starla said, "We've got to get through this year, Niles, then we're free to walk out of orphanages forever." Her dark hair fell away from her face, and her gaze softened her brother's fury.

"Tell us what to do, Leo," said Niles.

"Promise me you won't run away. Right now. Fast, and mean it."

"We promise," both of them said.

"Polycarp is mean," I said in a whisper. "A sadist and a psychopath. Learn to say 'Yes, Sister; No, Sister.' 'Yes, sir; No, sir' to the Count. He's a sweetheart. Get him on your side. Get those snotty looks off your faces. Try to smile once a year. You can work this place."

"How do you know all this?" Starla asked.

"When my brother died I didn't handle it well, so I was in a mental hospital for a couple of years. Had to figure out a plan to get out."

"Then you ain't no better off than us, numbnuts," Niles said.

"I ain't handcuffed to no chair, hillbilly," I said. "Why are you wearing those ugly jumpsuits?"

"They've got the word *orphan* stenciled on the back," Niles answered. "Sister had them specially made for us. 'Cause we're runaways."

"Why do you keep running away?"

"We've got a mama. And a grandma. They're looking for us," Starla said.

"How do you know?"

"Because we'd kill ourselves if we thought they weren't," Niles said.

Behind me, I heard the oak door swing open, and I turned to see Mr. Lafayette walking toward us with a set of keys in his hand. He walked around the table and unlocked Starla's handcuffs first, and then Niles's. Both of them rubbed their sore wrists.

Mr. Lafayette possessed a sunny disposition, but he looked careworn and harried as he addressed me. "I'll get fired, Leo, if these kids run away. I can't lose this job."

"Mr. Lafayette has four children," I told Niles and Starla. "Is your wife still on dialysis?" I asked him.

"Yeah. She's not well."

"We're not going to run away, Mr. Lafayette," Starla said.

"Speak for yourself," her brother said.

"Shut up, Niles. I speak for my brother too. We won't cost you your job, Mr. Lafayette."

"I'll watch out for you two," Mr. Lafayette said, looking back toward the library entrance. "I can help you in a million ways." He then walked back toward the main hall.

When I got up to leave, Starla Whitehead surprised me by saying, "Hey, four-eyes. Didn't anyone tell you how ugly your glasses are? They make your eyes look like two busted bungholes."

I blushed deeply, the blood rushing up to my face, soon to be followed by a blotchiness that would make my appearance all the more comical. I had inherited my father's shyness, his chalky paleness, and his tendency to redden from throat to crown when he was caught off guard. I learned the harsh lessons of being unattractive very early in my career as a child, but I never grew accustomed to it being highlighted or laughed at by my peers. But now I surprised even myself by tearing up, the most infantile and unwarranted reaction I could think of, and not the course I would have chosen in front of these newcomers to my life. I wanted to run and hide from my own face.

Then Starla surprised me by bursting into tears herself, crying hard, realizing the damage she had inflicted on me. It was the first time I think she truly saw me. "I'm so sorry, Leo. So sorry. I do it every time. I can't help it. I do it every time someone's nice to me. I say something hurtful, something no one can forgive. Something bad, evil. I don't trust it when someone's nice to me. So I say something to make them hate me. Tell him, Niles. I always do it, don't I?"

"She always does it, Leo," Niles agreed. "She doesn't mean it."

"Look," she said, pulling her long hair away from her eyes. "Look at my left eye. What a cross-eyed bitch. Look! What an ugly cross-eyed jerk bitch I am. It was because you were nice—but if you hadn't been nice, I would have said it anyway. It's what I am," she added helplessly, with a shrug, as if she couldn't properly explain.

I took off my glasses and wiped them with a handkerchief, then I dabbed at my eyes and tried to compose myself. Putting my glasses back on, I said to Starla, "I know an eye surgeon. The best in the city. I'll ask him to take a look at your eye. Maybe he can do something."

"Why would he look at her eye?" Niles said, protective of his sister. "She doesn't got a penny."

"Have," his sister corrected. "Quit talking redneck."

"She doesn't have a penny."

"He's a wonderful man, this doctor," I told them.

"How do you know him, big shot?" Niles asked.

"Because I'm a paperboy, and I know everybody on my route." I glanced at my watch and, with my mother's list in mind, stood and told them in farewell, "I have to go, but I'll get my father to invite you for dinner, okay? I'll call you about the time."

Both of them looked frankly astonished at something as simple as an invitation to dinner. Niles glanced uneasily at his sister, who offered as I turned: "And Leo, I'm sorry about what I said. I really am."

"I said something mean to my mother today," I admitted. "So I deserved it. It was God getting me back."

"Leo?" Niles said.

"Yeah, Niles?"

"Thanks for this." He held up his wrist. "When we met you, we were in handcuffs. When you're leaving, we're not. My sister and I won't forget it."

"We'll remember it the rest of our lives," she said.

"Why?" I asked.

"Because," Niles said, "no one's ever nice to us."

• • •

On the leisurely bike ride home, I congratulated myself for handling Sister Polycarp and the unruly orphans with some diplomatic skill. I was running an hour ahead of the schedule I had set for myself, and was thinking about the kind of cookies I would make for the new neighbors moving in across the street. My mother had ordered chocolate chip, but I was thinking of making cookies with more of a Charlestonian heritage and flavor. I was surprised to find my mother's old-model Buick parked in our driveway as I navigated my Schwinn into the garage. My father had built our house with his own hands in 1950. It had not a single suggestion of architectural merit; it was nothing more than a two-storied, five-bedroom home that many Charlestonians considered the ugliest house in the historical district.

"Hey, Mother," I called through the house from the kitchen. "What are you doing home?"

I found her in her orderly home office where she was writing a letter in her beautiful penmanship, her sentences all like well-made bracelets. As she always did, she completed the paragraph she was composing before she looked up to address me. "Normally, Bloomsday is a slow do-nothing day, but this one is heating up fast. I just received a phone call from Sister Polycarp, who said you handled the situation with the orphans well. So you completed directive number one. Your high school principal has several other directives for you."

"You've given me the other two directives: I'm to bake cookies for the new family, then meet the new football coach in the gym at four."

"There have been some events I must add. We are lunching at the yacht club. You'll dress appropriately. Noonish."

"Noonish," I repeated.

"Yes. We are meeting the two seniors who were expelled from Porter-Gaud this morning. And their families, of course. I want you to look out for them the first couple of weeks at school. Both are rather bitter at having to attend a new high school during their senior year. But under no circumstances do I want you to get close to any of these new students. Not the orphans, not the kids across the street, not the kids from Porter-Gaud.

Nor the coach's son, who you're going to meet this afternoon. All of them spell trouble in their own way, and you've already had enough of that. Help them, but do not make friends with them, Leopold Bloom King."

I put my hands over my ears and groaned. "Please don't call me that. Leo's bad enough. But I would die of shame if people knew you named me for a character in *Ulysses*."

She said, "I admit I had you read *Ulysses* at too early an age. But I refuse to allow you to denigrate the greatest novelist who ever lived or the greatest novel ever written on this special day. Do I make myself clear?"

"No other teenager in America would even know what this talk's about," I said. "Why would you name me for an Irish Jew who lived in Dublin and isn't even a real person?"

"Leopold Bloom is more alive than any man I've ever met. Except your father, of course."

"You could've named me after my father! I'd have liked that."

"I didn't because your father knew that he married a great romantic, and great romantics are granted lots of slack by the men we love. They understand our great hearts. For instance, your father balked when we named your brother Steve after . . ." Mother stopped, and her eyes flooded with tears at the mention of her son's name, which had rarely been spoken out loud within these walls since his death. Until memory rendered her speechless, she was about to confess that my father had balked at naming their first born Stephen Dedalus King, but my mother brought her gift for argumentative persuasion into play; she could have talked my affable, tongue-tied father into naming Steve "Hitler" and me "Stalin" had the inspiration seized her. My father was all red clay and alabaster in my mother's hands, and she had sculpted him into her imaginary perfect husband long before I had come onto the scene.

I was searching for the proper word of apology for my outburst against her, but the words fluttered into my head like a colony of luna moths, in disorderly, undecipherable array. I longed for the day when I could say what I meant to say and at the precise time the thoughts came to me, but it was not today.

Our entire household pivoted on the immense pride my mother took in her distinction as a Joyce scholar who had received her doctorate from

Catholic University for her unreadable (I tried once) dissertation, "On Catholic Mythology and Totemology in James Joyce's *Ulysses*," which was published by Purdue University Press in 1954. Each semester she taught a graduate-level course on Joyce at the College of Charleston that was both highly praised and fully subscribed by students as etiolated as egrets. On three occasions she had delivered papers on Joyce to enraptured Joycean scholars who acknowledged her deep affinity and rapturous nitpicking into even the most skillfully hidden minutiae as it related to Joyce's uneasy Catholic boyhood. It was my mother who had compared the menses of Molly Bloom to the blood-drenched Stations of the Cross and its relationship to the divinity of Christ, and it had won her enduring recognition among her stultifying peers. On many occasions, my father and I had prepared elaborate meals for Joycean scholars of the first rank who had come to Charleston to sit at the feet of my mother so they could practice intoning ponderous inanities to one another. I believe in my heart that my father taught me to cook so that the two of us could escape those killer nights when academe came to our house to speak of Joyce and nothingness and then Joyce again.

Mother gathered her papers in her briefcase, then checked my list of directives. "Your day is filled up. No idle time for you to get in trouble, young man."

"The banks are all safe from me," I said. "At least for today."

"You stole that line from your father. All your jokes came from your father. You should try originality. What do you and your father have cooked up for our Bloomsday feast?"

"Top secret."

"Give me a hint."

"Chicken Feet Florentine," I said.

"Another tired joke of your father's. You get all your attempts at wit from him. I've never said anything funny in my whole life. I think it's a waste of time. Tootles; I've got to go, darling."

"Tootles."

I walked to the kitchen to make a batch of cookies. Unlike any other family I knew, the kitchen was my father's bailiwick and his alone. Jasper King had cooked every at-home meal that my family had ever eaten, and he had turned his sons into table setters and sous chefs for as long as I could remember. I had seen my mother in the kitchen only during those times when she was passing through on her way to the garage. In a court of law, I could not swear she had ever lit the stove, defrosted the refrigerator, refilled the pepper mill, thrown out spoiled milk, or even knew the direction to the spice cabinets or where the oils and condiments were kept. My father washed and ironed the clothes, kept the sinks and toilets spotless, and kept the household running with an efficiency that I found astonishing. Over the years, he taught me everything he knew about cooking and grilling and baking, and we could make the crown princes of Europe happy to find themselves at our table.

I opened the copy of *Charleston Receipts* that my father had bought on the day I was delivered at St. Francis Hospital, and I turned it to the benne seed wafer thins, a recipe submitted by Mrs. Gustave P. Maxwell, the former Lizetta Simons. My father and I had cooked almost every recipe in *Charleston Receipts,* a transcendent cookbook put together by the Junior League and published to universal acclaim in 1950. Father and I placed stars each time we prepared one of the recipes, and the benne wafers had earned a whole constellation. I began toasting the sesame seeds in a heavy skillet. I creamed two cups of brown sugar with a stick of unsalted butter. I added a cup of plain flour sifted with baking powder and a pinch of salt, and a freshly beaten egg that my father had purchased from a farm near Summerville. As I was checking the brownness of the seeds, the phone rang. I cussed silently, because cussing was a flash point with both my parents, who wanted to raise a son who did not dare utter the word *shit.* A shitless son, I thought as I answered the phone.

"Hello, King residence. This is Leo speaking." My Southern race does politesse with thoughtless grace.

An unknown woman's voice spoke. "May I speak to Sister Mary Norberta?"

"Mary Norberta? I'm sorry, but no one lives here by that name."

"Excuse me, but I believe you're mistaken, young man. Sister Norberta and I were novitiates at the Sacred Heart convent many years ago."

"My mother is the principal of a high school. My high school. I can assure you that you have the wrong number."

"You are Leo," the voice said. "Her younger son."

"Yes, ma'am, I am Leo, her son."

"Except for your glasses, you're a very attractive young man," she said. "I suggest you remove your glasses when your father takes your photograph."

"He's photographed me my entire life," I said. "I don't know what his face looks like, but I know what his camera looks like."

"Your mother brags about how witty you are," the voice said. "You get that from your father's side of the family."

"How would you know?"

"Oh, I haven't identified myself, have I? My name is Sister Mary Scholastica. I called to wish your mother a happy Bloomsday. I bet that rings a bell with you, doesn't it?"

"Never heard of it," I said. "Sister Scholastica."

"She's never spoken to you of her time in the convent?"

"Not once in my life."

"Oh, dear, I hope I haven't broken a confidence," the nun said.

"Not that I'm aware of," I said. "Are you saying that my brother and I were illegitimate?"

"Oh, heavens, no. I'm afraid I must go gargle; it seems I have put my foot in my mouth. So, has she raised you a feminist? She bragged that she would."

My mother had, indeed, bragged such a thing, to everyone, since I was born. "My God in heaven," I breathed. "You do know her. Sister Norberta, huh?"

"She was the most beautiful nun I ever saw. Any of us, for that matter. She looked like an angel in her habit," Sister Scholastica said. "Will she be in later?"

"Let me give you her phone number at the school." And I did so, my rage a bile I could hardly control. But then I finished the task: added vanilla and the benne seeds, dropped them in dollops from a coffee spoon on a pan lined with aluminum foil, and placed them in a slow oven. Then I dialed my mother's number.

When she answered, I said, "Yes, I admit it: once I called you Mother. But from now on, you'll be Sister Mary Norberta to me."

"Is this one of your jokes?"

"You tell me, Mother dear, if this is a joke or not. I'm on my knees, praying to St. Jude, the patron saint of hopeless causes, that it is a joke."

"Who told you this?" my mother demanded.

"Someone with a dumber-sounding name than Norberta. Her name was Scholastica."

"She knows that she's never supposed to call me at home."

"But it's Bloomsday, Mother," I said with more than a pinch of sarcasm. "She wanted to share your joy."

"Was she drinking?" Mother asked.

"We were on a telephone. I don't have a clue."

"You get rid of that tone right this minute, mister," she demanded.

"Yes, Sister. I'm sorry, Sister. Please forgive me, Sister."

"I didn't really keep this a secret. Look at the photograph on my dresser, the one with his parents and your father. You'll see."

"Why couldn't you just tell me?" I asked. "And quit saying you're raising me as a feminist."

"You've always been strange enough, Leo. Steve knew all about my life as a nun. But you were so different and so difficult that I wasn't sure how you'd handle it."

"It's going to take a while to get used to this," I said. "It's not every day a boy finds out his mother's a professional virgin."

"My vocation was very fulfilling to me," she informed me firmly, then changed the subject in a sidestep unusual for her. "Have you taken the cookies to our new neighbors?"

"I'm baking them now. Then I'll let them cool."

"Do not be late. Lunch at the yacht club, then four o'clock to meet your new coach. And, Leo. I'm proud I'm raising you to be a feminist."

"No wonder everybody treats me like an oddball," I answered in amazement. "I was raised by a nun."

Just after three, I began packing the cookies in a tin as my father entered the kitchen carrying two bags of groceries.

"Benne seed wafers?" he said. "They're not mentioned in *Ulysses*."

"This is not part of the Bloomsday feast," I said. "A new family's moved across the street, remember?"

Jasper King put the grocery bags on the counter and said, "The sweetest boy in the world needs to be kissed by his father."

I groaned, but knew the folly of resistance. He kissed me on both cheeks like he learned to do in Italy during World War II. All during my childhood, my father made up excuses to kiss me and my brother on both cheeks. When we were young, Steve and I would practice the groans we'd make whenever he approached us.

With great care, I packaged the wafers in a rounded tin that once housed salted pecans. I tasted one to make sure it was worthy to enter a stranger's home. It was. "I'm going to run these over to the new neighbors," I said. "Sister Scholastica called, by the way."

"Haven't heard from her in a coon's age."

"You know her?" I asked, ignoring the subject of my mother's nunhood for the moment.

"Of course I know Scholastica," he said. "She was the maid of honor when your mother and I got married. By the way, I ran into Judge Alexander on Broad Street. He bragged about how highly your probation officer thinks about you. I told him how well you were doing."

The moving van had already departed when I crossed the street to the Poe family. The cookies were warm in the tin as I bounded up the stairs of the nineteenth-century house that needed a facelift and a touch of rouge. I knocked twice and heard someone moving toward the door in bare feet. It opened and I got my first rapturous glance at Sheba Poe, who became the most beautiful woman in Charleston the moment she crossed the county line. Everyone I met, male or female, remembers the exact place where they first caught sight of this spellbinding, improbable blond beauty. It was not that we lacked experience in the presence of beautiful women; Charleston was famous for the comeliness of its well-bred and pampered women. But as Sheba stood tall in her doorway, her presence suggested a carnality that took me to the borderline of a cardinal sin just because of what I thought about as I gaped at her. To me, it felt like no appreciation of mere loveliness, but some corruption of covetousness or gluttony. Her green eyes drank me in, and I noted flecks of gold.

"Hello," she said. "My name is Sheba Poe. I'm the new kid on the block. My brother, Trevor, is sneaking up behind me. He's wearing my ballet shoes."

"I'm wearing my own ballet shoes, thank you." Trevor Poe appeared beside his sister. I was struck dumb by both his composure and his elfin size. If anything, he was prettier than his sister, but thinking that seemed to rewrite the laws of nature. Trevor noted my silence. "Don't worry; Sheba strikes everyone that way. I have the same effect on people, but for an entirely different reason. I've played Tinker Bell in more class plays than I can count."

"I made you some cookies," I said, flustered. "To welcome you to the neighborhood. They're benne wafers, a Charleston specialty."

"Does it have a name?" Trevor asked his sister. It was an odd echo of my conversation earlier that day with the orphans, as if I weren't in the room.

This time, I answered: "Its name is Leo King."

"The *Kings* of Charleston? As in King Street?" Sheba asked.

"No, we're no relation to the famous Charleston Kings," I said. "I'm descended from the nothing Kings."

"A pleasure to be friends with one of the nothing Kings," Sheba said. She took the tin of cookies and handed it to her brother, then took my hand and squeezed it, as mischievous and flirtatious as she was lovely.

Then a darker, more menacing presence approached from the rear of the house unsteadily, like a dog with three legs.

"Who is it?" There was something wrong with the woman's voice. A lovely but diminished version of both her twins appeared in the doorway, parting her two children like a wave. "What do you want from us?" she asked. "You've already got your check for the move."

"The movers are long gone," Trevor said.

"He brought us some cookies, Mama," Sheba said, but there was a nervous, stilted quality to her voice. "From an old family recipe."

"It's from *Charleston Receipts*," I said, "a local cookbook."

"My great-aunt has a recipe in that cookbook," the woman said, and a note of familial pride entered the slurred speech of what I now recognized as a common drunk.

"Which one?" I said. "I'll cook it for you."

"It's called breakfast shrimp. My aunt was Louisa Whaley."

"I've cooked it often," I told her. "We call it mulled shrimp and serve it over grits."

"You cook? What a faggoty thing to do. You and my son are destined to be bosom buddies."

"Why don't you go back inside, Mama?" Sheba suggested, but with diplomacy in her voice.

"If you become friends with me, Leo," Trevor explained, "it's a kind of kiss of death to my mother."

"Oh, Trevor, Mama's just joking," said Sheba, guiding her mother back into the shade of the house.

"You wish," said Trevor.

"Would you like to subscribe to the *News and Courier*?" I asked the retreating figure of Mrs. Poe. "We've got a special introductory offer: the first week is free except the Sunday edition."

"Sign us up," she said. "If you're the milkman, we need milk and eggs too."

"I'll call the milkman," I said. "His name is Reggie Schuler."

Sheba appeared at the door again and said in an exaggerated Southern accent, "I don't know what my mother, Miss Evangeline, would do without the kindness of flaming assholes."

I laughed out loud, surprised by the profanity coming from such a pretty face and knowing the witty reference to Tennessee Williams, which seemed dangerous. Her twin was not nearly as amused as I was and chastised his sister. "Let's wait until we make a friend or two until we reveal our true trashiness, Sheba. My sister apologizes, Leo."

"I most certainly do not," Sheba said, mesmerizing me with her eyes. Her Southern accent was extraordinary for its depth, although it was certainly not a Charleston accent, which was gussied up with its own bold flares and Huguenot accessories. Her brother's voice was high-pitched, but hard to place in a geographical setting, though I would have guessed the West.

"My natural charm has captivated Leo, has it not, my little benne wafer?" Sheba had opened the cookies and was eating one as she passed another to Trevor. Their mother's sudden reappearance took them by surprise.

"You haven't left yet," the mother said. "I forget your name, young man."

"I don't think I introduced myself to you, Mrs. Poe. I'm Leo King. I live in that brick house across the street."

"I find it most undistinguished," she said.

"My father built it before the Board of Architectural Review got strong," I explained. "It's considered dreadful by most Charlestonians."

"But you're a King. One of the King Street Kings, I suppose."

"No, ma'am. We're the nothing Kings. I already explained that to your kids."

"Ah, you've met my darling children. A faggot and a harlot. Not bad for a single lifetime, don't you agree? And to think I came from the Charleston aristocracy. The Barnwells, the Smythes, the Sinklers, all that and more. So very much more, Mr. Nothing King. The blood of the founders of the colony flows through these veins. But my children are hideous disappointments to me. They poison everything they touch."

Mrs. Poe stopped in midstream that was half-genealogy and half-tirade and finished off a drink in a cut-glass tumbler. Then she placed her nose against the screen door leading to the piazza and said, "I think I'm going to puke."

She did not puke, but she did fall through the screen door and straight into my arms. I caught her, stumbled once, then righted myself and lifted her off the piazza floor, where she would have suffered some severe damage to her face. Sheba and Trevor both cried out, then together we carried their mother to her upstairs bedroom. The furniture we passed smelled newly out of the box, cheap copies of antiques, even the four-poster, rice-planter bed we laid her upon. The twins seemed undone that I had witnessed this humiliating event. But I was feeling heroic for catching their mother as she popped through her front door, invoking the infield fly rule and declaring her immediately out, and carrying her out of sight before anyone on the street could report the event.

Back at the front of the steps, Sheba grabbed my hand and asked, coming very close to begging: "Please, Leo, don't tell anyone what you just saw. This is our last year in high school and we can't take much more."

"I won't tell a soul," I said, and meant it.

Trevor said, "This is our fourth high school. Our neighbors can only take so much of this. Mom is capable of far worse."

"I won't even tell my mother and father," I said. "Especially not them. My mother's your new high school principal, and my father will teach you physics this year."

"You won't allow this to hurt our newfound friendship," Sheba said, close to tears.

"I won't let anything hurt our friendship," I said. "Nothing at all."

"Then let's start with some truth. Just a little dab," Trevor said. "My mother is from Jackson, Wyoming. We last lived in Oregon. You don't want to know a thing about my father. Mama doesn't have a drop of Charleston blood. And my sister is one of the greatest actresses who ever lived," Trevor continued.

That's when Sheba astonished me by falling silent, wiping her eyes with her fingers, and giving me the most dazzling smile. "But that's all part of the secret too. No one can know that either."

"I won't tell a soul," I repeated.

"You're an angel," the newly composed Sheba Poe said, kissing me gently, becoming the first girl ever to kiss me on the lips. Then Trevor kissed me lightly on the lips too, and sweetly, causing me much greater surprise.

At the bottom of the steps, I turned back toward the twins, not wanting to walk out of their presence just yet: "None of this happened. Simple as that."

"Some of it happened, paperboy," Trevor said as he went back into the house, but his sister lingered.

"Hey, Leo Nothing King. Thanks for being in the neighborhood. And by the way, Leo, it's not just my good looks that will make you fall in love with me. You're not going to believe how nice I am, kiddo."

"You could be mean as hell and ugly as sin, Sheba Poe," I said. "But I'd still fall in love with you." I waited several beats, then added, "Kiddo."

Floating back to my house, I realized I had never said anything like that to a girl, ever; I had flirted with a girl for the first time. A changeling self crossed that street as I skipped toward my house, having been kissed by both a girl and a boy for the first time.

CHAPTER 3

Yacht Club

It was the noonday hour, under a man-eating Charleston sun, the air so full of humidity it made me wish for a set of gills beneath my earlobes. I walked into the main dining room of the Charleston Yacht Club for the luncheon my mother had ordered me to attend. The yacht club was plush but threadbare and in need of renovation. For me, it carried the silent menace of enemy territory as I walked beneath the contemptuous stares of the club's founders. Their faces scowled down at me, disfigured by the ineptitude of their portraitists. The artists of Charleston made the movers and shakers of the river-shaped city look like they needed both a good dentist and an effective laxative. My freshly shined shoes moved across the Oriental carpets as I looked for a uniformed guard to halt my progress toward the inner sanctum of the club, but the few men I passed neither noticed nor spoke to me as I moved toward the murmurous conversations of the lunchtime crowd. Outside, the Cooper River was lined with white sails limp in the breathless air like butterflies trapped in a strange, city-spawned amber formed by buttermilk and ivory. Even behind the closed windows, I could hear the profanity of the stalled sailors cursing the lack of wind. Before I entered the dining room, I drew a deep breath and wondered again what I was doing at this lunch. Charleston could produce men and women so aristocratic they could smell the chromosomes of a passing tramp in the armpits of a tennis-playing Ravenel. It was a city and a club that knew exactly who it wanted, and I didn't fill the bill in any of its particulars. And I was well aware of it.

Across the room my father rose out of a chair and motioned for me, and I felt like a booger in a Kleenex as I crossed the room. But I noticed that the stillness of the river lent it a green, almost turquoise, shine; the slight movement of the tides cast moving shadows on the ceiling that passed like reluctant waves from chandelier to chandelier.

The table I joined was not a happy one, and my intrusion seemed welcome. "This is our son, Leo King," my father said to the table in general. "Son, this is Mr. Chadworth Rutledge and his wife, Hess. Sitting beside them is Mr. Simmons Huger and Mrs. Posey Huger."

I shook hands and said my howdy-dos to all the adults, then faced three teenagers about my age. Meeting my own peers had often been more intimidating than any introduction to adults. Since I was in a chair directly across from them, I couldn't help but be uncomfortable beneath their curious scrutiny. But these were my own internal demons and had nothing to do with the three young people who sat across from me.

"Son, the young man sitting across from you is Chadworth Rutledge the tenth," my father said.

I reached across the table to shake his hand. I could not help but ask, "The *tenth*?"

"Old family, Leo. Very old," young Chadworth said to me.

"And the lovely young lady sitting beside him is his girlfriend, Molly Huger, whose parents you just met," Father added.

"Hello, Molly." I shook her hand. "It's nice to meet you." And it certainly was: Molly Huger looked as though she had long grown accustomed to being the prettiest girl at the debutante ball.

"Hello, Leo," she said. "It looks like we're going to be classmates this year."

"You'll like Peninsula," I told her. "It's a nice school."

"The other young lady is Fraser Rutledge," Father continued. "She's a junior at Ashley Hall, the sister of young Chad. And Molly's best friend."

"Fraser Rutledge?" I asked. "The basketball player?"

The girl blushed, a deep one that rouged her porcelain skin. Her hair was shiny like a colt's; she was strong and tall and healthy and broad-shouldered, an Olympic athlete in repose. I remembered her lionesque presence under the backboard from a game I had witnessed the year before. Fraser nodded her head, but lowered her eyes.

"The game I saw was against Porter-Gaud," I said. "You had thirty points and twenty rebounds. You were great. Just great."

"State champs," her father, Worth Rutledge, said from down the table. "Ashley Hall wouldn't have won a game without her."

Hess Rutledge added, "Fraser's always been an incorrigible jock. She was doing cartwheels on the beach at Sullivan's Island before she was two."

"A lot of cartwheels," her brother said, "but not many dates."

"Leave Fraser alone," Molly said in an even-toned voice to her boyfriend.

"Do you like sports?" I addressed the question to Chad and Molly.

"I sail," Molly said.

"I'm a duck hunter, a deer hunter, and I ride with the hounds," her boyfriend said. "I'm a sailor too, because I grew up at this club. Played a little football at Porter-Gaud."

My mother then spoke to me, a brief summation of the day so far. "We spent the morning getting Chad and Molly registered for their classes. I thought, Leo, that you might be able to answer any questions they might have about Peninsula High."

As a nervous habit, I removed my glasses and began cleaning them with a handkerchief. The room blurred and the people across the table were almost faceless until I put my glasses back on. I felt like a guppy in a jelly jar as those people took my measure.

Mrs. Rutledge said, "It's so nice of you to meet us here on such short notice. Did I hear it right? Is your first name Lee?"

"No, ma'am," I said. "It's Leo."

"I thought you might've been named after the general. I don't think I've known a Leo. Who were you named after?"

"My grandfather," I said quickly. I heard my father chuckle, then flashed my mother a death's-head glance as a fair warning if she gave away the shameful provenance of my name.

"How's the cafeteria food, Leo?" Molly asked. I turned my gaze on this lovely, unapproachable girl, a type who seemed to spring so effortlessly from the city's upper-class homes—their hair, their skin, their bodies, all shone with a surprising inner light. They looked as if they had been put together with the casings of discarded pearls and the manes of palominos. Molly was so pretty she was hard to look at without feeling like a humpbacked whale.

"It's like cafeteria food everywhere: inedible. Everyone complains about it for nine months," I answered.

At the other end of the table, an officious and no-nonsense Worth Rutledge clapped his hands together and said, "Okay, back to business. I took the liberty of ordering for everyone—thought it would save some of our valuable time." He had established himself as a man of action and didn't wait for any better suggestions. His wife nodded her bleached-out face in agreement. On Molly's father's face, there was a look of resignation, even defeat. But Mrs. Huger also nodded, in an odd, faithful imitation of Mr. Rutledge's wife.

"It's been a rough morning," Worth Rutledge said. "Do you think we've covered everything? We don't want the kids to fall through any cracks now, do we?"

"I think everything's been taken care of," my mother said, checking a list beside her plate as a white-jacketed waiter produced several baskets overflowing with rolls, biscuits, and cornbread. Water glasses were refilled and drinks replenished around the table. My parents were drinking iced tea, but Mr. Rutledge was drinking a martini with three tiny onions on a toothpick. They looked like the tiny shrunken heads of albinos. The other adults were drinking tall Bloody Marys, each skewered with a celebratory stalk of leafless celery.

As my mother checked her list again, her voice droned over the barebacked details that she excelled in: "We've talked about health insurance, the policy for sick leave. The cost of a senior ring. The dress code. The penalties for drugs and alcohol found on any school property. The senior trip. The eligibility requirements for an extracurricular activity."

My mother was cut off abruptly by Worth Rutledge: "Why did you bring up the drug thing again, Dr. King?"

Simmons Huger, a pallid man who had barely spoken since I had arrived, said, "Oh, for God's sakes, Worth. We're all here because of drugs.

Our kids were arrested and thrown out of Porter-Gaud. The Kings have been very kind in helping us out."

"There must be some mistake, Simmons," Worth said, his voice edged with a withering irony. "I don't believe I directed the question to you. So I'd appreciate your silence if I can't count on your support."

"Dr. King is checking her list," Simmons replied. "You just asked her if we covered everything at our meeting. She was doing exactly as you asked. That's all I'm saying."

Mrs. Rutledge joined the debate. "In my day, we just drank and got in trouble. I don't understand anything about this drug culture. If Molly and Chad want to be bad, just go out to the beach house and get drunk. Sleep it off and come home the next day, and no one will be the wiser for it."

"If you don't mind, Hess," Simmons said, "we'd rather Molly not get drunk, and we'd much rather she sleeps in our house than your beach house."

From our end of the table, during the course of this low-key disagreement, I watched as Worth Rutledge drained his martini and sucked the onions off the toothpick. Another martini appeared by his plate without a hand sign or gesture being made. A waiter began ladling out a bowlful of she-crab soup as I heard the subject turn to me.

"Hey, Leo?" Mr. Rutledge said. "You had some pretty big problems with drugs when you were younger, didn't you?" With those words, Worth Rutledge altered the mood of our lunch.

"Hush up, Worth," his wife snapped. "For God's sakes."

"I don't think my son has anything to do with today's meeting," my father said. I had never appreciated his calmness under fire as I did then.

"I asked you a simple question, Leo," Mr. Rutledge said. "I think it's a fair one under the circumstances. Maybe you can give our kids some tips on your rehabilitation. I looked up your record: you were caught with a half pound of cocaine and kicked out of Bishop Ireland High School. So I imagine you can offer some good advice to Molly and my boy."

"Attacking a kid," said Simmons Huger. "You ought to be ashamed of yourself, Worth."

"I'd like Leo to tell us about his experience. It seems to have a lot of relevance to what we've discussed today," Worth replied.

"Yes, sir," I admitted. "I was caught and charged with possession of cocaine. I'm still on probation and have some community service to perform."

"So you're proof that this isn't the end of the world for Molly and my boy. Right, Leo?" Mr. Rutledge's voice intimidated me into confusion, if not silence.

"I've got a couple of more weeks of court-appointed therapy, then I'll—"

"Therapy? You go to a shrink, Leo?" Mr. Rutledge was staring hard at me, failing to notice my mother's arctic and dangerous silence.

"Yes, sir," I answered. "Once a week. But I'm almost finished."

"Son," Father said, "you don't have to tell Mr. Rutledge a thing about your life. It's of no concern to him."

Mr. Rutledge turned to my father. "Beg to differ with you, Jasper." When he pronounced my father's first name, there was mockery. I knew my father was sensitive about his name and wished his mother's father had carried a different one.

"Daddy, your tone of voice," Fraser said to her father, embarrassment reddening her cheekbones.

"I didn't hear anyone ask for your opinion, either, young lady," her father retorted.

Hess Rutledge entered the fray, but with trepidation. "She heard the anger in your voice, dear. You know how your anger upsets her."

Her husband threw up his hands. "All day I've been condescended to about my son, and what this does to his chances to get into a good college, and whether he'll even graduate from his class next spring."

Then I heard my mother say, "Who was condescending to you, Mr. Rutledge?"

"You were, madam," he answered. "And your schoolteacher husband, Jasper, over there. None of this would've happened if that goddamn prick of a headmaster over at Porter-Gaud would listen to reason. Pardon my French. I apologize for my language." Mr. Rutledge's blood was at full tide, a rage that excited his son, embarrassed his wife, and humiliated his daughter, who was near tears across the table from me.

Simmons Huger tried to defuse the tension, but again he sounded weak-willed and indecisive. "Our kids are in trouble, Worth. The King family is helping us all out of an unfortunate situation."

"Porter-Gaud should've handled this internally. We should not be here on our knees trying to get our kids into a crappy public school," Mr. Rutledge said.

"Are you quite finished, Mr. Rutledge?" Mother asked. Not one person at the table had touched a drop of the soup when the waiters came to clear the table.

"For now," he answered. "At least, for now."

The black waiters moved in phantom shapes around the tables, bringing a veal marsala for the second course with a mound of ghastly mashed potatoes and carrots cooked to lifelessness as accompaniments. It did us all good to concentrate on eating, letting the atmosphere around us decompress before the conclusion of the meal.

When the veal plates were taken away, Simmons Huger cleared his throat, then said, "Posey and I are very grateful to you, Dr. King, for handling this in such a professional manner. The last couple of days have been very traumatic for all of us. Molly's never given us an ounce of trouble in her life, so this has caught our family by surprise."

"I won't let you down, Dr. King," Molly added in a soft voice.

"I'm a changed man," the younger Rutledge said. "This has taught me a big lesson, ma'am."

"The males in the Rutledge line have a long history of being hell-raisers," his father explained. "It's sort of a way of life by now, part of a heritage."

Hess Rutledge interrupted to say, "But you'll see no sign of that, Dr. King. My son has sworn to me he'll behave himself."

"If he doesn't behave himself," Mr. Huger said, "he won't be dating Molly when she comes off restriction at the end of the summer."

"You're on restriction?" Chad asked Molly. "Why?"

"We were arrested the other night, darling," Molly said. "It didn't make my parents very happy, okay?"

"Kids are young once," Chad's father said. "It's their main job to go out and have as much fun as it's possible to have. The only mistake they made the other night was getting caught. Am I right? Yes or no?"

"An emphatic no, Mr. Rutledge," Mother said. "I think you're as wrong as a parent can be."

"Ah, Dr. King, again, that note of condescension. Grating and irritating at best. Infuriating at worst," Worth Rutledge said, shooting my mother a look that could have removed acid from a car's battery. "Let's just examine the facts: our two kids get caught with a couple of grams of cocaine. Granted, they did wrong. But we've got this principal who's raised a son who was once caught at a party with a half pound of cocaine. He's been part of the Charleston Juvenile Court system ever since."

"I was told we were coming here to talk about helping your son and Molly out of a bad situation," my father said, his innate gentility girded with body armor. "I didn't know you'd be conducting a seminar on my son's past."

In the sudden airlessness of the room, I kept my head down and my eyes fixed on the plate in front of me. The level of discomfort reached a boiling point. Then Molly's father coughed, but words failed him at this essential moment.

"I think what my daddy's saying is that Molly and I are amateurs compared to Leo here," the younger Chadworth said.

I burned with discomfort, but I knew that the willful contentiousness of Chad Rutledge would earn a measured but fiery response from one of my parents, if not both.

However, it was Fraser Rutledge, the great Ashley Hall basketball player, who broke out of a cocoon of shyness and said, "Shut up, Daddy. Shut up, Chad. You're only making it worse, and you're making it much worse for Molly."

"Don't you dare talk to your father like that, young lady," Hess Rutledge snarled through thin lips.

Posey Huger added, "He can't make it much worse for Molly. She's restricted for the rest of the summer."

"That so?" Mr. Rutledge asked. "Funny thing, I'm sure my son told me that he and Molly were going to a dance at the Folly Beach pier next weekend. Didn't you mention that, son?"

"My daddy was never one to keep a secret," Chad said, winking at the entire table and somehow coming across as a charming rascal rather than the darker creature that I felt staring me down every time he looked my way. His courtliness was the flip side of his aggression. It might not have been pretty, but it was masculine and, I thought, Charlestonian to the core.

"You're not going anywhere next Friday," Hess said to her son, evidently realizing what a spoiled figure he was cutting for my silent but appraising mother.

"Ah, Mama," Chad replied, "I was even thinking about getting my sister—old Muscle Beach down there—a blind date for the dance."

Fraser stood up with quiet dignity and excused herself to the ladies' room. The suffering of plain girls who were born with a duty to be beautiful to rich and shallow families was almost unbearable to me. I nearly rose to follow her, then thought I would look strange in a ladies' room. But Molly Huger did rise abruptly. Molly excused herself, shot her boyfriend a murderous look, then followed her friend out of the dining room. In her own beauty and straight-backed carriage, Molly had fulfilled the most pressing and necessary duties for a Charleston girl of her generation. For the rest of her life, she could sit around being beautiful, marrying Chadworth the tenth and bearing his heirs, rising to the presidency of the Junior League, and putting fresh flowers on the altar of St. Michael's. With thoughtless ease she could throw parties for her husband's law firm, sit on the board of the Dock Street Theatre, and restore a mansion south of Broad. I could write out Molly's entire history as she passed in hot pursuit of her bruised friend. Because she was pretty, there was nothing about Molly that was not a cliché to me. But I had no idea how history was about to manhandle Fraser, a girl with a man's shoulders, a twenty-rebound game on her résumé, and a future that contained uncertainty and, I was certain, great sorrow. In a flash, it bothered me that I was much more attracted to Molly than to Fraser.

"You shouldn't say things like that to your sister, Chad," Simmons Huger said, a gesture that seemed correct and timely. "You'll regret it when she's older." Fraser's mother followed the two girls.

"I was just teasing, Mr. Huger," said a contrite Chadworth the tenth. "She's never had much of a sense of humor."

"She's a sensitive girl," Mr. Huger agreed, then turned to my parents. "Dr. King? Mr. King? Thank you for your time and for the help you're giving Molly. I'm going to be late for an appointment if I don't get going."

"Certainly," my father said. "We'll let you know what's been decided."

"Thanks for arranging this, Worth," Mr. Huger said. "And thanks for springing for lunch."

No one had noticed my mother's tundralike silence as this small-time passion play between troubled families unfurled around her. It was a huge tactical error for Worth Rutledge to bring up my drug connection to defend the actions of his own son, but Mr. Rutledge was a well-known litigator in Charleston, which made him eager to engage whenever he smelled blood in the water.

Mrs. Rutledge and the two girls entered the dining room again. I followed my father's lead in rising from our chairs until the ladies were seated, their chairs held by white-jacketed waiters who hurried from the corners of the room.

"Ah!" Chadworth senior said. "The return of the natives." Looking to my mother for approval, he added, "That was a literary reference in honor of you, Dr. King. Hardy, I believe. What was his first name?"

"Thomas," Mother said.

"I understand from my research that you did your doctoral dissertation on James Joyce. *The Odyssey,* or something like that. Correct?"

"Something like that," she said.

"Fraser has something to say to everyone at the table," Mrs. Rutledge announced.

Fraser, red-eyed, began to speak. "I'm so sorry I caused a scene, and I want to apologize to my daddy and brother for embarrassing them in public. You both know how much I love you."

"Sure thing, sugar. The whole family's been under a lot of pressure," her father said.

My mother pulled out of her long period of near-silence and said, "Miss Rutledge, I've been noticing you with great interest today at lunch. It's my conclusion that you're a young woman of much character."

Fraser glanced around the table, her eyes glistening. "But I didn't mean to ruin the lunch. I had no right to speak."

"You had every right to speak," Mother said. "You are a woman of parts."

The silence of bivalves gripped the table until young Chad made a serious error by following my mother's praise of his sister with the most untimely joke. "Yeah. Big parts. Real big parts: big shoulders, big thighs, big feet."

"Hush up, young man," Mother said, rising out of her seat. "Just hush your mouth."

"Don't you ever talk to my son like that again, Dr. King," an enraged Worth Rutledge snarled. "Or you're going to find yourself looking at want ads."

"He's enrolled in my school," Mother flashed back. "If the superintendent doesn't like how I'm doing my job, then he can let me know about it."

"If you want to come back to my office after lunch, Dr. King, we'll put in a call to your superintendent," Rutledge said.

"The business of education at Peninsula High is conducted from *my* office, Mr. Rutledge," Mother said. "You're welcome to visit me there. Please set up an appointment with my secretary."

If the setting had been anywhere but the Charleston Yacht Club, with the sunlight shining on bone china and silver cutlery, I think Worth Rutledge might have exploded. Social forces I was only dimly aware of had brought anarchy upon that sedate luncheon which had begun as a function of bureaucracy, courtesy, and goodwill.

Across from me, a shell-shocked Molly Huger was staring at me.

"Ever had so much fun, Molly?" I asked. To my complete surprise, the whole table laughed, except for Chad, whose face was stony at the general loosening of the ghastly atmosphere. In the privileged world of young Chadworth Rutledge, when he chose to be the comedian, boys like me were born to be the audience. When Chad chose to be serious, my role was to play the admiring fool. When Chad declared a pronouncement, I was to be a midnight rider, delivering the message to the countryside. But that would be years in the learning.

My mother took her seat and the gathering grew cordial and pragmatic again. Lunch came to a swift conclusion over coffee and pecan pie. In parting, the gentility that is both the bedrock and the quicksand of all social endeavors in Charleston brought grace and quietude to the last act of that meal. There were handshakes all around, but no love lost among any of the major participants.

My parents and I made our farewells. We walked out of the Charleston Yacht Club, and the great heat met us at the doorway. Uncharacteristically, my mother kissed me on the cheek, and the three of us walked together toward East Bay Street and our city of many mansions, away from the yacht club that we would never be invited to join.

• • •

My meeting with Coach Anthony Jefferson awaited. I entered the gymnasium, which smelled like mildew and boy sweat and the stale air of inflated pigskins and basketballs. Through the office windows, I saw the coach studying a thick manila envelope that I knew was my file. He was obviously concentrating, and three uneven lines of wrinkles creased his forehead as he familiarized himself with the downs and then the deeper downs of my life. By my junior year, I thought I had turned myself into a reasonable model citizen of Peninsula High, but even I was aware that the bar I had set for myself was a low one.

Coach Jefferson's face was coffee-colored; there was gray in his sideburns, but his eyes were an impenetrable mahogany. He froze me in midstep as I entered his office. He had been a star halfback for South Carolina State in the early fifties and was one of the first inductees into that black college's athletic hall of fame.

"I guess you're Leo King." His voice was softer than I expected.

"Yes, sir, I am. My mother sent me down here."

His eyes moved back to my record. "You were arrested for having a half pound of cocaine in your possession."

"That's right, sir."

"So you're not denying it?"

"They caught me fair and square," I admitted. "It was my first party ever at a house south of Broad."

"But someone put it in your pocket so they wouldn't get caught. And you refused to divulge that person's name. Is that the story?"

"Yes, sir."

"Don't you think society depends on people like you—innocent people like you—cooperating with the police, Leo?" he asked. "Was this boy a friend of yours?"

"No, sir. I'd never spoken to him," I said.

"Then why not turn him in?" the coach asked. "It doesn't make sense."

"I admired him a great deal, sir."

"Did you tell the cops that?"

"No, sir, I didn't tell them anything about him. I didn't even tell them it was a guy."

"You told nobody this boy's name? Not your mother or your father, no friend, no shrink, no priest, no social worker? Why would you take the rap for some scumbag who set you up?"

"I made a decision. Spur-of-the-moment kind. And I stuck with it," I explained. "I'm sorry."

"You don't look like much of a player, King."

"It's my glasses, sir. They make me look weak."

"Do you wear them during games?"

"Yes, sir, or I couldn't see any of the other team. I'm blind as a bat."

"And you catch for the baseball team?" the coach asked. "Catchers are hard to come by."

"My father was a catcher for The Citadel. Since I was a little kid, he's taught me how to be in charge of a game."

"Yet you haven't played much baseball, have you?" he asked.

"I had some mental problems when I was younger, Coach Jefferson. They don't have baseball teams in mental hospitals. But I played a lot of pickup games with the orderlies and the janitors, and some guards always played too. They taught me some good stuff."

Coach Jefferson studied me as though he was trying to comprehend our go-around, taking my measure. I had never known a good coach who could not render himself unreadable. His face was blank; his rapt absorption unnerved me because he made it seem like a form of prayer.

"Leo," he said finally, "let's try to cut a deal between us. I think I'm going to need you this year a lot more than you need me. I've already had six white boys pull out of this school because they won't be coached by a nigger. You hear that?"

"Yes, sir," I admitted. "Some called me. They wanted me to go with them."

"This is going to be a volatile year. We could have everything from race riots to firebombs. And I need a white kid on the team I can trust."

"There are some nice guys already here, Coach Jefferson. It might be hard at first, but they'll get to like you."

He said, "I'd like for you to prove I can trust you. I need to know I can count on you through thick and thin."

"How can I prove that?"

Rising from his chair, Coach Jefferson walked out of his office and surveyed the gym. When he was assured the gym was empty, he returned to his small office, folded his powerful hands, and leaned across the table. "I'd like you to tell me the name of the boy who put the cocaine in your sports coat, Leo." I flinched, but his raised hand calmed me as his voice continued. "You give me that, and I give you something back."

"What can you possibly give me for that?" I asked. "I made a promise to myself that I would never tell anyone that kid's name."

"I admire you for keeping that promise. It's why I trust you," Coach Jefferson said. "But I want the boy's name and the reasons you kept quiet. Here's what I give you back: I'll never tell another living soul what that boy's name is. Not one—not my wife, not my daddy, not my preacher man, not even Jesus if he appears to me on a white cloud. And I'll never mention it to you again. It'll be like we never had this discussion."

"How do I know if I can trust you?"

"You don't, Leo. You got to look at me. Study me, and come to some decision about me. Is this a man I want to charge the sniper's nest with, or a Judas who will sell his soul for thirty pieces of silver? Or is this a Simon who will help Jesus carry the cross up to Calvary? You got to make a decision about me, Leo. And you got to do it fast."

I watched the face of Anthony Jefferson, then said, "His name is Howard Drawdy."

The coach whistled and I knew he would instantly recognize the name. "The best quarterback in the history of Bishop Ireland High School," he said. "But still, he screwed you good. He got you into big-time trouble."

"My brother, Steve, worshipped Howard Drawdy. Howard was always nice to my brother."

"Your brother who killed himself?" the coach asked.

"Yes, sir. And Steve once told me how poor Howard was, how his father was dead, and he lived in a trailer, and he couldn't go to Bishop Ireland without a scholarship."

"That guy owes you the bank, Leo," the coach said. "He's the starting quarterback at Clemson this year. Did he ever thank you?"

"No, sir, he didn't have to. But he's really nice to me every time I see him."

"So you got arrested. You get a trial. You get a police record. You go on probation, report to a probation officer. You do community service, you get kicked out of school. And the guy never thanks you?"

"I don't think he knows what to say, Coach."

"I think he's a perfect shit, Leo." He paused. "Okay." He stood up and held out a hand. "Shake on it. I'll never tell a soul what you just told me. I'd rather die than break that promise to you."

I stood up and we shook hands, his powerful and large.

"Now I have a problem I need help with, Leo."

"Anything, Coach Jefferson. Anything."

"You're going to be one of the leaders of my team. But you've got to help me with something. My son, Ike, is bitter about having to change schools his senior year. I graduated from Brooks High, so did his grand-daddy; his mother, her mother."

"What can I do?"

"Meet my son over at Johnson Hagood Stadium tomorrow at nine. Work out together. Get to know each other. I wrote up a conditioning program for him. It'll do you some good too. Just one rule for the sum-mer: if you ever call my son a nigger, I'll kill you."

"Not if my mother or father get to me first," I told him.

"They won't let you say that word?"

"Not even in a joke."

"My son's not allowed to call you 'honky' or 'cracker' or 'white mother-fucker,' either."

"What's he allowed to call me?" I asked. "In football, you always get mad at the guy who's just knocked you on your butt. Always. So you've got to call him something."

"I thought of that already. If my son makes you mad enough that you want to rip his head off and call him the worst name you can think of, then call him Dr. George Washington Carver, after the great black scien-tist from Tuskegee University."

"The peanut guy?"

"Yeah, that's the one."

"What can he call me?"

"He's got to call you Strom Thurmond. That's about as big an insult as a black man can yell at a white man."

"Sir, if I get mad at you at practice, do I call you Dr. George Washington Carver?"

"Call me Coach Jefferson. Anything else and I kick your ass. Hey, King? You think the other white boys'll play for me?"

"Yes, sir. I know they will."

"How are you so sure?"

"Because they love the game," I said. "And I bet they love those games on Friday night more than they do segregation."

At nine sharp the next morning, I was standing in the south end zone of Johnson Hagood Stadium watching Ike Jefferson walking across the north end zone. We walked slowly toward each other until we met at the 50-yard line, and a strange wariness set up shop between us. Ike did not smile or shake my hand or offer any greeting. He was chewing gum and flipping a football up into the air as a way of ignoring me. He kept flipping the ball, catching it with one hand, then flipping it again.

"Did you bring your father's workout plan with you?" I asked.

"Seem to have forgotten it, white boy." Ike looked at me for the first time.

"Gosh, Ike, ol' buddy, I didn't like the way it sounded when you called me 'white boy.' "

"I didn't mean it to sound friendly."

"Since you forgot to bring Coach's instructions, you want to run some laps to warm up? Or maybe do some calisthenics?"

"You do whatever white boys like to do," Ike said.

"I knew integration was going to be a pain in the ass, Ike," I said. "I really did. But I thought I was going to have to worry about my redneck boys a lot more than the black kids."

"Sorry to disappoint you, white boy."

"Hey, Dr. George Washington Carver Junior, you keep calling me 'white boy' and I'm going to start calling you a name with a long tradition in the South that rhymes with Roy Rogers's horse."

"You got quite a temper there, Strom Thurmond," he said.

"You've been screwing with me, Dr. George Washington Carver Junior."

"Just a little bit, Strom. You're a sensitive little soda cracker, aren't you? You were about to fight me, weren't you?"

"Yep. Sure was."

"Does it bother you that I could kick your ass?"

"A little bit. But I was going to throw the first punch when you tossed that football up in the air. Before that ball came down, I was going to break your jaw."

"Can you beat up any of those other white boys in that school of yours?"

"Not many of them," I said. "I'm not even sure I can beat up many of the white girls."

Ike surprised me by breaking out into an unexpected grin. He tossed me the ball. "You know something, Strom? I'm afraid I may even like you before this is over."

"I hope not," I said as I lateralled the ball back to him.

From his back pocket, Ike pulled out a piece of paper that revealed his father's workout plan. I read it over and whistled. "He's trying to kill us."

"His players are always in better shape than the other team," Ike said. "Let's start with ten laps, Strom."

"It'll be a pleasure, Dr. George Washington Carver Junior."

"I hope you enjoy watching my fat ass running ahead of you." He began to run.

"Here's what you and your daddy don't know about me," I said. "I look nerdy, but I run pretty fast."

I took off after him, and for an hour we ran sprints, did assorted agility drills, and performed push-ups and sit-ups at twenty-minute intervals. At the end of the session, we went up in the stands. I put Ike on my back and tried to run to the top of the stadium. I went twenty steps before I collapsed in exhaustion. We returned to the bottom of the stairs, and Ike put me on his shoulders. He reached thirty-five steps before he collapsed. In our exhaustion that first day, all we could do was laugh when we staggered on the stairs in a heap of sweat and panting and grass-stained clothes.

It was Ike who first called it "carrying the cross." That is what integration felt like for everyone after *Brown v. Board of Education,* when boys like me and Ike and men and women like my parents and Coach Jefferson were put to the noble task of making it work.

Panting in the shade of the lower bleachers, I said, "You are one fat-assed George Washington Carver Junior. Why don't you lose some weight?"

"Take off your glasses next time I carry your ass to the top," Ike said. "What do those things weigh—about twenty pounds?"

"You're just weak as water."

"Me? Weak? If the other white boys look like you, we're gonna get our asses whipped good this year."

"How many guys from your team are coming to Peninsula?" I asked.

"Maybe ten. My daddy would like to get another dozen or so, but a lot of guys wanted to stick with the high school in their neighborhood. Like me. But your old lady messed up my plans by making my daddy the coach."

"Instead of having to listen to you run your gums every day, Ike, why don't we go down and have a fistfight on the fifty-yard line? Let's just get it over with; then we can get on with working out."

"We can't have a fistfight until after lunch," Ike said. "We're having lunch at my house, and I can't have you bleeding on my mother's new rug."

"Who said I was eating lunch at your house?"

"My daddy," Ike said, in exasperation. "Our coach did. I ain't ever eat with a white boy, and I'll bet you make the food taste like shit."

"I'll try to make it a nightmare for you."

"You're already a nightmare," Ike said. "Please shut up. Here comes my daddy."

Coach Jefferson entered by the alumni gate and walked slowly toward where we sat at the bottom of the bleachers. "You boys look like you've been working hard. Your clothes are soaked. You two get along okay?"

"Your son wouldn't even shake my hand at first, Coach," I said. "Then we did great."

"We did okay," Ike said, a slight echo of insolence in his voice that Coach Jefferson caught in an instant.

"No lip from you, son." He studied Ike, then said, "Tell Leo why you didn't shake his hand, and tell him true. I'm not asking—he needs to know."

"I've been going to Brooks since kindergarten," Ike explained. "Thought I'd graduate this year from Brooks. I've always been afraid of white people. They scare me to death."

"Tell him why, Ike," the coach said.

"My uncle Rushton got shot by a white cop in Walterboro. He shot him in the back, killed him. Said he back-sassed him and threatened him. The cop got off with a warning."

"Go on. Tell the rest of it," Coach commanded.

"My uncle was a deaf-mute. Never said a word in his life," he said. Then he surprised both of us by tearing up, angry tears he was at pains to conceal.

I was taken aback by the tears and muttered, in perfect sincerity: "That's the worst story I ever heard in my life."

"It is that," the coach agreed. He put his arms around us and began walking us toward the north side of the field. For a minute we just walked, waiting for Ike to gain control of his emotions.

"I am naming you two young men as the cocaptains of the Peninsula High Renegades for the coming season," Coach said.

"Coach, a lot of guys are coming back from last year's team," I said, "who're a lot better football players than I am. Wormy Ledbetter is one of the best fullbacks in the state."

"King, I didn't say you were my first choice as the white cocaptain. In fact, I called Wormy's home to give him that high honor. He's a better football player than you. I watched all the films."

"What did he say?" I asked.

"Not a word, at least not to me. His father found out who I was and said no nigger son of a bitch better call his house again. So I assured him I would not. I called two other white players and I got the same results. We're going to be lucky to be able to field a whole team this year. But you are my white cocaptain, and Ike is my black cocaptain. And boys, together we're going to make history.

"Now, I want you two to meet at nine every morning of this summer, except Sundays. Coach Red Parker said we could use the weight room at

The Citadel. Chal Port's going to design a weight program just for you two guys, and I'm going to devise you a workout from hell. I'm going to practically kill you. I can't be here; it's against the rules. But I trust you two guys with my job and my heart. When football practice starts, you're the two studs who're going to take me across the finish line."

I looked at Ike and said, "I'll outwork you."

"That'll be the day, you honky cracker son of a bitch," he said.

"Start running, son," the coach snapped. "Five laps."

"I forgot, Daddy."

"Seems like Dr. George Washington Carver Junior doesn't have a very good memory, Coach."

"Kiss my ass," Ike said, then added, "Strom Thurmond."

We both laughed, and I started running with Ike.

"King, you don't run. You didn't screw up," the coach shouted.

"When my cocaptain runs, I run," I said. "That all right with you, Coach?"

"I'll be." He hurled his hat to the ground. "It sounds like the beginning of a goddamn team to me."

By the end of that summer, I could carry Ike Jefferson two times to the top of Johnson Hagood Stadium, and two times down. Because he was stronger, Ike could make it to the top three times, but collapsed on the top step. Though I had never been through anything like it physically, Ike and I were more than ready when practice began in August. The surprise of that summer was that I ripened into a strong and formidable young man. But the real shock to everyone was that Ike Jefferson and I would be friends for the rest of our lives.

CHAPTER 4

Downtown

A few days after Bloomsday, I walked down Broad Street and spotted Henry Berlin measuring the width of a man's shoulders with his measuring tape. I knocked on the plate-glass window of Berlin's clothing store. He made a notation with a piece of chalk, waved at me, then called out, "Hey, jailbird." That wicked yet good-natured salutation always made me laugh. I hadn't forgotten that Henry Berlin had been one of the first Charleston adults to embrace my reentry into life after my turbulent week as the most famous unnamed drug dealer in the county. Though the *News and Courier* could not use my name because I was underage, Leo King came up in even the most casual conversations on every street and restaurant that month. By calling me "jailbird," Mr. Berlin had offered the first exit out of my predicament by allowing me to laugh at myself.

Normally, I would have stopped and talked to him, but he was busy with a customer, and I was cutting it close for an appointment with my shrink, Jacqueline Criddle. She was as serious about time as a watch repairman, so I jogged to her office above an antique store. I passed through an alley, then took a flight of flimsily built stairs to the second story and entered an air-conditioned room that was an oasis of good taste and serenity there in the heart of downtown, sitar music playing on a stereo. When I had first come to this room, I was still fresh from my traumatic trial in juvenile court. It took me more than a year before I could begin to appreciate the rain-foresty tranquillity of the room, which smelled of hyacinths and ferns. After a rocky start, I had come to revere the skills of Dr. Criddle as she proceeded with infinite care to put my life in order again.

Soundlessly, a green light came on above her office door. I entered and went straight for the leather chair where I always sat facing her.

"Good afternoon, Dr. Criddle," I said.

"Good afternoon, Leo," she replied.

Though I was a teenage boy locked in that maddening, wet-behind-the-ears stage of complete social unease, I thought that all women over thirty years old were menopausal and approaching their deathbeds. But it was not lost on me that Dr. Jacqueline Criddle was a most attractive woman with an admirable figure and pretty legs.

"So, how goes it, Mr. Leo King?" She looked over some notes from my file.

I thought about it before I answered. "It's going great, Dr. Criddle."

She glanced up with a quizzical eye. "You've never said that to me in all our time together. What's happened, Leo?"

"I think I'm in the middle of living a good week. Maybe a real good one."

"Whoa. Back up. Hold your horses. You sound like you're on drugs for sure."

"I'm feeling so good . . ." I paused. "I'm even starting to like my mother a little bit."

My shrink laughed. "Now, surely that's a hallucination."

"I've found myself feeling pity for her. I've put my parents through a lot. Did you know my mother was once a Catholic nun?"

"Yes," she said. "I was aware of that."

"Why didn't you tell me?"

"It never came up, Leo," she said. "You never mentioned it."

"I just found out. Why wouldn't she tell me something like that?"

"She must've thought it'd only make things worse for you."

"I guess. But things couldn't have been much worse, could they?"

"They were pretty bad," said Dr. Criddle. "But you've come a long way. You're the pride of juvenile court."

I laughed. "Music for my mother's heart."

"She's actually proud of what you've accomplished," Dr. Criddle told me. "You've done everything the court has asked of you. And much, much more."

"Y'all kept me busy."

"Judge Alexander called today. He wants all of us to clean up our business with you this summer."

"I still have a hundred hours of community service to finish."

"He's cut it down to fifty."

"What about Mr. Canon? He needs me."

"I've called him, Leo. It's true that he fully expected you to be his personal manservant for the rest of his life, but he'll have to make do."

"He's told me as much."

"What a dreadful man," she said. "When they assigned you to him, I argued that it was cruel and unusual punishment."

"He's all alone in the world," I explained. "I think I'm all he's got. He's afraid to let people see his kind side. Always looking for trouble that never comes. I'm grateful to him. To all of you. You especially, Doctor."

"You've done the work, Leo," she said. I could feel her withdrawing into her shell like a box turtle you stumble on in the woods. "I've facilitated your therapy. Remember, I'm just court-appointed."

"Remember how I was when I first came to this office with my parents?"

"You were a big mess."

"How big?"

She picked up my file from the table that separated us. It was thick enough to strike an ominous chord in me each time she displayed it. In my mind, my file represented some cold-blooded book of hours compiled with malice by that most cunning enemy of my childhood—myself.

"Here is how I described you at that time. 'Leo King seems terrified, depressed, anxious, ashamed, totally confused, and possibly suicidal.' "

"Don't you miss that guy?" I asked.

"No, I don't. But it took a lot of work to get where we are today. I've never had an adolescent boy work as hard to make himself well. Your mother looked like she wanted to kill you that day. Your dad looked like he wanted to run far away with you and leave no forwarding address. There was such agony in this room. That was almost three years ago."

"You spotted my mother that first day," I remembered.

"She is a formidable woman," she said. "A good woman, but she overpowered you and your dad that day."

"Nothing's changed there," I told her. "We're still not in her league."

"But you've learned strategies to work around her. And with her. Do you remember what your dad did that day?"

"He cried for an hour. Couldn't stop. Said I blamed him for Steve's death."

"You did blame him . . . at least a little bit."

"It was the only clue I had, Dr. Criddle. The week before he died, Steve was sleeping when I heard him screaming, 'No, Father. No, please.' I woke him up and Steve told me he was having a nightmare. He laughed about it. Then he was dead."

"I've never seen a father love a boy like yours loves you, Leo," she said.

"You've never liked my mother, though."

"Don't go putting words in my mouth," she said.

"Fair enough, Doctor. But you've taught me to tell you the truth. Otherwise, therapy isn't worth a hill of beans. Your exact words. Here is what I think is true: you don't like my mother."

"What I think about her is irrelevant," she said. "It's what you think about her that counts."

"I've come to terms with her."

"That's a great accomplishment. Sometimes that's the best we can do. You've become patient and forgiving with your mom. I'm not sure I could do the same in your shoes."

"She's not your mother."

"Thank God," Dr. Criddle said, and we both laughed.

. . .

Heading north on King Street, I jaywalked to the other side, moving toward Harrington Canon's antique dealership across from the Sottile Theatre. Because I had the Southern boy's disease of needing to be liked by everyone I met, Mr. Canon had presented me with the dilemma of being impossible to please about anything. I never had to worry about whether Mr. Canon would be in a good mood: he lived out his whole life as an anthem to the pleasures of a bad mood. Our first weeks together had been nightmarish, and it took me a while to grow accustomed to his starchiness. It was not that he lived as though he were wearing a crown of thorns that bothered me, but that he cherished those thorns and would have it no other way.

When I approached the doorway of his shop, it was so dark my eyes had to adjust before he materialized, his head reminiscent of a great horned owl, at his English writing desk against the back wall.

"You're sweating like an up-country hog," he said. "Go wash up before your bodily fluids stain my precious merchandise."

"Hey, Mr. Canon. Why, I'm doing just peachy, sir! And so is my family. Thanks for your kind inquiries."

"You are white trash, pure and simple, Leo. A sad fact that you bitterly resent. I would never think of inquiring about your family. Because, sir, like you, they mean nothing to me."

"Does an up-country hog sweat more than the ones around Charleston?" I asked.

"Low Country hogs are too well bred to sweat."

"I've seen you sweat. Much worse than an up-country hog."

"You are a scoundrel even to suggest such a thing." He eyed me through glasses as thick as my own. "Charlestonians never sweat. We sometimes dew up like hydrangea bushes or well-tended lawns."

"Well, you sure do 'dew up' a lot, Mr. Canon. But I always thought it was because you were tighter than a tick and refused to turn on the air conditioner in this store."

"Ah. You are referring to my prudence, my admirable frugality."

"No, sir. I was referring to your cheapness. You told me once you could squeeze a penny hard enough to make Lincoln get a nosebleed."

"Lincoln, the great anti-Christ. The defiler of the South. I'd like to give him more than a nosebleed. I still think John Wilkes Booth is one of the most underrated of American heroes."

"How are your feet feeling?"

"When did you earn a medical degree, sir?" he asked. "The last time I looked, my feet belonged to me and me alone. I don't recall handing them over to you with a bill of sale."

"Mr. Canon," I said, exhausted by the subject already, "you know your doctor asked me to make sure you soaked your feet in hot water and Epsom salts. He's worried about you not taking care of yourself."

"It was a disgraceful breach of confidentiality," Mr. Canon said. "I'm still thinking about filing a report to the medical authorities and having him defrocked. He had no right to reveal such intimate details of my life to a common criminal."

I started weaving my way through a narrow path of bureaus and cabinets, until I reached the frayed drapery that led to a broken-down kitchen. I turned on the hot water, waited until it burned my hand, then filled an enamel washbasin half-full. I poured in a cup of Epsom salts, then made my way back to Mr. Canon's desk at a much slower pace. I had once spilled hot water on one of his overpriced dining tables, and he acted as though I had cut the thumb off the Christ child. His moods were predictable and ran from mercurial to stormy. Today seemed to be an easy day, and I predicted nothing but small-craft warnings for the rest of the afternoon.

"I will not put my feet in that lava," he said, his mouth set in a thin line.

"It'll cool down in a sec," I said, checking my watch.

"A sec. Is that a unit of time? I've been living in the South for over sixty years, and I've never heard of something called a 'sec.' Possibly you've taken up a new foreign language at that second-rate public school you attend."

I tested the water temperature with my index finger and heard Mr. Canon shout at me, "Please do not add your stockpile of school-yard germs to my footbath. I may be fastidious and old-maidish, but good hygiene I take with the utmost seriousness."

"Stick your smelly tootsies in here, Mr. Canon." I watched him slip out of a pair of elegant leather-tooled moccasins. He moaned with pleasure as his feet entered the hot water.

Again, I checked my watch. "Ten minutes, and then I'll be back to dry your feet with my hair. A Mary Magdalene kind of moment."

"Could you sweep out the shop for me today, Leo? And if there's time, I'd like you to polish the two English sideboards in the front. Do them right, and with great reverence. They speak volumes about the superiority of Mother England."

"Be glad to, sir," I said. "I'll be back to change your water in a bit."

"A bit? Isn't that something that's part of a horse's bridle? Or a small particle of almost anything? Or what a snake does to me in the past tense? If you insist on speaking English to me, Leo, I demand a modicum of precision from my employees."

I grabbed the broom and dustpan before I said, "I am not your employee. The courts of Charleston have punished me by making me your slave. I'm paying my debt to society by cleaning your foul antique store and washing your smelly feet. You seem to like slavery."

"I adore it. I always knew I would. My family owned hundreds of slaves for centuries. Alas, there was the Emancipation Proclamation. Alas, came Appomattox. Alas, Reconstruction. I was born into the Age of Alas. Then, when you thought life could get no worse—alas, came Leo King." He laughed a rare laugh. "I far preferred it when you trembled in your boots whenever you walked into this store. I love the smell of fear, glandular and base, given off by the servant classes. But then you figured me out, Leo. I've always rued that day."

"You mean the day I found out you were a pussycat?"

"Yes, that day, that damnable day. I let my guard down in a moment of uncharacteristic weakness," Mr. Canon said. "I loathe all base emotions, all sentimental claptrap. You caught me off guard, undefended. You did not know it, but I was under heavy medication that day. I was not myself, and you took advantage of my enfeeblement."

"I brought you a Father's Day card," I said. "You cried like a baby."

"I most certainly did not."

"You most certainly did. And Father's Day is coming up again. And I'm getting you another one."

"I forbid it," he said.

"Dock my salary." I headed up the stairs, where five pounds of Charleston dust awaited me; but Mr. Canon had assured me that I labored in swirls of dust made sacred and aristocratic by the history of families who had made my native city so lovely and fine.

Twice I changed the water and replenished the Epsom salts for the soaking of Mr. Canon's splayed, ungainly feet. I went into the bathroom and retrieved the various oils and ointments to massage his swollen feet. As a man of stupendous modesty, he always made me feel like a lower order of rapist when I pulled up a chair and dried his feet with his delicate, monogrammed towels taken long ago from a family long dead. But it was part of the regimen his doctor insisted upon, and I received no credit for community service if I failed to massage Mr. Canon's antique feet. He always made this part of our weekly ritual a moment of high drama.

"Leave my tootsies alone, rapscallion," he said.

"This is part of my job, Mr. Canon," I told him. "You always make it hard. Yet you and I know you like it. It makes your feet feel good."

"Don't go inventing words that never came out of my mouth, boy."

I caught his right foot then swung it up on my knee, where I dried it thoroughly. The intimacy unnerved him, and he placed a towel on his head as I turned my attention to his left foot.

"Next week we might need to work on the pedicure." I studied his toes. "Your pinkies look pretty good this week."

"This is what I live for, Lord?" he moaned. "For a common criminal to praise my feet?"

I then began applying a cream made of aloe and eucalyptus, and massaged his feet from the heels to the toes. Sometimes, he moaned with pleasure, and sometimes with pain when I applied too much pressure. My goal was to rub his feet until they glowed with a renewed, healthy circulation; or at least that was the goal his doctor required of me. Mr. Canon suffered from sciatica and a weak back and could not bend to touch his feet. He knew my ministrations were good for his physical health, even as I offended his overdeveloped sense of modesty.

"Dr. Shermeta called me last week," I told him.

"For the life of me, I cannot understand why I put myself under the care of a Ukrainian."

"The Ukrainian wants me to start giving you a full shower. I'm responsible for hosing down your whole body from here on in." I smiled at his towel-draped head.

"I would shoot you between the eyeballs if you attempted such a thing! How ghastly. So my life has come to this. Then, after I watched you suffer agonizing death throes, I would call a taxi, drive to Roper Hospital, and dispatch of this upstart Ukrainian. Then I would kill myself with a single shot to the head."

"So, you don't like the shower idea?" I asked. "Would you donate your body to science?"

"That's why God created paupers," he said. "My body will be buried in my family plot of distinguished ancestors in Magnolia Cemetery."

"Just how distinguished are your ancestors, Mr. Canon?" I teased him.

He caught the note of teasing and thundered, "Canon? *Canon?* Open any history book of South Carolina and even an illiterate would stumble across my family name. They would make your sorry family look like Haitians, Puerto Ricans, or even Ukrainians."

"Your podiatrist has to leave now," I said. "Remember to say your prayers. And always floss your teeth." Then I added in warning, "Soon I will have paid off my debt to society."

"What do you mean?" he asked.

"Judge Alexander has cut my community service to fifty hours, instead of a hundred."

"That's preposterous. I'll call the judge at once. You were caught with enough cocaine to satisfy the entire ghetto of Charleston for a week."

"I'll see you next Thursday. Can I bring you anything?" I walked toward the front door.

"Yes," he said. "You can, Leo. Try to bring me some sign of good breeding, a proper bloodline, a mastery of the small courtesies, and a much greater respect for your elders."

"Consider it done."

"You've been a great disappointment to me. I thought I could make something out of you, but I've been a dismal failure."

"Then why do you keep my Father's Day card in the top right-hand drawer, Mr. Canon?"

"You are a rogue and a blackguard," he cried out. "Never darken the door of this shop again or I'll have a warrant out for your arrest."

"See you next Thursday, Harrington."

"How dare you—the impudence of using my first name!" Then softening, he said, "Thursday it is, Leo."

CHAPTER 5

Raised by a Nun

I took Ashley Street north toward the medical college and St. Francis Hospital, where my brother and I were born. I took a right at the old Porter-Gaud chapel, then another right on Rutledge, and into the parking lot, where I locked my bike to a door handle of my mother's Buick. The sign that said PRINCIPAL ONLY filled me with a secondhand pride as I walked toward the school that had become a safe harbor. I had come to Peninsula High in complete disgrace. I knew that was what my mother wanted to talk to me about, with my final year approaching.

Sitting at her desk in her erect posture, my mother looked like she could have led a destroyer into combat. "I thought you knew I'd been a nun," she said.

"No, ma'am. You never told me that."

"You've been an odd enough boy," Mother said. "I guess I didn't want to say something that would give you an excuse to be even odder. Do you agree that you've been odd?"

"You've never seemed satisfied with me, Mother," I said, looking out the window at the traffic on Rutledge Avenue.

"Your erroneous theory, not mine. And look me in the eye." She opened up a permanent file on her desk, and then spent several moments studying a record that seemed odoriferous to her. "You have not distinguished yourself as a high school student, Mr. King."

"I'm your son, Mother. You know how I hate it when you pretend we're not related."

"I treat you just like I treat every other student in my school. If you get bad grades in high school, no good college will accept you."

"I'll get into some college," I said.

"But will I think it's a good one?"

"I could get into Harvard and you'd think the whole Ivy League had lowered its standards."

"No good college would touch you." She studied my grades, tsk-tsking with her tongue against her teeth. Tsk-tsking belonged to the native vocabulary of nuns and atrociously bad public school teachers. "Your grade point ratio is 2.4 out of a possible 4.0. Below average. You've scored less than a thousand on your SAT exams. You have great potential, but so far you have wasted the best years of your life. Your grades in ninth grade destroyed your grade point ratio."

"I had a bad year, Mother."

"Disgraceful, I would call it." She lifted out a sheet of paper and pushed it across the desk toward me. I recognized the paper and ignored it. "That's the copy of your arrest warrant issued on the night of August 30, 1966. The night when you were found carrying a half pound of cocaine in your sports jacket. This forty-page document is the record of your trial in juvenile court. Here are the yearly reports of your probation officer. These are from your shrink, that love of your life."

"Dr. Criddle has been a great help to me."

"These are Judge Alexander's letters describing your progress," she continued. "There are other letters describing the community service you performed to keep you from serving time in the juvenile prison system."

"I'm sorry that I put my family through that," I said. "But you know all that."

She cleared her throat, another nun's trick, and said, "That night will follow you forever."

"I made a mistake, Mother. I'd been in and out of mental hospitals after what happened to Steve. Six years had gone by since Steve."

"Would you hush up about your brother? He doesn't play a part in your screwup."

"I walked into Bishop Ireland as a ninth-grader. The whole school saw me as a nutcase. Kids were nervous around me. I was invited to a party, my first high school party. You and Dad were happy that I was going to be a normal kid again. Some drinking was going on, then a police raid. A guy on the football team put a bag of something in my pocket and asked me to keep it safe for him, and I said okay. I was flattered that a guy on the football team knew my name. So I got caught."

"Yes, and the next day your principal threw you out of Bishop Ireland, preventing you from getting a Catholic education, your parents' dream for you."

"You were my principal, Mother. You kicked me out of school."

"I was following school policy. I resigned my position that same day. So did your father. We both fell on our swords to support you. Then you betrayed us by not telling the police the name of that boy who planted the cocaine on you."

"I screwed up."

"If you'd have named that boy, nothing would've happened to you."

"It wouldn't have been right to name that guy." I said it for the hundredth time.

"But it was all right for a senior to plant drugs on an innocent freshman?"

"No, it was wrong of him."

"Well, you finally admit that—after three years."

"He shouldn't have done that to me," I agreed. "I see that now. I'm older, and I see it differently now."

"None of it had to happen," she said, her voice rising. "You didn't have any idea what drugs were. You were innocent. You were terribly used by an older boy. It was your stubbornness, your impenetrable stubbornness. The stubbornness you inherited from me. Damn it, you got it from me."

"Such vulgarity, Sister Norberta." But I pitied my mother even as I tried to joke her out of her distress.

She said, "Moving on to another unpleasant subject: Sister Scholastica told me you were impertinent to her on the phone."

"I was not. She caught me by surprise. She asked to speak to Sister Mary Norberta. I didn't know that was your code name."

"She didn't like the tone of your voice. She detected a note of sarcasm."

"I was nice to her," I protested. "I thought it was a wrong number."

"I'm always telling the nuns back at the convent that I'm raising you to be a feminist." Her voice glittered with self-approval.

"I'm the only boy in the world who knows how to work a Singer sewing machine," I said. "So you obviously wanted a daughter."

"I resent you even thinking that," she shot back. "I've taught you useful things, things they made me learn during my novitiate that I loathed doing. But they are useful."

"Yeah, the whole football team roared when they found out I made you a dress." I was still embarrassed by the memory.

"You made me a dress for Mother's Day your sophomore year. It touched me more than you'll ever know. It's still my favorite."

"Keep it up, Mother, and I'm going to sew another dress. Only *I'll* wear it to the prom."

She ignored me, and leaned down beside her desk to retrieve a framed photograph from her calfskin briefcase. She placed it upright before me and ordered me to study it. "You know that photograph, of course."

"It's on top of Father's chest of drawers. But it's up high. I barely could see it when I was a little kid."

"You were born uncurious. You could've asked to see this picture anytime. Do you see it now?"

"There's Father and his parents I never knew, standing beside a nun I don't know."

"Look closer at the nun."

I had seen this photograph a thousand times, but it had always struck me as a picture of my father as an impossibly callow young man standing at attention between two strangers who had died before my birth. A shadow cut across the nun's cowled, veiled face, a stick figure in her time-honored anonymity and medieval finery. Only as I studied it did my own mother's face materialize. I could almost experience a field of force drawing my parents toward each other. It was like observing a pornographic chapter of my own history that had been written in invisible ink. I felt like I was trapped in a half-told life, a world of semi-lies and baffling fractions of controversial half-truths. I was staring at a photograph I had seen every day; it nearly brought me to my knees when I realized I was privy to the translations of all its opacities and secrets for the first time. In black and white, here was proof that my mother had been a member of a convent. I was trying to unravel the complicated trigonometry of the radical thought that silence could make up the greatest lie ever told. But on that day, I was far too young and unformed to hold a thought that deep. It etherized around me as I found myself in the gunsights of my mother's withering gaze again.

"Mother," I said finally, "I never knew you were such a living doll."

"Thanks to the nth power, son."

"I did not mean it the way it sounded." I studied the photo with more attention. "You and Father were always so much older than the other kids' parents."

"I felt old when I had my first child," she said. "Much older when I had my second."

"Your second? I guess that's me."

"I guess it is," my mother answered in her blank voice, the one that didn't fire live ammunition or anything else that seemed real.

"So you just quit being a nun? I didn't know you could do that."

"You can't. Your father's going to explain it all to you. I left the job to him." She looked at her watch. "He's waiting for you now."

My father handed me two tackle boxes, our favorite rods and reels, and a bucket of live bait I had caught by casting a shrimp net into the estuarine lake off Lockwood Boulevard, a lake that flooded our backyard during heavy spring tides. We walked down to the harbor. He untied the ropes on the mooring of the city dock where we kept a small fishing bateau. Father pulled the starter of the modest fifteen-horsepower outboard, and we moved out toward the center of the Ashley River, which formed the western border of the Charleston peninsula. Both of us baited up and cast our lines on opposite sides of the boat as the moon appeared in the east, as bright as a spoon.

The Ashley was a hiding place and a workshop and a safe house for my father and me to be alone with each other, to bask in the pleasure of each other's company, and to cure all the hurts the world brought to us. At first we fished wordlessly and let the primal silence of the river translate us into no more than drifting shapes. The tide was a poem that only time could create, and I watched it stream and brim and make its steady dash homeward, to the ocean. The sun was sinking fast, and a laundry line full of cirrus clouds stretched along the western sky like boas of white linen, then surrendered to a shiver of gold that haloed my father's head. The river held the gold shine for a brief minute, then went dark as the moon rose up behind us. In silence, we fished as father and son, each watching his line.

In the pale light, my father was a luminous silhouette, an emperor incised on a strange coin. With the movement of tides and the stillness of gentle fathers and the heartache one felt in the death of hot Charleston days, the Atlantic called out to us. Fishing gave me time to think and to pray and to sit with the man who had rarely raised his voice to me in my entire childhood. Because he was a scientist, his method of being a father was explanatory, and he made being his son feel like a tutorial. Even during the terrible time of Steve's death, my father never employed a tone that did not convey a respect for every part of my boyhood. When I went crazy in the days following Steve's funeral, he considered it the most natural thing in the world. Though I was now entering a time when I could not remember what my brother looked or sounded like, I could study my father's face and see my brother sitting in the boat with us. His face was tender in repose, yet it often carried a haunted look, when I could tell that he was thinking of Steve too. His lips would grow thin, as though they were drawn with a ruler. His cheekbones were high and prominent, and though his eyebrows were thick, they were symmetrical and matched the strong curve of his nose. His glasses, as thick as mine, overemphasized his mahogany-brown eyes. He was a thoughtful man with a streak of mischievousness and an obsessive love of my mother. This fishing trip was arranged for him to tell me about it, and I waited for it to grow dark enough for him to talk. Only after dark did my father tell me the things that really mattered, and it had been on such a night, when I was a small child, and with Steve in the boat, that he had paused and reflected on the glories of the Charleston sunset, bathed in crimson, and sighed: "Ah. Boys. Behold: the Mansion on the River."

We were starting later tonight, the red drained from the horizon, the sky metal blue as we drifted near the docks of the coast guard base. I handed my father my fishing pole, grabbed the oars, and moved us back toward the middle of the river. I straightened the boat as we began our drifting passage before the houses along the Battery. They were lit up like theaters, and we could hear the voices of families talking on their verandas and porches. Downriver, a chamber orchestra was warming up before a small crowd that had gathered in White Point Gardens, which at this distance sounded like the conversation of field mice. Twice we dropped anchor, then floated toward Fort Sumter.

"Tell me about the phone call from Sister Scholastica, son," Father asked as we anchored for the third time.

"It wasn't much. She hit me with the news that she had attended a convent with my mother. I was surprised, that's all."

"After Steve," my father said, then had to catch himself and get his voice back. "After Steve, your mother always insisted that we remain silent about the early part of her life. Steve knew something about it, but not much. We wanted to emphasize us as a family, not your mother's life before we married."

"Don't you think it's a bit weird?"

"No. Like the moon up there, Leo, every life goes through different phases. It's part of natural law. And before we were together, the phase your mother went through was her years as an ordained nun. Granted, it lasted a long time. But still, you'd have to classify it as a phase."

"It explains everything. Jesus Christ, I've been raised by a nun! I bet that's why I call her Mother and you Father. Right? Here we are living in the middle of Mama and Daddy land, 'the South,' and I go around sounding like Prince Charles by saying 'Mother dear.' "

"Nothing wrong with that," my father, not my daddy, explained.

"She looks like a nun, acts like a nun, talks like a nun, and breathes like a nun. I was raised under false pretenses. Kids my age have always thought I was weird, and they've been right. Something's always been a little off about me."

"I think you've been perfect in every way."

"You're prejudiced."

"That's my job."

"The fact that I was raised by a nun and didn't even know it explains why I've been an altar boy for an early-morning Mass for practically my whole life. Why we say an endless rosary before we go to bed each night. I mean, c'mon, Father, what is it about the Hail Mary you don't get the first thousand times you pray it? I'd like to dig up whoever invented the rosary and desecrate their bones."

He chuckled, then paused and grew serious again. "The rosary is a spiritual discipline, Leo. It brings us close to God."

"It's a bore," I said, then added, "and a pain in the ass."

"Your language, son."

"Sorry. How'd you meet Mother? She said you'd tell me the story."

"It's a nice story." He said it with infinite shyness. "The very best a man like me could hope to have."

"What do you mean, 'a man like you'?"

He said, "You know what I mean: a homely man. An ugly man."

"Why do you think you're ugly?"

He grinned. "Next time you're near my bathroom, walk in and look around. I happen to own a mirror."

"You're not ugly, Father!"

"Then I need to buy a new mirror. Mine keeps lying to me."

He laughed at his own joke before pulling the rope and starting the engine again as I hauled in the anchor. Our eyes watched the families in the generous houses facing the river. We saw a ballerina practicing in an upstairs studio, two roller skaters moving without effort down the Battery seawall, sliding as though on ice, their hands behind their backs. Bicycles moved along the streets with headlights as dull as flashlights lighting their ways. Killing the motor as we drew opposite the Fort Sumter Hotel, we watched men order from menus by the glow of candlelight. Lovers promenaded the length and breadth of the Battery, some couples stopping to kiss at the exact point where the Ashley and the Cooper met to form Charleston's fragrant harbor.

We baited our hooks and cast our lines. "I knew your mother my whole life, Leo," Father said, "but I didn't even begin to know her until we were juniors at Bishop Ireland and I saw her sunbathing on a floating dock off a plantation on James Island. This was the summer of 1937, and the whole world was about to change. I was early to the party. Like you, I didn't date much in high school. I'm not sure I was as shy as you are, but it's a possibility. I was tongue-tied when a girl was waiting for me to talk. Something about seeing your mother on that dock changed all that. Something broke inside me and I felt a million words tumble out, and I ran down that plantation lawn toward that dock. On that run, I decided that I wanted to marry your mother."

"Oh, c'mon. Nothing happens that fast!"

"Who's telling this story?" He described my mother's pale blue bathing suit, her pretty legs and figure, and his surprise when she stood up and dove into the salt creek just before he arrived at his destiny. Backstroking against the tide, my mother saw him silhouetted in sunlight and asked, "Jasper, where is your bathing suit? We could go swimming together."

He grabbed an inner tube from the dock, removed his shoes, and dove into the water fully clothed, a gesture he considered the most romantic and spontaneous of his life. "Have you gone crazy or something, Jasper?"

My mother squealed with laughter as he replied, "Something like that. Crazy for you, I think."

"You've ruined your clothes!"

"My clothes'll be fine. But I'd like you to pitch in some money to help me replace a watch and a perfectly good leather wallet."

"That's what you get for taking leave of your senses, Jasper King."

"If you could see the way you looked from up there on that lawn, you'd know why I got a little jumpy, Lindsay Weaver."

"Looked? What do you mean, how I looked?"

"You looked like the queen of the world."

Drifting toward Charleston, she said, "I think I like that answer, Jasper King. I think I like it very much."

Staring at each other across the diameter of that inner tube, the couple began to tell each other the stories of their lives, the ones that really mattered, the ones that remain secret until the right boy comes around the corner, or the perfect girl comes walking down the street. Taking turns, they told tales of their innocent lives that defined who they were.

By the time Jasper's father had come by boat to retrieve the two swimmers, Jasper and Lindsay were in love and didn't care who knew it. Both their classmates and their families joked about their elopement at sea when they returned to the gathering sunburned and unable to take their eyes off each other. When a storm hit that evening, they remained on the dock holding hands as the entire party observed them from the dry safety of the plantation manor house, while the lashing winds leaned into the palmettos and worried the live oaks along the river's edge. The rain came in heavy sheets, and Lindsay and Jasper still sat holding hands, oblivious to the world and to the party playing out behind them. They talked to each other as though they had just discovered speech. Neither Lindsay nor Jasper had ever had a real boyfriend or girlfriend, and both expressed the thought that they had been waiting their whole lives for this day to happen. No one who saw them that day ever thought that Lindsay or Jasper would ever marry anyone else.

If you're deeply religious—and my parents were back then and still were as I sat with my father in the boat—you would have to know that they thought it was God who arranged that chance encounter. They were simply following His inexorable design for how He wanted their lives to be lived. During that summer, my mother and father thought they were living the greatest love story ever written.

A quiet man, my father spoke to me of his courtship of my mother as though he were praying. He kept his eyes fastened on the line that disappeared into the black waters and chose his words with care. Before this tell-all night, I had barely known that my parents had been teenagers together. They had been older than the parents of my peers, and had once been mistaken for my grandparents. As I fished and listened and took in my father's words, I realized he was introducing me to a passionate young couple I never dreamed existed.

That June, Jasper got a job at Berlin's clothing store. He ate Sunday dinner with the Weaver family after Mass each weekend. During that magical summer, Lindsay and Jasper would walk through Charleston's trimmed, ethereal parks and churchyards and avenues, talking about their bright future as husband and wife. They would walk holding hands from one end of the Battery to the other, waving to the freighters putting out to sea. Once, Jasper climbed a magnolia tree searching out the perfect blossom as an accessory for my mother's jet-black hair. When he pinned it in her hair and she caught her reflection in the side mirror of a parked Buick, they declared it their favorite flower and promised they would get married only when they could cover the altar with magnolias. Another night, they decided to kiss in front of all their favorite Charleston houses and almost didn't make it home for Lindsay's curfew.

"I don't get it," I said. "How did all this kissing lead to the convent?"

He chuckled. "I'm getting to that part."

Since Jasper and Lindsay were both daily communicants, they would meet on the steps of the cathedral every morning of the early Mass. Jasper had never known anyone, male or female, to surrender himself or herself to the transforming power of prayer the way his beloved did every single morning. She accepted the Eucharist in complete rapture as a feast shared with the godhead. She yielded to its mysteries with a submission that permitted no contention or rivalry. Where Jasper found impasses and obstacles that stood in the way of harmony with the spiritual world, Lindsay found its access easy. Jasper's view of Catholicism was simple— his job was to accept the Church's teaching and to attempt to live a good and decent life. Lindsay believed with all her heart that sainthood was the only logical pursuit of a good Christian. Not only did she want to join Christ in his suffering during his crisis in Gethsemane, she wished it to be a place with her footprints all over the garden, a refuge to which she could run barefooted with her arm outstretched to her Lord in agony. It was not just faith that Lindsay Weaver brought to the altar rail each day, it was a complete immersion and a perfect affinity with its mysteries. Jasper's love did not stand a chance against such immovable faith.

In the following school year, Jasper King lost Lindsay Weaver. In September, a young priest named Maxwell Sadler, fresh from his ordination in Rome, came to the Cathedral of St. John the Baptist to begin his vocation as a parish priest and a teacher of religion at Bishop Ireland High School. In the Catholic world, the priest's sermon at Sunday Mass was the only part of the service rendered in English. But it might as well have been spoken in Sanskrit for all the spiritual nourishment it provided. When it came to their homilies, there was nothing living that a Catholic priest could not put to sleep.

Maxwell Sadler changed that perception forever in the diocese of

Charleston. Jasper and Lindsay were sitting together when the strikingly handsome young priest strode to the pulpit to deliver his first sermon. For a long moment, he stared out at the congregation and waited until there was discomfort and fidgeting at this silence. Then, at that moment, he roared out: "Johnny Jones went to church every single Sunday." There was another long pause, a wait, and Father Max finished his couplet. "Johnny Jones went to hell for what he did on Monday."

The new priest spoke in tongues of Southern fire and began to fill the cathedral. In the first months of his priesthood, he drew down the jealousy of Bishop Rice, who found his preaching vain and somehow sinister. When he began to teach the seniors of Bishop Ireland that September, he called his course Theology 101, and he changed the way each of his students thought about their relationship to their loving God. It was like having a matinee idol put his handprint on your soul. It was Maxwell Sadler who first admitted to Lindsay that he believed she had received a call to the sisterhood. He told her he knew a perfect convent of a teaching order in North Carolina that she could attend. He insisted that he'd had a vision and witnessed the ceremony in which she took the veil.

Secretly, without telling Jasper, Lindsay applied and was accepted as a novice at the convent in Belmont, North Carolina.

Father Sadler also tried to talk my father into taking a long, serious look at the priesthood. In his innocence, my father told Father Sadler that he had already committed his life to marrying my mother and raising a good Catholic family.

On the Christmas break of their senior year, Lindsay broke up with Jasper and announced her intention to enter the convent the following June, after her graduation. He did not take the news well. He said things to Lindsay that he would be ashamed of for the rest of his life, and it all came back to him in a rush of emotion as we fished together in the Ashley River. He had accused her of leading him on and ruining his life for nothing but the most selfish reasons. For hours, he begged and pleaded with her to change her mind, but to no avail. For a month afterward, they did not speak to each other and could not even bear to catch each other's eyes as they passed in the hallways of Bishop Ireland.

Force of habit brought them together at the cathedral, and eventually their friendship survived the ordeal of their blasted love affair. At times,

Jasper's bitterness would rise up between them, but she would bring him back down to her by reminding him of his own devotion to the same God to whom she was surrendering her life and their future. When Lindsay left her family for Belmont, she asked that Jasper do her the favor of delivering her to the convent steps. He accepted with graciousness and resignation. On the morning of June 16, 1938, he drove the back roads, and they entered the convent grounds at nightfall. Lindsay had packed very little: all the worldly possessions she would need fit in the smallest of bags.

They both got out of the car, and Jasper lingered behind as she walked up and rang a bell that could be heard throughout the convent. A sister answered the door and made a motion for Lindsay to enter, where two other nuns awaited to ship her down a long hallway. Her new life was starting.

"Are you Jasper?" the first nun asked.

"Yes, Sister. I'm Jasper."

"She wrote me about you," the nun said. "My name is Sister Mary Michele. I am the mother superior here."

"Could I come to visit Lindsay? Not often, just every once in a while?"

"That doesn't sound like a good idea," Sister Michele said.

"Can I write her?"

"You can if you wish," the nun said. "I can't promise they'll be delivered. She belongs to this order now."

"Then can I do something for the convent? Is there anything you need? I could buy it for you."

The nun thought about it, then said, "Soap. We could use some soap for the sisters to bathe with."

The next day, Jasper drove into Charlotte and cut a deal with a manager of Belk department store to have ten boxes of a simple but elegant women's hand soap sent to the Convent of the Sacred Heart. In her first note to him, Sister Michele revealed to Jasper that the gift had been controversial from the start, some of the older nuns thinking the soap far too luxurious for convent use. But Sister Michele had reasoned with them and explained the nature of the gift as well as the sin of wastefulness and the importance of cleanliness in the convent's daily life.

It began an annual pilgrimage for Jasper King. He would show up at the convent door on June 16 of each year and ask Sister Mary Michele if he could visit with Lindsay, who had undergone her metamorphosis into Sister Mary Norberta. Though my father's visit often caught Sister Michele off guard, she was a practical woman.

"What does the convent require this year?" Jasper asked the mother superior one year.

"Laundry detergent," Sister Michele said, and the next day a year's supply of detergent arrived at the convent's delivery door at the backside of the building. The following year it was floor polish, the next year hand towels, and the next year shoe polish.

A small but important friendship sprang up between Jasper and Sister Michele, and they began to look forward to their June 16 encounters. She would give Jasper reports on Norberta's progress, and one time Sister Michele said, "She's got more natural talent than any young woman I've ever seen at this convent."

These reports both pleased Jasper and filled him with dread. Each time he approached the pretty convent, he hoped to find Lindsay waiting for him on the front steps, holding her small bag and wearing the same dress as the one she wore on the trip up from Charleston. Jasper wanted to see Lindsay rushing into his arms, declaring that it had all been an unfortunate misunderstanding.

That first September, he entered the gates of The Citadel, following in the footsteps of his father and grandfather, pleasing his family immensely. But he was well aware that he chose to attend The Citadel only because he had never taken the time to form a plan of his life that did not include Lindsay. He became a physics major, and soon understood that he was subject to the laws of inertia like all other objects on earth, and that Lindsay's abandonment had set him in motion toward an unplanned though ineluctable destiny. He found it easy to surrender himself to the codes of discipline of The Citadel, fell in love with the natural order of the regiment, and took a young man's pleasure in the care of uniforms, in marching in step to the beating of drums and the calling of cadence. As the convent was a hermitage of women devoted to prayer, The Citadel became a priesthood for Jasper. That priesthood turned into a caste of warriors on December 7, 1941, when the Japanese attacked Pearl Harbor.

When Jasper took his physical for the army, he had memorized the eye chart used by military optometrists and so passed the vision test with a perfect score. He entered the war as a second lieutenant and fought with distinction in the European theater, entered Normandy in the third wave on D-day, took part in the liberation of Paris, and had just spent his first night in Germany when V-E Day was declared. After a year with the occupation army in Germany, he was sent home to Charleston to begin his real life without Lindsay. Jasper had written her a letter once a week all during the war, but she had never seen a single one. Sister Mary Michele prided herself in possessing more than a layman's knowledge of human nature, and she could feel Jasper's love for Lindsay pulsing in every line. So she had kept the letters from the young woman.

During the war, Jasper insisted that his father appear at the doorway of the Sacred Heart convent every June 16 and ask Sister Michele about their needs for the coming year. My grandfather did not enjoy the commission, but he did it because he was superstitious enough that he believed his son might be killed in battle if he refused to perform a charitable act for a convent full of nuns. As requested, my grandfather honored the anniversary of Lindsay's delivery to her vocation and appeared without fail on the afternoon of June 16. On the battlefields of Europe, Jasper received four brief thank-you notes from Sister Michele and assurances that the young Sister Norberta was a rising star.

Her superiors were quick to identify Lindsay's intellect, and after taking the veil, she enrolled in Catholic University. In a rigorous accelerated program, she completed her work for her doctorate in English literature and already began writing her dissertation on *Ulysses*. On her first reading, she had discovered that the novel's action all took place on a single day, June 16, 1904. Because it was the same day that Jasper had driven her to the convent to begin her life in the sisterhood, the date acquired a magical significance to Lindsay. Often, she would think about Jasper. She knew from her parents that he was part of the war in Europe, and she prayed for his safe return as she took Communion every morning. When she received word from Sister Michele that Jasper had survived the war, it convinced her further that the power of prayer was a natural, unimpeachable force for good in the universe. In her heart, she believed it was her prayers and entreaties that had brought Jasper safely home from Europe.

He returned to Charleston, got a job teaching science at Bishop Ireland High School, and moved into his old room at his parents' house on Rutledge Avenue. He limited his social life to an occasional date with a new teacher at Bishop Ireland, or with the sisters of his classmates at The Citadel. He made an affable and at least acceptably attractive partner, and several women let him know that they were ready for a serious commitment if he had finally been cured of his famous case of puppy love. Whenever the subject came up, he made fun of himself for his constant infatuation with a woman who had made herself unavailable to any man. But he had promised himself he would never marry a woman unless he felt exactly like he had when he floated, fully clothed, on an inner tube caught in the tidal currents of Charleston Harbor when he was seventeen years old. He knew exactly what love was and how it was supposed to feel.

In the summer of 1949, he bought a two-acre lot on the saltwater lake along the Ashley River that was separated from the river by Lockwood Boulevard. With the help of friends, he built a two-story brick home that added little to the architectural significance of his city. The house was as functional and as homely as a Catholic church built in the Charleston suburbs of that era. He built a working science lab in an upstairs room in the back of the house, and even his mother teased him for building a five-bedroom house for what was likely to remain a bachelor pad. But Jasper had developed a long-range plan that he thought would take some of the sting out of bachelorhood and help with the mortgage payments: he invited other young bachelors teaching at the high school to rent rooms from him, and he always had at least three male teachers living there. He remembered it as a happy time because there was a house party almost every weekend, and the laughter of young men and women dancing together was a kind of music that the house needed badly.

Several of these young men became some of the best friends Jasper made in a lifetime rich in friendships. Even Father Maxwell Sadler spent six months in an upstairs bedroom after an electrical fire damaged his rectory. Jasper did not charge the priest for rent, and he was sorry when

Father Max moved back to the rectory when the repairs were finished. Few of his other housemates knew of his deep love of Lindsay, and he felt free to talk of his unquenchable love for her with Father Max. With infinite patience, Father Max never tried to talk Jasper out of his constancy toward Lindsay; instead, he introduced him to other pretty young Catholic girls whom he met in his work.

Because of Jasper's bachelorhood, false rumors of homosexuality made their way along the corridors of Bishop Ireland, which Jasper did little to eliminate as he resigned himself to a single life. After his first years back in the city, there were fewer and fewer sightings of Jasper at cotillion balls or dinners with eligible young women in downtown restaurants or in the back rows of the Dock Street Theatre. A fellow English teacher asked Jasper to cruise a gay bar with him one weekend, and Jasper never spoke a civil word to that colleague again. Instead, he grew more inward with the passage of each year, more judgmental and pietistic and rigid, and young teachers stopped being comfortable renting rooms in his house.

Living alone did not prove beneficial to Jasper, and his habits began to turn slowly into noticeable eccentricities. He took the effects of loneliness to heart, but failed to note the corrosion of his sunny personality. The silences of his house caused him to reflect and despair of a life that might have been perfect. Still, he wrote to his beloved nun once a week, and sent the letters to the convent in care of Sister Michele. He would sometimes tell himself it was high time that he met and fell in love with another woman, but the falseness of the words tortured him. Writing his former girlfriend, he invented stories of beach parties, sailing trips to Bermuda, art openings, a planned summer trip to Europe, the purchase of a golden retriever, a fishing trip to the Gulf of Mexico, a spiritual retreat to Mepkin Abbey, and a hundred other remarkable events that never happened. His letters were pure fiction. My father may have been the first man in history who lived in fear of boring a nun.

On June 16 of every year, he kept his appointment with Sister Michele in Belmont. One year, Jasper brought fifty pounds of fresh iced-down shrimp that he had collected off a shrimp boat at Shem Creek. Another year, he unloaded a hundred small azalea plants that he had cultivated and grown in a makeshift greenhouse in the back of his house. Always, Jasper brought bushels of fresh tomatoes, cucumbers, and corn from a farm on Wadmalaw Island. He brought boiled peanuts and jars of jellies, chutneys, and preserves he had put up himself. The mother superior enjoyed the young man's sense of humor and the romantic hopelessness of the cause he pursued in spite of the fact that she offered him no encouragement and would not allow him to broach the subject of his former girlfriend. Sister Michele never told him that Sister Norberta had not been in residence at the convent since 1940 and was spending that summer teaching literature at the University of Notre Dame. Nor did she once reveal that convent rules forbade her to deliver his letters to his former love. But she did break a convent rule by saving the letters and keeping them boxed in her office, tied with a white ribbon. That she saved his letters bothered her not at all. But that she had read every one of them with avidity and even pleasure, she considered a kind of minor-league sin.

On June 16, 1948, she treated Jasper to lunch at a downtown Charlotte restaurant famous for its steak. During the meal, he asked, "What does the convent need this year, Sister?"

The nun laughed. "You won't believe this, Jasper. But we need hand soap."

"That's what I gave you the first time I met you," he said. "You gals need to bathe more."

When Jasper left her that day, Sister Michele surprised him by kissing him lightly on the cheek and thanked him for all he had done for the convent over the years. The kiss was a strangeness and a kindness, and he had an entire year to interpret its meaning. At the high school, an accidental fire set by an incompetent student shut down his chemistry lab. His mother began showing the first signs of dementia, and his father was diagnosed with cancer of the larynx. He moved back home to care for his parents, and he rented his house to four bachelors who taught in various high schools. His house became infamous for hosting the wildest parties in the city. But he was too busy to care, and for the first time he almost forgot his June 16 appointment at the Convent of the Sacred Heart.

Eleven years after Jasper had delivered Lindsay Weaver to the door, a younger nun he had never seen before motioned for him to follow her to the visitors' room after he informed her that he had an appointment with the mother superior. The young nun nodded and moved out of the room, as silent as wood smoke.

Another nun appeared at the top of the stairs leading to the visitors' room. Sunlight poured through a Palladian window and framed the outline of the nun, who moved too gracefully to be Sister Michele.

The sunlight now hit the lenses of Jasper's glasses, blinding him. Squinting, he said to the figure on the stairs, "I was expecting my old friend, Sister Michele."

"Sister Michele died of a stroke over a month ago," the nun said. "I've been selected as the acting superior of the convent. That's why I'm meeting you here today."

"Why didn't anyone get in touch with me?" Jasper asked.

"Her death was very sudden and unexpected."

He said, "I'm so sorry. I'd grown close to Sister Michele." Still blinded by the bright sun, he turned his head, removed his glasses, and began cleaning them with a white handkerchief.

"Even though you can't see me clearly, don't you know my voice, Jasper?" the acting mother superior asked. She moved out of the sun and into the shadow of that funereal room where visitors and family members summoned the nuns of their lives from the mysterious upstairs hideaways. When Jasper saw her face, he fell to his knees and howled like a wounded animal. His shriek brought nuns running from all corners of the convent. Sister Norberta was now in the unenviable position of explaining why this out-of-control man had gotten to his knees in front of her. Sister Michele had been the only one who knew the whole story of this love-struck weeping man.

"Should I call the police?" asked the young nun who had led Jasper to this room.

"No, of course not. This is Jasper King. He makes a large donation to the convent each year. I just told him about the death of our good Sister Michele. They were close friends."

"Then should I call a priest?" asked another nun.

"No, no, Jasper will be fine. Can someone bring us a glass of iced tea? Do you still like sweet tea, Jasper?"

Several nuns helped Jasper to his feet and into a chair; his body appeared boneless and weightless. When the tea came, it seemed to revive him, and he thanked the nun who brought it. He was disoriented and now extremely mortified over the spectacle he had made. Quietly, the other nuns slipped out of sight.

"Sorry, Lindsay. I mean Sister Norberta," he stammered. "I'd given up all chances of ever seeing you again. You caught me off guard."

"Off guard, Jasper?" She laughed. "I guess I did. I had no idea you had such a theatrical side."

"Neither did I," he said, and they both laughed.

In our small boat, in the tangy, salt-brimmed air, I reeled in a nice-sized bass as my father described his elation at seeing Lindsay Weaver again.

"So you didn't recognize her?" I asked when I realized he was too overwhelmed to continue.

"She was in the light," he said finally. "The light came over her shoulder into my eyes."

"But her voice?"

"I wasn't expecting ever to hear it again. Nothing had prepared me for this encounter, Leo. I'd reconciled myself to never seeing her again. Didn't even know I'd done it. But I had."

"What did Mother say?" I asked. "After you settled down?"

Reeling in his line, my father put another live shrimp on his hook before casting it over toward James Island in a smooth, athletic motion. Then he continued his story.

As they sat in armchairs that faced each other, Jasper studied Sister Norberta's face and found himself dismayed that eleven years of separation from this woman had done nothing to dampen his boyish ardor for her. Lindsay's beauty had deepened with age and with the contemplative life she had chosen.

"I never got over you, Lindsay," he said.

"Please call me Sister Norberta."

"I never got over you, Sister Norberta."

"I know that, Jasper," she said. "Sister Michele told me about your visits. At first, she disapproved of you greatly. But she softened over the years. You got to her, Jasper, by your persistence, your generosity toward the convent, and your kindness. She began to cherish your yearly visits. And she loved your letters."

"Did you ever see any of them?"

"Not when they were written. But last summer, Sister Michele and I were on retreat together. A forest near the retreat house had beautiful pathways, and we'd take long walks. She started talking about you. She told me that she felt I had never really belonged in the convent. That night, she gave me the box containing your letters."

"Did you read them?"

"Yes, Jasper. I read every one of them."

"What did you think?"

"I'll have an answer for you someday. Not today. But soon, I promise."

Already Lindsay had initiated the convoluted and Byzantine process of being released from the vows of sisterhood. Her decision pleased no one, and she had to convince the head of her order in America of her seriousness, who forwarded that request to the order's headquarters in Europe, who passed it along to the world of men and all the way to the offices of the Pope himself. To Lindsay, the pace seemed snail-like and agonizing. But for her time and place in a church locked into the embers of its immovable laws, Lindsay's deliverance from her vows arrived in a timely manner. The See of Rome, exhausted by the travails of World War II, was dealing with the broken Catholic soul of a ruined Europe. It had little energy to waste on a Southern nun who had discovered late that she had other fish to fry. Her letter of manumission was signed by Pope Pius XII himself.

Lindsay Weaver was wearing the same clothes when Jasper King picked her up in the fall of 1949. In a small ceremony, they were married at the main altar of St. John the Baptist and Father Maxwell Sadler performed the ceremony with all the panache for which he had become so famous in the diocese of Charleston. Stephen Dedalus King was born ten months later in 1950, and I was born in 1951. Jasper's patience had earned him, at last, the love of his life.

"The wind is picking up, Leo," Father said. "Let's get back to the marina."

We reeled in our lines. I took care of the gear as my father cranked the boat and we made our way back up the river, the small motor strumming against the tide.

Trailing my hand in the warm saltwater, I tried to think of the strangeness of time when I was not a part of it; how unimaginable a world denied the coiled, itchy presence of Leo King. Yet my father had permitted my entry into a landscape where mothers were cloistered and celibate and fathers were handed back to lives of solitude, even bitterness. A week ago, I would have written out my autobiography and not even come close to approaching its central truth. If the beginning of knowledge is when you discover more gargoyles than realities in your past, then my father and I had spent a long and fruitful night together on the Ashley River.

At the marina, we tied up our boat and gathered our gear, treated our rods and reels properly, and cleaned the fish we had caught with dispatch and expertise; Father made a fetish out of performing tasks the correct way. There was an efficiency and economy of his motions that I always found a pleasure to watch and a pain to mimic. When we walked across Lockwood Boulevard and returned to the house, I walked to my mother's bedroom and knocked on the door as my father stacked the fish in the freezer. Not unbelievably, she was reading *Ulysses*.

"Did you catch any fish?" she asked, laying the dog-eared book on her bedside table.

"It was a good night," I said, going in and lying down beside her. I am not an affectionate boy by nature, and this was a rare gesture for me.

She put her arm around me and I nestled my face against her shoulder, a rarity for a woman not famous for her affectionate nature, either.

"Thanks for leaving the convent, Mother," I said. "You did a hard thing."

She did not say anything for a moment, then asked, "Why do you say that?"

"Because I know you. I bet you were happy in the convent. You felt safe there."

"I wanted to be a wife. I longed to be a mother. I wanted it all. Or thought I did."

"You didn't know about things like Steve," I said.

"I never wanted to know about things like Steve. We almost lost you because of Steve. Your father and I almost lost each other."

My father came into the room and could not hide his happiness in finding me in my mother's arms. "I'll leave you two alone."

"I was just going to bed," I said, jumping up.

"Good night, Leo," Mother said.

My father grabbed me and kissed me and said, "Good night, sweet pea."

"Night, Father." Smiling, I couldn't help myself: "Good night, Sister Mary Norberta." I escaped the room before the copy of *Ulysses,* flung at my head, hit my parents' door as I ran laughing to my room.

CHAPTER 6

Dear Old Dad

I lay in the darkness of the room, going over the events of the past week, amazed at their variety and complexity. The forces I had encountered during the week began to materialize as I set my clock for 4:30 A.M. In the country of dreams, I began my nightly voyage. Steve was there, as he always was. I got to tell him about the orphans, the twins across the street, the black football coach and his sullen son, the lunch at the yacht club, the fishing trip, and our mother's convent days. I woke when I heard screaming and crying and my father at my door, turning on the light. "Get up, Leo. There's trouble across the street."

I put on pants and a T-shirt and Docksiders. I reached for my glasses and rushed out of my room and encountered a sobbing Sheba Poe, her dazed brother, and their half-drunken mother. In the living room, my mother opened a gun cabinet, handed my father his shotgun and then me mine, the one I had inherited from her father. Goofy from the lack of sleep, my father slipped shells into the chamber of his weapon. I caught the box of shells Mother threw my way one-handed and was loading as my father said, "Someone's breaking into the Poes' house."

"We came here because we don't know anybody else," Trevor Poe said, his voice despairing.

"He's found us again, Mama," Sheba screamed at her mother.

"He always finds us," she muttered, half-coherently.

My mother in her nightgown was running for the telephone to call the police as Father and I raced out of the house in darkness. There were times I hated being Southern, other times I reveled in it, and this was one of the latter. Since my parents had wanted me skilled in the ways of the woods and streams, I could work a shotgun the way a majorette handled a baton. My gun was a comfort as I followed my father and we circled the Poes' house, watching for movement and listening for sound. We found no signs of forced entry. We made our way through old growths of azalea and camellia bushes, then came to the front door as sirens bloomed overhead all throughout the city. My mother had not just called the cops, but the chief of police, whose daughters she taught.

It was my father who saw the odd, grotesque sign painted on the front door—a smiley face painted in a large, scrawling hand, seemingly in blood. It had a single tear coming out of its left eye. My father got out a handkerchief and removed a small drop of it and put it to his nose.

"Fingernail polish," he said. The cop cars hit the yard like landing craft, and officers spread all over the house and yard. Father grabbed my shotgun and whispered, "You're still on probation, son."

"Forgot," I whispered back.

Neighbors began to drift out on their first- and second-story piazzas, sleep-dazed and curious. One police car had parked in front of our house, and I saw a policeman interviewing Trevor and Sheba and their mother. Belle Faircloth walked down the length of the street and reported seeing a stranger in a white car parked near Colonial Lake for two straight nights. The man was a chain-smoker and had blondish hair, but she could provide no other physical description. A basement window had been broken and the Poes' house entered beneath an untrimmed hedge. For more than three hours the police scoured the house for clues or explanations, but they could find nothing moved or disturbed or stolen. Only the grotesque smiley face painted on the front door merited their attention.

When the police left, my father and I returned home exhausted by the emotional night we had shared. Mother poured a shot of bourbon for her and my father, and made a cup of hot chocolate for me. As we sat at the kitchen table whispering about the events of the night, my mother motioned upstairs and said she had put the Poe family to bed in the extra rooms my father had once rented out.

"Something terrible has happened to that family," she said quietly. "Something traumatic. They think someone came to that house to kill them."

"Not likely," my father said. "It might be a random break-in."

"Leo," Mother said, "be nice to these kids. Be as nice as you can, but don't let them into your heart. You don't know how mean the world can be. You're so innocent, you don't know the dangers."

"Were you scared tonight, Leo?" Father asked as I finished my hot chocolate.

"Terrified." I stood up to return to bed.

"You didn't show it," Mother said.

"That's because my father was with me."

It was just after three when I went back to bed and the neighborhood was quiet again. Sleep came easily. I had traveled far into a dream when I felt a girl's lips touch mine, and I saw a naked Sheba Poe move into bed beside me. I had never been on a date or alone with a girl in a car, yet here I found myself naked with the most beautiful girl I had ever seen, her hands moving up and down my body. Slowly, she brought my lips to her breasts, then she took my hand and placed it inside her, and I learned how a woman could smell like earth; that her wetness felt like a place where fire could be born and brought to sublime life. Her tongue went down my throat and my chest and she taught me in minutes all the places a tongue could go, all the places I had ever dreamed a tongue could go. When I entered her I did it with her direction; I had never imagined the pleasure one body could derive from another. On top of me, she rose and pitched like a small well-made boat in a storm-tossed river as her hair came over her shoulders in soft, hot waves. She kept thanking me in a throaty whisper. When she came to me I was dreaming, then she pulled me into a life that was far greater and more sublime than any dream could be. After I came inside her, with her hand over my mouth to keep me from screaming, she slid out of my bed and disappeared into the night. Wordlessly, I lay awake, intoxicated by the life I was starting to live. As the sun rose out of the east, I thought of nothing but Sheba. Later that morning, I thought of her face with every copy of the *News and Courier* I threw onto the porches of Charleston. It would be years before I learned that my mother had witnessed Sheba Poe's withdrawal from my room that night. And my mother was not the only one.

On Sunday evenings, my parents made a domestic tradition of sitting on the screened porch off their bedroom to watch the sun set over Long Lake and the Ashley River. Though they could be steely-edged and ruminant to a fault about the life of the mind, I found them both loopy and unapologetic about their own sappy romanticism when it came to their love for each other. Whenever they put on their Johnny Mathis or Andy Williams albums after dinner on Sunday, it was time for me to skedaddle to the comforting solitude of my room. It caused me a high level of anguish to know that my parents took pleasure in each other's bodies, long before I knew anything of my mother's career path as a nun. After my single night with Sheba, it seemed like an abomination. Because of the Catholic Church, I would always feel paroxysms of guilt at any thought of sex, peckers, vaginas, intercourse, and the whole shebang. The teachings of the Roman Catholic Church would cover my soul like a condom for the rest of my life. Already, I could feel nothing but guilt for luxuriating in the pleasures of Sheba Poe's heaven-sent body, even as I wrestled with a great desire to see her again and tell her honestly, sincerely, and from the very core of my being that I loved her. It was an essential truth that I had been too thunderstruck to tell her that night; one that now shouted to be told. Loving her would square the guilt, ease my conscience, and go a long way in that futile Catholic exercise of Making Things Right.

My guilt seemed to have been contagious, as my parents called me out to the porch that morning soon after they were seated, their faces unusually serious and distressed. Facing me, Mother said, "We're worried about you, Leo. We think the Poe twins are in trouble. Your father and I are concerned about the whole situation."

I turned to my father, who was usually the voice of reason, but even he was thoughtful. "The break-in at their house the other night—it doesn't add up. Except for the broken window, the police found no sign of forced entry," he explained. "There were no footprints around the house except for yours and mine, and the mother has been so drunk they can't get a signed statement. Even the twins are vague. And that smiley face at the door? It was fingernail polish. They found the same shade in both the mother's room and Sheba's."

He paused then, till Mother prodded. "You're not telling him everything, Jasper."

"They found a bottle of the same fingernail polish in Trevor's room," Father added. "It seems he paints his toenails."

I listened with a rising fear and a wholly selfish desire to defend Sheba. "They're nice kids," I argued. "They've had a hard life."

"You don't know what a nice kid is, Leo." The sternness of my mother's voice irritated me. "You've never had a friend."

I stood up and began to pace the porch, like a lawyer at the bar defending a client. "That's not true. I had Steve, and I'll never have a better friend. I've made lots of friends in the past couple of years. Because of the drug thing, none of them are my age. That's my fault, and I'm not blaming anybody but myself. But the people I meet every day, the ones on my paper route, Harrington Canon, my shrink—they all like me. The orphans and the twins don't know about the cocaine, but I can tell they want to be friends with me. So does the coach's son, Ike, now that we're getting to know each other. You're wrong to say that I have no friends. I've spent my whole life lonely, but I've got some friends now. I plan to keep them. My whole life, I plan to keep them, and love them as long as they love me. I'll even love them if they quit loving me."

"That's our point," Mother said. "We're afraid the orphans and the Poe kids will use you."

"They won't," I said. "They need me. They need my help, just like those rich kids who got busted for drugs. Just like Coach Jefferson and Ike. I don't mind being needed. I don't even mind being used," I said, feeling a small strength that I'd picked up from Sheba, an unaccustomed boldness. "I'm sick of being lonely. I never mean to be lonely again."

I turned at that, and bolted off the porch and back into the house, half jogging to my room. Though I was close to tears, I fought them off and became resolute instead. I reached to my bedside table and pulled out a rosary, blessed by the Pope, that Monsignor Max had given me on the day of my First Communion. I tried to pray, but all the words turned to dust for me. Going to my closet, I retrieved my collection of Topps baseball cards. I kept my priceless card of Ted Williams on the top of one of the piles in the box, while Willie Mays, Hank Aaron, and Mickey Mantle crowned the other three. The box also contained the only photograph I had of my brother, Steve, and me. After his suicide, all photographs of my brother disappeared, as though his extraordinary light had not once illuminated the spirit of our household. As I lifted the photograph out, I noticed how it seemed to grow more fragile with the passing of time. But there I was in the snow-white suit of my First Communion finery with my brother's arm draped around me in a fierce, protective gesture. When my prayers rang truest to me now was when I prayed to Steve. Since his death, I had come to think of him as some fearless, irrepressible angel who watched over me, part Rottweiler, part guard at the Tomb of the Unknown Soldier, and part seer who would one day unlock the mystery of both our lives. In my worst moments, I could pray to Steve and not to the God who had stolen my brother and left me to face a terrifying world without my greatest ally by my side.

In the great timepiece that was my life, my dance card was filled up every hour, my routine as set as a well-made cake. I awoke when my alarm went off the next morning and performed my morning toilet in ritual and darkness, then pedaled my bicycle down toward Colonial Lake and watched as Eugene Haverford's *News and Courier* truck pulled up to our appointed corner and four bundles of newspapers were heaved to the sidewalk. His cigar smoke was the first proof of my being alive each morning; that, and the blood surging through my thighs and the warm air, thick as marmalade, and the first traffic sliding down Rutledge Avenue. Paper route, daily Mass, breakfast at Cleo's, five new vocabulary words: my life was overencumbered by habit.

As I took my wire cutters and freed my stacks, I breathed in the odor of fresh ink and could smell the richness of the shallow tidal broth thrown off by Colonial Lake. I worked fast to fold my papers as tight as furled flags. Inside the truck, I heard Mr. Haverford cuss the president, Mayor Gaillard, Chief of Police John Conroy, and the Atlanta Braves. Not a morning went by when Mr. Haverford did not cuss with inflammatory gusto all the major and minor players who appeared for his court of disapproval in the morning paper.

Off I went into the deep Charleston darkness, flinging the news of the world to the people of my route. Still, I thought of little but Sheba Poe, and the night she came to my room. Crossing Broad Street on the fly, I took a left on Tradd and did not work up a real sweat until I hit Legare Street. I would be back to some of these houses this very evening to collect for the delivery of next month's newspaper. I would learn the gossip and secrets and off-kilter and off-centered and off-putting history of my city. I was bound in a deep connection of appreciation and community to every reporter, editor, typesetter, secretary, ads man, publisher, columnist, and deliveryman who worked in producing the News and Courier every day. By tying my destiny with this newspaper, I had given myself permission to pursue a career I hoped to find deeply satisfying.

In a complete reverie, thinking of Sheba, I steered through the streets and could hear the mansions and the turned-in row houses whisper their stories to me. Toward the end of my route, I turned up Stoll's Alley, so I could do the south end of Church Street. In my life already, I had fallen in love with shortcuts, alleyways, secret passageways, and cut-through easements like Stoll's Alley and Longitude Lane. Often I came to Stoll's Alley because of its mystery and inwardness; its narrowness was like a form of perversity or flawed design, making it my favorite getaway in the city. The sun had not yet fully risen, and it was as dark as a confessional booth as I made my way with caution. A large man stepped suddenly out of a doorway, surprising me by blocking the lane. Then he shocked me by almost knocking me out with his fist.

The quickness of it, the brutality, and the fact that I knew an ambush had occurred frightened me to the point of paralysis. His strength awed me. His quickness and complete mastery of the attack took me a moment to comprehend. When I had recovered enough to scream, his hand covered my mouth, a hand that felt like a first baseman's mitt. Then I felt a knife at my throat, and not the fun kind of knife that kids throw at trees.

For a minute, he satisfied himself with the tactical accomplishment of his bold assault. As my eyes adjusted to the dark, I could see he wore a cheap Halloween mask with the eyeholes cut out larger. The mask was black, and I could smell spray paint. Then he whispered to me, " *'Stately, plump Buck Mulligan came from the stairhead, bearing a bowl of lather on which a mirror and a razor lay crossed.'* "

No words any stranger could utter would cause me such surprise and terror. Because of those words, I felt certain the man was going to butcher me in that alley. No one without the most intimate, diabolical knowledge of my past would know the indescribable impact those words would have on me at such a moment. I was most likely the only rising senior in the American South who realized that the man had just uttered, in a voice filled with mockery and grotesque insider knowledge, the first line of *Ulysses.*

"So, Leo, my boy, you and your parents love to go to church every morning. Isn't that nice? So goody-goody. So pious. So true to Roman Catholic doctrine."

My mind sped up, and I thought a Klansman with a college degree had tracked me down. His knife played across my jugular vein. His breath was fresh and his voice polished as I smelled a trace of Listerine as well as the scent of English Leather aftershave.

" *'Riverrun,'* Leo," the man whispered, taunting me with the first word in Joyce's silly-assed novel *Finnegans Wake.* "I could cut your mother's throat, Leo," he added. "She's alone in her office a lot. Or your father's. That's a nice little lab he has set up in the house. Or your new friend, that nigger Jefferson you work out with every morning. You choose, Leo. Which one?"

Too paralyzed to speak, I was having difficulty breathing when he continued. "Or how about you, Leo, right here in this alley? I could end your life now and no one, not even you, would know why you were killed. Or, let's get creative: suppose I dig up the bones of your brother, and you wake up one morning sleeping next to his bones? I like that one, Leo. You like it? No, I didn't think you would. Let's make a deal: I watched you fucking your new neighbor the other night. Let's not have that happen again. Is that a deal, Leo?"

I nodded my head.

"Tell anyone about what happened here, and I kill your mom and dad. I'll take my time and do it slow. Then I'll come for you. Now hold still, Leo."

There was a sudden click of a flashlight, blinding me, and the knife went away. I heard it moan back into its sheath. Then a greater fear than I had yet felt overwhelmed me as I smelled the distinctive odor of finger-nail polish and felt the man painting something on my forehead. He took his time. When he was finished, he said, "Don't move for five minutes. Promise me, Leo. Say, like Molly Bloom, *'Yes I said yes I will Yes.'* "

" 'Yes I said yes I will Yes,' " I said, strangling on my own black terror as the man rose and walked calmly down Stoll's Alley, leaving me with only the last line of *Ulysses* to keep me company.

For more than five minutes, I waited. Not until it was daylight did I move and walk my bike to Church Street. Moving toward a Mercedes-Benz parked on the street, I studied my face in the rearview mirror. My left eye was red, but it probably wouldn't blacken or close. The left lens of my glasses was shattered. But the disturbing sign was the one I was expecting—there on my forehead was the death's-head stigmata of the smiley face, with the single exaggerated tear beneath the left eye. With one of my remaining newspapers and my fingernails, I scraped off the disfigured painting on my head, then walked into a customer's spacious garden, turned on the spigot, and washed my face. Because of the threats made by the attacker, I could not tell anyone what had happened. To explain my broken glasses, I would have to fabricate an accident on my bike. I wondered what blighted, unspeakable world I had entered by accident.

My idea to entertain the twins after the frightening night they had been through was spontaneous and full of holes, but my father agreed to help me form a coherent plan. I called him from the Poes' house the day after my secret attack in the alley, and detected a quaver in his voice when I asked for his help. It was a quaver that nearly broke my heart; for in it, I could hear his eagerness to help, his earnest father's hope that even the slightest sense of happiness might be jaywalking across the street, heading in his only son's direction. He grasped my plan easily, and promised to have everything ready.

"Can I borrow your convertible, Father? The '57 Chevy." I knew I was asking a huge favor. "I'll take good care of it. I promise."

"Didn't I tell you? I don't own that car anymore, son. I got rid of it."

"When?" I was outraged. I had thought my old man would have sold my mother and me into slavery before letting his favorite car out of his sight. "Who'd you sell it to?"

"I didn't sell it to anyone. That car's too precious to sell. I'm giving it to you, son. I was always going to give it to you, but I have to wait until you get off restriction. You can borrow it; it'll be washed and ready to run when you get home."

I hung up without saying good-bye. I could not utter a word, not a single word, not at that time, not to anyone on earth. My father's approach to the world was narrow-gauged and shot through with modesty and diffidence; he lacked flashiness, boldness, and flair. Each day he approached as a formula he would study with assiduousness and solve with aplomb. His affection for swank, fast cars was an oddity for him, the one misfit sentence in a textbook of boilerplate, scientific prose. Never had he purchased a brand-new car off the lot, but waited with his granite-like patience until a car had aged enough to fall into the price range of a high school science teacher. He was now driving a black '56 Thunderbird convertible that he had pronounced a classic the moment he laid eyes on it, when it made its debut on the Charleston streets, now more than a decade earlier.

When Sheba and Trevor appeared in our yard, I was shy around Sheba. Trevor's lighthearted presence, however, made being with her a little less formidable. My father had apparently put aside his distrust of them, and seemed happy to entertain the only two people in town who had not heard the twenty-five canned jokes he carried in his measly repertoire. He chatted amiably with them while I ran to put on my bathing suit, a Citadel T-shirt, and an Atlanta Braves baseball cap Father had bought me when we caught a double-header the summer before.

When I came to the garage door, Father threw me the keys high in the air. I made the imaginary gesture of removing a catcher's mask, adjusted my glasses, and made the catch near my mother's prize camellia bushes. The twins cheered. My father bowed, then loaded a large inner tube into the backseat and instructed Trevor to hold on to it tightly as the convertible sped its way toward James Island.

"Does Mr. Ferguson know we're coming to his plantation?" I asked him.

"He does, and he knows why you're coming. I told him we'd pick up the Chevy tomorrow."

"Make sure you meet us when we make it to the Ashley," I said.

"I called Jimmy Wiggins at the marina. He's lending me his Boston Whaler. I'll be doing a little fishing when you come out of the creek."

"You fishing for whales?" Sheba asked.

"No, sweetie, that's just the name of the boat."

When I started the car, I had one great worry, but I had a plan for how to deal with it. I'd still told no one about the man in the alley, concocting a bike wreck to explain my bruised face. Since my attacker had taken on an aura of omnipotence and mystery, I worried about him following us, trailing after us like a mako shark following the scent of a wounded grouper through the grottoes of a coral reef. But if this man pursued us on this day, he would have to know the streets of Charleston as well as I did. I was both a native of the city and a paperboy to boot, so a map had imprinted itself on my brain.

I gunned the car down Lockwood Boulevard, then made a sharp right and shot through the streets beside the city's hospital before swinging left on Ashley Boulevard, checking my rearview mirror as I turned sharply down each street. By the time I reached the Savannah highway, I was certain we were not being followed, and I relaxed and joined the twins in their animated conversation as I turned south, psycho-free and happy to be a teenage boy, at long last.

I was light-headed as I listened to the twins talk nonsense. Trevor leaned between us from the backseat. When he felt me relax, he invited me into their country of delicious, ridiculous banter. In the life I had lived, the free-flowing chatter of teenagers was unfamiliar. I found it joyous and liberating as we made our way across the Ashley River Bridge and headed out toward Folly Beach Road.

"Leo, it's my thought that Sheba should marry Elvis Presley next year."

"Isn't Elvis married?" I asked.

"A mere inconvenience. One glimpse of Sheba and Elvis would be sprinting toward the nearest divorce court. I've never met the man who could put up the slightest resistance to my sister's pagan charms. Except for a man like me, of course. You know what I mean, Leo? Surely you know that I'm drawn to other compass points."

"Compass points?" I asked. Though I was desperate to be sophisticated, I lacked the foggiest notion of what he was talking about.

"Leo is a pure innocent," Sheba said. "You talk good, but you never know what you're talking about. And I disagree about Elvis. I don't see myself as a home breaker. More like a nurse or a goddess."

"Ah!" Trevor said. "She lays out her life in all its simplicity."

"I was thinking about marrying Paul McCartney. I can tell by his eyes that he's a soul mate. Through him, I could jump-start my acting career, play Juliet on the London stage, and meet the queen of England. I'd love to meet the queen. I sense her loneliness and it's obvious that Prince Philip was a marriage of convenience, not of passion. I could keep her confidences while guiding Paul into making the right career moves."

"I live for beauty," Trevor said, apropos of nothing. "I will always go where beauty leads me."

"I admire beauty," Sheba answered him, "but art is what drives me. I want to be the leading actress of my time. I'd like to marry three or four of the most fascinating men in my era. But I want to make the whole world laugh and cry and be happy to be alive because my acting has touched them so deeply."

"Well spoken," Trevor said. He turned to me and asked, "What are your grandest ambitions, Leo? Hold nothing back. You and your father took up arms to protect us the other night, so you've become heroic in our eyes."

Tongue-tied and uncomfortable, I found myself inadequate to utter a word to these otherworldly twins. My dream of being with Sheba again one night was beginning to seem like the most absurd thing on earth. Should I tell them that I planned to wed Sophia Loren or become secretary general of the United Nations or take my vows and become the first American Pope? My mind raced as we sped out on James Island and I thought about some burning desire to be an astronaut, to study the mating habits of blue whales, to convert all of China to Roman Catholicism.

All of these half-baked lies clustered around my tongue when I finally said, "I'm thinking about being a journalism major in college."

"He can write about us, Sheba," Trevor said, his voice animated. "He can spread our fame far and wide."

"We'll give him scoops," she said. "That's what a journalist needs more than anything: scoops." At that moment, I had entered the whimsical, make-believe world of two kids whose lives would have proven all but unbearable if they had not set their imaginations free. It was a world where all the rules of civilized life had been smashed into shards and remade.

Though I had never been to the Secessionville Plantation, my father had given me precise directions, and I easily found the dirt road that brought us within sight of the mythic plantation. It was set on high ground, presiding over a vast acreage of marshlands that stretched for miles, the length and breadth of James Island Creek and the Folly River. Mr. Ferguson waved from the porch and gave us a thumbs-up sign; his pretty wife called down to see if we needed anything before we began our adventure.

Trevor's bathing suit was so skimpy it looked as though it were made by sewing two yarmulkes together. "It's European," he explained. Sheba's bathing suit was a flesh-colored bikini revealing enough to make me believe she could have her pick between Elvis and Paul McCartney, had either been lucky enough to join us that day.

"Do you like my bathing suit, Leo?" she asked.

"What bathing suit?" I answered, and both twins laughed.

For the first time in my life, I set foot on the floating dock where my parents had fallen in love well over thirty years before. Since my father had revealed the story of their courtship, I started planning to make this watery trip alone. But I wanted to share it with two new friends, one of whom had pocketed away my virginity forever. I threw the inner tube into the retreating tide—it was the exact hour that the moon had issued the recall papers to all the waters of the marsh. As we stepped onto the dock, the tides turned, exactly as I had planned it. We dove into the warm, sweet waters and came up to the inner tube laughing, then began our long, slow-motion float out toward the Atlantic, which in its immensity and silence, waited for all things.

In the summertime, the saltwater that floods the creeks and bays and coves of South Carolina is warm and sun-shot and silken to the touch. It did not hurt or shock to enter the water, but soothed and washed away the frazzled nerves of our runaway week. The creek was dark with the nutrients gathered in the great salt marsh; you could not see your hand if you opened your eyes underwater. We were swimming in a part of the Atlantic that the state of South Carolina had borrowed for a while. Now the tide was hurtling back, drawing the essence of its marshes, the blue crabs lying in wait for stragglers who would soon be prey. As the tide receded, the oysters would be locked tight, retaining a shot-glass-ful of seawater that would hold them until the next full tide; the flounders hidden in the mudflats; the mullets flashing in quicksilver sea grass; the small sharks nosing around for carrion; the blue herons straight-legged and heraldic in their motionless hunt; the snowy egrets—the only creatures in the Low Country whose name invoked winter—staring at the shallows for the quick run of minnows. I let the twins take it all in, and we remained wordless for the first hundred yards, remarkable only in our stillness and the rightness of the moment.

Finally, I heard Trevor ask his sister, "Is this it?"

"Close. Very close. I can't be sure yet."

"You're right. We'll have to see how it ends."

"You could cut your foot on a broken beer bottle," she said. "Develop a case of tetanus, then die. Worse than dying, no one knows you here. There wouldn't be a soul at your funeral."

"I want thousands at my funeral, Sheba. That is a *must*."

"No tetanus, then." Sheba looked toward Sullivan's Island and then back to the white chessboard of the city. The marsh held the deepest green of summer, the green of vestments, chameleons, or rain forests. The spartina grass threw off a bright, show-offy green that could change its aura when a cloud passed between the sun and the creek, invoking jade or olive oil in the ever-shifting light. Its green was infinite in the moment we found marshes alive in our newfound friendship.

"This could be it, Trevor," Sheba said as we became part of the tide, the tube spinning in slow circles.

"What are you two talking about?" I asked. "No fair keeping secrets."

Both twins laughed, then Sheba explained, "You don't know us very well, Leo. And we don't know you. Your mother doesn't like us and she'll break up whatever friendship we might've had. We're too flamboyant for most people. We know that. And you've met our mother, a nut bag who gets knee-walking drunk."

Her brother interrupted, "But it's not all her fault. Our mom's had a hard life. Sheba and I weren't born in a rose garden, if you get my drift."

"When we were little kids, Trevor and I decided to live a world of total make-believe. We got stuck with a bad script. Too much Dracula, not enough Disney."

"You're talking in code," Trevor said to his sister. "As you've pointed out, Leo is one of God's innocents, and I think we should let him remain so."

"Might be a little too late for that," Sheba said, winking at me and confirming my earlier intuition: that to Sheba, sex wasn't ruled by notions of love and responsibility, and cast about with the shadow of the Stations of the Cross. To Sheba, sex was—and this was so bizarre that I could hardly fathom it—possibly a matter of *fun*. I was so astounded by the notion that I ducked my head underwater, where I thought even the fish might notice my blush.

When I rose to the air and the light, the particular magic of the tide's flow, the slinking sunlight, the turquoise blue of the sky, and the magisterial silence of the marsh had put the twins in a prayerlike trance again. We did not have to move unless we came too near the shore or had to kick away from sandbars. We were tide-carried and tide-possessed.

Then Sheba said it again. "This is it. You're right, Trevor. We're in the middle of it, and it's so nice to recognize it."

"What's *it*?" I cried out. "You keep talking about it, and I don't know what in the hell either of you are talking about."

Sheba said, "The perfect moment. Trevor and I have been looking for it our whole lives. We thought we had it before, but something always came along to ruin it."

"Quiet," Trevor remarked. "Don't jinx it. This all could fall apart on us."

"Last year we went out whale watching in Oregon. Our mother took us," Sheba said. "We were just along for the ride, but then the whales started coming. The ocean seemed full of them. They were migrating north with their babies. Trevor and I looked at each other. We'd been so unhappy. But then we were in the front of the boat, just the two of us. We held hands and looked at each other, then back at the whales, and said, 'This is it,' at the same time."

"That's before our mother vomited. She said it was seasickness, but we knew it was bourbon," Trevor said. "Needless to say, it did not turn out to be the perfect day. Didn't even make the cut for the top ten."

"Leo doesn't need to hear this, Trevor," Sheba said. "He's had a perfect life. He's so innocent."

"Ah, you're new in town," I said. "Have you heard about my brother, Steve?"

"We thought you were an only child," Trevor said.

"I am now. But let me tell you a little story. I had the nicest and best-looking brother in the world, and I thought the happiest. When I was nine, I found him in our bathtub after he'd slit his throat and wrists. I spent the next years talking to shrinks. I thought the sadness would kill me. It almost did. But I'm getting over it. Perfect life? I don't think so, Sheba. And just so you know: I have zero friends my own age. Zero."

Both twins reached over and touched me, Trevor grabbing my arm, and Sheba my hand.

"Two." Sheba said it with emotion.

"You got two now," Trevor said. "We can love you twice as well as anyone else because we're twins."

"Have you ever told another teenager about Steve?" Sheba asked.

"Not once," I said. "But everyone in Charleston knows about it."

Trevor said, "But we were the ones you chose to tell about it. It's an honor, Leo."

"A great honor," Sheba agreed. "Let's make room for Steve. Let's invite him to float down the creek with us."

She moved closer to me and so did Trevor. There was an empty space where my brother should have been.

"Steve," I heard Sheba say. "Is that you, sweetheart?"

"Of course it's him," Trevor said. "How could he refuse an invitation to this party?"

"I don't see him," I said.

"You've got to feel him," Sheba said, a patient instructor. "We're going to teach you all about the pleasures of make-believe."

"But you've got to believe in it too for us to make it real," Trevor said. "Is it in you, Leo?"

"Then Steve knows it," Sheba said quickly. "He's the one who's really nervous about this meeting. Speak to him."

"Hey, Steve," I said, my voice breaking. "God, I've missed you. No one ever needed a brother more than I did."

Then I cracked like a pane of glass, and the twins broke with me. They cried to see me cry, as hard as I did. My tears mingled with the saltwater of the tides, until there were no more tears, and all the tides of sorrow had drained the marshes inside me dry. We floated in absolute silence for the next five minutes.

Then I said, "I ruined your perfect moment."

"No, you didn't," Sheba said. "You added to it. You told us something true about yourself. That never happens."

"You gave us a part of your self," Trevor said. "Perfect doesn't just mean happy. Perfect can have lots of different parts."

"Do you know why I brought you to this dock today? Do you know why we're floating toward Charleston Harbor right now?" I asked.

"No," Sheba said. "Does Steve know this story? You've got to include him. We've taken you into our imaginary world, Leo. You've got to take it seriously."

I looked over at the imaginary spot where my brother lived in the running-down exit of tides. "Steve, you're going to love this story most of all."

And I told the story of the summer my mother and father fell in love. The twins listened to the entire story without interrupting me once.

"Now, that's a love story," Trevor said, finally.

We came out of the creek into the slightly rougher waters of Charleston Harbor, still prisoners of a tide that grew in strength and power once we hit the waters of the Ashley River. The sun was beginning to set and the river turned citron-colored before it deepened into a full-bodied gold. Panic set in briefly when I did not see Father or any boat, then I spotted him waving. He had tied the Boston Whaler to a buoy and seemed to be fishing with great pleasure, probably in no hurry for us to float into the pickup zone. I think Father was so happy to see me spending time with kids my own age, he might have left us floating until midnight if not for the safety factor.

As the tides moved us swiftly toward the rendezvous with my father, I told the twins something I felt I had to tell them, in spite of my resolve to keep it to myself. The day had been so special that I worried about spoiling it, but I didn't think I had much choice.

"Sheba, Trevor," I said with great tentativeness, "I don't know how to say this. I've never spent a more wonderful day than today. But just yesterday, a man attacked me. It was in an alleyway. That's how I got this black eye. He put a knife to my throat. He said he would kill me and my parents. He saw us together, Sheba, and knew that you'd spent the night at my house. He wore a mask. He painted one of those things on my face, just like the one on your door. I've never been so scared."

"You just ruined it, Leo," Sheba said coldly. "Ruined the perfect day."

"That's it. Puff. Gone, just like that," Trevor said, turning away from me.

"I didn't mean to spoil anything," I said. "I'm worried about you two."

"We can take care of each other," Sheba said. "Always have, always will."

My father started the engine and moved out toward the center of the river to meet us. He threw out an anchor, idled the engine, and pulled us aboard one at a time. For several hours, we had floated in the saltwater, and now it felt good to dry ourselves with the beach towels and slake our thirst with the iced-down Coca-Cola Father had brought in the coolers.

"Your mother drove me out to the plantation. I picked up the car and the clothes you left behind," Father said, as he handed us paper bags full of our summer clothes and flip-flops. In silence, Trevor and I pulled off our bathing trunks and pulled on shorts and T-shirts. I could not have been sorrier that I had mentioned the man in the alley. I thought I had lost the friendship of the twins forever by my indiscretion, though I could not imagine what my real crime consisted of or why they had both seemed so repulsed by the revelation.

From the marina, we crossed Lockwood Boulevard and turned up

Sinkler Street, where all of us lived. My father was still delighted and managed to sustain a conversation with both the twins. We walked them to their house, where we could see their mother watching television in the front room. When I told Sheba good-bye, she surprised me by hugging me and kissing me on the cheek. "It was a perfect day. I'll explain it to Trevor. But it could not have been better."

As she shook my hand, she passed me a note. I hoped it was a love note or a love letter of any kind. I had read about love letters in novels, but never had received one. My father put his arm around my shoulder, and the gesture seemed timely and right. We took our good time, then walked into the house talking about what we'd prepare for dinner that night.

As soon as I was alone, I read the note that Sheba had slipped me in secret. It was not the love note I had hoped for, but its shock value was high.

"Dear Leo, sorry about the way Trevor and I acted just now. We knew the man who attacked you. He is the reason we've made up an imaginary life together. The man who hurt you was our father. Yes, Leo. You met our dear old dad."

CHAPTER 7

Party Time

On the Fourth of July, I gave a party to celebrate the end of my probation. All morning, my father and I set up card tables and folding chairs we had commandeered from the high school. Mother decorated each table with a vase of multicolored flowers from her garden. Father had stayed up all night barbecuing a small hog, and he had spent the hours of darkness cursing both the neighborhood raccoons and the untethered dogs driven mad by the aroma of hickory-infused pork. Sheba and Trevor came over in the morning and spent the whole day making themselves useful: they polished the silverware and laid down tablecloths and set immaculate tables all over the backyard, heeding my mother's ironclad order that there would be no plastic knives or forks or paper plates at any social function at her house.

When Coach Jefferson and his family arrived just after one in the afternoon, he and Father began setting up a makeshift bar. It surprised me that it was going to be a full bar, ranging from the plebian to the exotic, from iced-down beer to Singapore Slings. Mrs. Jefferson and her mother brought huge containers of lemonade and iced tea. Ike and I were sent off to the ice house to buy enough ice to sink an aircraft carrier, according to Father's orders. I took my '57 Chevy and we headed out toward North Charleston on I-26.

We lucked out with the weather. July Fourth in Charleston was capable of being hot enough to blister the paint off moving vehicles, but the day was overcast and the breeze a cool one. Though nervous, I also felt a lightness I had not experienced in years, an exhilaration of spirit nearing floodwater marks. I was trying to gain small glimpses of myself that might help me know anything about the man I was in the process of becoming.

Ike broke my spell by asking, "Why do you have the top down in this car, white fool?"

"Because it is summertime, black dimwit. And the summertime is when it's most fun to ride in a convertible."

"What do you think it looks like to a white cop or a redneck seeing a white boy and a brother riding down the highway like they own the world?"

"It'll do 'em some good. Ike, shut up and enjoy the ride."

He adjusted his side-view mirror. "It'll be my black ass swinging from some rope. From an oak tree."

"If there's a choice, I sure hope they hang you and not me."

"They may hang both of us. You don't know the cracker mind like I do."

"Oh, really? Who you work for, cracker expert, Mr. Soda, Mr. Ritz, or Mr. Graham? Every time we get together, Ike, every time, you've got to turn it into a sociology class. We're going out to buy some ice. It feels like I picked up H. Rap Brown or Stokely Carmichael hitchhiking along I-26."

"Staying aware is staying alive," Ike said.

"Let me put you in the trunk."

"I like it fine up here. You just need to think about things a little more."

"That's why I made friends with a sharp guy like you."

"You thought about your guest list to this party, white boy?" Ike asked. "You got black people and white people coming to the same party, you dumb-ass son of a bitch."

"One black girl I want you to meet," I told him. "She's from the orphanage."

"The last thing I want to do is meet an orphan."

"You'll like meeting this one. She's awfully pretty."

"How you know everything in the world?"

"Cracker-boy just knows." Then I looked into my rearview mirror and started. "Uh-oh, Ike. Coming up on my left. Pickup truck full of rednecks. Oh, God, they've got shotguns and they're aiming them. Get down! Quick—get down!"

Ike threw himself to the floorboards. We rode on for thirty seconds then Ike asked, "They gone yet?"

"I made a mistake. They were kindergarten kids eating snow cones. False alarm."

"You lying white Strom Thurmond son of a bitch!" he said as I pulled the car off a ramp onto Remount Road and drove to a newly opened ice house owned by a man my father once taught. I had rankled Ike with my hoax and was feeling bad about it, but he finally broke a stony silence and said, "You tell any of these white folks today that you invited black folks to your getting-out-of-the-loony-bin party?"

"This party has nothing to do with the loony bin. This is to celebrate my coming off probation."

"You sure have led a good life. First, a lunatic, then a drug dealer. How did you manage all that?"

"I just caught all the breaks, Ike. Just like getting to know you. No, if the white people get upset at blacks being at the party, they can leave."

"Something wrong in your head, white boy."

I answered, "But I believe in the power of prayer. Oh Lord, have me wake up tomorrow thinking just like that wonderful, perfect black hero, Dr. George Washington Carver Ike Jefferson Goddamn Forward-Looking Junior."

"I'll be lucky if you don't get me killed this year," he mumbled, grimacing as I pulled the car onto the loading ramp of the ice house.

When Ike and I drove up with both the backseat and the trunk filled with ice, the orphanage school bus was turning the corner on tires as shiny as licorice, with Mr. Lafayette at the wheel. I saw that Sister Polycarp had dressed the orphans in orange jumpsuits with the words "St. Jude's Orphanage" printed on both the front and back of the uniform.

"Hey, Mr. Lafayette, why did Pollywog make them dress this way? Didn't you explain this was a party?" I asked.

"Sister Pollywog doesn't countenance well to advice, Leo," he replied with a snort.

As I made the introductions all around, I could read the humiliation of the three orphans in a form of secret graffiti around their eyes. "Betty Roberts," I said to the new girl I'd met the other day, "here's the guy I told you about, Ike Jefferson. I met him when I was in the state mental hospital."

"He did not," Ike said as he shook Betty's hand. "Though I think they made a bad mistake letting this boy out so soon."

There was the nervous laughter of teenagers as I turned to Sheba Poe and asked, "Sheba, you got any extra clothes that Starla and Betty could wear to this party?"

"Follow me, girls, and I'll fix you right up," Sheba said, and I could tell she knew exactly what it was I wanted. She took Starla and Betty by the elbows and led them in the direction of her house. "I know some makeup secrets you girls are going to love."

I said, "C'mon, Niles. You're now going to select something to wear from a real clotheshorse's closet. Naturally, I'm referring to me."

I dressed Niles in a new pair of Bermuda shorts, an old pair of Docksiders, and a Citadel T-shirt, of which I owned about twenty because of my Father's oxlike affection for his alma mater plus his painful neediness to see me follow in his footsteps.

"You look good, Niles." I folded his uniform and placed it on my dresser.

"Why do you have two beds in your room?" Ike asked as he conducted a brief survey of my bedroom.

"I used to have a brother, but he died."

"How'd he die?"

"He killed himself."

"Why?"

"Never got to ask him," I said. "Let's go to the party."

Niles asked, "Was he anything like you?"

"No, Steve was just a great guy," I answered. "Nothing like me."

We heard piano music coming from the living room, where I was surprised to find my mother and Trevor Poe performing a duet. Immediately, I could see that my mother's skills as a pianist were overmatched by the far more accomplished Trevor. He had long, perfectly manicured fingernails and beautifully shaped hands. My mother soon held up her own hands in a gesture of surrender. "I give up, Trevor. You didn't tell me you were a prodigy."

"It's a God-given gift," Trevor said. "Wait until you hear Sheba sing along with me."

"She's a singer?" my mother asked.

"Dr. King, you don't know it yet, but you will: Sheba Poe is a star."

"Do you play classical music?" my mother asked. When she had abandoned her duet, Trevor had begun to play "Hey Jude" by the Beatles. But when my mother mentioned classical, he transitioned to a piano arrangement of Beethoven's Ninth Symphony, his hands flashing with astonishing grace over the keyboard.

"Once I hear a song—just once—I can play it for the rest of my life," he explained.

"You ever play any football?" Ike asked him.

"How grotesque! What would be your guess?"

The girls returned from the Poes' house across the street, where Sheba had transformed Starla and Betty by applying makeup with a light but expert touch. Both wore sundresses and sandals, and Sheba had even figured out how to disguise Starla's unfortunate strabismus by fitting her with a pair of expensive-looking sunglasses. Starla was a pretty, happy young woman now, and she came up to thank me for giving her up to Sheba.

"You and Betty look like you're ready to party. Great job, Sheba. Some party music, Trevor," I shouted, and Trevor began blasting away at "Rock Around the Clock." My party for myself officially began.

In the small, insular world I had created for myself in Charleston, I had invited everyone who had played a significant role in my long struggle to get back to myself. I had experienced a lostness so profound that it seemed like a rain forest, impenetrable and inhospitable, had grown up around me one day; in that dispiriting forest, I had found no relief. But now I planned to leave its alien geography far behind me, and I could feel a child's pleasure every time the doorbell rang and I welcomed Monsignor

Max, or Cleo and her husband, or Eugene Haverford, who brought me an afternoon paper. Judge William Alexander and his wife, Zan, came; it delighted me that they brought my shrink, Jacqueline Criddle. Harrington Canon walked up the sidewalk, then came Henry Berlin with his wife and his two oldest kids; I introduced them to Chad and Fraser Rutledge and Molly Huger, who came in right behind them.

"I'd go out of business without the Rutledge family business. And the Huger family is just icing on the cake," Henry Berlin said. "So this is where my favorite jailbird lives!"

"Quiet, Henry," Mrs. Berlin said, but Henry winked at me.

"I tried to get a date for Fraser," Chad said, "but not much luck there."

"It's great to see you again, Leo," Molly said as we shook hands.

"Hey, Fraser," I said. "There's a guy I want you to meet. Come with me."

I took her by the hand, led her through the crowd in the backyard, and walked her over to a table where Ike and Betty were chatting with Niles and Starla.

"Hey, Niles," I said. "This is a friend of mine, Fraser Rutledge, and I thought you two might enjoy each other. Niles Whitehead."

"You seem to be quite the matchmaker, Leo," Starla said.

"I don't know, I've never done it before."

"Who you going to match me with?" she asked.

I looked around the yard and didn't see an obvious candidate, but my eyes came to rest on Trevor Poe.

"Hey, Trevor. Will you play some love songs for my friend Starla?" I asked.

Trevor said, "I find that prospect divine." He took Starla back into the house, then the prettiest music in the world started pouring out of our living room window into the backyard as the tide rose toward us, moon-summoned and spiced with summer.

Walking over to a table where Harrington Canon sat in solitude, I asked, "Want me to get you another drink, Mr. Canon, or refresh the one you have?"

"Sit with me for a second, Leo," he said. "I have some statements to make to you. Some are general, some provocative."

"Sounds like the Harrington Canon I know and love," I said, pulling a chair up beside him.

"Your parents don't own a single item of interest," he said. "I've never seen such an awkward display of tastelessness."

"They have simple tastes. Plus, they're teachers," I explained. "They couldn't afford much in your store. You even say that *you* can't afford to buy anything in your store."

"There are people of color here," he said, looking off toward the Ashley River.

"Yes, I invited them," I said. "They're friends of mine."

"I think it is disgraceful to bring colored and white people together for a party. I wouldn't have the first idea of what to say to any of them."

"You aren't talking to anyone, white or black. You're sitting by yourself staring at nothing."

"I'm admiring a river," he said. "God's handiwork at its most superior."

"You're being a teensy bit antisocial," I said.

"A convicted felon, calling me antisocial. I've never heard of such raw presumption."

I made my way across the backyard and greeted some of my favorite customers who stood in line at the barbecue pit. As I made my way toward Judge Alexander's table, my mother called to me from the far side of the yard, where I saw her hugging Septima Clark and her daughter. Septima had been a civil rights leader in Charleston for decades. It was a brave act to invite Septima Clark to any function in Charleston, but it was unheard-of for a white family to invite her to a purely social occasion. I felt a shiver of pride as I saw Septima and my mother embrace. I thought that one could entertain doubts about the personas my parents presented to society, but no one could doubt their courage. Monsignor Max rose and led Septima across the yard to eat dinner with him at his table.

But the spirit did not pollinate everyone in equal doses. I noticed that Niles and Fraser, Ike and Betty, and Starla Whitehead were on the fringes of Judge Alexander's group, laughing out loud at the stories he offered up in the late-afternoon air. Chad Rutledge broke away from Molly when he saw me retracing my steps back toward the judge's table. He got a firm grasp on my arm and led me toward the edge of the lake where we were all but hidden from view behind a water oak.

"What do you think you're doing, King?" Chad said.

"What're you talking about, Chad?"

"The niggers. You've invited niggers to your party! Are you and your parents nuts?"

"Why don't you go ask my mother and father if they're nuts, Chad, old pal?" I said. "I'd love to see their reaction."

"This is Charleston, son," he informed me.

"Thanks for the news flash."

"We don't do things like that here. We're too smart for that."

"Speak for yourself," I said. "Hey, Chad, this is only the second time I've met you, but *smart*'s not the first word I think of when I think of you."

Chad bristled. "What's the first word you think of, loser? Aren't we having this niggered-up party because you're coming off probation? Poor Molly and I got caught snorting a little coke, but they found enough in your cheap sports coat to get half the city high."

"I screwed up, Chad. So far, it's been the story of my life."

"So what's the first word you think of when you think of me?"

"My mother taught me not to talk in clichés. It offends the English teacher part of her."

"Give me a try. I don't mind clichés," he said.

"The first word that comes to mind is this: *asshole*. Yep, that's it, all right. The second is *flaming asshole*. The third is *flaming, fucking asshole*. That about sums it up, Chad. Need anything else?"

"One thing. Why did you set my sister up with a fucking orphan?"

"Well, you teased her about not having any dates at the yacht club. You made fun of the way she looked. I thought she was pretty, and very nice. I'd just met Niles, and he looked like he could use a friend or two. They seem to like being with each other tonight."

"I'll guarantee you it'll be the last time you see them together," Chad said. "My parents'll go nuts when they hear about Little Orphan Annie."

"I imagine so," I said. "But I'll bet Fraser and Niles'll have something to say to that."

"You don't know a thing about how the Charleston aristocracy thinks or works."

"But I've watched people a lot. They look pretty easy to predict."

"I'm leaving this party," Chad said. "And I'm taking Fraser and Molly with me."

"God, it was such a pleasure getting to know you, Chad," I said, not bothering to hide the mockery in my voice. "Don't go out for football, pal. A warning."

"You think I'm afraid of you?"

"You should be," I said, "because I plan to knock you on your pussy Charleston aristocratic South of Broad ass."

"You and your niggers?"

"Yep, me and all the rest."

"Keep your mountain nigger away from my sister," Chad warned.

"*Who?*"

"The orphan. He's out of the mountains of North Carolina, so he's a mountain nigger. Pure white trash, which is lower than a nigger."

"Bye-bye, Chad," I said. "What a swell guy. You make me even hate white people."

Chad stormed away, and I wandered through the yard, offering more helpings of barbecue and fried fish and calming myself down. Chad seemed both venomous and insecure, a flammable combination. I pulled a chair up to Judge Alexander to hear him ending a tall tale to laughter and applause because it seemed mannerly, what a good host should do. But my peripheral vision caught a serious argument being conducted in a whispered fever at the side of the house where my mother's prized camellias grew to unseemly heights. Chad and Fraser Rutledge were locked like dissonant enemies in one of those battles that often spring most violently between people who are supposed to love each other. One fact I was sure of was that Fraser was giving no quarter nor taking a foot-long hot dog's ration of shit from her brother. From a distance of twenty feet, I watched Niles and Starla witnessing the dispute, and I was sure they knew where the heart of the argument lay. I wondered how long these orphans had felt humiliation at the hands of the native-born citizens of towns where they would always be dishonored visitors. Fraser broke away from her brother's grip, and when he tried to prevent her from going back to Niles, I saw the exact moment when the leading rebounder among South Carolina high school women basketball players shot a well-placed elbow into her brother's ribs and sent him flying into a ten-foot camellia bush.

Chad and Molly left the party without any farewells. When Fraser joined Niles, she took his hand, and he gave her one of the most radiant smiles I have ever seen. It struck me speechless that I was instrumental in the coming together of this teenaged couple who instantly seemed to be completions of each other. Betty Roberts and Ike seemed to be getting along well too. What had Starla called me? For the first time in my life I could call myself a matchmaker. I now felt I possessed an innate power I had never realized existed. Looking around the yard, I saw that it was a good party.

I was surprised to see Molly, having remembered her manners, return to the party through the garden, flustered and red-faced. I arrived to back up Niles and Fraser, but recognized immediately that neither of them needed reinforcement. Molly still carried the markings and insignias of the Charleston society girl, an inoculation against the anarchy that had managed to break through her impregnable lines of defense. She was a Southern girl born to please rather than to think, to charm rather than to issue calls to arms. I loved girls like Molly Huger and always had. But she had returned to fight a battle her boyfriend had just lost. Instantly, you could tell that Molly loathed conflict in all its contentious forms. Also, I saw a flanking movement take place on my right, and noticed that my mother's wolflike attention to mayhem was guiding her to the scene of discord in her yard. I hurried over to cut her off. Although I could explain many things to Molly about what the gloss of unfamiliarity my Southern home represented, I lacked the time or energy to explain that she had entered the spectral garden of James Joyce.

I intercepted my mother before she could enter the fray. "Let me take care of this, Mother."

"What did that Rutledge boy say to you out there by the oak?" she asked.

"We were just getting to know each other."

"You're lying. He was attacking you."

"I fought back, Mother. I held my ground."

"Now you're not lying, so go stop the fight that's about to break out between Miss Fraser and Miss Molly." There was a sibilance that meant a mocking irony when she used the word *Miss*.

When I reached the group at the fringes of the party, I heard Molly saying to Fraser, "If you won't let me talk to you alone, then I'll say it in front of everyone. Chad's not leaving until you're in the car with us, Fraser. I wouldn't embarrass you in front of strangers for anything, you know that about me."

"I'm having fun, Molly," Fraser said. "I'm having a good time, maybe the best of my life. Why does that make you and Chad so unhappy?"

"Because it's not right. It's not who we are, or what we were raised to be. We shouldn't have come here tonight. Leo was wrong to ask us. He knew very well what he was doing."

Her tone irritated me. "Just what was I doing, Molly?"

"This party," she said, "is like a can of mixed nuts. It's all wrong. Everything about it. You know what Chad's father is going to say when he finds out Fraser was set up with a boy from the orphanage."

Someone came up beside me, and I turned to see Sheba. "If you don't like it, then leave the goddamn party. And don't you dare say one thing to my friend Leo King. He may be the nicest boy I've ever met."

But Niles intervened. "Go with Molly, Fraser. She's right; I'd only spell trouble for you. Starla and I don't have much to offer anyone. Heck, we had to borrow these clothes to come to this party. Guess we better get back to the orphanage."

"You've got a twelve o'clock curfew," I told him. "My mother called Sister Pollywog and arranged it."

"So you can kiss my ass, Molly," Starla said with all the sultry darkness and mystery of the Blue Ridge in her low-pitched voice.

Trevor Poe came up from behind. "Molly, you are such a vision of loveliness and spirit. Come into the house and I'll play love songs to you until my fingers fall off. Now, Sheba, Starla, you girls go easy on Miss Molly."

"Trevor, don't you see?" Molly said, pleading now. "We weren't raised like this. There's nothing here for people like us, nothing of value. Our values, I'm talking about."

"What about compromise?" I suggested. "I'll drive Fraser home before midnight. The orphans have to go back to St. Jude's in the bus with Mr. Lafayette."

"My family and I can leave right now too," Ike said.

"You are my guests, Ike," I said. "I hope me and my family have made you feel welcome tonight."

"I'm talking about Molly and Chad," he said. "They don't seem happy that we're here pretending that we're something else besides niggers."

"I didn't say that," Molly said, and now her body language suggested she had come up against an entire army of invasion she was not born to understand. "And I don't think that. I promise, that hasn't entered my mind. It's hard to explain to outsiders. We were raised with great privilege, but also with great expectations. Family is everything, the one holy word. The glue that holds our whole society together."

"So the orphanage and the Negro Marching Band got to you tonight?" Starla asked, her dark eyes glittering dangerously. She turned to Betty and Ike and told them: "Got to thank you two. Me and Niles've never got to feel like high cotton until tonight. I think Molly actually rates us higher than she does you. Shee-it, this girl's making me feel like high society."

"Put a lid on it, Starla," Niles snapped. "Chad's the idiot here, not Molly. He's put her in a bad situation." To Fraser, he said, "Go on, Fraser. A lot of stuff happened tonight. A lot can still happen."

"I'd consider it a personal favor, Fraser," Molly said. "I'd love you to death if you'd do it. Just this once. I'll never ask it again."

Fraser considered it a moment, then surprised us all by saying, "Is it okay with you, Starla? I'd rather be with you and your brother than with my brother. Ike and Betty, I've been made to feel like a freak by this phony Charleston society since I was born. But tonight, I felt good, and I like it. Y'all made me feel good."

Betty hugged Fraser and said, "It was great to meet you," and Ike added, "I got a feeling we'll be seeing each other again."

Then Fraser turned to me and kissed me lightly on the cheek. "You throw the best party of anyone in Charleston, Leo King. And I've been to all of them."

When Fraser and Molly had said their good-byes to my parents and to the other adults they knew at the party, I walked them to the front, where Chad sat in his car. He was not fuming and distracted, as I expected him to be, but coolly confident to the point of boredom. After they left, the party moved inside. Most of the older folks also made their farewells. But many stayed on, surprising me, and that's when Sheba and Trevor Poe took over. They made the memory of that evening belong to them, their spectacular debut in a very oddball demimonde of Charleston nonsociety. Trevor started out by getting all the adults slow dancing as he played the favorite songs of my parents' generation—songs that suggested the unknowable fears of the men and women separated by oceans during World War II. It was the first time we found that Sheba sang like a fallen angel remembering paradise, her voice rich and golden-toned and throaty. Because music is an inexplicable awakener of the dark engines of our immortal souls, I remember every song that we danced to during that magical night. When Sheba noticed that most of the party could not dance well, she turned the living room, the den, and part of the kitchen into an elaborate dance studio. Then she arrayed us in long, undulating lines as we learned to shag and twist and do the fish and the mashed potato. At center stage, Sheba and Trevor Poe found themselves exactly where they belonged. If Salome had danced half as sensuously as Sheba, I understood the severance of John the Baptist's head.

Sheba frequently ordered us to change partners. I would spin around and find myself dancing with Starla in her dark eyeglasses, then my shrink, Jacqueline Criddle, then once with my mother, then once, hilariously, with Ike, and we performed the dirty shag to the sounds of Elvis Presley's "Heartbreak Hotel." It was a joyous, miraculous, unrepeatable night.

After the orphans' bus disappeared behind the imposing iron gate of St. Jude's, my father asked me if I would take a short ride with him. He drove me to the Battery. We walked up the cement stairs, then moved to the point where the Ashley and the Cooper meet to form the beautiful immensity of Charleston Harbor. As always, you could feel the force and power of the collision of the two rivers. That fusion meant the extension of each river, yet neither seemed happy about it.

"My father took me to this exact spot when I was eighteen, Leo. His father had taken him here for the same ceremony. My grandfather's father had done the same thing. We don't know how far back the tradition goes. I'd planned to take Steve here when he was eighteen, but that didn't work out. When Steve died, I decided to let this tradition die with him. But I changed my mind tonight."

Father took two silver cups and a pint of Jack Daniel's from a pouch he was carrying. He poured a finger of bourbon for himself, then he poured a finger for me. "My father wanted to share my first drink. He told me how much I meant to him as a son, and that he hoped he had proven to be a worthy father. At the joining of these two rivers, he welcomed me to manhood. He asked me to be a fine man, the best man I was capable of being. I promised him I would. I ask the same of you, Leo."

"I'll never be able to be as fine a man as you," I said as I raised my cup and touched his. "But I'll give it a run for its money. That's a promise."

"No, I've put a study on you in the last couple of years," he said. The moon caught us in a sluice of its magical light. "You're not just going to be a fine man, son. You've got potential. You might even become a hell of a man."

"If I do, it will be because I've worshipped you," I said. "I want to grow up to be just like you."

We drank and the moment felt transformational. All I could do was hope that Father would prove right.

So began the time that would alter my vision of things forever. Many years later, the past is calling out to me in a canny, undermining voice, but the starting point was always on Bloomsday, the summer before my senior year. By the time I had my party of celebration on July Fourth, the cast of major characters had all made their entrances. The forces that brought us all together would take their good time in both tearing us to pieces and teaching us the subtleties and indiscretions and high-water marks that bring such pleasure to friendships. I thought I had discovered some friends who could not love one another more, and I was almost right. The following May, we left our graduation stage positive that we would live fascinating, self-actualizing, and amazing lives. We promised we would make a difference in the world we were about to storm. As a group, we did well; as friends, our love sustained us for a while. Then it began to lose some of its lustrous sparkle. But all of us came roaring back to one another in the middle of our lives, by something as simple as a knock on the door.

PART TWO

PART TWO

CHAPTER 8

Knock on the Door

There is a knock on my door. I check my calendar: it is April 7, 1989. I have written down no appointments on my schedule today. Everyone in the newsroom knows I close my office door only when I am writing a column, and I consider those hours of creation sacrosanct. On my door, I have a printed sign hanging from a picture hook that says, LEO KING IS HARD AT WORK ON THE COLUMN THAT HAS MADE HIM FAMOUS IN CHARLESTON WHILE THE REST OF HIS COLLEAGUES LABOR IN WELL-DESERVED OBSCURITY. IN OTHER WORDS, I AM BUSY WRITING LITERATURE THAT WILL NEVER DIE, AS LONG AS THERE ARE MEN AND WOMEN WHO LOVE THE HUMAN SPIRIT. KEEP YOUR SORRY BUTTS OUT OF HERE UNTIL I'VE FINISHED. Then I signed it with a flourish, "That godlike man, Leo King." My colleagues have defaced the sign with the vilest graffiti over the years, making it increasingly difficult to read. The knock grows louder and more insistent, and I can hear a crowd gathering outside. I stop typing, make a note to myself about the train of ideas that is now derailed, and walk to the door. I fling it open, fully prepared to shoo away the intruder.

A woman stands outside my door, and her presence in the newsroom could not have surprised me more. The woman's face is well known all over the world; her exquisitely proportioned body has appeared on dozens of movie posters half-clothed in both lingerie and animal skins, and in one infamous shot involving a rock python as she strutted her admirable stuff in her birthday suit. She has no appointment nor is she in the habit of needing to make them. She is wearing a white dress that barely seems sufficient to contain the voluptuous curves of a body that now seems old-fashioned when most actresses are intent on looking underfed. She had obviously vamped her way across the newsroom, attracting twenty or so curious souls, mostly rutting males, but several starstruck females who are mesmerized by all things Hollywood. If you do not know that Sheba Poe is a movie star in 1989, you are admitting to a monastic life. There is a very good chance you don't subscribe to the *News and Courier*, which reports every Sheba-related event, no matter how outlandish or scandalous. Sheba is the only major movie star who has ever come out of Charleston, South Carolina. We cover our dream girl with the reverence we think she deserves. Charleston never did Mexican food very well, but when we exported Sheba to the West Coast, we sent them a fiery jalapeño-stuffed enchilada.

"Excuse me, ma'am," I say. "But I'm writing a column, and I'm working on deadline."

Behind her, the reporters boo me roundly. The crowd has begun to swell as the rumor of Sheba's appearance makes its way through the building. I can think of nothing more combustible than Sheba and a crowd.

"How do I look, Leo?" she asks, playing to the crowd. "Be honest."

"Good enough to eat." I regret the words as soon as I speak.

"Promises, promises," she says, and the crowd roars in appreciation. "Introduce me to some of your friends, Leo."

I want to defuse the situation quickly, so I choose a few faces in the crowd.

"That horny one is Ken Burger, down from the Washington bureau. Beside him is Tommy Ford. Over there is Steve Mullins. That's Marsha Gerard who's about to ask you to sign her bra. Over there's Charlie Williams, who wants you to sign part of his body, but the part's so small you'll just have to initial it."

"I'll write a love letter on it, Charlie," Sheba says.

The movie critic, Shannon Ringel, cries out, "I better get a damn interview, Leo. Don't hog her."

"Are you the bitch who panned my last movie?" Sheba says, silencing the room. She possesses a voice that can meow or send a pride of lions out to hunt water buffalo. There is no "Here kitty, kitty" in her question.

Shannon gamely says, "I think you've done far more distinguished work."

"A critic," Sheba sneers. "I call pest control every time I meet one."

"Sweet Sheba," I say. "Please excuse me, ladies and gentlemen. Miss Poe has had a long day making lifelong enemies wherever she drifts. And I still have a column to write."

"Leo and I were high school sweethearts," Sheba says.

"We were not," I reply.

"He's hung like a rhino."

"I am not." I quickly lead Sheba into my office and shut the door.

Sheba has developed the planetary ego that keeps her star bright among the Milky Way of ambition that brings the prettiest girls and handsomest boys spilling into Hollywood every year, an endless river of hormones and wishfulness that is always for hire. But when I shut the door, Sheba sloughs off her diva role and transforms herself into the teenage girl who brought so much joy and mystery into my senior year of high school. She pinches me on the butt as I walk back to my desk, but does it in a playful, not a seductive, manner.

"You're still uptight about sex, Leo," she says.

"Some things never change," I say. "I haven't heard from you in six months. None of us has."

"I was making a movie in Hong Kong with my new husband, the moody auteur."

"I haven't met your last two husbands."

"Believe me, you didn't miss anything. I just came from the Dominican Republic, where I got the quickest of quick divorces."

"So Troy Springer is history?"

"His real name is Moses Berkowitz, which is fine, but he had a mother who made Mrs. Portnoy look like June Cleaver or that Swedish broad from *I Remember Mama*. The bitch changed her name to Clementine

Springer. I caught her sonny boy in bed with the sixteen-year-old actress who was playing my daughter in the movie."

"Sorry, Sheba."

"Men. Say something in defense of your sex," she challenges me.

"We'd be fine 'cept they gave us dicks."

The crowd has not broken up completely outside of my doorway, and I can still hear the murmuring of disappointment among the reporters as they begin to drift back to their desks. As I listen to Sheba, who begins to talk easily to me, I study her at my leisure. It is easy to forget about Sheba's thoughtless cargo of pure sex appeal. Her voice, husky and familiar, sounds like one of the most seductive forms that lovemaking can take. She has taken possession of the entire building by the simple fact that she entered it.

Only one person has noticed that her entrance was unauthorized. There is a peremptory knock on my door without a trace of caution behind it. Blossom Limestone, the gladiatorial gatekeeper who checks visitors in and out of the newspaper with all the efficiency of the marine drill instructor she once was, has muscled her way through the crowd and walked right into my office. She places a muscular black hand on Sheba's right shoulder, but looks at me when she scolds, "Your fancy friend did not go through proper channels—again."

"She hasn't been here in three years, Blossom," I say.

"She can sign in at the front desk just like everyone else."

"I love the feel of your hand on my shoulder, Blossom, darling," says Sheba, taking the large hand and holding it against one of her own ample breasts. "I've always loved the gentle lesbian touch. They and they alone know how to make a woman feel right. They get right to the point—no gamesmanship, no role-playing."

Blossom snatches her hand away as though it touched a burning coal. "Lesbian?" she asks. "I got three sons, and you's barren as a dump truck last time I checked. Now, sign this piece of paper and the time you got here."

Sheba signs with a flourish, her signature taking up four spaces on the log sheet, and there is boldness even in its illegibility. Then she says, "I came in where the delivery trucks load up. My brother and I used to help

Leo on his paper route. I was a regular here long before you came, Blossom, angel."

"So I've heard," Blossom says. "Sign in with me next time, Miss Poe, just like everyone else."

"I thought it was so cute the last time," Sheba says. "You sold my signature for fifty bucks. Or was it sixty?"

Blossom looks shaken by the revelation, then recovers. "I sell it or someone steals it."

Again, a small crowd has gathered at the doorway watching the fireworks between the two strong-willed women. Sheba has not noticed the audience until she turns around and sees their hushed, expectant faces. I prepare myself for the worst, and the worst comes as I am forming the thought.

"Let me sign your left tit, Blossom. No telling what you could get for that," Sheba says.

The reporters by the door exhale audibly. They would have laughed out loud except for their deep respect for Blossom, who fields the responses of the crazies who charge her reception desk at the first appearance of an article that offends their paranoid sensibilities. I can see that the remark has cut Blossom deeply. "She didn't mean that, Blossom. Sheba can't help playing to the crowd. She's a nice girl."

"She might be a lot of things, Leo. A nice girl is not one of them." Blossom snorts. "She's come back to you because she's after something. You watch yourself."

I clap my hands and order, "All of you, get out of here. I've got a column to write for Sunday and a deadline to get it in."

When we are alone again, Sheba looks up with the only expression of hers that can pass for shyness. Then both of us laugh and hug like a brother and sister. "I'm sorry I act like that, Leo."

"I'll get over it."

"I do it to everybody, I promise. You're not the only one," she whispers in my ear.

"I know, Sheba. You can be anything you want around me. I know who you are; don't forget that. Why are you in town?"

"Besides the fact that I'm washed up? Used up like a snot rag? My agent hasn't had a call for a starring role in over a year. I'm thirty-eight. For a woman in Hollywood, that's like being a thousand."

"That may all be true," I say. "But that's not why you're here."

"I came back to see my old friends," she says. "I need to get back to what I once was, Leo; surely you can understand that."

"But none of us has seen you more than ten times since we graduated."

"But I call. You've got to admit I'm good about checking in by phone."

I cover my eyes with my hands. "You phone drunk, Sheba. You phone stoned. Do you know you asked me to marry you the last time you called?"

"What did you say?"

"That I'd divorce Starla and gladly marry you."

"You and Starla aren't really married, and you never have been."

"I've got the papers to prove it," I say.

Sheba says with a cruel, bladelike quality, "It was a sham love affair. A worse than sham marriage. And it's caused you to live a sham life."

"You can't fool me. You came back just to inflate my ego," I say. "Before you arrived, Sheba, I was feeling kind of successful here in Charleston."

"None of my Hollywood friends has ever heard of you."

"Are they the same ones who quit calling your agent?"

"The same ones."

"You've been nominated for two Academy Awards for best actress," I say. "You won an Oscar for best supporting actress. That's a great career."

"But I didn't win best actress. A nomination means zip for your career. It's like choosing to sleep with the gofer or the best boy on location, instead of shacking up with the leading man."

"You've done okay with leading men," I say.

She smiles. "Married four of them. Slept with all of them."

"Can I quote you?" I ask, moving toward my typewriter.

"Of course not."

"Okay, Sheba. I ask very little of you. Just give me enough salacious gossip and unexpected rumor so that I can knock off a column for Sunday. Then we can blow this joint and get drunk with our friends."

"Ha!" she says. "You're using me. Exploiting my world fame."

"It hurts me you'd even imply such a thing." My fingers hang over the keys of my typewriter.

"No one knows about my divorce from Troy Springer. That's breaking news," she says.

"Was he your fourth or fifth husband?" I ask while typing.

"Why're you so fixated with numbers?"

"Accuracy. You'll often find that among reporters. Why're you getting divorced from Troy? *People* magazine called him one of the handsomest men in Hollywood."

"I bought a vibrator that has more personality and does its job better."

"Give me something I can use in a family newspaper," I say.

"Our careers had been growing apart, especially after I found him banging the kid in the hot tub."

"You took that as a bad sign?"

"Yeah, I was trying to get pregnant at the time," she says.

"Can you remember all of your ex-husbands' names?"

"I can't even remember what half of them looked like."

"The worst person you ever met in Hollywood?"

"Carl Sedgwick, my first husband," she says without hesitation.

"The best person?"

"Carl Sedgwick again. That's how illusory and contradictory that city is."

"What keeps you there?"

"The belief that I'll one day be given the best role ever handed to an American actress."

"What keeps you from going mad while you wait?"

"Big peckers. Strong drink. A ready access to pharmaceuticals."

"You can get the liquor here in Charleston."

"A martini tastes a lot better when you hear the Pacific crashing into the cliffs below you."

"Can I just say you're dating a pharmacist?" I ask.

"You most certainly cannot!"

"What do you miss most about Charleston?"

"I miss my childhood friends, Leo. I miss the girl I was who first drove into this city."

"Why?"

"Because I had not laid waste to my own life then. I think I was a nice girl then. Didn't you think so, Leo?"

I look up at her, and still see the lost girl she is talking about. "I never saw a girl like you, Sheba. Before or since." As I watch her, the journalist inside me wages war against the young boy who was Sheba's first friend in this city. The journalist is a cold man, bloodless in the pursuit of his profession, paid to be a voyeur and not a participant in the passion plays I enter with my notebook open. Detachment is my theme. As I watch her open up her wounds, I do not mourn for the girl she misplaced on the day we met, but instead for the disappearance of that offbeat, miserable boy who took a batch of benne wafers across the street to welcome a pair of long-suffering twins to the neighborhood. In turning myself into a reporter, I extinguished all the fires that boy displayed as proof of his worth and humanity. Though I can be objective about Sheba's life, I have long ago lost any ability in taking stock of my own. She continues to talk with a nakedness of spirit I have never seen in Sheba.

"And what did I do with that girl? The one you liked so much? The friend you came to love?" she asks.

"You answered the bell," I say as I type. "You had a calling and a vocation, and you never questioned it or looked back. No one could stop you or stand in your way. The rest of us followed our destinies, the way most of mankind does. You grabbed hold of your own dreams of yourself. You rode it out of town, took it to the limit. Few people do that."

Sheba lifts her hand above her, closes her eyes, and makes a motion as though she is erasing an invisible blackboard. "You make it sound noble. But you know that girl well, Leo. She considered acting to be a writ of the highest order, and there were times she was right. That girl became the toast of Hollywood. But then the crow's-feet appeared near the eyes, her skin began its coarsening, and she could not laugh during close-ups because of three distinct lines on her forehead. I've never had a husband who didn't suggest I have a face-lift. So the girl gets scared in the middle of the journey and gets so eager to please that she starts accepting every role they throw at her: bimbos and nymphomaniacs, shoplifters and anorexic soccer moms who turn into serial killers."

"I thought that was one of your best roles."

"The script was dead on arrival," she says. "But thanks, Leo. Remember London?"

"Never forget it."

"I played Ophelia on the London stage. I was twenty-four years old, and all of England went crackers when they chose this unknown American broad to play this suicidal Danish girl. All of you Charleston friends came over for the opening. Trevor flew out from San Francisco with his new lover. What was that boy's name?"

"I think that was Joey," I say.

"No, Joey never saw me in *Hamlet*," she says. "I think that might've been Michael the first."

"It was Michael the second. I never met Michael the first."

"Whatever. Trevor changed boys like flip-flops in those days," she remembers. "Do you remember the party you guys gave me after the first night? What was that restaurant?"

"It was called L'Etoile. I still go there when I'm in London. Remember when the reviews came in? The critics said there had never been an Ophelia like you before. Richard Burton and Laurence Olivier came backstage to congratulate you. It was one of the great nights of all of our lives."

Sheba smiles, then darkens again. "Last year, the same theater called from London. This time they wanted me to play Gertrude, Hamlet's bitch of a mother. I'm not yet a hag, Leo. Give me another year or two. Though I've abused them quite seriously, this face and this body can still play a young, beautiful woman with devastating wit and effectiveness. There are seven women more beautiful than I am in Hollywood today, but only seven. And I can bury most of those dwarves by the force of my personality and the power of my acting. Do I see the hag forming in this face? I do. I see everything in this face. Every flaw, every wrinkle, every imperfection that sneaks up on me as I sleep off a hangover or pretend to have an orgasm with the new Hollywood flavor of the month. I feel like I should approach every mirror with a gun in my hand."

"Whoa, girl," I caution. "We're sliding out of great acting into melodrama."

"I don't need to act with you, Leo. That's one of the reasons I'm back here."

"You'll be a beautiful old woman," I say, looking up at her again.

She throws her head back, laughing. "I'll never be an old woman. That is a promise. And that, sir, you can print."

"What's the real reason you're back?" I ask. "Is it to check on your mother?"

"That's one of the reasons. But there's one other . . ." She trails off, and then the phone rings.

"Hello," I say. "Oh, hey, Molly. Yeah, you heard right. She's sitting right here in my office. Everyone's going to meet at your house for drinks and dinner?" I place my hand over the phone and say, "Word's out. You got plans for the night? Molly's called the gang, and they're all rallying at her house."

Sheba says, "Tell her I wouldn't miss it for the world."

"She'd love to come, Molly. See you at six. I'll tell her the guesthouse is ready."

A knock at the door interrupts us again. I can tell the sheer weight of Sheba's celebrity is about to overwhelm us. The moment of intimacy has come and passed out of both of our reaches. I yell, "Come on in." The youngest journalists in the newsroom have summoned the courage to knock and ask me to introduce them to Sheba. Amelia Evans steps through the door first and says, after apologizing to Sheba, "Leo, I'm going to get fired if I don't get an interview with Ms. Poe before she leaves the building."

"Sheba, this is Amelia Evans, fresh out of Chapel Hill. Editor in chief of the *Daily Tar Heel.* Hottest young reporter we got. We're lucky to have her. This is Sheba Poe, Amelia."

"Is it true you dated Leo in high school, Miss Poe?" Amelia asks, before she gets permission to conduct the interview.

I can feel the tops of my ears burning as the blush catches my whole face off guard. I say, "No, we never dated. We were just friends."

A grin of mischief crosses Sheba's face as she watches my squirming. "Leo and his modesty! He just made love to me on his mahogany desk, and then he pretends we never dated."

"This newspaper is too cheap even to buy the publisher a toilet seat made out of mahogany. Amelia, take Sheba to meet her fans in the newsroom, then interview her in the library. I'll finish my column, then come get her. Behave yourself, Sheba."

"Since he was a very young man, Leo always had the sexual appetite of one of the great apes," Sheba says.

Ellen Wackenhut, who came to work in the newsroom the same year I did and who is now the science editor, hears the remark as she passes. She sticks her head in and says, "The sexual appetite of a great ape? What else haven't you told me about yourself, Leo?"

"That I made lousy friends in high school," I answer.

Ellen says, "What one word describes Leo in high school?"

Sheba pauses, then says, "Edible."

"Get Nathalie," Ellen calls out through the newsroom. "Where's the food editor when we've got a homegrown story?"

"Newsroom humor," I say to Sheba. "One soon tires of it. Get Sheba out of here, Amelia."

"These people are fine. I'd like to work up here," Sheba says.

"They're journalists, Sheba. These are poor, desperate souls. Working for starvation wages that couldn't keep you in makeup for a month."

Playing to Amelia and rising out of her chair, Sheba says to me, "I never wear makeup, dear. What you think is makeup is simply great acting."

After turning in my copy, I meet Sheba in the employee parking lot, open the passenger-side door, lean in, and throw empty drink containers, fast-food wrappers, half-empty popcorn boxes, and a catcher's mitt into the backseat. With a theatrical gesture, I motion for Sheba to enter. She gives it the once-over, then enters with that resigned look of a tourist who has just been offered a ride on the back of a mule.

As I turn onto King Street, she asks, more out of politeness than curiosity, "What kind of car is this anyway?"

"It's called a Buick LeSabre."

"I've heard of them," she says. "Not a single soul I know owns one or would ever even think about buying one. Don't you buy this kind of car for a servant? Or when you start getting social security?"

"I'm a Buick kind of guy. My grandfather sold them for a living."

"I never knew that. That might be the most boring fact I've ever heard."

"I have a wealth of boring facts," I say. "What do you drive in Holly-wood-goddamn-California?"

"I've got six cars," Sheba says. "One's a Porsche. One's a Maserati. Four are something else."

"Sounds like you're not much into cars."

"My new ex-husband's nuts for them. He talked to them when he polished them."

"Was he a nice guy? Before he started screwing starlets?"

She leans over and grabs my hand, a sweet and sisterly gesture. "I don't marry nice guys, Leo. Surely you know that by now. And you haven't exactly dazzled in your choice of women."

"Ouch," I say.

"You seen your wife lately?" Sheba is watching me carefully.

"She came back last year. Stayed for a couple of months. Then lost it again. We had some good times while it lasted."

"You need to Aretha Franklin that girl," Sheba says, then begins singing "D-I-V-O-R-C-E."

"They made me take vows," I say. "I took them seriously."

"I've taken those same vows—lots of different times. They talk about richer or poorer, better or worse. That kind of crap. Those vows don't say nothin' about being padded-cell crazy, do they?"

"I knew there were problems when I married Starla, so I didn't walk into that marriage blind. I believed in the power of love then."

"You were innocent, Leo. So were the rest of us. But not like you."

"But I've turned into the most sophisticated and worldly of men. I'm looked upon as somewhat of a Renaissance man here in this city."

"How is your mother, Sister Mary Gonzo Count Dracula Godzilla Norberta?" she asks.

"I still let her into the morgue each night. Want to swing by and see your mother?" I ask her.

"I had lunch with my mother today," Sheba says. "It's getting serious, Leo. Just like you told me six months ago."

"Let's drop the subject of mothers," I order. "Our friends are gathering South of Broad to celebrate your return to the Holy City."

We drive beside Marion Square, with the old Citadel anchoring the border, the statue of John C. Calhoun grimly surveying the harbor from the highest pedestal in town. Sheba insists that we roll down the windows so she can inhale all the complex aromas of the city and I acquiesce, even though I consider the inventor of the air conditioner the equal of the caveman who invented the wheel. Beside me, Sheba snorts and breathes in the smells of the port city. "That's confederate jasmine I smell. It's low tide in the rivers. That's the smell of the pluff mud."

"All you're smelling is carbon monoxide. The fumes of rush-hour traffic."

Sheba looks at me. "What happened to the romantic in you?"

"He grew up."

We shoot past Hyman's Seafood and the slave market, which is crowded with tourists in Bermuda shorts, T-shirts, and flip-flops, then we are stopped at the traffic light at the intersection called the Four Corners of Law. Catty-cornered is St. Michael's Episcopal Church in its starlight whiteness and all the assuredness that good taste can bestow on a house of worship. I once got in trouble with the Roman Catholic bishop of Charleston for begging him, in print, to hire only Anglican architects whenever he felt like erecting a new grotesquerie in the Charleston suburbs. My coreligionists who worship in those toadstools wrote me hate mail for weeks, but their vitriol did nothing to make their churches prettier.

As I pull south of Broad after the lights change, the siren and flashing blue lights of a police car catch me by surprise. Instinctively, I look at my speedometer and see that I am traveling at less than fifteen miles an hour. I go quickly through the list of items that allow me to drive as a free South Carolina citizen without a criminal record—insurance, registration, tax receipt, license renewal—and I am certain I have taken care of these responsibilities in an efficient and timely manner, a rarity in my life.

"You didn't moon that cop behind us, did you, Sheba?" I ask.

"If I mooned someone in South Carolina with my beautiful ass, there'd be lawsuits and fatalities. In L.A. only lechers and lesbians notice."

"Sir," a cop says as he approaches my car. "Put both hands on the steering wheel. Then slowly get out of the car. Let me see your hands at all times."

"Officer?" I ask. "What seems to be the problem?"

"I'll ask the questions," the cop says. I can hear the black inflections softening the ending of every word he speaks. "Place your hands on the hood of the car and spread your legs wide. There has been a reported kidnapping of a well-known actress by a local sex offender."

"Son of a bitch, Sheba," I say. "It's that living pain in the ass, Ike Jefferson."

"Ike!" Sheba screams. She leaps from her side of the car, they rush into each other's arms, and Ike spins Sheba in ever-widening circles, to the delight of the ladies who sell their tightly woven baskets of sweetgrass to tourists and locals alike. Ike has been a hero in Charleston's black community since he was a young man, and it is not a surprise to the basket ladies to see him whirling the most famous white girl in recent Charleston history. Because it always terrifies me in the most primitive fashion to be stopped by the police, no matter how innocent I am or how bogus the encounter, it takes me several moments to stop my hands from shaking. I take my hands off the hood, only to have the baton of another cop poke into one of my kidneys. A female cop, I realize as I hear her harsh whisper. "Freeze, white boy. I think you were given a lawful order to place your hands on the hood of your ugly, white-trash car."

"Don't hit me with that stick again, Betty," I say, "or we're going to have a fistfight in the middle of Meeting Street."

"Resisting arrest. Threatening a police officer," says Betty Roberts Jefferson, Ike's wife and a sergeant on the force. "You heard it, didn't you, Captain?"

"I did," Ike says. "Search his trunk, Sergeant."

"I hope you have a search warrant," I say. Of course, Betty puts one in front of my face, signed and sealed by Desiree Robinson, the first black judge in the history of the city courts.

"The worst year in American history was 1619," I say. Sheba is laughing at me, still enfolded in Ike's powerful arms. "First black slaves imported into the Virginia colony. It's been downhill for the South ever since."

When their cackling finally passes, Ike says, "Sheba, ride in my squad car with me. Betty, you ride with that cream-puff white boy."

"Not until I give this girl a hug," Betty says, turning toward Sheba. "Hey, Sheba, how's my favorite white bitch?"

The two women embrace fiercely. Sheba says, "Betty, let me take you west. I'd have casting directors creaming all over themselves to put you on the silver screen."

"Got to stay here and keep my eye on the new chief of police," she says, nodding in the direction of her husband.

"Chief?" Sheba cries loudly. "You're the goddamn chief of police in Charleston, South Carolina, Ike Jefferson? What happened to good old white racism? Segregated lunch counters? Whites-only drinking fountains? Where is it now that we really need it? Chief of police! I've never felt this much pride for anyone in my whole life."

I say, "It's amazing what a little graft, corruption, gun smuggling, and drug dealing can do for a bad cop's advancement."

"It won't happen for a few months," Ike says to Sheba, ignoring me. "Then there'll be a big ceremony, and The Citadel's going to throw a parade in my honor. It'd be an honor to me for you to be there."

"Wild horses and a role in the next Spielberg movie couldn't keep me away," she says. "No, I'm lying about the Spielberg movie. But only Spielberg could keep me away. That's a promise. Who're you going to invite?"

"Dignitaries. Big shots," Ike says, giggling. "Just the cream of white society. Hell, even Leo won't be invited."

"I'm buying dental floss that weekend," I say. "I don't have time to eat chitlins with social-climbing black traffic cops."

"Put that white boy in handcuffs, woman," Ike says. He opens his patrol car for Sheba, bowing elaborately as she sweeps into the front seat. "I'm tired of his lip."

Betty and I drive behind Ike's car. "Think my man's safe with Sheba?" she asks.

"A man's never safe with Sheba," I answer. "And there's never been a woman born who didn't know it."

"She's always looked like a movie star, carried herself like one. It's almost unnatural, isn't it? Oh, I almost forgot, the future chief ordered me to handcuff you, Leo." In an effortless motion combining experience and deftness, she cuffs my right hand to the steering wheel.

"Take the handcuffs off. I don't want to report you for police brutality."

I love Betty's high-pitched laugh. "It excites me to see you in handcuffs, Leo. Makes me feel like a dominatrix. You know, the old white-black thing, reversed."

"Race," I say. "At least it's not complicated down South."

"Yeah," Betty agrees. "We always have that. Complete ease and trust among my people and yours."

We turn into the driveway of the mansion on East Bay Street where we are gathering for the evening, the home of Molly and Chad Rutledge. Sheba rushes out, runs up the front stairs, and she and Molly hug, screaming on the piazza. Ike, Betty, and I watch from our cars below.

Leaning over to remove the handcuffs, Betty gives me a quick peck on the cheek. "Do you know what I love about Sheba coming to town?" she asks. "I always feel more alive. I feel that something big is about to happen."

"It's no accident she's here, Betty," I say. "Sheba will take us all to center stage tonight."

"She'll never be happy, will she, Leo? What does she want from us?"

"I'm sure she'll tell us. Nothing comes free with Sheba."

"Our girl's in trouble," Ike says.

"Did she say anything to you in the car?" I ask.

"Her typical Hollywood bullshit," Ike replies. "But I think she's in trouble."

"That girl's been in trouble her whole life," Betty says, shaking her head. "Are we really going to Chad and Molly's? Every time I walk in their door I feel like Cinderella going to the ball."

Ike laughs. "With your cop's uniform and those shit-kicker shoes?"

"Use your imagination," Betty says. "This is a ballroom gown and I'm wearing glass slippers. Leo, give me your arm. I'd like a white Southern gentleman with a sense of style to lead me into the Pinckney-Barnwell mansion."

With a smile, I escort Betty Jefferson up the winding exterior staircase of one of the twenty-five most distinguished private dwellings south of Broad. Molly comes out to greet us on the veranda.

"Hey, Molly Mouse," I say.

"Good golly, Miss Molly," Ike adds, and we all take turns hugging Molly.

I catch a glimpse of Sheba roaming toward the guesthouse. Molly says, "Sheba insisted on a quick shower and costume change before the other guests arrive. Let's go to the library, where Leo will be in charge of making drinks. I picked up some T-bones from the Piggly Wiggly. Do you and Ike mind grilling them if my absentee husband does not make it home from his office?"

"Chad's working late again?" Betty asks. "Am I wrong or does he spend more time at his fancy office than he does at home?"

"You're not far from wrong. Hey, Leo," Molly says as she holds me close to her. "I need more than a proper greeting from you. Do you mind putting a hickey on my neck?"

All of us laugh. "I was thinking about a more creative place. How about your right thigh?"

We enter the great house and walk past two hundred years of Charleston history in the shape of antiques too exquisite to sit on or otherwise use. In the center of the room, a chandelier hangs that looks like an ode to cut glass. An ebony grand piano stands guard in a corner overlooking the Cooper River, and a great fern-shaped harp stands in elegant attendance across the room. In all the years I have known the Rutledge family, I have never heard anyone play either instrument. I have never sat down on one of the priceless divans or chairs made by the earliest furniture makers in the colony. In its lackluster inertness, the room strikes me with the same pity I feel for an abandoned child; the piano and harp seem like they are dying from the absence of melody. Charleston is filled with such somber rooms maligned by lack of use. The large dining room with a mahogany table large enough for twenty-four shapely but fragile chairs finds use only on special occasions, and it too exudes a feeling of sterility and desertion. I would bet a month's salary that it has been years since someone has eaten breakfast in its forbidding shadows.

But in the library, the house springs to delicious modern life with its well-stocked shelves of books that climb from floor to ceiling along one wall, the huge TV where we gather to watch the Carolina-Clemson game that is a communal rite in our state, the comfortable chairs and sofas, some leather and some made from the most decadent fabrics, the wet bar with its tiers of bottles, the fireplace with its renowned grillwork by the great Charleston cabinetmaker Thomas Elfe. This is a room that carries happy memories for all of us, the place we come to party, relax, and sometimes fall apart. It was filled with the memories that attend the reef-like accretions that build up friendships. That is the necessary role Molly plays in all our lives, the first real grown-up our circle produced, a mother figure long before she even became a mother. Only her husband, Chad, seems incapable of appreciating his wife's goodness and wise counsel. But all of us are old enough to know that marriage is an institution that can breed hostility and indifference when none is justified.

Molly puts me in charge of distributing drinks. I have played bartender for this group ever since high school, when I was the only one among us who didn't drink. I pour gin and tonics for Molly and Betty and retrieve a Heineken from the small refrigerator bar for Ike. But he says, "Hey, you gossip columnist!"

I turn to him. "Excuse me, sir, I consider myself the conscience of this town. Its daily chronicler. Its heart and soul. Now, do you want me to get your sorry ass a beer or not?"

"I drank beer when I was a traffic cop. What do you think the new chief of police should drink when he steps into high society?"

"I got to put up with this shit for the rest of my life," Betty says. She lifts her glass to Molly, who touches it in a show of solidarity.

"Would his lordship like Wild Turkey on the rocks? A margarita with a salt-rimmed glass, or an old-fashioned, a Manhattan, or would you join me in a dry Beefeater martini, stirred like a son of a bitch, not shaken?"

"I love that double-o-seven talk," Ike says. "Yeah, give me that James Bond drink. He kind of reminds me of myself."

All of us look up when a figure in the doorway materializes without warning. Molly says, "What's the password, mountain boy?"

Niles Whitehead smiles and takes in all the faces. "Molly Rutledge is the goddamnedest broad in the history of Charleston."

"Not true," Molly says. "Your own wife is."

"Except for my own wife," Niles agrees.

"What about my damn wife?" Ike says.

"About time, husband," Betty says. "Niles, you quit that flirting with Molly."

"I'm allowed to flirt with my sister-in-law, Betty," Niles says. "It's almost a requirement in Charleston. But I make it a habit not to flirt with a woman who packs iron on her hip. Especially when her husband's in the same room and glad to provide backup."

"Hold your fire, Ike. Don't shoot the mountain boy when he runs his mouth. I like it when the white boys flirt with me," Betty says.

"Betty Jefferson is the goddamnedest broad in the city of Charleston," Niles says.

"I like the sound of it," Betty says. "You can tell the mountain boy's being sincere. He's not full of crap the way you Charleston boys are. Thanks, Niles. You made it sound real nice."

"It's the orphan factor," I say. "Niles always gets a break from women because of his Oliver Twist background."

"Oliver Twist. I've heard of him. We go to school with him?" Ike asks.

"I married an idiot," Betty says, covering her face. "Don't forget I grew up in an orphanage too, Ike."

"You guys go down and light the charcoal," Molly says. "I don't know where we're going to eat because Sheba didn't hand out a production schedule for the evening's events. By the way, Leo, your mother's invited too."

I stop dead as Niles and Ike laugh and head down to the yard. I groan, and there is not a person in the room who does not understand the authenticity of that sound. "Why did you do that, Molly?"

"Cowardice comes easily to me. So does human weakness. True Southern girls need to please, no matter what the consequences. Monsignor Max called and said he heard Sheba was in town and wanted to come see her. He offered to be your mother's chaperone. He caught me by surprise, Leo. I'm truly sorry."

"It doesn't seem like a good idea, Molly," I tell her. "Sheba and my mother aren't members of each other's booster clubs."

Molly comes up and kisses me lightly on the cheek. "I also knew you'd forgive me, no matter what I did. You always have, Leo."

"You've always been my weakness, kid."

"Weakness, my ass," Betty says, grinning at both of us. "Look at Leo's eyes. He's been in love with you since high school, Molly. The boy never could hide it. Still can't. Used to be cute, now it's just sick."

I ignore her, and ask Molly, "Did you tell Sheba that my mother's coming?"

"Yes, I did," Molly replies. "That's what I'm really worried about."

The doorbell rings, and I know that my mother and Monsignor Max have arrived. I shudder at the multifold possibilities the evening holds in its precarious balance. Since my father's death all those years ago, my mother and I have skirmished over the most trifling matters, and have even gone to war on several occasions when confronted by issues that neither of us felt to be paramount. A new combustibility has grown up between us that can easily turn a pilot light into an inferno. Recently, my mother threw a drink in my face while we were arguing the place of colons in an English sentence: Mother thought of them as elegant pauses and an artful way to let a sentence breathe; I thought of them as ostentatious. When Father died, my mother and I lost our referee and middleman, our greatest fan who could translate the hidebound idiosyncrasies that could drive us crazy in a moment's notice; we forever lost that demilitarized zone that kept us from each other's throats. Yet she is constantly searching for inroads to navigate our relationship, and I know that this party is the ultimate white flag she can use from her breached walls. I appreciate the gesture of goodwill.

I let my mother and the monsignor in the front door. Though I should've known better, I do not notice the gargoyles forming on the waterspouts or the trolls licking their lips under the boxwoods. "I know I was the last person you were expecting to see tonight," my mother says as I peck her cheek. Mother and I could give college-level courses in false displays of affection.

"I was delighted when Molly told me," I answer. "Hello, Monsignor Max. It's wonderful to see you."

"If that little minx Sheba thinks she's going to come to Charleston without seeing me, she's got another think coming," he says.

"You and Mother make a handsome couple," I say. "Come on in. I'll make you some drinks. The guest of honor is planning a grand entrance."

"The only kind she knows," Mother murmurs as she leads the way to the library.

As I pour drinks for the two of them—red wine for my mother, a dry vodka martini with two olives for the monsignor—I say, "This martini is Saharan or Gobi-like."

"It is the martini's job to bring me closer to God," the monsignor says, then sips with satisfaction. "It brings me halfway to God, then I must rely on the awesome power of prayer to take me to the summit."

"Then you must teach me how to pray in the proper manner, Monsignor." A man's voice comes from the doorway, and I look up to see

Chad Rutledge putting his briefcase on a bench. "The Anglicans teach that drinking is the fastest way to approach God. Charlestonians think it's the only way. What's wrong with our theology?"

"Join us in a drink and we'll talk about it, Chad," the monsignor says.

"Let me do the honor," I say. "I'll even bring it to your chair."

"I like it when you're sycophantic, Leo," Chad says. "It's so rare these days."

"I try not to make it a habit, Chad. You like it too much."

"I think it's the natural order of things." He winks at my mother.

I pull down the sterling silver cup, part of a set that Chad received the night he stepped down from his position as the youngest president in the history of the South Carolina bar. I pile the cup with shaved ice, then half-fill it with Wild Turkey.

"Where are your children, Chad?" Mother asks.

"Banished to their grandparents' house," Chad answers. "It still amazes me that my father—the guy who Fraser and I barely saw in our childhood—has gone bonkers over his grandkids."

Monsignor Max says, "I've seen it happen dozens of times. He probably realized he was a bad father, and this is his way of making it up to you and your sister."

I wait for Mother's onslaught, and don't have to wait very long: "Every night I pray for a grandchild."

"Can't have everything," I say as I carry a tray full of appetizers around the room.

"Look around you tonight, Leo," Mother says. We can hear the rest of our group coming up the back stairs. "It doesn't seem that hard to attract a real wife. One who lives with you, shares your bed, and devotes her life to your happiness. On the way over, the monsignor confided that he could get you a papal annulment with no trouble whatsoever."

"It'd take three phone calls," Monsignor Max says.

"Now is not a good time to talk about it," I say.

"Name a good time, son, and I'll be there," Mother says. "A tribe of cannibals couldn't keep me away."

"Drop it, Mother. My brother-in-law approaches from the west."

Molly enters first, and comes up short when she sees her husband, relaxed and sitting in his leather chair. She goes over to kiss him. "Darling! So good of you to come. How on earth did you find your way to our house?"

"Someone at the office lent me a compass and a street map," he responds good-naturedly. "Now, behave yourself, darling. I think this could be a famous Charleston evening, if we just let ourselves enjoy it."

"A night to remember," Fraser Whitehead says, moving in behind Molly. "Wasn't that the name of a movie?"

"Certainly was, sis." Chad's voice is as smooth and soft as a dropped silk handkerchief. "It was about the Titanic."

My mother whispers to me, but loud enough for most people in the room to hear, "It's funny talking about your marriage, then the Titanic. A perfect segue, don't you think?"

"Mother, I don't think this event's about you." My voice is strident.

"I disagree," Chad says. "This evening is about anything we decide to make of it. Don't let your son inhibit you, Dr. King. I'll always be grateful for how you helped me and Molly during our senior year in high school."

"You and Molly proved a gamble well worth taking," Mother responds.

"I told her at the time," Monsignor Max says, "if you can't trust a Rutledge or a Huger in Charleston, then we might as well all move to Myrtle Beach."

"Mother's always enjoyed helping millionaires out of tight situations, Chad," I say. "It's a hobby of hers."

"When did you notice that Leo was like this, Dr. King?" Chad asks.

"At a very early age, I'm afraid," she replies.

Again, a door opens and shuts in the rear of the house. Niles and Ike file into the den, Niles holding a bottle of frosted beer and Ike still working on his martini, bringing with them the smell of burning charcoal from the garden. They greet my mother and the monsignor. Niles then walks over to the television, turns it on, inserts a videotape into the VCR, and directs everyone's attention to the screen.

Ike says, "As you can imagine, Sheba is not just going to walk up here to have dinner. Since the day we met her, Sheba's been in the middle of a performance that had no beginning, and it certainly ain't going to end tonight."

When we see the movie flash onto the screen, all of us recognize the opening credits of Sheba's first big Hollywood break, *The Roar of the Girl Next Door,* starring Dustin Hoffman and Jane Fonda. As the credits roll, the camera establishes the setting as Manhattan, with a score by Thelonious Monk that sounds like sex being performed in three-quarter time. At the entrance to a posh women's boutique, the camera lingers. The door opens. A nineteen-year-old Sheba Poe, luscious, desirable, yet innocent and dewy in her own way, bursts out of that shop like an orchid opening up to sunlight. The same camera registers the almost heartless pleasure she takes in the effect of her own beauty on the men she passes on the street. She is wearing a low-cut white summer dress that clings to her body like a new layer of skin. The camera veers in front of her, capturing her dazzling walk down Madison Avenue, the ripeness of her figure strutting toward the lens like a force of nature as powerful as a tidal surge. There is a shot of her long, coltish legs and her sandaled feet and the dark red of her toenail polish, which had been enough to make me consider a minor-league career in foot fetishism when I saw the movie for the first time. The eye of the camera turns to the people on Madison Avenue watching her languorous passage, the wolf-whistling cabdrivers, the lunchtime construction workers yelling from high beams, teenage boys blushing, fashionable dowagers torn between envy and admiration. She stops suddenly and checks her makeup in the reflection of a plate-glass window that is decorated with shining tiers of diamond rings, brooches of ruby, amethyst necklaces, and watches that look like fancy collars for Chihuahuas.

A shot of her magnificent behind is captured from the point of view of a Middle Eastern cabdriver. Cars honk in appreciation as she moves away from the window toward the traffic jam that she has created. She smiles and winks at the cabdriver. He adjusts his rearview mirror, and she freshens up her lipstick as he counts his worry beads at a higher rate to match both his rapid heartbeat and the haunting music. She continues her walk down the runway that is Manhattan isle. There have been very few walks in Hollywood history that have achieved such attention or acclaim.

When the set designer's name appears on the credits, we hear someone entering the back door of the library, an entrance designed to not go unnoticed. We turn to see her in the flesh: the actress Sheba Poe, wearing

the same dress and the same sandals and the same pearls, the same shade
of lipstick and nail polish, and the same hairdo she wore in the movie we
are watching. Synchronizing her moves to the action on the screen, Sheba
walks through the center of us, and we applaud the pure imagination of
this homecoming. A natural ham, Sheba plays to her hometown crowd
by adding bumps and grinds as she struts to that throbbing sound track,
which sounds like it was written for some banned fertility rite. As our
eyes flicker from the screen to the live woman, it is not just a good figure
on a woman we praise but a body that helped define feminine shapeliness
for a generation.

As the young Sheba crosses Madison through the traffic that has backed
up to honor her beauty, the real woman weaves through the couches and
chairs in that paneled library. In the film, horses rear up with cops trying to bring their mounts under control; a distinguished-looking man
emerging from a florist watches her approach, then bows and hands her a
dozen white roses. Sheba curtsies to the gentleman, puts one of the roses
between her teeth, then begins passing out the others to a homeless man,
a young mother pushing a stroller with twins, and two sewer workers
who have popped out of a manhole to observe her passage.

Molly cut white roses from her own garden that day, and Ike seizes
the moment by stealing them from their Oriental vase and handing them
to Sheba with their stems dripping water on the rugs. Sheba puts one rose
between her lips, then passes out the others to everyone in the room, saving the last for the monsignor, who beams.

As the assistant producers are named in a passing trilogy, a crane
operator high above studies Sheba's walk through a pair of binoculars.
We turn from the screen toward the real woman, who has now walked
to the end of the room and is coming back toward us. I watch her approach, the lyricism of her promenade toward the friends who honored
her before she made this walk famous on movie screens around the world.
Not a single critic reviewed that movie without mentioning Sheba's con-
cupiscent walk in which she seemed to define sex itself as something
brand-new, some interior fire she had stolen and reincarnated in her own
image. In that opening sequence, Sheba Poe walked into the cold heart
of her complicated history by displaying an allure dangerous in both its
carnality and its innocence.

The opening score is slowing down, and Sheba's celebrated walk is ending. She vamps her way over to the screen as her younger self enters a high-end restaurant and spots Dustin Hoffman at a table, impatient and fidgety. Looking down at the younger incarnation of herself, Sheba waits as he stares at his Rolex over an empty wineglass, and says, "You're late . . . again."

Sheba the younger is joined by Sheba the older in the library on East Bay Street, with her high school friends around her, as she speaks her first line of dialogue in a film: "No one else seemed to mind, darling," the two Shebas say in unison. " 'Cept you."

The room explodes into applause, and Sheba curtsies demurely. After her ovation, she poses in front of the monsignor as though his delighted face were a mirror. For as long as I have known Max, he has been as comfortable with center stage as Sheba has, and he obviously loves that her last act is in his honor. It would have provided a perfect ending to her performance if Sheba had not repulsed my mother with the shamelessness of her performance.

"Oh, stop it, Sheba," Mother says. "You've made enough of a display out of yourself for one evening."

With wicked timing, Sheba says, "No one else seemed to mind, darling. 'Cept you." My mother's disapproval seems to both delight and disturb her, but the jawlines on both women are wired tight.

"You have a God-given talent," Mother says. "Yet you glory in playing the role of a tramp."

"That was the part I was hired to play," Sheba responds. "Would you like the scene better if they had dressed me in a garbage bag and combat boots?"

"I've read the stories about you in Hollywood," my mother continues. "I know the choices you've made and I know you were born with free will like the rest of us."

I try to think of a way to change the subject and the razorlike tension in the room. "Mother," I begin, but my voice is weak, "I'm trying to think of a nice way of saying shut up."

"Your mother is a guest in my house, Leo," Chad says. "Any of my guests has the right to free speech."

"Isn't that sweet?" I say. "Go fuck yourself, Chad."

"Easy, Leo," Niles warns.

"Why don't we get those steaks on the fire?" Ike adds.

But neither Sheba nor my mother is finished with the other. Sheba starts by saying, "Mother Superior, may I borrow a tampon? I left all mine at the Betty Ford clinic."

"I'd like to wash your mouth out with soap," Mother spits out. "How dare you say something like that in front of the monsignor?"

The monsignor pats my mother's hand. "Remember, dear, I've spent a good portion of my life in confessionals. It's hard to shock me."

Sheba's eyes do not leave my mother's. "It's acting, Mother Superior, just great acting. Lean back and enjoy the pure fraud of it."

"Not fraud, my dear," Mother answers. "I'd call it losing one's soul a little bit at a time. I would never twitch my body to arouse the lust of every man who passed by."

"Hell, Dr. King," Fraser says, trying to lighten up the room, "I probably would have, but it wouldn't work for me."

"It worked on me, kid," Niles says.

Fraser continues, "Sheba's a movie star, Dr. King. Being sexy's part of her job description."

"It's part of every woman's job description," Betty says with a laugh.

"Being sexy is one thing," Mother snaps. "Being a slut is another."

Without missing a beat, Sheba lifts a small linen cloth from the top drawer of a sideboard and pulls it over her head and shoulders like a cowl. She closes her eyes for a moment, then opens them suddenly, transforming herself by applying the strange alchemy of performance into something virginal and nunlike. Sheba turns her face toward us, as drawn in and sun-starved as a member of some cloistered order. The metamorphosis is extraordinary, a bird of paradise becoming a common grackle.

But the artist in our midst is not in a playful mood, and Sheba turns her newly minted Sister-of-the-Holy-Cross face on my mother and strikes out with no thought of mercy or restraint. "Mother Superior," Sheba says, "I too have dedicated my life to prayer and good work. I could play the role of a nun far better than you did on your best day in the convent. Because God endowed me with a gift, I remain true to that gift, and I can play the part of an accountant or an astronaut or a trapped housewife or a lesbian. But you're right; I can also play a stripper or a whore or a home wrecker or a lunatic."

"In some of those roles, you're a natural, Sheba," Mother says. "No acting necessary."

"Mother, would you kindly button your yap?" I cry. "Molly, why did you do this?"

"An error of judgment."

"Molly's good at those," Chad says, mock-toasting his wife.

"But only one of them really counts," Molly shoots back before Sheba regains control of the stage.

"Did it turn on Leo's sweet father to see you in a nun's habit, Dr. King?" Sheba asks. "Did it excite you that you kept poor Leo's daddy horny and heartbroken all those years you spent in the convent? When did you know that he was turned on by the shaking of rosaries on the nun's body hidden by ten pounds of black cloth? Some men like G-strings. What lit Jasper's fire? Was it enclosure? The untouchable girl in the convent? Did you ever think that you did to him the same thing I was doing to every man on the street in that walk down Madison Avenue?"

"You've gone far enough, Sheba," Betty says.

"I happen to be Sheba's lawyer," Chad says, ice tinkling in his silver cup. "She has broken no laws I'm aware of."

"The laws of polite society?" Fraser suggests.

"Sheba's never followed those," Niles says.

Betty says, "Sheba, all of us in this room check in on your mother from time to time, Leo more than anyone, so you shouldn't go after his mama. It's not right."

"Could we drop it?" Niles asks. "Or should I hog-tie the both of them? Leave Leo's mama out of this, Sheba. She's off-limits. Always has been."

"Not off-limits for me, Niles," Sheba says, "because Dr. King hated me from the first time she laid eyes on me. Isn't that true, Doctor?"

"No, it isn't," Mother says. I hear something deadly and familiar in her throat that I am sure no one else recognizes. I prepare for the worst, and the worst comes: "It took two or three months for the hatred to settle in," Mother continues. "I fought against it. But it came, Sheba. And you're right. It never left me. Everything was always about you; you were the center of the universe. I am certain you could find a spotlight in the darkest corner of hell."

Holding fast to her nun's habit, Sheba tightens the grip around the cloth. In a nunlike voice that makes the air seem murderous, she says, "I know your act, Mother Superior. I've known it from the beginning. I've been onto you."

The monsignor, who seems transfixed and fascinated, springs to sudden life. "I know the moment when an evening has arrived at a point of no return. I think we should let the young people enjoy the rest of the evening together, Lindsay."

"Who's Lindsay?" Niles asks.

"That's Dr. King's first name," someone answers.

"I always thought it was Doctor," Niles says.

"Just a minute, Max." Mother lifts a finger to fix the monsignor. "Sheba, do you remember what I told you the day before you graduated from high school?"

"How could I forget?" Sheba answers. "I was an eighteen-year-old kid who came up the hard way. My only crime was to befriend your lonely son, who was nicknamed 'the Toad.' Right, Leo?"

"Sounds right to me."

"So my brother and I took the Toad into our lives and hearts, and he took us into his. It was the same year the mountain boy came down from the hills holding his damaged sister at arm's length from the world. Remember her, Mother Superior? Anytime I do tragedy, I think of that mountain girl. If I have to do courage, I become that mountain boy. The actor is a natural-born thief, and I steal from everybody. For sweetness, I do Betty. For strength, I have Ike in reserve. See Fraser there? It's her integrity I steal for my characters. For beauty, I have Molly. For success and self-assurance, I conjure up Chad. For kindness, I've got the Toad. I've got your terrific son, the one blushing over there, the kid you could never quite bring yourself to love."

"Tell them what I told you that night," Mother orders. "Your speech was artful, but you changed the subject."

"You told me that I was the most talented girl ever to go through Peninsula High School." Sheba's voice nearly breaks from an emotion that has nothing to do with her talent.

"Go on," Mother says. "That was the first thing I told you. But I didn't stop there, did I, dear?"

"Could someone stop this?" Fraser asks, covering her ears.

Niles says, "Betty, you shoot Sheba. Ike, you take out Dr. King. It's the only way."

"You told me I could discover a cure for cancer or be the biggest whore who ever lived," Sheba says, dropping her linen veil to the floor behind her.

"I was only half right," Mother says. "Cancer is still a real threat to society."

"Jesus Christ, Mother," I say. "Monsignor, don't even bother taking her to the car. Pitch her off the balcony into the street."

Through tears, Sheba says, "I was a child."

"You were never a child," Mother shoots back.

"Well, be an adult now and forget it, Sheba," Molly says. "And you, Dr. King, need to settle down. Sheba's been through a lot, and no one knows that better than Leo. You and Ike, refresh everyone's drinks. Sheba, come into the kitchen and help me get dinner on the table."

Chad scoffs. "Who're you trying to kid, Molly? You and Sheba wouldn't know what to do with a kitchen if it bit you in the ass."

"Your language, dear brother," Fraser says. "The monsignor's here."

"And I think that's the perfect exit line," Monsignor Max says, rising. "I'll pretend to be highly offended by Chad's profanity and storm out of here with Lindsay in tow."

"I think that's an inspired idea, Mother," I say. "What you said to Sheba—you ought to be ashamed of yourself."

"She started it," Mother says. But I can see her temper cooling down as she surveys the damage she has wrought by studying the shocked faces surrounding her.

"I can only hope so," Sheba says.

Mother flames again. "Don't you think for a minute I don't know that you stole my son's virginity, you white-trash slut!"

"Jesus God almighty," I say, blushing to my very bones in abject horror at the deformity the evening has shaped itself into. I turn to the monsignor. "Please get my mother out of here."

Ike stares at Sheba in disbelief. "You nailed the Toad?"

"She stole the most precious thing Leo had," Mother says. "His innocence."

"No. No, Lindsay. No, Mother Superior. No, Dr. King," Sheba shoots back. "The one precious thing he had was the thing you loved best: the son you lost. Remember him, Lindsay? I don't. Never met the kid. Bet that he was a sweetheart like Leo. Stephen, Steve? Wasn't that his name? Seems he killed himself years before I got here. You can't blame me for Steve's suicide, but I bet you'd love to. I believe you always wished it had been Leo who slit his wrists, Leo who'd died. In your weird, screwed-up world, it's always the handsome boys you lose. The ugly ones are the keepers. You've always treated Leo like he was the second-place trophy you got for losing your golden boy."

"That's evil, Sheba," Fraser cries in horror. "Just pure evil."

Ike grabs Sheba from behind, lifts her in his strong, brown arms, and carries her through the kitchen and down the back staircase. Molly walks to open the front door, and Betty helps the monsignor get my mother down the stairs and into the monsignor's Lincoln Continental. The evening is finished, but it is not over.

I collapse into a leather couch, close my eyes, and let myself drift into the luxurious easement of the library with its tiers of well-selected books. The smell of leather consoles me, and it feels like I have rested my head inside a well-oiled baseball glove. As far as I know, no one has mentioned my brother's name in my mother's presence for years. Even now, in the toxic wake of this evening's passage, when I try to conjure up an image of my brother's face, I can summon only a ghostly, featureless portrait, half-sketched in sepia. All I remember is that Stephen was golden and beautiful, and that our losing him drove a stake into the heart of my family. Somehow we managed to survive that day, but none of us ever experienced the deliverance of recovery. I realize you can walk away from anything but a wounded soul.

CHAPTER 9

A Night of Fun

I hear a match strike near me, then smell the smoke of expensive cigar leaf. I open my eyes and find myself under the intense scrutiny of Chad Rutledge. He blows a plume of sweet-smelling smoke in my direction. "Now, that is what I call entertainment with a capital *E*."

"Glad you enjoyed it, Chad."

"Think of what Molly and I would've missed if we hadn't been kicked out of Porter-Gaud the summer before our senior year." He grins. "We didn't know anyone like you or Niles or Starla or Ike or Betty. It was a brave new world for us."

"We were your first experience with the underbelly of Charleston."

"You've always been so class-conscious," Chad says.

"Only since I met you. When we met at the yacht club, it was the first time someone had looked at me like I was a lower form of toe cheese."

"Not so. To me, you were the Camembert of toe cheese."

A large shadow appears at the kitchen doorway, and I look over to see Niles Whitehead. "What kind of toe cheese am I, Chad?" Niles asks.

"You're family, Niles. My much-admired brother-in-law. The husband of my only sister. The father of my handsome nephews."

"But surely you recognize that Leo comes from a much-higher-class family than I do. To refresh your memory, Leo found my sister and I handcuffed to chairs when he first met us."

"My admiration for the two of you is boundless," Chad says. "Both of you were ambitious young men. You've made your mark in the field of education, Niles. You married into one of the oldest families in Charleston, which was not the easiest thing to do for a boy from your background. Leo has become a famous journalist. His column is one of the first things everybody reads when they open the paper in the morning. No small achievement."

"Gosh, I feel like a shrimp boat right after the bishop blesses the fleet," I say.

"Wow," says Niles. "To think of having human worth in Chad's aristocratic eyes."

Chad laughs, then stares at his cigar with contentment. "Ah, Sheba, didn't she give us a night! If I hadn't met you, I would've missed all the melodrama of these lives you consider normal. I'd miss the discord, all the howls and barks you bring to every event. My people are high-class and civilized, which is another way of saying boring, I think. All the grunts and whines have been bred out of us. Tonight was high opera."

"Chad, I've always felt bad that I didn't kick the shit out of you when you were a kid," Niles says.

"I've got to get back to the office in a few minutes," Chad says, unperturbed. "Big case next week."

"Does Molly know?" Niles asks.

"Molly likes being in this house. She likes the life my law practice provides. She likes being married into my family's fortune, just like you do, Niles," Chad says.

"I told you this a long time ago, Chad," I say. "Don't screw with the mountain boy. It ain't safe."

"Tell Molly good night for me," Chad says. "I may work straight through the night."

"Molly's not going to like it," I say.

"Tough titty." Chad winks and salutes us as he skips out the front door.

Niles and I sit for several minutes in silence as we smell the steaks sizzling on the charcoal fire. Rising to walk to the bar, Niles says, "Can I make you another drink?"

"I was trying to think about how much I'd have to drink to forget everything that happened tonight, and still enjoy the rest of the evening."

"There's not enough liquor in the world for that," Niles says. "But Sheba and Chad have left for the night—that means the shitbirds have flown out of the cuckoo's nest."

"Sheba's in the worst shape I've ever seen her," I say.

"Bet your mama thinks so. That was brutal."

"Sheba's lost her way."

"Didn't she used to be sweet?" Niles asks.

"The sweetest girl in the world," Molly says, materializing in the kitchen doorway. "Where's Chad? Oh, let me guess! He went back to work on a big case. A big, big goddamn case. Don't tell me. I know the drill. He does it out of love for me and the kids. I couldn't live without this mansion and an armored car full of money. Could you go down and help your wife with the steaks, Niles? I need to beg Leo's forgiveness for bringing Sheba and his mama together."

"Fire and ice," Niles says. "Where are Ike and Betty?"

"Putting Miss Sheba to bed. She took the homecoming scene hard. It wasn't what she wanted."

"We'll be back with the steaks," Niles says, then I hear him taking the back stairs two at a time.

Molly walks over to the bar. "Sometimes a woman needs flowers, Leo. Sometimes she needs a massage, or to hold hands, or to cuddle. Sometimes she needs to call an old friend she hasn't talked to for years, or read a trashy book with a lot of dirt thrown in. Sometimes a woman needs to get laid. Or run a mile, or play three sets of tennis. But then there are nights like this one, nights when a woman needs to get drunk."

Molly answers by pouring herself a jigger of vodka and throws an ice cube in the glass. "Do you want me to fix you anything?" I ask.

"A cup of arsenic with a dash of Angostura bitters and, if it's not too much of a bother, a cigar box full of sleeping pills. That was as bad a scene as any of us has seen for a while."

"Don't say that, Molly," I warn. "God is listening. He likes challenges."

"God had nothing to do with what Sheba said."

"He had everything to do with it," I say.

"Did you really get it on with Sheba in high school?" Molly cannot quite suppress a smile at the thought of it.

"You saw me in high school. Did you want to get it on with me?"

"You got handsome late," she admits.

"I never got handsome."

"I've thought about putting the make on you a time or two over the years, Leo."

"That's not your libido talking," I tell her. "That's alcohol."

"Sometimes it takes alcohol to let your libido in on what you really want."

"That's the dirtiest thing you've ever said, Molly Rutledge."

"I think it is," she says, reflecting. "I liked saying it."

"What a shame we're both married," I say.

"We might be, Leo," she says, "but I'm not a lunatic on the subject."

"And I am?"

"You and Starla don't exactly have a traditional marriage," Molly reminds me. "She stays with you awhile, starts to lose it, goes off the deep end, and bang, she disappears again."

"I knew what I was getting into."

"Did you really?"

"No. I had no idea what I was getting into," I admit.

"Neither did I."

"Molly, you're married to one of the most successful lawyers in the city. He's from one of the oldest, most distinguished families in Charleston. You were destined to marry Chad Rutledge the day you were born."

"It's a pretty story." Her voice contains a dissident quality I've not noticed before. "But not a true one." She takes a chair opposite me. "Chad was sick of me a long time before we married. You know it, I know it; all of my friends know it. And most tragically, Chad knows it."

"Everyone who knows you is in love with you, Molly. Everybody knows that. Even Chad."

"Sweet Leo." She smiles. "But you don't lie well. Forget it. Let's talk about pleasant subjects, like tonight. Do you think any of us will ever get over what happened tonight?"

"The whole thing caught me by surprise," I say. "I didn't know that bad blood could run so deep. Or for so long."

"That wasn't bad blood." Molly fingers the rim of her wineglass. "That was hatred—of the Shakespearean variety. Sheba was a lot of things when we knew her, Leo, but she was never mean. It's her kindness everyone remembers most."

"I still believe in that kindness."

Betty comes charging up the back stairs carrying the first platter of steaks. She places the food on the large kitchen table, where the Rutledge family eats most all of their meals, then walks directly to the bar. "How can you two lovebirds sit around flirting after that scene? This shit ain't right. Give me a glass of white wine. This is what I get for hanging around you white folks. I like it better in the damn ghetto. We get that mad, we just shoot each other. Leo, honey, I never knew you had a brother. You've always seemed like an only child."

"I should've told you," I say. "It's hard for me to talk about Steve. And I don't think I'd know him if he walked into this room tonight."

"I'm getting worried about Ike," Betty says. "He's been there putting Sheba to bed for a long time."

"He'll be in soon," I say. "Thanks for helping get my mother to the car. I was too paralyzed to move."

"The monsignor did the real dirty work. I've never seen your mother so shaken up. But the good reverend was making fine use of his golden tongue. I got to hand it to the man: he's got a line of bullshit you could take to the bank. He sounds just what you think God would sound like if God was a Roman Catholic—which He sure as hell ain't."

"His sermons pack the cathedral," I say.

"And what an operator he is." Betty sits beside me and grabs my knee with one hand while sipping her wine with the other. "Before I came back to the house, the monsignor asked if Sheba could get four front-row tickets to *A Chorus Line* on Broadway next month. What's Sheba got to do with Broadway?"

Molly says, "She slept with one of the producers of the show for a while. At least, that's what I read in *People*."

"You subscribe to *People*?" I ask.

"Doctor's office," Molly says. "A guilty pleasure, but a pleasure nonetheless. And it's how I keep up with our girl Sheba."

"I've always wondered what you South of Broad girls read," Betty says. "I'm talking about the real reading—when you're on the commode. I used to think all you white girls jacked off when *Southern Living* came in, then you couldn't wait to get out to the gardens to plant dahlias and sweet peas and shit."

"Dinner is served," Niles calls out as he and Fraser bring in the remaining platters of T-bones along with potatoes and onions wrapped in aluminum foil.

The emotions that spilled out during the evening have left us famished. We have already half-finished the steaks by the time Ike comes in through the back door with worry lines furrowing his handsome brow.

"You get Sheba to bed, honey?" Betty asks.

"I should've come out to help," Molly says.

"Yeah, you should've," Ike says. "All of you should've. But not one of you did."

Fraser says, "Why do you say that, besides making us feel guilty as hell?"

"Sheba thought you were taking sides," Ike explains. "Choosing Dr. King over her."

"Both were jerks," Niles says. "I didn't feel like choosing."

"Let me fix you a drink, Ike," Molly says, rising out of her chair.

Ike washes his hands at the sink, considering Molly's request. "I think I'll have a Cuba libre."

"Rum and Coke," Fraser says. "I haven't heard of that since high school."

"My husband, Che Guevara," Betty says.

"Your husband, Pontius Pilate," Niles says. "Would you quit washing your hands?"

"Our girl's in trouble out there. Bad trouble," Ike says. "Sheba passed out in the bathroom. I went in there and found cocaine all over the floor, everywhere. I flushed two bags of it down the pot. She had a nosebleed that I had trouble stopping."

"You should have called us to help," I say.

"You should've arrested her," Betty says. The rightness of her words and their careful delivery shock the room into an edgy silence. "If you'd found a brother or a sister living in the projects with that much cocaine, they'd be in jail now."

"I thought about all that," Ike tells her. "Thought about everything. It'd've been the right thing to do. Except for us . . . all of us. Our past together. I decided to honor that instead of my badge."

Fraser says what the rest of us are thinking. "You could get fired, Ike. Right before you take over as chief of police. It'd be the biggest scandal in years."

"It'd make a great column, though," I say. Every eye in the room flashes toward me with unabashed hostility. "That is one of the drawbacks of having a world-class sense of humor: my literalist friends take me seriously when I've delivered my most hilarious line."

"Why is Sheba here?" Molly asks. "Did she tell you why she came back, Leo?"

"I think it's Trevor," I say. "I think something's happened to Trevor."

"Did she tell you that?" Fraser asks. "Or are you just guessing?"

"His name hasn't come up once," I say. "I find that strange."

"When's the last time you heard from Trevor?" Niles asks. "When did you get that postcard, doll baby?"

"Over a year ago," Fraser says. "He was visiting the Monterey Aquarium with his boyfriend of the month. He sent a card with a sea otter on it. But he'd drawn a picture of a huge dick on the otter."

"That's our boy," Molly says.

I say, "Trevor called me last year at about this time. He needed to borrow a thousand bucks. Some emergency. But he didn't tell me what it was."

"He borrowed a thousand from us too," Molly says. "I don't remember when it was, but it was a while ago."

"Did you idiots send him a thousand bucks?" Betty asks.

"Of course," Molly and I answer at the same time.

"What's our boy borrowing money for?" Ike says. "He's always made a great living playing the piano."

"The news isn't good for San Francisco," I say. "Especially in the gay community."

"Trevor's gay?" Fraser says it in an exaggerated Southern accent while fanning herself with her napkin.

"Do you remember when you brought Trevor out to my grandmother's house on Sullivan's Island, Leo?" Molly asks me. "I was sunbathing in my bikini. Leo and Trevor came walking down the path to the beach. Trevor took one look at me and said in that amazing voice of his, 'Molly's so lovely, Leo. It almost makes me wish I were a lesbian.' I'd never heard anybody talk like him. He and Sheba were originals. I don't think Charleston's seen anything like them before or since."

"Remember his phone calls?" Niles asks. "I dreaded answering when I heard Trevor on the other end of the line. He could talk for hours."

"It was impossible to get the little son of a bitch off the phone," Betty agrees. "He could talk about nothing and make it sound like the most interesting thing in the world."

"You think Trevor could have AIDS, Leo?" Fraser asks.

"Trevor's neither celibate nor cautious," Molly says.

"If he doesn't have it, it'll be a miracle," I say.

"It's not just San Francisco," Ike says. "It's come to Charleston to stay. I got two cops with it."

"We've got gay cops in the city?" Fraser asks.

"We've got everything in this city," Ike tells her.

Fraser thinks about it for a moment, then says, "When I was growing up, I thought the world was composed of white people and black people, and that's all I knew for certain."

"We were the girls of Charleston," Molly says. "They raised us to be the most charming of idiots. We're the sweet confections, the sugar dumplings who are the pride and joy of a dying society. I don't think my parents even know they were coconspirators in the scheme to erase my brain."

"I don't know about that," Betty says. "You white girls sure look like you live fine lives to me."

"But at what price?" Fraser asks. "The only thing that separates Molly and me from the girls we grew up with are the friends who are gathered here tonight."

"You're not a cliché, Fraser," Niles says. "That was a shallow creek you were fishing in when you decided to marry me. I wasn't on the A-list of too many debutantes the year we got hitched."

"Yeah, but I got the gold standard." Fraser smiles. "Though my parents still won't admit it." She then walks over and sits in her husband's lap. They fit together like two silver spoons, and kiss each other lightly on the lips.

"Damn, I'm glad your marriage worked," Ike says. "I almost died when Niles asked me to be one of his groomsmen."

"*You* almost died?" Betty says. "I was the first black bridesmaid in the history of St. Michael's Church."

"Y'all looked so beautiful that day," Fraser says. "I think you were the two best-looking members of our wedding."

"What about Trevor and Sheba?" I ask.

"They don't count. Sheba was already famous. And Trevor was always the prettiest belle at the ball," Molly says. "Trevor's words, not mine."

"This won't surprise any of you," Fraser says. "My parents weren't very happy with our list of bridesmaids and groomsmen."

"But be fair, honey bun," Niles says. "Their real problem was your choice of a husband."

"You weren't their first choice," Fraser admits.

"Hell, mountain boy," Ike says. "I think Mr. and Mrs. Rutledge would rather have seen her marry me instead of you."

Molly says, "I wouldn't go that far, Ike."

With that line, our group of friends, tested to the limit by this ferocious night, explodes with shared laughter, the way we always do when we gather together.

"Ike," Betty says, "let's tell the white folks how we felt going out to the wedding reception at Middleton Place Plantation."

"They're not interested in that crap, Betty."

"The hell we're not," Niles says. "I bet you didn't feel any weirder than I did. And I was the goddamn groom."

"You've got to remember the times," Betty says. "Before I met you white folks in high school, I thought all of you subscribed to the *Ku Klux Klan Weekly*. What did I know? I thought it taught you how to sew better-looking Klan outfits for your menfolk. Gave you tips on how to make picnic baskets attractive before you and the family went out for a lynching."

"I miss those lynchings," I say. "They were the high points of my youth."

"Me and Ike drove out to the reception thinking we were going to be strung up on an oak tree. Sort of like dessert," Betty says.

"How horrible that you thought that," Fraser says. "Did the guests treat you well?"

"They treated us fine—like we were invisible," Ike contributes. "Only one time all night did anybody notice me. The wedding party had our own table, and I went to get everybody a round of drinks. I was carrying them back to our table on a tray when white folks started grabbing them one by one. They thought I was the help."

"Then Toad got drunk and asked me to dance," Betty says. "I said, 'Get away from me, you crazy cracker.' But Toad lifted me out of that chair and dragged me to the dance floor."

"Starla said she'd never talk to me again if I didn't dance with you," I tell her. "She kept kicking me under the table to dance with your sorry ass."

"That's when Starla asked me to dance," Ike says. "What a nightmare."

Fraser says, "I knew I had pushed the social limits of Charleston with my marriage. But I never thought I'd introduce interracial dancing to society."

"Trivia time," Niles says. "What was the song playing when the crackers and the colored danced for the first time under a Charleston sky?"

"It was a slow song," Molly remembers. "I tried to get Chad to dance with me, but he would have none of it."

"The drunken Toad tried to dance cheek-to-cheek," Betty says.

"Lust does funny things to a man, Betty," I tell her.

"A pretty song," Molly says. "I know—it was 'Wonderland by Night.'" She rises from her chair and walks the length of the room. "Bert Kaempfert, right?" She opens a cabinet, places a record on the turntable, and we find ourselves shot back through time to our high school years. Ike and Betty begin to dance, melting into each other's arms; Niles and Fraser lift off their chair. Soon Molly and I are dancing cheek-to-cheek, as though we were born to dance with each other. She waltzes me away from the others into the mansion's great room, between the grand piano and the harp. Her body feels good against mine, and her breath is sweet against my ear as she whispers, "Did you really have a crush on me in high school, Leo? Everyone said you did, even Chad."

"No. I can say that honestly too."

"Liar," she says. "You know the answer I need tonight. And you know why I need it."

I was silent.

"Then tell me the truth. I need to hear you say it. You're the best friend I've ever had—male or female—Leo King. And you and I are the only ones who know it. As your best friend, I need the truth from you: did you have a crush on me in high school?"

"No, I didn't. And that's a kind of truth. The whole truth is this: I've been in love with you my whole life. It started at the yacht club. It ends with 'Wonderland by Night.' "

"Sorry, Toad," she says. "It begins with 'Wonderland by Night.' "

Then she kisses me, a long, deep kiss that I want to last forever, but the song ends and so does the kiss.

I look up and see a face staring at us through one of the tall windows that faces out to the piazza. Looking maddened, drugged, and a stranger to herself, I see Sheba Poe studying Molly and me with the concentration of an actress preparing for her next part.

CHAPTER 10

Hangovers

The next morning I wake in my solitary house on Tradd Street with a slight hangover and a sense of irritation when I realize it is five in the morning and the sun has not even begun to rise. Because I am married to a wandering and importunate wife, I never know when I will hear from Starla or where she might be calling from. I clear my head and let the phone ring four times before I answer it. Then I hear Chad's voice asking me with perfect control, "Leo, sorry to bother you so early in the morning. But could I speak with Molly, please?"

I switch on the lamp beside my bed and try to gather myself together to make some kind of sense out of this. As long as I have known Chad, he has never done anything so gauche. Though my brain feels like it is covered with mosquito netting, I answer him. "There must be some mistake, Chad, old chum. The last time I checked, Molly seemed to be married to you, not me."

"Try not to be a comedian this time of the morning." Chad's voice registers anger for the first time. "I'd like to have a few words with my wife."

Now my voice hardens. "Chad, I can't tell you how much I'd like for Molly to be in bed with me. I'd love to shake her gently, wake her up, and say, 'Sweetheart, it's Chad on the phone.' But Molly happens to be a decent woman and a fabulous wife. I know you've never noticed that. Molly's got it in her head that you're working too hard. She thought you should've stayed for all of Sheba's homecoming party. Fancy that."

"I do work hard for my family, Leo. I've got pressures that I keep from Molly. I let her fret over silver patterns, the place cards for dinner parties, the parties we will or won't attend, the cutthroat politics of the Junior League. She has a full life, and she plays an important social role because of the long hours I put in at the largest, most important law firm in this city. I don't do anything without thinking about the best interests of her and the kids."

"That's all peachy keen, Chad. But why're you calling my house asking to speak to the woman lucky enough to be married to such a swell guy?"

"Let's be grown-up about this," Chad says. "Just put Molly on the phone."

"Kiss my royal red Irish ass. How many ways can I say it, Chad? She ain't here. She's never been here, and she never will be, much to my regret."

"I envy you, Leo." Chad's voice rises a pitch toward meanness. "You've got a wife who's never there, and you write a gossip column that ruins someone's life every six days."

"Well, you're at least halfway to happiness, pal. Seems like your wife isn't at your house, either. Your sister's having a picnic for Sheba on Sunday evening. See you there."

"I can't promise anything. I'm up to my ass at work."

"I'd be there," I say. "That's advice from a friend, Chad, a guy who loves you, though goddamn, you make it heavy lifting sometimes."

"I didn't realize it was so early in the morning. I just panicked when I found out Molly wasn't here."

"You want to talk to Sheba?" I ask. "We just spent the night making passionate, animal-like sex."

Chad laughs loudly. "She's passed out in our guesthouse. I already looked for Molly there. I'm really sorry, Leo."

"I like waking up early on Saturdays," I say. "So I can gloat over all the lives I ruined during the week."

Chad hangs up. I fall into a brief but fretful sleep. At seven I hear the satisfying plop of the *News and Courier* as it hits the privacy door of my Charleston single house. It pleases me that I live in a house that I once served as a paperboy, the type of house I never dreamed of owning. When I step out onto the street, the first fingerlings of sunlight are waking the drowsy silver in the crepe myrtle trees in front of my house. The houses of Tradd Street always look like an exquisite yet mismade chess set to me, where one cannot execute a queen's gambit or a Sicilian defense because the maker of the set has lined the street with variations of rooks, bishops, knights, and kings, but has neglected to include a pawn. The original architecture resembles the finest lacework; the gardens are hidden but generous with delicious smells.

I read the paper in my garden with my first cup of coffee like I do every morning. First, I read my column, cringing with embarrassment when I come to any sentence that appears flaccid or lazy. My work for this Saturday seems tiresome, the attempts at humor forced. But I know the ebb and flow of column writing as well as I know the tides of Charleston Harbor. And I possess the secret that I will be the talk of the city when my article on Sheba runs in the Sunday edition.

I am checking the batting averages of my favorite National League players when I hear my back door open. I look behind me, and I'm surprised to see Ike Jefferson entering the garden. He has already fixed his own cup of coffee.

I check my watch. "You're an hour early, Ike."

"Needed to talk," Ike says as he sits down. "You're the only one I could talk to."

I can tell Ike is troubled as he starts to read my column instead of revealing what is on his mind. I breathe in the aroma of the sun-shot gardens that surround my home. As we sit in silence, I can feel the power of the earth's fertility enclosing us; you can almost hear things growing. The green roots are shouldering through the black earth of the peninsula. I walk to the end of the garden, where my yard receives the lion's share of the sun's exposure, and select three perfectly ripe beefsteak tomatoes I grow in a small greenhouse against the far brick wall. I retreat into the kitchen, wash and slice the tomatoes. They glisten with their red-faced, pink-seeded perfection. I bring a salt and pepper mill, and hand a plate to Ike. He forgets the news of the day once the first bite of tomato bursts along the seams of his palate.

"Damn, these tomatoes are good," Ike says, closing his eyes.

"Chief of police," I say, "in the most beautiful city on earth."

Ike grins. "Black folks couldn't even vote when I was born. You and I couldn't have bought a milk shake together at Woolworth's on King Street."

"Look at you now, big guy. Guess I'll be bringing all my parking tickets to you. You've earned the job, though. Nobody's worked harder than you. That's what worried me about last night. You should've arrested Sheba. She put you into a bad dilemma."

"Yeah, I know. I do know that, for sure. And if you're doing your job, you'll write a column about me not arresting her."

"That's not going to happen."

"I know, and so does Sheba." Then he says, "I do have something serious to talk to you about."

"Let me guess," I say. "It's about Chad."

"How'd you know?"

"I write a column five times a week," I say. "Eventually, I hear everything."

"Chad's dicking a secretary down at his law firm. She's got an apartment at Folly Beach."

"Is it the paralegal from Greenwood? Or the Brazilian girl?"

"It's the girl from Ipanema. His mistress," Ike says. "She's nineteen. Just out of high school. Comes from a nice family."

"How do you know?"

"Janitor at her apartment complex goes to my church. How'd you know?"

"Anonymous letter," I answer. "I get lots of those."

"Who you think sent it?"

"Someone who doesn't know whether the lucky girl's from Greenwood or Brazil."

"Greenwood was last year," Ike says. "You white folks are weird."

"Yeah, we need lessons from you black folks about how to live decent, fulfilling lives."

"Molly doesn't deserve this, Leo."

"She should be used to it. This ain't the first. You want another cup of coffee?" I ask, then add, "Chief?"

I walk back into the kitchen and see Niles pouring himself a cup of coffee. He has already made quick work of his plate of tomatoes. He turns his blue-eyed gaze on me, his eyes appraising and unreadable. He has also come too early. I know he has come either to give me advice I don't want or to tell me something I don't want to hear. His guilelessness is what I most admire in Niles, but his need to share truths that can contain the seeds of despair has frayed intimate connections. Basically, he is a quiet, intuitive man; the only time I fear him is when he becomes talkative.

"Excuse me, sir," I say. "But you look like mountain scum to me. Did you wash up here during a flash flood along the Appalachian Trail?"

"I always love to hear you talk, Toad." He sips his coffee. "It may be bull hockey, but it's bull hockey of a very high quality."

"Ike's in the backyard."

"Saw his car," Niles says. "I didn't like last night."

"I've been to better reunions," I agree.

"Sheba put on quite a show," Niles says. "So did your mama."

"My mother hates women like Sheba."

"Did Chad call you this morning?" Niles asks.

"Five A.M."

"What'd he want?"

"To know who won the Braves game." I pour another cup of coffee for myself, though I can tell my flip remark has angered Niles. "Go out in the garden. I want Ike to hear this."

Ike is still reading the paper when Niles and I join him. He looks up and nods. "You here early too, Niles," Ike says. "Why'd you want a private audience with Leo?"

"Chad woke us up early this morning. Fraser answered the phone. Chad believes that Leo here is sleeping with Molly," Niles explains.

"The Toad and Molly did go dancing off into the dark," Ike says. "You and Molly get it on last night, big fella?"

"We most certainly did not."

Niles sips his coffee slowly. "He's married to my sister, Ike. Starla called me this week, Leo."

"Thanks for telling me," I say.

"That's what I came over for," Niles says. "I didn't think Ike would beat me over here."

"I can leave," Ike snaps, "same way I came."

"No, stay," says Niles.

I ask, "You guys want any breakfast?"

"Yeah," Niles says. "I need to get my thoughts in order. I'm not fast-talking like you and Ike."

"You're a dumb-ass white boy from the hills," Ike says, going back to his newspaper. "Like you've always been."

As we eat, we talk about sports, the white noise that men use to express their abiding feelings of friendship but without the sense of violation that often accompanies deeper journeys. Of all my friends, Niles has erected more stop signs and warning signals along the pathway to his heart than anyone else. His hurt childhood made silence his first instinct and place of refuge. But when Niles talks, you can bet he has something to say. He is one of those dreadful gunnysackers who lets it build up inside him until he dumps its entire deposit on the floor for your inspection.

"Thank you for that mighty fine meal, Leo," Ike says, leaning back in his chair. "Now, why don't you spill your guts, Niles, and get it over with?"

"I think Sheba Poe's more trouble than she's worth."

"Let me run in and get my reporter's notebook," I say. "I can't let a news bulletin like that go unquoted."

"What's your point?" Ike asks him.

"Chad's over at my house raising hell with Fraser," Niles says. "He says he's going to throw Sheba out of the guesthouse as soon as she wakes up. He went nuts when he heard about the cocaine."

"Tell Sheba she's welcome to stay here with me," I say. "I've got a nice guest room on the third floor."

"She can also come to my house. Betty would love it, and so would my kids," Ike says.

"Hell, Fraser told Chad that Sheba could stay at our house for the rest of her life if she needs to," Niles says.

"Then who cares what Chad thinks?" Ike says. "That boy loves to run his mouth. He's always been about noise. All thunder, no lightning."

"Leo, Chad just found out that you call Molly every day and talk," Niles tells me.

"A small correction," I say. "We call each other. Sometimes I call Molly, but she often calls me. And this is not exactly top secret. We've talked to each other every day since we were in our twenties. By the way, Niles, I talk to Fraser and Betty all the damn time too."

Ike says, "He's always trying to fish for stories from our girls."

"Those girls know everything that's happening in Charleston," I say.

"Well, Chad doesn't want you calling his wife anymore." Niles's discomfort is obvious.

"Then Chad can tell me that face-to-face," I say. "And a small piece of advice, Niles. You don't need to be Chad's messenger boy."

"I did it because I thought you might beat Chad's ass if he said it to you. He was pretty strung out."

"About Starla?" I change the subject to an even more painful one.

Niles shakes his head. "You've got to ditch my sister, Leo," he pleads. "You've got to drop-kick Starla out of your life. It kills me to say it. But your marriage to my sister kills a little part of you every year. You deserve better."

"I've made my peace with it," I say testily.

"You deserve a normal wife. You'd like to have kids. All of us can see that. Nothing can be normal until you get rid of my nutty sister. It's getting worse, not better, Leo."

"What did she say?" I ask. "Where is she?"

"She didn't say. She was just checking in, like she always does. Wanted to know all the news. Wanted to know how you were doing."

"What'd you tell her?"

"That you were whore-hopping your way through every divorcée in the city. But she just laughed."

Ike asks, "Laughed? Why'd she laugh?"

"Because she knows Leo. That Catholic boy took vows. He still deposits money in her checking account every month. I told her to let go of you, Leo. Do you know what she had the nerve to say to me?"

"No," I answer, "but I'm curious."

"She'd let you go when you stopped loving her."

Ike whistles. "Your sister's a smart woman."

"But a stinking wife to the Toad," Niles says. "She's a fruitcake and you're an idiot. Divorce her, Toad. Your friends'll get you dates with the nicest women in the world. We're all sick about it and don't know what to do. Does begging work? Tell him, Ike."

"I just found out my little girl, Verneatha, doesn't know you're married, Leo," Ike says. "You know Niles is right. And you know it must be hard for him to say so."

"I bet we got your mother's vote locked up," Niles says.

"That's not fair," Ike says. "If Leo likes 'em, Dr. King hates 'em. And that includes all of us."

"My mother doesn't hate y'all." But I realize that Ike is uttering a truth he has carried inside him for a long time. "At least, not always."

"She loves us when she's asleep. Or unconscious. Or when we're asleep or unconscious. But she loathes Starla and has never made a secret out of it," Ike says.

"Yep. She hates your sister, Niles; she hates my wife," I admit.

"Starla's no wife. Never has been. Things happened to her when she was a little girl. To both of us. Things that shouldn't happen to anyone. Yet it started to seem natural to us. Our daily bread, Toad. We grew up thinking the world was the worst place a kid could be. Then we stumbled into the Toad's world. You took us in. You were just a kid yourself—an ugly kid. But you opened your heart to us. Did the same thing for Ike. You did enough. You didn't have to marry my screwed-up sister. No one can save her but herself."

In the silence that follows, the three of us sit around the table as I pour the last of the coffee. We avoid one another's eyes, and I watch two ruby-throated hummingbirds skirmish over a feeder hanging from the Japanese maple.

"Ike?" I finally ask.

"I agree with everything Niles just said. If Betty were here, she'd second the notion," Ike says. He reaches over and presses my shoulder with the tenderness a large man can show in a delicate touch.

At last I ask: "I was that ugly?"

"As homemade diarrhea," Ike replies.

"Those glasses you wore," Niles explains. "They looked like two see-through hubcaps."

"Your hair stuck straight up in the back," Ike says.

Niles says, "That was hair?"

Ike looks at his watch. "Gentlemen, we've got fifteen minutes. I say we get a move on."

"My turn to play quarterback," Niles says.

"My turn, mountain boy," Ike says. "You were quarterback last week."

"Why don't I ever get to play quarterback?" I ask.

"Because you're the Toad," Niles says.

Ike adds, "Toads never get to play quarterback. That's just a fact of life."

Every Saturday at ten, Ike, Niles, and I gather at The Citadel practice field for a fierce game of touch football. Whoever shows up can play, but the numbers vary each week. Usually, we can depend on rounding up a group of cadets or a ragtag squad of assistant coaches from the various athletic teams who guide the Bulldogs' sportsmen during the academic year. But today, the three of us end up alone and left to our own devices.

This morning, we all get to be quarterback, even the Toad.

CHAPTER 11

Evangeline

I try to pay a visit to Evangeline Poe's house at least once a week to make an amateur's judgment on the state of her health and the relative order or anarchy of her household. When I knock on her door that Saturday afternoon, I realize I have not visited her in almost a month. Always when I come to this door I can imagine the ghostly presence of the Atlas moving van that brought the twins cartwheeling into the dead center of our history, changing the directions of all the lives they touched. Across the street I can see the house my father built, the one where I grew up— such a haphazard, unsuccessful mess of a boy. I admire the two towering magnolia trees that were my parents' symbol of their love for each other, or had been until my father's fatal heart attack. I know my mother will hear that I've visited her enemy across the street and will hold that against me. She considered Evangeline Poe far less than a horse's ass the day she met her, and nothing my mother has witnessed in the intervening years has done anything to heighten her opinion.

When Mrs. Poe opens the door, she stares out into the harsh light through a series of four chained locks that would make a Greenwich Village apartment proud.

"It's me, snookums," I say. "The favorite."

"I could sue you for dereliction of duty." She unlocks the door in slow motion. "I thought you might be dead."

"You read my column," I remind her. "You disagree with almost everything I say."

"They never print my letters to the editor." She opens the door, and I kiss her on the cheek as I pass on the way to the kitchen.

"I bought you some groceries at Burbage's," I tell her.

"You need to help me find my reading glasses while you're here, Leo," she says as she enters the kitchen behind me.

"They're on top of your head, sweetie." I see her surprise as she reaches up into her abundant gray curls.

"I'm getting so forgetful lately," she says. "I lost my car keys again."

"You haven't driven a car for two years. They revoked your license, remember?"

"Those bastards. I do now. I called that Negro all of you are so crazy about, and he was of no help at all."

"You hit or scraped over twenty cars parked on King Street, ran a couple of red lights, then crashed into the front door of an antique store—George C. Birlant and Company, if memory serves me right. And you didn't exactly ace the sobriety test." I put up Burbage's homemade soup. "Let me get some of these dishes into the dishwasher before Sheba arrives." I begin collecting random glasses and plates spread haphazardly throughout the rooms on the main floor. "Did Miss Simmons come this week?"

"She quit on me a couple of weeks ago," she replied. "I've given up on the Negro race. I'm looking for a Serbian woman to cook and clean for me. I read that Serbians are all the rage among the finer households in New York City café society."

"Café society? I don't think I've ever met a Serbian."

"I prefer them because they're white people. I've discovered that I get more and more knee-jerk white as I grow older, if you know what I mean."

"Were you mean to Miss Simmons?" I ask her.

"That's her story. If you value her opinion over mine."

"She claims you hurled racist epithets her way."

"None that she hasn't heard before." Mrs. Poe snorts. "Look, I was very polite to her. She got irritated when I referred to her as a Negress, which as you know is a term of great respect. When she snapped at me, I flipped. I admit it."

"I'll keep my eyes open for a Serbian housekeeper."

"I hear good things about Mexicans too," Mrs. Poe says. "Except I'm too old to learn a new language."

"Do you mind if I run the vacuum cleaner in the living room?" I ask.

"Be my guest. I saw Sheba yesterday. Did she tell you we had a fight?"

"I knew you saw her," I say, but Mrs. Poe doesn't hear me over the drone of the Hoover.

"Both my children always made me want to take a long walk," she says.

"Really? Where to?" I yell over the noise.

"To the liquor cabinet. I talk to Sheba, and I want to get drunk. I talk to Trevor, and I *need* to get drunk."

She walks to her liquor cabinet, which she keeps fully stocked, and pours from a cut-glass Waterford decanter. I haul the vacuum cleaner into the hall closet, grab a dish towel, and try to wipe layers of dust from all the side tables and cabinets. Then I hear Sheba entering through the back door. After the hijinks of last night, I thought she would look the worse for wear, but she walks in looking refreshed and stylish. For her mother's sake she is dressed like the daughter of a Charleston matron of the old school. She is taking her mother to dinner at the yacht club, courtesy of her hostess, Molly.

"You look positively radiant, Mama," Sheba says. I note she has toned down her whole persona in her mother's presence. Gone is the starlet of the night before, vamping for her high school friends. She and Trevor have always gone to extremes to try to please their hypercritical mother, and neither has ever succeeded, as far as I know. Evangeline is one of those oddball mothers who stop raising their children once the kids reach the exact age at which they can begin the thankless task of taking care of their mothers. Drinking vodka straight from a glass, Evangeline studies her famous daughter and says, "You appeared naked as a jaybird in your last movie. I couldn't show my face in Charleston for a month." Then she adds meanly, "Your tits are starting to sag."

"They looked mighty good to me, Sheba," I say.

Sheba curtsies. "I've always depended on the kindness of the best friend I've ever had."

"I hate that Tennessee Williams crap," Evangeline says. "Speaking of faggots, when did Trevor drop off the face of the earth?"

"I talked to him about six months ago, Mama," Sheba tells her, and I catch an off-key note of insincerity that makes me realize she is lying. "Trevor finally got a lucky break in his music career. Some fat cat commissioned him to write a concerto for the Omaha Symphony. A friend lent him a house up in Mendocino, California, and he promised not to come back to the city until he has produced a work he's proud of. He told me his working conditions were austere. A Steinway piano, a stone fireplace, and a melody that's haunted him since childhood. It's the break he's been waiting for, Mama."

"I knew he was a pervert when he was a year old. A mother's got a sixth sense about those kind of things. I prayed that it wouldn't be so, but you can't make apples out of applesauce or . . ." In midsentence, Evangeline loses one of those lines of thought that have always distinguished her ruthless dismissal of her children's careers, but I see a panic invade her eyes that I have not seen before. I wonder if the years of abusing vodka are finally catching up with her. She takes another hard swallow from her glass and tries to cover up that she has lost the demoniacal fury of her attack.

"Leo, I was in the middle of saying something of vital importance. Do you remember my subject or predicate?"

"You were discussing tits," Sheba says.

"I could see baring them in your twenties—when they were perfect," her mother says. "But now that they're sagging like circus tents . . ."

In another gulp, Evangeline finishes her first vodka of the day, a drink without ice or tonic or lemon peel or vermouth or accompaniment of any kind; just the pure firewater that is her reason for living. I can read Sheba's face and transcribe the full horror as she witnesses what all the rest of us have known for more than a year: the drinking has begun to kill

Evangeline Poe and has taken a deadly serious turn. Despite her heavy makeup, a slight yellow pallor has taken up residence in a complexion that was once her most noticeable feature. That is her liver barking with displeasure at an eighty-proof bloodstream. When I last talked to Sheba, I warned her of a darker premonition of mine—something, and I didn't know if it was the liquor, the depression, or the despair of Evangeline's unlucky life, but something had begun to play havoc with those soft tissues that control the wiring of the brain itself.

"I have a lot more to say, and I won't be condescended to . . ." Again, she stops in midsentence. Evangeline gets up and walks with great strength of will, but not much steadiness, and pours herself another drink. "Leo? Be a gentleman and help a lady back to her divan."

"Will you cancel our reservations at the yacht club, Leo?" Sheba asks quietly.

"Molly never made them," I tell her. "We all check in on your mother. We know the scene."

"You should've called me earlier," Sheba says. "At the first sign of trouble."

"I called as soon as I heard your last movie wrapped. And the first sign of trouble happened on the day you moved into this house. Do you have Trevor's number in Mendocino?"

"Ah! Trevor. Yes, the concerto. Tomorrow night, we meet at Fraser and Niles's house. Will you be taking your mother to church in the morning?"

"Of course. My mother's still my mother. I'm still her chicken-hearted son."

"Just checking, Leo dear. There's always the chance you could do the unexpected thing and grow up." As she walks me to the door, she says, "I didn't like the way that sounded."

"It's okay, Sheba. Take care of Evangeline. She's about to become a big problem for everyone. Especially herself."

I have taken the most pleasure in my lifelong study of the Broad Street lawyer, among all the opalescent inhabitants of Charleston. I first became enamored of the group as a whole during my days as a paperboy, when I would witness their languorous drift from their houses to their offices, a seersuckered tribe who make their living sweet-talking judges, always approachable when a settlement offer comes across the table. A radical among them might sport a bow tie or wear a Panama hat or believe in mixed marriages (a union between an Anglican and a Unitarian), but generally they attend the same law school, marry the same kind of woman, sire identical children, raise the same breed of dog, attend the same church, drive the same car, belong to the same clubs, and golf in the low nineties (they all cheat in golf), and all of them subscribe to the *News and Courier*.

Once a year I parody the Broad Street lawyer in a Sunday column. My editors prepare for a firestorm of hot-tempered letters denouncing me for my buffoonery and naïveté in disseminating the stereotype. Some of their responses are brilliant and disputatious, and I publish the best and funniest of them the following weekend. I admire their tribe, but with some caution. The caution comes from my deep friendship with and intimate knowledge of Chad Rutledge, and the portion of darkness he carries inside, like a rumor of bad weather.

It is a quarter of six when I try the front door of the sumptuous offices of Darcy, Rutledge, and Sinkler in one of the prettiest buildings on King Street. A guard comes to the door to tell me the firm will not be open until Monday. I give him my card and a five-dollar bill and ask him to ring Chad's office. The guard makes the call, keeping a close watch on me, then he points me in the direction of a small elevator that I take to the top floor. I emerge into a realm of thick law books, Tiffany lamps, and comfortable leather chairs that lend a faintly liturgical smell to the offices. I walk to his office and knock at the door. Chad has spread out five books of case law and is writing with painstaking concentration on a legal pad. His reputation for hard work is well deserved, and I hear other lawyers speak in awestruck terms about his fastidious preparation for any case he tries. When he finishes recording his thoughts, he looks up and studies me in the doorway.

"Sorry about the phone call this morning, Leo," Chad says. "I was worried about Molly. It turns out she had driven out to her grandmother's house on Sullivan's Island."

"Hey, what're friends for?" I ask. "I like being awakened by my friends at five A.M. Especially when they accuse me of adultery with their wives."

"I was worried. I panicked."

"You shouldn't've left the party."

"I'd seen enough of the party," he says. "I had work to do. Still do."

"You've been working here all day?"

"I'm an ambitious guy, Leo. And a successful one. I got that way by outworking everybody in my profession. Nothing ever surprises me in court. But your appearance in my office does. To what do I owe the pleasure?"

Chad leans back in his swivel chair, puts his hands behind his neck, and appraises me through his green-flecked eyes. He means for the gesture to be disarming, but it reminds me of a copperhead poised to strike from a nest of leaves. "Since I'm working hard on a case that is damn important, tell me your business and then get your ass back down on Broad Street as fast as you can. I bill my clients at fifteen-minute intervals, and I'm granting you fifteen valuable minutes."

"But, our friendship, Chad? You don't seem interested in *me*. In what *I'm* thinking or feeling, or in my ideas and concepts and the direction I think the world is heading."

"What do you want, Leo? We're going to see each other at the picnic tomorrow. Couldn't this wait?"

"There's some whispering around town that you're screwing around again, Chad," I say. "Hey, nice hunting print. Very rare and unusual to find in a Charleston law office."

"Sorry to disappoint you," Chad says, "but the rumor is false. Now, be a good boy and run along. Go say a rosary, or do a novena. Whatever you Catholic boys do."

"I get around, Chad. Goes with the territory. I'm not hearing this from a single source. And this has been going on for a while."

"What sent you today?"

"Ike made the request."

"My favorite cop." A twitch in Chad's right eyebrow is the only outward sign of discomfort he reveals. He seems bored by my allegations. "Niles brought it up a week ago. He's a coach, I believe. Didn't he and his white-trash sister grow up in a Negro orphanage somewhere? You knew his sister, I believe. Didn't you marry the little bitch?"

"Aw, shucks, Chad," I say. "You're just trying to get my goat, you old rascal, you."

"What I do is none of your concern," he says with an air of finality. "Nor anyone else's."

"I think your wife's getting a little antsy on the reservation. At least that's what she told me when we were making love last night."

Chad laughs out loud at this. I have always admired his resolute coolness under fire. "Thank you, Leo. I can handle my own affairs, and I can certainly handle my wife. Now, run along, little gossip columnist. Let me finish here, and see you at my sister's tomorrow. Maybe I'll even corner Ike and Niles and tell them to mind their own business."

"Chad, Chad, Chad. Lots of people know about this. You're getting careless about the rendezvous points. Your baby-blue Porsche has been seen parked outside her condo at Folly Beach."

"Time for a new car. Look, Leo, I've lent my car to a young woman in the firm whose car threw a rod. I generally walk to work and back."

"You need to treat this seriously," I warn.

"These kinds of rumors have followed me around since high school. Let's face it, Leo, I'm not hard to look at. I've got a great job, money to burn, and am descended from the first families of Charleston on both sides. I've been part of Charleston's jet set since the day I was born. There's always going to be gossip about me."

Chad's manner and voice can be intimidating, and he is gifted in selecting his weapon of choice when the critical occasion arises. He surprises me by reaching into his desk and bringing out an ornate eighteenth-century Bible that he waves in my direction as both heirloom and movie prop in the drama we are acting out.

"Here is my word of honor, Leo," he says. "Here is a Bible. In this court of pure bullshit where you have set yourself up as the hanging judge, I, Chadworth Rutledge the tenth, do solemnly swear an oath that I've been faithful to my wife and the vows I spoke in the summer of 1974 at St. Michael's Episcopal Church. I do believe that the pain-in-the-ass Catholic boy Leo King was present and accounted for on that solemn occasion."

"The bride was beautiful, and the groom was handsome."

Chad studies me for a second, then says with a flat edge, "You don't fool me, good buddy. You could wrap yourself in altar clothes and go to Mass every day in a leap year, and I still know you find yourself in bed with some strange pussy sometimes. I hear as much about you as you do about me, friend. But I'm a bit more discreet and tolerant than you are, because I know you're still married to a certifiable lunatic who spends her life running away from you."

"I get lonely, Chad. I end up sleeping with women who're my friends. Single women, divorcées, widows, even a few gals who're still married. But as you say so eloquently, none of them happens to be my wife."

"You goddamn hypocritical son of a bitch." His voice all but performs a victory lap around a crowded stadium.

"Nothing hypocritical about it," I say. "I just admitted to sleeping with women I'm not married to. You swore on a Bible that you'd been faithful to Molly since the day you got hitched. Me, the hypocrite? Sorry, pal, but I can name eight women I know you slept with. I'm trying to help you, Chad. You're coming up to an avalanche. Let's try to change direction while we can."

"Let's talk about the avalanche that's already happened," says Chad. "Your goddamn wife. Divorce the lunatic. I'll draw up the papers right now. Won't charge you a cent. For old times' sake."

Of all the friends I have, I think that Chad Rutledge and I understand each other along every latitude and longitude of our melancholy hearts, and along the breathless equator of our poor, lacerated souls. We like each other less than our other friends, yet we share a respect for the talents and flaws of the other; we acknowledge the kinship of our charged, imperfect brotherhood. Neither of us fears a thing about the other, yet knows there is much to fear about both of us.

I have always withheld the respect that Chad thinks he is owed as his birthright. Chad holds all the face cards of opportunity, rank, and family, yet he never underestimates the cumulative powers of those of us who rise out of the lower orders; he always thinks we will hurt him if the chance presents itself. Chad is arrogant, and lacks all the talents of camouflage that can put a pretty face on his sense of entitlement. Nevertheless, if I am ever in serious trouble, I will beg for an immediate audience with Chad Rutledge. He is the kind of man you cannot trust with your women, but one who will rise out of the warrior caste, holding fast to ancient creeds if you find yourself face-to-face with the ruin you bring to your own door.

"I'd like to help you," I say. "I've done my best to quash the rumors as they've come to me. But this carelessness is not like you."

"But sticking your nose where it isn't wanted . . . sniffing other people's assholes, that's your life's work, isn't it, Leo?" Chad asks. "The nasty rumor turns into the column of the week."

"I've never written about you like that. And you know I never will."

"You didn't show the same restraint to my friend Banks Prioleau."

"Banks brought a five-million-dollar lawsuit against his wife's lover for alienation of affection. Once it hits the public record, it's open season, which Banks learned the hard way."

"You got him disbarred," Chad says, and I know the cross-examination is on full throttle.

"He got himself disbarred, Chad. He hired a private eye who wire-tapped his wife, her lover, her lover's ex-wife, his own parents, and the family dog. He also kept a mistress in the Fort Sumter Hotel and had freely stolen money from the estate of Gertrude Wraggsworth, who'd caught herself a bad case of Alzheimer's. The IRS came sniffing and discovered an offshore account in Bermuda, and the fact that Banks owed a couple hundred grand in back taxes. Banks turned into a mess, Chad, and he did it all by himself. He didn't need my help or anyone else's."

"How did you feel when Banks killed himself?"

"Like a million bucks, you sorry bastard. I felt horrible. He was a very nice man who found himself trapped in all the worst parts of the human dilemma. At the end, he felt like he dishonored himself and his family. Shooting himself was the only way he could figure out to make it all right again. He was wrong, of course."

"His children can't seem to get over it. I don't think they ever will," Chad tells me. "I think you helped load the gun that killed him. Disgrace is one thing. Public disgrace is another."

"That's what I'm here to warn you about. You're about to face public disgrace that'd be your worst nightmare, and I don't think you're gonna like it much. I wouldn't have come here if Ike hadn't asked me. And as you said, Niles is furious about it."

"The mountain nigger." Chad shakes his head. "And the real one."

"Niles isn't that fond of that nickname," I say. "It doesn't get much of a laugh from Betty or Ike or Fraser, either. And Ike would kick your ass if you ever called him that."

"Even you can see the irony in all this. An orphan boy from the Blue Ridge comes to Charleston and marries my sister because she was horse-faced and pimply, and built like a left guard for Clemson. Niles pulled himself from the outhouse to the manor house in a single generation. It makes me want to stand up and sing 'God Bless America.' "

"Niles and Fraser are two of the good people in our lives. You and I both know it. We're lucky to have them."

"God, you're so much like your mother it's a crime. You've inherited the starched piety she brought straight out of the convent. But with your mother, it's real. With you, it's phony and makes me want to vomit all over my understated but well-appointed office. Can I talk about you and me and this town—at this hour, at this moment, the here and now? Can I tell you the truth, Leo?"

"Be my guest." I am fearful but also curious about what Chad is capable of saying.

"Right now, I feel like you're both my jailer and my father confessor. I'm the chimp to your organ grinder, then you let me dance for the applause of the good people. I've come to hate the good people, Leo. I can admit that to you because I think you're a shit, just like me. I've come to hate being good, dressing up for church every Sunday, going out to the club for dinner twice a week, putting on black tie for every goddamn charity in this city. But it's for a good cause, you say. Of course it's for a good cause. Who would pay money to support a bad cause? So I dress up and I write a big check for the kidney foundation. Or the heart association. Or diabetes. Or multiple sclerosis. Or cancer of the belly button . . . all wonderful, all life-affirming. Let's play name the cliché, Leo. I live it. I wake up to it. I breathe it. I gorge myself with it . . . family, that's what it's all about. The be-all and end-all . . . community. I just want to give something back. If I hear that statement from one more self-satisfied prick in this city, I'll scream. Just give something back. 'Charleston's been good to you, Chad, old chap, and it's time to give something back.' Leo, I hate this world, and it's got me by the throat and I'll never escape it. I know that stranglehold. I know it all too well. Yet, now . . . now . . . I wake up each morning and find I want to give back something to myself. I want to give back to Chad Rutledge, who is slowly dying from being nothing more than Chad Rutledge. I'm dying of being what I was born to be."

I try to take in everything Chad has just revealed to me. Chad would be an easy man to hate, except that he often surprises me with these scorpion-tailed revelations that speak of a tortured interior life, of a troubled man with an odd but genuine depth. What he says moves me and makes me experience a pang of solace for his wife. I say, "I delivered the message, Chad. I didn't ask for the job and I didn't want it. It's none of my damn business. Do with it what you will. If you continue your affair, I'd advise discretion. You need to tell your girlfriend not to discuss your situation with Tommy Atkinson's secretary." I fish a notebook out of my pocket and open it to a marked page. "Her name is Christine Aimar, and she's the one doing most of the talking. It's not like you to go after a secretary."

"She's not a secretary." Chad has a metallic glint of dismissal in his eye. "She's a paralegal. What else do you know, Leo?"

"A lot. I checked her out. She seems like a really nice girl from a very nice family. But she chose the wrong confidante in Miss Aimar. The word is out that you're leaving your bitch of a wife by the end of the next school year. Then you'll get married in Las Vegas and honeymoon in Hawaii. Chad, I get a hard-on just thinking about you doing the hula. But Las Vegas? *Las Vegas?* A Charleston Rutledge getting married in one of those sleazy red-velvet chapels?"

"I'm getting awfully tired of you, Leo," Chad says, and I sense a fresh current of anger in his words.

"Tough titty. This is out in the open now. It's up to you to figure out how this story ends."

"I already know how it ends. I've always had more imagination than the rest of you put together. I won't be coming to my sister's house tomorrow, Leo. I'll call at the last minute, of course, just to piss off Molly a little bit more. Just to make Fraser and Niles go into a slow burn. The case I'm working on is the biggest one in the history of this law firm, a lawsuit that involves maritime law on three continents and most of the major port cities of the world."

"I bet I know where to find a blue Porsche when this long grind ends."

There is a soft knock on the office door, and I can tell the unknown visitor catches Chad by surprise, though he is valiant in his attempts to mask his displeasure. "Please come in."

A lovely young woman of Latin descent enters, walks briskly to Chad's desk, and says, "Mr. Rutledge, I made copies of the three depositions you requested. I've also reviewed the translations from the lawyer in Naples and the one from Lisbon. So far, I see no discrepancies."

"Sonia Bianca," Chad says, "I'd like you to meet my old friend Leo King. Leo and I went to high school together."

I had risen to my feet when she entered and took in her exotic, astonishing beauty in a glance. We shake hands, and her handshake is firm and unapologetic. I have an intuition that she knows she was the primary subject under discussion before her businesslike entry.

"Mr. King." She smiles. "What a pleasure. I read you every morning."

"Where are you from, Miss Bianca?" I ask.

"I was born just outside of Rio de Janeiro," she answers. "But my father was in the diplomatic corps, so I was raised in a dozen countries."

"Sonia's fluent in five languages," Chad announces.

"Will that be all for the day, Mr. Rutledge?" she asks. "I've got a dinner date tonight."

"Who's the lucky guy?" Chad asks.

"He's just a guy. I hope to see you again, Mr. King," Sonia says.

"Please call me Leo."

"Good night, Mr. Rutledge," she says. "Good night, Leo."

She leaves, and we hear her heels clicking against the wooden floor of the eighteenth-century building. Chad and I are left to our own precipitous devices as I sit down again and we resume our unsavory task.

Chad asks, "When was the last time you made love to a woman and she began screaming out of pure pleasure? When's the last time a woman had more orgasms than you could count?"

I look at my watch and say, "A couple of hours ago. I forget the woman's name, but that girl really knew how to have a good time."

"Very funny."

"So if I tell Molly to scream and yell a whole lot, wake up the kids and all the dogs in the neighborhood, and have more orgasms than you can count, this marriage might be saved?"

"No one has to pretend anything—not anymore. I owe that to myself," he says. "Has it occurred to you, Leo, that you're loving every minute of this because you've always had a thing for my wife?"

I push away from his desk and our eyes lock onto each other. Our faces are blank, like gin rummy players who have been counting cards and know exactly what the other holds. Chad's eyes are fixed and dark.

"It must be difficult being a homely man," he says, taking my measure in his most exaggerated pretty-boy manner. "Not that you haven't improved greatly in that department over the years. Henry Berlin has taught you how to dress with at least modest distinction. And thank God someone invented contact lenses that could correct your batlike vision. Someone's seeing to your hair, but it still looks as kinky as a wire-haired terrier. But to be born ugly in a city that prizes beauty—in its men as much as its women—that's a real tragedy. From the first day I met you, I've never heard a woman say she wanted to sleep with you. Of course, it never occurred to me, or anyone else, that you'd become a celebrity in this town. Remember the poll that came out last year in the newspaper? You were the fifth best-known person in Charleston. This is a different city than the one I grew up in."

"Vive la différence," I say. "Should I call Sonia back up here to translate that?"

"But I'm not being fair to you, Leo. I'm not telling the whole story. I know perfectly well that the women who'll be at dinner tomorrow night love your fanny. And they're the ones who love you best—my darling wife, my homely sister, Man-o'-War, and the cutest Negress ever to carry a gun for the highway patrol. You've been nice to all of them, Leo, I give you that. For a long time over a period of many years, and I'm even starting to think it's sincere. You're nice to their husbands and you remember their kids' birthdays, you bring bones to their dogs and chocolates to their maids. You've got a way of making your friends feel special. It's a gift. One that I truly envy, Leo."

"What about you? How do I make you feel, Chad?"

"Special. I include myself in that illustrious category. Not many people like me. That caused me some pain and has taken some adjusting to. I've learned to live with it because I have no choice."

"Have you ever thought about being nicer to people? Friendlier?"

"No, I leave that to the superiors of the world, like you. The grovelers. The bootlickers. That's not part of my makeup. But I'm more successful than almost all my contemporaries. Most men who have loathed and underestimated me have come to fear me. I take great satisfaction in that. I breathe their fear, Leo. It's pure oxygen to me. But you seem to have taken joy in my success. This puzzles me. I've always wanted to see you fall flat on your ass. I waited for you to fizzle out, to reach the burned-out end of a very slender talent. Yet I've got to admit you've helped me out in my own career. You brag about me in your column. People ask me about our friendship all the time. How it started, what kept it up—what they're really asking is how a good guy like Leo King could like an asshole like Chad Rutledge."

"A noble and fair question," I say. "And a question I've been asking myself with more and more frequency. What's your answer?"

"Silence," he replies. "I answer them with pure silence."

"Got some advice for you. Call up Molly and surprise her. Take her out to dinner tonight. Then come to the cookout at your sister's tomorrow."

"I'll see what I can do."

"Here's some more advice," I say. "If you come, try to put on a happy face."

On Sunday morning, I walk my mother up the steps of the Cathedral of St. John the Baptist, in a bright sunlight that makes the red sandstone building look as though it is bleeding in tones of irregular gold. As we enter the vestibule, the inside of the cathedral shimmers with the overripe beauty of a European church. Our trek through the believers passes the sightless eyes and tongueless faces of the saints who preside over the side altars in unnoticed postures of religious ecstasy.

When Mother and I take our seats, I hear a disconcerting murmuring of the congregation behind me. I turn and almost laugh out loud when I spot Sheba Poe, wearing sunglasses and the most shapeless and demure suit in her repertoire. That shameless queen of entrances tries to catwalk her way into the cathedral without being noticed, to slip unobtrusively down the side aisle to the confessional.

With perfect timing and a sense of theater that matches Sheba's own, Monsignor Max bolts out of a rarely used doorway in the rear of the cathedral, magnificent in the gold and ivory finery of his Sunday vestments. He moves like a bird of paradise beneath the towering altar candles, arriving at the confessional booth at the precise moment that Sheba disappears behind the burgundy curtain as a gasp of incredulity explodes from the parishioners. Because of Sheba's notoriety among the tabloids, the churchgoers of St. John's can be forgiven their response to the electrifying sight of one of the most brazen sinners of our time entering a confessional with the humility of an Augustinian hermit.

"If she's honest, she'll be in there a week," Mother says, loudly enough to get a muffled laugh around us until I elbow her into silence.

"I could face the Lord today at the judgment seat, look him in the eye, and tell him that his humble servant did her best. What're you going to say on Judgment Day, Leo?"

"That my mother was a pain in the ass," I whisper.

"How dare you speak profanity in this sacred sanctuary?"

"The good Lord would understand. He was once flesh and blood like me. But he picked the Virgin Mary to raise him. I got you."

Mother notices a commotion to her left and says, "My Lord, she's coming out after only five minutes. Who does she think she's fooling?"

"That is between her and God and her confessor."

"Oh, Lord," Mother gasps, "she's coming straight this way. I'll leave if she tries to sit with us, and that's no idle threat, son."

A simple black veil covers Sheba's hair, and she appears beatific as an usher leads her to our pew. I move over to make room for her, meeting stiff resistance from my mother, whose body goes rigid. But I put my shoulder into it and make room for Sheba, who shoots me a collusive wink as she kneels to say her considerable penance.

In her own uncontrollable outrage, my mother rises up, as obvious as a humpback whale breeching near a cruise ship, demanding that I allow her to sit elsewhere and to humiliate Sheba in front of a goodly percentage of Catholic Charleston. I hold her wrist in a grip and I whisper, "Sit down and pray, Mother. We should rejoice. Sheba's come home to her faith. Look at her. She's kneeling at the foot of the cross, looking up to the crucified Jesus."

"Bad acting," Mother spits out as she resumes her seat. "Her career's tanking fast. She's had two face-lifts already."

"Three," Sheba says, but she does not open her eyes.

As Monsignor Max follows his altar boys onto center stage, the congregation rises as one. I listen with admiration as he glitters his way through the opening prayers of the Common of the Mass. Even back when I served as his altar boy I was a passionate fan of the showmanship he brought to the task of worship. There is a lot wrong with the Roman Catholic Church, but I have to admit that my people sure know how to put on a show. Though my faith has suffered a watering-down over the years, I still cherish the imperishability of its rituals, and I will always find myself a prisoner to the divine sublimity of the Eucharist itself.

I begin a prayer that dismays and frightens me because it issues out of a black place inside me, unbidden and surprising in its forcefulness. But it comes, and I can do nothing but listen to its urgent message. "Let me help my friends, Lord. But I need something else, and I need it from you: Let those same friends help me. Grant me the humility to let them do it. Let them save me from my darkness, my terror, and my sadness. I've held them inside me for too long. I ask for your help—all the help you can give me. I need something to hold on to, to anchor on, to save myself with. I ask you for a sign. A simple one, but something clear. I ask for a sign."

When I open my eyes again, a terrible fear consumes me because the prayer felt like a nervous breakdown instead of a conversation with God. So I try to control my breathing as I await the usher's call to the Communion rail. To my surprise, Sheba stands up before that call comes, and the usher is at her side as she leans over and kisses me on the cheek, whispering, "See you later, handsome."

With perfect timing, she takes the usher's waiting arm, and he leads her to the far right side of the Communion rail as Monsignor Max sweeps down to meet them. Sheba kneels and he places a Communion wafer on her tongue. She takes it, prays, makes the sign of the cross, then lets the usher lead her out a side door as the entire congregation watches the drama unfold before their eyes. Then the platoon of overstarched ushers begins to invite the front rows to partake of Communion as a flock of sparrow priests enters, their chalices overflowing with the ivory-white wafers.

Mother presses her mouth against my ear and whispers, "Our monsignor is an egomaniac. That was disgraceful and unnecessary."

"Great theater," I whisper back.

"This is a temple to praise God, not Sheba Poe's plastic tits," Mother says. We walk to the altar and receive the host from the priest who married my parents and baptized me. Then we follow the crowd out to Broad Street. My mother still cannot let the subject of Sheba go. "That girl's the whore of Babylon. Her birthplace is at Sodom or Gomorrah."

"She sure is cute, though, isn't she?" I cannot help teasing my mother, who is always volatile when aroused.

"I find interior beauty far more attractive. Spiritual beauty, I'm talking about, like Saint Theresa, Saint Rose of Lima, or Saint Francis of Assisi."

"Not me," I say. "I like plastic tits."

When she punches me on the arm, we both break down laughing on the steps of the cathedral. Though it is nice to see my mother laugh, I am positive it is for all the wrong reasons.

CHAPTER 12

Niles and Fraser

The 1974 marriage of the mountain boy Niles Whitehead to the Charleston debutante Fraser Rutledge, with her lineage unimpeachable and her bona fides in order, shook Charleston society with the force of an earthquake that went off the charts on the city's inflexible Richter scale. The shock waves that rippled through the drawing rooms of my mannerly city lent proof that the tumultuous era of the sixties had managed to breach the city limits of Charleston: when a penniless orphan born in anonymity could win the heart of a bride whose ancestors included one of the signers of the Declaration of Independence and whose grandfathers on both sides served as presidents of the St. Cecilia Society, the rules of order and civility had taken a direct hit. Though there was nothing in Fraser's background to suggest either a revolutionary or a contrary leaning, she recognized the incomparable nature of Niles's character on the night they met. As one of the best female basketball players in the state, Fraser knew all she needed to about establishing a strong position and holding on to it for dear life. Her decency and fineness of spirit had floored Niles, who had never been to a dance when I introduced them the summer before my senior year.

Worth and Hess Rutledge mounted a fruitless campaign to break up the couple, but the clumsiness and meanness of their attempts only strengthened their daughter's resolve and Niles's ardor. Even Charleston families began to discover that when a young man and young woman fall in love, and that love proves rugged and fire-tested, all the social rules and laws of heraldry are flung aside. Niles and Fraser needed only the laws of their own uncommon passion. Fraser took his hand and together they crossed that line of distinction called South of Broad. He carried his bride across the threshold of the Thomaston-Verdier house, which her mother and father had presented to them as a bridal gift. In their hearts, both parents hoped that the marriage would be brief and childless. It would be years before Fraser's mother, Hess, could admit that her daughter's love affair with Niles was the kind that could not be washed out or towed away with the morning trash.

From my house on Tradd Street, I walk west to Church Street as the Charleston heat hits me with a body blow that is part humidity and part horse latitude. The houses along Church are set like gemstones against the sidewalk; the honeybees are working overtime in the flower boxes overflowing with lantana; the scents of jasmine and lilies of the valley catch me off guard, but the lush fragrance of a mock orange makes me happy to be alive.

I arrive early at the Thomaston-Verdier house to help with the preparation of the meal and to try to find out if Fraser has heard the rumors about her brother. I find her deveining shrimp in her spacious kitchen, which looks out into a garden perfectly composed and tended.

"Hey, Fraser, you look scrumptious in lavender. Can I make love to you before the others arrive?" I ask, kissing her on the cheek.

"Talk, talk, talk." Fraser smiles. "All you ever do. Never any action behind your words."

"It'll have to be a quickie."

She says, "Then a quickie it will be."

"I heard that, woman," Niles says, coming in from the den, where I can hear a baseball game playing on the television. He lifts me off the ground in his strong embrace, spins me around once, then lets me down gently to the floor. It is Niles's way of saying hello, and he performs the gesture with both men and women.

"Hey, kid," I say. "Did you catch any fish last night?"

"Enough red drum to feed everybody. Also, the kids pulled up a couple dozen crab."

"What's my role?" I ask the hostess.

"If you'd make your she-crab soup, that would be lovely."

"Let me go clean the crabs now," I say.

"I already did that, and gutted the fish while I was at it," Niles says.

"We sent the kids over to their grandparents' pool, Leo," Fraser says. "Did you talk to Chad? Ike said you would."

I look over at Niles, unsure of how much Fraser knows. He says, "It's all over town, good buddy. Fraser was the one who told me about it. I was not surprised that both you and Ike had gotten wind of it."

"I think Chad and Molly are coming today," I say. "Have they called?"

"They haven't canceled," Fraser says. "Chad must have listened to you."

"I didn't say that," I say. "He sure as hell wasn't pleased that I knew so much."

"We're sick about it," Fraser says. "I think Molly's gone if she hears about it. I don't think she's going to take it sitting down this time."

Niles says, "I'm thinking about cutting his pecker off and using it as bait for a billfish or a mako."

Fraser, still working at the shrimp, says, "I didn't tell you this, Niles, but I went to Chad's office and had a talk with him last week."

"I bet he wasn't thrilled by that sisterly visit," Niles snorts.

Fraser laughs. "I thought he was going to throw me out his window onto Broad Street. He denied everything, of course. He was working hard for the good of his family. The same old shit he always says."

"How'd Chad react to your visit, Leo?" Niles asks.

"Like I was a horse turd someone had shoveled into his room. But, to give Chad his due, no one would like to have such a conversation."

When the guests begin to arrive at five, all we have to do is grill the fillets and serve the meal. Ike and Betty bring a salad large enough to feed the Citadel football team, which Ike carries in, pretending to stagger under its weight. Sheba dances in wearing tight shorts, a yellow blouse with the top three buttons undone, a jade-colored belt, and ballet shoes. Unable to enter a room without some degree of showmanship, she whirls through the kitchen doing an impromptu and improvised ballet. When she kneels in homage to our small crowd, we play our part and cheer her performance.

We walk to the second-story piazza as a group. A delicious, unexpected breeze springs up from the harbor as we watch a cruise ship moving through the channel, riding low on the incoming tide. Niles and I serve gin and tonics all around, and we clink glasses and make toasts, all of us aware that each toast pays some commission of reverence for Sheba's return to our midst. Under our lavish attention she grows animated and tells us privileged insider gossip about the fey and nutty world she inhabits in Hollywood. She tells us which actor has the largest penis in the world of cinema, and the macho action star with by far the smallest. Though all of us find ourselves riveted, we all lack the guts to ask how she was sure of the accuracy of those measurements.

A horn sounds in the driveway, two gentle taps that denote familiarity. We rise up and see Chad and Molly, both nattily dressed, getting out of the blue Porsche with its top down. Both wear rakish hats and fashionable sunglasses—they are well groomed, combed over, and oiled down as they make their way through the wrought-iron garden gate. They enhance each other's good looks by the refinement each brings to the other, the rightness of their union, as though they are a matching pair of candelabra.

When Molly appears at the top of the stairs, she is regal yet self-effacing in her carriage. She is soft-spoken and reserved, so her loud infectious laughter always comes as a surprise. Molly possesses a lush head of hair, close to the hue of an Irish setter. Chad appears beside her, and I think they look more like brother and sister than husband and wife. But it is not unusual to think that in the rarefied, inbred corridors of Charleston.

"Chad!" Sheba cries out. "I haven't seen a hair on your head for over twenty-four hours. You've been hiding from your one true love."

"The damn law's my one true love these days, Sheba," Chad says as Sheba runs into his arms. "You can ask Molly about that."

"Amen," Molly agrees.

From a large purse, Sheba then pulls out a director's beret and a pair of sunglasses and throws a showy ascot around her neck. "The show has just begun," she says in a peremptory voice. "Everybody down to the lawn. Move double-time, extras. If we have to pay you union fees, you can sure as hell double-time to your next marks."

"C'mon, Sheba. Just let us get drunk," Ike sighs.

"Silence the Senegalese prince," Sheba barks.

Grumbling, we make our way down to a small swatch of lawn the size of an average putting green. Sheba claps her hands in a commanding manner and orders us to line up, women in front and boys bringing up the rear, saying, "Now, with brio and gusto and great savoir faire, we are going to perform the great 'Renegade Love Call.' "

There is a moaning in the choir, but Sheba halts it by bringing up an imaginary baton, then force-marches the women to the far side of the lawn. She separates them in intervals of three feet, then poses them all in the provocative stance we recognize from the beginning of football games when an unseen announcer named our starting lineup. With a brush of her hand, Sheba sweeps a wing of hair over the right eye of each woman and then she positions them in the sexiest cheerleader stance of all—the love call of the Renegade girls for the Renegade boys of Peninsula High. Sheba invented the choreography and the words of the cheer as one of the gifts she brought to our school life when she appeared out of nowhere for our senior year. The packed stadium always went into a zone of scriptural silence when those pretty girls brought the players out onto the field. Sheba starts things by slinging out her hip and pointing her finger directly at me. She flicks her head, tossing the wing of hair behind her, then begins her loud, passionate chant: "I champion Leo, can all of you hear—I call him forth for the victory cheer!"

Hearing my cue, I jog toward Sheba. In high school, she would peck my cheek, and I would run over to my place, facing the home crowd. But, of course, on this occasion Sheba surprises me with a French kiss that puts her tongue somewhere in the vicinity of my tonsils. So completely has she caught me unaware that I begin gagging and choking, to the high hilarity of my assembled friends. I shoot them all the bird as I stagger to my place.

Then Betty steps forward, also tossing her hair. No one can do sexy like Betty Jefferson as she points downfield to her man and cries out: "I champion Ike, and I feel him draw near—he'll stand by Leo in this victory cheer."

Ike jogs to his wife, they share a nice kiss, then Ike comes slowly toward me. After our foreheads touch, he turns to the crowd that disappeared from our lives nineteen years ago. We lock arms together as Fraser steps out, unsure of herself, a better athlete than any of us boys were, but a newcomer to the cheerleaders' art. She says: "I stand by Niles and I see my man clear; if he's not worthy, there'll be no victory cheer."

Niles runs up and kisses his wife, and they hold the kiss until the rest of us begin wolf whistling and catcalling. Then Niles runs over, and he and I touch foreheads, then he and Ike touch foreheads, and we lock arms together.

Molly begins her chant, "But I champion Chad, and I'll do it all year—if he will stand with us, then all Renegades cheer. We're right in the middle of a championship year."

As I listen to Molly's voice, I am moved by this collision of events that brings back so many memories—some that I embrace with a tenderness that surprises; others that can bring me to a boiling point of the spirit, the very threshold of agony. In high school, the cheer seemed endless and pointless when I was nervous and chafing for the game to start. Now, at this moment, I wish the cheer could last forever so I can have an excuse to lock arms with these essential men in my life and to watch the sensuous movements of those hair-tossing, pretty women for all time. Their voices seem to call out to me in the lostness of all my days; the nostalgia is close to overwhelming.

I watch Chad jog toward Molly when her cheer ends. It is easy to remember that Chad was all style then and is all style now: he seems to make his way across the yard in slow motion, all comfort in every inch of his aristocratic bones. As he approaches Molly, he puckers his lips in exaggerated fashion and throws the guys a conspiratorial wink at the same time. The mood is good and jocular.

All of us are caught by surprise when Molly Rutledge makes a fist and busts her husband's nose with a punch that is astonishing in its ferocity and effect. Drops of blood fly through the air, spattering Molly's face and blouse. The astonished group stands in a frozen, airless tableau. No one speaks until Sheba says, "I guess that's the end of the pep rally."

Then Molly explodes with a rage she has long held in quarantine. "You rotten son of a low-life bitch! You dare humiliate me in front of my best friends, my family, the town we grew up in! You conduct an open affair with a nineteen-year-old girl and flaunt it by inviting her to our parties, paying her rent, keeping a room at the Mills-Hyatt house for when you feel like a quickie. I thought I'd married one of the finest men to ever come out of Charleston society, and I find out I married the worst piece of shit instead."

"This is all a mistake," Chad says, but he directs his voice at us, not at Molly. "This can all be explained."

"They all know about it," Molly screams. "You've been so goddamn indiscreet, I bet the seagulls are talking about it. It's everywhere. Four lawyers in your firm have called, three of their wives. But my best friends— these fine, fine people—haven't said a word to me. And I've been able to tell for a month that they knew something terrible was happening in my life. Real friends would've said something. All of you owed me that much . . . at least."

Molly turns and runs out of the garden. She takes a right toward East Bay, and disappears from sight.

"She's imagining things," Chad says to us. "It's something mental. I'm going to have her tested next week."

"Start telling the truth, Chad," Betty says. "After doing that, you can quit humping that broad in your office."

"Molly's having a breakdown," Chad insists, but it is difficult to take him seriously with his nose bleeding. "I guarantee she'll call all of you next week to apologize. She's been having these symptoms for a long time now. I'm going to need the help of all of you."

"Chad, why don't you go after Molly and have a serious talk with her?" Fraser suggests, then she goes over to an ice chest and soaks a dinner napkin in the freezing water. With great care, she begins to wash the blood from her brother's throat and nose. He snatches the napkin from her hand and presses it to his nose. We know from experience that Chad has a temper that is flammable and dangerous when ignited.

Fraser says in the softest, most sisterly of voices, "Just go home, Chad. You can make everything okay. It's not too late. Molly wouldn't be so crazy if she didn't love you so much."

"Shut up, Fraser. For once in your life, just shut up," he snarls like a treed bobcat. "You've always taken Molly's side in everything."

"I'm just trying to help," she says. "I love you as much as she does."

"Then show it. Start believing me. Take me at my word," he shouts at her, then makes a tactical error by adding, "piano legs."

If Ike and I had not both lunged for Niles at the same time, I think Chad would have suffered grievous physical damage far greater. Though Ike and I are heavier men than Niles, he is taller and rangier and more menacing when aroused. I slow Niles's headlong charge toward his brother-in-law by catching hold of his belt, allowing Ike to grab him in a bear hug.

"If I get my hands on you," Niles says to Chad, "I'll bite your nose off. I swear I'll bite it right off your face."

Fraser runs between her brother and Niles, shielding Chad from Niles's charge.

"Should I get the cuffs for Niles?" Betty asks Ike, her voice professional and take-charge.

Ike answers, "Naw, honey. Niles'll be fine. Get my nightstick out of the truck and break both of Chad's knees instead."

"My pleasure." Betty walks without haste toward their vehicle.

"Chad," Ike says, "you don't seem to be in the mood for advice tonight, but I've got some for you."

"Bad time for advice, Officer," Chad snaps. The word *Officer* has never been uttered with such contempt.

"Advice is this: Run, you son of a bitch. Run your ass off. I don't think me and Leo are strong enough to hold Niles much longer."

With those observant words, Niles bursts free from my grip. Ike falls to his knees as Niles tries to kick away from his grip. Niles makes one sprinting gallop across the yard before Ike and I bring him down with an open-field tackle from behind. We tumble to the earth, but it takes us ten long seconds to pacify our formidable pal. By then, Chad has ingested the wisdom of Ike's advice, and he runs to his Porsche, the bloody rag still pressed to his nose. His car roars to life, and he screeches off in dramatic fashion. We are expecting Chad to take a left on Church Street, following Molly, but he hits second gear, takes a right at Meeting Street, then guns it past Tradd at a speed too reckless for Charleston.

Betty says it first. "After all that, he's still going to see his girlfriend."

"Tell you what," Sheba says, a woman who discovers her greatest joy in the center of the most uncontrollable chaos. "You Southerners really know how to give a party."

CHAPTER 13

Sheba Asks a Favor

At first, the conversation after dinner is directionless. It wanders from subject to subject as Sheba plays the piano, the show tunes she and her brother introduced to us when they appeared in the dead center of our lives. Then the dancing starts and I pour a glass of Cognac and lean against the baby grand. It is hard to believe that Sheba is only the second best piano player in her family, and that her skill is amateurish compared to her brother's simple mastery. But her voice is a lovely thing.

When the dancing is over, we sit on the welcoming, overstuffed furniture beneath the tiers of books that go floor to ceiling on three sides of the room. Niles is solicitous in bringing glasses of port and snifters of Cognac, the candlelight tossing a jeweled pallor on the room as the evening starts to wind down. The couples sit on couches holding hands with a naturalness I envy. Sheba and I sit on chairs across from each other. She is about to say something to me, but I see her choke back the words.

"There's something poison about me," Sheba says finally, and the room becomes still. "Always has been. I do this to every room I enter.

I can never leave my unhappiness behind me. It follows me, tracks me down—it was waiting for me here tonight."

"Nonsense," I say. "Molly and Chad are fully capable of screwing up their own lives. We were all pulled into it tonight. It doesn't change the fact that we've all missed you, darling."

"You haven't missed a thing," she says. "I haven't been worth knowing for the past ten years. True confession time. I'm not just bragging." She laughs, but it is too loud and of the mirthless variety that soon turns to something darker. Then she begins crying softly. The women in the room move as one to surround, comfort, and caress her. As men, we sit paralyzed in our seats, undone by the ninjalike power of a few tears from the eyes of a woman we have cared about since we were boys. Sheba regains a small measure of her composure as Betty hands her a handkerchief from her large purse. "I'm so sorry. So sorry," Sheba sobs.

"You never have to apologize to us," Fraser says. "That's the kind of friends we are. Or that's the kind we'd like to think we are."

"I've been afraid to ask you something," says Sheba. "And it's what I came back to ask you."

"Ask," says Niles.

"Anything," Ike seconds.

"When's the last time any of you heard from Trevor?" she asks. Her crying begins again, but this time there is an opening up, a spillage out, and several moments pass before she can collect herself.

We all look at one another as Sheba puts her face in her hands. Niles is the first to speak.

"He called here collect about a year ago."

"Did you accept the charges?" Sheba asks.

Niles nods. "Of course I accepted the charges. It was Trevor. But he was so drunk I couldn't make out what he was saying, so I put Fraser on the phone."

Fraser says, "It was mostly liquor talk. You know the kind: 'I love you' slurred in a hundred different ways. 'I miss all of you' slurred in a hundred others. Classic Trevor. If he'd been born straight, he'd have married me or Molly. If he'd been born a girl, he'd've married Leo. It was drunk talk sure enough, but pure Trevor. I tried to call him the next day at his flat on Union Street, but his phone was disconnected. I wrote him a letter, but it came back with address unknown. So I figured he'd moved."

Sheba says, "He was evicted for not paying rent."

"Why didn't he call us?" Betty asks.

"The question is this," Sheba says: "Why didn't he call his famous sister?"

"Can you answer that?" I ask her. "We can't."

"Trevor's hated me for a long time," she says. "Remember my first gig in Las Vegas? I had to beg him to come and play the piano for that. The only reason he came was because of the chance to see all of you. He wrote me off his list of favorites a long time ago."

"But why, Sheba?" Fraser asks. "You were so close. I've never seen a brother and sister as close as you two. Maybe Niles and Starla at one time. Chad always acted like I was created in Frankenstein's lab. But you and Trevor were devoted."

"Trevor resented me for lots of reasons. Start with my success, go to my self-destructive behavior. He said he couldn't stand to watch me slowly killing myself. And I wasn't very nice to Trevor. Or anyone else, even you guys. The one thing I can do well is be a perfect shit. Trevor got on my nerves when I was strung out on coke. I said some things I shouldn't have said. One of my husbands beat him up and almost killed him."

"Blair Upton?" Betty guesses.

"Yep, that guy. I knew he was the most famous actor I was ever going to get to meet me at the altar, and I wasn't going to give him up for my fairy princess of a brother."

I said, "Trevor called me a year ago; he sounded scared. Of course, then he told me if I'd been gay, he'd never have needed another boyfriend. I would've satisfied his most lascivious needs. I haven't heard from him since."

"Where did you send the check?" Sheba asks.

"It was a money order. A P.O. box on Polk Street."

"I put a private eye on the case," she says. "I heard some bad rumors: Trevor's dying of AIDS."

"Have you called his friends?" I ask. "They'll help us find him."

Now it is time for Sheba to fish around in her commodious purse. Some tubes of lipstick and jars of cosmetics spill out, as does a sandwich bag full of marijuana.

"Oregano," she says to the officers of the law. "I've developed a passion for Italian food." Ike shuts his eyes and Betty rolls hers and motions to Niles to refill her glass.

Finally, Sheba pulls a photograph out of a side pocket and hands it to me. In a picture taken in 1980, there I stand in Trevor's dining room with my arm flung around him and his lover at the time, Tom Ball. Twelve other gay men mug for the camera, and I remember that ecstatic evening as one of the best in my life. I flew into the city with enough shrimp, fish, crabs, tomatoes, and corn to feed all the true believers and the hangers-on at the Sermon on the Mount, and Trevor and I fixed a Low Country feast for all of his best friends in San Francisco. Trevor was at his magical best that night, and the conversation was brilliant, hilarious, and over the top. After dinner, Trevor played the piano for hours. Every man there had a passable singing voice except me, and some had the loveliest voices in that part of the world.

"I'll start calling those guys tomorrow," I say. "I bet they don't even know that Trevor's in trouble."

"I've tried to call all of them," Sheba tells me.

"Had they heard from him? Any of them?" Ike asks.

"Worse than that, Ike: every one of them is dead. Every single one of them."

"Where do you think Trevor is, Sheba?" Niles asks, walking over and sitting on the arm of her chair.

"I think he's like a sick cat and has gone off to the woods to die. I don't know what else to think. A producer I know is lending me his house in Pacific Heights. I'm here to ask you all something I've no right to ask. I'd love it if one or two of you would help me find him."

"I'm due some time off," I say. "But I can't go till after the Fourth of July weekend."

"We were going to take the kids to Disney World," Ike says to Betty.

She suggests, "Your parents would love to take them. They actually like Disney World."

"Niles, we can do it, can't we, baby?" Fraser asks. "We can do that for Trevor."

"Couldn't come at a better time for me," Niles says. He's the athletic director for Porter-Gaud, and the school year will have just ended. "I'll get tickets tomorrow."

"We can find Trevor and bring him home. Bring him to Charleston," I say.

"We can be around him when he dies," Fraser says. "We can help him die."

"I've got a plane," Sheba says. "A Learjet. Another gift from the producer."

"Just what're you doing for this producer?" Betty asks.

"Enough to get a house in Pacific Heights," Sheba says. "Enough to have a Learjet waiting for us at the Charleston airport."

"The first weekend after July Fourth," I say. "Does that work for everybody?"

"Yeah," everyone agrees. When our words rise in the air like white papal smoke, Sheba bursts into tears again. Fraser hugs her from one side, Niles takes care of the other, and Sheba rocks forward as she weeps.

Ike says, "Why're you crying, girl?"

"Because I knew that all of you would say yes," Sheba says. "I just knew it. And I've been a perfect shit to every one of you."

I walk over to the Battery instead of going straight home. Whenever I want to think hard, I need a river to help me lighten the load. The return of Sheba has set something loose inside me, and I have to fight through the barricades and impasses and dead ends I've erected as defenses to the overwhelming solitude I accept as an orderly way of life. As I walk south along the Battery's wall, I notice the crescent moon, sparking the trellises of a nervous tide. As a Charlestonian, I am a connoisseur of tides, and can almost tell you how high or low the seawalls of the harbor are at any given moment. The deep heat of the day has surrendered to a cooling wind from the Atlantic. The air gives off the scents of honeysuckle, turmeric, and salt. My head clears and I make an attempt to figure out what all the events of the night signify. I also take an honest inventory of my own life, and do not like the results.

My marriage to Starla Whitehead has been both a joke and a hoax from the very beginning. Going into that hasty and ill-planned marriage, I knew everything about Starla's fragility and volatile nature. What I misjudged was the extent of her madness and the strength of those interior demons that made her nighttimes sleepless and the daylight hours a time of exhaustion and despair. When I am honest with myself—and I can be honest with the Cooper River surging back toward the sea to my left and the governess-like serenity of the mansions along East Bay Street on my right—the thoughts come out true and hot to the touch. I once thought I married Starla for love, but now I am looking at it with a harsher lens, and consider that love came to me in a diffused and scattershot form: I had trouble with the whole concept because I never fully learned the art of loving myself. For most of my life, the way I loved was another form that awkwardness took in me. My attraction to women has always depended on the amount of damage I could detect on the surface, how much scar tissue I could uncover when I started to finger my way through the ruins. I mistook Starla's instability as the most fascinating aspect of her personality. Her madness I translated into a kind of genius. Though I heard my friends lament the fact that they had found out too late that they had married carbon copies of their mothers or fathers, I was even more fearful that I had married my childhood, the one that found me in straitjackets during the years following my brother's suicide. That was also my darkest fear about Starla—that I had married my brother, Steve, because I could never condone my appalling failure to give my parents a reasonable facsimile of their lost son when I knew they wanted that from me more than anything. When I became aware of Starla's great lassitude of spirit, and the flimsiness of her hold on sanity, my greatest fear became that she would take her own life and send me staggering off into the infernal country where I once earned citizenship after Steve's funeral. But the river is beside me and saltwater has always fed my soul like a truth serum. I can say to myself, with the river's full acquiescence and support, that I would love to live with a wife who loved me, who shared my house and bed with me, who would look at me the way Fraser looks at Niles, who would treasure my company and our house together the way Ike and Betty do with such ease. And yes, I'd love to have a child—a boy, a girl— one of them or five of them; I want to be a father and take out photos of my kids and pass them around the office the way the other daddies do at the paper. I turn and look out toward Fort Sumter, Mount Pleasant, and James Island. The air comes to me in drafts of hothouse roses, and the harbor is traffic-less, the stars as pale as moths.

The walk has helped me straighten things out, and I head home with out thinking. I rejoice in the prodigal charm of my palm-haunted city. Though I've written love letters to Charleston hundreds of times in my columns over the years, I don't think I've ever come close to touching on the city's uncaptured mysteries. Walking back north along the Bat tery wall, I realize words are never enough; they stutter and cleave to the roof of my mouth when I need them to blaze, to surge out of my mouth like an avenging hive of hunter wasps. As I go back to my house, I let no sensation pass without my appreciation—on this night, this amazing night that brought forth imaginary cheerleaders, fight songs, screaming, bloodshed, a quest, a gathering of our own aristocracy of the elect and the chosen. It has been a rich and satisfying night, and I am bursting with something I have to describe as joy.

Tradd Street is a European street, not an American one. The houses push their stuccoed façades up against the sidewalks. If not for the street lamps, darkness would give the night a sinister and claustrophobic cast. The outside light at my house on the south side of Tradd is lit, but I don't remember flicking the switch on my way out. Such inattention to de tail is not common to me. I unlock the privacy door that leads onto my first-floor veranda and see a light on in the living room that I never use. I hear music coming from my third-story study.

"Yoo-hoo!" I call out. "I hope you're a friendly burglar and not a Charles Manson type."

I hear Molly's clear, unmistakable laughter, and it relieves me that she can still laugh. I walk upstairs and find her sitting in one of the leather chairs that look out over the rooftops of the city. Because I have a clear view of the steeples of both St. Michael's and St. Philip's, I consider myself a lucky man.

"Could I change into something more comfortable?" I ask. I see Molly's pretty feet propped up on a footstool.

"Sure. It's your house." She smiles.

"If I get in my birthday suit, would that be bad form?"

"Yes, it would. But it might make the evening more interesting," she says, and again, the good Molly laughter, not the sorrowing kind that can break your heart in an instant.

"You helped yourself to the wine, I hope."

"Emptied the open bottle, got a head start on a second."

"Why do we drink so much in Charleston?" I pour myself a splash of Hennessy.

"Because we're human," she says. "Like everyone else. And the older we get, the more human we get. The more human we get, the more painful everything becomes. That was a bad scene today, wasn't it?"

"It was memorable."

"What happened after I left? I'm terrified to know the answer. But I need to know."

"Chad bled to death in his sister's arms. Fraser was like the Virgin Mary, holding Chad in the pietà style. Before he succumbed, he looked at me and said, 'Leo, thou has a very small peter. And upon this rock I shall build my church.' Ike and Betty are patrolling the streets hunting down the murderess. Bloodhounds are roaming South of Broad."

"Why'd I ask you a serious question?"

I take a seat in the chair beside her. Both of us stare out the Palladian window at the rooftops that run together until the steeple of St. Michael's interrupts their irregular march.

"Your punch was a good one. At first we thought Chad's nose was broken. As you might expect, he did not handle public humiliation well. He denied that he was having an affair. Claimed you were crazy. But the good news is he's having you tested next week, and you'll soon be getting shock treatments and living in a padded cell."

"He said that?"

"No, but those were the implications."

"Did he go to the hospital?"

"Don't know. But he went somewhere. In a big hurry."

"He went to see that Brazilian bitch, didn't he?"

"He didn't leave a forwarding address."

"How long've you known?" Molly asks, still not looking at me.

"Unfair question. I'm a columnist. I hear every rumor, true or not. If Mayor Riley wears a dress to a city council meeting. If the head of the NAACP has a sex-change operation. If your father turns his house into a whorehouse. I hear it all."

"Sarah Ellen Jenkins saw you going into Chad's office yesterday," she says, looking at me with enough fury to put me on fair notice that I need to change my tactics. "Did you discuss his affair?"

"I told him the rumors that I'd been hearing."

"Why didn't you come to me? Our friendship's a lot stronger than yours and Chad's has ever been. Tell me that's a lie."

"That's the Lord's truth."

"You've never liked Chad," she says.

"That's not true," I defend myself. "I had to get accustomed to him."

"Which part?"

"The asshole factor. It's a strong genetic trait that runs in all males in the family. He denied having the affair, by the way."

"Did you meet the Brazilian girl?" Molly asks.

I flinch when I nod my head.

"Was she beautiful?"

"She had the loveliest mustache. It covered her harelip quite nicely. She could use a better-fitting set of dentures. Her breath smelled like a bag of shrimp left out in the heat for a month."

"That pretty, huh?"

"Made me wish I'd been born in Brazil."

She slaps my hand hard, and we both laugh. We look out again at the white steeple and hear the bells of St. Michael's tolling the midnight hour. In her chair, she shifts to the left and props her bare feet on my ankles. The shock of her flesh on mine sends a jolt right through me.

"Do you remember our dance Friday night?"

"No," I lie.

"Do you remember how we kissed once we got free from the others?"

"No," I say again.

"Sheba saw it," Molly says. "She thinks we kiss pretty good."

"I was drunk. I don't remember a thing."

"Let me tell you about it, then, Leo. You kissed me like you meant it. Like I was the only woman in the world you cared anything about. You kissed me like you wanted my mouth around yours forever. You're only the second man I've ever kissed. I liked it a lot. Now you say something."

"I'm glad you liked it." I rise to pour a little more Cognac. "It was one of the great moments of my life. I've dreamed about kissing you since we met. Never thought it would happen. But we're both married. Both of us. Me in name only, but you're really married, and I happen to know you still love Chad. I know something else that you probably can't even imagine now: he still loves you, and he always will. He's a guy, Molly. He's got a dick. It makes us all act nuts."

With surprising grace and speed, Molly rises from her chair and sits in my lap. She sets her wineglass down, wraps her arms around my neck, and puts her face close to mine. Her eyes are clear and pale and determined. The whole scene feels dangerous and wonderful, like a prayer I threw at God in high school has finally arrived in his range of hearing.

"Do you think Starla is ever coming back to you, Leo?" she says. "A year is a long time to be gone. She used to run off for a month or two. It's gotten serious, and I know it bothers you."

"She calls me every week, Molly. No, that's not true now. It was true at first. Now she calls me once a month, sometimes two months. Cries a lot. Feels guilty. Asks me to wait for her. I say, 'You're my wife. I'll always wait for you.' Which makes her mad for some reason. As though that was the last answer she was waiting for. Lots of times, she'll start screaming. Tells me the number of men she's sleeping with. Tells me their names. Their professions. Their wives' names. Then she catches herself. She comes back to herself. The real Starla. Cries again. Feels guilty. And on it goes into the night. It always ends the same way. She passes out."

"Leo." Molly kisses my nose. "What a darling, foolish man. No, let me change that. Let me be a little more accurate: what a stupid, stupid, *stupid* man."

"I knew what I was getting into," I say, then think better about it. "Or I was foolish enough to think I did."

"I need you to answer a question," Molly says. "I'd like a serious answer."

"Go ahead."

"Are you in love with me?"

I twist uncomfortably in the chair and try to get up, but she pins my shoulders and glares at me with an expression that brooks no opposition.

"I thought I answered that Friday night. Why do you keep asking? Why now? Why tonight? Ask me on the happiest day of your marriage with Chad. Ask me on the day you think you have the perfect marriage with the finest man in the city limits. But it's not right to ask it now. Look, you just smashed his nose, got blood all over his Porsche, and canceled his trip to Brazil for Mardi Gras."

She hits me on the shoulder, then cries out in pain. She used the same fist to bust open Chad's schnozzola, and I think she is going to weep from sheer pain.

"Let me see that hand." I lean over and turn on a lamp. Her hand is swollen and turning purple. Gently, I feel for broken bones, but cannot tell if there has been real damage. I did notice that Chad was lucky Molly had punched him with her right fist: the two-carat wedding ring she wears on her left hand could have put out one of his eyeballs.

"You'll need to get that X-rayed tomorrow," I say.

"Are you really in love with me?" she insists. "Answer my damn question. Everyone has always teased me about it. Especially Fraser, and even Chad. Hell, Starla used to tease me about it in the early years, when she actually lived with you."

"I've loved you since the day I first met you, like I told you the other night," I tell her.

"Why? That's stupid. That's unheard-of. You didn't know me, or one thing about me."

"I knew your style. The way you carried yourself. Your courtesy and attentiveness to everything going on around you. I loved your defense of Fraser the day I first met you. I knew you were a match for Chad. A match for anyone. I felt your strength. Then there was your beauty, your extraordinary beauty. Does that answer your question, Molly, you pain in the ass? Does that mean you won't punch me again?"

"If I punch you again, I'll use the other hand."

"Why are you sitting on my lap?" I ask her.

"Gosh, Leo," she says, laughing. Reaching over, she turns off the lamp and we are staring at each other in dim moonlight. "Let's put our heads together and try to figure this out as a team. Let's look at the evidence. I have a fight with my philandering husband in front of my best friends. I bloody his nose and run home to wait for him. Silly me. I thought he'd come and apologize for putting me through such hell. But no, time goes by, and I realize he's gone over to seek comfort in the arms of his piña colada. Do they drink piña coladas in Brazil?"

"Never been there."

"So then I realize there'll be no tender reconciliation, none of the sweet crap. So I take a walk to clear my head, and walk straight to your house. Like all of us, I know where you hide your spare key in the gutter spout, so I let myself in. I grabbed a bottle of wine, crawled into your bed, and slept for two hours. I felt safe. Relaxed. I got up and took a shower, washed my hair, made myself at home. At Starla's dressing table, I used her cosmetics and makeup and perfume. Then I turned on the Braves game and waited for you to come home."

"Who won the game?"

"Shut up," she says. "The question in the air is still in the air. Why am I sitting in your lap?"

"You go first," I suggest.

"Friday night, when Sheba caught us making out, she went back to the guesthouse. She came over for lunch. We talked a little girl talk. Turns out that Chad sneaked back to the guesthouse to hit on Sheba. Sheba told him it was one of the highest compliments she ever received. But she thought it a bit tacky to bang him while staying in his and his wife's guesthouse. He admitted she had a point, and skulked back to his office. Big case, you know. Big, *big* case."

"A gentle rebuff from Sheba. Chad, ever the gentleman."

"We all know who Chad is," says Molly. "We always have. He's the only one among us who never pretended to be good. I always admired that about him. Chad's view of the human race is a dark one. He's finally convinced me. Now his Molly has changed. Ergo, you thick-skulled son of a bitch, that is why Molly presently finds herself on your lap."

"Good forensic argument," I say. "Bad idea."

"Have you noticed lately, Leo, that I've been looking at you in the same way you've always looked at me?" She kisses me sweetly on my lips, on both cheeks, on the tip of my nose.

"I don't want your anger at Chad to get hooked up to your feelings about me—in any way, shape, or form."

"You don't know a thing about women."

"I know a few bad things about them," I say. "I even know some good things."

"No, listen to me. You're a blank, a zero, when it comes to what makes a woman tick. Or what turns them on or off or puts them in neutral or overdrive or on cruise control or whatever the hell I'm trying to say."

"Chad's putting you through a hard time. May I make a suggestion?" I ask.

"Ah, an invitation to your boudoir at last."

"No. Here's what I'd like you to know: if Chad leaves you, if Starla leaves me as she's threatened to do a thousand times, I'd rather be married to you than anyone in the world. I'll never be good enough for you, and I know that better than anyone. But if that kiss the other night was the beginning, then I'd like that feeling to last the rest of our lives. Together."

"What do we do in the meantime?"

"Let me make you some coffee," I say. "Let's go down to the kitchen. Because I have something important to tell you, something that's going to change all our lives. I think it'll prove whether Chad's right about humanity—its darkness, its hopelessness—or it might prove that there is reason to hope, that we can be better than we were born to be."

Molly kisses me a last time, but this one is sisterly, the sealing of a friendship, a door opening to the future. "Give me a hint. What's going to turn us all toward the light? Where does this path to goodness begin?"

"San Francisco," I say. "The Renegades ride again. We're going out to find Trevor Poe. He's dying of AIDS. We're going to bring him home, Molly. We're not going to let him die alone."

PART THREE

CHAPTER 14

Pacific Heights

The West is both a great thirst and a dry, weatherless curiosity. In California, the mad, deep breath of deserts is never far away. The sky above San Francisco is often so dazzling a blue that it merits the overripe description of cerulean, or comparison to lapis lazuli. Its clouds are sea-born and formed in the odd depths of its mysterious bay, where the fog moves inland in a billion-celled, mindless creature, amoeba-shaped and poisonous, like a stillborn member of the nightshade family. Southern fogs calm me as they paint the marshes with their milk-stained fingers. The San Francisco fog is a silver-lined hunter of the predator class, and I always find it troubling. When I awaken to its fog horns, they sound like the exiled whimpering of a city in endless sexual distress.

As a Charlestonian, I know I am not supposed to bend a knee in admiration of a hill country of such amazing, brittle wildness. But San Francisco seduced me on my first visit to Trevor Poe's flat on Union Street. In its profusion of roses and eucalyptus and palms, the city seems voluptuous and decadent in its very pores, a place that revels in folly and rolls around in the carcasses of human vice. The whole place feels graded, uplifted, maxed out; the views are all spectacular and aha-inducing. San

Francisco is a city that requires a fine pair of legs, a city of cliffs mis-named as hills, honeycombed with a fine webbing of showy houses that cling to the slanted streets with the fierceness of abalones. You can spot a whale sounding in the waters between the Presidio and Sausalito in the morning, buy a live eel for lunch in Chinatown, see the Shakespeare Garden at Golden Gate Park in midafternoon, catch a wave in the Pacific along the Great Highway, inhale the unforgettable farts of sea lions on Pier 39, catch part of a gay-lesbian film festival at the Castro Theatre, get a book signed by Lawrence Ferlinghetti at City Lights Books, buy a drink at the Top of the Mark. Trevor Poe gave us this astonishing city as a gift, once he abandoned us to our less glitzy lives in Charleston.

His place on Union Street served as a home away from home for all of us, a vacation wonderland. He opened his doors to us and proved an in-defatigable lover and sightseer of his adopted city. So it feels like a home-coming to us as the jet lands in Oakland and a limousine transports us to the mansion on Vallejo Street owned by the producer, a man named Saul Marks, which he has offered to Sheba in her search for her twin. The house is Italianate with a view of the bay, the Golden Gate Bridge, Sausalito, and the white linen majesty of the city itself. The laconic Irish chauffeur tells us to call him Murray.

"What did you have to do to get the producer to give you this house?" Betty asks Sheba, whistling as Murray helps us get our luggage inside the ornate entryway.

"I had to play with his little weenie," Sheba replies. She gives Murray a lavish tip, then directs us to our various bedrooms. She apologizes as she sends me down into the entrails of the house, where I have a bedroom without windows, then says, "I've ordered in some Chinese. Meet up in the dining room after you unpack."

When I make my way upstairs, I find my noisy group of friends gath-ered in front of a massive window watching the sun set against a cloudless Pacific in a wilderness of blue. The sun blisters the waters with a seething gold, then a flare or red, followed by a pink-fingered, rosy exit left.

Betty says, "Sunsets make me believe in God."

Molly adds, "They make me know that one day I'm going to die."

"Tell me why we brought Molly again?" Fraser smiles at her best friend and sister-in-law.

"Comic relief," I suggest.

"It's one more day we'll never see again," Molly says. "One day closer to our own demise."

"I just think it's prettier than shit," Ike says, pouring a drink over at the bar. "I always noted that white people thought too much."

As we feast on the takeout that is far superior to any Chinese food I've tasted in the South, we moan over dishes that we never had until Trevor brought us out to San Francisco in the early 1970s. Niles reminds me that I once outraged the minuscule Charleston Chinese community by claiming that all people of Chinese ancestry forgot how to cook as soon as they crossed the South Carolina state line; this was after my first two-week visit in Trevor's flat, which served as my honeymoon with Starla.

Fraser says, "I'm wearing down. The liquor's good, the vino's great. But we're out here for a reason, and I already miss my kids. Give me a job, Sheba. Tell me what to do tomorrow."

Sheba hands us all copies of a long list of names. Her efficiency at this is real, and it's moving. With rare patience, Sheba has waited for the proper moment before she springs into the business side of this hunt. From a beautiful doe-skin briefcase, she hands us each a folder filled with hints and possibilities and rumors that have accrued around the last sightings of Trevor.

"Betty and Ike, I'd like you to present yourself to the police department, tell them what you're doing here, and ask them for any assistance possible. Leo is meeting with his columnist friend Herb Caen. The list contains the names of all the gay men who've been friends or lovers of Trevor's over the past fifteen years. Or musicians who've played music with him. Or hostesses who hired him to play piano at their parties. I'd like my Junior Leaguers, Molly and Fraser, to track down any clues from this list. Let me show all of you something. This is a photograph of the last time I visited Trevor here."

"Did you stay with Trevor?" Ike asks, studying the photograph.

"I'm a movie star, honey," Sheba snorts. "I don't do flats. I do penthouses at the top of the Fairmont."

"What a peasant loser you are, Ike," Molly teases. "To think that a movie star would even think about parking her butt in a flat."

Sheba ignores Molly. "Remember, Trevor and I haven't been close all these years. He kept in much better touch with all of you. We reminded each other of a hideous childhood we were both in a hurry to forget. I've pinned all of your assignments on your pillows. You've got the necessary maps and the folders. Some of you'll be pounding the pavement for the first couple of days. That's you, boys. One of the worst things about dying of AIDS is that you're penniless at the end. You end up in a fleabag hotel at the end of the line."

Fraser gets down to business again. "Who was the last person to see Trevor?"

"His doctor at the AIDS clinic in the Castro," Sheba responds. "He told me Trevor had lost twenty pounds in the last two years."

"Jesus!" Betty cries. "He was such a puny thing anyway."

"Then he dropped off the face of the earth," Sheba continues. "The last time he saw him the doctor treated Trevor for Kaposi's sarcoma."

"Oh, no," Molly says. "That's not good. That causes those sores and scales on the face."

"What about Ben Steinberg? Georgie Stickney? Or Tillman Carson?" Betty asks. "They were three of his running buddies when Ike and I were here a couple of years ago."

"All dead," Sheba says. "All kids, and all dead."

Molly rises from her chair and walks over to one of the extravagant windows that take in the lit-up grandeur of the nighttime city. Her silhouette is forlorn and round-shouldered, looking like one of those helpless witnesses who watch the Passion of Christ play out in those innumerable Renaissance paintings. Our group gathers in quiet solidarity around her. The city glitters beneath us like a prodigious swarm of fireflies. My eye catches the Golden Gate Bridge, which looks like a piece of jewelry linking two music boxes. A stringed trio of architecture, art, and hopelessness all gather up in perfect unity as we hover near our damaged friend.

Sheba looks at each of us and says, "Why don't all of us go beddy-bye now?"

Ike says, "I haven't wanted to bring this up, Sheba. I've been waiting for a good time, but there's not going to be a good time: where's your goddamn daddy?"

I watch as Sheba's face contorts into sudden hatred, then she catches herself. "I don't like to talk about that bastard. You know that, Ike."

Ike says, "But you know why I have to ask, and you know why it's important."

I say, "We all got to know about your daddy over the years, and none of us has enjoyed it much."

"If it hurts too much to answer, Sheba," Molly says, "then don't."

"Not good enough, Molly," Niles tells her. "We've got to know at least where he is."

"You're right," Sheba says. "Here's the short story: after my graduation from high school, he followed me out to L.A. I didn't know it. But he is brilliant, smarter than anyone. I started working soon as an actress. He found me living in an apartment in Westwood. He raped me."

"Don't tell us any more," Fraser says.

"No, the boys are right, all of you need to know. He held me prisoner, did lots of stuff, but no different from when I was a little girl. I learned to dissociate then. I did it again. Then he let me go, went to San Francisco, and did the same thing to Trevor. Next movie, I hired a bodyguard. My dad almost killed that poor man. What name was I to give to the cops? What description? He's used a hundred names. Had red hair, gray hair, no hair. Wore beards, mustaches, goatees. Brown-eyed, blue-eyed, green-eyed. Turbaned. Yarmulke. Beret. Baseball cap."

"Now. Where is he now?" Ike demands. "He's stalked all of us over the years."

"He's dead, thank God. He finally made a mistake. Five years ago, I made that movie in New York. By then, I had enough bodyguards to take on the Secret Service. I was staying at a fancy high-rise. My dad came in disguised as a deliveryman. When he was stopped and questioned by the doorman, Dad killed the man by stabbing him in the heart. An alarm was sounded. He was overpowered. The murder was caught on security tapes. Jack Cross pleaded guilty to murder and was sentenced to life without parole at Sing Sing. He went nuts. Got transferred to a high-security nuthouse, where he jumped off the roof. End of story. No one knows to this day that Jack Cross was my dad."

"How do you know?" Betty asks. "We've got to know this for certain."

"Jack Cross wrote me from prison," Sheba says. "Almost every day."

"Was that your dad's real name?" Molly asks.

"No," Sheba says. "When Trevor and I were born, he was named Houston Poe."

"But you're sure he's dead?" Niles asks.

"I have his ashes in a vase in my place in Santa Monica," Sheba says. "I should've said something to all of you before this. I try to pretend he never lived."

"To bed," Betty says, and we hug each other good night.

"Do you mind if I check that story out?" Ike asks as he bear-hugs Sheba.

"Not at all, Ike," Sheba says. "But I've got his ashes."

"You've got someone's ashes," Ike says. "You may even have Jack Cross's ashes. That doesn't mean they're your daddy's."

When I enter my windowless, claustrophobic quarters in the basement, I am pleased to discover good lighting and a comfortable bed and a wall full of carefully selected books. Sheba has typed out my instructions on a piece of heavy personal stationery and I read them as I undress.

1) Meet with Herb Caen at 9:00 A.M. for breakfast at Perry's on Union Street. (Sheba will attend the meeting.) Very important he helps us.

2) Go to Trevor's old address at 1038 Union Street and meet the new tenant, a lawyer named Anna Cole, to see if she knows anything about Trevor or his disappearance. Be flirtatious with her, Toad. Use the charm you claim you don't have. Make notes of everything, whether you think it's important or not.

3) Meet the group back at Washington Square Bar and Grill at one for lunch and comparison of notes.

Your favorite movie star, Sheba Poe

I turn out the lights and climb into bed, into a darkness that seems more than dark, living a life that feels much the same way.

When Trevor first moved to San Francisco, he would tease us poor mortals who were doomed to live out our boring lives in South Carolina. He has always been a conversationalist of rare gifts, and in his first years in the city, he would call and talk to me for hours. I would marvel at his easy command of language and his jeweler's eye for the precise and necessary detail. His first job was as a piano player at a bar called the Curtain Call in the theater district. To the surprise of none of us, he was a sensation from his first night. The great columnist Herb Caen authenticated Trevor's success by visiting the Curtain Call on the first anniversary of Trevor's hiring. He wrote that "a young Southern wizard has been tickling the ivories and has become legendary for his witty one-liners and flashing repartee." Being written up in Herb Caen's column was a defining moment in Trevor's career. Trevor sent Herb's columns to me so I could learn how a truly accomplished writer defined his city with wit, sophistication, and flair.

The next morning I walk into Perry's and see that Herb Caen is already holding court at the best table in the house. He has surrounded himself with a dewy-eyed bunch of low-key sycophants, two ecstatic owners, and tourists snapping pictures of him. His aura creates a swarm of emotion that is something more than hero worship and a bit less than a Zen Buddhist satori. I have my work cut out for me this morning. Before we left Charleston, I contacted Herb and asked for his help. But now I have to try again to convince him to write a story about Trevor Poe's disappearance and the search party of his high school friends from South Carolina.

When he catches me studying him, he motions me to his table. "Sorry I didn't use your friend in Sunday's column, Leo. Not much of a story there, *bubeleh*. We've got thousands of guys dying of AIDS in this city. I spotted six guys with AIDS in this restaurant this morning."

"How do you spot them?" I ask.

"You'll be an expert in a couple of days. Pretend you're a Russian soldier and you've just arrived at the gates of Auschwitz. That starved, haunted look. That look is a death warrant in this town."

"But you remember Trevor Poe," I say. "You've written about him before."

"He's a great guy. Funny as hell. Hell of a piano player. But you've got to get me a story. No hook, no story. A gay musician who's got AIDS? Big deal."

"Seven of his high school friends flew in from Charleston yesterday to hunt for him. One of them's just been named the first black police chief in the history of Charleston."

"Nice story. Maybe if I was a cartoonist doing Mary Worth."

I laugh and enjoy Herb, as I always did on previous visits. But he goes even further by saying, "You were the best town guide I ever had when I visited Charleston. But I already paid you back for that one. Your story might play in Charleston; it's old news in Baghdad by the Bay."

"You're right," I say. "Let me buy you another Bloody Mary, Herb. For old time's sake."

"You're not telling me something," Herb says. "What do you got? What're you holding out on me?"

"It may be nothing. Big guy like you. Big city. Big names everywhere you look. You don't need anything from a guy like me. I've got to be going now."

Herb grabs my arm. "Before you go, I need to know the bone you were going to throw me."

"Got to get it into your column, Herb," I say. "Got to get a little special attention from you. Otherwise, I fly back South with it."

"After all I've done for you," Herb grumbles. "Hell, there's nothing you've got I could use. The best scoop in your life wouldn't make the last line in my column. We play in different leagues, Leo, and you're smart enough to know it."

"You're a symphony orchestra, Herb," I say. "I'm an ocarina. I got all that. But I'd never let a story walk out the door like you're about to do. I need you, pal. You're the best at what you do in the country, but I gotta go now, Herb. Enjoy your breakfast."

"You'll get one line tomorrow," Herb says. "What you got, Leo? Better be good."

"I need half a column."

"You're wasting your time. And mine," Herb scoffs.

"Bye, Herb. Here's a number where you can reach me." I hand him a piece of paper.

"You're playing me. You're actually playing me, greenhorn," Herb says, but with vague admiration. "Tell you what, Leo: half a column. But it better be great. If it's not, you don't get *bubkes. Comprende?*"

"I speak many languages. Including Yiddish and Italian."

"Spill it."

"Trevor Poe is the brother of the Hollywood actress Sheba Poe. She organized the search. She came to Charleston to ask for our help."

"You son of a bitch."

"I was taught by a master. He taught me to always hold a few cards in reserve. Show them the hat. Never the rabbit."

"How do I know you're telling me the truth?" Herb asks.

"Two ways. First of all, I give you my word."

"Not good enough, Southern boy," he says. "Who do you think you're dealing with, a card-carrying member of the Sons of the Confederacy?"

"I'll ignore your slur on my background."

Herb says, "Hot air sells balloons. Not newspapers."

I remove the perfect stalk of celery from Herb's Bloody Mary and bite off the leafy top of it. With that signal, a woman dressed demurely in a black leather jacket and silk slacks removes her sunglasses. She rises from a table near the end of the bar, and unties her Armani scarf. She unzips her jacket, and reveals a scant, silvery blouse, as flimsy as a sandwich bag. With a shake of her head, a cascade of golden curls falls around her shoulders. Her stride across the room, however, is purposeful, without the unstudied voluptuousness she brought to every role she played. The entire restaurant is mesmerized by this transformation of a woman who has been sitting in anonymity. The words "Sheba Poe" pass from table to table as she strides with her green eyes affixed on the appreciative gaze of Herb Caen.

"You got yourself the lead tomorrow, Leo," Herb says as I rise to leave. "Done with class and brio, baby cakes."

"I would like to introduce you to the legendary Sheba Poe, Herb. Sheba, this is the equally legendary Herb Caen."

"I'll take it from here, Leo," Sheba says. "See you at lunch." With perfect timing, she adds, "Baby cakes." But to Herb Caen, she says, "I've lost my brother, Mr. Caen. I need your help."

I flag down a cab that delivers me to Trevor's old flat at 1038 Union Street, on Russian Hill. More than half of his Charleston friends have visited Trevor in his well-equipped guest room that overlooks the everlasting busyness and traffic of Union Street. Trevor exploited his large gift for friendship by sharing his place with anyone who could prove an even tenuous relationship with his core group of Charleston admirers. We paid him back by treating him to overpriced meals in the newly acclaimed hotspots that opened with astonishing frequency in a city that lived for sundown. At the beginning, Trevor force-marched all of us to the Castro to show off the gay community. He took enormous pride in serving as a Southern ambassador to his gay demimonde. The South provided him with both cachet and color commentary. Over the years he introduced me to so many gay Southern men, from the Tidewater of Virginia to the Arkansas Ozarks, that I thought I could hang their accents out to dry on a clothesline, separated only by geographic idiosyncrasies and slurred syllables of every stripe. Though his high school classmates knew that Trevor had lived in Charleston for only a year before he lit out for the Castro and its unspeakable pleasures, we had to admit he had developed one of the most authentic Charleston accents any of us had ever heard. His brilliance at mimicking had served him well.

In his garden one summer, I remember him telling a convivial group of gay men from Chicago, "The gay men from the South are always the most fascinating members of our tribe. They are the best conversationalists, the most inventive cooks, and they hold their liquor almost too well, I'd say. And they are wicked to the point of criminality in bed. No party in this city is worth its salt without the inclusion of at least one gay man of negligible character and unquestioned provenance from somewhere in the old Confederacy. I've been severely criticized by gay activists with bad breath and British teeth for maintaining my friendships with all my straight friends from Charleston. But they bring me news of that stodgy, asexual world I left behind, where even the missionary position is considered a revolutionary deviation. They remind me that life is a smorgasbord, not just a box of Ritz crackers. And besides, these were my sandbox friends. Metaphorically, of course, but you never desert or dishonor the delicious boys and girls who played in the sandbox with you. Even philistines from Chicago, with your souls frozen by the winds off Lake Michigan, can understand the power of a friendship that goes all the way back to the sandbox. Or do you Midwesterners make your best friends in snowdrifts?"

Then Trevor winked at me with marvelous affection, and I winked back, locked in my colorless, unimaginative straightness. But I could laugh at everything Trevor would say or think or conjure. He always made me and his friends think we were living fuller, richer lives by simply dwelling in his romantic, overeroticized presence. He made Fraser feel like she was watching a Broadway play and Molly feel as though she were starring in one. Trevor brought out the protective side of Niles, the maternal side of Betty, the competitive nature of Chad, and the melodramatic part of me. Only Ike looked sideways at Trevor's bravura performances, and the accent grated on Ike's sensibility. "Lose the accent, Trevor. You ain't from Charleston. You ain't from the South. And, at best, you sound like a third-rate Negro houseboy," he once told Trevor.

"My accent sounds like the tinkling of an eighteenth-century chandelier," Trevor replied. "I've been told that by ladies with the name of Ravenel and Middleton and Prioleau, yard jockey."

As the cab leaves me at 1038 Union Street, I have no idea if I will ever see Trevor Poe again or enter this charming space that has meant so much to me over the years. Cars whip by going much too fast; others jolt past driven by unsure-footed drivers tapping the brakes again and again, surprised by the steepness of the grade on Union as it makes its incursion into North Beach. I move up to the door and ring the bell, expecting nothing, but putting a Southern smile on my face if I am wrong. Sheba has written the woman letters and received no reply; neither has the new renter responded to a series of phone messages from Sheba's secretary. The renter's name is Anna Cole, and she's a young lawyer from Duluth, Minnesota.

"Anna Cole," I shout, calling up to one of the shapely bay windows that look out from the living room. "I'm a friend of Trevor Poe's from South Carolina, and I need to talk to you. Will you please open the door?"

A nervous but flashy young woman opens the door with unnecessary ferocity and studies me through the space left by a lock and chain.

"What the fuck do you want?" Anna Cole asks. "Why're you following me?"

"Ma'am," I say, "I've never seen you before. I'm not following you. My good friend Trevor Poe used to live here, and I'm with a bunch of friends who're looking for him."

She looks past me with wild, distrustful eyes. "I thought you were the pervert who's been tailing me for the past week. What's with the 'ma'am' shit?"

"I'm Southern," I explain. "It's instilled in us at birth. Sorry if it offends you."

"I've always thought the South was the weirdest place in the nation."

"I couldn't agree with you more. But I've never been to Minnesota," I say.

Again, I arouse her paranoia. "How do you know I'm from Minnesota?"

"We did research on the Minnesota chick who got our friend thrown out of his home."

"Look, George Wallace, or whatever your damn name is, I'm on edge here. I picked up a bad guy in my life. I've called the cops, but they can't do anything until he rapes me and disembowels me and dumps me into the bay. And I did not get your friend evicted from this flat. He didn't pay his damn rent. How's that my fault?"

"You're right, Garrison Keillor. It's not your fault."

"You're stereotyping me, and I don't like it worth a shit."

"We George Wallaces tend to stereotype ice fishermen from Duluth who stereotype us."

"I shouldn't have said that," she says. "I apologize. Now, please get out of here."

"I need to find my friend," I insist. "I just have a few questions for you, Anna Cole."

"Oh, Jesus!" Her terror is real. "There he is. He's in that ugly Honda halfway down the street. He's ducked back down now. You can't see him."

She reveals a pistol that she is carrying behind her. She handles it inexpertly like a girl handling a copperhead for the first time—or a boy, for that matter.

"Do you know how to use that weapon?" I ask.

"I point it at his balls, I pull the trigger. And presto, no balls. How hard can that be?"

"May I borrow the gun, Anna?" I ask with great politeness. "I know how to use one. But if I succeed in running your friend off, I'll insist you answer some questions about Trevor."

She studies me as though noticing me for the first time. "Why should I trust you?"

"Do you trust that guy more?"

"You could rob me. You could rape me. You could kill me and the cops would say, 'What a dumb fucking broad. She gave him her own gun.' "

"Yes, ma'am, that's one scenario," I say. "But I think I can get rid of him for you. I have a great imagination."

"How does that help me?"

"Because now we'll find out about your own imagination, if you've got one or not. We'll also find out if you're a good judge of character."

"I don't like your face." She stares hard at me.

"I don't, either. Never have."

"I'll be watching from the bay window," she says.

With understandable nervousness, she slips me her small twenty-two pistol, which I notice is unloaded as I place it in my jacket pocket. I knock on the door again and she is clearly irritated when she cracks it open.

I ask, "Did you buy any bullets for this gun?"

"I don't believe in violence or bloodshed or even the death penalty," Anna Cole says with a spiritual certainty I find off-putting.

"What if your pervert kills me? Will you hope he fries in an electric chair? Or gags to death in a gas chamber?"

"I'd hope he'd get life with no chance of parole," she answers.

"So you think he'd be better off making stop signs and license plates the rest of his life? You think he should take correspondence courses from a community college or enroll in a poetry course taught by some beatnik on Telegraph Avenue?"

"I believe that human life is sacred," she says.

"Garrison Keillor."

"Don't you dare call me that," she snarls.

"My wife is dying of cancer as we speak. Will you promise to take care of my twelve children if they are orphaned in the shootout on Union Street?"

"It won't be a shootout," she says. "You don't have any bullets."

"The pervert may have some. Do you promise to help support my orphan children if they need help?"

"Haven't you ever heard of birth control down South?" she asks, then relents and says, "I promise to do what I can."

"Now, Anna Cole, go to the bay window. Showtime. The latest install-ment of *A Prairie Home Companion* is about to begin."

I walk across Union Street and head down the hill, passing the Honda without giving it a sidelong glance. But once I am past it, I circle behind it and write down his license plate number, and the fact that it is a brown 1986 Accord. As I write down this general information, I watch the man's head rise up a second time. As I approach his car from the driver's side, he disappears again, dropping all the way to the floorboards along the front seat. When I knock on the window to attract his attention, he lies motionless.

I knock harder. "Sir, open the window. I'd like to talk to you."

"Fuck you, Officer," he squeals to the floorboards. "I haven't done any-thing. This is a legal parking space."

"You're scaring a young lady across the street," I say. "Open the win-dow, sir."

" 'Fuck you' still sounds good to me. Yep, sounds even better the sec-ond time," he says.

I take the handle of the pistol and break a hole in the window. Then I kick the rest of the window in with my right leg, coming at it from an uphill angle. It is a large leg, and the window shatters in an immensely satisfying fashion. I'd once been a Citadel cadet, and I could play the tough guy.

"That's it! Now you're a dead man." He brushes shards of glass from his clothes and body. He jerks upright, red-faced and furious, and I take in his plain, unspectacular features as he adjusts his wrap-around sun-glasses. If I am forced to describe him in a court of law, I'll say his face is modest and plain and functional, just like a Honda Accord. I place the pistol against his forehead, but keep my good humor and wave to passersby to let them know I have the situation in hand. I remove his sun-glasses and deposit them in my pocket. His brows are thick and march above his eyes like one large caterpillar. His eyes are brown, a similar shade as the car, and he is wearing a cheap black toupee.

"Your wallet, sir," I order. When he gives me his wallet, I say, "Thank you for your extraordinary level of cooperation, Mr. John Summey. Ah! This must be the lovely Mrs. Summey. And your three handsome sons. And gee whiz, you've been a member of American Express since 1973. And your Visa card's still valid. Though I must tell you, Mr. Summey, you've allowed your Discover card to expire. I'll just keep your wallet for a month or two. By that time, we'll see if you can quit stalking that nice young woman who lives across the street. She's been seeing your ugly mug everywhere she goes. But now that I have your driver's license and know that you live at 25710 Vendola Drive in San Rafael, you might be looking at my ugly mug more often."

"I know the mayor personally," he says. "I'll have your badge, asshole. You'll be looking at want ads tonight."

"Hear that sound? That's my teeth chattering. But you got it all wrong, pal. I'm no cop. I'm that woman's husband, and I just got out of San Quentin. Got your car keys, Mr. Summey?"

"Yes, sir," he says.

"You got any problems with me just letting you go? I promised my wife I'd kill ya. But you know how broads are? Sentimental as hell. I'll tell her about your three boys, tug on the old heartstrings. See where I'm coming from?"

"Yes, sir." He fumbles with his key, trembling as he tries to insert it into the steering column.

"I'll mail you your wallet in a month," I say.

"I'd appreciate it."

"Now, Summey, we got to make the next part look good for my wife. I'll need your help here. You've got twenty seconds to get out of here. Then I'm going to start shooting at your head. Two seconds have already passed." I never saw a car outside of the Darlington 500 cover such a distance in such speed.

I return in a leisurely fashion to the doorway of 1038 Union where I once again ring the bell and again hear Anna Cole's strained voice through the locked doorway. "You're a bigger nut than he is," she says. I can see her outline against the antique lace curtains that had once belonged to Trevor Poe.

"He was more difficult to get rid of than I thought," I say.

"Why'd you kick out his window?"

"He refused to talk and I thought it might get his attention."

"Leave now, this very moment, or I'll call the cops. You're obviously a lunatic. I don't want to talk to you, and I don't know what happened to your friend. If I did, I'd tell you. Just go."

"Okay," I say. "Thanks for your help."

I turn again and walk down the short flight of steps and back onto Union Street, then hear the door open.

"May I have my dad's gun?" she asks.

"No. You don't believe in bloodshed or violence, remember? By keeping the gun, I'll be helping you live a pious, liberal life. You can't have the gun, nor can you have the stalker's license plate number, nor his wallet, which is chock-full of information about his degenerate life."

We stand facing each other in a hostile standoff, but she is thinking fast. "Would you like a cup of herbal tea?"

"No, I would not," I say. "Do you have coffee?"

"I don't like coffee."

"I don't like herbal tea," I say. "Look, I've got to be going. Here's your dad's gun. Buy some cartridges for it. If that guy's not a sexual pervert, then he's missed his calling. Here's his wallet. Send a copy of the driver's license to the cops."

"Would you like a glass of V8 juice?"

"Yes," I answer. "I'd like that very much."

I receive a shock when I enter the living room: she has barely changed a thing in Trevor's space. She has placed photographs of her own Minnesota family on top of Trevor's piano, where there had once been pictures of his best friends and the celebrities he met along the way. When I mention to her that she is in possession of every piece of furniture and work of art that once belonged to my friend, there is alarm in her voice as she explains, "I didn't steal any of it. I rented the flat furnished, and was delighted to find it furnished by a man of impeccable taste."

"Why would he leave all this behind? He loved every single piece of furniture, every book, every piece of silver."

"I've no idea. He was evicted five months ago, I think. I've been here for three months. He had not paid a penny of rent for over a year. It killed his landlord to evict him, but Mr. Chao felt he had no choice. Trevor never told Mr. Chao he had AIDS. Never even told him he was sick. Mr. Chao broke down and wept when he admitted this to me, and he insisted that I keep all of Trevor's furniture exactly the way it was. It still belongs to Trevor. I'm the caretaker." Then she asks, "You got a name?"

"Leo King. I went to high school with Trevor."

"He was in pretty bad shape when he left here, evidently. The neighbors talk a lot about him. They hate me because they think I stole his apartment."

"Where are his photograph albums?" I ask. "I'd like to take them with me so my friends and I can study them."

She opens a drawer and takes out the albums, then asks me curiously, "Are you married, Leo?"

"Yes, I am."

"You're not wearing a wedding ring," she notes.

"My wife wants a divorce. The last time I saw her in Charleston, she stole it while I was taking a shower. I haven't seen her or the ring since."

"Children?"

"I've always wanted some. Starla never has," I say.

"Starla?" Anna says. "What a strange name."

"I think it's from the Cherokee language."

"What's the translation?" she asks. "I'm interested in all things Native American."

"A strict constructionist would translate it this way: 'By the shores of Gitche Gumee.' "

"Another Minnesota joke."

"Last one," I promise.

"Thank God. Not one of them's been funny. Tell me everything you know about Minnesota."

"The Vikings. The Twins. St. Paul's the capital. Minneapolis hates everything about St. Paul. And vice versa. The Mall of America. Ten thousand lakes. Paul Bunyan. Babe, the Blue Ox. Mayo Clinic. Lake Superior. Lampreys. Beaver. Loons. No poisonous snakes. By the shining Big-Sea-Water. The wigwam of Nokomis. Canadian geese. A million Swedes. Lots of Norwegians. F. Scott Fitzgerald. Lake Itasca. Lake Wobegon. And though I hate to say it because it seems to piss you off—Garrison Keillor."

"Not bad, Leo. I'm impressed."

"Good. You heard from the gander. Let's hear it from the goose. Tell me everything you know about South Carolina."

"Didn't you start the Civil War or something?" she asks with some tentativeness.

"Very good. You know about Fort Sumter?"

"The Research Triangle. Duke University. The Tar Heels."

"That's North Carolina," I say.

"It's all the same thing to me. I've never given a shit about the South."

"Strange. Minnesota is a constant subject of conversation in Southern drawing rooms. Listen, can I take these photograph albums with me?"

"Of course. What about all the other stuff?"

"What other stuff?"

"Over thirty boxes. I packed it all up and put it in a storage room down in the garage. His clothes. His personal effects. And his unmentionables."

"We'll send for the boxes. What are his unmentionables?"

"Some of it . . ." she begins.

"What?"

"Some of it is the vilest pornography I've ever seen. I don't care if a guy is gay or not. Hell, I live in San Francisco. But some of that stuff could land you in the federal pen."

"Trevor liked his porn. He called it his 'foreign film collection.' We'll pick all that stuff up too."

"I watched some of it. You don't want to carry that stuff across state lines."

"We'll take our chances. Why were you looking at Trevor's porn?"

"Curiosity," she admits. "I thought it might turn me on. It had the opposite effect."

"It didn't do much for me, either. Trevor used to show it to me when I was out here visiting. Told me he was trying to entice me over to the dark side."

Then a thought hits Anna, who has the type of expressive face that registers every message she receives from her interior. "Do you know the photograph that Trevor has in the bathroom? Is that Charleston?"

"Yes, it is. Mind if I look at it while you're getting my glass of V8 juice you promised?" I walk down the long hallway before taking a right into the tiny toilet area, where I see the blown-up photograph of the row of sumptuous mansions that line South Battery Street. The houses glitter in the rich overtones of a perfect sun-shot afternoon. It always got a laugh from his South Carolina visitors because Trevor would shout to us through the closed bathroom door, "I always think of Charleston anytime I find my body urging me toward excretion."

Taking the photograph with me, I walk back into the living room and tell the story to Anna Cole as I drink the V8 that she has spiked with Tabasco sauce and lemon juice. "May I take this photograph, Anna? It'll give a big lift to the people I'm meeting for lunch."

"Yeah, sure," she says, but with some reluctance. "But I'm going to miss it. Which house did Trevor grow up in?"

I was going to tell her the truth, but I think that people often need the mythologies they create. "He grew up in this one. On the corner of Meeting and South Battery," I tell her.

"I knew he came from a life of privilege."

"You were right on the money," I say. "By the way, Anna, can I write down all the information about your stalker? I'm traveling with two cops, and I'd like them to run it through the system."

I copy all the information in his wallet, then thank her for her help and give her our address. "If you remember anything that might help us locate Trevor, you can find us there. Sorry about the guy's window. I surprised myself there, and it must have scared you."

"I thought you were a nutcase," she agrees. "Do you know how weird all this is, Leo?"

"Tell me."

"I've gotten two letters from someone who claims she's Sheba Poe. Also, phone calls—but I can tell it's a female impersonator. Can you believe that?"

"Save the letters. They'll be collector's items someday." I rise to my feet and collect the albums and photograph. "Thanks for your help. Here's the phone number and address of where we're staying. Keep in touch, kid."

On the walk down to Washington Square, I think about my encounter with Anna Cole, and her reaction to me as a Southerner. I never knew how strange a breed of cat a Southerner is until I began to travel around the country. Only then did I learn that the Southerner represents a disfigurement in the national psyche, a wart or carbuncle that requires either a lengthy explanation or cosmetic surgery whenever I would stumble upon the occasional Vermonter or Oregonian or Nebraskan in my journeys. I could grow testy when I met up with folks whose hostility toward the South seemed based on ignorance. I once compiled a list in my column about the reasons people seemed to hate the South, and I invited my readers to add to the literature of contemptuousness a Southerner might encounter on the road. My list was fairly simple:

1. Some people hate Southern accents.

2. Some fools think all Southerners are stupid because of those accents.

3. Some dopes still blame me for the Civil War, though I remember killing only three Yankees at Antietam.

4. Many black people I have met outside the South blame me personally for Jim Crow laws, segregation, the need for the civil rights movement, the death of Martin Luther King, the existence of the Ku Klux Klan, all lynchings, and the scourge of slavery.

5. Movie buffs hate the South because they have seen *Birth of a Nation, Gone with the Wind, In the Heat of the Night, To Kill a Mockingbird,* and *Easy Rider.*

6. A man from Ohio hates the South because he once ate grits at the Atlanta airport. He admitted that he put milk and sugar on them and thought it was the worst cream of wheat he'd ever tasted.

7. Many women who married Southern men, then divorced them, hate the South, as do any men who married Southern women and divorced them. All men and women who married Southerners, then divorced them, hate their Southern mother-in-laws—ergo the entire South.

8. All liberals based in other geographies hate the South because it is so conservative. They refuse to believe that any true liberals could also be Southern.

9. All women not from the South hate Southern women because Southern women consider themselves far more beautiful than women of the lesser states.

10. All Americans who are not Southern hate the South because they know Southerners don't give a rat's fanny what the rest of the country thinks about them.

That column struck such a nerve in the community that I received more than a thousand letters pro and con, so Anna Cole's reaction to the South was not unprecedented.

From his first days in the city, Trevor Poe laid a claim as principal eccentric among the variegated tribe who frequented the Washington Square Bar and Grill. In all of its understated oddity and eclectic decor, it always struck me as a gauzy snapshot of the soul of San Francisco. Because of Trevor's prominence as both a patron and a frequent performer, the place feels like a home away from home for us. Trevor had been given a window seat to welcome him to the neighborhood, and in many ways, he never surrendered that honorary table as he watched the great carnival of the city pass by in all the fey surrealism that North Beach has to offer.

When Leslie Asche—the greatest waitress on earth, in Trevor's phrase— came to take his order, he pointed out the windows toward Coit Tower poised erotically on the summit of Telegraph Hill and asked her, "Darling, do you believe Coit Tower is an exercise in phallic symbolism, or a literal rendition of an erect penis?"

"I'm just your waitress, honey," Leslie said. "I'll get you what you want to eat and drink. You'll have to hire your own tour guide."

"There's nothing I love more than a witty, unexpected answer from a sassy woman. Can your bartender make me a Bloody Mary I'll never forget?"

"Mike, we got a rube in town. Wants to know if you can make a Bloody Mary."

"A bloody what?" asked Mike McCourt (the world's greatest bartender— Trevor's words again). "Let me look it up in my bartender's manual."

That marked the beginning of Trevor's long association with the Washbag, which became his headquarters, his refuge, and his hideaway from the home he never had.

Today, I am the first to arrive. Leslie puts me into a bear hug, then kisses me on the cheek like a sister. Mike McCourt blows me a kiss and makes me a Bloody Mary. The whole restaurant has marked Trevor's sudden disappearance and all have been worried about both his disease and his whereabouts. It moves me when Leslie brings my Bloody Mary to Trevor's table and motions for me to take a seat.

She tells me, "We'll keep you posted on anything we hear about Trevor. If the little bastard was in trouble, he could've come to live with me."

"You know how cats go off in the woods to die alone," I say.

"Everybody who comes in here is looking for Trevor. We've got eyes all over this city."

"Then we'll find him," I say.

Soon, the Charleston crowd begins to drift in, and the scene with Leslie and Mike repeats itself over and over. Our group has thrown parties for both of them when they visited Charleston with Trevor in the early eighties, before the AIDS epidemic detonated its quiet poisons through the bloodstreams of an unsuspecting gay population. By now, the newspapers across the Bay Area have become dense and swollen with the obituaries written by the partners and survivors—many of whom carry the virus themselves. It makes me weep to read them, and I always see the face of Trevor Poe in the rawness of the wording. It is a new and terrible literature delivering an ache of loss and a hopeless mourning over the death of boys.

We order light lunches and begin to compare notes from our morning's work. Sheba enters the restaurant in her impenetrable disguise of everydayness and no one recognizes her. It surprises me that she did not greet either Mike or Leslie, and I let her know that.

"I've never met them," she says. "I've never been here."

"How'd the meeting with Herb Caen go after I left?" I ask. "It looked like the beginning of something sinful."

"Full-page column. Tomorrow morning. Herb's going to tell the story of the famous actress and her high school friends from Charleston who've come to hunt for her brother dying of AIDS. He loved the angle of Ike and Betty being black, Fraser and Molly being society broads, Niles being an orphan, and Leo being a brother columnist."

We cheer, but Niles is clearly miffed. "Why did you have to tell him I'm an orphan? Why didn't you tell him I'm the athletic director at Porter-Gaud or teach honors history?"

"Good copy," I explain. "A pathetic orphan boy searching for a childhood friend dying of AIDS? We newspaper guys love hooks."

Sheba has grown frustrated by this argument. "Leo's a hermaphrodite, and Molly's a lesbian whore, and I'm having an affair with President Bush. I just want to find my brother, okay? I didn't mean to hurt your feelings, Niles. You know what we all think about you."

"I have no idea how you think about me, Sheba," Niles says.

"The same thing everyone else does: you're the best of us. The very best, Niles. You've got character that comes from walking through fire when you were a kid. Your sister's a nutcase for the same reason. Me and Trevor are both borderline cases because we didn't do so well in the fire. But you and Betty—the fire made you stronger. It showed your mettle and proved your steel."

For the next few moments we eat and drink in silence. Then Ike clears his throat and says, "Here's what me and Betty found out: the chief of police handed us off to a cop whose beat has been the Castro for years."

"But Trevor lived on Russian Hill," Fraser says.

"Don't worry," Betty says. "Our boy's well known in the Castro. This cop was fascinating. Told us right off he was gay. Had a dossier on Trevor. In fact, he said they once had a flirtation and he thought it might go somewhere. Trevor admitted he had a thing for guys in uniform."

"I bet that's why he always liked Ike," I say.

"Shut up, Toad," Ike says. "Trevor's been picked up two or three times for public drunkenness. Got caught once for DUI. Paid a fine. Had to attend some classes. He was found in possession of pot four or five times, but that's like being picked up for parsley in this town."

"The most serious thing in Trevor's file is he was picked up once for possession of cocaine with intent to distribute," Betty reads from her notebook. "Again, he was fined for possession, but told the judge he was not guilty. And I quote here, 'Your Honor, I plan to use every damn gram of it for myself.' It got a laugh from the judge."

"That's our boy." Niles grins.

"We called the cop who arrested Trevor for the DUI," Ike says. "Cops are funny. He could've been pissy about it, being called out of the blue and everything. But I explained who we are and what we're doing. He said that Trevor was the most gentlemanly, courtly, and comical drunk he'd ever picked up. Trevor told him, 'Officer, it's men like you who're taking all the fun out of drunk driving. I'd be ashamed of myself if I were you.' "

"Jesus Christ." Fraser puts her face in her hands. "If you had told me when I was fifteen that one day I'd be hunting for a sick homosexual who did drugs and had sex with a hundred other men, I'd have signed an affidavit that you were crazy as hell."

"You were born with a silver service stuffed up your ass, Fraser," Sheba says, her sudden fury silencing us into an abnormal discomfort.

"But you were born beautiful, Sheba," Fraser says, shaken. "I'd trade for that any day of the week."

"Do you think it's made me happy? Do any of you think it's made me happy, a single day of my life? Do any of you think of me and say, 'God, I wish I were Sheba Poe?' "

"Leave Fraser alone, Sheba," Molly says with an authoritative voice. "And let's hear what Leo learned at Trevor's flat."

I pass around the four albums of photographs and mementos, which have turned out to be treasure troves. I see dozens of men I met over the years, smiling through time in the sheer enjoyment of their ineffable handsomeness.

"Jesus Christ," Betty says as she and Ike turn pages. "Is there any such thing as an ugly gay man? These are the best-looking men I've ever seen."

"Tell us about Anna Cole," Molly reminds me. "Did you learn anything from her?"

I give an edited version of my encounter with Anna Cole and the lecher she had picked up. Already, I am feeling sheepish and uncertain about my outburst of machismo. I come up inadequate, if not quite wordless, when I describe my encounter with the beetle-browed stalker. I do not mention the pistol, but I do read out the license plate number, the Social Security number, and the number on the driver's license of John Summey. I think my exploits will win me a round of well-deserved applause from my friends, but their full-frontal assault catches me off guard.

"You impersonated a police officer, you dumb son of a bitch!" Ike yells.

"You kicked in his window." Molly is unable to hide her disgust.

"Have you lost your mind, Toad?" Niles asks.

"We'll be lucky if John Summey doesn't go straight to the cops," Sheba says.

Fraser jumps in. "How do you know the guy was stalking her, Leo?"

"Because she told me," I explain. "He was lying down on his goddamn floorboards. Why would anyone do that?"

Betty rushes in. "Lying down on his floorboards? I don't know of a statute in a single state where that's against the law. You kicked in his window. Intentional destruction of personal property."

"You're a journalist, Leo," Molly says. "And the *News and Courier* would fire you if this story makes the local news."

I say, "The hell with all of you. None of you were there. I did the best I could."

"Were you trying to get laid, Leo?" Betty asks. "Was this gal pretty?"

"What difference does that make? I ran the goddamn guy off. The woman's glad, so glad she let me into her flat and gave me these albums. She tells me that she's got thirty boxes of Trevor's stuff stored in her garage and she promised to help in any way she could. I think I did pretty well, to tell you the goddamn truth."

"You're right, Betty," Molly says in disgust. "Leo was flirting, trying to get laid."

"What is it with you women? Does every damn thing on earth revolve around sex?"

"Yep," says Betty. The other women nod in agreement.

Niles says, "We're operating in strange waters out here, Toad. All of us are in over our heads. We've got to make good, smart decisions. You screwed up, pal. But learn from it. All of us can learn about how not to do it just by listening to how you made a horse's ass of yourself."

Fraser says, directing the attention away from me, "On Monday, we start delivering lunches to indigent AIDS patients for a group called Operation Open Hand. The woman in charge told me and Molly that Trevor probably found himself living on a welfare check and got a room in some squalid hotel. Most likely, in the Tenderloin. We'll be delivering lunch to the worst dives in the city. She told us we needed to be in the company of some of you guys because it's so dangerous. A lot of times these gay men use aliases to avoid people like us who're trying to find them. So we'll deliver meals to those guys, then interrogate them. We'll get addresses, phone numbers, everything. And sooner or later, we'll find Trevor."

CHAPTER 15

The Tenderloin

S unday falls upon us not as a day of rest but one of drowsy, melancholy, or, at best, enforced leisure. Since I was a child, God's day has felt anxiety-fraught; the Sunday afternoon willies always leave a handprint on the middle of my stomach. I go to an early Mass and get back to a household gathered around the breakfast table. Opening the Sunday *Examiner and Chronicle,* we turn to Herb Caen's column and read his piece, "The Queen of Sheba." He is as good as his word, and his whole column praises the heroic efforts of the sex goddess Sheba Poe to locate her twin brother, Trevor, who has disappeared into that stricken underground world of AIDS.

Sheba opens a huge package of circulars that had arrived from L.A., featuring a photograph of Trevor in his dazzling prime that touches me to the core. "I hired a Boy Scout troop to put these up all over town," Sheba says. "It's a beautiful photograph. He looks just like me, don't you think?"

Outside the limo driver honks three times. "Murray is going to ride us over to Powell Street," I say.

"Why don't we just stay around here and get drunk by the pool?" Sheba asks. "I hate when the Toad makes us go on field trips."

"It'll be interesting," I promise.

"What's on Powell Street?" Fraser asks.

"A surprise," I say, "but one I promise you'll like."

On Powell Street, Murray rolls his eyes when he hears I am forcing my friends to take a cable car ride through the city to Fisherman's Wharf. I think there might be a mutiny among my friends, who groan as they depart the luxurious limo and join a crowd of camera-laden tourists awaiting the arrival of the next cable car. In the storming of the cable car, I barely make it onboard, grabbing on to a back railing and hanging on for sweet life. The crowd is high-spirited as our car labors up the hillside. When we reach the summit of Powell Street, I look out toward the white-capped bay alive with the pretty slippage of sailboats and yachts. But I feel an uncomfortable danger when I realize that I do not have enough room to change hands or find purchase with my dangling right foot on the step I balance on. It is only after we pass through Chinatown, which smells like wonton soup and soy sauce and egg rolls, and begin a headlong dive toward the bay, that I have fears of my bright idea of a cable car ride turning life-threatening.

In the middle of the steepest lunge back down the hill, with the cable still humming beneath the streets like some living thing, I hear a woman's voice screaming out in fury. Even worse, I recognize the voice: "Get your goddamn hand out of my purse, you smelly son of a bitch!"

The crowd, the gripman, the conductor, and I all freeze. She screams again: "Are you deaf, you worthless bastard? I told you to get your goddamn hand out of my purse and drop my goddamn wallet. Quit pretending you don't know who I'm talking to, bozo. Let me be more specific: get your goddamn *black* hand out of my purse. That narrow it down enough, asshole?"

Sheba Poe's voice is as unmistakable as any in movie history—breathy, sultry, iconic, and, at this disturbing moment, unstrung. When the cable car reaches the next intersection, almost every rider leaps off, sprinting in all directions in helter-skelter flight from the drama Sheba has unleashed. The passengers who remain onboard have known one another since high school, except for the largest black man I've ever seen: wild-haired, frantic, six feet five inches tall, three hundred pounds.

"Little woman," he says to Sheba, his voice gently controlled, considering the circumstances, "you gonna get yourself hurt if you don't hush your mouth and lower your voice. I can't get my hand out of your purse because you got it so tight around my wrist."

"Let go of my goddamned wallet and I'll loosen the purse, you smelly black son of a bitch."

"I'd lose the references to smell and color," Molly suggests in a soft Charleston accent.

"Uh-oh," the big man says, emboldened. "I believe I found me some cracker-girls a long way from home. You cracker-girls could get hurt when I pull a knife out of my pocket, which is what I'm about to do to improve Miss Goldilocks's manners."

"You got worse than cracker-girls to worry about, tiger," Betty answers smoothly, pulling out a thirty-eight and laying it against his head. "You got the law."

With no assistance from anyone, she goes into professional posture, flipping out handcuffs and passing them to Ike in a move as showy as a behind-the-back pass. Ike snaps them, then steps him off the cable car and into an alleyway as our group follows. The gripman and the conductor appear from where they'd ducked down in front, as do six or seven curious passengers who materialized out of nowhere. Soon the cable car continues its interrupted journey down toward Fisherman's Wharf as the seven of us face the wrath of a man whose eyes are murderous. "I didn't know you were cops," he says, taking us all in with his wild-eyed gaze, but addressing only Ike and Betty.

"We're part of an exchange program," Betty says. I recognize that she and Ike have no idea what to do with their prisoner now that he is cuffed and in their illicit custody. By the looks on their faces, I can tell that what they did was every bit as illegal as the theft of Sheba's wallet.

"You heard that woman call me a nigger," the man shouts. "It was a racial incident, plain and simple. I'm the victim of a hate crime."

"Shut up, mister," Betty orders. "Give us time to think."

Sheba possesses a gift for making a bad situation worse. "You're absolutely right, loser: it is a hate crime. I've always hated bastards like you. Look at the size of your ass. Why don't you get a job sawing down redwoods in the national forest or something?" For reasons unclear to us Sheba delivers these words in a drop-dead perfect Charleston accent that only exacerbates the racial tension. I also notice that Sheba has ventured out in her disguise of everywoman, with sunglasses, scarf, and loose-fitting clothes, rendering both her fame and her beauty invisible to the naked eye.

"Officers, listen to these white folks," the man says. "These is cracker rednecks. Hell, they're Klansmen for all we know. I know what I'm talking about; I grew up in Carolina. I know a racist bastard when I see one, and I sure as hell know it when I hear one."

"Which Carolina?" Ike asks. "South? Where 'bout?" By now, all of us have calmed down enough to hear the familiar rhythms of this stranger's voice.

"You ain't never heard of it," the man says.

"Try me," Ike replies.

"Gaffney."

"Gaffney?" several of us scream.

It suddenly hits me when he turns to me that I have seen those eyes before. "We know this guy," I say in wonder. To Niles and Ike, I say: "Get rid of the greasy hair, erase the beard. Make him twenty years younger and fifty pounds lighter. Pure muscle. The state semifinal in Columbia."

"Son of a bitch—you're right," Ike says in disbelief.

Niles obviously doesn't see it yet, and murmurs, "What?"

"Think, Niles, think," Ike says. "We should've beaten Gaffney. Why didn't we? We had the better team and were favored to win. Look at those eyes."

"You know South Carolina?" the man asks with hope.

"Macklin Tijuana Jones!" Niles exclaims at last, astonished by the recognition.

"We were on their five," I remind the women, who are staring at us as if we've lost our minds, "down by six. Fifty-eight seconds left to play. Those eyes. We drove our fullback into the line three straight times, and this was the guy who stopped us each time. The last play, Ike, Niles, and I had the same assignment. To knock this guy out of the play. Our job was to give Wormy a shoulder to get into the end zone. After our last time out,

Macklin Tijuana Jones shoved all three of us back and tackled Wormy for a three-yard loss. The last play of the game."

"My daddy still thinks you're one of the best five football players ever to come out of the state," Ike says. "Take off the cuffs, Betty. We got us a homeboy on our hands."

"Not till he promises to behave himself," she grumbles.

"You guys played for Peninsula?" Macklin asks. "I kicked the shit out of you."

"You sure did," I agree. "Then you played for Georgia."

"You played pro," Niles says. "But you got hurt—your knees, right?"

"Both knees by the time I was finished. The Saints traded me to Oakland. That's how I ended up out here. I was already finished."

Ike says, "Man, did you go from sugar to shit in a hurry."

"I had back luck," Macklin says. "Anyone can have bad luck."

"What are we developing here? Skills in the art of conversation? Shoot him in the kneecap and let's go to lunch," Sheba says.

"Tell me I didn't rob the wrong broad," Macklin says, which gets a laugh from a few of us.

"You've got no clue, my friend," Niles says.

"Where do you live now, Macklin?" Betty asks, though she doesn't let down her guard.

"In the Tenderloin," he says. "In a deserted car owned by a friend. It's parked in the backyard of a building he owns. He was a Raiders fan. Helped me out."

"You a crack addict?" Ike asks.

"That's what they tell me," Macklin admits.

"You were a magnificent athlete." Ike shakes his head, then studies Macklin for a long moment. "You know the Tenderloin well?"

"I *am* the Tenderloin," Macklin brags. "It's my base of operations."

"You want a job?" Ike asks.

"Have you lost your ever-loving mind, Ike?" Sheba cries.

"No, but I just had me a bright idea," Ike says. "Macklin Tijuana Jones is going to help us find Trevor Poe."

"That's the dumbest idea I ever heard," Sheba says.

"C'mon, Ike," Niles says in protest.

"This is going to be hard enough," Molly says. "Let's try not to make it harder."

"What's a soul brother and sister from South Carolina doing hanging around pig, honky motherfuckers like these?" Macklin snarls.

"That's it, Macklin: screw up just when things are going your way," I say.

"I don't get the Tijuana," Fraser interrupts to ask, speaking for the first time. "Is that a family name?"

"Jesus," I groan. "If Charleston were a snake you couldn't kill it with a stick."

"My mother's old man was Mexican," Macklin answers her calmly, as if it were the most natural question in the world. "My daddy's people were the Joneses."

Ike lets out a bark of laughter at the exchange and says, "Take off the cuffs, Betty. This is a South Carolina Jones."

"He still hasn't promised to be a good little soldier," Betty says. "He's got to give me a sign."

"I'd still like to coldcock that bitch." He looks directly at Sheba.

"He must like the handcuffs, Ike," Betty says.

"Threaten my friend again, Macklin," Ike says, "and I'll take my pistol and break one of your kneecaps. Because I'm a fair man, I'll let you decide which one."

"I ain't gonna do nothing," Macklin says. "Just talking. Always just talking."

"Shut up and listen for once. In Charleston, Betty and I know the streets. All of them. We know people who can tell us everything: the rumors, the dealers, drug shipments arriving on freighters. But we don't have dog shit in San Francisco. Until now. Now we've got Mr. Macklin Tijuana Jones. Everybody see what I'm talking about?" Ike speaks directly to each of us.

"One thing I know," Macklin says in the quiet that follows Ike's explanation. "None of you ain't never seeing my black ass again. Nice meeting this interracial pep club, but I'll be on my way if it's okay with you nice folks."

"If that's your final decision, we'll be on our way," Ike tells him.

"What about these handcuffs?" Macklin asks.

"They're yours now," Betty says. "They belong to you. Enjoy them."

As a group we begin walking away from Macklin. He screams, "You can't leave me here handcuffed. We're from the Palmetto State."

Our laughter infuriates him, and he begins cursing us with creativity and panache, which tickles rather than frightens us. The sheer outrageousness of the encounter is taking a giddy toll on all of us.

Then Ike spins around and grabs Macklin by the throat. "We need your help, Macklin. Do we get it or not? Be quick, make a fast decision. And try to make a smart one."

Macklin takes it all in, then calms himself. "What can I do for you fine ladies and gentlemen?"

Betty turns him around and removes his handcuffs, and Ike says, "Sheba—give me your wallet."

With reluctance, Sheba passes her wallet over to Ike's outstretched palm. He does not take his eyes off Macklin Jones as he removes three hundred dollars and presents it to Macklin with a small flourish. "There's more where that came from. We're out here looking for a man named Trevor Poe. He played piano in the city for a lot of important people. Here's a flyer, Macklin. He's got AIDS. You find him for us and we'll give you five thousand bucks, no questions asked. On the flyer, I wrote down everything you need to find us while we're here. If you want to start your shitty life over again, we can help. Thanks for robbing us today, Macklin. I think God brought us together."

"I think it was Satan," he mumbles.

"I'll second that," Sheba says, taking off her sunglasses and glowering.

Macklin stares at Sheba. They are evenly matched in their capacity to attach hatred to their glaring. "I've seen this twat before," he says at last, looking away from Sheba to the rest of us. "She was in a Nike commercial or something."

"Or something," Sheba says, and we rush to catch the cable car returning down Powell.

Every city has its Tenderloin. It's the part of town where you can feel the air change as you break through some invisible epidermis of squalor, a down-at-the-heels, joyless place where a city has gone wrong and can't figure out a way to right itself. Though the Tenderloin is in the heart of the city, it seems like a bad piece of fruit, left too long in the sun and attracting the attention of flies and hornets. Although the Tenderloin was once lovely, and much of its architecture is still a pleasure to behold, it has spent itself with all the intrigues required by dissipation. In San Francisco you know that you are entering a rough neighborhood because no room has a view. In the Tenderloin, all vistas are worthless and disheartening; all alleyways smell of urine, strewn garbage, and cheap wine. On Monday, we are to deliver meals to seven hotels, more than a hundred meals. Our plan is to stick together and work with the utmost speed as we enter the Hotel Cortes. Sheba pacifies the deskman as the rest of us spread out through a hotel that does justice to the word *fleabag*. It smells of the kind of mold that grows on expensive cheeses, but also of a darker variety that has metastasized in dampness and air shafts and crawl spaces, untouched by disinfectants.

With six boxes of lunches, I sprint up a flight of steps that seems in danger of collapsing beneath my weight. Molly brings up the rear, with Niles and Fraser matching her step for step. I knock at the first door and hear a faint stirring, but the movements seem overcautious. A weakened voice finally asks, "Open Hand?"

I call: "Lunch is served."

The man laughs as he unlocks the door. Thus I make my first acquaintance with a human skeleton so ravaged by AIDS I do not think he will see the next sunrise.

"Are you Jeff McNaughton?" I place his food on an unpainted desk. He looks translucent in his thinness and I watch blood flowing through the veins in his forehead. His flesh looks like it is made of onionskin.

"I ordered beluga caviar with blinis. Also a bottle of iced Finlandia to wash it down. I do hope there were no mix-ups," he says.

"I can't lie to you, Jeff. Someone substituted sevruga at the last minute. It was an outrage. But I'm just a delivery boy. My name's Leo King. You'll be seeing me for the next couple of weeks."

The man begins a spasm of coughing. "I won't last a week, Leo. I've got the Pneumocystis pneumonia. It's come back to me."

"You need me to call anyone?" I ask. "Your parents? Your family?"

"All the calls have been made," he says. "None of them answered."

"I'm looking for a friend." I pull out a circular. "His name is Trevor Poe. You know him?"

"The piano player." Jeff studies the photograph. "I used to see him play in bars in the Castro, but we were never formally introduced."

"If you hear where he is, will you call me?" I ask. "You can reach me at the number below his picture."

"No phones at the Cortes," Jeff tells me. I help him over to the desk and open his lunch for him. "I won't be leaving this room, Leo. And you're the only name on my dance card, sweetheart. Thanks for lunch."

On the next door I knock loudly, and it is answered by an older man, who is in much better physical condition than his younger companion. Rex Langford is the older man and Barry Palumbo the younger. Barry's eyes are open but offer no sign of greeting; he could have been a mannequin if I could not hear his raspy breathing.

"You're early. Unprecedented," Rex says.

"First day. At the rate I'm going, I'll get lunch to some of these guys by midnight."

"New on the block, huh?" he asks. "Somebody at Open Hand hates your guts. No one lasts long delivering meals to the Cortes."

"My name's Leo. Anything I can do for y'all?"

"Y'all. Music to my ears. A concerto at last. A country cousin come to town."

"Where are you from?"

"Ozark, Alabama," he tells me. "It's not far from Enterprise, which boasts a sculpture of a boll weevil on its main drag."

"You're joking, right?"

"Sadly, I'm reporting the gospel truth. The Louvre has its Venus de Milo, but Enterprise, Alabama, has its boll weevil. Both represent something essential about the souls of each place."

"It must be odd growing up in Ozark, Alabama," I say.

"Growing up is odd, no matter where you do it. That's my only piece of observed wisdom. It's yours for free," he says.

"I like it. I accept it as a gift."

"Where are you from, cracker-boy? Do I detect the slight memory flaring of Mobile in that accent?"

"Charleston, South Carolina. There's a Huguenot influence in both accents." I place a circular in his hands. "I'm looking for a friend. Trevor Poe's his name. You ever run across him?"

"Did he go to the Baths?" Rex asks.

"Trevor lived at the Baths."

"Then our lives may have abutted," Rex says. "If you get my drift."

"If you have any friends who visit, would you ask them about Trevor Poe?"

"Most of my friends are dead. Except Barry over there. Say hello to Leo, Barry. He brought us lunch; isn't that nice?"

"Hello, Leo." His voice sounds half-human.

"Barry's blind," Rex says. "I feed him. Then he throws up. Then I feed him again, and he throws that up too."

"I can't help it, Rex," Barry whispers.

"It's nice of you to do for him, Rex," I say.

"Not nice at all. It's all I've got to do," he says with a shrug. "He'll go, then I'll go. But there won't be anyone to help me."

"Do you have any money, Rex?" I ask.

"Of course not. Both Barry and I get welfare checks, but that goes poof into the wind. Medicine, rent for this penthouse, and so forth."

From the bed, Barry calls out, "Will the guy who brought lunch call my sister Lonnie?"

"I'll be glad to call Lonnie," I tell him.

"We were so close when we were growing up. No sister ever loved a brother like Lonnie loved me."

"I'll call her tonight, Barry."

"Her husband hates me, so hang up if he answers the phone. I'd love to have her visit me one last time. Give him her number, Rex."

Rex writes on a piece of paper and hands it to me as I exit. I walk down the hall toward my next delivery and open the paper: "Don't bother," it reads in a barely legible scrawl. "She says it's God's will he's dying—calls it a pervert's death. But thanks anyway."

Each day we return to our elegant quarters on Vallejo Street spent and defeated. We follow up leads that come in by the hundreds based on Herb Caen's column. We received three letters from men who claimed to be

Trevor Poe, as well as five ransom notes from people claiming to be holding him hostage. I speak to kooks, weirdos, five private detectives, dozens of Trevor's former lovers, his masseuse, his barber, his neighborhood grocer, and three psychics who promise to discover his whereabouts.

At the first week's end, we gather on Saturday evening for a serious conference. We have been efficient, yet we all agree that we are no closer to finding Trevor than we were before leaving our jobs and homes in Charleston. We vow not to give up yet, but to dedicate ourselves to one more week. We go to bed exhausted and praying for a break.

The next day, I am not expecting what I find in room 487 at the end of still another lightless hallway in the Devonshire Hotel. I notice that none of those hotels give much room for hope to hide in, and the Devonshire is worse than most. I know something is wrong as soon as I knock on the door of room 487.

I am greeted by a silence that unnerves me, with no stirring or rustling about or shuffling of unsteady, slippered feet. I try the doorknob and it comes off in my hand, but the door swings open on rusted hinges. Inside a young boy is sleeping, his blond curls and full lips giving him the look of a figurine trapped in an unnatural stillness. He cannot be more than twenty years old, but his attractiveness is offset by the smell of excrement that seeps through his silk pajamas and the cheap sheets that cover him. I place his food on a dresser, then touch my hand to his forehead. When my hand feels the coldness, I know he has been dead for hours. The peaceful expression on his face is an act of mercy that death can sometimes bestow on someone in unbearable pain. His clothes hang neatly in a filthy, mouse-befouled closet, and I find his wallet in the back pocket of his best suit. His driver's license contains a picture of him smiling with some coyness and impish humor. His name is Aaron Satterfield, and he once lived in an apartment on Sacramento Street.

Inside his wallet, I discover several photographs of interest. There is a series of photos of Aaron and four of his friends dressed as cowboys at a Halloween party in the Castro. The same group of five mug for a camera in one of those lamentable curtained booths you find in cheap bus stations. On the back of the photo, Aaron has written these words: "All dead, except me."

In the top drawer of his bedside table, I find two letters, one from his mother and one from his father. Because I am present at their son's deathbed and they are not, I feel I have a right to read those letters. A part of me has to know the story of why this gorgeous child died alone. It is the Satterfield family of Stuart, Nebraska, who should be standing over the body of this blond, wasted boy, and not me. As that thought preys on me, I wonder how long the tears have been running down my face, and if they are tears of pity or rage or a molten combination of both at the same time.

The father's letter could not have been pithier or more to the point: "Faggot. If you are dying as you claim, I declare it God's will. That you have been something foul and unclean in the eyes of God is no surprise. It is Bible written and Bible promised. I would not send you a penny I made from working on my farm. May God have mercy on your soul. I have none. Your father, Olin Satterfield."

After I finish the father's letter, I sit there trembling and tearful while I pray to God and ask him not to allow me ever to think like the people of God if it requires me to be anything like Olin Satterfield. No matter what your Scriptures say, Lord, I will not do it. I open his mother's letter and read, "Dearest Aaron, this hundred dollars is the last of the nest egg I have saved since the day I married your father. I don't know what he would do if he found out I'd been sending you money all this time. I wish I could be beside you right now, taking care of you, cleaning up for you, making sure you were eating right, holding you and telling you stories you used to love as a child. I kiss you now, and it carries all my love and all the hurt I feel for you. By the power of prayer, I believe that Jesus will cure you. He died on the cross for people like you and me and especially for people like your father. Your father loves you as much as I do, but his stubbornness won't let him feel it. At night, he wakes up crying and it has nothing to do with the wheat or the cows. I love you as much as Jesus does, Mom."

The death of this pretty half-child proves to me that I have come to one hotel too many in this beleagured city. If I wished to spend my life working miracles among the dead and the dying I could have gone to medical school, but I was born to write frivolous, witty columns about the pulse rate of Charleston. My time among young men dying of starvation because of some ruthless virus loose in their bloodstream is starting to wear me out. I want out of San Francisco, and the sooner the better. At this moment, I don't give a damn whether we find Trevor Poe or not. I want to sleep in my own bed and work in my own garden and walk down streets where every house is familiar to me. Mostly, I want to run away from the presence of this dead Nebraska boy, and yet I sit beside him on his bed, staring at his lovely, inanimate face. Then I smell his shit again and spring into an action that surprises me.

I remove his sheets and pajama bottoms and clean him up with a towel I find in his sink. Gathering the towel and the sheets and the pajama bottoms together, I open up a window and hurl the fetid pile into the alley below. I find some Paco Rabanne aftershave lotion in his shaving kit, and after I shave him, I liberally sprinkle him from his cheeks to his thighs with the sweet-smelling cologne. Carefully, I comb his hair and style it the way I found it in his wallet photograph. I cover him with a blanket he had kicked off the bed, and I feel a certain satisfaction when I have completed my assignment. To me, Aaron Satterfield is ready for anything—a baptism, a laying on of hands, or a meeting with the godhead. When I finish I burst into tears, and of course, that is when Molly Rutledge finds me.

"We've been looking all over for you," she says, then realizes the situation. She goes over and touches Aaron's face with remarkable tenderness and says, "Oh, my God. What a beautiful boy."

I hand her the two letters and she reads them without emotion or commentary. "He looks as though he died while dreaming something nice, Leo," she says afterward.

"Yeah, I had the same sickly sentimental thought when I first saw him too."

"I guess what I mean is that I'm glad his suffering is over," Molly says, choosing not to react to my acidulous tone. My weeping embarrasses me and I wish I could've finished it before she entered the room.

"We'll have to call the police," Molly says. "They'll take him to the morgue. We can let his parents know tonight."

"Why weren't they here?" I ask. "Or why didn't they bring him home?"

"Shame. Pure human shame on his father's part. Fear of the father on the mother's. I bet the father tormented this poor kid from the time he was born. Come on, Leo; we'll do your last floor together. They're waiting for us. If we were all as slow as you, these boys in the Tenderloin would starve to death." Molly takes my list and adds, "Just three more rooms then we're through for the day."

She touches Aaron's face again with her soft, manicured hand. "What've we gotten ourselves into, Leo? This time out here will change us forever. It'll mark us in ways we don't know."

"Was it hard downstairs in this dump?"

"It was awful. We're not going to find any nice death by AIDS. It's like all of them, every one of them, have been nailed to their beds."

"We're not going to find Trevor, are we?" I say. "We're just putting on a show to make ourselves feel better. Make Sheba feel better."

Molly wipes the tears from my face with a handkerchief. "Remember who we are, Leo. We're folks who get things done. We're going to find Trevor and take him home with us. We might lose him in the end, but he's going to be surrounded by people who love his ass when he dies. We aren't gonna let him die like Aaron Satterfield. Get the picture?"

"Yeah, girl. I get the picture."

And Molly licks the last tears that roll down my cheek.

I try to regain control of the situation, that terrible moment of time. "Why did you do that?"

"Because I wanted to. It tasted good. Like an oyster. Or a pearl from an oyster. Salty like the ocean off Sullivan's Island. I liked it that you cleaned this boy up," she said.

"How did you know I cleaned him up?"

"Ike and Betty were standing near the alley when you threw all the stuff out the window, then Betty ran up to tell me you needed some help. Ike gathered up all the stuff and put it in a Dumpster. Said it smelled like hell."

"Why didn't Betty come find me?"

"She thought I could handle it," Molly says. "Plus, Betty's calling the cops. An ambulance is on the way. Let's finish and get out of here."

"Good idea. Sorry I took so long."

"You're forgiven, Toad," she says, smiling. "Just this once."

That evening I pick up the phone in the small office off the kitchen and dial for information in Stuart, Nebraska, where I ask for the number of Olin Satterfield. With the compassionate telepathy that made her famous among her friends, Molly Rutledge enters the room behind me carrying tumblers with two fingers of Jack Daniel's on the rocks.

The phone rings twice and the father answers.

"Mr. Satterfield," I say. "This is Leo King calling from San Francisco. I'm calling with news of your son."

"There must be some mistake," he says. "I have no son."

"Aaron Satterfield is not your son?"

"Do you speak English? I just told you that I don't have a son."

"Do you have a wife named Clea Satterfield?" I ask, studying the name on the second letter I hold in my hand.

"I may and I may not," he replies.

With some effort I control my temper, and say, "If Clea Satterfield has a son, sir, I would like to talk to her."

"Clea Satterfield is my wife." The man's voice is glacial. "And I assure you that neither of us has a son."

A brief but furious argument breaks out on the plains of Nebraska, in a state where I have never set foot, and it is muffled yet hard-fought. Then I hear the voice of a woman, clearly agitated and at the end of whatever short rope she is tethered to in the small acreage of her life.

"This is Clea Satterfield," she says. "I'm Aaron's mother."

"I'm afraid I've got some terrible news for you, ma'am," I say. "Aaron died today in a hotel in San Francisco."

I would have continued, but I hear a scream of purest sorrow, and for several seconds, her voice is something primal and ancient and inhuman. "There must be some mistake," she says between terrible sobs. "Aaron's always been a healthy boy."

"Aaron died of AIDS, Mrs. Satterfield," I say. "He was probably too embarrassed to tell anyone."

"You mean cancer," she corrects me. "Aaron died of cancer, you say?"

"They say it was AIDS. I'm no doctor, but he was diagnosed with AIDS."

"Cancer is such a killer," she says. "I don't know a family in our community it hasn't touched. It's such a scourge. Did Aaron say anything before he died? I didn't get your name."

"Leo King," I answer. "Yes, he said to tell his parents that he loved both of you very much. Both of you. His mama and his daddy."

"Such a sweet boy," she says. "Always thinking of others. Where is he now? His remains, I mean."

"In the city morgue. Here's the name of a funeral home that you can call and they'll prepare the body to ship home for burial."

I give her the name and number of a funeral home that specializes in the preparation of corpses who died of AIDS.

"Wasn't my boy beautiful?" Mrs. Satterfield asks.

"One of the best-looking men I ever saw," I say.

"Even the cancer couldn't touch that."

I hear something strange in the background and ask, "What's that?"

"That's my husband, Olin. Aaron's father. He's crying, so I have to go. You sure Aaron told you he loved me and his father very much, Mr. King?"

"Those were his last words," I lie. "Good-bye, Mrs. Satterfield. I'm Roman Catholic and I'll have a Mass said in memory of your son."

"We're Pentecostal. Please, no Masses for us," she says. "Let us do the praying. Let us do the burying. We'll do it the old way, and the right way. You wouldn't understand."

"Mrs. Satterfield." Again, my blood is up. "That should've been you and your husband with Aaron when he died. Not me. That's the old way. That's the right way."

She hangs up on me and I put my face in my hands. "I had no right to say that to that poor woman," I tell Molly.

"The hell you didn't," Molly says. "She's lucky it wasn't me who called her. I'd've told her exactly what I thought of her and her god-awful husband."

"He was pretty torn up."

"It's easy to be torn up in Nebraska," Molly says. "It's harder in room 487 in the Hotel Devonshire. Let's go feed the troops."

· · ·

Just past midnight, my bedroom door opens. I reach up to turn on the lamp by my bed. Molly Rutledge enters, trailing her beauty like something that can damage a man or change his life forever. She is carrying two glasses, and I smell the Grand Marnier as she sets them on the table. She removes her robe to reveal a silken, diaphanous gown that makes me praise God for the shape of women. I do not like that Molly is putting us in such an awkward situation, but I don't hate her for it, either. Even so, our friendship holds a richness and a power and a completeness that I do not wish to risk because her misguided husband has developed a taste for long-legged Brazilians half his age.

While Molly's prettiness is classic, imperturbable, natural, I sport a face that has no business coming anywhere in the vicinity of hers. She is one of the great beauties of her Charleston generation, and I am just a foot soldier in society who knows his place in the order of things.

Molly looks at me, and takes a sip of her drink. "Well?"

"I can think of a thousand reasons not to do this, Molly."

"That all you got?"

"Your sister-in-law is upstairs sleeping with my brother-in-law. It seems tacky to have a romp in the basement under those circumstances."

"Seems natural to me," she says. "What does a nice girl have to do to get laid around here?"

"We're both married. I'm the godfather of your daughter. I was a groomsman in your wedding."

"Tell me that you don't love me, and I'll leave."

"I'm not in love with you, Molly. I've always had a thing for Trevor Poe."

"I knew you'd make one of your stupid jokes. I was expecting it. Now I'm going to lie down beside you."

"I'm afraid for you to," I say.

"Why? I'm up on my rabies shots."

"I'm afraid the world won't ever be the same."

"I don't want the world to be the same." She walks over to the bed, and turns out the light.

On this night I rediscover why all the great religions condemn the sweet, enchanted crime of lust. When I am inside Molly's body, when the cells of my flesh light up in ecstasy with the fiery truth of her flesh, I feel the creation of a whole new world as we move together, purr together, moan together. My tongue becomes her tongue, our lips burn in congruence, our breasts lock into each other's heartbeats. When I come in a burst of fire and flood, she roars in behind me. Words pour out of me that I had thought for twenty years but had never believed I would whisper in the ears of this woman, and she accepts them with forbidden words of her own. With a cry, I fall off her. Then, she kisses me a final time. In darkness she gathers garments that are feathery, and in nakedness she leaves me. What began in mere sin ended in sacrament, and as I lie there alone, I know that she was right: my world will never be the same.

CHAPTER 16

The Patel Connection

When we finish our work for Open Hand on Tuesday, a police car is waiting for us, parked in front of the Vallejo Street house. Ike and Betty go over to flash their badges and speak with a detective. Rather than the break we are hoping for, it turns out to be a surprise: the police want to interrogate me about a murder for which I am a prime suspect. That's when I see Anna Cole walking toward me.

The homicide detective is named Thomas Stearns McGraw, the son of two poetry-loving parents. His father teaches American literature at Berkeley and his mother's father is a third cousin twice removed of the author of *The Waste Land*. Since it is a new experience for me to be a suspect in a murder case, I do not learn this fascinating autobiographical detail at our first encounter, but later, since Tom McGraw is a gifted conversationalist and a man with a curious nature.

I introduce Anna Cole to everybody and explain who she is. Anna is obviously deeply shaken by the recent turn of events, and her hands tremble visibly. She turns to me in a sudden white fury and says, "I knew I shouldn't have opened the door for you."

"Let's go inside to discuss this, Detective McGraw," Ike says. Tom

McGraw's unexpected arrival breaks up the rhythm of habit that has sustained us in our search. Everyone wants to be present when the detective questions me. But Ike assumes control and sends the others to the phone bank in the dining room, ordering them to remember the hundreds of leads that need to be followed up.

Sheba kisses me on the cheek. "If Leo King committed murder, Detective, I'll jump off the Golden Gate Bridge and let you film my suicide. You'll have worldwide rights to my death."

"How can you joke about something so horrible?" Anna Cole asks, then breaks down crying.

"Because none of us knows what this is about," I tell her. "I've never murdered anyone, so at this moment I am fairly relaxed."

"Shouldn't we get Leo a lawyer?" Sheba asks Ike.

"He doesn't need a lawyer," Ike says. "He's never even gotten a parking ticket."

Anna Cole is completely unstrung, and we have to wait for her hysteria to ease before the interrogation can begin. "Ma'am, could I get you a glass of water?" Ike asks softly. "We could get this done a lot faster if you could get control of yourself."

Anna says, through tears, "All I did was send the cops a photocopy of the man who was stalking me like you told me to do, Leo."

"He was from San Rafael, right?" I ask. "I forget his name."

Detective McGraw helps me out. "His name was John Summey. He lived at 25710 Vendola Drive in San Rafael. He worked as a physical therapist at a retirement center here in the city."

"And he had picked up a bad habit of stalking young women from Minnesota," I add.

"That's what Miss Cole said," the detective says. "But a problem came up."

"What's the problem?" Ike asks.

"John Summey turned up dead in the trunk of his car in a city parking lot, day before yesterday. The back of his head was caved in by a blunt instrument. There was some noticeable decomposition of the body—in other words, a bad odor led to someone making a complaint. It took us a day to run the tag number. We interviewed the distraught Mrs. Summey, who filed a missing-person report last week. Then, voilà, Anna Cole's complaint comes up. We visit and she gives us your name, Leo King, as the last person who saw Mr. Summey alive."

"It's all because I opened the door for you," Anna screams. "I've never opened the door to a stranger in my life. And then you stalk that man down and kill him?"

"Whoa," Ike says. "Let's not jump too far ahead of things here."

"Miss Cole said you threatened the man with a gun," Detective McGraw says to me. "It was Miss Cole's, a twenty-two revolver. You asked for it when you went over to confront Summey."

"Anna seemed frightened by the guy," I explain. "She had a pistol in her hand when I rang the doorbell. She told me about the man stalking her. I borrowed the gun in case I had to bluff him, which I did."

"Miss Cole said you kicked in his window," the detective says. "This was corroborated when we searched the car. Could you explain why?"

"He wouldn't roll down his window, and I wanted to get his attention. I also wanted to find out who he was."

"So you threatened him with a gun."

"Yes, I threatened him with a gun."

"Leo, you dumb, dumb-ass white boy." Ike sighs.

"Then you stole his wallet? And his sunglasses?"

"I confiscated his wallet hoping that he would leave Miss Cole alone," I say.

"You succeeded," Mr. McGraw says. "And the last time he was seen alive, you were aiming a gun at his face."

"Yes, I was, but Mr. Summey was seen by me and Miss Cole racing up Union Street at a high speed, very much alive."

"Actually, we think that Mr. Summey might have been dead at that particular moment in time, Mr. King," the detective says. "According to our time line, Mr. Summey may have already been killed and stuffed in that trunk. Could you give a description of the man driving that car?"

"White man, six feet tall. Black hair," I say.

"Could the hair have been dyed?"

"I don't know. I'm not a hair colorist," I say. "It was a wig. A toupee. A cheap one."

"Don't be smart-mouthed, Toad," Ike says sharply. "The man deserves serious answers."

"I'm sorry, Detective McGraw," I say. "I didn't get a good look at the man."

"How old would you say he was?"

"He looked like an older man trying to pretend he was much younger. He had deep brown eyes. Bushy eyebrows. He was a powerfully built man. But he had seen better days."

"Mr. Summey was born in New Delhi, India. He was on a student visa when he married Isabel Summey. He changed his name legally from Patel to Summey to sound more American. He was five feet seven inches tall and weighed a hundred forty pounds."

"Not the same guy I met," I say emphatically.

"The driver's license has been doctored. We think that photo is the murderer." He passes me a copy of the license and I study the photograph I gave only a cursory glance during the incident on Union Street.

"I can't tell if it's the same guy or not. I just got a brief look at him, then sent him on his way."

Detective McGraw hands me another picture, this one of a small-boned Indian man. "That's a recent photograph of Mr. John Summey, formerly Anjit Patel."

"Not the guy driving the car," I say. "Not even close."

"How long ago did you notice the man following you, Miss Cole?" asks Detective McGraw.

"Two days. He followed me to work on Thursday. I noticed him while I was waiting for the bus. Then I was shocked to see him when I got off near my office in the financial district. He was waiting when I got back home. Then, the same thing on Friday. He would leave for the night, but was there when I woke up the next morning. Just parked, waiting. I'd called the cops and reported it on Friday. Then Leo rang the doorbell the next day."

"But he never approached you or threatened you?" the detective asks. "Am I correct in assuming he never spoke to you or accosted you? Could he have been following someone else from your neighborhood?"

"He was staring at me. I was the one he was after," Anna says, trembling with conviction.

I tell the detective, "When I went out to take down his license plate number and tried to confront him, he lay down on the floorboards. Unless he spilled some peanuts, it sure looked like he was hiding from someone."

"Do you have a license for the pistol you used, Mr. King?" the man asks.

"I borrowed the pistol from Miss Cole," I say.

"It was a gift from my dad," Anna says. "He didn't give me a license. I don't own any ammunition."

"Could either of you pick this man out of a police lineup?" Detective McGraw asks.

"No," Anna and I answer at the same time.

"If you see the man again, will you report it to me immediately?" He hands us each a card and also gives one to Ike. Before he leaves, Detective McGraw asks me, "Do you still have those sunglasses?"

"I think I do. Let me run down and check. I tossed them into a drawer on my bedside table."

McGraw says, "Let me go with you. It may have a good set of this guy's fingerprints."

In my catacomb of a bedroom, I turn on the light switch and am astonished to find my room torn apart. Before I can go on to assess the damage, Detective McGraw stops me with a hand squeezing my shoulder. He pushes me back outside my room, then enters the room with caution. He takes out his notebook and writes several things, then asks me, "Is that the table where you put the sunglasses?"

The table is smashed and the drawer is lying on the bed, which a knife has slashed clean through. In a mansion filled with Picassos, Monets, and Mirós, overstocked with silver services and candelabra and movable antiques, priceless even on the black market, it is a surprise to find the most modest room in the house vandalized.

"He came to find those sunglasses," the detective says. "How did he know you were staying at this house?"

"I don't have a clue. Hell, the Herb Caen article, maybe."

"I'm going to tape this door shut. I'll have the boys from the lab come out here tomorrow to take a look-see. I don't like this. I'm going to look in the bathroom. Does anyone use it but you?"

"No, sir."

"My name is Tom. No need to call me 'sir.' " He takes out a handkerchief and pushes against the half-opened bathroom door. I can see the contents of my shaving kit strewn everywhere.

"Could you come in here, Leo?" Detective McGraw asks. "Please do not touch or disturb anything. But explain this to me if you can."

It angers me to see the contents of every vial of medicine I own spread across the floor. The intruder has emptied my shaving cream into the sink and broken my bottle of aftershave lotion and squeezed out the last worming loop of my toothpaste. The bathroom mirror covering the medicine cabinet is open wide and the fancy contents that the producer left for guests have been flung. But the disturbing nature of this visitation does not overwhelm me until McGraw shuts the mirror and I see the flyer notifying San Francisco of the disappearance of Trevor Poe. It is the drawing that freezes my cells in all the dread of memory and history, in the secret mythology that forms the grotesque substrata that lies at the center of this search that has just turned deadly.

"Can we get police protection at this house," I ask, "starting tonight?"

"If there's a good reason," Detective McGraw says.

"Could we get Sheba and Ike and Niles in here," I ask. "None of the other women, please."

Ike and Niles arrive first. I hear Sheba protesting as she is led by the arm by Tom McGraw. "What's up, Toad?" Niles asks.

"Who the hell did this to your room?" Ike adds.

I can hear Sheba at her most put-upon as she enters. The violation of the bedroom shocks her, but she almost falls to her knees when she sees the fluttering piece of paper with her brother's photograph taped to the bathroom mirror.

In bright red fingernail polish, someone has drawn the image of a smiley face. Sliding out of the left eye is a tear rolling down the featureless cheek.

"Jesus Christ," Ike says.

"Holy shit," Niles gasps. "What does that mean?"

I say, "Sheba, your dad's still alive. He was the guy in the car."

The following day, Ike takes command of our embattled unit, now exiled and afraid. By sunrise there is a San Francisco cop patrolling the front of the house like a Praetorian guard. The intruder entered through the backyard fence, which the lifeless body of a poisoned Rottweiler proves. The police find no fingerprints, no hair follicles, and no evidence of forced entry. They discover a single footprint of a size 11 New Balance running shoe on the lower terrace. For two hours, they question Sheba and hear the details of a tumultuous family history that includes every essential piece of the puzzle we had all been trying to solve through the years. All of us had known something; none of us had known everything.

I pour Sheba a cup of black coffee when she joins us for breakfast. Tension shimmers in the sunless fog-bound air. It is cold in the city, which seems to have no real attachment to or belief in summertime. A disputatious silence grips all of us. It seems like a corporal act of mercy when Ike takes charge and draws up a plan.

"Last night changes everything, Sheba," Ike says. "You know that better than anybody."

"I wouldn't put any of you in danger," Sheba tells us. "I can only hope you believe that."

Molly is the most visibly shaken of all of us. She has not once mentioned our evening together, nor has she made any effort to speak privately to me, or so much as touch my hand. Her cool avoidance is difficult to understand, as Molly isn't a cold woman. She is caring, devoted, loving, and loyal, and it has only gradually dawned on me, these last few days in California, that she is also a compartmental kind of woman. She has a drawer for family, a drawer for friends, a drawer for house repairs, and a drawer for Leo, her faithful servant and devoted lover. I think her silence comes from the fact that she hasn't yet decided what to do with the Chad drawer: Throw it out? Reorganize? The uncertainty of it all seems to have paralyzed her, and the reappearance of Mr. Poe has only added to that feeling of creeping chaos.

It is clear that her enthusiasm for the trip has considerably waned, and her voice is sharp when she tells Sheba, "Coming out here to find Trevor was a lark. It was a pleasure. It gave us all a chance to prove something to one another, to have an adventure together. You didn't say a thing about our dying in the process."

"I thought my old man was dead," Sheba says.

"We've got kids to think about, Sheba." Fraser states it in her most matter-of-fact manner.

"Then all of you get the fuck out of here and I'll find my goddamn brother by myself." Sheba seems to scream it out of a despondency that comes from some dark place inside her.

"I'd like to suggest a plan of action," Ike says. "I think the risk is minimal. Betty and I worked this out last night."

Betty adds, "It's not perfect, but it's a plan."

Ike says, "Let's give it till Sunday. That'll mean we've been out here for over two weeks. We've busted our asses. We've put ads in the newspaper, circulars all over the city, got a column out of Herb Caen. Sheba's been interviewed by every radio and television show in the city. All of the gay newspapers have covered why we're out here. We've given it our best shot."

"I was with Fraser—ready to get on a flight this morning," Betty says. "But Ike's plan seems better. He always keeps a cool head."

"He's not a mother," Molly says. "Neither is Sheba. And Leo is not a father. I'd rather OD on heroin than let Chad and that Brazilian twat raise my children."

"Don't forget that Chad happens to be my brother," Fraser says. "He loves those kids as much as you do."

"We don't need a catfight," Niles says, trying to defuse the situation. "We got problems enough."

"I saw you sneaking up from the basement the other night," Fraser says to Molly. "I was using the hall bathroom so I wouldn't wake Niles. I guess you and Leo were discussing the need for economic reform in Sri Lanka?"

"I warmed up a cup of milk in the microwave." Molly's lie lacks conviction. "I couldn't sleep."

"You smelled a lot like sex to me," Fraser says.

The whole room gasps. I have never known such words to come out of Fraser's mouth; if I had not heard them with my own ears I wouldn't have believed it. By her expression I can tell she has even shocked herself.

"So the Rutledge family closes ranks," Molly says. "Little Chad does whatever he wants, and Molly and the kids have to hold their tongues and smile for the camera while the house burns down."

"Apologize to Molly," Niles says to Fraser, his blue eyes glittering.

"I have nothing to apologize for," she replies. "You'd have to be blind not to see what she and Leo are up to. And I didn't come out here to make orphans out of my kids."

"What do you have against orphans?" Niles asks his wife. Now the room seems to be spinning out of control, a molecular planet freed from its own minimalist laws of gravity.

"Nothing at all, darling." Fraser is gaining a measure of control over herself. "It's just not the fate I choose for our children, no matter how character-building it might seem to you."

"I've never thought of it like that," Niles says. "It was the most terrifying thing in the world. I woke up scared every day. I went to school scared, and so did my sister. It ruined her whole life. Your loving me saved my life, Fraser. My sister got hurt so bad that even Leo's love couldn't come close to touching her heart. So Leo ruined his life by loving someone who couldn't be fixed. But as scared as I was, and as scared as Starla was, I don't think that either of us were scared like Sheba and Trevor were. I didn't have much of a daddy, and that was a bad thing. But they had one who wanted to terrify them and hunt them down through the years. I don't know the whole story, Sheba, not by a long shot. But I know it's a bad story, a real bad story."

Ike stands up, his voice peremptory yet calming. "Here's the plan that works for Betty and me. We promised Open Hand we'd deliver food to those hotels until Sunday. But we're changing the way we do things now. Betty and I won't be making deliveries. We'll play cops instead. We'll all move together, one hotel at a time. The San Francisco cops will guard this house day and night. We'll finish this job up, and we'll do it right. Toad, will you fix dinner tonight?"

"Be happy to."

"We'll eat all our meals inside with shades drawn and curtains pulled. No more swimming, no more hot tubs."

"What about my honeymoon with Leo?" Molly asks.

"Shut up, Molly," Ike commands.

"I got scared," Fraser explains. "I ran my mouth."

"For the first time in your life you sounded mean, Fraser," Niles says, staring at his wife, who refuses to encounter his gaze. "My God, if I didn't know better, I'd say you sounded like a goddamn orphan, the scum of the Western world."

"That's not fair, Niles," Molly says, surprising everyone in the room, but especially Fraser. "She just told you she was afraid. We can all be forgiven that we're scared."

Sheba unexpectedly supports her, hugging her knees in a chair at the periphery of the room. "My dad is perfectly capable of killing us all," she says. "I caused all this; I can repair all the damage. I swear I can."

"First we've got a job to do," Betty says. "We've got to deliver meals to these poor guys. They'll be waiting for us."

"I don't feel like moving a muscle," Sheba says. "I feel like staying in my bed, getting drunk, and watching old movies I've made. Maybe it'll help me forget that my old man, who I thought was dead, is a psycho ax murderer who knows my address."

Ike says, "Feed us good, Leo, your fanciest shit. But we need to get all this stuff between us cleared up. Sheba, you get yourself ready, girl. Tonight, every one of us in this room is going to know the whole goddamn story, from A to Z. You came into our lives like gangbusters, about twenty years ago. None of us knows where you came from or why you showed up in the house across the street from Leo. We don't know anything about your mama except she was born to cause trouble. We've got to know everything. You can't hide anything from us, because this guy has scared all of us before. Your daddy is Count Dracula and Cyclops and Frankenstein and Charles Manson to us, yet I don't think any of us would know him if he walked into this room. I don't know his name. I don't even know your daddy's name."

Sheba surprises us by saying, "I've told you: neither do I, Ike. Neither does Trevor."

"Tonight, Sheba Poe," Ike says, "you're coming clean. You're going to lay it all out for us. I don't mind dying for you. I really don't. But I'd sure as hell like to know why."

That night, Sheba takes center stage in her scrumptious bedroom, which stretches the length of the top floor. It has a sitting area made bright with an infestation of pillows and comfortable chairs, an overdone realm dedicated to comfort. All of the women look tiny on their observation perches, except Fraser, who sits tall next to Niles. Molly and I sit ten yards apart, pretending we do not inhabit the same world.

"Trevor and I don't know where we were born or when," Sheba begins.

"You've got birth certificates?" Ike asks.

"Several," Sheba says. "On one my name is Carolyn Abbott, and my twin brother is Charles Larson Abbott. The birthday remains the same. But we were born in St. Louis on the first birth certificate and in San Antonio on the second."

"Your dad?" Ike asks.

"He changed his name and job every time we moved."

"Why on earth?" Molly asks.

"Don't have the foggiest. When you move every year, when you go from town to town, when everyone you meet is a stranger, you get confused about everything. When we lived in Cheyenne, Wyoming, Dad was called Dr. Bob Marchese. He spoke with an Italian accent and spent that year as a veterinarian whose specialty was beef cattle. In Pittsburgh, he called himself Pierre La Davide and sold Jaguars. In Stockton, California, he was an insurance salesman. I don't even know if my real name is Sheba Poe. Trevor once claimed he found four or five fake birth certificates and three passports for my dad, using three different surnames, none of them Poe."

"Didn't you ask your mother questions?" Fraser asks.

"Not many. If it was strange for us, it was a nightmare for her. When we got old enough to know better, we could tell she was scared of him. Of course, by then, we knew she had every reason to be."

Ike asks, "Did he beat her?"

"Not where it showed, but he could devise a thousand ways to torture her. Sometimes he would torture her by not giving her any money for food. We'd always lived out in the country with no one around. No radio, no television, no neighbors, no cars. My dad was the only connection we had with the outside world."

Fraser cries, "Stop it, stop it right now! None of this adds up. This isn't an American life you're describing to us. No one grows up this way.

Where were your grandparents, your aunts and uncles? What did they say when they came to visit?"

"Grandparents? Aunts? Uncles? If I have them, Fraser darling, they haven't stepped forward. Don't you think I've fantasized about that a million times? Don't you think I hoped that someone would see one of my films and say, so that's what happened to Sheba? But what if these mythical folks never heard of twins called Sheba and Trevor? What if they know us as Mary and Bill Roberts of Buffalo, New York? What if our mother just fell in love with our dad and said farewell to her family? There are a million scenarios, Fraser, and it's your tragedy that you only think there's one."

"That's not my tragedy," Fraser says. "I have the luxury of knowing exactly who my family is and where they've lived for three hundred years. Stability was the most important gift of my childhood. I'm giving that same gift to my kids."

"You don't know where half of your children's family comes from," Niles reminds his wife. "They're half mine. They've got hillbillies and moonshiners and mountain girls who didn't make it past the third grade in their backgrounds. Our kids have got as many ghosts in their family tree as Sheba and Trevor do. My mama stabbed someone and so did my granny, and both her and my mama went to prison. That's one of the few things I know for sure."

"That sad story has nothing to do with our children," Fraser insists.

"It's got everything to do with our children," he says. "It's the central story of their whole lives; they just don't know it yet."

"I've protected them from everything about your history," Fraser says.

"My history'll find them," Niles says. " 'Cause that's how history works."

"That's how it worked for Starla," Fraser admits. "But I've protected you from that past."

"There's no such thing as protection from the past," I say.

Ike puts up his hand to end this. "The subject is Sheba. It's Trevor. It's her dad. It's her past we are trying to figure out now. We can talk about this other shit when we get back to Charleston."

"The smiley face?" Molly asks Sheba. "I don't understand why that became the theme of your dad's presence, his evil."

"When I was a small girl, I loved smiley faces." Sheba shrugs. "We had no money, so I would clip smiley faces out of newspapers and magazines. I found them everywhere for a while—on cups and paper plates, on ribbons and balloons. My dad didn't believe in hobbies, except for the piano. He was the one who taught Trevor and me to play. Otherwise, he had to be the center of our world. I came home from school one day and he had painted a red tear on every smiley face I owned. He used my mother's fingernail polish. But by that time, everything was clear. My mother had already made plans to escape."

Molly asks, "What was clear?"

Sheba says, "He'd already started in on me and Trevor. Especially Trevor. I always thought he liked little boys better than girls, but he had a taste for both."

"Enough," Fraser cries. "I can't even pretend I want to hear the rest of this. And I think I speak for all of us."

Silence can be measured out in shot glasses of time or it can take up space in half-gallon bottles. This one lasts to the point of making Fraser feel both isolated and defensive. Her eyes glint as hard as those of a lioness that has caught the scent of hyenas moving toward her cub. Sheba's confession is unsettling to us all, but it is taking a horrific toll on Fraser's famous self-composure. In the elaborate collage that our friendship has patterned itself into over the years, Fraser has taken the high ground of normalcy. You could always depend on her to be both a solid citizen and a good egg, no matter how powerful the disturbances became in the airstreams around us. It is painful to watch her world turn to quicksand.

"Niles, are you coming with me?" Fraser asks. "I've had enough. My imagination can provide the details."

"I want this thing finished," Niles says, not unkindly. "We all need to close this loophole in our lives, especially Sheba."

"Sheba, there's no use in dragging us through every sordid detail of your dad's abuse of you and Trevor," Fraser protests. "We get it already. We're in the middle of trying to live decent lives. We don't live in a world where kids get sexually abused by the adults in their lives. That's alien and disgusting, and I don't think it helps us find Trevor."

Niles says, "In an orphanage, anything can happen to a kid, Fraser.

I was butt-fucked by two men before I was ten and survived it. Me and Starla survived. That was the only thing."

"Your sister didn't survive anything, Niles. Your sister is human wreckage and we never know where she's going to wash up," Fraser spits out.

"Niles and I know what an orphanage can do to a kid's spirit, Fraser," Betty says. "We've made good lives for ourselves, but we have a long way to go."

"Good night, everyone," Fraser says. We hear her footsteps as they bound down the stairs with the athletic grace that remains her trademark. A door slams on the floor beneath us.

Ike asks, "You okay, Sheba?"

"No," she answers. "This is starting to make us hate one another. So I would rather stop. I'm sorry that my dad did that to me and Trevor, but these are the facts of my life. I didn't even know it was wrong when it was happening. Dad told me that girls and boys owed their fathers sex. It was how they paid for their upkeep. How were we to know different? Now I know it's sick. But I didn't know it when I was five or six."

"Sheba?" Betty slides off the couch and kneels down next to a distraught Sheba, taking her hand. "Same thing happened to me. My mother's boyfriend. He did me till social services moved in and got me out of there. I got to Charleston the same year as you and Trevor, same orphanage as Niles and Starla. We all helped save one another a little bit at a time. I was lost so deep inside myself I thought I'd never get out. Let's put an end to this, sweetheart. I ever get your old man in my gunsights, I'll send him over into the next world. So will Ike and Niles and Toad."

Molly interrupts. "I feel the same, but I don't think I could kill him. I just don't think it's in me to kill anyone."

Sheba says, "Don't worry about it, Molly. I couldn't do it, either. For the stupidest reason on earth, one that you will hate me for admitting."

"You can tell us anything," Ike says. "We're not capable of hating you."

"Because he's my goddamn father. And here's how screwed up he's made me: I still love him because of that, and only that. He's my dad and he's Trevor's dad. I'd love to see him disappear, but I don't want to see him die."

As she weeps, I observe Sheba and think that she has invented herself out of masks so numerous she can no longer select her own legitimate face out of the museum she has cultivated to hide herself in. Because she is an actress, she has fashioned an entire career out of identity theft. Sitting there, I find myself believing her completely, yet not really knowing if she has spoken the truth. It is difficult to trust a woman who has built herself out of a house of exits and not marked a single entrance.

"What else do we need to know?" Ike asks us as a group. "We'll make this as fast as we can, Sheba. This has been terrible for you, for all of us."

"Knowing your dad, why did you believe he was really dead, Sheba? Even with what was supposed to be his ashes?" Betty asks.

Sheba shrugs. "That's what they told me in New York. They found his ID. I got the ashes."

"When did this happen?" Ike asks.

"A few months ago," she says.

"So how does he know you're out here?" Niles says.

"Herb Caen told him Sheba's address," Molly says. "Sheba's father was staking out Trevor's old apartment. Hell, Leo's written a bunch of columns about Trevor's apartment, too."

"That's enough for tonight, Sheba," Ike says.

"But there will be more?"

"Why the obsession with you and Trevor?" Molly asks.

"A simple game. One of absolute control. One that brooked no rebellion," Sheba says. "My dad called himself master. He called us slaves. He said it was the simplest and most ancient and most honorable game on earth. And he once said, 'Here's my promise to you: it will never end.' When he raped me in L.A., he confessed to me that he only had children because he wanted someone to fuck for the rest of his life. 'Having twins was a surprise,' he told me. 'Double the pleasure, double the fun.' "

CHAPTER 17

New Denizen of the Washbag

On Friday we begin the difficult process of saying good-bye to the dying men we have been bringing lunch to for almost two weeks. The farewells are trying and emotional for all. Though Open Hand warned us about the dangers of growing too attached, the nature and seriousness of the duties have changed everything about us. We spend much of the day weeping as we make our departures. Already, we have found four dead men in the hotels we serviced in the Tenderloin. That we have failed to locate Trevor weighs heavily, that sense of imminent failure causing despondency in most of us and surliness in Sheba. None of us has ever encountered such indomitable courage, relentless wit, and passion for life as we have since our lives intersected with these disease-ravaged men.

My soul feels tired as we head into the Washbag. The waitress Leslie greets us with a hug; word has spread among the regulars that there still have been no sightings of Trevor.

"I wasted everybody's time coming out here," Sheba says. "I've put everybody's life in danger. And we still don't have jack-shit to show for any of this." She stops herself and collapses into tears. There is no acting here, only despair, and she begins whimpering like some small, soft nocturnal creature. Before we can respond, Leslie comes running to our table from the front room, breathless.

"Something odorous and homicidal this way comes," Leslie says.

"What do you mean?" Ike asks, rising out of his seat.

"A huge black guy. Obviously homeless. Says he needs to talk to you guys."

Sheba has gained some control of herself, and it is she who first makes the connection. "That creep on the cable car! The one who tried to steal my purse."

I say to Leslie, "Make the biggest steak you've got with all the works. Bring it out to that first bench in the square."

Niles and Ike are already on the street, talking to the only linebacker for the Oakland Raiders who lives in the backseat of a junkyard car.

"Maybe he has news," I say to the women following me as I reach the tense convocation taking place on Powell Street. "I ordered dinner for our man here," I tell Ike and Niles.

"They threatened to call the cops on me when I tried to go inside," Macklin Tijuana Jones says, with true indignation.

"You don't fit their client profile," Ike says in his most appeasing voice.

"You promised five grand if anyone found your little faggot." Macklin is sitting on a park bench as the rest of us stand. "Where's my money?"

Ike says, "Where's our friend? The money doesn't change hands until we're shaking hands with Trevor Poe."

"I found him," Macklin says. "Like I said I would. I proved myself trustworthy. Now I want my money." He takes out the flyer that we spread over the length and breadth of San Francisco and studies it as though it were a treasure map of infinite worth. "That's him, okay. I've seen him with my own eyeballs. Saw him yesterday."

Leslie comes into the park carrying a tray full of food and a six-pack of beer. With some solemnity, she places the tray on Macklin's lap and says, "We fixed the steak medium-rare. Is that okay with you, hon?"

"Just the way I like it, ma'am," he says. "My compliments to the chef and please add a thirty percent tip to my bill."

We watch as Macklin begins to eat dinner with surprising delicacy and enjoyment. Then I remember that he was once an NFL star and knew how to conduct himself in the best restaurants of any city. "Gentlemen, ladies, this is a fine, fine meal."

"You've seen Trevor Poe?" Ike demands impatiently.

"With my own two peepers," Macklin answers between bites.

"Can you get us to him?" Ike asks.

"Your boy's in trouble, lawman," he replies. "Yeah, I can get you to him. But getting him out's going to be hell."

"Where is he?" Sheba cries.

"Bunny's got him," Macklin replies.

"Who's Bunny?" Ike asks.

"You don't even want to know," he says, concentrating on his food. He points his fork at us. "Tell you what. Meet me at eight in the morning on Turk and Polk Street."

"You'll take us to see this Bunny?" Ike asks.

"Hell, no. Bunny'd kill me if he knew I was leading cops to his place."

"You afraid of somebody?" Ike asks. "That don't sound much like you."

"Bunny played for the Raiders a few years before I did," Macklin says as he resumes eating. "Bunny Buncombe, wore number eighty-nine. White boy who played for Florida State. He weighed three hundred pounds then. Bet he weighs in at four hundred now. He's mental. Bad crazy. Not cute crazy, but mean crazy. He'd kill his own mother and sell her used Kotex for a cough drop."

"What a beautiful image," Fraser says.

"Watch your language around my wife," Niles growls.

"We came out to San Francisco for a vacation and a few laughs," I say. "And we get to meet our friend Macklin again. Sheba's dad shows up for another go at the father-daughter dance. Now we find out Trevor's developed a friendship with a four-hundred-pound whacko named Bunny."

"Why would Trevor stay with someone like Bunny?" Betty asks in bewilderment. "He's always hated that kind of man."

"You've got it all wrong, ma'am," Macklin says. "Your friend Trevor's a prisoner of war. Like the rest of the pansies locked up in Bunny's house. He can't leave. Not allowed to."

"He's an adult," Fraser says. "He can leave if he wants to."

"Hey, society lady, I've seen people go low in the Tenderloin. Hell, *I've* been low in the Tenderloin. But Bunny has built his own kind of hell there. It may be worse than hell. I'll have to die to find out, won't I? Anyway," he says, finishing his meal and laying his napkin on the tray, "I'll meet you nice folks at eight in the morning, and we'll see what we can do. There's a coffee shop run by a Mr. Joe on the east side of Polk near Golden Gate. Meet me there."

"How do we know you'll be there?" Ike asks.

"Five thousand reasons. You come ready to rumble. Bunny'll kill every one of you if you try to interfere with his little lifestyle. By the way, your particular faggot ain't doing so good. And I'll bet one of you's gonna get killed by Bunny."

In the meanest part of the Tenderloin, we meet Macklin Tijuana Jones for breakfast at a place where the proprietor, who identifies himself as "Joe Blow," is an elderly Vietnamese man. Macklin sleeps in Joe Blow's backyard, in a rusted-out Mazda up on cinder blocks.

"Order everything," Ike says, and we do. "Another steak, Macklin?"

"A steak is a fine way to start the day," Macklin says.

"Where's Trevor Poe, Macklin?" Ike demands. "You said you knew."

"I'm a dead man if Bunny finds out I snitched," Macklin warns, his eyes on the room, watchful.

"No one has to know you're involved," Betty says.

"You bring my five thousand?" Macklin asks.

"We got it," Sheba answers. "Where's my brother?"

"The little faggot's your brother?" Macklin asks. "Well, he ain't gonna be much longer. He's eaten up with that AIDS shit. Been to the Castro yet? That's where all the candy boys hang out. When I really get hard up, I go mug me a candy boy up near the Castro."

"What an inspiring life," says Sheba.

"Racist bitch," Macklin mutters.

"Black fucking bastard from planet motherfucking hell," Sheba says. "I wouldn't give you five thousand dollars if you delivered my brother in a top hat and golden cane."

"Get Sheba out of here," I order Molly. "Where's Trevor, Macklin? And why do you think it's him you saw?"

"I told you Bunny was crazy, didn't I?" Macklin says. "But he's also smart. Bastard majored in business at Florida State. Son of a bitch graduated too. But got hurt in the pros right away. Used his bonus to buy a run-down boardinghouse in the Tenderloin. He does a little of everything. I buy my drugs from an addict he sponsors. No one cheats Bunny. Guys that do have to grow gills real fast."

Ike is writing down everything that Macklin speaks. "Meaning?" he asks.

"It's hard to breathe at the bottom of San Francisco Bay," Macklin explains.

"Back to Trevor," Niles says, growing agitated.

"Bunny was smart enough to see he could make money from AIDS. When the candy boys started getting sick, he got up a plan to take their money."

"The ones we came across were impoverished," I say. "They might as well be homeless."

"But they get welfare checks." Ike turns to Macklin. "Just like you do, I suppose?"

"Yeah, but mine's gone in a jiff. That's why I think drugs should be legalized," says Macklin.

"Christ, now he's a social reformer," Niles breathes.

Macklin ignores him. "Bunny knew he couldn't talk body lice into living in his boardinghouse. But if he found enough candy boys with AIDS, guys on their last legs, no family, no friends, nothing but a welfare check coming in every month? He gets himself twenty candy boys and twenty welfare checks. He gives them a room, enough food to keep them alive, no way to get in touch with the outside world. You don't have to major in business to see that'd make a tidy profit, after all."

"AIDS patients die," I say. "That's the hole in that theory."

"Yeah, they die. But he just goes out recruiting for a new candy boy. He gets another welfare check. Bunny's got a partner in the welfare department whose beat is the Tenderloin. He's the one that monitors all the checks over to Bunny's place on Turk Street. Bunny gives the cat a kickback on every check. I told you he was smart."

Niles asks, "How do you know Trevor's living there?"

"After y'all offered me money to find Trevor Poe, I went to Bunny for some drugs so I could nosy around. Bunny already knew about some folks searching for Trevor. He took me to meet him, bragging about having him, you know. Bunny said, 'Say hi to Macklin, piano man.' He calls him that 'cause there's an old piano in his room which the little faggot plays sometimes. 'Hey, Macklin, you're cute,' the piano man said. 'Men like you make me thank the Lord I was born gay.' It made me want to puke."

"That's Trevor," I say.

"That's our boy," Niles agrees.

"That goddamn Herb Caen article," Ike says with a shake of his head.

Macklin says, "Yep. Bunny reads Herb Caen first thing every morning. He's been keeping a close eye on you folks."

"We need to have a meeting with just us, Macklin," Ike says, taking a hundred-dollar bill out of his billfold.

"Where's my five thousand?" Macklin demands.

"That's when we get hold of Trevor. This is a down payment. Anything else you can think of that might help?"

"One: there's a broken door on the roof of Bunny's house. I've smoked a little dope up there with the janitor a time or two. How do I know you won't just skip town when you get your candy boy?"

"Because we're nothing like you, scumbag," Niles says to him.

"I may go tell Bunny that I just talked to you," Macklin says. "Maybe he'll work out a better deal for me. A man's always got to look out for himself first. That's my business philosophy."

"Bunny'd kill you in a flash," Ike says.

Macklin considers the wisdom of this observation, and tells Ike: "Your faggot lives on the third floor. His door is painted blue."

"Go drink a bottle of Thunderbird," Niles says. "We'll get in touch with you after the dance."

Macklin salutes us and Joe Blow, then hurries out to face his sad, disheveled life.

"I'd like to help that guy," Ike says.

"Put a bullet in the back of his head," Niles says. "You'd be doing the whole world a favor."

. . .

Bunny's house is a crumbling Victorian, two doors down from the Delmonico Hotel. We've passed by it dozens of times while delivering meals for Open Hand. The squalor of the Tenderloin gains resonance by the presence of these run-down houses that were once beauties. Its front door looks like the entrance to a small-town jail; all the windows are barred. There are no signs of life. The five-story house would fetch millions in Presidio Heights, but I wouldn't have paid a silver dollar for it in the sad-faced Tenderloin.

Niles and I pretend to sleep on either side of the house, both dressed as homeless men in bad shoes, stocking caps, and scabrous coats from a Goodwill store. Molly and Sheba, looking well dressed and efficient, walk up the front steps and ring the doorbell. For a long minute, nothing happens. They ring the bell again. It hits a deep, rich tone that sounds clearly through the house.

The gigantic figure of Bunny appears at the door. Though pretending to sleep, I keep my eyes fixed on the doorway, the world made bizarre through a squint. Bunny is terrible-looking, deranged.

"What the fuck do you want?" he asks. He has a surprisingly high-pitched voice hiding in his gargantuan body.

Sheba has made herself up to be a plain, mousy woman, and she allows Molly to take the lead role. "Hello, sir," Molly says. "We're from the Ladies' Auxiliary Guild of St. Mary's Cathedral, and we're doing a census of the entire parish. The bishop wants to make sure that the Catholic Church is doing all it can to meet the needs of its parishioners. We were wondering if we could come in and ask you a series of questions? We promise not to take up too much of your time."

"Fuck you," Bunny says.

"Are you Roman Catholic?" asks Sheba.

"Yeah, I am," Bunny says. "I'm the fucking Pope, his own self."

Phase two of our makeshift plan now rolls down the street in the form of a police car. What appear to be two San Francisco cops double-park across the street in front of a sandwich shop. Ike and Betty get out and look over at the two women interrogating the ex–Oakland Raider. Every single inch of them speaks the word *cop* with exhilarating conciseness.

"Should we invite the police over to speak with you, Mr. Buncombe?" Molly asks.

"How did you know my goddamn name?" Bunny asks, his eyes on Ike and Betty.

"The whole street is proud that a former lineman for the Raiders is one of their neighbors," she answers.

"Who gave you my name?" Bunny asks. "I'll kill them."

Molly ignores the threat. "Your neighbors said you take in quite a few boarders. Could you give us an exact figure, Mr. Buncombe?"

"Who told you that?" Bunny's paranoia is gaining speed at a breath-taking rate.

"We just need a number for our records," Molly says, writing down every word he speaks. I take a measure of the man from my reclining position on the street, and I think it likely that he can kill Niles, Ike, and me with ease and without breaking a sweat. He exudes a dreadfulness and the fragrance of an evil that seems to come naturally to him. I fear for the lives of our two women.

"Are you familiar with Operation Open Hand?" Sheba uses a voice that is affectless and untheatrical. "They think you're taking care of some gay men. They're very grateful to you, but wondered if you might need help feeding them."

"I hate faggots, and I live alone here," Bunny says. "Now, you two broads, make like nice cunts and continue on your way. For your infor-mation, we never had this conversation, and you never saw me. What are those two eggplants looking at?"

He shields his eyes from the sun with a hand the size of a dinner plate as he stares across the street. Ike and Betty stare back. I cannot tell if their fearlessness is something you learn to fake as a cop, or something natural that runs deep in their characters.

"Tell Open Hand that I hope every fag in the world dies of AIDS. Tell your fucking bishop that I hope he dies of AIDS."

"Have you ever been a practicing Roman Catholic, Mr. Buncombe?" Molly asks.

Then, from somewhere deep in the rear of the house, we find the proof we finally need that Trevor Poe is alive, even if he is not well. We hear the sound of a piano playing, and it is not the beauty or the flawless artistry Trevor brings to the task of his deft musicianship that tells us we have come to the right place. He is giving us a sign that he knows we are there by playing a song that he made a centerpiece in all of our lives. Deep inside that decadent, deflowered Victorian house, the secret piano plays an old song, "Lili Marlene." I see Niles sit up in recognition, and I watch the subtle changes in the expressions of Ike and Betty as they stand fast in their sentinel-in-the-night poses across the street.

"Why, Bunny," Sheba cries. "You must own a player piano. Since you live alone, and all that."

"Shut that fucking piano up," Bunny yells back into the house, directing his voice up the stairs. "How'd you know people call me Bunny?"

"Everybody on the street calls you Bunny," she says.

"Thank you for your time, Mr. Buncombe," Molly says. "Both the bishop and the ladies' auxiliary thank you for your time."

The two women walk down the stairs, then go across the street and into the sandwich shop, passing by Ike and Betty, who are heading straight for a confrontation with Bunny. Niles and I limp our way into the Delmonico Hotel. Niles lays a fifty-dollar bill in front of the guy at the front desk.

"We're going back to South Carolina tomorrow," I say. "We wanted to say good-bye to some of the guys again."

"For fifty bucks, you can say good-bye to the whole city, for all I care," he says, kissing the money with overdone affection. Niles and I race up the first landing of stairs. Niles takes the stairs two at a time, sometimes three. When we reach the top floor, the door to the rooftop is locked, but the door breaks into three sections when Niles throws his shoulder into it. He reaches into his bag and arms himself with a hunting knife the size of a rhino's tusk, then he hands me a tire iron. We sprint across the rooftops until we are directly across the street from the sandwich shop. Sheba comes out of the store flashing a thumbs-up sign, and we hear Bunny screaming at Ike and Betty. Ike is screaming back, and that does not augur well for Bunny.

Niles says to me, "I'm going down to get Trevor. Then I'm going to bring him back upstairs, out onto the roof, and take him over to the Delmonico and down to the street. If Bunny comes up the stairs, you've got to give me some time to get Trevor out of there. You hear me, Toad? You've got to hold him off. If you have to use that tire iron, don't hold back. Hit him in the face. He may weigh four hundred pounds, but his jawbone's breakable just like anyone else's. Can you believe how smart Trevor is? 'Lili Marlene'!"

"It was like he wrote his name in the air," I say, still moved by the sound of the song. All teenagers develop a list of those totemic, signature songs that define their coming of age, but this was a bit different: the World War II song made famous by Marlene Dietrich became the clarifying song of our group because of the arrival of the Poe twins into our lives. As a team, Trevor and Sheba entered a talent show in the first month of school, and their winning performance of a song we'd never heard, "Lili Marlene," was the talk of the town for weeks.

There is a cheap, flimsy door leading into Bunny's house. Niles grabs the tire iron from me, demolishes the door handle with a single swipe, then kicks the door in. But the noise is loud, and Bunny's profane yelling at Ike ceases in an instant. I hear Ike yell even louder to cover our illicit entrance: "I'm going to have to call me all kinds of cops, Bunny. I'm going to have cops crawling all over your house, you fat blimp."

"Hurry," Niles says to me. "We've got to get to the third floor before Bunny does."

Niles sprints down the stairs at a pace I can barely keep up with, but my adrenal glands are pumping away as the pure terror of our situation begins to overwhelm me. The lawlessness of our actions hits me as an afterthought as I see Niles throwing his shoulder against a blue door on the third floor. When the shoulder fails to achieve the desired result, he kicks the door in, splintering its hinges, then he races inside. He lifts a skeletal figure into his arms like a child, and I hear him say, "I told you that sucking dicks would get you into trouble, Trevor Poe."

"My hero" is the response I hear. Though it does not look like Trevor Poe, I would know that voice anywhere in the world. Then I hear heavy footsteps lumbering up the stairs.

"Hold him off, Toad," Niles says as he races past me.

I take my position at the top of the stairs. When Bunny starts up to the third floor, I pray to the Old Testament God who gave David the strength to slay the giant Philistine, Goliath. I pray for the strength granted to blind Samson when he brought the temple down on the heads of Delilah and her cohorts.

When Bunny lifts his eyes and sees me, he says, "You are a dead man, motherfucker. Who the fuck are you?"

The ex-Raider is coming at me one step at a time, but with caution: I am wielding the tire iron like I know what I am doing. My answer surprises me. I scream back: "I am Horatio at the Bridge, you fat son of a bitch. And you, pal, shall not pass."

"You are one crazy bastard," Bunny says, still advancing. "Who are you?"

"Horatio at the Bridge," I yell again. I have not thought about that lost, elemental fragment of my childhood for years. When I was a young boy, my father used to read poetry to his sons before we went to sleep. Steve became enamored with "Horatio at the Bridge" by Thomas Babington Macaulay, and he and I memorized parts of it. A stanza comes back to me as I face this gargantuan man inching up the stairs. I scream the stanzas and stop him on the middle stair. I appear deranged as I spit out poetry to him in that shameful house full of dying men. From the corner of my eye, I see several of them stagger out of their rooms to witness our drama playing out. I begin to recite maniacally:

> Then out spoke brave Horatio,
> The Captain of the gate:
> "To every man upon this earth
> Death cometh soon or late.
> And how can man die better
> Than facing fearful odds,
> For the ashes of his fathers,
> And the temples of his Gods."

I wish I had memorized more of the poem, but it makes little difference because that is when Bunny makes his charge. His mistake is trying to take my feet out from under me with his massive arms, which exposes his face, and I hit his right cheekbone with a short, deadly flick of the wrist. The tire iron rips into his face with a savagery that surprises us both. He stumbles backward, breaking his fall by catching onto the banister, which collapses under his weight. He falls into the stairwell, the right side of his face covered with blood.

That is all Horatio sees, because Horatio has begun some serious ass-hauling. It startles me how fast I can run when I think a four-hundred-pound killer is in pursuit. I can hear the sirens of police cars bearing down on the Tenderloin from points far and wide. Flying down the stairs of the Delmonico, I feel like something winged and fleet and uncatchable. Murray is waiting for me, and I leap into a door that Molly holds open. When the door closes, the driver steps hard on the gas, and we shoot away from the Delmonico and head for a hospital on California Street that Sheba has already alerted about Trevor's imminent arrival. Niles holds Trevor in his arms, wrapped in a warm blanket. Sobbing, Sheba holds her brother's hand. I hug him and kiss his cheek, too spent to speak.

"Did I hear you reciting poetry to Bunny?" Niles asks.

"Shut up, Niles," I say, trembling all over.

"You've always been weird, Toad," Niles says. "But reciting poetry to a psychopath . . ."

"I won't let you say a discouraging word to Leopold Bloom King, the only one of us to be named after a fictional character in an unreadable novel," Trevor says weakly.

"Shut up, Trevor," I say hoarsely, getting my voice back. "I just hit a man with a tire iron. I'm a respected columnist for a decent newspaper, and I just hit a psycho with a tire iron. I could end up in prison being butt-fucked by weight lifters."

Trevor says, "Sounds like heaven to me."

Sheba laughs. "Some things never change."

"I've missed your depraved wit, Trevor," I say. "This has been terrible."

"We'll be back in Charleston tomorrow, Trevor," Molly says. "We're going to take care of you. We're taking you home."

On our last night in the city of San Francisco, we gather late in the Redwood Room in the Clift Hotel to perform the sacrificial rituals to mark our final hours as Californians. For more than two weeks our souls have belonged to and suffered in the most golden city in the most myth-intoxicated and most improbable of states, the one that shoulders an entire continent against the tides of the Pacific Ocean. The Redwood Room is always the final stop that Trevor insists upon as a last rite of passage when any guest of his leaves San Francisco to live out their sullen and lesser lives in duller towns.

I am the first of our group to arrive at the Redwood Room, dressed in my best clothes according to the strict laws of protocol Trevor Poe had once cut in stone about leave-taking from the great city. Tonight, we will all assemble in this place of farewell as though nothing has changed. But we did not make this trip for pleasure the way we always did when we came to visit Trevor. This time we came to see if we could still love in the simplicity that gathered our fates together as teenagers, to measure ourselves against the innocence of those kids who once found themselves caged by time in the same soft prison cell in Charleston. When we leave San Francisco tomorrow, we won't be leaving a city recognizable to Trevor, nor will we look back on the way to the airport. Trevor's city of gold and laughter has turned into our city of the voices and terrified eyes of lovely men who await a firing squad that lacks rifles or an appointed hour. Tomorrow, we leave behind those desperate eyes, which changed everything about us.

Someone kisses me lightly on the lips, then takes a seat beside me. By the faint scent of Chanel No. 5, I know it is Molly before I open my eyes.

"Just got the word. Trevor's pretty good for all he's been through," she tells me.

"Wonderful," I say, and concentrate on my drink.

Molly and I have still not spoken privately since that blissful night she came to my bed; we've been too caught up in the desperate search for Trevor. But even now that we have him, there is still hesitancy between us, more on her part than mine. We have not talked about it, and I do not know if the bafflement is due to second thoughts, or because she has decided she loves Chad after all, or because Fraser so publicly revealed our secret. I do not know and do not ask; I am too terrified of her answer.

For the night, it is enough that we have Trevor, and we sit there like strangers at a bar, sipping our drinks till the others, except Niles, make a clamorous entry behind us, pouring through the giant doors and swarming all around us. Sheba begins to weep as she kisses and holds each one of us tightly. Ike wraps me in a bear hug and dances me around the dance floor. Betty, flushed with excitement, fills in the events of the day for Fraser. A piano player performs "Try to Remember" as Ike waltzes me along the polished wooden dance platform.

"People are going to get the wrong idea about us, Ike," I say.

"Let 'em." He grins. "This is the only city in the world where you and I look like a normal couple. Relax and enjoy it."

"Where's Bunny?"

"Jail, baby. It's going to be his home for the rest of his life. They also arrested that social worker who was his partner in crime, and that guy started singing like a mockingbird as soon as the cuffs went on."

"How'd Bunny get Trevor?"

"Found him wandering the streets. According to Trevor, Bunny may have accidentally saved his life."

"Ike, I don't want to hurt your feelings. But could we stop dancing?"

Ike roars with laughter. "I was starting to like the way your tits felt crushed against mine."

We both laugh and make our way back to the table, then enter into the rapid-fire conversation of the girls of our lives. Betty is holding court, telling in rich detail about the interrogation of Bunny Buncombe. "Here's the funny part, Toad," Betty says. "Bunny insisted that the San Francisco police conduct a dragnet of the city to find you, the lunatic who assaulted him in the sanctity of his home. He kept referring to you as a lunatic. He said you were huge and out of control and were screaming obscenities at him. Bunny thinks you hit him with brass knuckles."

Ike laughs. "He kept saying 'the sanctity of my own home.' Betty and I liked to have bust a gut when he said it. When our friendly detective asked for a description, he said you were at least six-ten, weighed three hundred pounds, and a fat-assed white boy. And I swear to God, Leo, I'm not making this up: he said you had crazed eyes that reminded him of a hoppy toad."

Our table screams with laughter, and I find myself joining, in sheer relief. All of us feel release from the dissonance of our time in the city.

"Trevor's in better shape than he has any right to be," says Sheba. "The doctors worked him over from head to foot. He's dying of AIDS, but not right now. Do any of you remember David Biederman? He was a cute little guy in ninth grade when we were seniors. He had a crush on me, but of course he was only human."

We hiss and jeer at Sheba, but she continues on. "Dr. Biederman is sending an ambulance to meet our plane tomorrow night when we land in Charleston. He is going to take on Trevor's case personally. I just got off the phone with him."

"So it's over," Molly says, with dense, complex emotions. "It's really over."

Ike raises his hand and says in a soft voice, "There's the slight problem of Sheba and Trevor's old man. The cops think he skipped town."

"Thank God," says Fraser.

"That's the good part," Betty tells her. "But here's the part that's scary. They have a theory that Ike and I agree with, that he's on his way to Charleston. That he'll be waiting for Sheba and Trevor because he knows they'll be going back to their mother's house."

"All of you can stay with me," I say. "I've got plenty of room. I'll buy a Doberman, a king cobra, a flamethrower, and I'll have nine ninja warriors to guard the perimeter."

"My men are already patrolling Mrs. Poe's house," Ike says. "We can come up with a plan when we get back. Let's go get some sleep. Tomorrow's going to be a long day."

"By the way, we put Macklin into a drug rehab center today," Betty tells us. "Ike promised him a job in Charleston if he cleans himself up. I called Macklin's aunt, who lives in the projects near the Cooper River Bridge. She'll give him a place to stay."

"Could I ask where my husband is?" Fraser asks quietly. "Is that a fair question amid all the celebrating?"

Sheba rises from her seat, walks over to Fraser, then sits down beside her to embrace her. "He refused to leave Trevor's side. When I left the hospital tonight, Niles had put a mattress on the floor beside Trevor's bed. Both of them were asleep. Here was the sweetest thing I ever saw: Trevor's hand had reached down and Niles was holding it. Both were sound asleep, but they were holding hands."

"That's my sweet boy," says Fraser.

"I talked with Anna Cole today and made arrangements to send for all of Trevor's stuff. She said something sweet: she had never seen a bunch of friends as close as we seemed to be. She wanted to know how it had come to be," Sheba says.

I feel a great discomfort. I finish my drink and look up, surprised that all five of my friends in the top-drawer elegance of the Redwood Room are pointing their fingers at me. Brushing their gestures aside, I shake my head in furious denial, but they continue to point. I can do nothing to stop them as my thoughts storm out in the high air currents over San Francisco and send me reeling twenty years past, into the airlessness and joyfulness of what all of us still refer to as the Bloomsday Summer.

PART FOUR

CHAPTER 18

The Renegades

The first day of school had always felt like a small death, a long dark fall into some wordless void. Because I was a plain boy, I always dreaded facing the piercing judgment of kids who had never encountered an odd, off-centered face like mine. Though the black horn-rimmed glasses gave me a look of some yet-to-be-discovered species of amphibian, they also gave me something to hide behind, a mask that preserved a sense of detachment, if not anonymity. But I was now a senior, and Peninsula High had begun to feel like an extension of my own home. Though I had managed to make only a few friends because of an instinctual shyness and my citywide notoriety as a drug dealer, I was on familiar territory and thought I knew all the ropes and tricks and how to keep myself out of trouble.

I could not have been more wrong.

On the way to school that first morning, my mother assigned me the unwanted task of patrolling the breezeway, a no-man's-land where the hoods and rednecks and no-goodniks of both sexes gathered because they were far from the gaze and interference of teachers. It was lion country for a boy like me, the dreaded realm where Wilson "Wormy" Ledbetter ruled over his fierce pride of man-eating rednecks, who worshipped him. I had attached the nickname "Wormy" to the Ledbetter family tree; it was the reason Wormy had beaten me up during my freshman year. In the era before desegregation, every white school produced some variation on the theme of Wormy Ledbetter. At Peninsula High, Wormy was the *Tyrannosaurus rex* of the classic Southern redneck. He had beaten me up often and taken pleasure in doing so. Last year, he had broken my nose. My mother scared the bejesus out of Wormy and his parents by letting him know she would throw his sorry butt out of school if he ever dared to look cross-eyed at another student. Wormy was also racist, peerless in his hatred of black people.

That day Wormy was gathered with his usual mob of flat-topped cretins. But that was not what alarmed me when I turned the corner on the breezeway. All the new black kids had also gathered on the far side of the breezeway—an unexpected and historic gathering on the first day of school. Muscle for muscle, they looked equal to Wormy and his gum-popping posse, both groups languidly sizing each other up. The air was electric as I walked between them. It was supposed to feel like the first day of school, but I felt like a French peasant carrying a pike outside of the Bastille. I was close to terror till I caught a glimpse of Ike, standing with a group of the new kids. I caught his eye, then raised my hand in a gesture for him to keep his ranks in order, and he nodded. Then I turned to face the boy who had served as both my nemesis and my nightmare through high school.

"Hey there, Wormy!" I said with false bonhomie. "Gosh, I missed you this summer. Your friendship means so much to me."

"We ain't never been friends in our fucking lives and we ain't never gonna be," Wormy said. "And don't you ever call me Wormy again."

"Everybody calls you Wormy," I said. "They do it behind your back. Why don't you come out for football?"

"I ain't playing for no nigger coach," Wormy said, but in a modulated voice that made certain he was not heard by the swelling rank of black kids behind us.

"Yeah, that's what you told me when I called," I said. "But the team needs you, Wormy. You were an all-conference fullback last year. We could make you all-state this year."

"Don't you understand plain English, Toad?" Wormy said. "I ain't playing for no nigger."

"Today's your last chance. Coach Jefferson'll let you on the team if you come out today."

"Tell him to suck my white dick," Wormy said. The crowd behind him erupted in cheers, and he smiled.

"Here's why I think you're not going out for football, Wormy."

"I'm all ears, Toad."

"You're a big talker, but yellow as canned chickenshit." I thought I would be killed in the next several seconds. I waited for Wormy's charge and was taken by surprise when he did not lunge for my throat. Instead, he shifted tactics and looked past me down toward the motionless, expressionless sea of black faces, with Ike Jefferson a yard in front of his companions.

"I smell a *gar*," Wormy screamed out. His white mob was ready and waiting to shout the time-honored reply: "What kind of gar? A *cee-gar*?"

"No," Wormy yelled. "A *knee-gar*."

I immediately disengaged and went down the breezeway and faced Ike, who was grim-faced and about to lead half the football team in a headlong charge into the center of the heckling mob.

"I can handle this," I promised, shouting so all the black kids could hear me. Ike didn't look too convinced, and I shouted around him to the others, "My fellow students! My name is Toad, the good-hearted white boy. Stand back and watch me kick Wormy's cracker ass."

I said it to break the tension, but it had gone too far, and Ike's face was immobile as he suggested: "Do it fast, Leo. We don't have to take their shit."

"No problem, Ike," I said, though my try at defusing the fight was complicated by the entrance of yet another group of new students who appeared in the breezeway with the cadence and tramping of inexpert marchers. We all turned and, to my horror, I saw Mr. Lafayette bringing in his contingent of twelve orphans wearing those bilious orange jumpsuits stenciled with the ugly logo of St. Jude's Orphanage. They looked like a dozen pumpkins lined up in a supermarket aisle on Halloween. Wormy and his crew hooted at them in unfeigned hilarity.

I ran up to Mr. Lafayette, red-faced and angry at this new complication to the already overburdened first ten minutes of my senior year. "At ease," Mr. Lafayette said to his squad, but he didn't allow them to break formation.

"My mother told Sister Pollywog not to make these kids wear these ugly uniforms," I told him, and caught Starla smirking at me behind the sunglasses Sheba had given her on the night of my Fourth of July party.

"Polycarp's my boss, Leo," Mr. Lafayette said. "I do what she orders, and this is it."

"Hey, orphans!" Wormy shouted. "Nice threads. I see they even got coons in the orphanage."

I had endured my fill of the drawling slimeball, and I turned to confront him, striding toward him in what I hoped was an intimidating fashion. He readied himself to punch me through the brick wall of our high school. That's when Peninsula High, both black and white, got the surprise of our young lives: emerging from the white crowd, a diminutive, parakeet-like white boy, fragile as an elf, rushed toward Wormy. With a slight leap, he slapped a startled Wormy Ledbetter with an open-handed blow that echoed the length and breadth of the breezeway. Thunderstruck, I halted my timid charge, waiting for Wormy either to kill poor Trevor or to simply devour him like a gumdrop.

"Who the hell are you?" Wormy roared.

"How dare you make fun of those kids, you dumbo-brained lout!" Trevor said. I made a mental note that I would have to train Trevor in the indelicate art of cussing out a redneck.

Wormy gained control of himself and his cheering section by saying, "Hey, queer bait, you want to suck my white dick before I knock your block off?"

The second slap against Wormy came from an embattled Sheba Poe, who had fought through the crowd to defend her twin brother. Her slap couldn't have hurt him much, but the humiliation of publicly taking a well-delivered backhand from a girl made Wormy truly dangerous.

"You want your dick sucked?" Sheba asked loudly. "I'll suck your white dick, you fucking asshole from hell. But only if I think it's big enough. Pull it out. Go ahead, you scum-sucking fat pig of an asshole."

On Southern schoolyards in 1969, whether black or white, this was an extraordinarily rare, if not unparalleled, use of language. It drove it home to me that Trevor and Sheba were a lot of things, but they were not even remotely Southern. Not even Wormy, at his most profane and arrogant in the enclosed privacy of locker rooms or shower stalls, had ever descended to Sheba's level of coarseness. Observing Wormy's expression, I knew that a conversation about the size of his genitals was particularly unnerving. Though Wormy had the heart of a thug, he was rendered speechless by the two irrational twins. Both Sheba and Trevor rushed him again, as fearless as gladiators. Wormy hit Trevor with his fist, a glancing blow that knocked Trevor to the ground. But Sheba clawed his face with her fingernails. Wormy slapped her face hard, and her mouth was bleeding when she hit the pavement. When he hit Sheba, Wormy drew down on himself the unappeasable wrath of the orphans.

I was aware that the moment was upon me to summon up the physical courage I did not think I had or would ever have. In the chicken-hearted depths of me, I turned toward Wormy and prepared to get an ass-whipping. Women have little idea of the fearful world their sons grow up in, populated by pin-headed, mean-spirited lunatics—the countless legions of Wormy Ledbetters. Putting up his fists, Wormy smiled as he watched my trembling approach.

But Wormy was having a bad day. He was not expecting the all-out charge of orange furies as Starla and Betty leaped on his back from behind. St. Jude's Orphanage made an official entry into the fray, and their onslaught brought Wormy to the ground. Both girls were clawing at his face, and Starla was trying to put out his eyes. On the ground, wrestling and kicking, Wormy knocked both girls off him. I helped them both up, then pushed them into the vicinity of an unnerved Mr. Lafayette, who had his hands full holding Niles in restraint. Betty's participation in the attack had made it racial again, and I turned when I heard the crowd of black kids about to charge. Again, I held up my hand and pointed to Ike, who had taken several steps forward with his fists clenched, his huge hands ready to break the jaws of some loose-lipped white boys.

"Stay where you are, Ike. Please. Let me see if I can handle this," I pleaded.

"It isn't working out for you, Strom," he said. Before any of us could move, however, Niles Whitehead broke free of Mr. Lafayette's grip. He got directly in Wormy's face and gripped a handful of his shirtfront.

"Get your fucking hands off me, orphan," Wormy sneered. "You don't know who you're fucking with."

"Wrong, pal." It was his perfect control of himself that made Niles seem so dangerous. "I know exactly who you are. You don't know who *I* am."

"I'll know better after I kick your ass, fart blossom," Wormy said.

"You ever touch my sister again, and I'll slit your throat, numbnuts," Niles said. There was not an ounce of fear in his voice. "And if you hit me, I'll find out where you live, and I'll slit your mama's and daddy's throats while they're asleep. Then you'll think twice about calling me an orphan again."

"Let me take it from here, Niles," I said. "You get back in line."

"I can break his ass in front of his friends," Niles said to me as matter-of-factly as if he were informing me of a changing traffic light.

"You done good, son. But go back. Please. We've got to get this school year started," I said. "Wormy, take your gang of dimwits to the front of the school." It surprised me to see Chad Rutledge and Molly Huger watching this drama take place while sitting on the hood of Chad's car in the parking lot.

Itching to salvage what he could from a morning that had turned sour, Wormy threw a right-handed punch that would have knocked me unconscious if it had landed. But that summer had done something to me. I had grown three inches and had spent months lifting weights at The Citadel, running Ike up stadium stairs, and working my bicycle hard on my morning paper route. My father had toasted my brand-spanking-new manhood on the Battery at the exact point where the Ashley and the Cooper meet in all the violent nature and communion of rivers. Because of my father's gesture, I had known a transfiguration as though I had received an invitation to join a sacred order of knights. I was not the same boy that Wormy had beaten up the previous year. I knew it, but Wormy Ledbetter did not. He threw me his best punch, the same one that had put me on the ground the three previous years. Repetition was not always the brightest stratagem. I stepped back, blocked it with my left hand, then delivered a punch to his face that seemed driven by the Lord himself. Wormy's nose exploded with blood, making him collapse in on himself, which he did to the cheers of the black students.

By then, teachers had appeared on the periphery, so I held up my hand in an attempt to silence the noise. "Ladies and gentlemen," I said to the students, "welcome to Peninsula High."

With those words, the bell rang, a merciful sound. And where some things ended that day, many more began. Many more.

Being the principal's son did not always work in my favor at Peninsula High School. My craving for anonymity was thwarted anytime a kid learned that I was the son of the regal and sometimes censorious principal. And today, the whole school was already on edge during my first-period French class when my mother began calling on the loudspeaker for students to report to her office. Unsurprisingly, she first called out the name of Wilson Ledbetter. Before long, the loudspeaker crackled back to life, and she called for Trevor and Sheba Poe. Five minutes later she requested an audience with Betty Roberts, Starla Whitehead, and Niles Whitehead. Then she called for Ike Jefferson. Finally, in her frostiest tone, she called for me.

In the funereal setting of the principal's office, I reported to my mother's secretary, Julia Trammell, as I saw the main players on the breezeway lined up awaiting their interrogations.

"Hey, Mrs. Trammell. How was your summer?"

"Way too short, honey bun," Julia said. "But I've got to admit, this joint has been hopping since I got here this morning."

"Please inform her royal majesty that her prince has signed in," I said.

"Boy, talk about the village weirdo," Wormy said, holding a bloody handkerchief to his nose. "No one talks like the Toad."

I asked, "What's that you're holding on to, Wormy, what's left of your nose?"

"Your old lady just kicked me out of school," he said. "For the whole year."

Coach Jefferson burst into the room, his dark eyes smoldering. He walked over to his son and towered above him. Keeping his head low, Ike did not meet his father's glower of pure disgust.

"You get called to the principal's office in the first hour on the first day of school, son," Coach Jefferson growled. "Remember our talks this summer about discipline and keeping control?"

"He didn't do anything, Coach," Sheba said.

Trevor added, "There would've been a race riot if it hadn't been for your son."

"Leo?" Coach Jefferson asked, turning to me.

"Ike saved the day, Coach. He was heroic out there."

"Ike kept the black kids from charging the greasers, Coach," said Niles.

My mother stepped out of her office and said, "I hear Ike was the ringleader of the black students."

"No. He was their *leader,* Mother," I said. "There would be blood all over the breezeway if it wasn't for Ike."

"Call me Dr. King at school," my mother said, infuriating me. "Get in the office and I'll hand out your punishment."

"Dr. King," I said, "I'd like you to ask me questions about the fight in front of these students here."

"I've already punished them," my mother said. "Now it's your turn."

"The twins should not be punished. And the kids from the orphanage should not be punished. They were great out there, Mother. They were nothing less than great—Ike too."

"Call me Dr. King," my mother reminded me.

"The only ones who deserve to be punished are me and Wormy," I said. "You ought to give medals to those other kids. They stopped a race riot."

"I hear Sheba and Trevor physically attacked Wilson Ledbetter," she said.

"They did, and for a good reason," I said.

"They used unprintable, vile language," she said.

"They did, and it was very effective."

"The two girls from the orphanage tried to put out Wilson's eyes. Look at how scratched up his face is."

"It hasn't been Wormy's day, Mother—I mean, Dr. King," I said. "But I think even Wormy will admit he asked for this."

"Yes, ma'am," Wormy admitted, surprising me. "That's fair of the Toad."

"And you shouldn't kick Wormy out of school for a whole year," I said.

"When did the school board appoint you principal?" my mother snapped at me.

"I saw what happened, Mother. But Wormy doesn't deserve to be expelled for just being Wormy."

"Your thinking is unclear to me."

"What you taught me my whole life: that a man or a woman is simply the product of their childhood. All their standards and every shred of their characters are formed in their homes by their parents. You've told me over and over that the man I become will be a reflection of who my parents were. If it's true for me, it's true for Wormy, and it's true for Ike. But what do you do about kids like Sheba and Trevor, who don't have a daddy around to guide them? Or what about Betty and Starla and Niles, where do they fit in?"

"What's your point?"

"Wormy was raised to do exactly what he did today. His parents taught him to hate black people. He wasn't raised by Martin Luther King or the Archbishop of Canterbury. He thinks like ninety percent of the white South thinks, and you and I know it. You can hate the way Wormy thinks, but you can't blame him for it. I know the trailer park where Wormy lives. It's not much."

"So you think nothing should happen to Wormy, or to anyone else in this room? I have eyewitness accounts of you being in the center of the brawl and having a fistfight with Wilson on the breezeway."

"I was trying to keep some order," I said.

"And you failed?"

"No, Dr. King, I didn't fail. I succeeded. It was you and the teaching staff who failed. None of you were there to help defuse an explosive situation."

"I had called a meeting to discuss the school year," my mother said.

"We needed a large presence of teachers," I said. "If that thing had broken, I think some people might have been seriously hurt."

"I'll be out there tomorrow morning," Coach Jefferson said.

"I'll send all my male teachers out there," my mother said. "Make a note of that."

"It's done," Julia Trammell said.

"About Wormy?" I asked.

"There's nothing to be done about Wilson," she said. "I've already made a decision."

"Then change it," I said. "Here's what I would do, Mother—"

"Dr. King," she corrected.

"Dr. King. I think everyone in this room has learned a lot this morning, including Wormy. Am I right, Wormy?"

"If you say so, Toad," he muttered.

"Let Wormy back in school under one condition," I said.

"This better be good," my mother said.

"He has to play for Coach Jefferson's football team, and he has to bring all the white boys with him who don't want to play because Coach Jefferson's black."

Catching Coach Jefferson's curious eye, I watched him walk over and study the muscular physique of last year's star fullback.

"You're Ledbetter?" Coach Jefferson asked.

"Uh-huh," Wormy said, not looking up.

"Put a 'Yes, sir' on that," Coach Jefferson barked.

"Yes, sir," Wormy said.

"I studied the films of last year's games," Coach Jefferson said. "I thought you were going to be the stud in my backfield."

"I thought so too, sir," Wormy said. "It's just that my parents . . ."

"See what I mean, Dr. King?" I said.

"Would you play for me, son?" Coach Jefferson asked. "Tell me the truth now."

"I guess," Wormy said.

"That's not good enough," Coach Jefferson said. "Would you play for me?"

"Yes, sir," Wormy said. "If Dr. King gives me a chance, I'll play for you."

"Son," Coach Jefferson asked Ike, "will you play with Ledbetter and other white boys like him?"

Ike was clearly uncomfortable, but he finally said, "If I played all summer with the Toad, I guess I could play with any white boy."

A howl of laughter broke the considerable tension in the room. Sheba said, "Dr. King, could I marry your son?"

My humorless mother was caught off guard by Sheba, and she answered, "Leo hasn't even been on his first date yet."

"Don't listen to her, Sheba," I said. "I accept your proposal."

"There will be no punishment for what happened this morning, then," my mother announced. "But I want no trouble out of any of this crew for the rest of the year, or I'll hammer you. Understand?"

"One other thing," I said. "These orange jumpsuits have got to go, Dr. King. Please. And could Pollywog be talked into not having the orphans marched over here by poor Mr. Lafayette?"

"You'll have to clothe them, then," my mother said. "I've already had this discussion and she was adamant that she had no funding for clothing."

"Then, we'll clothe them," I said. "Sheba, can you dress Starla and Betty for tomorrow?"

"It's as good as done," Sheba said.

"Ike, Wormy: you got some spare clothes that Niles can wear? I got a couple of khakis and shirts," I said.

"You girls will look like you stepped out of *Vogue* before we're through with you," Sheba said.

"I'll do your hair tonight, girls," Trevor said.

"Jesus!" Wormy said.

"Quiet, Wormy," I said. "You got to forget that you're Wormy Ledbetter. Pretend you're someone wonderful and fabulous. Go wild and pretend you're the finest, most splendid man you've ever met. Pretend that you're Leo King."

"Oh, puke," Ike said.

In single file, we marched out of the principal's office and straight into the history of our times. Later that afternoon, Wormy Ledbetter and seven integration-resistant white boys joined the football team.

In the world of high school football in South Carolina, nothing scared a young man any worse as he strapped on his shoulder pads than the knowledge that he was about to face the awesome and storied Green Wave of Summerville High. The legendary John McKissick coached the Green Wave, and his teams were famous for being ferocious between the lines. The year before they had crushed us, 56–0. I had never felt as humiliated as when walking off that playing field.

But Coach Jefferson had brought a slick defensive scheme and a complicated offensive one from his days at Brooks High. His playbook looked like a branch of advanced calculus, and I had to study hard every night before I began to feel any mastery. His practices were disciplined, hard-hitting, and utterly exhausting. The Charleston sun had been a brutal star in the exotic heat of August. It took an effort of will to survive the first week of two-a-days, and I would often go straight to bed after supper. A couple of guys quit each day, and our team was down to twenty-three players when Wormy and the seven other latecomers showed up at practice.

Though I thought Coach Jefferson would go easy on the eight white boys, I couldn't have been more wrong. He singled them out, screamed obscenities at them, and generally ran them into the ground. Ten minutes after their first practice, Coach Jefferson had terrified them into a lamblike submission. His defensive coach, Wade Williford, was a young white man I had watched play in the defensive backfield at The Citadel. He surprised me by putting me at linebacker, pairing me with Ike Jefferson, who had looked like an All-American to me since summer practices had begun. I had never played defense, but found out I loved it far more than offense. With Wormy and the boys back, I thought we might have a pretty good football team. The only thing we lacked was a quarterback, and that was like a Catholic church lacking a tabernacle.

Late one afternoon, Coach Jefferson had an inspiration. He called out to Niles, "Hey, mountain boy! You ever play quarterback?"

Niles said, "No, sir, just played end. Just went out and caught the ball."

"Throw it for me, son," Coach Jefferson ordered.

"Where you want me to throw it, Coach?" Niles asked, standing with the team near the 50-yard line.

"I don't give a damn," Coach said. "I just want to see how far you can throw it. I saw you tossing it around with Toad yesterday, and you throw a nice pass. Can you go deep?"

"Don't know, Coach," Niles said. "Never had any reason to."

"Throw the damn ball, boy."

Until I saw them wrap around that football, I had never noticed the size of Niles's hands. They were large, magnificent hands. He placed the ball behind his ear, and threw that football out of the end zone and between the goalposts.

"Jesus God Almighty, son, can you do that with any accuracy?" Coach Jefferson yelled, as the team murmured with admiration.

"Have no idea, Coach."

"Looks like we've got us a quarterback," Coach Williford said.

And so we did. Since Coach Jefferson had played quarterback at South Carolina State, he spent long hours with Niles, practicing snaps, the three-step drop and the seven-step drop, and hand-offs. With each day, Niles grew in his role and became more and more proficient at calling the game and running his team. He improved every time he touched the ball, infusing his teammates with great hope for the coming season.

From the locker room beneath the stadium, we heard the noise of the crowd gathering above us. We had already heard that the Summerville game was a sellout. The ignominy and completeness of our destruction by Summerville last year still ached in the psyche of last year's players, especially Wormy Ledbetter, who had been held to a season low of twenty yards rushing by an awesome Green Wave defense. But most of that defense had graduated, and we knew very little about their replacements. Coach Jefferson came in to deliver the pregame pep talk, and I could not wait to see if he brought any natural gifts to that art form.

The coach walked into the locker room with a pride that was contagious. For a moment, he was silent as the hum of the crowd grew thunderous outside in the stands. Then he began to speak. "I want to talk about integration. Just one time. After that, no one on this team is going to mention it again. I've never coached white players or coached against a white coach. But I'm doing both tonight. I've always wanted to coach against John McKissick to see how good I really am. With you young men—I believe with all my heart that we can kick the Green Wave's ass all the way back to Summerville. I think this team is that good."

My teammates roared their approval. Then Coach Jefferson continued. "When the white players didn't come out for the team because I am a black man, it hurt my damn feelings. It damaged me in ways I don't even realize, and in places like my heart and my soul. That's why I was so hard on Wormy and his friends when they came back. I tried to kill you boys in this Charleston sun. I tried to break your spirit. I couldn't do it, and I gave it my best shot. Now what I have left is a team. I think it's a team with character and mental toughness. Look around you. Look at your teammates. If you see black faces or white faces, you get the fuck off my team. No white. No black. No more. The time for that is over. We walk the world as a team, and we're going to have fun kicking a little ass this year. I've studied McKissick's game films, but he doesn't know what the hell I'm going to do. He has no idea that we're going to kick his team's ass this year. People in this whole state are going to know about Peninsula High School when they drink their morning coffee tomorrow. We believe in this team with our bodies and souls. Repeat that in one voice."

"We believe in this team with our bodies and souls!" my team roared out in unison.

"We *will* kick Summerville's ass!" he said. "Repeat it."

"We *will* kick Summerville's ass!" we shouted.

"Then go do it."

We stormed out of that locker room, with Ike and me leading our fired-up teammates into the blinding lights of that stadium and the thundering applause of that sold-out crowd. The ten cheerleaders sprinted out ahead of us, breaking out fast like a spooked covey of quail—five white girls and five black girls, as my mother had demanded. The great surprise of the crowd was the presence of the frail-boned boy who led the cheerleaders, Trevor Poe, the first male cheerleader in the history of my state. Not surprisingly, Sheba Poe took to the sidelines as head cheerleader, with Molly Huger and Betty Roberts trailing behind her.

As we ran toward the home-team bench, Ike surprised me by grabbing my left hand with his right one, then lifting his other hand into a fist and pumping it at the home crowd. I lifted my own free fist and pumped it at the fans. To my surprise, it drove our crowd into a frenzy. Ike's hand felt good in mine. It began a tradition that still exists at Peninsula to this day: the cocaptains of the football team clasp hands and pump their other fists as they emerge from the locker room.

I turned and looked across the field at the huge and menacing Green Wave of Summerville. They had dressed out sixty-six players, while us poor Renegades could manage to dress only thirty-one. Their line outweighed us by twenty pounds per man. Their entire offensive backfield had returned after being second-best in the state. The quarterback, John McGrath, was being recruited by all the great college programs in the country; he was leaning toward Alabama or Southern Cal, which at that time was as big-time as big-time got.

Ike and I walked out to the center of the field. We shook hands with their captain, John McGrath, who handled himself with the princely carriage all great athletes have as their birthright. The referee flipped the coin, and Summerville won the toss. We told the ref we wanted to defend the south goal. Then Ike and I strapped on our helmets and ran back to join our teammates.

Coach Jefferson gathered us in a huddle. "Summerville doesn't think we have a chance. Play clean, boys, but play mean. When Chad kicks off, let the Green Wave know they're in a game."

It had been Chad Rutledge who had surprised me most in the brutal football practices of August. I had taken a poisonous dislike to him when I first met him at the yacht club. Over the years, I had met a thousand boys just like him—a candy-assed, cookie-cutter type with a last name for a first name thrown in for the grand pretension of it all. But Chad had proven resilient, versatile, and fast on his feet. He could punt and kick field goals and showed good hands as our starting wideout receiver. On the first day of practice, Coach Jefferson put him in the safety position on defense, where Chad displayed a nose for the ball and was, I thought, our best open-field tackler. Though it would take some time, Chad would prove to me that it was a serious mistake to underestimate those boys of privilege who emerge from the pampered world South of Broad.

As we lined up, waiting for Chad to deliver the signal that he was about to kick off, I yelled to Ike, lined up beside me, "Bet you I beat you downfield and make this tackle, Ike."

"Dream on, Toad. You'll be fifty yards behind me when they're calling for an ambulance to scrape that poor boy off the field."

"I can feel this one," I screamed. Chad approached the football and kicked off. A Summerville back received the ball on his own 15-yard line.

In a blur of light and color, I sprinted downfield. A Summerville lineman tried to take my feet from underneath me, but he dove too low, and I leaped over him. I experienced the illusion of swiftness as I set my sights on the running boy, who wore number 20. He was sprinting up the left sideline when he saw his blocking breaking down. He reversed his field and started coming in the direction that brought him face-to-face with me, with nowhere to go. I hit him at full speed, driving my right shoulder into his chest and knocking him back five yards before I brought him crashing to the turf. I didn't know the boy had fumbled and Ike had picked it up until I heard the note of wild joy erupt from our side of the field, and I saw Ike holding the ball aloft in the end zone before handing it off to a referee. I had hurt the boy that I had tackled. He lay on the field, and I kept asking him if he was all right. Soon, a trainer and some coaches were around him, and they helped number 20 to his feet.

"I didn't mean to hurt you," I said.

"It was a good, clean tackle, son," a man said to me, the first and only time in my life that the great coach John McKissick would speak to me.

Chad kicked the extra point between the goalposts with Niles holding. As we lined up for the second kickoff, I looked up at the time clock: it had taken us only twenty seconds to score.

When Chad kicked off again, Ike and I both tackled the kickoff returner on the twenty-five. Then Summerville lined up and began to show us why they had one of the most feared programs in the state. John McGrath led them downfield in a timely fashion, throwing beautiful and accurate passes to his ends and backs coming out of the backfield. Whenever he handed it off to his big fullback up the middle, Ike and I would close the holes fast; twice we dropped the kid for a loss. But still, Summerville drove us down to our own thirty. Coach Jefferson kept screaming, "They know they're in a game now. They goddamn sure as hell know that."

Ike called his own number for a linebacker blitz on a third down and long. The ball was snapped. The quarterback dropped back, looking toward that hole in the pass coverage that was left after Ike charged through the center of the line. No one blocked Ike, and he was going at full speed when he made a spectacular sack on McGrath, who never saw him coming. McGrath fumbled the football, and Niles leaped on top of it.

Though we were not half the team that Summerville was, things broke our way that night, and our coach had delivered a clever and strategic game plan to offset the superior talent of the Green Wave. When Niles called the first play of the year on offense, I thought it was a mistake to start off a season with a trick play. I hiked it to Niles, who kept the ball himself and sprinted out toward the Summerville sidelines. The left guard and I pulled from our positions to lead the blocking in front of Wormy. I stopped a Summerville linebacker from getting to Niles in our backfield, but our blocking was breaking down badly. Niles was about to get in trouble when he stopped suddenly. He looked far down to the other side of the field, where he saw Ike standing alone, calling for the football. Ike had pretended to block his man but let him through, allowing Ike to slip unnoticed down our own sideline. He was still alone when Niles hurled him the ball.

After Chad kicked the extra point, we were leading a stunned Summerville by a score of 14–0.

It was a joyful and rapturous night, one that happens all too infrequently in the brief transit of human life. I can remember everything about that night, every play that either team ran, every block I missed or made, every tackle I was in on. I remember the feeling of complete, transported bliss that one can get only from athletics or lovemaking. I fell in love with the heart of my team as we fought against the strength of an infinitely superior team. Because we had worked out so hard during the summer, Ike and I stuffed their running game the whole night. We would jump up, slapping each other's helmets, pounding each other's shoulder pads, trusting each other, and, by the end of that game, loving each other. A bond formed between us and our teammates that I thought would last for the rest of my life. We screamed at one another and fought with lion-hearted courage against Summerville all night long.

The score was tied, 14–14, with a minute left to play. I blitzed and hit McGrath the moment he set up to pass; Ike recovered the fumble on Summerville's 28-yard line. Our home crowd turned lunatic. I looked up to where my mother and father sat with Monsignor Max and saw that they were leaping up and down and hugging one another. My James Joyce–loving mother was actually gyrating like a cheerleader over a football game.

Niles was cool and no-nonsense in the huddle. Before he called the play, he yelled to us over the noise of the crowd, "Boys, I want to win this goddamn football game. I won't fuck up; I promise you that. But none of you can fuck up, either. You promise me that."

"We promise!" the team screamed at him.

"They stopped Wormy tonight," Niles said. "Now I want my goddamn line to open some holes for him."

I knocked their noseguard on his back and took out their left line-backer as Wormy ran for fifteen hard-earned yards and a first down on the 13-yard line. On the next play, Wormy went ten yards up the middle to the three. With twenty seconds left, Niles called for Wormy to run it off-tackle.

I snapped the ball. I blocked the man on my left and was looking for a linebacker to bring down when I was hit from behind and found myself lying on my back in the end zone. The world slowed down, and time was stillborn and the movement of all stars and moons sat frozen as I watched something float out of the night air toward me. I reached up to grab it, to touch it. I caught it before I realized it was the football Wormy had just fumbled, which had popped straight up into the air and straight back down into my waiting arms. I secured the ball in the end zone and then felt the entire weight of the whole Green Wave leap on top of me, trying to steal the ball from me in the pileup.

When the referee signaled that Peninsula had scored a touchdown, the stadium approached meltdown. There were five seconds left on the clock. We lined up for the extra point, and I snapped it back to Niles. He did not put the ball down for Chad to kick, but instead danced around in the backfield for the five seconds it took to end the game.

Then the fans moved in a great flood toward us, surrounding us, pummeling us, just about hurting us in their ecstasy and surprise. Then they went for the goalposts. I retained a sight from that perfect night that could bring me to tears for the rest of my life: I watched in amazement as my mother and father and Monsignor Max helped an out-of-control mob of football fans pull the goalposts to the earth. I howled with laugh-ter when I watched Betty Roberts kiss Wormy Ledbetter on the cheek in her sheer exuberance. I laughed harder when I saw Wormy wipe that kiss off with the sweaty sleeve of his jersey.

I turned and watched the moment when Coach Anthony Jefferson shook hands with Coach John McKissick. Both were models of sportsmanship and made me proud to be part of such a game. History was changing all around me.

I watched the swaying goalposts, watched my father get lifted up to the crossbars to direct the surging, unstoppable fans, watched my mother whip off her shoes and hurl them backward, deep into the crowd, into that lost night. She was trying to get better traction as she rejoined the crowd that finally brought those stubborn goalposts crashing to the earth.

In Charleston that September, a heat wave put a stranglehold on the city. The sun seemed parboiled as it made its slow transit across the peninsula. Because of our nearness to the Atlantic, the humidity seemed man-killing and inescapable as I made my torpid way from class to class. It had pleased me immensely when I found myself in the same classes as the twins, the orphans, Ike Jefferson, Chad Rutledge, and Molly Huger. And, yes, I recognized my mother's handiwork in the arrangement and understood that she had drafted me as her watchdog over a group that still seemed flammable to her. Of course, Sheba Poe, with her incandescent, voluptuous beauty, was a natural enemy to my mother's intellectual sensibilities, and Trevor seemed like a creature imported from an undiscovered planet. Starla carried her woundedness like a weather report issued by her damaged, wandering eye. Niles played his role of guardian angel to his sister, but to my mother he seemed unanchored, a young man turned inward because of too many responsibilities given him at too young an age.

"That boy never had a childhood," my mother announced at dinner one night.

"Niles is a fine young man," Father said, simply.

"Too bad his sister's a head case," my mother said.

"She's a nice girl, Mother," I protested. "Why don't you cut her some slack?"

"I don't like the way she looks at me," my mother explained.

"That's because one of her eyes is looking due west, while the other is looking straight ahead. That's not her fault."

"I'm talking attitude, not strabismus or whatever malady she has."

"Dr. Colwell has agreed to operate on that eye," I said. "I bet that changes everything about Starla. The eye makes her self-conscious."

"How on earth will she pay for it?" Mother asked.

"He's doing it for free."

"Did you tell Dr. Colwell about Starla?" my father asked.

"Yes, sir. I told him this summer, one night when I was collecting from him for the newspaper. He's already examined her, and he'll operate when he has an opening."

"So your nice boy set this up, Lindsay," my father said with pride.

"That girl's personality is set in stone," Mother said. "She's a head case. Moving her eyeball isn't going to change a thing. Mark my words."

By the end of October, my football team was still undefeated. But Coach Jefferson made us well aware that we had been luckier than we had been good. He swore we could be in better shape, and he made us outhustle every team we played that season. I would feel half-dead after one of his practices.

Fate has its own quirks and defiances and accords, as I was to learn one night after I got home from such a grueling practice. When I walked into the house, my father said, "Your dinner's in the refrigerator, son. And that pretty Molly Huger called."

"Molly?" I asked. "Why'd she call?"

"Don't know," Father said. "It wasn't me she wanted to talk to."

I picked up the phone in my bedroom, then I found myself almost faint with fear. I realized I had never called a girl. My distress came not from being unnerved but from feeling unmanned. My hands trembled and felt clammy. It became clear to me why I was suffering from this un-expected panic attack: the reason I had never called a girl was that I had never dated one. Even to me that seemed like an odd and illogical fact in the life of an eighteen-year-old boy.

Molly and I had developed an easygoing friendship in the first month of school, and we sat next to each other in three of our classes. So I sum-moned up a small reserve of courage and dialed Molly's number. Her mother answered on the first ring. When I gave my name, her voice turned frostbitten and brittle.

"Molly isn't here, Leo. Good night," Mrs. Huger said, then hung up the phone.

I was rising out of my chair when the phone rang immediately. I answered it as my parents had taught me to do: "King residence. This is Leo speaking."

I heard Molly laughing at the other end of the phone. "Do you always answer the phone like that?"

"No," I said, "sometimes I say, 'This is Leo King and you can kiss my ass, whoever you are.' Of course, I always answer like that. You know my mother now. This house has ten thousand rules."

Then fiery words broke out between Molly and her mother. Because Molly's hand covered the receiver, I could not make out the words, but there was genuine fury in the muffled exchange. Finally, Molly said, "Mama, I think I deserve a little privacy. Thank you very much. Leo, are you still there?"

"Still here," I said. "Anything wrong?"

"Yeah, there's a lot wrong," Molly said. "Chad and I had a fight, and he broke up with me today. In fact, just a few minutes ago."

"What an idiot," I said. "Is he nuts?"

"What makes you say that?"

"Because you're you," I said, flustered. "You're everything in the world."

"I was hoping you'd say something like that," Molly said. "That was one of the reasons I called."

"What was the other?"

"To ask if you could take me to the dance after the game Friday night."

I blushed so deeply and suddenly that I thought my face might have a crimson hue for the rest of my life. I hunted for words but muteness had turned my tongue to stone. I prayed for an electrical storm to bring down the phone lines of the city. In wordless shame, I awaited Molly's intercession.

"Leo? Are you still there?"

"I'm here," I said, grateful that my voice had returned to the stage.

"Well, what's the answer?" she asked. "Will you take me to the dance or not?"

"Molly, you're Chad's girlfriend. I know how much he thinks about you. I know how proud you make him."

"Is that why he asked Bettina Trask to the dance?" she said. "Is that why he asked that big-titted tramp to the sock hop?"

"Bettina Trask," I gasped, stunned at the news. "Does Chad have a death wish? She's Wormy Ledbetter's girlfriend. That's like committing suicide."

"I hope Wormy beats the snot out of him."

"We can plan Chad's funeral if you like. I know how this story is going to end."

"I don't want to talk about Chad. Will you take me to the dance or not?"

"Molly, I've never been on a date. I wouldn't know what to do or say or how to act," I said, each word coming out as slowly as an extracted tooth.

"I can teach you all that stuff," she said.

"Then I should ask you to the dance, shouldn't I?"

"That's the normal procedure," she said.

"Molly Huger, would you go to the dance with me Friday night after the game?"

"I would be most honored, Leo," Molly said. "I can't thank you enough for the invitation."

"Can I ask you a personal question?"

"Ask away."

"Have you ever dated another boy besides Chad?"

"Never." She burst into tears and hung up the phone.

In a reverie composed of both terror and ecstasy, I moved out toward the kitchen, where I began to warm up the meal my father had cooked for me. When I sat down to eat dinner, Father joined me as he did every night, to discuss the events of the day.

"Did the chef do a good job, son?"

"He can work in my kitchen anytime," I replied. "The flank steak's delicious. The squash and asparagus couldn't be better. The mashed potatoes, perfect."

"Balance is the key to everything. What did Miss Molly want from our boy?"

"The strangest thing in the world," I said. "She wants me to go to the dance with her after the game."

"*Strange* is not the appropriate word," Father said. "How about *fabulous* or *splendiferous* or *prodigious*? It's not a bad thing when one of the prettiest, nicest girls in the world wants to go dancing with you."

"Molly's way too pretty for a boy like me," I said. "Chad broke up with her today, so she's feeling hurt. Chad asked Bettina Trask to the dance."

"Uh-oh," my father said. "We know what that boy's after. Bettina has quite a reputation."

"I've gotten to know her a little bit this year. Her family's poor, and her father's a no-account. In fact, I heard he was in prison. But Bettina's really smart and, I think, ambitious."

"Wormy Ledbetter doesn't get you very far on the ambition scale," Father said.

"But dating Chad Rutledge will improve her social standing in a heartbeat," I said.

Father laughed and dropped his hands. "I bet Chad's stuffy mother goes nuts when she hears the news."

"Molly's mother didn't like it a bit that I called. She couldn't even pretend to be nice."

"South of Broad is a conspiracy of platelets, son: blood and breeding are all that matter there. No, that's not true: there's got to be a truck full of money somewhere near the blood bank."

"No wonder Molly's mother is upset. We don't have money. My God, we're Catholic. Not much family to talk of. Zip for aristocracy. Zip for clubs. From Chad Rutledge to Leo King. Molly's in a freefall."

"I bet this is the first original thing that Molly's ever done," Father answered. "In a way, it's her declaration of independence."

"What'll I do if Molly wants to dance?"

"Then, you dance with her. Dancing with a pretty girl makes it fun to be alive."

"I don't know how to dance, not really. Sheba tried to teach me at my party this summer, but that's it."

My father slapped his hand against his forehead. "Damnation. We used to dance all over this house, with you on my feet and Steve on your mother's feet. That's it, Leo; that's the cause. We stopped dancing after Steve died. We let our house die around us. The music died. We lost sight of you completely. We came close to losing you. Jesus, you've never been on a date! What in the hell were we thinking?"

"None of us did well with the Steve thing," I said.

"Tomorrow night when you get home from football practice, put on your dancing shoes, son. This joint is going to be hopping."

And my father was as good as his word. After practice the following afternoon, I was driving Niles back to the orphanage when he surprised me by saying, "Your father invited Starla, Betty, and me over for dinner. He said something about dance lessons."

"Holy God, Father gets so carried away," I said.

"You're lucky to have him," Niles said. "I wish he was my father."

"Do you know who your father is, Niles?"

"Yeah," Niles said. "Enough said."

"Enough said," I agreed.

I could hear loud music pouring out of my house when I pulled up in the driveway, and I noticed that my mother's car was gone. My father was in the backyard grilling cheeseburgers and corn on the cob, and Betty was serving everyone coleslaw and potato salad from huge wooden bowls. Sheba and Trevor were throwing their trash into an aluminum can when Niles and I walked into the backyard.

Sheba said, "Hurry up, slowpokes. We've got to teach you boys some foot-flogging. The party's inside."

Trevor was dragging Starla and Betty into the house. Father shut down the grill, removed his apron and showy toque, and hurried in to play his role of disc jockey. He was grinning with pleasure he could not contain.

"Where's Mother?" I asked.

"She wanted no part of this," he said. "She was mad as hell that I set it up on a school night. So she got huffy and went down to the library."

Inside, Sheba and Trevor gave lessons in the basics of rock and roll, the shag, the fish, and even the stroll. The twins danced with the natural-ness of trees moving with the wind. As they held each other, all the congruence and elaborateness of dance became clear to all us voyeurs who watched those bodies at play in their own divine gracefulness.

But we were not there to observe, but to learn to dance. Trevor took the boys to one side of the room and began teaching us steps of great simplicity. "Don't be afraid to make a mistake. You learn by making mistakes. You get better by making mistakes. Let yourselves go. Don't think. Just dance. Just let your bodies go. Dancing is just the body loving itself."

For three hours, we practiced steps and jumped around in a comedy of clumsiness and error. But because of the patience and goodwill of the twins, we ended up performing a rote imitation of the spirit of the dance. I started to loosen up and enjoy myself, and that night I was set free from my danceless body forever.

Then they taught us the waltz, the pure finesse of the slow dance where you hold a girl's hand and put another hand on her waist and pull her close to you. "The slow dance is really what all teenage boys and girls want to do," Sheba said. "You get to hold someone you adore, and hold them close. Your cheek touches their cheek. You can breathe into their ear. You can let them know how you feel by how you touch. Or cling to them. You can tell each other secrets without saying a single word. When a bride and groom get married, they always begin that marriage with a slow dance. There's a reason for that. Leo, let's show them that reason."

Sheba lifted her hand toward me, and I took it as though I were handling a stick of dynamite. My father put on a record called "Love Is Blue," an instrumental as pretty as a Charleston street. Putting my arm around Sheba's waist, I pulled her to me, and we began to dance—not think, but dance, and Sheba made it look as though I could. I wanted that song to play on forever. But the record stopped and time stopped and Sheba and I stepped back from each other. She curtsied, and I bowed. I felt blooming and handsome and un-toadlike.

The phone rang, and I walked over to answer it.

"Is this Leo King?" a female voice asked.

"Yes, it is," I said.

"This is Jane Parker, Dr. Colwell's assistant. We had a cancellation, and Dr. Colwell can operate on Starla Whitehead at eight in the morning this Friday, at Medical U. Can she be there?"

"Starla Whitehead will be there," I said, then returned to the dancers and announced to the room: "Starla, Dr. Colwell's gonna fix your eye!"

The room cheered. Starla went to Niles, and brother and sister wept together in the quietest and most tender way. Their cargo of sadness always seemed unbearable, even on the night when both of them learned to dance.

CHAPTER 19

Pilgrims

Because I recount a past of utmost importance to those of us who survived it, I find myself trying for an exactness that might be unreachable. But color, smell, and music have always opened the rose windows, blind alleys, and trapdoors of the past in ways I find astonishing. My route as a paperboy has now retreated in memory as a related series of smells, barking dogs, early risers, joggers along the Battery, the discussion of the news with Eugene Haverford, my luxuriant daydreaming as I pedaled and slung and thought about the good life I was riding out to lead. My memories seem evergreen and verdant, so I am always comfortable walking through the front door of my past, confident in the shape and certitude of all that I carry from those days.

On the day of Starla's operation, I delivered my newspapers with uncommon efficiency and speed. Afterward, I skipped going to Mass with my parents at the cathedral and having breakfast at Cleo's, and drove directly to the orphanage, where Starla and Niles awaited my arrival. Mr. Lafayette opened the gates with a key the size of a switchblade, then hugged Starla, wishing her the best of luck. It was the first time I realized that Starla had not taken off her sunglasses in public since Sheba had presented them as a gift. She and Niles both got in the front seat of the car, and I noted that Starla's hands were trembling as her brother tried to calm her fears.

"Starla's terrified," Niles said, speaking for her, as he often did in times of distress.

"So would anyone else be," I said. "It's natural."

"She wants me to go into the operating room with her," Niles told me.

"Dr. Colwell said they have strict procedures for surgery. They won't let you."

Starla managed in a small, shaky voice, "I don't think I can do it without Niles. The idea of someone cutting through my eyeball is more than I can take. I don't want to go."

I tried to allay her fears. "Dr. Colwell says you're going to have beautiful eyes when the operation is over. Do you want to have to wear sunglasses the rest of your life? Do you wear those things when you sleep?"

"Yes," she said, surprising me with quiet candor. "I only take them off in the shower. I want to hug Sheba every time I see her for giving them to me. You don't know what it's like to be a freak."

"You won't need 'em after today, I promise," I said. "Starla, listen to me. Dr. Colwell can fix all that."

"You didn't hear her, buddy-roo," Niles said. "She don't want to do it, she said. We ain't going to the hospital."

"I heard you, buddy-roo," I said as I slammed on the brakes. "I'm taking Starla to the best eye surgeon in Charleston. He's operating for free. Now, I know what your sister's going through. My nickname's the Toad, because my glasses are so thick they make my eyes look froggy. I know that. I own a mirror. If there was an operation for my eyes, I'd throw your sister out of the car and have Dr. Colwell do me instead. So if you don't like it, Niles, get out of here. Leave us alone. In a couple of hours, this is gonna be over with. Done."

Niles looked at his sister, who said: "He's right, Niles."

"I'm only going along with this because you asked me to," Niles said to her. "And of course he's right. He's the fucking Toad."

Relieved, I told Niles, "My heartless mother said you and I could wait outside the surgery room during the operation."

"That's mighty nice of her," Starla said.

"She'll never tell you this, but she's rooting hard for you two. She thinks God gave you a raw deal," I said. "Here we are. You two get out, and I'll park the car. Go on up to the surgical unit. They're waiting for you, Starla."

"Has Dr. Colwell ever done this kind of operation before?" Starla asked nervously. "I wanted to ask him during the examination. But he was so nice to me that I chickened out."

"Well, he's operated before, but never on anybody's eyeball. Until today, that is," I said. "His specialty is removing plantar warts."

"You sorry son of a bitch," Niles snarled. "Joking around at a time like this. I'm going to whip your ass when we get to the waiting room."

"Joking? Thank God he was joking," Starla said. "I needed a joke. I need to laugh." She took a breath and murmured, "I can do this."

"Then do it, mountain girl," I said. "I hear they don't make girls any tougher."

"Never mess with me, Toad," Starla said as she punched me on the shoulder and got out of the car. "Promise me if this operation doesn't work, you won't call me Cyclops, though."

"Promise," I said.

An hour passed in the waiting room, and Niles began to pace like a caged panther, his muscles taut and his eyes burning. A door opened, and Fraser Rutledge made a surprise entrance, going directly over to Niles, giving him a sisterly hug. The hospital was a block south of Ashley Hall, the private school Fraser attended; she had gotten permission to skip her study hall to visit a sick friend. She whispered a few words to Niles, and though I could not hear them, I could see his shoulder muscles relax as she got him to sit down. She walked over to me, gave me a rough hug, and said, "You've been the talk at our dinner table for the past couple of nights, Leo."

"Why on earth?" I asked.

"Chad admitted that he'd broken up with Molly. Man, it hit our house like an A-bomb. Molly's mother called my mother and said Chad had asked that slut Bettina Trask to the dance."

"Bettina's not that bad," I said. "She's up from crap, but she's smart as hell and tries hard. She's in my mother's advanced English course. Ask Niles."

"Bettina's been nice to me and Starla," Niles said. "Even after we got into a fight with her boyfriend on the first day of school."

"Well, I hear she puts out like a Pez dispenser," Fraser said. "And Toad, I hear you're playing sloppy seconds for Chad."

"Do your parents know you and I are dating yet, Fraser?" Niles asked.

"Not yet," she admitted nervously. "And the time certainly isn't now."

"The orphan and Bettina Trask," Niles said. "Too much shame for your parents to bear in one week."

"Don't go feeling sorry for yourself again, Niles Whitehead," Fraser said. "I won't rich-girl you to death if you don't beat me with the orphan stick, okay?"

At that moment, Dr. Gauldin Colwell entered the waiting room, wearing his scrubs and that maritime calmness that seemed to be his greatest asset as a physician. He was a handsome, aristocratic man who looked like he was bred to wear a stethoscope. His very presence calmed me, but more important, I saw a visible relaxation in Niles's ruffled demeanor.

Gathering us around him, Dr. Colwell spoke in a soft, authoritative voice. "I believe the operation was a success, but we won't know for sure for about forty-eight hours. Everything looked good. I'll be over each morning this weekend to check on the progress of her healing. We'll keep her groggy and sedated the whole time. I don't let my patients suffer pain. Before you go, you'll need to learn how to apply eye drops."

"I can do that, Doctor," Niles said. "I'm her brother."

"So I hear," Dr. Colwell said, turning to Niles. "You owe a debt of gratitude to Leo King here. He's the one who asked me to do this operation."

"He's got it, Doctor," Niles answered. "For as long as we live."

"You've got something too, Dr. Colwell," I said.

"What's that, Leo?" the doctor asked.

"Free newspapers the rest of your life."

"That's unnecessary," he said. "But very gracious."

His young assistant, Jane Parker, as pretty as a cornflower, came out into the waiting room and asked, "Who needs to learn how to apply eye drops?"

"Teach all of them," Dr. Colwell said. He began to leave, then stopped to say, "Mr. Whitehead, your sister is going to have something new come into her life, I expect."

"What's that, Doctor?" Niles asked.

"Gentleman callers," he said. "Lots of gentlemen callers."

"I don't get it," Niles said.

Jane Parker laughed. "Your sister's a pretty girl. A darling girl. This is going to change her life."

In the locker room that night, an undercurrent of discord was loose as the players laced up their shoulder pads and strapped hip pads to their waists. Something invisible had sucked the spirit out of our team, and we seemed lethargic as the crowd filled the aisles of Stoney Field, fired up by our undefeated season. The Hanahan team seemed like it was marching in step to some nihilistic death march that would bring our bright season to a demoralizing finish. The fiery love of competition that had carried us to a ninth-place ranking among the largest high schools of our state had either called in sick or decided to take a Friday night off. I could feel the first loss of the season adhering to our record before I had even finished dressing. Luckily, I was not the only one to notice it.

Ike looked around. "What's wrong, Toad?"

"We seem dead," I said. "We all need to be on an IV."

"Hey, Renegades!" Ike yelled as he got up, fully dressed and ready to go. He went down the line pounding shoulder pads and slapping boys on the ass, trying to light a fire in a room without kindling or oxygen. "Let me see some fight in your eyes!" he exhorted. "You're acting like scarecrows. Barnyard chickens. You guys forget who we are? We're the goddamn Renegades. We've beaten the Summerville Green Wave, the Beaufort Tidal Wave, the St. Andrews Rocks. And tonight we're playing a tough-as-shit Hanahan team that hasn't lost a game, either. Where's the fight in you guys? Tell me where it went to hide, and I'll get up a search party to go find it."

A voice answered Ike, rebellious and unappeasable. "Sit down and shut up, boy. You're beating a dead horse." The voice came from Wormy Ledbetter, who sat by his locker half-dressed.

His challenge to the cocaptain seemed cancerous to team unity, so I went to where Wormy sat and brought both my fists down hard on his shoulder pads. He jumped up with fists clenched, ready to fight me and Ike at the same time.

Niles intervened by pulling me back by my jersey. "Call a team meeting before the coaches get here," he told Ike.

Ike ordered, "Everybody dress on the double! One minute, then we meet in the conference room."

This decree caused some grumbling among both the white and the black players, but at least it was an audible sign that the team was no longer brain-dead. In less than sixty seconds, our entire team faced Ike and me as we stood in front of the blackboard, which was Coach Jefferson's personal realm of power.

"Let's finish this thing," Ike said, "whatever it is. I don't know who this team is."

"Guys," I said, "what's wrong with the Renegades? We've gone through so much together."

The silence was complete, unbreakable. I was about to say something else inane in the vocabulary-stunted limitations of sport when Niles spoke up. "Wormy's pissed off because Chad's dating his girlfriend after the game tonight."

Ike whistled. "Chad, are you a plain fool or what? From what I hear, Bettina and Wormy've been going together forever."

Chad, nervous and uncertain, said, "I think Bettina just wanted to try a little white meat from the other side of the tracks."

From knowing Chad, I understood his response was part bravado and part an unstrategic use of his sense of humor. As I was trying to think of a funnier response, I watched the rhinoceros-like charge of Wormy leaping over three of his teammates to get to Chad, who was sitting next to a cinder-block wall. Amid the flailing fists and bursts of creative profanity, we managed to separate the two combatants. Chad was lucky for the success of our intervention—I thought Wormy would have severed Chad's carotid artery with his crooked, yellowed teeth in the fury of that headlong charge. Ike and I got unsteady handholds on Wormy's uniform, and he was guided back to his seat with far less relief than Chad felt. When Ike and I gained control of the atmosphere, you could feel an agitation that had replaced the spiritual hollowness that had infected my teammates.

As Ike began to speak, Coach Jefferson and his assistant entered from the coaching office. I ran down the cement aisle to intercept them and said, "We need five minutes, Coach. Got to clear some things up. Team trouble, but we can handle it."

Though Coach Jefferson was surprised, he was immediately responsive. "Four minutes." He and his assistant retreated to his small, airless office. I ran back to the front of the blackboard.

"Wormy," Ike said, "we can't sacrifice this team for our love lives. We've all worked too hard. All of you know how I feel about Betty, but if my feelings for her ever got in the way of this team, I'd drop her, or at least during the season. All you guys got girlfriends. We're football players, and girls like us. All of us, except the Toad."

Even Wormy Ledbetter laughed along with the rest of my teammates. I roared too, admiring the brilliance of Ike's strategy.

Chad's voice rang in anger above the laughter. "Hell, that's why I asked Bettina to the dance—the Toad asked Molly out! Bettina's been calling me for weeks."

Ike said with pure sarcasm, "Chad, you don't mean to tell me you got snaked by a fucking amphibian?" Again, the team screamed with laughter, Wormy leading the way.

"Women can't keep their hands off me," I said. "It's been a problem since I was a kid. You guys call me the Toad, but women call me the Mink."

"Shit, bet you never kissed a girl," Chad sneered.

"That'll change tonight after he takes out Molly." Niles grinned, earning a big laugh from everyone but Chad, till Ike raised his hand to silence the room.

"That's enough. We got enough juice here to kick the living hell out of Hanahan. Wormy, use your anger about Bettina and Chad to have your best game of the year. The offensive line will make holes that you could drag a dead mule through. But we got to find a way to stay angry and hostile against our opponents. This thing called team is a holy word to me. I'll beat the shit out of anyone who brings their poison to this locker room again. You hear me, Wormy? You hear me, Chad? Now, let's take all this bad feeling—all of it—and make Hanahan High feel bad, real bad."

A cheer went up as Coach Jefferson and his assistant entered from the rear, sensing a team incorrigible in its will to win. What Ike had let loose among us was the dream-stuff of worthy coaches.

Hanahan was the game that provided my team with the limitless momentum that would carry us to the state semifinal in Columbia. As we lined up that night, I could feel the first cool tinctures of autumn in the Low Country air. When we kicked off, I had a footrace with Ike down the field, and we both avoided two of their blockers. We both hit the ball carrier at the same time and drove him out of bounds on his own 25 and into the midst of his team. Ike and I rose screaming before being overrun by our jubilant teammates. Whatever incubus or disease had invaded our locker room had received its banishment on that first play and would not return that season. A fierce tenacity remained our trademark.

Wormy Ledbetter ran the ball more than thirty times, many times coming right up the middle, where I had my best night of blocking that year. The offensive line moved like a pride of lions as we fired off that line with aggression and certitude. I pancake-blocked four of their linemen, putting them flat on their backs as I watched Wormy crashing into defensive backs with his head lowered and his legs churning like an eggbeater. When Niles faked to Wormy going off-tackle, it opened the field for Chad and Ike, who both scored long touchdowns after Niles laid it in their hands as though he were tossing loaves of bread high into the night air.

That night, Wormy set a school record by scoring five rushing touchdowns and gaining more than two hundred yards on the ground. Niles completed ten of twelve passes. Our defense played as though there were a forest fire in the end zone behind us. Hanahan didn't score until the final minutes of the game, when our second string gave up a harmless field goal. When the final whistle blew, we had defeated the fifth-ranked team in the state by an amazing score of 56–3. Our fans flooded the field after the game, but this time there was no pulling down the goalposts. A most miraculous thing had occurred—our long-suffering football fans were becoming accustomed to winning.

Drifting through that boisterous crowd was an entrance into wonderland for me. I had longed for a normal life for so long that it seemed like an unobtainable ideal. But here is what it was at last—my taking leave of a football field, shaking hands with my Hanahan opponents, receiving the congratulations of fans and teammates, being hugged by girls whose names I didn't even know, by cheerleaders whose uniforms were as sweaty as mine—yes, this was now my new normality, not being hand-cuffed to a bed at a mental hospital, paralyzed by drugs. I liked being part of a team with a game plan and a way of deliverance for a boy who knew how much he needed it. I drifted toward the locker room, believing I was savoring the ecstasy of the moment, until I realized I was postponing the inevitable. The real reason for my hesitation to join in the jubilation of my teammates was my fear of taking Molly Huger to the sock hop after the game.

When I entered the dimly lit gymnasium, the awful reminder hit me like a well-aimed meteorite that I had never been to a high school dance before and had no idea how to conduct myself. Nor was I sure how to set my face—a confident smile, an easy nonchalance, a cocky watchfulness. I found myself simply defenseless as I felt my face congeal into a dewy lostness.

I saw Molly approach from across the gym. She had changed out of her cheerleading uniform and was dressed in a simple skirt and blouse and the white socks that the basketball coach required for even the most soft-footed dancer. She rushed forward to meet me, and surprised me by hugging me and kissing me playfully on the cheek. "What a great game, Leo. This team has a chance to go the distance."

"It already has, for me," I told her.

A song ended. The disc jockey for the evening and the rest of the year was the unflappable Trevor Poe. I heard him say, "One of our all-stars, Leo King, has just entered the room. I'd like to call on him and his beau-tiful date, Molly Huger, to lead off the next dance. I'd also like to call on his cocaptain, Ike Jefferson, and his pretty date, Betty Roberts, to join them in the first slow dance of the evening. Slow dance! Doesn't it just make your toes curl to think about? Now, let's hear some well-deserved applause for our cocaptains. Ah, that's it. Last year, Peninsula High was ranked last in the league and here we stand undefeated beneath the eyes of man and God. I call this the Cocaptain Dance. The floor is theirs until

I give the signal with my tambourine. Now, let the deejay work his showmanship."

Trevor set the needle down and Bert Kaempfert's "Wonderland by Night" flooded the gym with notes so sensuous and romantic that each one seemed honey-flecked. Taking Molly into my arms was one of the defining moments of my life. Her cheek touched mine and her hand pulled me close. Her breath was minty and fresh when she whispered, "I love this song." I wished I could force her to spend all eternity whispering in my ear. As we danced, the hushed crowd watched us in breathless silence. I caught Ike's eye and he winked at me. Feeling one-tenth sexy for the first time, I winked back with the palmy confidence of a world-famous womanizer or a Left Bank boulevardier on the prowl in Paris, instead of a loser on his first date. Molly smelled like the climbing jasmine that overwhelmed the trellises in my mother's summer garden. I could breathe in sunshine and balsam in her hair, and her breasts felt soft and yielding, yet untouchable.

Trevor tapped his tambourine, and the rest of the school joined us. "Wonderland by Night" would be my favorite song for the rest of my life because of Molly Huger's bright eyes, shapely lips, pretty face, lovely body—because I felt my soul leave my own fortressed country of hurt and surrender in the time it took for a ninety-second song to begin and end. I was dizzy with my love of Molly when I spotted Niles and Fraser motioning to us from the front door. Taking Molly's hand, I led her through the frenzied dancers who were dancing to the Beatles' "Sgt. Pepper's Lonely Hearts Club Band."

Though it shouldn't have surprised me, Fraser and Molly threw their arms around each other and began silently weeping. They excused themselves and rushed to the ladies' room on the other side of the gym, leaving me and Niles alone.

"We just visited Starla in the hospital," Niles said. "She's still groggy as hell, but we told her all about the game. She laughed when she heard that Chad was dating Bettina and that Molly sought revenge by asking you to the dance."

"Why'd she laugh?"

"Starla's always had a thing about mischief," Niles said. "She loves to see things stirred up, everything simmering, right to the boiling point."

"Why aren't Chad and Bettina at the dance?" I asked.

"Fraser's positive that Chad has taken her to the beach house on Sullivan's Island, trying to get laid."

"Ike handled the crisis well tonight," I said.

"The cat's a leader," Niles said. "It comes natural to him."

"Why did Fraser and Molly start crying when they saw each other?"

"They've been best friends for a long time," Niles said. "Fraser started crying as soon as she saw you dancing with Molly. She can't remember a time when Chad and Molly weren't sweethearts."

"I think Molly really likes me," I said. "I really do."

Niles studied me for a moment, and I could study him in return as he tried to form the correct words in his mind, truthful words but not ones that would injure an already wounded spirit.

"Toad," he said, "we're not in these girls' league. We're playthings to them. We're not the boys they're going to turn to when they get serious about life. Chad's convinced Fraser that she's the homeliest girl in the world. She needs me now because I think she's the nicest girl I've ever met, and she's a doll too. I've always had to pick out girls who thought they were ugly as homemade sin, and they're always grateful for my attention. Then Starla gets a wild hair up her ass and tells me we're running away from another orphanage."

"Why do you always go with her?" I asked.

"She couldn't survive without me."

"Why don't you talk her out of it?"

"You checked out my sister's listening skills?"

"No, I guess I haven't."

"That's because she ain't got any," Niles said.

"Why do you put up with it?"

"She's all I've got," Niles answered. "Maybe all I'll ever have."

"Nah," I said, "you're the star quarterback. Star quarterbacks get anything they want."

"This year's going too good," he said. "It's scaring the shit out of me."

"Then enjoy it."

"Can't. Here's the one given of my and my sister's life: we're not allowed to have a good time." Niles brightened. "Look there, Toad: two pretty girls looking for us. It doesn't get much better than that, does it?"

"It's at the top of my list."

Molly took my hand and led me back out onto the dance floor where we danced every dance, slow or fast or in between, for the rest of that magical evening. Dancing with Molly Huger became the standard by which I measured all the rare incursions of magic into my life. She was a high-spirited dancer with a natural gracefulness that came wrapped in sexy undertones. That night as I listened to Trevor announce every song with a brief, witty, and sometimes bawdy introduction, I learned that I loved to dance, and could feel myself grow better at it as the night wore on. Looseness was the bright essence of the dance, the prominent ingredient necessary to let the bloodstream join the rhythm of the music and the girl whose hand you held: two bloodstreams, two bodies conjoined until looseness took command and swirled you into a zone of comfort where you'd never been before.

There was a commotion at the front door. Sheba Poe made one of the cinematic entrances that would become her trademark, and her brother announced the noteworthiness of the moment. In his beret and sunglasses, Trevor beat time on the palm of his hand with his tambourine as Sheba danced into the middle of the floor. Of course, she could not just date the president of the National Honor Society or the captain of the basketball team. No, Sheba Poe had brought the regimental commander of The Citadel as her inaugural date of the year.

"At center court, ladies and gentlemen, is the undiscovered starlet of stage and silver screen—that sultry siren of the forbidden night, that unforgettable vixen known to all of you as the delectable Sheba Poe. Her date is the redoubtable regimental commander of The Citadel, Cadet Colonel Franklin Lymington, from Ninety Six, South Carolina. You know Ninety Six? It's right next to Ninety Seven and just down the road from One Hundred, South Carolina."

The audience booed Trevor with good-natured relish and marveled that he had been a South Carolina resident for such a short period yet had already milked the comedy from one of the state's most oddly named towns. Trevor then put on Bill Haley and the Comets' "Rock Around the Clock." He pulled Sheba up on the stage with him, and the twins performed the sexiest, most orgasmic dance I had ever seen. It drove the black kids at the dance wild, and the twins' gyrations freed them from the inhibitions they had carried to a formerly all-white high school. The poor regimental commander from Ninety Six stood watching his date perform a sinuous, leopardlike dance that looked part Zulu and part nervous breakdown.

As Trevor put on the next record, he said, "There are people who are not dancing in this gym. Bashfulness is banned. Get bold. Everyone here is going to dance to the next song. So get ready. Sheba and I will show you how it's supposed to be done. Then you follow our lead."

"The Stroll" blasted through the speakers, and Trevor leaped in a graceful, featherlike jump from the stage. I remembered my brother, Steve, trying to teach me that dance when we were both small boys, and how we would strut and show off in front of my parents as they applauded every exaggerated move. Molly took my hand, and we began our own version of the stroll down the center of the gymnasium. We added jerks and shakes and spontaneous throes that were brand-new to both of our bodies, and people began to clap in appreciation of our unpracticed duet. In front of us, I watched as Sheba and Trevor separated and went trolling along the front line of the crowd to pull out the shiest, most unnoticed students and make them join the dance.

Being a failed teenager is not a crime, but a predicament and a secret crucible. It is a fun-house mirror where distortion and mystification lead to the bitter reflections that sometimes ripen into self-knowledge. Time is the only ally of the humiliated teenager, who eventually discovers that the golden boy of the senior class is the bald, bloated drunk at the twentieth reunion, and that the homecoming queen married a wife beater and philanderer and died in a drug rehabilitation center before she was thirty. The prince of acne rallies in college and is now head of neurology, and the homeliest girl blossoms in her twenties, marries the chief financial officer of a national bank, and attends her reunion as the president of the Junior League. But since a teenager is denied a crystal ball that will predict the future, there is a forced-march quality to this unspeakable rite of passage. When a girl feels the first drops of menstrual blood, how is she to know that this is the sacred stream of life, the stir of her blooming fertility, the world's thunderous answer to decay and death? And what is a boy to think when he studies the great surprise of semen in his hand, except that his body has become a firestorm and undiscovered volcano where lava is made in the furnace of his loins? It is an unforgivable crime for teenagers not to be able to absolve themselves for being ridiculous creatures at the most hazardous time of their lives.

As the dance broke up, Molly stood on her tiptoes and whispered to me, "I'm starved. Let's go get a barbecue sandwich at the Piggy Park."

"Sounds good to me," I said.

"Don't you think the Piggy Park has the best barbecue in town?" she asked.

"Never tasted better," I lied. Since I'd never been out on a date before, I had never ventured near that legendary national park of Charleston teenage bliss. It could also be a dangerous, hormonal gathering place that competing high schools wanted to claim as home territory. The undisputed kingpin of the Piggy Park was Wormy Ledbetter, with his greasy sycophants with their big muscles and borderline IQs. But I would have taken Molly Huger to the Berlin Wall if she had asked me in her sweet voice.

Niles and Fraser approached us at the same moment that Trevor came skipping up to us, working his tambourine like a gambler rolling dice. Before we could silence the noise, Ike and Betty entered our circle. Ike asked, "You going over to the Piggy Park, Toad?"

"Molly just gave me the marching orders."

"I've never seen any black people over there," Molly said with a worried look.

Ike laughed. "I'd rather go to a Klan rally. But Wormy invited me and all the black guys on the team. Said it'd be okay."

"Trevor, why don't you ride with Ike and Betty?" Fraser suggested. "Is Sheba off with her regimental commander? By the way, that's quite a catch."

"She'll dump him tomorrow," Trevor said. "She already thinks he's a hick, and he dances like some alien life form."

"Why don't you follow me in my car?" I said to Ike. "We can park together and watch out for each other."

"Good plan," Ike said. But I could sense his uneasiness, a little sick of desegregating one Woolworth's lunch counter after another as they appeared in infinite succession. "But if anything happens to Betty . . ."

Betty scoffed. "You worry about yourself, Ike Jefferson. Put a Coke bottle in my hands, and I can handle the three best white boys at the Piggy Park."

"You talk big, girl," Ike said, smiling for the first time.

"I talk truth, son."

"I find sexual tension so provocative," Trevor said, rattling his tambourine as we all laughed and headed for the parking lot.

At the Piggy Park on Rutledge Avenue, a stone's throw from Hampton Park, I drove to the far corner of the drive-in, leaving room for Ike to pull up beside me. Molly proved that she was a regular at the place by immediately ordering a Coke with a barbecue sandwich platter. Suddenly, it hit me in a flash of blazing insight that Niles lived in an orphanage and did not have a nickel to his name. "Let's get four of those," I said. "My treat, Niles and Fraser."

"You're a good man, Toad," Niles said, and I could hear the relief in his voice.

Wormy Ledbetter strode out to greet us, accompanied by some of his lowbrow entourage. I stiffened at his approach. There was always a trace of the lynch mob in Wormy's eyes. But he entered our realm as a teammate tonight. As Niles and I got out of the car, he embraced us fiercely and said that our defeat of Hanahan made for the best day of his life. Then he looked over at Ike and said, "Get out of the fucking car, Jefferson."

Ike did, and Wormy rushed over to hug him in full view of white Charleston. In that single gesture, something broke forever in the mystery that was the South. "Goddamn, you were great tonight, Ike," said Wormy. "So were Niles and the Toad. Goddamn, all great."

"But my father gave you the game ball," Ike said. "He hasn't done that all year."

"The biggest honor of my life," Wormy said, as emotional and vulnerable as I had ever seen that flesh-eating redneck. "Tell your daddy I said so, you hear?"

"I'll tell him," Ike said.

Wormy walked back to the realm of his Wormydom, and our trays came out. The carhop fixed them expertly on our windows and the smell of hickory-smoked hog filled the car like an anthem to hunger itself. I wolfed down my sandwich in record-setting time and so did Niles in the backseat. We had just played a forty-eight-minute football game and danced the night away, and our primitive, almost desperate hunger caught us both by surprise.

Niles said, "I could eat that whole hog, including his eyeballs and asshole."

Fraser looked shocked, then answered, "That's the crudest thing I've ever heard anyone say. Don't you think, Molly?"

"It ranks high," Molly said, but she was giggling.

Just as suddenly she wasn't giggling, and her expression turned fearful and cold. Following her eyes, I turned and saw Chad Rutledge's old-model Chrysler LeBaron pulling into the Piggy Park, doing a slow circumnavigation of the drive-in and doing it twice, so he would be sure to be noticed by all present. Twice, he passed directly in front of us and tooted his horn, trying to get Molly's attention. But he failed to get her to look up from her sandwich. Beside him, Bettina Trask rode in triumph, the smile of a low-rent, cut-rate Cleopatra lighting up her face.

"That bastard," I heard Fraser say in back.

Niles groaned. "Jesus, he's mocking Wormy to his face."

Chad had chosen the parking spot nearest to the picnic benches, where Wormy and his troop of no-goodniks hung out with their cigarette-smoking girlfriends and beer-drinking buddies. Though I felt like a voyeur to some kind of disaster, my eyes were riveted to the scene of the skirmish that was about to take place. I did not hear Ike get out of his car or make his way to my window.

"Let this one go, teammates," Ike said. "This is like taunting a king cobra. Whatever happens, Chad is asking for it."

"Why is he doing it?" I asked.

"Because he knows his place in this city," Molly answered. "He's untouchable, and he wants to prove it to Wormy. And to you, Leo and Ike. And to you, Niles."

"I'm curious, Molly, Fraser. What does Chad think of us, really?" Niles asked.

"Actually, he likes all of you very much," Molly said. "He's grateful how you've accepted him on the team."

"Deep down?" Niles pressed. "How does he feel deep down?"

Fraser closed her eyes, then said calmly, "He thinks you are all beneath him. Way beneath him."

"It's fun to know you're appreciated," Ike said. He kept his eyes sealed on the action near the front of the drive-in.

When it happened, it happened with quickness and contained the devastating power of surprise. Wormy leaped off the picnic table and rushed to Chad's car, opened the front door, and pulled Chad out by his hair. Chad's scream found itself muffled by the jeering laughter and the applause of Wormy's friends, who'd been alerted to the imminence of the attack. Backhanding Chad twice on the face, Wormy challenged him to a fair fight and put up his fists in a boxer's experienced stance.

If Chad had just fought Wormy, man to man, I think the outcome of the evening might have had a more honorable end. But instead of raising his fists, Chad answered in a loud voice, audible, I think, over most of the peninsula: "Wormy, my father taught me never to lower myself by fighting white trash."

"Oh, he did, did he?" Wormy said. "My, my. Well, I have a different theory. I think you're chickenshit from the bottom of your feet to the top of your head. A South of Broad pussy too scared to defend himself."

Wormy stepped forward and, with his open palm, began to slap Chad's face hard—slap, slap, slap—until Chad screamed, "I'd kick the shit out of you, Wormy, but my parents taught me to always take the high road and never let a common redneck drag me down to his level."

"Defend yourself, pussy. This ain't no fun. This ain't no fight. How do you fight a man without no pride?" Wormy said to the crowd, then surprised everyone by ripping off Chad's expensive and well-tailored shirt, leaving Chad looking as naked as a slug in a summer garden. It is difficult for a shirtless man to be taken seriously in a parking lot where every other man is wearing a shirt. Until that moment, I had never considered that possibility.

Viewing his domain and his options, Wormy looked around the Piggy Park, then down at the shirt he had torn from Chad's body. In a moment of rare creativity for him, Wormy blew his nose into Chad's swell shirt, then threw it on the ground and kicked dirt and debris all over it. Without a pause, Wormy walked around Chad's car, opened the passenger door, and offered his hand to Bettina Trask. To my surprise, Bettina took Wormy's hand and let herself be led by the arm in a garish triumphal march into the parlor beside the barbecue pit.

In a humiliation as complete as I had ever witnessed, Chad watched this event unfold, trembling with helplessness and rage. He shook his fist heavenward and shouted toward the open door, "Hey, Wormy, you fucking shit-bird redneck! I'm going home to lift weights for a year. Then I'm coming back to whip your goddamn ass. One year from tonight. That's a promise. And I'm a man of my word. I'm a descendant from one of the signers of the Declaration of Independence, so you know I'm a man of honor. One year, and I come back to kick your ass up and down and all over the Piggy Park."

Wormy walked out for a final time, shaking his head sadly. Then he backhanded poor Chad to his knees. "Shut up, Chad," Wormy said. "I'm eating a sandwich with my girlfriend now."

The laughter was unbearable. In my car, we watched as Chad got into his car, backed it up, then headed our way instead of exiting on Rutledge Avenue. When he got in front of my car, he shook his fist at me, then sat on his horn, maniacal and unhinged. I heard something to my right and turned to see Molly getting out of my car, shutting the door, and walking calmly to Chad's car. He flung the door open, motioned for her to enter, and Molly sat down in the place she was born to sit.

Though I struggled with a restless exhaustion for most of that night, I slept hard in the last hour before the alarm sounded at four-thirty, when I awoke to the starlit world of paperboys. I rode my Schwinn slowly down to Colonial Lake, every muscle in my body burning with fatigue and every cell of my body nearing collapse from the humiliation of Molly's public desertion of me. As I pedaled slowly, the thought occurred to me that I had just suffered through the most unsuccessful first date in the history of the sexes. Caught up in a maelstrom of an obsession I could not shake, I tried to recall every salient detail of how I had behaved with Molly from the moment she kissed me on the cheek to her measured, purposeful departure from the front seat of my car to the more familiar one of Chad's.

What had hurt me most keenly was the unnatural coldness of Molly's leave-taking. It was breathless in its wordlessness, the lack of farewell or a blown good-bye kiss or any attempt of an explanation. I wished that she had aborted our evening with a little more finesse and allowed me to take her home, endure my unbearable awkwardness at her front door, then called Chad for their tender reunion. That she left me publicly, with my whole team as eyewitnesses to my mortification, was nightmare enough, but to do it with Niles and Chad's sister in my backseat lent a touch of malice or inattention I didn't think I deserved.

In the backseat, Niles and Fraser had sat paralyzed, bee-stung into silence.

Finally, I had said, "You know, I thought we were double-dating. Now it seems like I'm your chauffeur."

But there was a knock on the window and Trevor jumped in to occupy the space just vacated by Molly. "I saw the whole thing. It was pure Elizabethan drama with a little barbecue sauce thrown in. We live in a town that is provincially bigoted against the culturally astute, effeminate young men such as myself. Allow me a minute to explain. Since I have arrived in the city limits of Charleston, I have been variously described as a faggot, a queer, a cocksucker, a fudge packer, a fairy queen, a sodomite, a pervert, and a wide assortment of other unpardonable slurs. Of course, in my case, such slurs are perfectly applicable. I can make all your mean thoughts about Molly go bye-bye, Leo."

Niles said from the backseat in a tone of innocent wonder: "How have you gotten this old, Trevor, without somebody killing you?"

"I have my tricks of the trade." Trevor said it so good-naturedly that I started to laugh.

I said, "Trevor, I don't even know what gay people do to each other."

"And I don't want to know," Niles said.

"Ditto," Fraser said, putting her hands over her ears.

"It involves meat hooks and razor blades and flamethrowers and dildos made from buffalo penises."

"What's a dildo?" Niles asked.

"Poor mountain idiot." Trevor sighed.

"I don't know, either," I said.

"Look, Leo. After what just happened to you, I'm going to give you a free introductory lesson, and I'll waive the usual initiation fees as a personal favor."

"Thanks, Trevor," I said. "Just by getting in the car, you saved me from an embarrassing situation. I'll never forget it."

"You baked me cookies," Trevor said. "First day in Charleston, and I'm eating benne wafers baked by the loneliest kid in the world. Molly shouldn't've treated you that way. She should be ashamed."

"Leo doesn't expect a girl like Molly to go with a boy like him," Fraser said.

"Why the hell not?" Niles asked.

"Oh, don't get defensive on me, Niles," she flashed back. "The differences are too great, and as a Charleston boy, Leo knows that. Charleston society keeps in the shadows, but it's still the most important force in this town."

"Got your word on that?" Niles said.

"You're walking into a trap, honey," Trevor warned Fraser.

"You can always trust the word of someone related to a signer of the Declaration of Independence," Niles mocked with a reptilian cold-bloodedness. "I learned that from a great man tonight. A guy who could run his mouth, but couldn't use his fists."

"Chad was trained to be a gentleman," Fraser said defensively.

"Cut, my dear, cut. This scene is getting out of hand," Trevor advised Fraser.

"I come from people who never heard of the Declaration of Independence, who couldn't read a word of it if they had to," Niles said. "My folks wouldn't read a book if you put a gun to their dicks. But they can read people all day long and always get it right."

"You're going to say something you don't mean, Niles," Trevor said. "Let's change the subject to the price of mangoes in Argentina or the life expectancy of a no-see-um."

"You were bragging about your people's ability to read other people," Fraser reminded Niles.

"Your brother, Chad, is not half the man the Toad is, or Trevor, or Ike," said Niles. "And this will be the shock of the night for you, Fraser. Or me.

He's had every opportunity in the world, and he still ain't worth a shit. Could you drive Fraser home, Toad? I'm going over to the next car to be with the niggers, where I belong."

Niles left my car even as a distraught Fraser tried to grab his arm. Then I heard him ask Ike, "Can I catch a ride back to the orphanage with you and Betty?"

"That's not what I meant to say," Fraser murmured tearfully as she watched Niles climb into Ike's backseat. "It came out all wrong."

"Why don't you tell that to Niles?" Trevor said. "Honey, the tongue is the most powerful and destructive organ in the human body."

But Ike had already cranked his car and was heading toward Rutledge Avenue. I followed and drove Fraser home. Trevor escorted her to the door with his matchless sense of the dramatic, then performed an elegant soft-shoe back to the car.

I parked my bicycle by the *News and Courier* truck, lifted the first bale of newspapers, and cut through the steel binders with my wire cutters. I began to fold the papers quickly, securing them with a new and stronger rubber band. Mr. Haverford's immense hulk made a shadow behind me, and I wished him good morning without looking up.

"You ever go out with women, Mr. Haverford?" I asked.

"Broke that bad habit years ago."

"Why?"

"Played the law of averages. Went out with a lot of women when I was young. One hundred percent of them were assholes or heartbreakers. I could take the assholes, but the heartbreakers could inflict some real damage."

"I can't imagine you heartbroken."

"I was married once," he said. "I ever tell you that?"

"No, sir," I said, surprised. "Who'd you marry?"

"Mrs. Haverford, you little bastard," he said, smirking. "We even had a kid, a boy. The kid would be in his late twenties by now. My wife fell in love with a welder in the navy. They moved to San Diego. Never heard from her or the boy again."

"You never heard from your son?"

"I don't even know if he's alive," Mr. Haverford said. "He's ignored my every attempt to stay in touch with him. What kind of sorry kid wouldn't want to get to know his own daddy?"

"An asshole, Mr. Haverford," I said. "Anyone who wouldn't be proud to have you as an old man isn't worth a shit."

"I thought you'd killed that Hanahan halfback last night," he said. "That was your best tackle of the year."

"You were at the game?"

"Got a season ticket."

"We got Wando High next week," I said.

"You'll cut their asses," he said. "I like this colored coach of yours. You guys have only jumped offsides twice this season. That's good coaching. And his kid, Ike: he's a bearcat."

"A great guy too," I said.

"Be careful of humanity," he said. "It's a bad breed overall."

"Eugene Haverford: the philosopher," I said.

"Eugene Haverford: the realist. Anytime you want to talk to me about the girl, I'll be happy to."

"Girl? What girl?"

"The heartbreaker," he said softly. "It happened last night, didn't it, kid? Take your time. I'm here every morning. Half-drunk but always ready to talk with an assful of life behind me and a nickel's worth left to live. Now, go deliver the news of the world to Charleston."

CHAPTER 20

Pygmalion

The following Sunday, while I nursed my wounded ego and obsessed over Molly's abandonment, I went to check on Harrington Canon. His coloring had displeased me last time I visited him, and he had been in bed for the past week. I had noticed that his listlessness had come to rest in the corners of his dried-out eyes. The only thing he had said to me was, "I forgot to get my flu shot, Leo."

"Let me get you to a doctor," I had pleaded, alarmed.

"Get out of my house, interloper," he had responded.

When I approached his house on Tradd Street that morning, I could sense a dissolution of a place and a civilization. I opened the gate and was immediately surrounded by a dozen neighborhood cats that over a long period had become both a hobby and the objects of Mr. Canon's most sustained devotion. They surrounded me howling and meowing and impatient. Mr. Canon's life was systematic and almost metronomic in its sense of order; his clocks were set with grim precision. But I could tell that some sort of breakdown was in motion, and I had to feed a pride of aggravated cats before I could walk upstairs to check on Mr. Canon. The smell of excrement nearly overpowered me halfway up his circular staircase, but I stiffened my resolve and knocked at his bedroom door.

"Leave me alone, Leo," he said in a weak voice. "I don't need your help."

"I don't believe you, Mr. Canon. Just let me in to clean up a bit."

"This is very personal," he said. "I've got too much pride to let you see me like this."

"Pride's great. I can't wait until I get me a little bit. But I've noticed it's hard to have much pride when you've got shit running down your leg."

"I couldn't get up," he said. "I just couldn't. I think I ruined my four-poster bed."

I opened the door and Mr. Canon began to cry. I worked with efficiency and speed, getting him out of his bed and into the bathroom, where I pulled off his pajamas. When he was naked, I turned on the water of his shower, and then walked in with him even though I was fully clothed. I soaped him down from head to foot, then washed him until his skin shone as red as a baby's.

"I order you to stop this. This is none of your concern," he said.

"It's my sole concern. Please notice I'm the only person here."

Drying him off with a fresh towel, I dusted his body with talcum powder, then helped him to brush his teeth and shave. Sitting him on the commode, I made sure he balanced himself against the sink and the claw-footed tub, then I went into the disaster area of his bedroom to find a fresh pair of pajamas and a set of fur-lined slippers. Though it took the moves of a contortionist, I finally got Mr. Canon into his fresh garments. Only then could I feel a slight diminishment of his abysmal fear.

"Now you've got to help me do something, Mr. Canon," I said.

"I don't follow the orders of wannabes," he said, his fighting spirit returning.

"It's going to take a couple of hours to get your room in shape. Let me put you in your guest room while I'm getting this done."

"Sounds like a good idea," he said. "I'm exhausted. Will you get me my pills?"

"Yes, and I'm going to make you some breakfast," I said. "Then, I'm going to call Dr. Shermeta."

Mr. Canon's bedroom had the feel of a surgical tent after a ruinous battle, and it was good to pull back the clean sheets of the smaller bed in his guest room. I brought him his pills and supervised his drinking several glasses of water for his dehydrated body.

Back in his room, I gathered his pajamas, sheets, blankets, and pillow-cases into a heap, then carried it downstairs and soaked it all in two great sinks that I overloaded with soapsuds and disinfectants. Then I returned to attack that room with mops, sponges, towels, and citrus-scented clean-ers. For a solid hour, I removed deposits of shit, vomit, and blood from every corner.

When I needed a break, I went down to the kitchen and put on a pot of coffee. I also fried bacon, poached eggs, made biscuits, and brought a glass of orange juice to Mr. Canon. I placed a call to Dr. Shermeta. The blood had frightened me. The doctor's wife said he had been summoned to the Medical University on an emergency, but she promised he would call as soon as she could reach him.

I felt overwhelmed. I called my house, delighted when my father an-swered. "Father, listen to me. I need you with me at Mr. Canon's house. I'm in over my head. I need you. Do you hear me? He seems like he's dying."

"I'm there, son," he said. "Right now. You and Mr. Canon hold on, and we'll get this thing done right."

"There was blood all over his bed," I said. "That doesn't sound good, does it?"

"I'm calling for an ambulance," my father said.

"It might make Mr. Canon mad," I said.

"He's too weak to get too mad."

I fed Mr. Canon his breakfast, spooning as much food into him as he could take. He was asleep in the guest bedroom before the ambulance arrived, and I was feeding a dozen more cats while the paramedics car-ried the stretcher upstairs. My father came through the front door as the men were carrying Mr. Canon out toward the ambulance, where a small crowd had gathered.

In the next two hours, my father and I cleaned Mr. Canon's house from top to bottom. When we went to lock up, my father said, "Those cats are your responsibility until Mr. Canon's well enough to take care of himself. Now, let us get ourselves home to relieve your mother of her clubhouse duties."

My father and mother had taken charge of Starla's recovery, bringing her and Niles to our house while she recuperated from the eye operation. When we got to our house, there were enough strange cars parked up and down our street to make it look like a main thoroughfare instead of the backwater side street it was; there was something about the term "sick orphan" that got to the hearts of the parent-teacher association.

Our house remained filled all day with visitors who brought slain gardens of flowers up to Starla's room and enough candy for Starla to start her own chocolate shop. My mother's eyes were frantic and undone when my father and I returned home. "You take over," she said. "I can't take another minute of this."

"You go back to our room," my father said. "Put in some earplugs. Take a nap. Leo and I will deal with the hordes."

I skipped up the stairs to check on Starla's condition but found that her sick room had been transformed into a makeshift beauty parlor by Trevor and Sheba Poe. All of the Peninsula High cheerleaders except Molly were reclining on the floor with cotton balls stuffed between their toes as Trevor went around giving pedicures and painting toenails in a color he called "gaudy fire-engine red." He had already done their fingernails, and both the twins had already cut, washed, dried, and set the hair of every girl on the squad, black and white. Sheba was in the process of applying makeup to the girls, transforming them into stunning creatures who looked nothing like the girls I went to class with every day.

Sheba said, "Get on out of here right now, Leo. This is the Palace of Perfect Beauty, where Trevor and I are turning these Renegade girls into goddesses."

"I wanted to find out how Starla was doing," I said.

"They're going to do me last," Starla said. "But I'd rather face a firing squad. I've never been to a beauty parlor."

"You won't believe how pretty we're going to make you," Trevor said.

"God's going to think he put a new angel down on earth," Sheba said. "Now, beat it, Leo. Skedaddle."

"Take me with you, please," begged Starla.

I found Ike and Niles out in the backyard. My father had assumed the role of disc jockey again, and I heard the sound of the Rolling Stones pouring out of the windows, startling the fiddler crabs.

"I need to ask you boys a question," I said. I took a seat beside them and looked north toward The Citadel. The tide was spilling in fast, moon-swollen and moon-timed.

"Ask away," Ike said.

"How in God's name did Trevor learn to cut a girl's hair, style it, give her both a manicure and a pedicure, then apply makeup like he was an expert in the field?"

"I bet he's never thrown a football or caught a baseball," Niles said. "And I bet he doesn't give a rat's ass, either."

"I've never seen a cat like him," Ike admitted. "He seems three-quarters girl to me."

"What's the other quarter?" Niles asked.

"That's girl too," Ike said.

"Yet he's such a great guy," Niles said. "He makes me laugh. He's involved in everything in school. He and his sister have made quite a mark on the school—hell, on all of us."

"My mother says their IQs are off the charts." I turned back to the house and said, "My father needs to be sending some of these kids on their way."

"I've noticed something," Ike said. "Kids love to hang out at their principal's house. It's like getting to see a part of them that is secret or forbidden. I used to see that when my old man had his football team over for a cookout. Guys would be going crazy to see that he had an actual life off the field and away from his office."

"My mother has never let a student into her house until Sheba and Trevor came on the scene," I said. "They gave her no choice. They forced their way into her front door. But not into her heart."

"Why do you say that?" Niles asked.

"My mother doesn't like the twins, and I can't figure out why," I said. "She's always loved artistic kids, and even she admits that they're both the most talented artists she's been around. I think she believes they draw trouble to themselves and to anyone who hangs around with them."

"They got no daddy?" Ike asked.

"Not that I've met," I lied.

"You got a daddy, Niles?" Ike asked, but with some unease.

"Virgin birth, pal," Niles said. "You ever heard of 'em?"

"Yeah, one," Ike said.

"I'm your second."

"It doesn't seem like Niles wants to talk about his family, Ike," I said.

"Very perceptive, Toad," Niles said. "Good call."

"I'd like to know how you and Starla got yourself into this position, is all," said Ike testily.

"You asked Betty how she got to the orphanage?" Niles asked.

"She cries every time I ask her," Ike said. "So I don't bring it up anymore."

"Take a hint," Niles said. "You don't want to hear my story. Neither one of you."

"Why not?" I asked. "We're your friends."

"If you're my friends, then listen to me: I don't want to tell you. It's a lousy story with some bad luck and mean people thrown in. I like you guys too much to tell my story."

"How will we really get to know you," I asked, "if we don't know where you came from or who your people are?"

Niles grabbed me hard by the back of the neck and pulled my face close to his. "Don't you understand, Toad? We don't *know* who our people are. Why do you think we're in this mess? Because we don't know anything, not a goddamn thing. I was five when I was put into a goddamn orphanage. Starla was four. Someday I'll tell you two what those first years were like. I'll tell you what happened to my mama and daddy. But I'll start with this: my mama was thirteen when I was born. Can you imagine having a mama all of thirteen years older than you? Starla and I've been looking for her all our lives. That's why Starla keeps running away. She thinks Mama must still be alive, but just doesn't know how to find us."

"She could check records and documents," Ike said.

"Ike," Niles said, shaking his head. "Poor Ike. You don't understand: Mama can't read or write. She couldn't have filled out any documents."

"That's all terrible, Niles," I said. "Sorry we got so personal."

"I'll tell you the whole thing someday," he promised. "But I'll want to have Starla with me."

"Why's that?" Ike wanted to know.

"Because this is the last year of it," Niles said. "Next year I don't even have an orphanage to run to because I'll be too old. We've run every place we can think to run, and now we're out of places. We spent so many years looking for our past, we didn't once worry about our futures. Now that the future's here in our face, that's something really scary, man. Scarier than anything we've faced."

"You need to get a plan," I said.

"Plan?" Niles said. "Life goes around in circles, and Starla and I catch on when it slows down. That's always been our plan."

"Toad and I are going to apply to The Citadel next year," Ike said. "You could come with us."

"Takes money I ain't got," he said.

"Red Parker likes the way you play football," Ike said. "I heard him tell my old man that."

"There'll be some scholarship money lying around," I said. "I'll bet the monsignor will know where to find some too."

"So that's what a plan sounds like," Niles said, his eyes pensive as he stared out against the still-rising tide.

My father leaned his head out the back door and called us all back inside, excitement in his voice. The house had the isolated feel of an abandoned village, yet the sheer number of flowers stuffed in vases or crammed in empty jelly jars made it smell like a florist's greenhouse. As ordered, we took our seats facing the stairway. Even my mother had left her roost in her bedroom, lured by my father's uncontrollable jubilance.

At the top of the stairs, there was a stirring, some whispering, then a disturbance as Trevor glided down the stairs with his elfin gait and sat at the piano. He was followed by Betty, whom Ike escorted to a nearby chair. Next, Sheba floated down, swanlike. Her eyes turned toward the top of the stairs and she gave a hand sign to her brother. Trevor began to play the "Triumphal March" from *Aida* in lush, subdued notes.

We all stood there, faces lifted, as Starla Whitehead made her shy appearance into the downstairs world of light and anticipation. When she crossed the point of no return between the slant of shadow caused by the banked stairway and chandelier light in the dining room, she paused for an instant, allowing time for her newly healed eye to adjust.

The rest of us observed the commemorative transformation that the twins had performed on Starla, who made no attempt to hide her discomfort in the spotlight. Slowly, she came down the stairs with an awkward grace, Trevor adapting his march to her reluctance. The patch was gone and so were the ubiquitous dark glasses. Her glossy black hair was now in a short, swingy cut that was stunningly attractive. She looked like a French actress I had developed a crush on, whose face I always looked for in movie magazines when my father took me to get a haircut, but whose name played hide-and-seek with me as this girl of absolute invention made her way down the stairs. The name broke free and my tongue held it like a prize—Leslie Caron. How many secret lovers had Leslie Caron collected by the millions as projectors took her gamine face into dark theaters all over the world, I wondered?

But it was Starla Whitehead's eyes that caught and held my attention. Her gaze was straight and direct and perfect. She would have to adjust to walking the world as a beauty, and I could not have been more proud. Sheba began the round of applause and the rest of us joined in, even my mother. Starla's dark eyes dazzled, and her steady, brown gaze seemed able to register passion or rage with equal forcefulness. Between the twins' constant obsession with high drama and my own need to make corrections in a flawed and dangerous world, we had turned a wallflower into a knockout.

"Have you ever seen such a precious girl in your life?" Sheba asked. "She's a sight for horny eyes. Oh, excuse me, Dr. King, Mr. King! I got carried away."

My mother turned an icy stare on her, leaving my father to try to make amends. "All you kids have to stay for dinner. Leo and I'll rustle up some vittles."

"Vittles?" my mother asked with disdain.

"Food," my father said. "In cowboy movies, they call it vittles."

"I abhor cowboy movies," she said, and returned to her room.

There was moonlight on the water as we ate our meal by the small acreage of marsh that cleaved to our yard. The moon had a silken, electric effect on the Ashley River, prowling through the tides like something active and with a story to tell. It was a happy meal, one of the happiest I could ever remember. When my father said grace that night, he prayed for the boys in Vietnam and for Harrington Canon's recovery. He thanked God for making Starla's operation so successful, and he thanked Him for the success of the football team. It was a comprehensive prayer, and he even thanked God for making me his son and for finding Lindsay Weaver as his wife. "Ah, yes, Lord, and last, before I forget, thanks for the vittles we're about to enjoy."

As he finished, we heard the train coming up the Ashley River, going straight through the Citadel campus. Ike said, "I've grown up with the sound of that train."

"Trains have always given me hope," Sheba said. "That one especially."

"Why that one?" Betty asked.

"Because that's the train that's going to take me into a new life," Sheba said. "That's the train that's taking me west one of these days. To Hollywood."

"But that train is heading due north, sugar," my father said.

"No, no. You're wrong, Mr. King," Sheba said, closing her eyes. "It's heading for the Pacific. It's moving west."

"I'll never make you a scientist," Father said, smiling.

"You don't have to," Sheba said. "I'm already an actress."

CHAPTER 21

Prayer Book for the Wilderness

It was almost midnight when I walked down the institutional, crepuscular halls of the Medical University looking for room 1004, where the night attendant told me Harrington Canon had been assigned. My tennis shoes made rodentlike squeaks as I neared the nurses' station, announcing my presence as effectively as though I had an agitated magpie squawking on my shoulder. Feeling self-conscious enough, I felt yet more mortification as I observed the curiosity of every night nurse on duty at my noisy approach.

"Yes, young man?" one nurse asked, wearing a name tag that identified her as Verga.

"I'd like to look in on Mr. Canon," I said. "He doesn't have much family, and I wanted him to know he has some people looking out for him."

"Are you Leo King?" she said, going over a list.

"Yes, ma'am."

"You're the only one he has on his visitors' list," she said.

"His family's all in nursing homes," I said. "They are too infirm to visit."

"I see. And your relationship to Mr. Canon?"

"I help out in his antique store on King Street," I said. "Ever been to it?"

"I'm a nurse, not a millionaire," she said. Some of the faceless nurses looming over their charts laughed in appreciation.

"Is Mr. Canon going to be all right?" I asked. "It's nothing serious, is it?"

"Dr. Ray will examine him tomorrow," the nurse replied. "We'll know a lot more after that."

"What is Dr. Ray's specialty?" I asked.

"Oncology," she answered.

I couldn't believe a four-syllable word had escaped inclusion in my mother's indefatigable five-word-a-day vocabulary list, and this one had a barbed, ominous sound. "I don't know what that means, ma'am."

"Cancer," she said, and I was faced with the horrifying word at last. "He's in that room over there. We've got him medicated, but he's been restless all night."

It took several moments for my eyes to adjust to the prisonlike darkness when I peeked into his room.

"Who're you staring at like I was some kind of polecat, boy?"

"I thought you'd be asleep, Mr. Canon. I thought they'd give you something to help you sleep."

"I'm too worried to sleep."

"What're you worried about?"

"Just the little things. Incontinence, dementia, paralysis, unbearable pain, and then death itself."

"Don't worry. They'll all come in good time."

"You're just the person I don't need to see," he said. "Why did it take you so long to get up here?"

"I went back over to your house to feed your cats."

"They'll be fat as hogs if you stuff their guts twice a day."

"I didn't know. I've never owned a pet," I said. "My mother's allergic to animal fur."

"Once a day is sufficient," he said.

"I'll take care of it," I promised.

"A housekeeper will need to be hired," Mr. Canon said. "I left that four-poster bed a mess, I'm afraid. I was filled with shame that those sweet boys in the ambulance had to encounter me in such a situation."

"Those guys've seen everything," I said. "That's what my father told me as we were cleaning up your place."

"You cleaned up?"

"It's good as new. We couldn't save the sheets, but we saved everything else. We dusted, we polished, we cleaned. We made a good team. We even brought flowers in from the gardens."

"Thank you, rapscallion," he said. "Please thank your daddy for me. Neither of you were required to do it."

"My father said we were the only two people in a position to do anything. You were unconscious and fighting to live."

"I don't remember a thing about it," he admitted.

Nurse Verga stuck her head into the room. "Is this boy bothering you, Mr. Canon? We can send him on his way."

"You and your incompetent cheerleading squad of nurses are what's really bothering me," Mr. Canon grumbled. "This boy just fed my cats and cleaned my house. Why am I not asleep? Are you feeding me placebos instead of using effective drugs of sufficient potency?"

"It's time for a shot that will put you out for the night," she said. "I can get rid of the boy."

"I need him for another couple of minutes," Mr. Canon said. "Leo, I'll need you to place a call to my lawyer, Cleveland Winters, tomorrow. I've got some important decisions to make, and I'll need to make them in a hurry."

"The doctor will see you in the morning," I said. "He'll fix you up fine. You'll be back home in no time."

"That's how it works in books and movies," Mr. Canon said. "But something broke in me this morning. Something broke deep inside me, and whatever it was is going to kill me. Get that pussyfooting look off your face. I'm going to make up a long list of things for you to do. Customers to call. Scoundrels with accounts receivable, and other dealers who have things I own on consignment. I'm going to donate all my books to the Charleston Library. I need to talk to a curator at the Gibbes Museum of Art. You'll need to call the rector of St. Michael's, so he can come give me the last rites. I'd like you to bring me the Book of Common Prayer that's in the first drawer of my bedside table. My great-grandfather Canon was carrying it when he went down at the Battle of the Wilderness."

"No," I said, devastated. "I won't do it. I refuse to accept this. Dr. Ray is going to take care of all this tomorrow. You'll see. We'll be laughing about this tomorrow night. I'll tease you about this conversation for the next thirty years."

"Leo, Leo, I've told no one this. I'm not close enough to anyone to tell them. I chose a reclusive life because it seemed to fit me best. I was a bitter disappointment to both my mother and father. An only child never outgrows that. That's a wound that suppurates through the years; there's no healing, and not even time can touch it. I've told no one in Charleston, not even my beloved rector or my lawyer: I was diagnosed with leukemia two years ago. I'll never leave this hospital."

"Don't say that," I said. "Giving up's the worst thing you can do!"

"What in the hell am I listening to you for, Mr. Nobody? You've never even had a head cold."

"But I know all about giving up."

"Yes, I sometimes forget about your bouts with insanity," he said. "It gave me great pause before I took a lunatic into my store. But my Charleston values overcame my fears of the asylum."

"That there are saints like you who walk among us."

"You should be getting on home now," he said. I could see he was tiring.

"I'm staying here with you tonight," I said. "I'm sleeping in this chair."

"Preposterous! I'll not have it."

"My mother and father don't think you should be alone. At least for the first night."

"I've been alone my whole life," he said. "I'll make a deal with you: go sleep in your own bed tonight. But bring me my newspaper on your way to school in the morning."

"You sure you don't want me to stay?"

Mr. Canon exploded, "What must I do? Send up a smoke signal? You need to be home with your family, and I need to be alone with my thoughts."

"Call me in the middle of the night if you need me," I said. "I'm just ten minutes away."

"I snore," he said.

"So what?"

"It's such a low-class thing to do, snoring. Pipe fitters snore, used-car salesmen snore, welders snore, union members snore. Charleston aristocrats shouldn't snore. It seems unforgivable for a man of my stature to snore."

"The nurses were talking about it when I asked to visit," I said.

"What did those fishwives and scoundrels say?" he demanded.

"Said you were noisier than a volcano. Noisier than rain on a tin roof."

"I'll have their jobs," he stated, offended that his private life had been the subject of vile gossip. "Those magpies'll be sorry they ever heard the name of Harrington Canon."

There was a rattling sound at the door, and Nurse Verga brought a tray in with a small paper bonnet filled with pills and a serious-looking syringe. I knew that Mr. Canon was not a big fan of shots, so I was not surprised when he wailed, "My God, that shot could put a blue whale to sleep!"

"Probably," she said. "And it'll certainly put you to sleep."

"Do you know who to call, boy?" he asked.

"Your lawyer, your rector, someone at the Charleston Library, a representative at the Gibbes Museum of Art. Feed your cats."

"Once a day. Not twice. Change their kitty litter."

"Bring you your Book of Common Prayer that your great-grandfather carried with him into the Battle of the Wilderness."

"That's all I can think of now. I'm exhausted to the bones."

The medicine acted fast, and Harrington Canon was asleep in a matter of seconds with his hand in mine. Despite his insistence, I slept in a chair beside his bed. Of course, he snored throughout the night, a soft funny growling noise. Once, he woke and asked for a glass of ice water, which I gave to him, holding his head in my hand. At four-thirty in the morning, Nurse Verga woke me for my paper route, as I'd asked. I kissed Mr. Canon on the forehead as I whispered to him good morning and good-bye. I was lucky to have met him, and I knew it. I had many duties to perform for him that morning.

The following Friday, at the end of my first-period French class, a language I spoke with no facility and wrote in just a notch above idiocy, a message came from the principal's office. I went to my mother's severe bailiwick in the front hall. I tried to think of what I might have done to raise her ire, but could come up with nothing.

My mother was writing, treating the document with the same significance as though she were penning the final words of the Magna Carta. It was a very nunlike gesture of intimidation. When she finally spoke, she still did not interrupt her writing.

"Harrington Canon died this morning, Leo, not long after you left him. They think he had a heart attack. So he went fast and died in peace. His lawyer, Cleveland Winters, called and said you're the head pallbearer. Mr. Canon put it in his will that he wanted you to choose the other five pallbearers."

I lay my head on my mother's desk and began weeping softly.

My mother sniffed with displeasure. "Don't take it so hard, Leo. You knew he had to die. Everybody does someday."

Ignoring her, I continued to cry.

Finally she said, "I found him to be a most pretentious, unpleasant man."

"He was nice to me, Mother," I said. "At a time when not many people were."

"You made your own bed there, mister."

"So you've reminded me a few million times."

"Try not to be disrespectful in your grief," she said. "Mr. Canon was famous for being penurious. You worked for years for him without wages. He enjoyed slave labor."

"Why is it so disappointing to you when someone seems to like me? Why does it make you so angry?"

"You're talking nonsense, son."

"I don't think so, Lindsay." I heard my father's voice as he entered the door behind me. "So there's nothing our sweet boy can do to please you?"

"My standards might be higher than yours are, Jasper," she said. "My expectations for Leo are exacting, and I'm not ashamed of that."

"Or they might be too high for anyone to achieve," he said.

"He hasn't been a perfect son," she said. "Even you can admit that."

"I never wanted a perfect son," he said. "A human one was good enough for me."

"Harrington Canon was a crank and a leech on Leo," my mother said. "I don't see why his death merits such grief."

I cried out, "Mr. Canon was a sweetheart to me, Mother. You had to be around him awhile to understand him."

"I think there might have been something prurient in his interest in you."

"You mean you thought Mr. Canon wanted to screw me?" I asked, as incredulous as I had ever been in my life.

"You'll not use such language in the principal's office," she snapped.

"That's what the principal implied."

"She certainly did," my father agreed.

"I've always loathed old degenerates," Mother said.

"Mr. Canon was a gentleman," my father said. "And we have no reason to believe he was a degenerate."

"You just became one of his pallbearers," I said.

"A high honor, son," he said.

That same afternoon, after a grueling football practice, I rode my bicycle down Broad Street in a crisp darkness that carried the first signature of a cold winter to come. The wind was delicious on my face with the air as life-giving as a salt lick. I locked my bike around a parking meter and then entered the law offices of Ravenel, Jones, Winters, and Day. It was after hours, but Cleveland Winters had sent word that he would be working late that evening and needed to have a word with me.

His office was on the third floor of an antebellum mansion, and it had that harmonious, leathery smell that all the white-shoe law firms seemed to exude. Mr. Winters was a splendid example of a Charleston aristocrat, with a shock of thick, white hair and the serene, regal bearing of a prince of this watery Low Country realm.

"Hey, Leo," he said, smiling, as I walked into his office. "Let me finish reading this document, and I'll be right with you."

When he finally looked up and closed his Waterman pen, I said, "I bet you bought this desk from Mr. Canon."

"Harrington claimed I stole this desk from him over forty years ago," Mr. Winters said. "But actually, my parents bought it for me when I graduated from law school. I think they paid Harrington a hundred dollars for it."

"They did steal it," I said. "I bet it would go for four or five thousand in today's market."

"So Harrington taught you some things about antiques?" Mr. Winters asked.

"He told me he taught me everything he knew," I said. "But that's not even close to being true. Mr. Canon was a walking encyclopedia on antiques. I got to really like him."

"He felt the same," he said. "Do you know why I called you down here tonight, Leo?"

"I figured you wanted to talk to me about pallbearers," I said.

"No, I called you to my office for a very different reason. I am the sole executor of Harrington's will. He wants an auction company in Columbia to auction off the merchandise in his store. He would like you to take inventory of everything in the store and compare it with the auction company's inventory."

"That won't be a problem, sir," I said.

"He has some distant cousins living in nursing homes. Mostly in the up-country. He has made generous provisions to take care of those women until they die."

"I can't wait to tell my mother," I said. "She always said Mr. Canon was a cheapskate."

"She won't be saying that after tonight," Mr. Winters said with a smile.

"No one's ever succeeded in shutting my mother up," I said.

"I promise you that I will," the lawyer said with a chuckle.

I looked up at him in surprise, his physical attractiveness only heightened by his certainty.

"Harrington has left you his store on King Street, Leo. He has also left you his house on Tradd Street with all the furnishings in it."

"Great God Almighty," I said.

"He knows you do not have the means to take care of the store or the house, so he has left you $250,000 in bonds and another $250,000 in cash to give you some start-up money when you get out of college. What school do you plan to attend?"

"The Citadel," I said.

"That'll be taken care of," Mr. Winters said. "It's in the will."

"Jesus Christ," I gasped. "Why? I worked at his store under court order."

"He thought of you as the son he never had," Mr. Winters said.

"But I wasn't anything to him," I said. "Nothing real."

"Real enough to make you a fairly rich young man," he said, reaching into his humidor to hand me a cigar. "It's Cuban."

"Aren't they illegal?" I asked.

"Yep." He nodded, lighting one of his own. "That's what makes them taste better."

He leaned across his desk, retrieved my cigar, and cut the tip with an elegant guillotine instrument. Then he took out a pearl-handled cigarette lighter and lit the cigar, imploring me to puff hard. The penumbra of blue smoke made my head disappear from view. Several moments later, I was vomiting in Mr. Winters's private bathroom. When I emerged, I felt like my lungs and eyes had just endured a house fire.

"They take some getting used to," Mr. Winters said.

"No wonder they're illegal."

"An acquired taste," he said. "Like Cognac or martinis. You'll get some money from this rather quickly, Leo. I'll pay the estate taxes. It might take three to six months for the property to revert to you. There's always the possibility that some woebegone fifth cousin could challenge the estate."

Leaning across the desk, I shook Cleveland Winters's hand. "You're hired, Mr. Winters. If Harrington Canon trusted you, then I trust you. Sorry about your cigar."

"Cuba's not going anywhere," he said.

From that night forward, I never went to Canada or Europe without bringing back a box of Cuban cigars for the humidor of my Charleston lawyer. It gave me a smuggler's thrill at all border crossings and entry points, and nothing pleased Mr. Winters more. When he died in 1982, I inherited his humidor and the desk where I signed the papers that would change the direction of my life. I moved that desk to my office at the *News and Courier,* and I have written my columns on it ever since, always thinking of Cleveland Winters, and always sending up a prayer of thanks to Harrington Canon.

I parked my bike in front of Mr. Canon's house on Tradd Street and tried for a moment to imagine it as mine. Looking back, I think I can figure out what that boy was trying to decipher as he stared at the mansion he now owned. Though he could not articulate or arrange his thoughts in an order that would make sense out of this unexpected night, I believe he was trying to discover some obscure figure in the carpet from the randomness of his own fate. No matter what angle he chose, this majestic house would not be his had he not refused to tell the police officers who had planted cocaine on him during the first week of his freshman year. What was a boy supposed to do with that cache of forbidden knowledge? How is that supposed to help him fashion a philosophy so he could go out to live a worthy, self-actualized life? What do you do when you learn for certain that fate can lead directly to the ownership of one of the finest residences on Tradd Street? It did not look like the work of God, but it might have represented the handicraft of a God with a joyous sense of humor, a dancing God who loved mischief as much as prayer, and playfulness as much as mischief. That was why Leo King stood outside the home that struck into the middle of his life with all the suddenness of a meteor. He could think of no explanation for it, no reason for it—for an ugly boy who had spent much of his childhood in mental institutions and found his brother's self-slaughtered body in a bathtub, it seemed too much to have his direction restored and his luck changed in such an amazing fashion.

CHAPTER 22

Number 55

After practice for our semifinal against Gaffney, we showered, dressed, and walked over to Coach Jefferson's house for the oyster roast he had promised at the beginning of the year if we made the playoffs. The owners of Bowens Island were catering the affair, and my parents had raised me thinking that Bowens Island fixed the best steamed oysters in the land. The backyard filled up with my football team and their girl-friends and parents. I waved to Starla Whitehead, who was dating Dave Bridges, a starting defensive end.

Since her operation, Starla had attracted the attention of scores of young men, including me. I had called to see if she wanted to be my date for the party but discovered I was the fourth player on the team to ask her. She seemed perplexed and self-conscious at finding herself so sought after.

"What do you think they want with me?" she asked, perfectly honest.

I wasn't about to give a straight answer to such a loaded question, nor would I lie. "Ask Sheba," I told her, making her laugh unexpectedly, a lovely sound not so frequently heard before her operation.

I took a turn at the oyster table, wearing a heavy glove on my left hand, and prying the oyster loose from its shells with the blunt-nosed knife. Soon, Niles and Ike were on either side of me. Betty walked up to be beside Ike, which made me wonder why Fraser wasn't standing beside her boyfriend. "Why haven't I seen Fraser?"

"Said she couldn't come," Niles said.

I loped over to where Molly was sitting at a table full of cheerleaders. Since reuniting with Chad last month, she had studiously avoided me, even in class, where we sat across the aisle from each other. I had gradually come to accept that she was part and parcel of a life that I would never be part of, but even in my disappointment, I couldn't bring myself to hate her. She was too vulnerable and too basically decent, in spite of what she'd done to me, for me to work up any great fury against her. My voice was more patient than accusing when I asked: "Where are Chad and Fraser? They get sick or something?"

For the first time since that night at the Piggy Park, she met my eyes and lifted a shoulder. "I don't know, Leo. I don't think their father wanted them to come."

"You think, or you know?" I demanded.

Looking guilty, she said, "I know."

"Why?" I knew the answer before I asked.

"Mr. Rutledge put his foot down when he heard there was a party at a colored family's home," she said with another shrug.

"What about your family?"

"I told them the cheerleaders were having a special practice," Molly said, meeting my eyes levelly. Her gaze seemed to be asking for a return of the close friendship we'd once had.

Flustered, I turned quickly and went to the kitchen, where Mrs. Jefferson was preparing huge bowls of coleslaw and baked beans. I asked her permission to use the phone.

She said, "Sweetie, there's one in the back bedroom where you'll have a little privacy."

I dialed Chad's number. As I was expecting, his father answered.

"May I speak to Chad, Mr. Rutledge?" I asked, my anger veering off past courtesy.

"May I inquire about the subject of this call?" Mr. Rutledge asked. I

realized that I had never recovered from my visceral hatred of him after
that first meeting at the yacht club.

"It's sort of personal."

"So are all phone calls. But I am screening Chad's and Fraser's phone
calls tonight. It's a father's prerogative. You'll understand someday when
you have your own kids."

"I'm sure I will. But can you leave Chad a message for me?"

"I'll tell him you called, Leo," Mr. Rutledge said.

"No, I want you to deliver a message."

"Go ahead; I've got pen and paper ready."

"Tell him he won't be playing in the state semifinal this Saturday," I
said. "He can turn in his uniform tomorrow. Would you like me to repeat
that?"

"No, you little bastard. I got down every word," he said. "You know I
can make a couple of phone calls tonight and get your mama and daddy
and that nigger coach fired."

"Make those phone calls," I said. "But your son isn't playing in that
game against Gaffney."

"You don't have that kind of power, Toad." Mr. Rutledge added my
nickname sarcastically.

"I'm cocaptain of this team," I said. "If my other cocaptain agrees that
Chad is bad for the team's spirit, we can go to the coach and have that kid
kicked off the team."

"My son doesn't socialize with niggers."

"Then he doesn't play football with them, either," I said.

"You don't need to have me as your enemy in this town, Leo."

"We've been enemies since the day we met," I said as I hung up the
phone.

Returning to the party, I suddenly doubted the wisdom and hothead-
edness of what I had just done, and gathered Coach Jefferson, Ike, and
Niles to tell them about it. I tried to replicate the entire conversation I'd
had with Worth Rutledge, then awaited Coach Jefferson's wrath, which
could be intimidating in both its ferocity and its suddenness. But none
came. Ike and Niles looked troubled but not offended.

Then Coach Jefferson surprised me: he looked at his watch and said,

"I bet that Chad gets here in less than five minutes. I know boys and I know dads. All boys and all dads want to play in championship games. Do you know what is hilarious about this? You know who's having the most fun at this party?"

We looked around, and I heard Ike laughing, then Niles. And they both said the same name together: "Wormy Ledbetter!"

In less than ten minutes, Chad's car pulled onto Coach Jefferson's street. Chad and Fraser were both running as they came through the back gate. Chad walked up to Coach Jefferson, gave me an executioner's look, then said, "Sorry I'm late, Coach. Had a little car trouble."

"Can happen to anyone, Chad," he said. "You and your sister, get yourself some oysters." He then turned and winked at the three of us. "Boys," he said, "what you just saw was good coaching. Mighty fine coaching. We need Chad for this Gaffney game."

And need him we did. The Gaffney fullback and linebacker whom we had studied on film all week looked five times bigger in real life. He was wild-eyed, possessed, and stacked with muscles in places it didn't look like muscles were supposed to grow. He scored four touchdowns in the first half, and Gaffney led 28–0 when we went into the locker room. On the blackboard, Coach Jefferson made the necessary adjustments, inventing five misdirection plays that would offset the overaggressiveness of the Gaffney linebacker. His number was 55, and his satanic, all-seeing eyes would enter my personal country of nightmare for months. He ran over me like I was a toddler in his driveway. When I tackled him—a rare event that night—it felt like I had slammed into the side of a mountain. We scored three times by air in the second half, and Wormy broke loose for two long touchdowns, but we lost the game, 42–35. It was, by far, the worst game of my career.

I would repress number 55's name and trained myself not to think of him, even after he became a star at Georgia and in the pros. But I would eventually recognize those flame-throwing eyes when I encountered them once again twenty years later, in an alley in San Francisco when I met Macklin Tijuana Jones for a second time.

• • •

On the first Saturday in my final January of high school, I drove my car over to St. Jude's Orphanage and parked in the gravel lot next to Sister Polycarp's Chevy station wagon. I signed the guest registry and jotted down my time of arrival, then ran the stairs two at a time to the recreation room. Ike and Betty were shooting a game of eight ball when I walked in. Starla was reading *The Cat in the Hat* to a young girl I had never seen before.

"Pick up a cue, white one," Ike said, grinning at me. "And I'll show you how to use it."

I hated the game of pool because it was manly and supercharged and carried an aura of tough-guy danger. Plus, I couldn't play it worth a damn. But Ike looked like he was practicing an art form when he applied blue chalk to his cue stick and lined up his shot. Then Betty ran the table on him, while he watched with a connoisseur's admiration for her game.

"Where's this place Sheba and Trevor are the star attractions tonight?" Betty asked.

"Big John's," Ike said. "It's on East Bay."

"You going?" I asked.

"You seem to have trouble with this concept, so listen up, Toad. I am a soul brother. Great rhythm, great style, great looks, great moves. I mean, I'm the whole package, just like Betty here. But we got one big hang-up. We live in the South, where our people have had a tad of trouble with your people. Your people seem to like to hang our people from trees. So my people have gotten into the habit of not going near yours. You follow me? Big John's is a white bar. We aren't going to hear Sheba and Trevor play shit."

"I know Big John. He's an ex–pro football player. A great guy. I've been in his bar, and black guys come in. My father and I were in there one night when three of his teammates came in, all black. It'll hurt the twins' feelings if we don't go."

"Are you and Niles going?" I asked Starla.

"Niles is taking Fraser," she said.

"So, can I take you?" I asked, trying to sound casual.

"Is he suave," Ike said, "or what?"

"Are you asking me out on a date?" Starla looked at me in surprise. When I'd asked her out before, she seemed to think it was out of friendship.

"No, I'm a taxi service."

"Tell her you're asking her out on a date, Toad," Betty demanded with a sigh.

"I'm asking you out on a date," I said. I had found myself thinking about Starla a lot lately, since Molly had drifted back to society's herd. Quite a lot.

"A date," she said. "It sounds so normal, doesn't it? Why, yes, Toad, I'd love to. Thank you," she said. "Do you know they're tossing me and Niles out, right after graduation? Sister Polycarp just gave us the big news. The second we get our diploma, we're on the streets. She keeps bugging us about how old we are, and we don't know. We can't even guess. Hell, I might be forty. No one's ever found our birth certificates. The only thing I know is that Niles has always been around. He's always been there."

"Where is he now?" I asked.

"He's been tight as a tick with Chad ever since we got back from the senior trip," Ike inserted from the pool table.

Betty snorted. "And I don't like it. I don't trust Chad. He's got that white-boy chip on his shoulder. Even when he smiles, I can feel that mean streak."

"You two want to double-date with me and Starla?" I asked.

"Sure thing," Ike said. "I'll pick you up at seven. You sure about Big John's?"

"I'll have Father call Big John," I said. "We'll make sure."

"My parents will be pissed if they have to identify me at the morgue," Ike said.

"Mine won't," Betty and Starla said at the same time, and it cracked up all the orphans in earshot.

A bell rang. We joined the procession of orphans down the dark stairwell that led to a large, slatternly garden, though it was elegantly designed and must have once been a showcase. The brickwork was harmonious and pleasing and had been laid with expertise and a gift for order. St.

Jude's garden made Mother crazy and distressed, but she knew the cost and hard labor involved in revising a garden of such stature. The garden was now used as a venue for exercise where the orphans stretched their legs by walking the brick pathways every day as one of the younger nuns stood guard at the library window. At the first sign of carnality or hand-holding, she would blow hard on a referee's whistle, its piercing voice putting an instant stop to any scrimmage of hormones disturbing the peace in the garden below.

Ike and Betty walked about ten feet behind as the eagle-eyed nun watched over us. At first, Starla and I walked in silence in the out-of-season, hibernating garden. Because of Mother's passion for flowers, I understood that we were passing over a blind world of roots and bulbs and seeds that would burst into the bright fire of spring. The earth was sleeping beneath us, but waiting with the infinite patience of taproots and stems for their April run to the light. Now we moved through paths where nothing was green and the city paid homage to the necessity of withering. In silence, we passed over a nation of ferns and stalks.

"I need to talk to you about Niles," Starla said as we turned down the pathway that bisected the garden.

"What about him?"

"Something's wrong," she said, in obvious distress. "He's hanging around too much with Chad. Betty's right: it's creepy."

"He's nuts over Fraser," I said. "No mystery in that."

"It's something else," Starla said, shaking her head. "Niles has always told me everything. He's got secrets now. Things he's keeping from me."

"You don't know that."

"I know it as well as I know how to write my name in blood on that wall," she said, pointing to the mud-red brick chapel attached to St. Jude's.

"Niles can take care of himself," I said. "You know that better than anyone."

"He goes out every weekend. He and Fraser double-date with Chad and Molly. You know that Chad and Molly are back together, don't you?"

"Of course," I said. "They walk so close together at school that you couldn't separate them with a piece of cigarette paper."

"I never trust it when couples are that affectionate in public," she said. "It's like they're hiding something. A cover-up for something else."

"I wouldn't know. Me and Molly—we never got to that stage. We never got anywhere."

She nodded, her brown eyes unreadable. Before I could ask what she was thinking, Starla took me by surprise. She reached over, lifted my chin, and kissed me on the mouth. It was not a sisterly kiss. It was a kiss I felt all the way down to my toes.

She drew back and asked, "You've been wanting to kiss me, haven't you, Leo? Did you like it?"

I couldn't speak so I nodded, dumbfounded.

She laughed, her hands on my shoulders. "Then why don't we fall in love with each other? Like Niles and Fraser? Ike and Betty? Bet we could be happy like them too. Look at them." I turned to see Ike and Betty in a passionate embrace, locked into a full, lip-smacking kiss that seemed just right.

The centerpiece of the garden was a live oak that must have been well over a hundred years old. I thought it hid them from the watchtower in the library, but the whistle blasted out in all its shrillness. Ike and Betty reluctantly parted, then resumed their promenade, not even holding hands, but smiling brightly for all the world to see. Starla was right: they looked happy.

Starla and I joined them, and the four of us exchanged conspiratorial smiles.

The bar at Big John's was small enough to fit in a railroad car, and it was filled with Citadel cadets when we arrived. It looked like a whites-only crowd for sure, and Ike cast me a glance as though I had invited him to be an honored guest at his own lynching. Then two black cadets came in; coincidentally, Charles Foster and Joseph Shine, the first two blacks to integrate The Citadel. They were delighted to hear that Ike had just won a football scholarship to their college. Outside, we joined their table while inside Big John's seethed with beer-guzzling pods of cadets with a high percentage of plebes. On the other side of the small courtyard I spotted Chad and Molly with Niles and Fraser. They were sitting at a table with two couples I didn't recognize, but they had those telltale tans that signi-fied yacht club and regattas and a working knowledge of coconut palms during Christmas breaks in Martinique. Big John's was crowded enough to draw the attention of the fire chief, who stood at the front door, blocking the entrance to any latecomers. As Ike had predicted, the news of Sheba's beauty had spread like a virus through the Corps of Cadets.

Trevor came through a back door by the kitchen, and made his way to an upright piano. He sat down and began playing The Citadel alma mater, which sent all the cadets scrambling to stand at attention and place their caps back on their heads. Sheba came through the door and sang the alma mater in a breathy, sexual manner that was unprecedented in the history of that song. The bar was suffused with a strange combination of shock fringed with lust. When Sheba came to the last line of the song and all the cadets lifted their caps and waved them in the air, Trevor changed the tenor of the whole evening by blasting away at the piano keys with the most rousing version of "Dixie" I'd ever heard. You could barely make out Sheba's voice above the roar. But then she quieted things with her haunting interpretation of "We Shall Overcome." A full-bloom knowledge of the music of our time was one of my generation's identifying legacies, so we realized she had fooled us into an American trilogy that she would end with "The Battle Hymn of the Republic," bringing the respectable number of Yankee cadets to their feet.

As Sheba held the crowd in thrall, Starla turned to me, put her arms around my neck, and began kissing me. Fabulous though it was, I was self-conscious about making out in public. My face was red when I pulled back from her and surveyed the crowd to see if anyone had witnessed the scene. As far as I could tell, the only one who saw it was Molly, and she clapped her hands in slow, mock applause when she caught my eye.

"It's okay, Leo," Starla told me. "Lots of people kiss in public. I've watched them."

"People like us?"

"People just like us," she said. "By the way, you going to the junior-senior prom?"

"I didn't go last year," I said.

"You're going this year," she told me. Sheba began her rendition of "The Ballad of the Green Berets," which sent the cadets into a frenzy once more, and Big John raised his huge right hand to restore some modicum of order in his joint. It was a shameless playing to the crowd, but that came naturally to Sheba and Trevor.

"I hadn't thought about it," I said. "It doesn't even happen till May."

"Ike's already asked Betty."

"Oh. So, you wanna go with me?" I asked.

"No, I can't," she said.

"Why all this hinting around, then? Why won't you go with me?"

"I could never afford a prom dress," she said.

An idea struck me with the force of a thunderbolt, and I blurted out, "I can make you a dress."

"What?"

"Mother raised me to be a so-called feminist, whatever the hell that is," I said. "I made her a dress a couple of years ago, for Mother's Day. Sheba sews great too. She can help me."

"What about shoes?" Starla asked. "Your mama teach you how to be a cobbler?"

"Sheba's got a closet full of shoes," I said. "Don't worry, we can work out the details."

Starla reached over and touched Betty on the shoulder. "Leo asked me to the junior-senior prom!"

Betty and Starla embraced, then Betty punched me hard on the shoulder with a fist that could boast of power. My shoulder hurt for a whole day and it affected my aim on my paper route the next morning. Ike turned around and congratulated me, then asked me if I wanted to double with Betty and him. I had stumbled into normal teenage life by accident, and everything about it felt right. The Toad years were leaving me behind. I was saying farewell to the boy who had been tortured for years by the accuracy of that name. It had never occurred to me that a girl as cute as Starla could like me as much as she seemed to. We kissed some more, and when I pulled back, I could feel the loosening and the possession take place. Staring into Starla Whitehead's melancholy eyes, I fell in love that night, and inadvertently began the long, agonizing process of ruining my life.

• • •

In the winter, when Father built a fire, he began with wood shavings as transparent as shrimp shells and coaxed it toward its crackling glory, laying the firewood with its veins exposed to the rising flames. I would inhale the aroma, close my eyes, and think that smoking wood was the darkest perfume on earth. In his workshop Father had built us three perfectly proportioned desktops that we could lay across the arms of our leather chairs. I could do my homework on mine, and in front of the fireplace Mother could catch up on her correspondence and Father could read his scientific journals and take copious notes. The fire itself made an amazing noise and Father kept it well tended until it was time for bed.

One late winter night, the phone rang. Father answered it and talked quietly into the receiver. After hanging up, he said to me, "That was Sheba. Go across the street and check on Trevor. He's really upset about something."

I took my jacket out of the closet by the front door and went out into the cold Charleston air. The smell of smoke from the chimney of our house was stronger than either the rivers or the marshes and made the airwaves above the neighborhood as dark-scented and fragrant as a night garden. I could hear Trevor sobbing while he sat on the first step of the veranda as I approached. Sheba was holding him tightly. I climbed the stairs and sat on the other side of my sobbing friend. I grabbed his hand and he squeezed it as I asked Sheba, "Lovers' quarrel?"

"Worse than that," Sheba said. "Cry it out, darling. Cry as much as you need to."

When she ran into the house to get her brother a glass of water, I put my arms around him until Sheba returned. The water helped, but it was several minutes before he could speak, and his whole body trembled. Finally he said, "A month ago, Niles and I were nominated for membership into a fraternity. Guys from high schools all around Charleston, public and private, try to get into it. It's a big honor."

"You never said a word to me," Sheba said.

"They swore us to secrecy. The organization began in the 1820s."

"The Middleton Assembly?" I guessed.

"How did you know that?" Trevor asked.

"Mother has long suspected it's been a presence at the high schools in town, even Peninsula, but she's never had any proof."

"Chad Rutledge nominated us, and tonight the induction ceremony took place. I was excited. Niles couldn't believe his good luck. He and I were both amazed that this honor had come to us after we'd had such shitty lives."

"Why do I think things went badly?" Sheba said.

Trevor continued. "They took us to a place on Meeting Street, some Confederate hall or something. There were about a hundred guys our age there. They were dressed in tuxedos and wore black masks. They looked like fucking extras in a Lone Ranger movie. All were silent as the inductees were led in to a pimply-faced guy at the desk. There were eight inductees. The first six were approved with no problems. The assembled members voted aye, with their thumbs raised. Their qualifications were impeccable. The usual Charleston bullshit: the Prioleaus, the Ravenels, the Gaillards, the Warleys. The first six were related to everybody, and it was a fucking cakewalk. Then the gears shifted and the fun began."

"Where was Chad?" I asked, my voice cold.

"I guess he was in the crowd," Trevor said. "I never saw him. He may not have been there at all."

"Oh, he was there," I said. "Go on, Trevor."

"Well, they get to me. I'm thinking I'm about to be inducted into an old part of Charleston history and I was caught up in this sense of brotherhood that was completely unfamiliar to me. Then the guy at the desk said, 'Mr. Trevor Poe is the first openly homosexual to be nominated for membership. His mother is a common drunk, his sister is a common whore, and he has no family that we can find. How does the assembly vote on the known faggot, Trevor Poe?' A thunderous nay went up from the membership, all thumbs pointing down. Then they went to work on poor Niles."

"At least they got the part about your sister right." Sheba trembled with a rage she could barely contain.

"That's not true, Sheba," I said. "Don't say things like that."

"The pimply-faced guy at the desk—God, he was an ugly fuck!—read from a piece of paper, in this awful, serious drone: 'Niles Whitehead has spent his life going from orphanage to orphanage looking for his mother, Bright Whitehead, and his grandmother, Ola Whitehead. But in our research we found obituary notices for both of them in the *Chimney Rock*

Times. Mr. Whitehead evidently does not know the name of his actual father. He was born in a shack in the Blue Ridge Mountains. At Peninsula High School, he has earned the nickname of "the mountain nigger." How does the assembly vote on the mountain nigger, Niles Whitehead?' Again, the roar of nay and the thumbs pointing down. Niles and I were led out of the hall by four guys who took us out to Meeting Street like we were the morning trash and left us there, too stunned to speak."

"Where's Niles now?" I asked.

"I fell apart and started to walk home, but when I looked around for Niles, he was gone. My crying may have upset him as much as the ceremony itself."

"No," I said. "They told Niles something he didn't know. Starla and Niles have always kept going because they believed their grandmother and mother were still alive. Do you know Niles was born when his mother was only thirteen years old? His grandmother was twenty-seven when Niles came into the world. Those bastards killed something in Niles when they announced those women were dead."

"I'm going to ask Chad Rutledge to fuck me," Sheba said. "Then I'm going to chop his dick off with garden shears."

Father walked onto our front porch and yelled from beneath the towering columns of our two magnolia trees, "Everything okay, kids?"

"Things are awful," I shouted back. "Could you come over here?"

Father sprinted across the street. With rare economy, I sketched out the events of the night. I could see his anger as the lines in his forehead deepened. "Come over to the house and sit by the fire. I need to make some phone calls," he said.

I sat by the fire with the exhausted twins and it moved me that they held hands as they watched the flames. When Father came in to stoke the fire, he brought them each a snifter of Cognac to calm their nerves.

"It's been a rough night, Trevor," Father said. "But it's going to be a rougher morning for Chad Rutledge. Here's a promise to you: Chad's going to have no trouble with constipation for the next couple of weeks. I'm going to chew His Highness a new asshole. I think his principal is going to chew him a matching one on his other cheek."

Sheba took a sip of Cognac, then said to the fire, "I've never felt safe in my whole life, but I feel safe in this house."

Hearing a noise, I went to the front door. Looking through the curtains, I saw the solemn face of Fraser Rutledge through the pane. When I opened the door, she rushed in and ran straight to Trevor, who stood to meet her. Trevor looked like a toy when Fraser lifted him off his feet to hug him. He looked like a fragile, harmless invertebrate.

Fraser cried, "I just slapped the living hell out of my brother. When I heard what those guys did to you and Niles, I went crazy. I said I was sorry that I had a drop of Rutledge blood, then I spit in Chad's face."

"So Chad was a part of this?" I asked.

"I heard Chad and my father laughing so hard it brought me downstairs. Chad was telling our father what happened tonight at the Middleton Assembly. Something in me died listening to it, Trevor. Sheba and Leo, you've got to believe me. Chad said he did it for the family name. No Rutledge was going to marry a mountain nigger."

"Why'd they do it to Trevor?" I asked.

"Trevor was thrown in as a plum. He was dessert. Also, it set Niles up good. He wouldn't suspect anything because he and Trevor were being inducted together."

She threw a mask at me, and I caught it in surprise. "There's a souvenir from Chad's big night. He just humiliated the only boyfriend his ugly sister ever had."

"You're not ugly, doll baby," Sheba said, taking Fraser into her own sweet embrace. "Knock that word out of your vocabulary. Hey, Leo, do you get a hard-on when you think about Fraser?"

"Every night."

"Fraser brings out the half-tenth of the one percent of me that's straight," Trevor said.

As we heard the sound of Fraser's laughter again, there was another knock at the front door. On my way to the door, I said over my shoulder, "Let me know if you're ever going to join a club again, Trevor. This is beginning to feel like a house party."

Under the outside lights, Starla cast a large shadow across the yard. I hugged her, led her to the fire, and she went over to kiss Trevor on the cheek. As Father came back into the room, Starla announced, "Niles called me from a truck stop on this side of Columbia. He told me to tell all of you thanks and good-bye."

"Did he tell you where he's going?" Father asked.

"No," Starla said. "But he didn't have to. I know where he's going: he's headed for North Carolina. The boy's going home, to the house where we were born."

"Do you know where that house is?" he asked.

"It's twenty miles from some big rock," Starla said. "I was a little bitty kid when they came to take Niles and me away."

"Chimney Rock?" Father asked.

"That's the one," Starla said. "How'd you know?"

"Leo," Father said, "a field trip to the mountains tomorrow. You're going to bring Niles back."

"I'll walk to Chimney Rock if you don't take me," Fraser said.

"I'm a runaway," Starla said.

"We want to come too," said Trevor and Sheba.

Father shook his head. "Too many," he said. "Let's limit it to Starla and Fraser. Take your mother's Buick, Leo. I'll call your substitute, Bernie, to do the paper route. You sure you can find him, Starla?"

"Pretty sure," she said.

"I'll call Polycarp," he told her. "You and Fraser, go to the guest bedroom, and I'll call your parents, Fraser, tell them you're okay. Now, let's break this up. Get some sleep. We're going to bring that boy back where he belongs."

"He's going to where he belongs, Mr. King," Starla said.

My Charleston-loving father just smiled. "Charleston's in Niles's blood now," he said. "He's been home a long time. He just doesn't know it yet."

At six in the morning, I eased Mother's car out of the driveway and made my way through the waking city's dark streets until I mounted the ramp that took me to I-26, where I gassed the pedal and headed west through the heart of South Carolina. Starla sat with me in the front seat, sleeping as we passed Summerville. The sun began to rise out of the sea behind us. In the backseat, Fraser slept on one of the pillows Father had provided, along with a cooler of sandwiches, deviled eggs, a baked ham wrapped in aluminum foil, and a bag of chocolate chip cookies. He handed me two crisp hundred-dollar bills before I left the house, in addition to my shotgun with a new box of shells.

"For emergencies," Father had said to me. "I packed your fishing rod and gear."

"We'll be back by Sunday," I said. "Whether we find Niles or not. If we don't find him, I don't know if Starla will come back or not."

"She won't," Father said.

Outside of Columbia, I pulled the car into a gas station and announced a pit stop. My fellow travelers stumbled out and stretched their limbs in the cold sunlight. I studied a map of the Carolinas and compared it with the one Father had traced with a yellow marker that guided me through a maze of backwoods that would begin our climb into the North Carolina mountains. He had circled a blue smudge of a place called Lake Lure, which seemed to be the entryway to Chimney Rock. Once I hit Chimney Rock, Father had warned me, then I'd enter the land of pure detective work. We'd have to spread out to ask questions of the mountain people, who were noted for their ambiguity and their complete distrust of strangers. Seeing a look of distress cross my face, Father reminded me that Starla was returning to her native land and would be back among her own people.

After leaving Spartanburg, we entered into that haunted country that always represented the real South to me, the God-fearing truck stops and the small whitewashed churches that worshipped a fiercer Christ than I did. We had entered the kingdom of snake handlers and clay eaters and moonshiners, where the farmland itself was stringy, stone-pocked, and unforgiving. We passed through Lake Lure just before noontime, and the tension in the car mounted as we went over the game plan we had devised in ignorance of the terrain and the mumbling people of few words whom we were certain to encounter.

"What're the mountain folk like?" I asked Starla.

"Like everyone else," Starla said. "A lot nicer than Charleston people."

"I resent that," Fraser said. "Charleston's famous for its civility."

"How do you think Trevor and Niles liked Charleston's famous civility last night?"

"It's a tradition," Fraser said, looking straight ahead. "There are always two guys who are picked because they won't make it. It's even written into the by-laws of the Middleton Assembly. Chad said it would be the most boring ceremony in the world if not for the eviction of the unfit."

"It was so thoughtful of Chad to let Trevor and Niles share that experience," Starla said. "Chad's cute to be such an asshole. I like for God to mark assholes. You know, make them ugly as sin, their meanness written all over their face. I thought Wormy was like that, but hell, I like him better than Chad."

"White trash charm," Fraser said.

Starla fired back, "Niles and I are a lot lower than white trash, Fraser. For us, white trash is a step up."

"You might be," Fraser said, "but not Niles. He has some pride, at least."

I heard a small noise like a cricket turning over on its wings in a bait bucket. I looked over and saw a glitter of metal in Starla's hand. She held the knife up for Fraser to see.

"Jesus, Starla," I breathed.

She told Fraser levelly, "I've thought about cutting your throat all morning because of what your brother did to Niles. So drop the lectures about pride, you Charleston bitch. You better think twice before you fuck with a mountain girl."

I steered the car to a screeching halt on a pullover designed to let faster traffic pass and yelled at the girls, "The purpose of this trip is to bring Niles back. I don't want to hear another word about the debutante-versus-the-mountain-girl shit, or you can both get out. Now, give me that goddamn switchblade, Starla."

She folded the knife and handed it over to me. I jammed it in my pocket, then eased the car back out onto the road. When we passed over a bridge, I threw the knife into a creek.

"There's Chimney Rock." I pointed to a towering outcropping that looked capricious and out of place, as though an imbecilic creator had fashioned it when he tired of making stars. The town of Chimney Rock was a place to buy a Cherokee tomahawk, an Indian headdress, a leather bullwhip, or jars of honey taken from beehives in mountain laurel country. Without tourism, Chimney Rock would be a lonesome stretch of mountain road beside the boulder-strewn Broad River. Several of the stores were closed for the winter, but many were open, trying to lure wayward travelers like us as they climbed the mountains on the way to Asheville. There were storefronts on both sides of the street, and all looked as though they were selling duplicates of the same merchandise. I dropped Starla and Fraser off in front of one, and they scrambled out like beagles as they went door to door asking for any information about the Whitehead family.

On the other side of town, I parked the car and went into a barber-shop. As the barber trimmed my hair, I asked about the Whitehead family. Though the name was familiar to him, he wasn't sure if he had ever actually met a Whitehead, but he had certainly heard the legends; they were mountain people who had a reputation for being disputatious and stubborn, and they had a particular antipathy toward officers of the law. He thought they were part Cherokee, and there was nothing in the physiognomies of Niles or Starla to disprove that theory. But he was fairly certain they had disappeared from the area, probably trickling down to Charlotte to look for work. Though he said there were a lot of hard-up mountaineers, it was hard to find a low-down one, and that's where you had to look to flush out the Whiteheads.

I went to look for my search party when I spotted Starla and Fraser racing across the street in my direction. "The lady in that souvenir shop made a phone call, and I got me a third cousin once removed who's coming down to see us," Starla told me, breathless.

Later, as a pickup truck drew near us, we saw it as our best chance to make any connection with Niles. The man wore a strange fedora and overalls, and he studied us before he spoke. Then he spoke only to Starla. "You're the Whitehead," he said, then gave me and Fraser a look of disapproval. "Who're they?" he asked her.

"I brought them with me," Starla said. "We're in this together. Do you know where my family lived?"

"Back there." He pointed behind him with his thumb. "Way up in the hills. You can't get there now."

"Why not?" Starla asked. "I want to see the place where I grew up with my brother."

"It's a dirt road. Goes near straight up. Scary at times. I only been there once. There was a rock slide a couple of years ago during a storm. No one's seen those houses since."

"How do we get there?" Starla insisted.

"Take the Asheville Highway. You're on it," he said. "Start climbing. The Broad River's on the left. When a trout stream enters the Broad, look for a dirt road leading up the mountain. The angle's steep. Be careful. Drive to the rock slide. You'll have to climb over that, a mile to the houses. It used to be called Whitehead Road."

"Thanks, cousin," Starla said.

"Anything for family," he said, then he touched his hat in a fine salute and drove off.

I've always admired people who have the ability to give accurate directions, and their tribe is small. Starla's third cousin once removed provided directions so accurate it was like he had drawn a map. We began the steep incline up the mountains as soon as we left the city limits of Chimney Rock, and soon were struggling in a land of hairpin turns as we made our way through a rain forest while the sun began its decline. I was driving as fast as I could, trying to make it to the Whitehead compound before dark, the Buick climbing and groaning its way upward, until Starla shrieked when she saw the trout stream cascading into the Broad River. We had entered a land of mountain laurel and waterfalls with veils of milk-fed foam careening off house-sized boulders.

I turned off onto a road that looked unfinished. I slammed the car into second gear as we wove our way to an uncertain finish. As we climbed, we left the trout stream below us, one hundred feet, then a thousand, and the road grew more perilous. Then we started back down toward the stream, with the car so close to the edge that I laughed when I looked into the rearview mirror and saw that Fraser had her eyes tightly closed.

"I never liked Niles this much," I said.

I slammed on the brakes when I reached the rock slide that caught me by surprise, then maneuvered the car as we drew close to the river again. The severe cave-in looked as though the entire mountain had exercised a flanking movement to the left.

I put the gear shift in park. "Let's get to that stream and walk to those houses. They've got to be close by. Fraser, grab the fishing pole. I'll get the food."

In the last light, I saw an ancient path or deer run going down to the stream, and I headed down it, shouldering the cooler. When I reached the water's edge, I followed it toward its source. As it grew darker, I heard Starla say these glorious words: "I smell a wood fire."

We hurried into the setting sun until we saw the silhouettes of four unpainted shotgun houses on stilts built over the stream. We walked toward the wreckage of those abandoned homes, and followed the smell of that Blue Ridge smoke to the last house. I opened the door and we walked into a house undermined by spores and mildew and lack of attention. A lone man sat by the fire.

"Niles?" Starla said.

"What took you so long?" he asked.

It was the saddest voice I ever heard.

In front of a stone fireplace, we sat by a towering fire, eating sandwiches and listening to the impatient movement of the stream beneath us. Niles ate three sandwiches in a row without uttering a word. It occurred to me that he had not eaten a thing since he was tossed out of his induction ceremony. Fraser took up a position near him but seemed almost afraid to touch him. The fire, the cold, the dampness of this imperiled house, lent a sense of foreboding among us as we waited for Niles to break his eerie silence. He rose from the floor and threw on a couple of logs he had collected in the surrounding forest. The fire rose higher, crackling into sudden light as the wood surrendered to the devouring cunning of flames. Silence itself began to seem like a series of partitions driving us even farther apart from one another.

Finally, it was Fraser who broke all the treaties that made us silent and unforthcoming. "So this is where you and Starla grew up?"

"I was born here, but we grew up in the first house you passed," Niles said. "It doesn't have a floor."

Fraser looked around in a gloom so impenetrable the fire had little effect on it. "It's nice. I really like it."

Starla and I cracked up in unguarded laughter. There was even a thin smile that crossed Niles's clouded face.

This was not the effect Fraser had planned on, and in her nervousness she kept removing a sapphire ring from her right hand, then putting it back on again. "What I meant was," she said, "that didn't come out right. I was just thinking—talk about exotic. Talk about waterfront property."

And again there was convulsive laughter from Starla and me above the trout stream as the fire made grotesque, jerking shadows on the wall, and the evening fell deeper into discomfort and incoherence. My irritation with Niles was growing, though. I had always thought the quiet man was the most overrated form of human life. "When does the welcome wagon arrive?" I asked, more to break the silence than anything else.

"Why'd you come?" Niles finally said.

I said, "Because we heard it was a great time to visit the mountains. Chance of snow. Luxury accommodations. Room service. Feather beds. Hot showers. A sauna. Great talks with old friends."

"We want you to come back, Niles," Fraser said. "We're not complete without you."

"Your family can always get me again," Niles said to her, "because I love you."

Taking her cue, Fraser pulled Niles into her arms and stroked his hair with a delicacy that moved me. A gust of wind blew through some broken panes of glass, moving us all closer to the fire. I threw on some more wood.

"I won't let them touch you again, Niles, I swear," Fraser said. "I slapped the shit out of Chad when he came home with his little story. My parents were upset when they saw me fall apart. Charleston society is so cruel, yet none of them can see it. The Middleton Assembly almost folded twenty years ago. The ceremony was so boring, and they were losing membership. One year, only nine members showed up for the induction ceremony. So someone came up with the idea that two boys be nominated as jokes. My parents have never been happy that we're dating, Niles. You've always known that. By leaving Charleston, you played right into their hands."

"That's all very beautiful and touching," Starla said, "but I've got to pee."

"Use the outhouse across the road from the second house," Niles said. "There's some newspaper in there."

"I want to pee, not read," she said.

"You've been gone from the mountains too long," Niles said. "C'mon. I'll show you the way."

When Niles returned with Starla, Fraser and I told him everything that had happened since his and Trevor's humiliation. He laughed at our story about the cousin in the pickup truck. One memory sparked another until Niles was taken up by a flood of them. Soon, it was only Niles's voice that was heard in that dilapidated house. I think our arrival had shaken something loose in him, had touched him in a long-buried place, so he decided to open up in all the protection that fire and cold and darkness could provide when a soul has a butterfly-like moment and decides to soar toward the high, urgent places. That night, his soul was a living thing born by firelight. He told us his history, one he had never told even Starla.

He was born in the house we were now in; his thirteen-year-old mother, whose name was Bright, had walked over to her mother's house at noon when her water broke. Bright's husband, a solid, big-chested guy, worked as a janitor in an insane asylum in Asheville, and didn't get home very often. He was Bright's third cousin from the Asheville Whiteheads. They named Niles after the river in the Bible after hearing the preacher mention it in church, although he did not know why they made it plural. When Starla came a year later, they named her after the star that shown over the stable in Bethlehem.

His grandmother was twenty-seven when Niles was born, and she was a midwife. Niles's two uncles lived in the middle houses, both sullen, hardworking men. The sons of Niles's grandfather, Pickerill, made the best moonshine in that part of North Carolina, and had a prison record to back it up. Niles's mother was a sweet woman who had cried when Starla was born because now she had a perfect set of dolls to play with, a boy and a girl, never having had a doll to play with in her childhood. Niles and Starla agreed that their mother had adored them and spoiled them, as did their grandmother. No one in the family could read or write, but they spent the evenings entertaining one another with tall tales of hunting and mayhem and family feuds. Uncle Fordham played the banjo, and they would sing the old church songs as well as the mountain songs passed down for generations, songs that brought news of life's hardships.

Niles had little memory of his father, none of it good. He often arrived drunk on his rare visits to the creek. By the way, Niles said, its official name was Whitehead Creek, and he guaranteed he would catch us all a trout for breakfast.

"If we're still alive," Fraser said, as we huddled in a tight circle. I fed the fire with more wood.

Their father would cuff their mother around, bringing the menfolk into the mix to defend her. Niles recalled the arguments along the creek as red-hot and vile. Usually, his father would stay the weekend, then hitch a ride back to Asheville. His visits became less frequent, which was fine by him and Starla. His mother, Bright, raised enough honeybees to support herself, and jars of her honey sold in stores as far away as Raleigh. There were two cows that provided butter, milk, and cheese, and they raised pigs that they slaughtered for their meat. Their grandmother was a marvelous cook. On Sunday, they would take a mule, hitch it to a wagon, and ride two miles down to Chimney Rock to the Church of God. After the service, there was a luncheon in the churchyard, which provided their social life.

"As kids, you don't know if you're happy or not," Niles told us. "Starla and I were just in the business of being kids, but strong in the knowledge that we were cherished and loved and well fed. Mama was sure that we'd be the first kids in the family to get an education. It was a bitter blow to lose her, but we've had to wake up to that bitterness for more years than anyone should count. It's when you fall in love with your life that some demon force decides to take it all away."

His father returned from the city again. Niles did not know his first name because he and Starla called him Daddy and his mama called him sweetheart and those kinds of names. He brought papers written up by his lawyer to divorce his wife. He wanted Bright to put an X on the paper, so he could go ahead and marry another woman. She went crazy and ran to her own mama's house and got her daddy's shotgun out of his closet, and was heading back to her house when she spotted her husband running as fast as he could, being chased and bitten by the pack of dogs that served as an alarm system for strangers coming up the road. Because she was afraid of hitting the dogs, she unloaded the shotgun into the creek just to scare the sorry son of a bitch and make him think twice about bothering her again. But Bright took it harder than she let on, which Niles knew in his heart, though she never uttered a word against his daddy. That was not part of the Whitehead code.

Several months later, their father died in Asheville. The family preacher had received a call from Asheville, so he drove his car up to the White-head compound to bring the grim news. His mama let out a howl, and the Reverend Grubb offered to drive the family to the funeral, which was gratefully accepted.

"We were in our Sunday finest when we waited for the preacher on the Asheville Highway to pick us up," Niles told us. His grandmother was the only adult to accompany her daughter to the funeral, since the menfolk had reached the conclusion that the husband was worth less than their egg-sucking dog with mange. On the ride to Asheville, Starla and Niles both got sick on the curves.

The church was too fancy for their mama's country taste. Bright had never met a Presbyterian. Though hesitating, she and her mother both drew shaky Xs in the guest book, then went up to view the body.

It was hard for Niles to tell the rest of this story. He tended to the fire before he continued.

His mama began wailing and keening in the ancient way—decidedly not in the Asheville Presbyterian way. People were looking at Niles's family group like they were from outer space. A woman approached Bright when she started planting kisses on her dead husband's face. In a curt tone, she asked Niles's mama, what did she think she was doing? Bright turned on the woman and screamed out so everyone in the church could hear: "I'm crying for the death of my husband here, the father of my two children. That okay, city girl?" Niles appreciated the danger of Bright's outburst when he saw a look of horror pass over the Reverend Grubb's face as he conferred with an usher. Before the Reverend Grubb could get back to Niles's mother, another woman approached her and said, "I was married to that man in this same church eighteen years ago. Those are my three sons in the front row. We ask that you leave this house of worship. You have no place here."

"Reverend Clyde Grubb married me to this dead man under the sight of God and in the presence of my family six years ago when I was pregnant with my son, Niles," Bright responded. "And this here is his daughter, Starla. So don't you go telling me I ain't got a place here. I'm his lawful wedded wife."

Then Mrs. Asheville Whitehead made a serious mistake when she said to the head usher, "Throw her out of here. Make as little noise as possible." Though Asheville was in the mountains, the city had long ago lost its deep knowledge about the psychology of mountain women. Pride grows as dense as the laurel in the high mountains, which Mrs. Fancypants Asheville learned the hard way when Niles's distraught mother took out her hunting knife and put it into her rival's retreating back. It made a terrible, but not fatal, wound. Then Niles watched helplessly as two ushers grabbed his mama from behind. Soon, one of the ushers was on the ground with his grandmother's hunting knife protruding out of his shoulder. Bedlam was set loose in that very proper church.

"We never saw our mama again. We never saw Meemaw either. That night we began our lifelong tour of orphanages. Starla and I always thought they were going to find us. We heard they both went to prison. We knew that when they got out, they wouldn't quit until they found us. That dream kept us going for all these years. That dream and nothing else," Niles said.

"I've still got that dream," Starla said. "I need them to hold me again."

"I'll show you their graves tomorrow," Niles said. "They're in the family plot up the hill a ways."

The wail that echoed through that house was mountain born. It told of mountain sorrow with an awesome eloquence, and it rose out of Starla like a storm assaulting her heart. We took turns comforting her, but some wounds are not healable, and some hurts are born with inhuman powers of endurance. Fraser took Niles into her arms that night and wouldn't let him go.

Before we left the next morning, we visited the graveyard and said prayers over the bodies of the two women who had grown in my mind until I felt I had approached the tomb of goddesses.

Niles and Starla let us take over the details after that. I drove them to a restaurant in Lake Lure and told everybody to order everything. From the restaurant, I called my parents with the good news that we were heading back to Charleston with Niles. Mother assured me that Niles was cleared with the orphanage, his high school, and the police force. There would be no repercussions for his running off. She had suspended Chad Rutledge from school for a week and had almost come to blows with Chad's parents in her office. Drive safely and great job, son, they both said. I felt giddy and coddled by their love. By a long shot, I had the best parents of anybody riding in my car.

Later, Niles would reveal something to me that he had left out of his story. After a fruitless search for her children when she was released from prison, his mama hanged herself from a tree not far from the house we had stayed in the night before. After her funeral, his grandmother visited her daughter's fresh grave and put a bullet through her own head. Niles thought Starla was too fragile to take in that horrifying tale. I agreed, and never revealed that part of her mama's story to her, even after we married and began our disastrous life together.

Because of what happened to Starla, it still fills me with dread and astonishment that I never told her the details of her mother's death.

CHAPTER 23

Fog and Mist

One night soon after we returned from the mountains, the doorbell rang. Father had been helping Ike Jefferson with his trigonometry and Betty Roberts with her physics homework, and got up to answer the door. At the piano, Trevor was playing Schubert because he said it was "a Schubert kind of night," one of those lines that we had come to expect from Trevor, and that we'd repeat to one another for the rest of our lives. Working side by side at two sewing machines, Sheba and I were concentrating on the prom dresses we were making for Betty and Starla, who interrupted their homework every once in a while to let Sheba measure them with a tape measure. The dresses would be lovely—"Showstoppers," Sheba declared with confidence. Niles was studying in silence at my desk in the bedroom. The music had an ache to it, bringing with it all the accounts of melancholy you would ever need.

Father opened the door. Chad Rutledge stood in the light, flanked by his sister and his girlfriend. Sheba and I were concentrating and didn't look up, but we got distracted when the music stopped with unnatural abruptness. Chad, Molly, and Fraser stepped into the room just as Mother emerged from her bedroom at the back of the house. An awkward silence settled on us all. Niles, sensing the mood of the house, came downstairs and froze at the sight of Chad.

Mother said, "I asked Chad and the girls to drop by. Everyone here has quit talking to Chad since you got back from the mountains. At school, Chad is isolated and shunned by his fellow students. He did something stupid, something almost unforgivable. But there isn't any crime that lies beyond forgiveness. That's what literature teaches us, as does art and religion. Chad?"

Chad stepped forward, visibly shaken by our enemy stares. He began to say something, then stopped, cleared his throat, and started to speak again, all the Rutledge arrogance purged from his quavering voice. "I owe everyone here an apology. I don't deserve forgiveness from any of you. I wanted to tell you face-to-face, and I wanted you to hear me say it. Niles and Trevor can spit in my face like Fraser did, and I'd deserve it. I can't explain what I did, even to myself. Niles, you haven't called my sister since you got back. We hear her crying in her room every night. It's driving my parents nuts. She didn't know anything about the Middleton Assembly. I'm sorry. I apologize. I don't know what else to say."

I turned my back on Chad and continued to work on the hemline of Starla's prom dress. Sheba did likewise, and Trevor resumed his Schubert. Niles walked back to my room, and Chad stood in the middle of the room looking thunderstruck.

"Just a minute," Mother said. "Niles, come back here! Trevor, knock it off. Leo, you and Sheba look at me. You can choose not to accept Chad's apology, but tell him so to his face. Your rudeness I will not tolerate. This is not about Chad, really. It's about the kind of people you are."

"Niles, why haven't you called me?" Her voice breaking, Fraser cried out to Niles when he reluctantly came and joined us. "I went up to the mountains to find you, so I thought everything was good between us."

Niles looked at the floor, his fists clenched. "How can I call your house again? What if your mother answers, or your dad? Or even your brother? What do I say to those people? 'Hi, this is Niles, the neighborhood orphan. May I please speak to your daughter, Fraser, who lives in a mansion and whose family hates everything I am or ever will be?'"

"It's not what *I* think," Fraser said. "I don't care what they think."

"You say that now," Niles said. "But let's look at the future. What if we got married? Can you see the looks of your parents and their snot-nosed friends when they see a Charleston Rutledge marrying the mountain nigger? Ike and Betty, I mean no offense to you, and wouldn't use that term to hurt you."

"We dig," Ike said, looking hard at Chad.

"Mr. and Mrs. Rutledge feel terrible too," Molly said. "They wish none of this ever happened."

"If Trevor forgives you, I'll forgive you, Chad," Sheba said. "I've thought about what you did to my brother and to Niles. What I hate about your sorry ass is that you picked on the two sweetest and most vulnerable boys in the world. What do you think it's been like for Trevor to grow up? Always the sissy boy, the sensitive one, the effeminate little pansy boy. He's been a magnet for bullies like you his entire life. And they're everywhere, in every town and every school, waiting for my brother. To beat him up. Or strip him bare and take his money."

"I liked it when they stripped me bare," Trevor said, winking at the room, causing a slight break in the tension.

"So along comes Chad Rutledge," Sheba continued. "Handsome, vain, aristocratic, born with a silver spoon so far up his behind it looks natural. Chad—who doesn't know a thing about suffering, about misery. The worst thing that's ever happened to Chad is when he finished third in a fucking regatta."

"Your language, Sheba!" Mother interrupted.

"Sorry, Dr. King," Sheba said. "So you take my sweet, tortured brother and you mock him as a faggot in front of a hundred young Charleston assholes in Lone Ranger masks. You let my poor brother believe that he was being inducted into an old Charleston society because his talent had amazed the city. Trevor and I got us a daddy too, Chad. Now, he's a piece of work: a lunatic, a rapist, and even a murderer, we think. Only the King family knows about our daddy. And you know what we learned? This goddamn family'll fight for you. That guy over there you call the Toad? Yeah, that one, Leo. My father came all the way to Charleston to hurt us right after we moved here. He tracked us down again. We've been running from him forever. But he found us, and we ran to the Kings for help.

Know what? Mr. King loads his shotgun and throws another one to Leo, and they're out in the night hunting that son of a bitch down."

"Sheba," Chad said, "I can't help how you were born. I can't help what Niles and Starla have gone through. I can't even help that Fraser and I are Rutledges. All I can do is be sorry for something truly awful that I did. I can't take back what I did. But I can beg your forgiveness for it."

"If Dr. King and Mr. King ask me and Trevor to forgive you, we'll do it. We owe them that much, and so much more. But the guy you call the Toad has to go first," she said.

"That goes for me too," Ike said.

"Second that motion," Betty said reluctantly.

"I didn't do a damn thing to the Toad," Chad said, flaring and resorting to his old form.

Starla then broke her silence. "What you did, Chad, hurt your whole school. You hurt every one of us."

"I didn't mean to," Chad said. "I didn't think it through. It was a mistake made by someone who was never taught to think about anyone else. I was the center of my parents' universe. Even made my only sister feel ugly. That's one thing I'll never be able to forgive myself for."

"Does anyone have a vomit bag?" I asked. "I'm about to heave my dinner."

"Words are easy, Chad," Ike said. "It's action that's hard. How come Betty and I don't even know where you live?"

"Our parents won't let us invite you to our house," Fraser said, speaking for her brother. "They don't believe in integration, and they never will. But Chad and I don't think that way."

"Is it what you used to believe?" Betty asked.

"Yes," Chad said. "We were raised to believe that."

"That's how I was raised too," Father said. "People change. That's one of the nice parts about growing up."

"Father," I asked, "do I have to forgive Chad tonight? Or can I go on hating him for another month or two?"

"Here's what you don't know about time, son," Father said. "It moves funny and it's hard to pin down. Occasionally, time offers you a hundred opportunities to do the right thing. Sometimes it gives you only one chance. You've got one chance here. I wouldn't let it slip out of your hands."

Under my parents' withering glare, I went through the motions and Chad and I embraced. It was during that awkward, fumbling moment that I recognized the depth of Chad's suffering, and that the shunning he had endured by the cold silence of an entire school had devastated him. Until then, I had never seen Chad suffer through an authentic human moment.

Then he turned toward Niles and Trevor and Starla and put his hands out, palm up. It was like a white flag, and his voice was a high-pitched whimper, and a cry of surrender. "I keep looking for a motive, Niles and Trevor, some reason that would explain to me why I did that to you guys. The only motive I can come up with is that it was the meanest thing I could think of. And that you two guys were so far removed from the society I grew up in that there couldn't be any payback. It was the meanest thing I've ever done. And here's what's horrifying: I loved every minute of it. Until I heard that Niles had run away, that is."

Ike and Betty walked over to embrace Chad and welcome him back into our hurt, fragmented band. Sheba skipped across the room and kissed Chad on both cheeks with the chasteness of a European nun. "Be nicer, Chad. If you were nice, you'd be almost perfect."

"I'll try, Sheba. You guys gotta teach me the steps."

Niles took his time as he moved nearer to Chad, his eyes hawklike and unforgiving. Leaning close, Niles stared into Chad's eyeballs as though he were decoding a cipher that would reveal what Chad's heart was thinking. Finally, Niles said, "I'll let this pass, Chad, but it has nothing to do with you. I love your sister. Have since the day I met her. There's another reason. Because I ran away, I found my mama at long last. Found my granny too. Me and Starla been looking for them since we were little kids. At the Middleton Assembly when that asshole mentioned the *Chimney Rock Times*, it was the first clue I ever had about where to look. So now me and my sister can quit looking. When you spend your life as an orphan, you don't believe in happy endings."

"Niles," Fraser said, "I think you and I can have a happy ending."

"We'll see," Niles replied. "In our world it's bad luck to believe in them.

And Chad, I can save you some trouble—Starla won't forgive you and will die hating you, so don't even ask it of her. It's just the way she's built."

"Fair enough," Chad said. Niles went over and embraced Fraser, who began sobbing on his shoulder.

"Well said, brother," Starla admitted.

The attention of the room shifted to Trevor, who had sat through Chad's entire performance with his back facing the room and his hands covering the keys, as though he were going to play something in B-flat minor. His eyes never wavered from the keys, but he had taken in every word that had ricocheted around that room. He rose in theatrical splendor, ready for his moment in the spotlight. He approached Chad light-footed and flamboyant; Trevor always gave the appearance that he was walking across a pillar of air. On his face, he wore a crafty look, like a jack of clubs in certain decks of cards.

"I'm sorry, Trevor," Chad said to him. "I don't know how else to say it."

"It's all right, darling," Trevor said. "Let's just kiss and make up."

Trevor launched a surprise attack on Chad by kissing him right on the mouth, driving his tongue far into his throat. Chad backpedaled until his rear end collided with the front door, then he grabbed an ashtray and began to spit in it as though he'd been snakebit on the tongue. The rest of us doubled up with laughter.

"I can always spot a closet queen," Trevor said. He returned to his piano and started playing "One Last Kiss" from the musical *Bye Bye Birdie.*

Then my parents opened the back door for a mystery guest. Monsignor Max swept into the room, his biretta rakishly angled on his head. He removed it and hurled it like a Frisbee at me as Father handed him a dry martini.

"The King family has asked me to perform an exorcism, and there's nothing I can refuse this family. Will the miscreant introduce himself? Who is the poor sinner who needs to have the devil driven out of him?"

Chad came forward. "Sir, I think you're looking for me."

"Let's make this quick, son. Boil it down for me: I want the essence of what you did. And, my title is monsignor," Max cried out with great style and bluster.

"Monsignor," Chad said, "I think I was something of an asshole."

"Language, Chad," Mother warned.

"Forgiven," the monsignor said. "Your soul is wiped clean. Being an asshole is only another phrase for the human condition. It means that you are mere flesh and blood like the rest of us. Go now and sin no more."

Monsignor Max blessed the room with a sign of the cross, and the night ended with a sense of recovery and fresh joy.

April of that year is a blur, and May is fog-bound. But I have some photographs from that time to lend me guidance. At the junior-senior prom I am sitting at a round table holding hands with Starla, who is radiant in her new dress. Sheba and Trevor came with each other, and the camera seems to have settled on the lush beauty of the twins and refuses to move toward the other people at the table. Niles is unsmiling in his eternal gravitas as Fraser sits on his lap, elegant in a designer dress she and her mother purchased at a New York boutique; until I studied this photograph, it never occurred to me that Fraser had the prettiest shoulders and most flawless complexion I had ever seen. Ike and Betty are looking at each other instead of at the camera, and so are Molly and Chad. As I looked at the framed photo twenty years later, I was struck by the group's wholesomeness, by the remarkable youthfulness of our faces. We looked like we could never die. It struck me as amazing that all the couples present at that fateful table, except for the twins, of course, ended up marrying their dates.

Had Starla and I already exchanged the sweet words that would eventually lead us to the altar of the Summerall Chapel, where Monsignor Max would bind us in holy matrimony on the day I graduated from The Citadel? Ike and Betty got married in the same chapel later the same day, and we took turns being in each other's weddings. Sheba and Trevor flew in from California to be members of the wedding party, with Sheba serving as maid of honor for Starla. Niles and Fraser got married at St. Michael's the following Saturday, and Chad and Molly followed suit the next weekend. We partied long and hard that summer.

But I return to the forgetfulness of April 1970, and the oblivion of May. I picked up another photograph and smiled at the memory of my father taking it. Though we had nearly killed ourselves getting into position, Father had insisted we listen to his commands, and the photo turned out to be a treasure for all of us. We were in our caps and gowns after a rehearsal, and Father made us climb the magnolia trees that stood majestic guard of our porch. The trees were lush with their snowy, showoff blossoms that perfumed the Charleston air for a hundred yards. We clambered up the trees with some difficulty and much grumbling, the girls struggling up the tree to the left, the boys to the right. Father insisted we poke our heads out into the open only when we had picked a perfect magnolia blossom and placed it between our teeth. It took us more than fifteen minutes of cussing and positioning, but in the resulting picture we all look like new varieties of wood nymphs, our faces wild-eyed and starry, balanced precariously as we leaned out in what felt like mortal danger so Jasper King could take his ridiculous photograph. The photo turned out to be an artifact of that sublime and magical year. It made strangers laugh out loud when they saw it, and we came to an appreciation of its whimsical humor and, of course, the fact that Father had conceived the idea and had the patience to see it through to the end.

Joseph Riley Jr., a fiery up-and-coming politician, delivered that rarest of historical events, a memorable graduation speech, which electrified my class and made us want to race out and change the world. Molly invited her whole graduation class out to her grandmother's beach house on Sullivan's Island, black and white, rich and poor; Molly made it plain that she didn't give a damn and neither did her parents. She invited all the teachers, and again it was black and white together. I heard Mother say to the Hugers that Molly's gesture was the greatest act of leadership she had seen in her career as an educator. It thrilled the Hugers, and Molly did a polite curtsy in Mother's direction, but I thought I saw a dark cloud forming in Chad's green-flecked eyes. But I don't carry much of that evening with me. I remember swimming in the warm surf, and the swiftness of the high tide and the crash of the waves. The water was salty and fine. I loved Starla's mouth on mine, and the party lasted all night. I had to drive back as the sun rose and was late starting my paper route.

When I arrived, Eugene Haverford barked at me. But then he softened and presented me with a graduation present, wrapped in an old copy of the *News and Courier.* I unwrapped a brand-new Olivetti electric type-writer that must have cost a fortune.

"I know you want to be a journalist one day, so I want to see you working for this newspaper," Eugene Haverford said. "And I want to be able to deliver your goddamn shit around the city."

I'm still using that same typewriter when I write my columns today.

At noon, a large gathering of the graduates assembled at the train station for the departure of Sheba and Trevor Poe to the dream-filled state of California. Sheba would take the southern part of California as her trophy; Trevor would satisfy himself with possession of the northern sector. Their mother, Evangeline, was there at the station, and I think my parents were as well. I remember the roar of the crowd as the twins blew us kisses and the train pulled off toward Atlanta, but it is moving away from me now, losing clarity, fading out of range.

Instead, in my memory I am back hurling papers beneath starlight again, the gardens blooming in secret. I am riding through darkness, the streets feel honeycombed and spiritual again, and the sun is rising over the rouged and columned city as I pedal down Church Street and over to East Bay and right on Meeting Street. I could finish this route with my eyes closed or sound asleep, and I hated to give it up.

After I threw my last paper, I rode down Broad Street to join my parents for the morning Mass. I was a couple of minutes late, but I saw that Monsignor Max had a full complement of altar boys at his service, so I slipped into the front row beside Mother. It was then that I noticed Father's absence.

"Where's Father?" I asked her in a whisper.

"Feeling poorly this morning," she replied.

It wasn't until after the Gospel was read that an unexplained but electrifying sense of dread came over me. I jumped up from my seat and sprinted down the central aisle of the cathedral. I leaped onto my bike and rode like a madman to my house. Only later did the neighbors tell me I was already screaming even as I unlocked the front door. I raced to my parents' bedroom and found my father lying facedown on the floor. When I turned him over, he was already stiff to the touch, but I tried to revive him by breathing into his mouth and punching his heart. When

I breathed into him, pinching his nostrils closed, it was like blowing air into a torn paper bag. My air did not return from his lungs, but remained there in the darkness and quiet that was death itself. Then I found myself in our neighbor's arms. Evangeline Poe called the ambulance as I sat there on the floor wondering what I was going to do for the rest of my life.

When Monsignor Max finished the rosary at the viewing on Friday night, I went up to the opened casket. I kissed Father on both cheeks and silently thanked him for all he had done for me, for loving me at times when even I found myself unlovable. I removed his Citadel ring from his right hand, and I put it in my jacket pocket.

Mother observed this and asked, "Why don't you wear it?"

"Because I haven't earned it yet," I said. "After I earn it, I'll wear it the rest of my life." I am looking at my father's ring at this moment as I type these words on my Olivetti.

Much of the town turned out for Father's funeral. Half the doctors and nurses in the city had taken his science classes in high school. Monsignor Max came through with flying colors and started his eulogy by saying, "Jasper King was the finest man I've ever met on earth. I will wager that Jasper King will be finest man I will meet in heaven."

A huge crowd was present as he was interred in St. Mary's churchyard in a grave beside his son Steve. I thought my mother would collapse when she saw Steve's name on his tombstone, and I realized she had never been to visit her oldest son's grave. I had been there dozens of times, and it never failed to break my heart.

PART FIVE

CHAPTER 24

Home Again

When the Learjet taxies down the runway in Charleston, Ike spots the ambulance awaiting our arrival. The pilot parks the jet twenty feet away, and two orderlies rush out. With the steps lowered, Niles carries down Trevor, who slept the entire cross-country journey, and lays him out on the stretcher. Dr. David Biederman walks out on the tarmac to greet our disheveled, exhausted group. We look like a lost squad of soldiers that has been in the field and under fire for too long.

I shake hands with him. "Hello, David. I haven't seen you since I handed over the receipt book to you when you took over my paper route. Now you're a hotshot."

"My God," David says, "this plane is filled with the gods and goddesses of my freshman year in high school. Sheba Poe, I had such a crush on you."

"Of course, you were David," Sheba says. "Can you help my brother?"

"AIDS is a puzzle," he says, "but yeah, I can help him. I'll do everything in my power to keep him alive."

"You keep Trevor alive, I'll give you a toss in the sack every year," Sheba says.

"I'm married now, Sheba," he tells her. "Two kids."

"Did marriage turn you into some kind of nutcase?" she says. "I'm not talking about spending the next fifty years together, just a friendly roll in the hay."

"Leave David alone," Betty tells her. "Hey, Doc, good to see you again. You remember my husband, Ike?"

"The new chief of police." David shakes Ike's hand.

"The pig of pigs," Ike says. "Thanks for meeting the plane."

Niles asks, "Want me to ride in the ambulance with Trevor, Doctor?"

"No, that's my job. I want to check him out before we even get to the hospital. It sounds like he has not been on any medication."

"None," Molly says.

"He wasn't getting the best of care," Fraser says.

"It's a miracle he's alive," Dr. Biederman says.

Sheba says, "It feels like we spent ten years in San Francisco. And now, because God obviously hates my guts, I get to go take care of my bitch of a mother. Anybody got any cyanide?"

"Is it for you or your mother?" Betty asks.

"I haven't decided yet." A limousine pulls up beside the plane, and the pilots begin moving the luggage out of the hold.

"Go rest now," Ike says, "but we need to have a powwow Sunday."

"Let's go to my grandmother's house at the beach," Molly suggests.

After we drop off the others, I drive with Sheba to her mother's house. I walk across the street to visit my own mother. The dutiful son called her with a report of each day's activity in San Francisco, and she did a superb job of keeping me current about the high and low life in the city. After her retirement, Mother discovered that she had both a talent and a relish for gossip, especially of the salacious variety. I wrote several columns from hearsay she gathered during discussions at her garden club; it delighted her to be the unnamed source of some of my more controversial columns. Instead of viewing her spy work as rumor-mongering for her reputation-killing son, she considered her purposes to be Joycean: she had her ear to the Charleston ground as James Joyce did when he covered the streets and waterfront of Dublin.

The University of South Carolina Press is publishing a book of her essays on Joyce the following spring. She shows me the acceptance letter after we embrace in the doorway, and she leads me to a seat in the living room. Nothing ever changes in this house: the same furniture remains in the same position as when I was a child. Going home is like walking into a dream I have entered a thousand times before.

"Congratulations, Mother," I say. "I'll throw you a publication party."

"Of course you will," she says. "I've already talked to the Charleston Library Society to see about having it there."

"Do they let you bring liquor and food into the society? I've never been to a party there."

"That is under serious negotiation," she responds. "And we have plenty of time to plan."

"Pretty impressive. Your second book published when you're eighty years old!"

She doesn't rise to the bait, but tells me wearily, "Fix your mother a drink. I'm depressed."

"Why are you depressed?" I rise and walk to the bar. "You're getting a book published."

"Monsignor Max got some bad news," she says. "His lung cancer came back."

"I'm sorry. I thought they got all the cancer the first time."

"So did he. But he is taking it well. After all, he is a man of God, and he knows what his heavenly reward will be."

"Does lying about your age keep you out of heaven?" I tease her.

"Not if you're a woman," Mother says. "Now tell me all about the syphilitic Whore of Babylon and her brother."

"Sheba's across the street with her mother," I say. "Trevor's in good hands at the Medical University. Sheba is not syphilitic, and she is not the Whore of Babylon."

"You could've fooled me," Mother says. "Evangeline is a mess, Leo. She keeps getting worse. They need to put that woman in a home."

"That's what my friends all say about you."

"Invite them to my publication party," she says, "and I'll wow them with a lecture on the intellectual complexities of Dublin street slang in *Ulysses*."

"I'd rather shoot them than have you bore them to death," I said. "It'd be more humane."

"It's the final essay of my book, the illumination of my life's work."

"Studying the pages of the worst novel ever written in this great world," I tease her, as I always have.

"You got a 499 on the English section of the SAT," Mother shoots back. "Mediocre."

"Is there a statute of limitations on those damn tests?"

"They'll follow you to your grave. You never tested well. It's held you back."

"How has it held me back?"

"You could be a novelist," she says, "instead of a smut peddler."

Though it is hot in the city, I decide to walk over to Colonial Lake and toward Broad Street, letting the palm-filtered light welcome me back to Charleston. When I take a left on Tradd Street, the humidity of late afternoon makes my clothes cling to my perspiring body like some primordial skin. There are days in Charleston so hot it feels as though you are dog-paddling across a heated pool. A wind comes in from the harbor and I can smell the Atlantic again, the real ocean, the one that filled my nostrils in my boyhood. I slowly maneuver down the manicured, intimate narrowness of the street that has become my place of residence. I have returned to my home waters, and its un-sea-lioned depths, and its lukewarm shallows un-dungeoned by crabs. The Pacific is darker and grander and colder; I would choose a Gulf Stream over a Humboldt Current any time of year. As I make my way, I take in the good clean smells of the harbor welcoming me back to my birthplace.

As I near the Cotesworth-Canon house I think about the extraordinary circumstance that brought me a job to work off my obligation of community service in the glooms of Harrington Canon's antique shop. The outraged but distant relatives of Mr. Canon contested the will with a ferocity that surprised me, but I received the deeds to his house and his store two years after the case went into probate. I immediately rented the store to another antique dealer, who was pleased with my condition of retaining the name Harrington Canon Antiques.

His generosity gave me a jump start in the world. While I was a cadet at The Citadel, I rented out the first and second stories of the Canon house to young teachers at the College of Charleston. Mother was generous with her time and labor to be sure my garden was flourishing. In a large, spacious fountain, I raised Japanese koi and watched them swim, breaking to the surface through the lily pads, whose white blossoms were perfect complements to the gold and obsidian ballet of the fish.

I water the garden and check on the health of the koi before I let myself into my house. But the key I keep hidden on a hook attached to a drainpipe, and obscured by azaleas, is not where I left it. Nor has it fallen on the ground. My best friends all know where I keep the key, but they have just flown in with me from California.

Then it hits me in a bolt of pure knowledge, and I settle in for a long, recriminating night: Starla has come home for the first time in more than a year. I walk through a door I know will not be locked and into an air-conditioned house cool enough to preserve corpses in the morgue. Most of the liquor in the house will be feeding Starla's bloodstream. The kitchen looks like someone has tried to clean it with a grenade. I find her in the den listening to her favorite country music station. I don't think she has begun drinking yet, which can be either a good or a bad thing. With Starla, I know she is capable of presenting me with a whole array of women, all warriors, all hurt, and many of whom still love the man who found her in an orphanage chained to a chair.

I can tell she is taking psychotic medicine again because it always makes her gain weight. The story of every drink she has ever taken is written deep in her face. "Hello, my darling husband," Starla drawls. "Glad to see your loving wife?"

"Nothing like it." I walk over and peck her on the cheek.

"You don't look that happy to see me," she says.

"You've made it difficult the last two times you were home," I say. "Want a drink?"

"I've gone through your white wine," she says. "Let me kill a bottle of red now."

"Coming right up," I say. As I open it, I offer, "You look good, Starla."

"I look like death warmed over," she answers, turning and eyeing the room as I open the wine.

There is something in the order of my house that is capable of bringing to the surface my wife's most vicious insights—some accurate, some absurd; always painful. She takes a step to the window and looks out on the peaceful vista of the side garden: fountain, draped crepe myrtle, koi pond. When she turns back to take her wine, her eyes fall on a small ocher and crimson icon on the wall. She says with incurious flatness, "You really are such a pious little son of a bitch, Leo. I always forget how your professional niceness can set me off. I find it overwhelming."

"No doubt," I answer. I've learned not to argue with her and pour my own wine. My detachment is my form of armor that draws a long stare of her dark eyes—still lovely, as they were when we were young.

Above all, Starla cannot endure being ignored, and with the skill of a master fencer, she continues in that dry, conversational voice, "More than anything else, it was the thing that I most detested in you. It drives me away, and it always has. My family always loved their little church, but I've always preferred the asshole to the Good Samaritan; liked Judas more than Jesus."

She is openly baiting me now, and there was a day when I valiantly would have responded. But history has shown that waiting out the storm is more peaceful than flailing against it. And in any case, she has lost her edge with age. When we were young to marriage and she still had a grip on normalcy, her attacks were subtler and harder to withstand. This reduction to good and evil is symptomatic of a sad deterioration, and I stand there marblelike in my inability to be wounded, as she makes her case in an increasingly drunk, querulous voice. "I always have. I like shit better than ice cream. Breakdown better than the Rotary Club. I like the darkness," she says, and in some ways, I know she is being nothing less than sincere. "I trust it."

We have gone through many rounds of psychoanalysis and none of this is new to either of us. I nod, but my patience infuriates her, making her dig deeper, feeling for a soft spot. "I'm pregnant, Leo," she confesses abruptly, with calculated nonchalance, and though I try to hide it, the news brings a flicker of reaction to my face.

Her ability to read me is undiminished, and her face almost softens as she shares the details. "A guy from Milledgeville, I think. I don't know his name. I don't know him. I saw the clinic doctor and he scheduled an abortion, but I don't know," she says, her face suddenly wistful. "Something in me also wants to have this child," she says, and in the strange interior world that is my wife's, there is a bit of honest, wholly unfounded optimism in her words.

I am almost drawn in. I almost mouth the inevitable words of support or worry or whatever it is you say to people like Starla when they make an outrageous claim. She sees her opening and, with catlike precision, lands her blow in the form of a casual confidence. "Face it, Leo—it's the only kid I'll ever have. You know, I aborted two of yours. Two boys," she adds. "I asked."

An eerie paralysis makes its way through the vast network in my body, and the veins in my face react as if she has set them on fire. In three Charleston households I walk the world known as Uncle Leo; I served as godfather for a dozen children over the years and have always honored that title. I take so much pleasure in the term *godfather* because I secretly believe I will never father a child with the doomed, hurt woman I chose to marry. In my own arrogance, I thought I could make Starla happy by offering her entrée into a life without want or malice or conflict. Never did it occur to me that some people make an early acquaintance with a dark, disfiguring anarchy so strong that they cannot consider a day complete without the music of chaos roaring in their ears. Starla is such a girl. She was a lost soul on the day I met her. I now know that the most dangerous words in the English language are the ones I once uttered in all innocence to Starla: "I can change you."

As I sit in my den struck dumb by her callous admission of aborting our unborn children, I can feel nothing but a sadness that seems immortal. For a brief moment, I want to beat her head in with a fireplace tool. But that passes quickly as I look over and see the lostness in her eyes, which is her most chilling calling card. It is also the signature of an incurable madness that a shrink in Miami once diagnosed as borderline personality disorder. When I asked what that meant, the doctor told me, "It means you're fucked. She's fucked. I'll load her up with drugs, but that's about all I can do. The borderlines are mean, egomaniacal, relentless. Their job is to make everybody around them miserable. In my experience, they perform their jobs very well." I cannot mention the word *borderline* to a shrink without noticing an involuntary flinch in their reaction. I experience an involuntary flinch in my whole body.

As is usual in our encounters, once Starla has inflicted a sufficient amount of pain, her voice takes on a conciliatory note that is not to be trusted. "Are you mad at me, Leo?" she asks. When I don't immediately answer, she puts down her wineglass and says, "Please, Leo! Don't be mad. I didn't mean to say that to you. I hate it when I hurt you. I've ruined everything for you, and you've got to hate me for it. I beg you to hate me. To hit me. To kill me. To free me from all this. I'm crazy, Leo. I'm completely nuts. And I don't know what to do about it."

This is Starla reaching the boiling point, which is the time she becomes the most dangerous woman on earth. She is feeling around deep inside her, trying to resurrect the ghost of the young woman I fell in love with. But that woman ceased to exist long ago, and so did that exuberant young man who fell in love with her and promised to spend his life with her.

"Hate you, Starla?" I echo. "Can't do it. I can do a lot of things, but not that."

"Toad, I can make you hate me. I've got powers that I haven't used yet. The affairs I've had? I've had dozens of them. But no. Hey, I've got one— your kids! Abortion number one. I remember the nurses counting his arms and legs to make sure they cleaned everything out."

As I take this soul-killing tirade into my already shut-down nervous system, I hear footsteps coming fast up the stairs. Then I hear Starla's loud sobbing as she throws herself into her brother's strong arms. Niles is always her safe house, her hermitage of last resort. How great to have a brother like Niles, I think.

And then the memory of Steve rises up in the room. It troubles me that I cannot even summon up the palest image of him. His face is lost to me forever, as though he never really lived at all. Even Steve's photographs seem stillborn and shapeless to me. My memory has come to a terrible point, passing a statute of limitations from being able to call out my brother's face from the void. While Starla weeps as Niles comforts her with a tenderness I seem to lack, I wonder where my brother would've lived in Charleston. I believe in my heart that he would've married a local girl, a good Catholic girl, and they would have a houseful of kids, living on James Island or maybe over in Mount Pleasant. I would be a real uncle many times over, and my nephews and nieces would love me, and I would volunteer to coach their Little League and soccer teams. They would grow up knowing everything about me. My brother's kids, Steve's kids, would be the ones to take care of me when I began to die. Yes, Steve's kids, that noisy, chattering gang that lost all chances of being born when time and life went dark for Steve. I think of my own son, the one whose arms and legs were counted by an unnamed nurse—"One, two, three, four: all accounted for, Doctor"—and think of playing catch with him or taking him fishing in the Ashley River where my father fished with me.

I have an affinity for choosing the tightrope walk across the abyss and have developed a genius for the wrong turn. I chose a woman so broken along the soft tissues that she took me to her house of ash and veils. When did she disappear forever? What was the moment when I turned over in my marriage bed and found myself staring at the deadly black widow with the red hourglass on her abdomen? That hourglass keeps time for me.

Niles manages to calm his sister down. I catch his glances, feel the full weight of his great pity for me. I see him trying to make a decision about how to bring this enriching evening to a close.

Starla breaks away from Niles. She comes over to sit on my lap and weep hard against my chest. It would be becoming of me if I comforted her or hugged her or tried to ease her suffering in any way. I do nothing but let her feed on my coldness.

"Poor Leo. Poor Leo. You never should have married me! I knew the moment I heard you say 'I do' that you had destroyed your life."

"It didn't work out as planned," I finally say, as her hysteria will not abate till some response is given.

"Let me take her to our house," Niles says. "We'll talk about this tomorrow. We all could use some rest."

"I lied about the abortions," she says as her brother leads her out. "I would never hurt you intentionally. I didn't mean to have the abortions, Niles. I'm scared to death to have a kid like me. Leo, I stole ten thousand bucks from the wall safe. Take it back." She throws her purse at me. It glances off my chair and hits the floor.

"I keep that money there for you, Starla," I tell her. "That's your money. You can always come get it, whether I'm here or not. You know where I hide the key. This is your house, and you can stay here anytime you want. You can live here forever. You're still my wife."

"Get me a goddamn divorce from the Toad!" she yells at Niles. "If you love me, get me out of the paws of this Roman Catholic fanatic."

"We Catholics take this shit seriously, Starla," I say wearily.

As Niles takes her out, her profanities resound through the gardens and courtyards of Tradd Street.

I sleep late the next morning. It is about eleven when I awake to the smell of fresh-brewed coffee. Niles is waiting for me in the kitchen, badly shaken from the evening before.

"Starla took off sometime in the night," he says. "I wish it didn't turn out this way, Leo. I wish we'd all never met. We had no right to poison someone's life like we did."

"We're all innocent," I say as Niles and I embrace. Neither of us is embarrassed to cry about Starla's ruined, thrown-away life.

I wonder how many more times we will have to weep for her.

Always, it takes weeks for me to recover from these blitzkrieg encounters with Starla. But I see a truth in the latest one that I have not faced before. I think I have come to an endgame at last, and a deal breaker. As I drive out to Sullivan's Island, I try to figure out why I have stayed married to Starla for far longer than anyone thinks possible. My religion has certainly played in my stubborn choice not to take her through the divorce courts. Sheba and Trevor have always treated my unshakable faith as some teenage problem I failed to outgrow, like acne. I think I hold tightly to my religion with the same rigorous inflexibility as I hold the sacredness of my laughable marriage. The form of my faith appreciates the hardness and unapologetic rigidity of my church. It gives me rules to live by, and it demands I follow them twenty-four hours out of every day. It offers no time off for good behavior. The power of prayer has enabled me to survive the suicide of my only brother. And though I walked straight into a poisonous marriage with my eyes wide open, I take my vows to Starla to be permanent and sacramental even when I strayed. But something broke in the center of me when Starla flaunted the bloody arms and legs of a son I never knew I'd conceived. It is an image that holds mythical sway over me. I look at the water below me and try to think of what a life without Starla might bring.

As I turn into the driveway of the home I have always called Molly's grandmother's house, I realize that her grandmother, Weezie, died a good ten years ago. I park my car behind Chad's Porsche convertible and leave my keys, in case anyone needs to leave before I do.

Sheba's limo pulls in directly behind me, and I rush over to open the rear door for her. She swings her legs out of the backseat with the casual elegance of a vacationing queen, and tells the chauffeur she will catch a ride back to the city.

"How long do you keep the limo?" I ask.

"As long as I keep giving the producer blow jobs."

"Forever seems like a long time," I say. She holds on to my arm while I lead her toward the back steps.

"That's my plan," she says. "One that I can live with. The woman I hired to look after my mother is wonderful. She's so patient she can even put up with my bitchy ass."

"My God, she must be a saint."

Sheba punches my shoulder. "Shut up. I've never been a bitch to the Toad."

"You've always been great. I saw Trevor this morning. He looks better."

"He's getting stronger every day," Sheba agrees. "I talked to David, and he thinks he can come home in a week."

"Send him to me, Sheba. You've got your hands full with your mother."

"Mom's a lot worse than she was when you last saw her," Sheba says. "No short-term memory at all. Sometimes she doesn't know me from a Buick station wagon. And here's the odd part: I thought people with Alzheimer's are gentle and malleable. My mom's gotten mean as hell. She bit my chauffeur the first night home, and she scratched my arm today. Look."

Sheba unbuttons her blouse to show me four bloody lines running from her collarbone to her elbow. But that is not what I notice first: as usual, Sheba is braless. I stare at her magnificent and world-famous breasts.

"Sheba, I'm looking at your tits," I say.

"So what? You've seen them before."

"Not for a while."

"I heard about Starla," Sheba says. "You sound like you could use a soft body to lie down with."

"I probably could," I say.

"Why don't you ask me to marry you?"

"Because you've dated Robert Redford and Clint Eastwood and about a thousand other movie stars. I don't want my little wing-wang following those boys."

"Oh, that," Sheba scoffs. "They got me through some bad nights and more than a few jobs. Now ask me to marry you, Toad."

"Sheba," I say, dropping to one knee in a posture of grotesque overacting on the balcony of Molly's grandmother's house, "would you marry me?"

Surprising me, Sheba says, "I accept your nice proposal. And yes, it's time for me to have a kid, and I bet you and I could have a sweet one."

"What?" I echo, startled. But then Sheba makes one of her patented entrances for the crowd that awaits us. I stop at the refrigerator and open up a beer, then move into the sitting room where Sheba has just announced her engagement "to the Toad, of all fucking people." She kisses me with real feeling, which takes me by surprise, and my friends laugh at my obvious discomfort, with the exception of Molly, who raises her eyebrows, and Niles, who doesn't laugh at all. Despite his exhortations for me to leave Starla, the subject still carries the power to hurt him deeply.

"Sheba's just kidding, Niles," I assure him.

"I hope not," Niles says. "That scene the other night was a nightmare."

"Amen," Fraser says. "You don't know how bad it got when Niles brought her to our house."

"Starla's lost," Niles says. "It's over for her."

Molly doesn't allow herself to get drawn in, but says lightly, "Get on your bathing suits, everyone. The chief of police gave us permission to go swimming before he conducts his doom-and-gloom session."

"I forgot to bring a bathing suit," I say.

"I've got an extra one in the bathroom downstairs, Leo," Chad says easily, with no sign of jealousy, no indication that he's picked up on any clue that his wife's friendship with me has changed. "It'll be a little big in the crotch, but fit otherwise."

"The last one in has the shortest pecker and the littlest tits in Charleston," Fraser says, racing out the front door. She and Niles have a footrace to the beach. Both are still superb athletes and in perfect shape. Their sons are all ferocious competitors and eating lesser rivals alive in their sports teams.

I put on Chad's swimsuit, then leave the basement on the run, onto the sand and into the ocean until I reach a depth safe enough for me to dive in. The heat of the day vanishes in a heartbeat as I swim underwater until I burst out into the sunlight, then a wave crashes over me. I look back at the house and feel a deep gratitude to that disheveled, shabby cottage with its sprawling rooms and comfortable furniture. The house has become a fixture in some of our lives, a place of safety and refuge for the others. Due to Molly's generosity, I have always used the beach house as a place of escape and spiritual healing. She has always let me stay here at the house on Sullivan's Island whenever Starla embarked on one of her desperate walkabouts. The first time Starla ran out of our house on Tradd Street, she stayed away for a month. The second time she stayed away for six months, the third a year. Then I stopped counting. On each occasion, Molly brought me the key to this house, and I went out and stayed here. It is a place of comfort in a falling-apart life. I know every inch of this beach the way I know the oddities and markings on my own body.

Swimming into deep water, I am blessed by the warm currents of the Atlantic. My body feels as though I am swimming through a bright veil of silk in the green caress of the waves. Looking out onto Fort Sumter, I watch as the last ferry leaves for the return trip to the city. The island seems much too small to have started the deadliest war in American history. But I am old enough to remember when it would've been against the law for Ike and Betty to swim in these waters or to set foot on these beaches.

Molly swims out to me. She balances herself against my shoulders as

I stand on my tiptoes, and we ride the waves that answer some internal timepiece set by the laws of moonlight. This is the first time we've been alone since my bed in San Francisco, an evening that seems an eon ago.

"Cat got your tongue?" she asks. "Why are you being so antisocial?"

"I'm sorry," I say. "I don't mean to."

"Why didn't you call me about Starla?" she asks.

"Bad night, Molly. The worst. And, I think, the last."

"And your engagement to Sheba?" she teases.

"A joke. How else could Sheba grab center stage with all you pretty girls out here? She's a pro. She knows how to do it."

"I don't think she's joking."

Sheba is riding the waves with Betty, Ike, and Chad. The tides are strong and moving us quickly, already three houses down from Molly's grandmother's house. Sheba waves to Molly and me, and shouts: "Keep away from my fiancé, bitch."

Chad shouts, "Stay away from my wife, you horny bastard."

He says it with a smile, and it occurs to me that Chad isn't worried. The day has yet to come when a man of Leo King's ilk steals anything from a man like him, his expression tells me. I glance at Molly for confirmation and it is written on her face, which is resigned and even a little comforted. I can feel a density in her sadness, but also resignation to the case-hardened life she was born to lead. We have lost the ease of communication we enjoyed when we first arrived in San Francisco, where the sun set over an alien ocean, far enough away that we could put aside the responsibilities that lay in ambush for us in Charleston, and say things to each other we could never utter in our South of Broad lives. We are now shy around each other; a dark star has grown between us. Words have gone on holiday. Molly swims ashore and walks into the house.

When Molly calls us in, we go inside wordlessly, and go about helping, laying out food on a sideboard. The food is simple and perfect for a summer day. Niles made coleslaw and potato salad and baked beans, while Ike brought take-out pork barbecue and ribs. Molly puts out a stack of her grandmother's finest china and her best silverware and insists we use it, even as we raise our voices in a collective complaint and argue for paper plates and plastic utensils.

"I'm not a paper-plate kind of person," Molly insists, her face strained, but always the perfect hostess. "So kill me."

We spend a half hour listening to reports about news of the children and how the various sets of grandparents have managed to spoil them, to set them on the path to ruin, all the disciplined and well-trained children of my friends.

"My father took our kids over to our house on Edisto Island and went on a fishing trip that lasted a week. None of them brushed their teeth that week. Or changed their clothes. Or took a bath. He managed to turn them into savages in the time it took us to find Trevor," Fraser says.

"They had a blast," Niles says.

"Let's call Trevor," Molly suggests.

"Great idea," I chime in. Molly dials the main number for the Medical University. Sheba talks to her brother first, and I talk to him last. When I take the receiver from Betty, Trevor sounds exhausted. I say, "Just wanted to say hi, Trevor. Get some rest."

"Come see me and I'll promise to talk dirty to you," he says. "I think I'd be dead now if you guys hadn't found me."

"Old news. Now you've got a whole bunch of tomorrows to get ready for."

After I hang up, Ike rises. His innate authority brings the room to a hushed, patient silence. Though he is dressed in shorts, a billowy Hawaiian shirt, and flip-flops, his carriage lends him a gravity that is inseparable from his character. He clears his throat, takes a swallow of beer, and checks several handwritten notes on note cards. "As Betty and I see it," he says, "we still got one big problem. We don't know where Trevor and Sheba's daddy is. But we think it's a pretty good bet he'll end up in Charleston."

"How can you be so sure?" Fraser asks.

"We can't," Betty answers. "The guy may be a psycho, but he's a sophisticated one and a weirdly obsessive one. We've been looking at case studies today. We can't find anything like this in crime literature. This guy's special and he'll go to extreme measures to get at the twins."

"Betty and I are convinced that he will come here. From everything Sheba has told us, he started out as a run-of-the-mill pedophile; this usually stops when the kids hit puberty. But something snapped in this guy, and Sheba's fame as a movie star clearly drove him around the bend. We're lucky he didn't kill one of us in San Francisco. The authorities at Sing Sing sent his mug shot and fingerprints and his psychiatric evaluation when they transferred him to a mental hospital. They don't like to send their prisoners to a mental hospital; otherwise, all of them would act crazy, just to get out. You've got to be a special nutcase with a real gimmick to be transferred."

"I give up, Ike," Sheba says. "What was my dad's gimmick?"

"I wasn't going to tell you this," Ike says reluctantly, "but since you asked—he had a bad habit of eating his own feces."

The room fills with howls of disgust. Betty passes out copies of the mug shot, and we study the face of a moderately attractive middle-aged man who looks far more quizzical than monstrous. Sheba explains that when she was growing up, her father seemed like a hundred different men inhabiting the same face. There was no role he could not play with the mastery of a born actor, except he never let anyone know the moment when the games ended and the man himself stood facing the world without artifice. He had a flair for accents and costumes and personas. He forced Evangeline Poe into home-schooling the twins as he rented country houses and farms, and they sometimes found themselves living in homes with no address. He was a jack-of-all-trades and he would come home dressed as a minister, a rural surgeon, a veterinarian, a TV repairman. For each role, he perfected different mannerisms; he dyed his hair so many times that the twins used to argue over its natural color.

They moved every year, sometimes twice a year. In isolation, they grew up terrified and abused. Finally, their alcoholic mother made contact with someone in her family. Evangeline discovered that an aunt she'd never heard of had left her money and a run-down house in Charleston, South Carolina. It took her two years to make a break, but she finally summoned the courage to leave. She took the money the aunt left her, plus what she'd hoarded for years waiting for the chance to escape. She got a moving van to take them across the country for the chance of a renewed life. They were living in Oregon then and, of course, their father tracked them down because of the van. Sheba said her mother had always managed to make such small errors of tactics and judgment.

Now Evangeline is sick of running from this creep and can accept whatever fate is due her. Sheba Poe has returned home, and she is certain that her father will be making his way south. Besides, Sheba says, she is dead set on marrying the Toad, having a couple of kids, and settling down for the rest of her life. She has known too much chaos in her life and has caused too much of it in the lives of others.

"Sheba, would you knock it off about our marriage?" I ask. "You know I was fooling around."

"Actually," she says, "I wasn't. You proposed to me and I accepted. It seems simple to me."

Fraser is worried, though, and ignores both of us, addressing her question to Betty and Ike. "What about our children and our families? Are we placing them in danger?"

"We think everybody surrounding Sheba and Trevor are potential targets for this guy," Ike says. "He doesn't seem to set any limits."

"Then we can't help you anymore, Sheba," Fraser says. "We went to San Francisco gladly. But the stakes have changed. This is asking too much."

"Speak for yourself," Niles says. "I'll guard your house at night, Sheba."

Chad scoffs. "Don't be ridiculous, Niles. Our children and families are the most important things here. They trump everything."

Betty says, "Ike had an idea and I like it."

Ike asks, "What about Macklin Tijuana Jones?"

"No fucking way!" Sheba says.

"He's in rehabilitation," Betty says.

"Betty and I both talked to him today," Ike says. "Part of his rehab is taking a course. He's studying to become a bodyguard."

Betty says, "So, we hired him to be your bodyguard, Sheba. He can live in your basement room. A former Oakland Raider wandering your grounds at night is not the worst idea in the world."

"He came through for us. He delivered Trevor," Ike reminds her.

After a moment of deliberation, I say, "Do it. Or I'm calling off our wedding."

And the meeting ends in a relieved laughter that we all know might not last long.

CHAPTER 25

Parade

On the first Friday of September, The Citadel Corps of Cadets marches onto the parade ground from the four battalions to the rhythm of drums and bagpipes and in fine order. Captain Ike Jefferson had been sworn in as the new chief of police by Mayor Joe Riley earlier in the day at a moving and heartfelt ceremony that seemed both historical and familial as I watched my friend take his oath of office. Now the Corps was moving out in the reckless eloquence of soldiers on the march to honor the first Citadel graduate ever to become Charleston's chief of police. In his dress uniform, Ike stands at strict attention beside The Citadel's new president, General Bud Watts. The rest of Ike's large and vocal entourage sit in a red-ribboned section of VIPs. It is the largest crowd I have ever seen gathered at a summertime parade, and it gives simple testimony to how beloved and respected Ike has become in his native-born city. His parents, wife, and three kids seem delirious with pride, and Coach Jefferson cries whenever his son's name is mentioned, from the moment the marching band begins the music that calls the Corps to the field till the last cadet passes in review.

"Suck it up, Coach," I tease him.

"Sometimes you've got to take a stand and be a man," Niles adds, throwing back the words he'd screamed at us at every practice.

"You boys leave me be," Coach Jefferson manages as he wipes his eyes with a tear-soaked handkerchief. "Who'd a thought such a thing could happen?"

"Who would've ever thought my hard-assed coach was such a cry-baby?" Niles says as he walks over and embraces the old man, his own eyes wet. It is impossible to remain unflappable on such an amazing day. It seems like fully half of our Peninsula High School class is in atten-dance, and a rowdy contingent of our Citadel class of '74 has filled the reviewing stands.

I watch as Sheba's limousine pulls through Lesesne Gate. Niles and I drift over toward the front of the Padgett-Thomas Barracks. When the limo stops, I open one back door and Niles opens the other. Sheba wears a clingy yellow dress and a white sun hat that looks like a piece of archi-tecture attached to her head. She almost starts a riot among the cadets on guard duty. "Fashionably late?" I ask.

"Early for me," Sheba answers.

"Take this cadet's arm, and he will lead you to your seat," I tell her. "I'll help your mother to her seat. Trevor's waiting for you."

I walk to the side of the limo. "Evangeline? I'm Leo King. Remember me? I lived across the street."

"You brought us cookies. Such a lovely gesture. This man has tried to molest me," she says, her eyes fearful and confused. "Where are we?"

"The Citadel," I say. "Where the cadets go to school."

"Oh," she echoes faintly, "cadets."

"This one will take you to your seat." A young sophomore approaches Evangeline. I thread her arm through his, and as he begins to guide her toward the VIP section, she turns and looks at the perfect stranger lead-ing her through the restive crowd. I see the flicker of terror in her face, and before I can reach her, she seizes the boy's hand and bites it, hard. The cadet does not whimper or utter a sound, but continues to lead her to her seat, despite a bleeding hand. When she takes her seat between Sheba and Trevor, she settles down. The parade itself, with the cadets in their summer whites and the surging music of the band and the skirted polish of the bagpipes, seems to calm her roiled spirits. Niles hands the cadet a clean white handkerchief from his pocket, and suggests he go to the infirmary.

"Mom, you bit that poor boy," I hear Sheba say to Evangeline.

"What boy?" she stammers, her face taking in the crowd and trying for civility. "How pretty this, thing, is."

"Easy, Mom," Trevor tells her, with a pat of his hand. "Just enjoy the parade. Doesn't Ike look handsome? Yum, yum. The Corps of Cadets, let me at them, Lord. Just one night in the barracks."

"I knew it was a mistake to bring you," I say to Trevor. He is still too ill to be without the use of a wheelchair, but he is gaining strength by the day. It was a landmark day when he could brush his teeth unassisted; two weeks later he could comb his hair. He pitched a fit and told me he was going to crawl like a serpent through the streets of Charleston if I did not agree to let him attend the Citadel parade honoring Ike Jefferson. Under duress, I agreed, but soon regretted it when it took me an hour to get him into a coat and tie. Because he had lost so much weight, he could not wear any of the clothes that Anna Cole had forwarded from his former flat in San Francisco. The movers had stashed all of his earthly belongings in my attic. Trevor had forced me to unpack his impressive collection of LPs and to set up a stereo system in the downstairs guest room, where he fought valiantly to get back his health and buy a little more time on this earth. None of his records were scratched, and my house swelled with the heady genius of Brahms, Schubert, and Mozart.

"You're still so uptight about sexual matters, Catholic boy," Trevor complains. "I didn't mean to imply I wanted to sleep with the entire Corps of Cadets. Half of them would do fine."

"I'll take the other half," Sheba says. They flash each other the thumbs-up sign.

"The goddamn twins," Niles sighs.

"I'll second that," I say.

Before the cannons go off to announce "The Star-Spangled Banner," Niles and I try to warn everyone in the VIP section to brace themselves for the earthshaking report. But Evangeline begins screaming and clawing at the air like a wounded cat. Niles and I have to escort her back to the limo with Sheba in rapid pursuit.

"I'll take her home," Sheba says, jerking off her hat. "Guess this wasn't such an inspired idea."

"Put her in a nursing home," Niles says.

"I can't do that," she answers, fanning her face with her hat. "You ought to know that better than anyone."

"I do know that, baby. It's one of the reasons I love you."

"What about my legs?" Sheba winks as she enters the backseat beside her mother.

"They are the first reason."

Niles and I turn back toward the parade ground, and place our hands over our hearts as the band plays the final bars of the national anthem. We walk back to our seats, but barely get comfortable when two sharp cadets approach and ask me and Niles to follow them to the general's box. Surprised, we do as we are told, and find ourselves standing at attention beside Ike and the general, both of us confused about the meaning of this unscripted moment. Since I am closest to Ike, I whisper, "What's this about?"

"Fuck you, Toad," he whispers out of the side of his mouth. "This parade is to honor my ass. So shut up and let me enjoy it."

"I hope you fall off the jeep when you review the Corps and break your sorry ass," I say.

"You're riding with me. So is Niles," he says, unable to suppress the note of triumph in his voice.

"That's illegal."

"It ain't now," he says.

A military jeep pulls up in front of us, driven by a cadet who glitters in his well-groomed sharpness—a poster cadet if I've ever seen one, and I have seen swarms of them in my day. General Watts marches smartly in front of me and introduces himself.

"I'm General Bud Watts, Mr. King. Class of '58."

"Leo King, General," I answer, shaking his gloved hand. "Class of '74."

"Niles Whitehead, General," Niles says. "Class of '74. We were Ike's roommates."

"I know," General Watts says. "That's why Ike insisted you two have the high honor of reviewing the Corps with him. Mr. King, you take the shotgun seat beside Cadet Sergeant Seward. Mr. Whitehead, you'll be on my left: The chief of police will stand on my right."

I wish that my father had lived to witness this overpowering moment. The jeep moves crisply along the trimmed greensward. I look toward Bond Hall, where I had taken my chemistry and physics classes early in my Citadel career. Turning sharply left, the jeep passes the Battery salute team, then veers left again as we pass T Company, and then our old Company Romeo, who give Ike a scream of pride in his passage. Because it is Romeo, Ike, Niles, and I are all allowed to salute the company that had escorted us toward manhood. In front of the entire Citadel family, we inspect the whole Corps of Cadets, who appear surpassingly well drilled to me. The jeep drops us off at the general's box, and Niles and I return to our seats, but not before we embrace and thank our roommate on one of the best days of all our lives.

Then the Corps passes in review, in beautiful, faultless order, in the glory of the companies and the cadenced precision and bright flutter of battalions on the march—it is all surreal and disciplined and perfectly choreographed, and the parade goes off without a hitch. Only later do we learn that every person at the parade that day had been in grave and mortal danger.

The following Monday, I finish writing a column about Ike's swearing-in ceremony and the full-dress parade in his honor. I read over the words I'd written in praise of Ike, and somehow they feel inadequate. I brighten a sentence here and tone one down there, striking a middle ground that contains the seeds of both gravitas and humor. I read it again with a critical eye and decide that it will do.

I take the column out to the newsroom and hand it over to Kitty Mahoney, who had been hired on as my assistant the same day I became a daily columnist. She possesses a Catholic schoolgirl's brilliance in grammar, punctuation, and spelling, and she edits my work with a critical eye for pretension or overstatement. She is one of the crown jewels in my life, and we are both lucky enough to know it.

"Hey, Kitty," I say. "Another masterpiece. I don't know how I do it every day. Could you cut it to shreds, change every single word of it, then sign my name when you finish your butchering of my flawless prose?"

"Be a pleasure, Leo," she says. "Since you're writing about Ike, I can already smell the sentimentality."

"You're a hard woman, Mahoney."

Kitty's phone rings and I watch as she listens to a voice I don't recognize, but I see the alarm in her eyes. She puts the caller on hold. "This guy wants to talk to you, Leo, but won't identify himself."

"You know the rules. He doesn't give his name, I don't take his call."

"He says you'll want to talk to him," Kitty says. "He says to remind you of sad smiley faces."

I ask in a whisper, "Do you have a recording device on your phone?" She nods. "Can you still do shorthand?"

"It's like riding a bicycle."

"Then record this call—and take it down in shorthand," I say, sprinting across the newsroom to my office. I catch control of my breathing before I push the lit-up button and pick up the receiver.

"Hey, Toad," the voice offers immediately, in oily familiarity. "Long time, no see. The last time was in Frisco. I believe you had a pistol pointing at me on Union Street."

"I get a hard-on when I think of putting that gun to your head, Mr. Poe," I say. "I hope to get the chance again sometime."

"Name ain't Poe, friend. Never has been. It's not the twins' name, either. Nor their mother's."

"Let's do lunch."

The man laughs and it is the normal, relaxed laugh of a man with a working sense of humor, not the madman of my nightmares.

"I've got to talk fast, Toad. I'm killing you first. Then Niles. Then Ike. I'm saving the twins for dessert."

"I should be easy," I say. "Ike and Niles may prove a problem."

"Like shooting cabbage in a field," he rejoins with a laugh. "Yesterday, I had all three of you in the crosshairs, out taking your joyride in the jeep. I thought about taking out the regimental staff just to let them know I was back in town."

"The Citadel gets nervous about guys with rifles roaming the campus," I say. "I don't believe you."

"The eagle on top of Bond Hall? No one's on duty there during parade."

"There's an eagle on top of Bond Hall?"

"I was going to put a bullet through your brain, then had a better idea," he says. "I thought it'd be more fun to let you know you're being hunted."

"You're known for your sense of fun, Mr. Poe. We talk about it all the time. When did you know you were a pedophile?"

"My name ain't Poe," he snaps. "And I'm not a pedophile. I don't care what my kids say."

"Pedophile is about the nicest thing they say about you. And just for the record, did you enjoy screwing Sheba or Trevor the best? You started in on them when they were five. Or at least that's what my notes say."

"Hide your house key better, Toad," he rejoins, his tone no longer bantering, but menacing and foul. "I paid you a visit last night and watched my faggot son sleeping in the guest bedroom. Check your china. See you soon. Sweet dreams, Toad."

The voice, the threat, and then the secret man hangs up. I am drenched in sweat when Kitty bursts through the door and says, "I got it all. Word for word. Shorthand and on tape. Jesus Christ, what've you gotten yourself into, Toad?"

"Mahoney, never forget about your inferior status at this newspaper. You are a lowly secretary who is expected to call me Mr. King in a voice of reverence. I'm a godlike figure in the newsroom, revered in this great city."

"Fuck you, Toad," she says. "What've you got yourself into? That sounded like Count Dracula on the phone."

"Give me that tape," I say. I place a call to the new police chief and relate the conversation before handing the phone to Kitty so she can read him her notes. Then I race down the stairway to my car in the parking lot. I travel down Meeting Street at a breakneck, reckless speed, hoping to attract the attention of a city cop, but all I get are middle fingers shot at me from endangered tourists. When I reach Tradd Street, there are two police cars already there with cops searching the premises. Molly had let them into the house. I forgot it was her day to sit on guard duty, watching over Trevor.

I take her out to the garden, and am whispering the news of Mr. Poe's return when Ike joins us, his gait quick and harassed, and asks me to go over the details of the conversation, one word at a time. Instead, I motion for them to follow me into the house, to my den on the second floor, where I pop the tape in the recorder I keep in my home office and press play. Molly listens with horror, Ike with care, periodically scribbling notes to himself.

The phone rings, and I lift the receiver to my ear. "It's for you, Chief," I say. He takes the phone and listens with that same controlled intensity that I had originally noted on the football field. When he hangs up the phone, he looks thoughtful, but aggravated. "One of my guys found three cartridges on the roof of Bond Hall. No fingerprints, of course, but they were shells from a sniper's rifle. Where's your china, Toad?"

"In the dining room."

"Let's have a look."

"This is Charleston," Molly says. "This isn't a New York movie. Stuff like this doesn't happen here."

"You'd be surprised what happens here," Ike tells her as we go down the stairs.

"Not to people like us, Ike," she insists.

In the den, I open up the secretary where I keep Harrington Canon's finest china. I start lifting the light and delicate pieces of Rose Canton, which had become one of my favorites of the three complete sets that he had bequeathed me. But Ike interrupts to make me wear thin latex gloves. He too puts on a pair as I begin to inspect the china, one piece at a time. As I turn over the first dinner plate, I see it immediately. Molly lets out a small shriek of surprise as she spots it—the tearstained smiley face— knowing the history of that appalling signature.

"He's got your key, Toad," Ike says, looking grim. "It's lock-changing time. You know who to call."

I look up locksmiths in the yellow pages and dial the number next to Ledbetter's Lock and Security Company. A familiar voice answers and I tell it, "I'd like to speak with the owner—the dumbest, meanest, sorriest excuse for a redneck white boy I ever saw in my life."

"You got him. How you doing, Toad?" asks Wormy Ledbetter.

"Got a big problem," I tell him. "Had an intruder last night. Need to get all my locks changed."

"You got a security system?" Wormy asks.

"An old one. Think it's time for a change?"

"Damn right. And I got one. State of the art. Goes off if somebody farts in the rosebushes."

"Put it in, son," I say. "And when you finish here, how about doing the same thing to Sheba Poe's mother's home?"

"I'll do it for free if Sheba wears a bikini while I'm installing it."

"Consider it done," I say.

"I'll get all my guys over at your house right now," Wormy promises. "We'll get it done if we have to work all night. I'm gonna charge you twice what I usually do, Toad."

"Anything else would be an insult," I tell him. "And Wormy—thanks."

A policewoman comes in when I'm done and hands a note to Ike, who reads it with some puzzlement before he reads it to us: "A cadet named Tom Wilson skipped Friday's parade, but watched it from the roof of the fourth battalion. In the middle of the parade, he spotted a man walking across the roof of Bond Hall. The two men waved to each other. The odd thing to young Wilson was the man carried a golf bag full of clubs."

Ike ponders the note several moments, his brow wrinkled with concern. He tries to frame the words, then says to me, "Toad, here's what bothers me. And it really bothers me. Why is this guy telling you the truth?"

Molly surprises me by answering. "He's instilling the fear of God in all of us. He's ruining our everyday lives, and he knows it. He wants to punish us, all of us, for loving his children."

CHAPTER 26

Evil Genius

The city of palms and tea olive and unseen gardens turns overnight into a place of galvanic nightmare. The narrow streets with their houses riding sidesaddle, which have always brought me comfort and pleasure, now make me shiver with apprehension. Water oaks frame themselves into ogres, and Spanish moss appears as hang knots. Crepe myrtles come disguised as the bones of dead men. Though I have always loved Charleston at night, it now assumes an incurably sinister cast when the sun sets in the west. I wouldn't have gone for a walk beneath the streetlamps for the promise of either wealth or beauty, nor stepped foot in any of its storied alleys. Without my knowledge, Charleston has put on a grotesque mask that fate designed when an Atlas moving van pulled up to a house across my street more than twenty years ago.

Wormy and his crew of locksmiths descend on my house. Wormy promises both of us he will not leave my house till I return. It surprises me to see how solicitous and gentle Wormy is with Trevor. With genuine feeling, he recalls the talent show in high school when Trevor played the piano and Sheba sang "Lili Marlene," and, as Wormy phrased it, "blew the fucking socks off that school." Ike and I leave the house with the sweet noise of men working with tools sounding out on every floor. Ike waves to the cop he placed on duty in front of my place. When we drive past Niles and Fraser's house, Ike rolls down his window to talk with the cop he assigned to protect the Whitehead family.

Two squad cars are parked in Sheba's mother's driveway as we pull in front of the house. Sheba rushes out to greet us. "I've had a rough day with the Bride of Frankenstein. It's great to see you boys. The worst thing about this job is being bored off my ass."

"Don't throw open the door like that again," Ike orders her. "Your daddy's in town."

Inside, Ike strides through the house, untying the draperies of every window on the first floor, and instructing me to do the same upstairs, where I find Evangeline Poe sitting in a recliner beside her bed, vacant and unresponsive. Ike brings Sheba to her room and delivers a brief thumbnail sketch of the day's highlights. When he begins to play the tape, the uncommunicative Evangeline goes berserk at the sound of her husband's voice. Her shriek is unworldly and haglike, and loud enough to draw the attention of two cops on duty in the squad cars outside.

Sheba shuts off the tape recorder in an instant, and her mother is restored to the baffled vacancy that will be her natural dwelling place forever. When Sheba takes her by the arm to lead her to bed, she tries to bite her daughter, lunging like a dog at Sheba's arms and face. With surprising nimbleness, Sheba holds her mother at bay and succeeds in calming her down, then walks her to the bed to lay her down for the night, sending Ike and me downstairs to wait.

Fifteen minutes later, she returns to the living room with a bottle of Chardonnay, and pours each of us a glass. "I'm going to have to take a course in kung fu if she gets any meaner."

"She's a handful," Ike agrees.

"Mom tried to put my eyeball out with a bobby pin the other day," Sheba says. "So no more bobby pins. She hid the scissors under her pillow. I have to put her down a couple times a day, like a cop with a perp."

"Was that your dad's voice you heard on the tape?" I ask.

"No. It's Satan's voice. But unfortunately for me and Trevor and my mom, it's also my father. If you listen well and you're an actor and know about these things—it's his voice. It's a bottomless evil. I don't know a single actor who could pull it off."

She begins to weep when Ike plays the tape in full, as her father's demonical voice lays waste to the air around us. The menace in his undertones could throw a scare into a highland gorilla. It paralyzes me as I watch its effect on his daughter and study Ike's worried and careworn gaze. But when Ike reaches over and hugs Sheba when the tape is over, his calmness and professionalism is bracing.

"What can you tell us from the tape?" Ike asks her.

She shrugs. "That he's lost all control of himself. Control used to be his strength. He could push you to the point of breaking, then pull back. He would go from killer to lover of all mankind in a single breath. But he prided himself on his utter mastery of every situation. Now he's aiming his rifle at a bunch of kids at a parade. He's gone. He's finished. He's toast. Bye-bye, Dad."

"Do you have any pictures of your father?" Ike asks. "Any documents or birth certificates or anything that can help us get him?"

"Nothing. I've looked through all of Mom's things. There's nothing. Mother named me Sheba the day we escaped Oregon. The year we finally got away, I was Nancy. Trevor was Bobby. Or maybe he was Henry that year. Trevor was Clarence one year, and he hated it. When I was about six, Dad named me Beulah," she says, wrinkling her nose at the memory in a way that makes her look young and vulnerable.

"What perfect training for an actress," I say.

"I've been playing make-believe since the day I was born," she says with a small smile. "You get good at pretending you're other people, in other places, living with someone like my father."

"Well, you can't stay here alone," I tell her. "Pack your things, and your mother's. Both of you can stay with me."

"Isn't my fiancé a sweetie?" she asks Ike. "What did I do to deserve a man like this?"

"I'm not your damn fiancé," I tell her. "Quit playing around and get serious, Sheba. The guy on that tape's a fruitcake. And he has a rifle. You are not safe here."

"My dad may be crazy, but he's crazy like a fox," she says with another shrug. "He didn't like jail time, obviously. He won't make a move with those cop cars parked outside. Besides, I can't bring my mother to your house, Leo, or anywhere else. I've just gotten her settled down."

"Let's sleep on this," Ike suggests. "I need to come up with a plan. I'm beginning to think this cat may be smarter than all of us."

"He's an evil genius," Sheba says. "But a genius nevertheless. When's my lovable bodyguard getting here? If that guy doesn't scare the bejesus out of my old man, then it can't be done."

"Betty's picking Macklin up at the airport on Monday," Ike tells her. "The director of the school told me Macklin's the pick of the litter. Tops in his class."

"Can't believe I'll be glad when he gets here. I cleaned out the basement room for him this morning."

Before we leave, I give it one more try, but Sheba won't budge, unable to deal with the idea of moving Evangeline. Ike and I drive back to my house in a stoic, uneasy silence. The day has exhausted and terrified me. I have no particular gift for courage, and I don't mind sharing that juicy fact with anyone. Wormy is waiting for us, sitting on the curb, talking to the on-duty cop as we drive up. He comes ponderously to his feet to give us a hug. He tells us to take care of Trevor, and promises to kill anyone who touches a hair on the head of anybody he'd loved in high school. He says he wants to read about himself and his company in my column, and I give him my word of honor.

"I'll do Mrs. Poe's house in the morning," he says as he climbs into his truck. "I moved it up on my calendar. Just for Sheba."

I am fixing Trevor breakfast in bed the next morning when someone pounds on my front door. I open it to find Ike standing there, in terrible emotional shape. I have seen him in tears before, but I have never witnessed him so close to collapse. At first, I think something has happened to Betty or one of his children. When I grab his arm and ask if his family is all right, he nods with such emphatic fury I realize he is having trouble speaking. Leading him by the arm, I take him to the nearest couch. When he sits down, he drops his head and starts to wail like a beaten child. The sound chills me to the bone. I sit down beside Ike and hold him in my arms, but I cannot comfort him. Standing, I open a drawer for a box of tissue so he can blow his nose and wipe the tears from his face. He holds a tissue over his eyes, but the more he tries to gain control of himself, the harder he falls apart. Finally, he excuses himself in a voice I don't recognize, then stumbles down the hall to the bathroom. I hear him washing his face. Soon, he has gained control, and the hysteria subsides with each breath drawn. When he comes back into the living room, he returns as the police chief of Charleston.

"Can you take a ride, Leo?" he asks. "Just the two of us. Leave Trevor here."

"Of course," I answer, but with dread.

Ike waits till we are in the patrol car before he says a single word: "Sheba."

"What about Sheba?" I ask, but Ike nearly loses his composure when he hears the question. He waves me off, unable to say more, so I grow silent as he drives us to Broad Street. I glance his way when he takes a right on Ashley as Colonial Lake shimmers in the morning light. He drives to Sheba's mother's house, which looks like a used-car shop for squad cars. Yellow crime-scene tape circles the yard. It occurs to me then that something has happened to Evangeline. Ike parks in my mother's driveway.

"Is your mama home?" he asks me, staring straight ahead.

"I don't know," I answer weakly. "She's probably at Mass. What's happened at the Poe house? Goddammit, Ike, if it's Evangeline or Sheba, you better tell me."

"I can't. I'll have to show you."

We walk across the street. Ike lifts the tape and motions me to go under it. Solemnly, he nods to his fellow officers as several of the younger ones salute him smartly, but it's obvious there isn't a policeman or policewoman on the scene who is having a good time. When we get to the open doorway, we encounter two detectives who eye me with some suspicion. After I flash my press card, the suspicion transforms into open hostility.

"He's with me, Mac," Ike says.

"Tough scene for a civilian, Chief," Mac says.

"Tough scene for a cop," Ike says. "Brace yourself, Toad. I'm about to ruin your life."

As I enter Evangeline Poe's bedroom, I step into an abattoir. The sight and smell of it hits me, and I make a run out the front door, gagging. Taking deep breaths, I force myself to return to the bedroom. I go into shock the moment I take in the bloodbath, extraordinary in its grotesqueness. Sitting calmly on her bed is Evangeline, dressed in pajamas, holding a butcher knife and covered with blood. On the floor, unrecognizable if you didn't know her, lies the hideous, mangled corpse of the radiantly beautiful American actress Sheba Poe. She has stab wounds all over, even to her face and both eyes. One of her breasts has nearly been sheared off her body.

My eyes move away from Sheba, for I will never look at her violated body again. The sight of Evangeline is mythic in its dreadful power. She sits there still holding the knife in her hand. In her confusion, she sweeps the air with the bloody knife at anyone who approaches her. Her daughter's blood covers her hair, tangling it in bizarre kinks and curls. Her pajamas are drenched in Sheba's blood. Her face is a red mask.

"I thought she might recognize your voice, Leo," Ike says with great gentleness.

"Hey, Mrs. Poe," I make myself say. "Do you remember me? I'm Leo King from across the street. All the kids called me the Toad. I brought cookies over to this house the day you moved in."

She stares at me, a stare as vacuous as an open well. "Glasses?" she asks finally.

"Yes, ma'am. That was me. I wore horn-rimmed glasses then. I've been wearing contact lenses for years."

"Toad," she says. "Toad?"

"That's me, Mrs. Poe."

"Poe?" she questions.

"That's your name. Evangeline Poe."

"No. No," she says. "Mark. Mark."

"What mark?" I ask. "Is that Trevor's real name."

"Where's Sheba?" Evangeline asks. "She promised not to leave me. Mark?"

"Sheba's not here," I say, my voice breaking. "Sheba's not coming back."

Evangeline's eyes grow mean, and she flashes the knife at me in a quick cutting movement. I back up, even though I am already a safe distance from her. There is a policewoman both recording and writing down every word that comes from Evangeline's mouth.

Ike says, "See if you can get her to drop the knife, Leo. Otherwise, we're going to have to jump her, and I'd hate to do that."

"Mrs. Poe?" I ask. "You want to see your son, Trevor? Trevor's over at my house. He wants to play the piano for you."

"Trevor. Trevor," she says. Her face brightens in a surge of recognition, then freezes again. "Trevor?" she repeats without affect.

"Trevor wants to borrow your knife. Big surprise. He's cooking you dinner tonight. He needs your knife."

"No knife. I don't have a knife, Mark. Where's a knife?"

"In your hand. Is that a spider on your head, Mrs. Poe?" I suddenly remember a phobia of hers. She won't even walk in my mother's garden at springtime because of her incurable fear of spiders.

The knife slips out of her hand, and she begins swatting her head violently. The policewoman reaches over and grabs her arm. Evangeline bites the woman's hand so hard that she draws blood.

"Okay. Finish it up," Ike says. He then leads me out of the room, holding me by the elbow. I collapse against him when we make our way outside into the hot sunlight. Neighbors have gathered in clusters around the crime scene, curious, attuned, hoping for the worst in their malevolent gawking. At that moment, I hate them all, then instantly forgive their open show of raw humanness and innocent curiosity.

"My cops think the old lady did it all," Ike says.

"No. It was him," I say.

"Maybe, but we'll have to prove otherwise. They can't find another drop of blood in the house. If her father killed her, he would have to be covered with blood himself. He'd have been dripping with Sheba's blood, and we'd have found it all over the place as he made his getaway."

"The guy is slick," I say. "And from what I just saw in there, he's pretty committed."

"I want to ask a favor, Leo," Ike says. "Would you write a column about all of this? The threatening phone call you got at the office, the father stalking the twins all those years, and the commission of the perfect crime. I mean, Leo, I think this guy pulled it all off without a flaw. I bet my evidence guys will find nothing to prove there was another person in that room."

"Then, why do you want me to write a column?"

"I think it'll flush him out," Ike says. "And after seeing how he cut Sheba up for bait, I'd like the chance to kill him face-to-face. But don't write that part."

"I won't," I promise. "But I love you for saying it."

I stand up on the porch and stagger, but Ike is watching me. He catches me as I lean against one of the columns.

"My God, Ike," I say. "That was beyond horrible."

The curious neighbors will receive an immense measure of satisfaction when they get to report to friends and family that they witnessed a newspaper columnist and a police chief weeping helplessly in each other's arms.

In my column, I describe the shock of seeing Sheba's mutilated body and the dementia-addled mother who had recently grown violent, sitting on her bed standing guard, her knife and clothes covered with her daughter's blood. If Evangeline Poe had killed Sheba, I wrote, there would be no crime scene because no crime had occurred. I was witness to a great tragedy and nothing more: Alzheimer's disease had rendered Evangeline Poe incapable of either crime or rational act. I talk about the day Sheba and Trevor moved into the house across the street from the one I grew up in and my welcoming them to the neighborhood with cookies. And about the night the twins and their mother flooded into our home undone by fear of an unseen intruder, the same month I was attacked by a masked and fearsome man in Stoll's Alley on my paper route. I tell of the mournful smiley face as his emblem and calling card, of his constant predatory stalking of his two terrified children. I write about how in New York City, he was finally caught when he killed a doorman at a Park Avenue address where Sheba was staying. He was sentenced to life in prison, where he faked insanity, then faked his own suicide after his transfer to a mental hospital. I describe his journey to San Francisco, and the dead Indian man in the trunk of a car, and the break-in at the house on Vallejo Street.

I call him the man with no name, and I reveal that even his children had no idea about the true identity of their father. He made up a multitude of pseudonyms, changed jobs each year, rented houses deep in the country, insulated his children, raped them at will, brutalized them in every conceivable way.

While she was being raped, Sheba Poe dreamed of being a great actress, starring in tragic roles, speaking lines so powerful she could bring the whole world to its knees. When Trevor Poe's turn came, he imagined himself on the great orchestra stages of the world, bringing people out of their seats with the indescribable delicacy he brought to the works of the great composers. Out of the unimaginable ruins of their childhood, they both had managed to craft lives of exceptional beauty.

For the first time, I admit that Sheba Poe was the first girl who had ever kissed me. For a homely, bashful teenage boy, it was like kissing a goddess. And a goddess, I wrote, is what Sheba Poe set out to become as she took off for Los Angeles the day after graduation. And that is what she had become: a goddess of film and the limelight, with a body of work that will grant her a portion of screen immortality.

The *News and Courier* produces the photograph taken of her father when he entered Sing Sing to serve his prison sentence. A staff artist also creates a macabre version of that weeping smiley face that has made a guest appearance in all my nightmares.

Because Sheba Poe was famous, my column goes out over the wire services and is printed in newspapers around the world. On the day it comes out, the switchboard at the paper is overwhelmed by a deluge of phone calls. Readers call with leads, tips, hunches, coincidences, sightings of the father, and every other kind of minutia. We write down the name and phone number of each informant, carefully notated and checked for accuracy. Blossom Limestone at the front desk becomes unsettled by the onslaught of men and women who appear with handwritten notes or typewritten letters to me, describing the effect my column had exerted on them. A cop from the bomb squad has to intercept and check these letters before they can be sent up. After Kitty Mahoney vets them, she brings them into my office by the armload.

Ike rides over to see me when he can't get through the overburdened switchboard and takes the back stairs to my office. He wears an alarmed, impatient expression as he looks through the mounting stack of letters on my desk.

"We think we got something," Ike says. "An old lady who lives in the Sergeant Jasper Apartments read your article. She lives on one of the top floors. Can't sleep. Likes looking over the rooftops of Charleston. Saw a middle-aged man running out of a backyard and getting into a car in the parking lot. Says she thinks it was three in the morning, the night Sheba was killed."

"She give a description?"

"No. Too dark."

"The car?"

"She wouldn't know a Pinto from a Maserati," he says. "We need a bigger break."

"We'll get one."

"What makes you so sure?"

"Ego," I say. "This guy's going to get off on the publicity."

The letter comes in the next day, and Kitty lets out a scream loud enough to bring reporters sprinting from their desks. When she hands me the letter, I read it over twice before I put in a call to Ike. I check my watch and it says Friday, September 8. Time rushes by me without leaving footprints or any signs of its passage, and I am lost in the days. I hear Ike's voice on the phone.

"Something came in," I say.

"Whatcha got?"

"A letter. No handwriting. The words are all cutouts from magazines and newspapers. There's a picture of a toad at the top right of the page."

"A love letter."

"It says, 'One down. The cops are idiots. You're an idiot. I've never been a child molester. My kids love me. Next week hunting toads.' "

"That's it? Did he sign it?"

"Oh, yeah. His best yet, the most elaborate. He took his time with this one. The smiley face, the single tear."

"Red ink or fingernail polish?"

"Neither," I say. "I think this one is drawn in blood."

And indeed, tests are done that very day to prove that Sheba Poe's blood had provided the paint for her father's latest work of art.

On Monday, September 11, the funeral of Sheba Poe is held in the Cathedral of St. John the Baptist on Broad Street. Monsignor Max is pale and pained by the loss, but can't quite resist enjoying his finest hour as a man of the cloth. Resist as he might, he clearly revels in the attention he receives from the national news media. He sponsors a dinner held at the bishop's quarters for the many Hollywood producers and directors and stars who fly in on a fleet of private jets. The *News and Courier* presents a roster of headshots listing the celebrities who are swarming into the city to honor the slain actress. Meryl Streep is tearful in her news interview with Bill Sharpe and Debi Chard on Channel 5. Clint Eastwood is manly, Paul Newman shaken, Jane Fonda emotional, Al Pacino testy, and Francis Ford Coppola affectionate.

Living as I do in the backwaters of South Carolina, I had not fully appreciated the corroding effect of the celebrity obsession that has taken hold in America, leading to a maggoty and fly-spotted culture. But I catch my first glimpse of it at Sheba Poe's funeral when five thousand people surround the cathedral and violently press in for their right of entry. These are Sheba's fans, not her friends, and they have come from as far away as Seattle and Mexico City to sign the guest registry: the funeral home goes through seven guest books, and her fans stand in line till two the next morning so that they can record their fulsome, sentimental praise of their "favorite actress." Outside, the cathedral is a mob scene and Ike's police force has its hands full controlling this combustible crowd. Trevor has chosen the pallbearers—Ike and Betty, Niles and Fraser, Molly and me—and has asked my mother to push his wheelchair and sit with him at the front of the church. Devastated by his sister's death and the role his lost mother played in it, he is as frail as a wraith. As the pallbearers bear Sheba's body up the cathedral steps, I fear the crowd will overwhelm us.

"Let us touch the casket," a girl screams.

"We have a right to see her!" another cries as the crowd surges forward dangerously, nearly blocking the aisle.

"Oh, yeah, that's a great idea," I whisper to Molly wearily.

A fire marshal has cut the crowd to a lucky thousand people, but the place is overflowing as we make our way down the center aisle. The six of us are weeping openly by the time we take our seats in the first row. The search for Trevor in San Francisco has transformed our friendship into something deeper and finer than anything I've ever let myself feel before. The covenants between us are now unbreakable, writ in stone, and will be part of our self-definition for the rest of our lives. Sheba came back to us and asked us to accompany her on a quest, and all of us responded with an unhesitating answer of yes. But now, because of dark forces set loose on that journey, we are readying ourselves to bury the woman who bid us to travel west with her. During the funeral, all of us fall apart, and hold on to one another like lifelines.

Monsignor Max conducts a solemn and majestic ceremony, hovering over the Mass of death with an actor's natural attraction for center stage. His voice is spellbinding and I can tell he is well aware that most of the dignitaries of Hollywood are watching. I can almost hear my mother saying, "Max should've been the first American Pope," and I have to admit that there is something royal about his carriage.

The pallbearers have their first surprise when Wormy Ledbetter rises and walks toward the altar, where the monsignor leads him to a huge, embroidered Bible. Wormy reads the epistle in a Southern accent strong enough to have won him a minor part in the movie *Deliverance.* Trevor told me how Wormy had come undone when he learned the news of Sheba's death. He moaned that he and his men should have worked all night long to install a security system in her house. Wormy thought they could have saved her life. Trevor assured him that nothing could have saved his sister's life.

After the epistle, the six pallbearers give Wormy a round of silent applause as he returns to his seat, tears streaming. Chad rises up next and reads from the Gospel according to Luke. In his noble bearing and mellifluous reading, one could understand how breeding and aristocracy have played such a central role in the formation of the city's gentry. Chad's voice is silken and polished, and he reads the Gospel as though he'd written it. When he returns to his seat, he nods his head as he too receives a round of silent applause from the pallbearers.

When it comes time to receive Holy Communion, Molly grabs my arm and whispers, "Am I allowed to receive Communion? I'm Anglican."

I realize that I am the only practicing Roman Catholic among the pallbearers. I look up at Monsignor Max and he motions for all of us to come.

"The monsignor is saying everyone is welcome to the Lord's feast," I say. And I lead the pallbearers to the Communion rail, though Ike and Betty are reluctant, as only the best Southern Baptists can be. Letting me lead them through the ceremony, Ike and Betty make their First Communion at Sheba's funeral. It seems fitting to me that my mother, the purist, hits me with one of her most scabrous stares.

Outside the cathedral, the monsignor has enlisted six other priests of the diocese to serve the Eucharist to the boisterous crowd. With their chalices gleaming and loaded to the brim with hundreds of sanctified wafers, they plunge into the crowd. It mollifies and tames the mob as they are tended to by the priests. For the rest of their lives, they will be able to say: "I received Communion when I attended Sheba Poe's funeral in Charleston."

Then the wizardry of Monsignor Max flies into high, imaginative gear. After the Eucharist has returned to its tented lockup in the tabernacle, he lifts his head to give a special signal to the projectionist in the choir loft. At the dinner for the Hollywood guests the evening before, Max met and charmed Sheba's Hollywood agent, Sidney Taub, who had discovered her at eighteen and had proven faithful and honest to Sheba her entire career. I always thought Sidney was half in love with Sheba, but this caused me no concern; so was I. Sidney dug up all the glamour shots, modeling gigs, and movie stills that he could find. He arranged them as a slide show for the evening before, but the monsignor had an inspired idea. He suggested the slides be shown at the end of Sheba's funeral.

The first slide, of Sheba Poe in the full flower of her radiant youth, takes the crowd's breath away. How could a woman be more beautiful, I think, as I look at her green glittering eyes and golden hair, her perfect oval face, her full ripe lips, and a figure formed by the love of God for the shapes of women. In the second slide, Sheba is posing for the camera, petulant, sexy, and brand-new to town. And the third, a lost angel in a big city. Soon, with each slide, a gasp of pleasure bursts from the crowd. A muffled cheer goes up when she makes her first cameo appearance with Clint Eastwood. She is fresh-faced, joyous, Madonna-like, vixen, street-walker—and the funeral crowd falls into a rapture as we witness the slow, inevitable changes as her face matures. We watch in astonishment as she ages from girl to ingenue to young woman, her beauty deepening, her countenance more knowledgeable, more severe. Until finally, there she is in a Los Angeles restaurant dancing with Al Pacino. Again, she is dazzling, lit up from the inside, still possessing that unnameable something. That flawless look that only a cameraman can discover, a face and a body the whole world wants to make love to—to see and watch and adore again, again, and again. When the last slide is played and the camera snaps off, the crowd waits for the pallbearers to move the casket to the hearse.

As we take our positions, Molly says in an aside to the rest of us: "You boys will never know how hard it was to be in the same high school as Sheba Poe."

Niles replies, straight-faced, "Molly? We know everything about what it was like to be hard in a high school with Sheba Poe."

It was the sole bit of conversation we were allowed before starting down the aisle, and I know Sheba would have loved it.

A silence descends on the drive through the mob to the burial until Molly, always the nurturer, attempts to break up our grief and silence with small talk. Even though I know what she's doing, it almost irritates me that she is trying to divert our attention to a report from the evening news.

"Did you know there was a storm in the Caribbean?"

"Haven't had much time to watch the news," Ike says, distracted.

"They name it yet?" Niles asks.

"A couple days ago," Fraser says. "Starts with an *H*, and it's a boy's name. Herbert or Henry? Something like that."

"Hugo," Molly tells us. "They named it Hugo."

Like Sheba, it is a name we will carry with us for the rest of our lives.

CHAPTER 27

Guernica

It is the morning of September 21, 1989. The dogs of Charleston have begun to whimper in collective terror while the cats of the city are languorous and unconcerned. The windows of the great houses wear plywood eyeglasses as folks gird their homes against a storm still four hundred miles away. The air in the city is ominous and strange and illuminated from the outside in. A pretty lady plays the harp in the window of a mansion on East Bay. When she finishes, she rises and curtsies to a gathering of swells that have gathered for a hurricane party. Hugo will crash this party with his terrible dark fist. By tomorrow, the people of South Carolina will know all there is to know about the rules of the storm. The rules are biased and hard.

The great storm Hugo acts of its own lethargic, devastating volition. In an emergency meeting at the *News and Courier,* the journalists receive a briefing from a grim-faced meteorologist who has tracked the storm for days. He refers to Hugo as "monstrous, lunatic, and unpredictable." This is the worst news he offers us—and that the combined wisdom of all the weathermen on earth cannot guarantee what path the storm will take. It depends, he says, on the temperature shifts, fronts moving in the storm's path, the attraction of the Gulf Stream, and a thousand other things that fall outside the precincts of available data. It can still hit Savannah or Wilmington, or it could be swept northward and out to sea.

"Where do you think it will hit? What's your best guess?" a reporter asks.

"Sir, I think it's going to hit Charleston," he replies. "It's coming right at us."

Since I live south of Broad, my assignment is to cover any damage to that distinguished but vulnerable part of the city. Molly and Fraser have already packed their kids off with Chad to their summer house in Highlands, North Carolina. But both women have decided to ride out the storm at Fraser and Niles's house on Water Street, near the bend in Church Street. The parents of both Chad and Fraser have adamantly refused to abandon their city during its hour of greatest need. Neither of their children can talk them out of the decision. According to the parents, these houses had weathered storms from the Atlantic for centuries, and it was pusillanimous at best to ask them to hightail it to the mountains. Fraser has a furious argument with her parents that leaves them both outraged and helpless, and their daughter in tears. It has become a city of frayed nerves and temperamental exchanges.

I am writing a prestorm column when I receive a phone call from my mother, who is in the middle of one her patented dithers. Molly has arrived at her house and is insisting that my mother accompany her back to the house on Water Street. She demands to know that I acknowledge her to be of sound mind and body, fully capable of making decisions on her own accord, and that she is not about to abandon her home and garden to a storm named after an overrated and melodramatic French novelist. Echoing conversations that are taking place all over the city, I remind her that she lives next to a saltwater lake. If Hugo strikes the city, he will come in at night, at dead high tide, with a storm surge as high as twelve feet, and that will put her house, her garden, and herself underwater. As her only son, I order her to accompany Molly, and promise to meet her at Niles's house later. Advising her softly, I tell her to pack up her most precious possessions and all the food and water she can carry. When she asks if I think she is some beast of burden, I can hear in her voice the early warning signals of a madness that will soon possess the whole city.

All the roads and avenues of escape are clogged up with a manic traffic too eager by half to escape. By early afternoon, the wind is up and the river stutters with whitecaps as they merge in fury. Small craft warnings are posted everywhere, but are completely unnecessary. I drive out to where the surfers have clustered on Folly Beach, riding the greatest waves of the century. While eating the last oysters served at Bowens Island before the owners close shop and head for Columbia, I write down my impression of a routed, battened-down city. The radio and television have reduced our world to a single, malignant name: Hugo. I make my way into a traffic-less downtown at four in the afternoon. One thing I can report with certainty—there is no one driving into the city, but a whole army of folks is fleeing it. I cannot imagine a more apocalyptic scenario.

Driving down an emptied-out East Bay Street, I notice that the birds have stopped singing and the seagulls have taken cover; that the koi in my garden pond have sunk to the bottom, their gold-flecked backs hunkered down as the air begins to gust and sweat at the same time. I park my car in Mr. Canon's old garage in the alley behind Tradd Street; I give neither the car nor the garage much chance of survival if the storm hits. Inside my house, I drift from room to room trying to select items that elicit notes of ecstasy or nostalgia, but I discover I love the whole house and everything contained within its comforting walls. This house has represented something precious to me, a solid reminder that life could hurl good luck at you as easily as it could devastation or ruin. I have no rights or claims on this house, yet it has reached out to possess me; it has turned itself into a bright, lush hermitage of spirit. I cannot bear the thought of it being hurt or damaged. I place duct tape over all of its beautiful windows. I lock its sweet doors, and in her time of greatest peril, I abandon her, that love of my life, and walk over to the Whitehead house. I say a prayer for my house and ask the ghost of Harrington Canon to inhabit it in my absence.

"I have no children," I whisper to myself as I walk down Church Street, whose palmetto trees are rattling and whose oaks shake with the ancient grief of storm. "My life is half-gone. How did I get here, at this moment?"

The light is unearthly, surreal, almost an antilight; the city gives off a scent of resignation from its stones. About a quarter of my neighbors are riding out the hurricane in their homes, and there is a party atmosphere emanating from many of the houses I pass. The music of Vivaldi rides the growing winds out of one house; Emmylou Harris sings about the "Queen of the Silver Dollar" from another. Television sets blaze in the sonic lights of dens, where Hugo is the only subject under discussion. I have never before seen Charleston hunkered down or fearful, not once in my life. The city must have felt something like this during the Civil War when the Union navy was bombarding it relentlessly. I can feel the approach of the storm in every cell in my body, as though my body has transformed itself into some dark gauge of the planet's mischief.

A window shatters in a second-story piazza, and I look up to see a middle-aged man, his faced tied with a bandanna, breaking into an abandoned mansion. He may be the first looter sighted in the city, but he will not be the last. I flag down a police car and give the cops the necessary information, but the two policemen offer no proof that my fingering a burglary in progress is of any particular interest to them. Their radio cackles with directives streaming from headquarters. I hear an ambulance crossing the city in fingerpaintings of sound. For a brief instant, I wonder where Starla is, and I pray she is far away. Then I shut her out of my mind completely, the one thing I have learned to do best.

I turn the latch to the gate on Water Street, then open the door to a maelstrom, in whose creation I had played a part. The wind slams it shut behind me. I enter a formal parlor where the inhabitants of my own endangered ark cluster around a television. The satellite images of Hugo are breathtaking. It looks bigger than the entire state of South Carolina.

"It will never hit Charleston," Worth Rutledge announces to the room at large. I had forgotten that quality of know-it-all certainty in his cultivated voice. "It'll turn north when it hits the Gulf Stream."

Worth recently broke his hip while playing golf at the Charleston Country Club, and is still clumsy with his wheelchair. His irascibility is innate, but the accident has made it worse. Instinctively, I have always kept away from Chadworth Rutledge the ninth, and I do not look forward to spending what could turn out to be a memorable night in close quarters with the blue-blooded jerk. In the kitchen, Molly is busy preparing supper while Fraser passes around appetizers to the worried listeners as the Channel 5 news team keeps issuing disconcerting updates. Several wind-blown reporters, with their carefully coiffed locks a-flying, shout information about the wind velocity with a nation of whitecaps boiling behind them. It is 7 P.M., and our eyes are turned toward the terrible eye of Hugo as it moves its malignant powers and its prodigious vortex toward Charleston at its own dark leisure.

"Mark my words," Worth repeats. "The Gulf Stream will turn it."

"Darling," his wife says, "could you please hush your mouth? Only God knows if this storm's going to hit us or not."

"Don't be afraid, Mama," Fraser says, leading her mother to a chair and settling her, as she is trembling with terror.

"I always thought I'd die in one of these," Hess Rutledge says.

"Nonsense. Only sharecroppers in shacks and poor whites in trailers ever die in hurricanes. More people have been killed hunting deer in this state than have been killed by hurricanes." Worth holds his glass up for a refill, and I walk over to take it from him.

"What's your pleasure?" I ask.

"My pleasure is that my daughter make my drink and not you, Leo. I didn't realize the village gossip had arrived."

"I'll get it, Leo," Fraser says, hurrying to the elaborate wet bar in the corner of the room.

Molly peeks her head out of the kitchen, and calls, "Worth, behave yourself. Fraser and I already talked to you about being nice."

"I should have stayed home," he grouses. "My house is built like a castle, of heart pine. It is hard as granite. It would survive a nuclear attack."

"It's beside the harbor," I say. "The surge could cause waves higher than your house."

"The Rutledge-Bennet mansion has survived two hundred years without listening to the advice of a Roman Catholic," Worth replies, bringing my mother into the fray, a woman well able to defend herself.

"Worth," she tells him with great frosty languor, "I know that Christ died on the cross to save the souls of all men, but I can't believe he'd do it to save a bastard like you."

"Lindsay," Hess Rutledge murmurs in a tone of wounded dignity. "That was unnecessary. Worth lashes out when he's worried or scared."

"Scared?" he scoffs. "Of what? A little rain? I tell you, the damn hurricane will turn. How many times do I have to say it?"

"Tell Leo that you're sorry," Fraser insists.

"Sorry, Papist," he says, but laughs when he says it, and I know he is trying to make a joke to save face. The gesture is insincere, but I accept it in the spirit of a night's distorted reality.

Niles joins us after finishing the job of X-ing all the windows with duct tape. Then Fraser says, "Trevor, will you play the piano? The most beautiful music you know. Nerves are on edge here."

"Is AIDS an airborne disease?" Worth asks his wife, not bothering to lower his voice.

While Trevor plays, Molly serves us plates of oxtail soup, pork and steamed asparagus, boiled potatoes, and salads. We form a line and pass things hand over hand until everything is on the table. As we sit down to dinner, Fraser asks me to say grace, and we all take one another's hands around the mahogany dining room table that had once belonged to Mrs. Rutledge's great-grandmother. Trevor halts his rendition of Mozart in the middle of a piano concerto, but isn't ready to join us at the table. Four candelabra ignite the charged air with pearly, comforting light as I pray.

"O God of wind, O God of storm, we place ourselves in your hands on this night of mystery. This night of fear. There is a reason you brought this group of people together, and that is a mystery we will understand at daybreak. We ask that you be kind to this city, and this home, and these people. Because of our worship of you, we understand the calamities that can befall the world, the nature of whirlwinds, the power of words, and the glory of the Last Supper. We trust in your mercy, and tonight we hope you will justify that trust. I am sorry Worth Rutledge doesn't like Roman Catholics, and I trust you will torture him in everlasting hellfire for that grievous sin. Amen."

"Amen," the others say, and even Worth utters a stiff laugh.

"I hate showy, overelaborate prayers," my mother comments pointedly as she picks up her spoon.

"We need one tonight, Dr. King," Molly says as she prepares a plate for her father-in-law. "Leo, roll Trevor to the table."

"I'm not hungry, dear heart," Trevor tells her. "Just let me waste away over here while I tickle the ivories and trip the light fantastic."

"The music comforts me," Mrs. Rutledge tells him, with a wan smile. "I feel like Noah's wife. Before the flood."

"It's a hurricane," her husband says. "Rain and wind. It's not a flood."

"How are the children?" I ask Molly.

"Safe in Highlands. Chad says every inn is packed, as is everything else there. If things get bad, we may have to go to your place, darling," she tells Niles. And to the rest of us, "Ike's parents are already there; so are the kids."

"If I went north, I'd stay at Grove Park Inn," Worth says, concentrating on his meal. "A plush luxury hotel in Asheville. Know what I call camping now? A Ritz-Carlton."

My mother clears her throat and throws her napkin to the table. "I cannot spend a hurricane with this vulgar man."

"Be quiet, Mother," I command.

"We'll always have Paris, Dr. King," Trevor says, and begins to play "As Time Goes By" from *Casablanca*. He knows my mother reveres it.

He finishes with a flourish, and in the moment of silence, Molly murmurs, "My God, listen to that wind!"

"We should have stayed home," Worth Rutledge repeats. "If we die here, we won't even be dying in an important house."

"Shut up, Worth," his wife answers, standing up suddenly and heading for the guest room in the back of the house. She is followed quickly by Fraser, who spends ten minutes calming her down.

When Trevor finally tires at the piano, I carry him to the couch and tell him I won't rest till he drinks a milk shake, at least, before he falls asleep. The one great illogical result of AIDS is that Trevor keeps losing weight, no matter how many calories I manage to stuff down his gullet. He constantly accuses me of overloading him, like a French farmwife in the Dordogne force-feeding a goose. I try a hundred sneaky ways to get him to eat the most fattening foods I can conjure from a lifetime of cooking, but the food is not nourishing him.

I bring the milk shake to Trevor, then stand over my mother, who can't break away from the television, with its lifeline of information and advice. Hugo now looks like a gunsight with its crosshairs trained on our city. I pull on a rain slicker to go outside and take a look, and tell my protesting mother, "I'm covering the hurricane for the paper, and South of Broad is my beat. I've got to see what the water looks like," I insist.

"I'll come with you," Molly says.

"You most certainly will not," Fraser tells her. "Think about your children."

"Okay," she says as she pulls on her slicker, "I thought about them. Let's go, Toad. Before it blows any harder."

It takes our combined strength to force the front door of the beleaguered house open, then it slams shut with a fierce bang when the wind gains control of it. Debi Chard just reported wind gusts up to eighty miles per hour as Molly and I make our wind-blinded sprint to the Battery wall. A strange emerald light unnerves us both as we hold hands and struggle to stay upright while we run toward the hurricane. Climbing the steps leading to the seawall, we both grip the steel bars where tourists usually look out toward Fort Sumter and admire the mansions of East Bay. The rain stings my eyes and a sudden wave, crashing over the seawall, comes close to washing us into the street behind us.

"I get the idea," Molly shouts over the wind. We straighten ourselves up and watch Charleston Harbor turn insane and deadly. The water frightens me. I thought I had seen it in every shade of green and brown and gray. But now I watch the Cooper River leap out of the channel in a pure, undone white.

Hand in hand, we make our way back to the house with the wind behind us, making us feel like world-class sprinters. We are laughing hysterically as we are met by Niles at the front gate. "Go to the back door, kids," he shouts. "Front won't open. Went out to lock the shed and a crepe myrtle flew by my head—scared the shit out of me."

"You risked your life for a tool shed?" Molly says, the idea tickling her.

"Name a more embarrassing death," I shout as we round the corner of the house.

"There is none," Molly says.

Our laughter continues as we go inside, shaking off the rain and describing the harbor. It is extinguished in an instant when an explosion erupts nearby, somewhere on the street. The flame of a burning transformer flares the sky briefly, and the house is plunged into total darkness.

We make our way inside by feel, to the living room, where Trevor calls, "It's as dark as God's pocket in here."

"Storm lanterns?" Molly asks Fraser, who is feeling on the sideboard for matches.

"Light the candelabra," she tells her, "and get out the flashlights."

She speaks in a slightly raised voice, as Hugo has begun roaring into the city with its demonic winds, snapping pine trees as though they are chopsticks, sending them hurling through the illuminated darkness, crashing through windows. A water oak is blown over next door and more electric transformers explode like bombs up and down the street. Niles and I peel back a corner of a storm shutter to stare out of a small corner of a window on the leeward side of the house, amazed by the shine of the turquoise-green light that allows us to watch cars and yachts fly by, airborne and seemingly weightless. A dachshund flies by the window, screaming. More transformers blow in the next block and wires come down, coiled like spaghetti. A stop sign razors into the trunk of a palmetto. Giant gusts of wind almost lift the house from its foundation, but the old house holds firm, like a barnacle against a rock.

When Molly finds us by the window, she screams, "Are you nuts? If the magnolia falls, it'll take off your heads."

"Good point," I say. Niles and I retreat to the living room. Our ears begin popping and our mouths are dry as the air pressure plummets. Soon we are gasping for breath as we pass around iced-down bottles of water and beer.

"The house is holding," Niles offers in a cautious optimism that my mother quickly squashes.

"Beware of unwarranted optimism," my mother warns.

"Goddammit, Lindsay," Worth snaps. "You always talk like an English teacher."

"Not true, Worth," she answers acidly. "Sometimes I'm seized by idiocy. Then I talk like a Broad Street lawyer."

Worth can't answer, as the extraordinary noise of the hurricane is rising, the house shaking so hard the light from the candelabra shakes. "We shouldn't have stayed!" Molly calls over the roar. "The house is giving."

"This house is two hundred years old!" Worth shouts back. "Our ancestors built these houses to last. They'll withstand any disaster."

"Your ancestors didn't build anything," Mother says. "Their slaves did."

Worth is readying himself for a rejoinder when Mother's voice rises another notch. "Water," she cries. "My God, Leo—it's the surge."

As we'd sat there, water had begun to leak into the house from every doorway and window. At first it was slow-moving and methodical. Then the wind ripped the plywood off the windows and glass began popping all over the first floor as the pressure of a high tide and a thirteen-foot surge of ocean water leaned against the house with the full force of its unbearable weight. I was ankle-deep in water before I moved a single muscle.

"Can rain do this?" Fraser shouts, her face incredulous.

"It's the ocean paying us a visit," Niles shouts back in reply. "I always wondered why they called this Water Street. Let's move it!"

I get my mother to her feet and direct her toward the stairs, while Fraser picks up all eighty pounds of Trevor and meets me at the bottom of the stairs, where the water is swiftly rising. I shout at her, "Can the best basketball player in the history of Ashley Hall get my friend up these stairs?"

"You're goddamn right I can," she shouts back. "Can you get my parents up?"

"You're goddamn right I can. Niles? You got Mrs. Rutledge?"

"Coming out with her," Niles calls, all darkness and hallucination as he passes with her in his arms. I fight my way through the water to get to Worth Rutledge in his wheelchair.

"Where are you, Mr. Rutledge?" I shout at the room.

"Here, Leo," he answers in a quavering, hopeless voice.

When I reach him, groping through the rising, turbulent water, I find him up to his neck in seawater and completely unhinged. He grabs me, and in his desperation, pulls my head under the black, unquelled surge. I lift both of us into the air and shout in his ear, "Worth! I'm going to float us over to the stairs. Don't fight me! We've got to keep our heads above the water."

I hear Niles splash into the water behind me, then two lines of light from two flashlights catch our heads as I struggle to keep both my head and Worth's in the air. I realize that there are actual waves, wind- and tide-driven, rolling through the antique-strewn drawing room. Niles reaches me, and it is his strength, not mine, that gets us to the stairway. Worth screams in agony as we lift him into the stairway, his broken hip almost broken a second time—and get him to the landing. There, we put his arms on both of our shoulders, and carry him up to his grandson's bedroom. He is delirious with pain, groaning loudly when Mrs. Rutledge comes into the room, her unpinned hair streaming down her face. By flashlight, she searches through her soggy handbag and finds a vial of pain medicine.

"Mrs. Rutledge," I say in admiration, "in all this mess, you remembered to save your handbag?"

"A lady never goes anywhere without her lipstick," she raises her voice to answer. She taps out a few pills and tells her husband, "Eat them, Worth. There's no water." He promptly obeys.

The second story appears to be holding, and we towel off and clean up as best as we can. Niles and I sit on top of the stairs with flashlights and candelabra and monitor the rising water in case we have to make an emergency evacuation to the attic. A depletion of body and soul overwhelms me as Niles and I sit there in astonishment, watching the water rising stair by stair. Around three, we notice that the water has stopped its radical ascent. It stands still for half an hour, two stairs away from the second story. Then visibly, it begins to recede.

Outside, the winds have slowed, as Hugo begins to muscle his way out of town. The candles are nearly extinguished in the candelabra when Niles says, "It's over."

He surprises me by reaching over and grabbing my hand. In the eerie darkness and beauty of returning water, he simply takes my hand. I think it is just something he needs to do. As we sit there watching the water recede, I think about Niles in the orphanage on the day I met him, and guess he had wanted someone, anyone, to hold his hand during the long, dreadful forced march of his childhood. It was the least I could do, as he had long ago taught me a lesson about the great inner strength sometimes granted to the most wounded of men. And how those men can sometimes grow up to be heroes.

We fall asleep on the top of that stairway, and when I wake just after dawn, it is to a stillness that is more than still, a calmness that is more than calm. I go to a window and look over the stricken city: roofs have been blown completely off, piazzas felled, trees decapitated and uprooted. My city looks firebombed and unsalvageable, as if Hugo had taken it with a perverse sense of artistry, and turned Charleston into Guernica.

Niles wakes not long after me, and we descend the mud-blackened stairs. The ruin of the first floor is complete and unimaginable. Every piece of furniture, every antique, every Oriental rug, two chandeliers, portraits of the Rutledge ancestors, every Spode plate—all of it violated, or gone. A foot of mud covers everything. The food that was in the refrigerator and freezer is scattered, hidden by the ubiquitous mud, already beginning to rot. For the next few days, the city will reek like a cesspool.

I make my way to the window where Niles and I had watched the storm. It is now open, the double panes shattered. A 1968 yellow Volkswagen convertible sits in the middle of Niles's front yard, crumpled like a tuna fish can. Beside it lies the bloated corpse of a golden Labrador retriever. Fish are everywhere. The smells of sewage pervade the unrecognizable, un-Charleston city.

Niles joins me there, and puts a hand on my shoulder. "Go ahead and cry."

I cry, but it grants me no release from the sorrow I feel. The city of the rarest man-made delicacy is on its knees, all putrefaction and carrion.

"We can't stay here," Niles says. "Let's see if your house did better than mine."

We pick our way with great caution across the yard. "Goddamn," he says as we gingerly step over a downed, wrought-iron fence, "the shed held better than the house."

Indeed, the padlocked shed looks sturdier than the house, the water marks almost to the roof. "Worth's ancestors built that," I comment drily, making Niles utter a bark of laughter.

We climb over what is left of the fence and slowly make our way up Church Street on the east side of the street. It looks blighted and firebombed, but we reach the spot where the surge ceased its incursion, the mud line. Dead birds are everywhere, a dead cat, a yield sign torn in two equal parts, an Exxon sign blown in from God knows where, a smashed car, a downed live oak, an entire piazza in a yard, ruined gardens, ruined gardens, ruined gardens. To add insult to injury, the day has dawned hot and beautiful, the heat of the relentless South Carolina sun speeding up the awful odor of corruption.

Turning the corner of Tradd Street, we encounter even more destruction. This is not the place where I have lived my entire adult life. We shuffle with extreme caution through a street full of broken glass until Niles stops me when we arrive at my house.

"It looks good," Niles offers cautiously.

"Where's my garden gate?"

"Gone with the wind," Niles answers drily. "Do you have a key?"

I hand him a key and he unlocks the front door. We enter. Everything looks the same. My house stood firm against Hugo. The roof lost some tiles, the attic sustained water damage, and there were windows broken here and there. But my home had endured the worst of the storm and come through it as well as any house in the city. I cry, and again, it brings no relief.

"Take off your clothes, Toad," Niles says.

"Why?"

"Because they're filthy," he says, retrieving some towels and a couple of bars of soap from the bathroom, and running shoes from the closet.

"Glass," he says as he puts on a pair and heads for the rear garden toward the birdbath that overflows with new water. He splashes himself down from head to foot, then lathers up with soap. I do the same, my hair as stiff as an osprey's nest, then silken as the sun warms my desolate garden. Walking to the koi pond as I towel off, I mourn their death, then watch a small miracle as three survivors make their way to the top and flash the golden password of their miraculous survival.

"I have to go to work," I say.

"Of course you do," Niles says, "but I wouldn't go like that."

Looking down at my nakedness, his nakedness, we both laugh until we become giddy, sounding more like the noise you would hear coming from an asylum than from a Charleston garden.

After I dress, I make my way down a forlorn, wrecked-in King Street in a daze, walking over broken glass while avoiding the tangles of downed wires as though they are pit vipers. I climb over and through the branches of fallen trees. A policeman stops me and tells me I could be shot as a looter. I roar with laughter for a second time that morning, then show him a very soggy press card.

"You're Leo King, the columnist," he says. "Fancy that. I'm Sergeant Townsend."

"Could you do me a favor?" I ask.

"No, I couldn't," he says. "I'm on duty. You may not have heard. We had a storm last night."

I explain that I am a close friend of Ike Jefferson and need to get a message to the chief. I tell him Niles needs help transporting some folks from his home up to some cabins in the mountains.

"Why should Chief give a shit?" Sergeant Townsend asks. "He's up to his ass in alligators."

"His parents and his kids are already up there," I say. "Ike didn't order you to arrest looters, did he?"

"Naw. The jail is packed. Said to beat the shit out of them instead."

"That's my guy," I say. "Your name will be in the paper tomorrow, Sergeant."

Ike sends a station wagon to Niles's house and we load everyone in, except Molly and me. Niles does not like the thought of leaving Molly behind, and argues that she can't do anything for anybody until the National Guard clears the debris and power is restored. He points out that the damage to the Rutledge home and her own home is so devastating that she can't even begin to repair it without a construction team. But Molly remains adamant about staying, and she surprises me by saying, "Leo and I are going to find out what happened to my grandmother's house on the beach."

Niles says, "They're not letting anyone onto Sullivan's Island. The National Guard is keeping everyone off. The bridges are impassable."

"I found a boat," Molly says. "A bateau with a motor. It's ready to go."

"What will I tell Chad?" Fraser asks. "And your kids?"

"Tell them I'm in Brazil," Molly answers drily.

When they finally leave, Molly and I walk to the remains of the marina. We stop by my mother's house and find it wrecked and sad, the

Poe home nearly collapsed. But Molly is set in her mission and has no time for reminiscence or emotion. Ike has found her a boat, and it is tied to a remnant of the devastated marina. Boats and yachts are strewn across Lockwood Boulevard in cruel studies of wreckage; the sleekness of a million-dollar yacht is turned to mockery as it lies smashed and disfigured on a Charleston roadway. But Molly is single-minded and unreachable as we inch our way through a slain nation of boats to get to a small bateau that survived Hugo in Ike's neighbor's garage. I start the engine and Molly points a finger out toward Sullivan's Island. I tell her I know the way, and if I get my ass shot by a National Guardsman, our friendship is off. She does not laugh or say a single word as we cross Charleston Harbor and witness the devastation of the city as we pass by the great houses on the Battery. Because the boat is small and the tide is running high, it takes more than an hour to reach the southern edge of the island. Two shrimp boats are marooned in the middle of the salt marsh.

Then we begin passing beach houses, or what used to be beach houses.

"The poor Murphys, gone. The poor Ravenels, gone. Claire Smythe will be sick over this. But good for the Sanders and the Holts; they're still standing. The poor St. Johns, and the poor Sinklers," Molly murmurs. The litany of names continues as we make our way toward her grandmother's beloved house. Weezie's house. The summer house. Coming soon, coming soon.

"Where is it, Leo? Where's Weezie's house? Why would God take Weezie's house? It's gone. It's all gone!" Molly bursts into tears as I turn the boat toward the gap-toothed space that Weezie's house once occupied. I pull the boat up in the sand and secure it as Molly faces the negligible ruins of her childhood. She is on her knees in the sand, weeping, screaming, and out of control, not much giving a damn who witnesses or hears her grief. Only a pathetic remnant of the house is left, a half-wall beneath the house and a cement floor where we once played Ping-Pong and danced to the music of the Seeberg jukebox. The jukebox is gone and the Ping-Pong table demolished. There is a cheap Naugahyde couch that miraculously survived the deluge, but the water has moved it to the one remaining fragment of a far broken wall. There is a floor lamp, a dryer bag,

and a forty-five record, the sole survivor of the missing Seeberg. I pick up
the record and read the label: Johnny Cash, "Ballad of a Teenage Queen."
My God, I think, that song told Sheba's story long before she got here.

I hear a man's voice yell, "Halt!"

Looking up, I see two painfully young National Guardsmen with
their rifles locked and loaded and aimed at us. I drop the record on the
cement floor and raise my hands in the air.

Molly rounds on them. "Get off my fucking property!" she screams.
"You've got no right to be in Weezie's house. Get out of my grandmother's
house and never come back. Unless I invite your asses, which I never
will!"

She trips in the sand and sinks to her knees. One of the guardsmen
shouts, "We've got our orders, ma'am. No one can come on the island.
We're trying to prevent looting."

"Looting?" Molly shouts. "You think I'm here to loot? What would I
fucking *loot*? Hey, there's a Ping-Pong ball. Let me loot that. A beer can.
Do I see an old license plate over there? Do you know what I really wanted,
young man?"

"No, ma'am," both guardsmen answer, lowering their rifles.

"The photograph albums. Pictures of my family coming here every
summer. Five generations of us. Priceless photographs. Lost! Gone forever!"

"Gentlemen!" I call. "I'll take care of the lady. I'll get her off the island.
Give us a few minutes."

"That'll be fine, sir," one of the men says. Then they leave. Molly, the
Charleston aristocrat, had intimidated the boys from the up-country.
When I last look, they are running for their jeep.

It is lost on Molly, who has begun wailing again. I let her wail, because
there are some emotions beyond comforting. The privilege of sharing
such an intimate moment with Molly is not lost on me. We are standing
on sacred ground, a monument from her childhood. Though the house
can be rebuilt, it will take another fifty years for it to be sacred ground
again. Molly stops weeping only when we both hear an unearthly breathing somewhere near us. We walk wearily to the waterlogged couch that is
facing away from us, and find a six-foot porpoise lying on the cushions

as if placed there by the hand of God. It is miraculously still alive, and without breaking stride, Molly orders me to find something that will enable us to carry the porpoise down to the sea.

I find a fragment of the splintered Ping-Pong table that looks large enough for the job. With extreme care, we load the porpoise onto the slab of wood. We labor and grunt and sweat as we bear the porpoise to the waves. We look like foot soldiers bringing a fallen comrade off a battlefield. The porpoise is heavy, deadweight, and Molly and I are still weak from the same ordeal that almost killed the porpoise. I fall to my knees, then rise in time for Molly to fall to hers. But we keep the porpoise steady, and move him toward the high tides the moon is bringing to Charleston.

As the sun is setting, we reach the water and walk out till we are waist-deep. Cradling the porpoise, we let the fragment of table go. We continue to walk the porpoise through the sun-shot harbor as Molly's complexion turns to gold in the fresh, dazzled waters. For fifteen minutes, in our exhaustion and the peril of our brother mammal, we walk that damaged porpoise, going with the tide. We splash it with seawater and exhort it to live; finally demand it. We both need a sign that Hugo could not take everything from us, that a spirit lived in this land and in these waters that no hurricane could touch. Eventually, the porpoise's breathing grows stronger, and it starts to move beneath our hands. Its skin becomes shiny. It looks like a gold slipper in the last light of the sun. When I think I can go no farther, when I believe I will drop into the ocean and die myself, the porpoise suddenly knocks me over with a kick from its powerful tail and leaves us forever, with Molly and me shouting, tears streaming down our faces. We fall apart at the seams again. But that is all right. Our friendship is a bright ring between us.

On Monday morning, I write about the trip to Sullivan's Island and Molly's terrible story of finding her grandmother's house completely destroyed; but these stories are told a thousand times this awful season in Charleston. It is the porpoise that gets to my readers. By saving the porpoise, Molly has saved something in the soul of Charleston. I describe Molly Huger Rutledge's beauty, and I confess that I have loved her since the day I first saw her. Though I didn't intend it to be, the column is a love letter to Molly. In the final paragraph, I admit that I looked at her in a new way when that porpoise ignited to life and kicked away from us. This was a woman I had never known before. This Molly Rutledge had turned herself before my eyes into a sea nymph, a goddess of the storm.

CHAPTER 28

Seven Percent

On the Friday after Hugo, Molly and I drive to the North Carolina mountains to retrieve our storm-tossed families. Molly has succeeded in having three separate work crews begin the cleaning and repairing of the damage at the Rutledges' mansion, her own house on East Bay Street, as well as Fraser and Niles's house on Water Street where we had unwisely chosen to ride out the worst storm in the history of Charleston. I have managed to find a construction team from Orangeburg to start cleaning out the foot of black mud in the house where I grew up. I feel as though someone has put me through the rinse cycle of a washing machine for an entire week. Molly has spent the last seven days on her hands and knees cleaning the ubiquitous mud and scattered debris from her house; she and Chad owned some of the most valuable antiques in Charleston when the waters leaped the Battery wall. I discovered that Water Street had once been a creek bordered on both sides by salt marsh, and a favorite place for Charlestonians to fish and shrimp, in the early eighteenth century. Though the city filled it in and killed the marshes, the river preserved a memory of superb integrity and chose an ancient, dishonored path in its headlong charge into the city. You can bury all the streams and creeks you want to, but salt waterways remember where they came from.

Molly falls asleep as soon as we turn onto I-26, and does not awaken till I make the sharp, upward turn on the road that leads to the four shotgun houses where Starla and Niles were born. For years, I have heard that Niles was restoring these cabins of his childhood, but I was not prepared for the excellence of the carpentry and the shrewd attention to detail. He and Fraser have restored these ramshackle, unsafe shells into houses pretty enough to sit in the French countryside. On strong, fortified stilts, the four houses still hang over a pretty trout stream, and that clear water rushing over rocks becomes our white noise and our sleeping partner for the rest of the weekend. Chad has brought his and Molly's two children, as well as Niles and Fraser's kids, on his way from Highlands to Chicago. They rush out to greet Molly. The Jefferson kids pile out of their house. They all charge me at once and almost knock me down in their headlong joy and cries of "Uncle Leo!"

Mother walks out of the fourth cabin, and the sight of her moves something deep inside me. She looks like an old woman for the first time in her life. We embrace and hold each other and refuse to let each other go, and in that clinch of blood and family, we share a rare moment of connection as we listen to the stream rushing below us.

"My magnolia trees?" she asks.

"Standing tall," I say.

"The house?"

"The first floor flooded. Ruined. Got a bunch of guys cleaning it up. You can live with Trevor and me till we get it cleaned up."

"Your house?"

"A few scratches."

She answers, "Then God does answer some prayers."

"Very few in Charleston lately."

Trevor is sitting on a screened porch playing a harmonica, of all things; but Trevor could play Rachmaninov tapping a butter knife on a drain spout. The harmonica seems congruent with these rough mountains and their swift, coursing streams, and he sounds like he's been playing the instrument his whole life. He is playing "Barbara Allen" when I enter the house behind him and I wait until he finishes. I give him a glass of white wine and lean down to kiss his forehead.

"A little light making out before dinner?" I ask.

"You've always been such a tease," he complains. "All talk and no semen."

"Forgive me for unleashing that beast," I say, looking back at Mother in the doorway.

"Beast? I find that a brazen come-on," Trevor says.

"How do you know how to play a harmonica?" I ask. "I once heard you say a harmonica is to a piano as a sardine is to a sperm whale."

"Oh, a sperm whale," Trevor says. "By far, my favorite kind."

"You and Mother getting along?"

"She's been a peach, Leo. A living doll. Hugo changed her," he says. Then, with a nod at the harmonica, "Let me explain the instrument to you, Leo. You control the sound by covering these holes with your tongue. I'm an artist with my tongue, if you really want to know."

"I'm sorry I asked."

"But wasn't the answer fun?" he says. "I've always loved the suggestion of filth. The mere hint of the obscene with a small drop of malice has always been my favorite form of humor."

"I smell charcoal burning," I say. "Niles is ready to cook. Where's Chad?"

"In Chicago, on business. You think he was going to babysit his kids for a whole weekend when there's money to be made?" Then, abruptly, "I dream about Sheba every night, Leo."

"I can't talk about Sheba yet," I warn him. "I'll be able to soon, but not now. We haven't had a chance to mourn her yet. But we've got the rest of our lives to do that. I may write a book about Sheba. About all of us. About this."

"It won't sell a copy if I'm not the main character," Trevor says. We are laughing when we hear the dinner bell ring.

Our first meal in the mountains is celebratory, even sacramental. Niles cooks steaks for everyone and Fraser makes enough salad and baked potatoes and fresh vegetables to feed a changing of the guards. Coach Jefferson plays bartender and keeps the glasses filled all night. Mrs. Jefferson tries to coax any news we might have about Ike and Betty, but the only information I have received is that they are working around the clock and both have performed heroically during and after the assault of Hugo. Molly tells of her walks through the city and the sheer massiveness of the destruction. She has made the amazing discovery that a palmetto is more likely to survive a hurricane than a hundred-year-old oak tree. Her theory is that the palmetto tree has more natural flexibility and can bend all the way to the ground and still survive, but an oak knows only how to stand firm against the amazing blasts of wind, and makes itself susceptible to the perils of uprooting. She reports that the Citadel campus has lost more than fifty oak trees and she believes that there is not a single flower left blooming in the city. I say that the *News and Courier* has reported only thirty-two people killed in South Carolina, a number that seems incredibly low to me after what we endured on Water Street. Modern communication has enabled people on the coast to remove themselves from danger, and most citizens heeded those warnings. A few dumbos, like us, waited it out in our homes, and paid a stiff price for our hubris.

"Leo, I know you're talking about me," Worth Rutledge says. "I plead guilty as charged. I demanded that my wife stay and, of course, that meant that Niles and Fraser and Molly had to stay behind to care for us. If anyone had died, I'd never be able to forgive myself."

"We all made it, Worth," Mother says, "and had that rarest of all things in life: we had an adventure."

"I hope it's my last," Mrs. Rutledge says.

"We were happy to miss it," Coach Jefferson says, and his wife laughs in agreement. "It's like those football practices in August. Remember the two-a-days, Leo?"

"Never forget them."

"Hell, looking back, I can't believe what I put you kids through. But I also can't believe I went through it myself."

Mother says, "That football season led to a lot of things."

"On your first day at Peninsula High," I say, "could you ever imagine spending a night like this? The guests of Niles Whitehead and the Rutledge family of South Carolina?"

"That was a good team," he says, ignoring my question. "Good leadership."

"Especially the white cocaptain," I say. "That kid was hell."

"Was my daddy on that team?" Little Ike pipes up to ask his grandfather.

"Your daddy and Uncle Niles were the stars of that team," Coach Jefferson says. "And Uncle Chad surprised me more than any player I ever coached."

"What about Uncle Leo?" one of the kids asks.

"He would get knocked over on every play," the coach says. "But a lot of great linebackers would trip over his body as he was lying there on the ground." He pauses at my noise of outrage, then admits, "Naw, son—truth is, Leo didn't have much talent, but he got after it. By God, he would get after it."

"Let's talk about the cheerleading squad that season," Trevor inserts with a spark of his old passion. "Talk about groundbreakers: I was the first male cheerleader at Peninsula, and had the best legs on that team, by far."

"I beg your pardon," Molly says.

Our group moves inside as the chill night air takes control of the mountain. Niles lights an oak fire with fluid, expert movements, the glow of the fire sweet to the flesh. The house is packed as tightly as a bus, the kids littering the floor, or sitting in the laps of the seated adults. Little Ike sits on one of my knees and little Niles on the other. I know I will sleep deeply that night.

I am beginning to get drowsy with the fire when Molly and Chad's delectable fourteen-year-old, Sarah, speaks up. "Mama, we want to hear about the porpoise."

"How'd you know about the porpoise?" Molly asks.

"Daddy called and read it to us," her son, Worth junior, answers. "From up in Chicago," he adds, with a childlike wonder.

Molly looks perplexed, and I explain, "It went out on the wire."

"Leo referred to you as a sea goddess, my dear," Mrs. Rutledge tells her in her earnest formality, with a small note of fondness toward me, unheard-of before the storm.

"Leo was overwriting as usual," Molly says, though her eyes are shining with pleasure.

I disagree. "I was underwriting," I assure her.

The children insist on hearing the story from her own lips, and I sit there by the fire and listen as Molly's clear, drawling voice takes us back to the roofless, storm-damaged city we left behind. Her account is straightforward and accurate, but when she comes to the part about the porpoise, the story pulls up lame.

She hurries to finish, her voice drifting toward ennui, even disinterest. She ends with the flattest note imaginable, saying, "We carried the porpoise to the water and let it go."

There is a beat of silence when she is done, then young Sarah offers with the brashness of extreme youth, "It sounded better when Uncle Leo told it."

"Molly lacks my son's ability to exaggerate," Mother says in Molly's defense.

"What she lacks," I correct, "is truthfulness." I ask the children, "Have any of your parents' dull, witless, and boring friends ever told you any stories? No, of course not. The only man in this room who ever told you fabulous, wonderful stories is your old uncle Toad—the greatest guy of all time. Right?"

"Right!" they agree. But then instantly begin amending themselves—"Except for my daddy."

The bright, happy children of my friends have offered a secret source of pleasure for me over the years. My childlessness is an inner wound and a point of unrelenting tension between Mother and me, so I turned this lovely troop of children into willing substitutes. I made up bedtime stories for them that I refined over the years. I wanted to dazzle their imaginations, and I never told a story in which they themselves did not have leading roles; I cast them as kings and queens and Knights of the Round Table, as Green Berets and French Foreign Legionnaires. Together, we route the nighttime terrors by fighting beasts and giants and bad-tempered dragons. The children and I take on crooks and scoundrels and highwaymen and any bullies they encounter on the school yard, or any teacher who brings misery instead of learning into their lives. Though we always fight fair, our enemies always die. That is one of my rules of storytelling: the bad guy always has to get it, and his death is slow and hard. When they go to sleep, the evil lost in a frontier of night lies vanquished and still in the dust as I say, "The end," and kiss them good night.

"Let me tell the real story of finding the porpoise," I say. "It'll be your bedtime story for the night."

"I'm too old for a bedtime story," Sarah says.

"You're never too old for a bedtime story," I tell her. "The story's too important for that. Your father read my column in a Chicago newspaper," I say as example, "and the reason it made it so far was that the story was good."

"I'd accept that in a court of law," Worth says.

Fraser asks, "How many people in this room think Uncle Leo will exaggerate this story?"

The entire room full of doubters and scoundrels and humorless literalists raises its hands in the air, and the children's laughter skitters through the room like hurled marbles.

I say, "Betrayed by my own mother, the parents of my best friends, the children of my best friends, and then my best friends themselves. It's a low point in my life. Does anything I tell you sound true?"

"No," the children squeal in unison.

"Twenty-seven percent is true," young Sarah offers from her place next to her mother. "Some of it's true. Then you start adding things."

"Nineteen percent," Little Ike offers to the floor. "Uncle Leo's had me killing dragons since I was born, and I've never even seen one."

Amid the squeaking of the kids, I am moved by Little Ike. "When the lights went out and you were a little kid, alone in the bed, did you ever feel that there were things loose in your bedroom?"

"Yes, I still do," says Niles junior.

"But after I told a story, what happened to all those awful things that made kids afraid to go to sleep?"

"Dead," the kids say.

"Twenty-seven percent dead?" I ask. "Nineteen percent?"

"A hundred percent," the older kids say.

"Let me tell the story of Molly and the porpoise. Listen carefully, kids, so you can tell me where I made up things. Then you've got to be able to tell me what is real, what I didn't invent," I say. "Kids, I'm teaching you to tell a story. It's the most important lesson you'll ever learn."

Standing in front of the fire, I speak a single word, "Riverrun," the first word of James Joyce's novel *Finnegans Wake*. I wink at Mother, who greets my joke with a scowl.

As the river runs beneath us, I dive deeply into the sweet-water fathoms of story itself. "When news of the death of the great actress Sheba Poe flashed around the world, the first person to weep was God. He had taken great care in the shaping of that exquisite woman and thought that Sheba was one of His most flawless creations. As He wept one of His tears fell into the Atlantic, near Africa, and a wind began to move. It was an angry wind and it asked God what it wanted, and God said, 'Gird yourself for battle, wind. Grow strong and fearful. I will hollow out an eye for you in the center of your brute majesty. Go to Charleston. They let my Sheba be killed there. I name thee Hugo.'

"So Hugo rose out of those waters and twisted himself into bizarre and funneling shapes and he began his fearful trek to Charleston, holding a single tear from God's eye. When he reached Charleston, he crushed the city. His weapons were the winds and rains and tides of God. He chopped down houses and blew away roofs and flooded streets. The only place that Hugo did not touch was the grave of Sheba Poe, which was as dry as a prayer book. Every flower ripped from the gardens of Charleston fell from the skies to honor her, sent to her grave by the hand of a loving and merciful God.

"This merciful God spared the lives of some people who waited out the storm on Water Street. He let them live for reasons all His own, and we will never begin to understand them. One of them was the lovely Molly Rutledge, who was born a princess in the Holy City and who grew up to become one of its queens. Her childhood was a cakewalk and a dream, and she had most loved her summers spent at her grandmother's house on Sullivan's Island. Queens often feel things that normal people are not allowed to feel. Molly feared for her grandmother's house, for Weezie's house. She went out to her stable and grabbed a peasant boy named

Leo, who worked in the stable taking care of jackasses and chickens. She grabbed Leo by the ear and demanded he find a boat and take her to the island. Leo ran to commandeer a boat stolen by an evil police captain.

"As the crisp air rushed through the queen's golden hair, she looked back at her hurt city with tears in her eyes. Then she smelled something foul and thought to herself that the peasant boy smelled exactly like a jackass. At the same time, Leo thought this queen smelled like tea olive or jasmine. As they neared the island, something stirred in the water. Molly found her boat surrounded by a magnificent but troubled school of porpoises. When she asked the porpoises what was the matter, a solemn voice called out that the pod had lost their queen during the storm. The queen was stranded on dry land but they could hear her crying out. Molly made a solemn vow to help. When a queen makes a pledge, it carries the rule of law.

"The boat rode the waves into the place where Weezie's house had once been. Molly wept when she saw that the storm had taken Weezie's house. But she called to the peasant boy, Leo. They ran together and found the stranded porpoise lying on a white couch in the ruins of a flooded, imploded house. The porpoise's name was Sheba, and she looked lost and forlorn and abandoned. She had given up all hope of rescue and had resigned herself to a slow death in the fog now lifting off the waters. But another queen and a peasant boy who smelled like a jackass placed her on a piece of wood, and they struggled and grunted as they staggered beneath the weight of that lovely mammal. They tripped on sand dunes and their muscles spasmed in agony as they made it finally to the waves.

"The school of porpoises was watching the effort and began applauding. They danced across the waters with their tails; in a language that was not interpretable, a language known only to animals and very small children, they commanded that Molly and Leo remain strong and save the pretty monarch.

"In the ocean, Queen Sheba stirred to life. Then her king appeared beside her, and her honor guard rushed around her in the ecstasy of her survival. Molly cleaned the sand from her blowhole. Arching her beautiful tail, Sheba dove out into the great ocean, which was both her palace and her home.

"Queen Molly took Leo home and left him with the jackasses and the chickens; she went to her castle. She thought that the loss of Weezie's house was more than made up for by the recovery of the porpoise Sheba. 'Always choose life over possessions. Always!' Queen Molly said, as she climbed into her bed for the night.

"Good night, Hugo. And farewell."

As soon as I bowed my conclusion, Sarah announced, with conviction: "Twelve percent."

"What about the goddess of the storm part?" Fraser asked. "That was my favorite part."

"I've already written that," I say. "What's important is that a story changes every time you say it out loud. When you put it on paper, it can never change. But the more times you tell it, the more changes will occur. A story is a living thing; it moves and shifts. If I had each one of you tell me the story the same way I just told it, no one could do it. Now, is it time to get you rascals to bed?"

"No!" the kids chorus.

"Past time," Fraser says.

When I go to bed on the couch, I find myself agitated and sleepless. I pour a glass of Grand Marnier and quietly tiptoe past the bedroom where Mother and Trevor sleep. The moon is out and it proves a bright comfort as I walk the road higher up the mountain until I find a shelf of exposed granite I can sit on to think about the rest of my life. I am thinking about the awful way Sheba died when a penny hits the rock beside me and bounces into the mountain laurel forest below.

"For your thoughts," Molly says, sitting beside me and hooking her arm through mine. She takes the snifter and drinks a sip. Her breath grows orangey and sweet, like it was the night in San Francisco when she came to my bed.

"Sheba," I say. "I wonder if she really wanted to marry me or was just joking around."

"She thought her career was finished, Leo," Molly says. "She wasn't a big fan of Hollywood men. She wanted a kid. She wanted to settle down."

"Sheba settling down? I don't believe it for a second."

"Me, neither. She had a restless spirit. A tormented soul. And a dreadful end."

"You don't know how dreadful."

"Speaking of endings," Molly says after a moment, "thanks for your story. I guess I can quit worrying about how to tell you. You let me know you already understood."

"The queen always goes back to the castle," I say. "I always knew you'd never leave Chad. And if it helps anything, I think it's the right thing to do."

"Please don't go noble on me, Toad," she says. "I can't stand that. But I belong with Chad. I belong with my house and children. I belong where I was born to be."

She isn't telling me anything I didn't already know, and I just nod. We sit there another moment in silence, then I bring our brief glimmer of forever to an end with, predictably, a joke. "If Chad ever beats you up or farts too loudly or just wakes up with bad breath and body odor, you can always come to me, Molly."

She smiles, but her smile is sad. "If I leave, then your story won't be true. And your story is true," she says. "One hundred percent true."

Molly kisses me, then walks back down the hill crowned by moonlight, now a goddess of these hills.

CHAPTER 29

Locked Doors

I return to a hurt city with the sound of chain saws echoing over the alleyways and cobblestones. Squat brown Dumpsters line the streets of the old town as workers fill them with waterlogged furniture. Whole libraries have died on their shelves and bookcases. Paintings of the founders of the colony find themselves tossed on junk heaps, sodden beyond recognition or hope of restoration. The shrimping fleet of Shem Creek has disappeared from the face of the earth. The corpses of sleek yachts lie marooned in the green flanks of the great salt marsh. A red fire truck lies upside down in the marsh behind Sullivan's Island. Insurance agents who have lived quiet, low-key lives find themselves the busiest, most harried people in town, spending sleepless nights.

The reporters at the *News and Courier* do not lose their early grit and resolve. I consider myself lucky to have lived through my paper's finest days. We hit the ground running every day and deliver the goods to our readers the following morning. Before, reading the *News and Courier* was a perfunctory, sometimes compulsive habit to start the day. But after Hugo, it has become a necessity, a road map to survival in the humid, haunted days that have followed the storm.

In the first week, a decadent, putrescent smell hangs over Charleston, caused by the rotting of sea life that Hugo had tossed ashore in its great tidal assault, stranding all varieties in ivy and honeysuckle vines. Molly finds a five-foot sand shark behind her guesthouse, decomposing in the bright sun. Some sewage lines have broken and the smell of excrement adds itself to the air we have to breathe. As I walk the city from north to south, east to west, covering all the neighborhoods, looking for human interest stories, I become conscious of a slight nausea I can't shake. The bloated corpses of dogs and cats, raccoons and possums, seagulls and pelicans, add their decomposing stench to the miasma of foul smells that have hung over the city like a mist for a week.

On Monday morning, South Carolina Electric and Gas makes heroic progress in restoring power to the city. Because the telephone lines are mostly underground, the phone service returns with astonishing speed. After finishing my column, I check on the progress of the work crews who are cleaning up the houses of my mother and my friends. I drive to my mother's house just in time to see the bed and mattress where my brother and I were conceived hurled into a Dumpster. The begrimed workers are making significant progress at the Rutledge mansions on East Bay Street. But as I walk up Water Street toward Niles and Fraser's home, I smell the foulest odor I have encountered yet. I introduce myself to the crew chief, who is waiting outside the house, sitting in his idling pickup truck. He motions for me to get in the shotgun seat. I am grateful he has his air conditioner running on high.

"How's the work going, Mr. Shepperton?" I ask.

"Not worth a damn," he says. "I sent my men home early."

"Why's that?"

"You want to work in this stink?" he asks. "I've had two men throwing up today."

"Where's it coming from?"

"Not sure," he says, looking over the steering wheel and holding on to it as though he were driving. "These houses are packed so tight, like Vienna sausages in a can. But we think it's coming from that shed in the back of Niles's yard, and a neighbor is missing a collie. Thing is, Niles has it padlocked—we can't get in."

"Break it down. Find out what it is."

"Got to hear that from Niles or the missus," he says. "Or even Miss Molly, if she's around."

"She's not coming back till Wednesday. Can I authorize it?"

"No, sir, you can't. And I can't do any good for anybody till we get that dead animal out of there. Might be a raccoon."

"Smells like a whale rotting on the beach."

"Get Niles to call me."

Walking to my house on Tradd, I notice that a brand-new civilization has sprung alive on Church Street as a small nation of contractors and subcontractors begins a long and fruitful season of renewal and salvage. The interior of every house on the street hums with the concentrated activity of repairmen of every stripe. Painters and roofers stare out at me from high scaffolding as I pass them in the street below. A friendly city at the worst of times, Charleston's innate cordiality informs its sensibility after the disaster. People wave and shout greetings to one another, whether an apprentice carpenter or a descendant of a signer of the Declaration of Independence. It is a fine time to renew my love affair with the city, which I do gratefully as Charleston begins its irrepressible resurrection in its kingdom of mildew and rot. When I get home, I call Ike Jefferson at his office, no easy task. He does not return my message for more than two hours, and when he does, his voice is lifeless and exhausted. "Hey, Toad. Sorry it took so long to get back to you. How's my family?"

"I got to see them in the mountains. That's the good news. The bad news is that they're all dead."

"I don't need this, Toad," he snaps. "I just don't need this shit right now."

"Sorry," I tell him. "I got letters from everyone. I'll take them by tomorrow and put them on that rocking chair by your front door."

"Everybody else all right?"

"Couldn't be better. How's Betty?"

"Working her ass off. Just like everybody else. This is a hell of a time, Toad."

"I agree. I was over at Niles's just now. Something is stinking up the place bad."

"I'll get somebody to go by and check," Ike says.

"Do the best you can. Can I do anything for you?"

"Come over and cook me and Betty something good whenever we catch a break."

"It's a date," I say. "Consider it done."

"Thank you guys for taking care of my family." I can tell Ike's bone-tiredness has made him emotional. "I love you, Toad."

"I wish I felt the same way about you," I say, then hang up the phone.

The next afternoon my office door opens and Ike Jefferson walks into the room carrying some unspeakable disturbance in the deep pools of his brown eyes. He slumps into the visitor's chair. For several moments I think he has fallen asleep at that very spot.

"Liquor?" he finally asks, eyes still closed. "I need a pop."

Later, I learn that he has not gone off duty since two days before the arrival of Hugo, and that he has eaten, showered, and shaved in his office.

I remove a bottle of Maker's Mark from my top drawer, pour a jiggerful, and pass it across my desk. He eyes it with the appreciation of a whiskey priest over his morning portion of wine. In a swift motion, Ike downs it with pleasure and asks for another. I refill the jigger and the motions repeat themselves. When he's done, he takes my measure with the concentration that has always seemed like a form of thirst to me.

"I sent a cop over to Niles's house—rookie woman cop. Too young to know it was a bullshit assignment."

"Was it coming from the tool shed?"

"Yep," Ike says. "There was a man inside."

"That's impossible. How could anyone get in there? It was locked."

"When was it locked?" Ike asks.

"I don't know—Niles went out before the wind got up. About six, I think. Molly and I went out to look at the storm."

"Idiots."

"He was afraid of looters," I tell him. "He didn't know someone had hidden out in there—why wouldn't they come to the door? God, this is all Niles needs," I mutter, and Ike apparently agrees.

"Can you take a little ride with me?" he asks, getting to his feet.

"Let me type a last sentence." I type it fast, then follow him out.

We drive slowly south on King Street. Ike asks me about his parents and his kids, his manner shell-shocked and somber as he pulls his squad car into the parking lot of the Sergeant Jasper Apartments. Several other police cars are lined up nearby, and Ike salutes the on-duty clerk as we walk to the elevator bank. We ride one to the top floor without Ike giving away a single clue as to the purpose of this visit. When the elevator doors open, he walks me toward an apartment where a crime team is still at work.

"Don't touch anything," he says, "and don't ask any questions. Just look around, then tell me what you think later."

I gasp as I take in the strange decor: the room a virtual shrine to the career of Sheba Poe. One whole wall is covered with publicity shots, taken at various stages of her career. There are Sheba Poe ashtrays and match boxes and pillowcases and a bedspread. Sheba Poe lamp shades from all her movies surprise me, because I never knew that my friend's career had induced such a bizarre degree of fanaticism. In the bathroom, I find bars of soap with her picture on them, Sheba's shampoo, her mouthwash, and her photograph on a row of hand lotions. The room is obsessional, and bizarre in the extreme.

Ike hands me a dime-store photo album filled up with photos taken by a camera with a long-range lens of Sheba getting out of cabs and limos, entering and exiting streets and hotels, holding hands with dates and boyfriends, many of them world-famous actors. Ike hands me another album. "Brace yourself," he says.

In the album are the police photographs of Sheba after someone had butchered her, mounted with special care. Evangeline Poe, in her frightful vacancy, is posed on her bed holding her knife, covered with blood, making me shiver. When I come to the final and most macabre photograph, I shiver: there is the wicked effigy of the smiley face with its lone tear, immaculately rendered. I put my nose to the bloodied image and smell the fingernail polish.

Ike grabs my elbow and takes me to a window that commands a splendid view of the Ashley River. I see my house and Sheba's house and Peninsula High School and police headquarters and The Citadel. I even see the rooftop of Ike and Betty's house. When I have taken in the full strategic importance of this view, Ike makes a noise that I interpret to be an invitation to follow him away from this grotesque crime scene.

Wordlessly, he drives us to his house, then goes upstairs and showers. I go to the refrigerator and pull out a couple of beers. I am sitting in his den when he comes out wearing the bathrobe he wore as a cadet and Citadel-blue flip-flops. He sits in his reclining chair, and opens the beer I brought him. He drinks it with eagerness, then falls asleep a moment. When he wakes up, he asks me what I am doing there, then goes back to sleep and sleeps for another hour. It is dark when he wakes up, and I am cooking bacon and eggs to go with cheese grits and an English muffin that I'd toasted, slathered with peanut butter, and topped with a banana crushed with a fork. We eat in silence like evacuees from a famine.

"Let's get drunk," Ike says when we're done, going over to the bar. "You can spend the night in Little Ike's room."

"Sounds like a plan."

"Tell me what you're thinking," he says, and I don't bother stating the obvious.

"How did you find him?" I ask.

"The guy who drowned in the tool shed," Ike says. "We found a key in his pocket. It was on a key chain that said Sergeant Jasper Apartments."

"Fingerprints?"

"They match the ones we got from New York. Same guy. But we still don't know his name. We found six passports, all with different names. Six credit cards. Three driver's licenses from three states."

"Should we get Trevor down for an identification?"

"Nothing to identify. The autopsy says he drowned. His lungs were filled up with stinky seawater. His face was unrecognizable—the rats got to him before we did. He had two handguns, both thirty-eights. Enough ammunition to kill half the city. I think he planned to kill all of you once the hurricane got going good. In all that noise, no one would've heard a gun going off."

Thinking hard, I try to recall the events of the day when Hugo came to town. "Fraser!" I say. "He must've followed her when she got Trevor and wheeled him down to her house."

"My theory too," Ike says. "He was normally a clever planner, a good strategist, but he was also an opportunistic son of a bitch. He learned about my parade at The Citadel from your column. Because he always knew what you were doing, he also knew what the rest of us were doing too. We found a golf bag in his closet and a sniper's rifle hidden among the clubs."

"The view from his apartment?"

"Perfect. A nice assassination lair, if it came to that. His neighbor said he was a courteous man who was away for large stretches at a time. Thus, the Los Angeles photographs. The neighbor claims he had a beautiful Southern accent."

"He wasn't Southern," I say.

"How do you know?"

"Because he's too damn grotesque, even for the goddamn South."

Ike didn't agree. "You ought to be a cop for a while, Leo. Nothing too strange for a human being. A human being is a fucked-up concept. Humanity is best described as inhumanity." He pauses, then adds, "Another thing in the autopsy: he had stomach cancer. I think he was wrapping things up. In his pocket, they found a bottle of fingernail polish and a key to Niles's house." He shakes his head at that, and says, "There might be other stuff to tell you. I can't think of it now. But the paper will report that an unidentified man was found drowned in a tool shed south of Broad. Police speculate that he was taking shelter during the storm."

"What was his name?"

"Bill Metts," Ike says, and confesses, "I did something bad at that apartment house. The presence of Sheba everywhere shook me up, so I stole a photograph from the crime scene. I've never done anything like that before; it's a terrible breach of professionalism. But I couldn't help myself."

He stands and shuffles over to his uniform jacket and pulls out a photograph encased in a small silver frame, and brings it back for my inspection. It is a picture of the twins, Sheba and Trevor Poe, captured in their inimitable beauty when they were five or six years old. They look angelic, rapturous; a stranger would think they were the happiest children on earth.

"What would my life be like if they'd not moved across the street?" I ask.

"Not as fun. Not as exciting. They were like prophets who brought the news of the outside world to the rest."

"He died hard, that sack of shit," I say, "and it couldn't happen to a nicer guy. What is that apartment all about, that Sheba theme park?"

"When obsession goes bad," Ike says, "it goes very bad."

When Betty comes in later that evening and finds us sitting half-drunk in the den, she says, "I'm tired of saving the whole world. I need to get laid tonight."

"Sorry, honey," Ike says. "I went one bourbon too far."

"Leo?" she asks. "I know I can depend on you."

"You know I get horny when I hear your name."

"So what's the dish?" she asks. "Anything interesting happen today?"

A long time passes before Ike and I can stop laughing.

CHAPTER 30

Lightbulbs

On March 1, 1990, six months after Hugo, I sit in my office thinking about the column I am going to write. It is one of those times my mind feels like a waterless basin. Every thought I manage to coax into daylight seems clubfooted and lackluster, when a column presents itself out of the void of time, and I receive a phone call from a sheriff in rural Minnesota. He asks me if I am the husband of Starla King. When I tell him I am, and ask if she is in trouble, he tells me in a gentle voice that they have recovered her body from a hunter's cabin not far from the Boundary Waters near the border of Canada. The deputies found an empty bottle of scotch and an empty vial of sleeping pills on the floor beside the bed. The owner of the house discovered her body when he drove up from St. Paul for the annual spring housekeeping. The corpse was in bad shape, and it was obvious she had broken into the cabin sometime after the fall hunting season. Starla was in the late stages of pregnancy and, of course, the fetus was dead too.

"Of course," I echo, as if I am hearing a weather bulletin instead of the news of my wife's death. I feel a profound sense of nothingness, but still retain some fragments of human decency that make me regret not feeling anything else. I ask the sheriff to arrange for Starla's body to be flown home to Charleston, and give him the phone number of the J. Henry Stuhr funeral home on Calhoun Street. He apologizes that Starla left no suicide note, and expresses sympathy at the unnecessary death of my son. I see no good reason to explain that I had not been responsible for placing the lost embryo in the body of my deceased wife. He tells me that Starla had left a manila folder on the kitchen table full of my columns from the past year, and that that's how he knew whom to contact. I thank him for that grace note, then tell him I've been awaiting his phone call my entire married life.

In a daze, I write a column about my wife, from our original meeting to the Minnesota phone call. How that when I first met her, Starla was handcuffed to a chair in St. Jude's Orphanage. I tell about Dr. Colwell performing an operation for free to fix her wandering eye, and how she walked the world as a beautiful woman after the success of that operation. I tell how I fell in love with her slowly, a little bit at a time, the way shy boys always fall in love with shy girls, in baby steps and small increments. Though I did not recognize it at the time, I am one of those unlucky men who are destined always to fall in love with women with sad stories, that love seemed a real and hard-earned gift to me. I describe her lifelong war with a mental illness that maddened and drove her to drugs and despair, and explain that because I am a devout Roman Catholic, I would never grant her desire for a divorce. I believe I am responsible for her death as much as anyone. I mention that she was pregnant when she committed suicide. I speak of my shock and my lack of grief, and my dread that I have to rise from my desk and drive across the Ashley to deliver the news to Niles Whitehead that his beloved and fragile sister is dead. In the integrity of his grief, I am sure Niles will pay high honor to the life of his sister while all I have to offer is the disgraceful gift of nothingness. I try to describe what nothingness feels like, but I turn mute and wordless, and prove unworthy of the task. I turn my column in to Kitty, then go to see Niles.

I find him in his office on the lovely campus of the Porter-Gaud School, which fronts the marshes and commands a magical view of Charleston's severe and disciplined skyline. We walk toward the river and I can't find the words that will change Niles's world forever. I talk about the Atlanta Braves and the damage Hugo had caused at The Citadel and everything I can think of that has nothing to do with the death of his sister. Finally Niles tells me that Porter-Gaud is a job, not a hobby, and that the school fully intends for him to earn his salary. So I tell him the news of Starla. He roars like a wounded beast and falls to the ground sobbing. He places his face against the earth and cries as hard as any man I've ever seen.

"She never had a chance, Leo," he says, weeping. "Not a fucking prayer. She was so hurt, nobody could fix it. Not you. Not me. Not God. Not anybody."

His sobs are so loud they bring teachers and students running toward us from the main campus. They engulf Niles and hold him tightly, stroking him and wiping away his tears as I walk back to my car, still uneasy with my new citizenship in the country of nothingness. On my drive home, I wonder if I will ever feel anything again, and if I really want to.

Starla's funeral is a low-key but heartbreaking affair. Monsignor Max gives a moving sermon, displaying his intimate knowledge of both Starla's charms and her insurmountable demons. He speaks of suicide with compassion and a deep philosophical understanding of mental illness. He explains that he thinks God holds a greater love for his hurt and suffering children than he does for those who lead privileged and graceful lives. His words soothe me and I taste their sweetness as they flow over me like the mountain laurel honey the wild bees make in the mountains where Starla was born. I appreciate Monsignor Max's words even more as I study his gaunt, emaciated face. Mother whispers to me that his lung cancer isn't responding to chemo this time, and his prognosis is grim. Because of his illness, his performance is elevated from brilliant to heroic. When I ask how much time Monsignor Max has left, Mother cries for the first time since the service began.

In St. Mary's cemetery, we bury Starla next to the graves of my brother and my father. The city shimmers in a pearly, illuminant light as the sun shoots through the high thunderheads of a cumulus cloud bank. St. Mary's is bone white in the austere economy of her symmetry. I try to pray for my lost wife, but prayer refuses to come. I call on God to explain to me the ruthless life he granted to Starla Whitehead, but my God is a hard God, and he answers me with a silence that comes easily to Him from his position of majesty. But the terrible silence of God can offend the violated sensibilities of a bereft and suffering man. For me, it does not suffice. If the only feast my God can provide me is a full portion of nothingness, then prayer dries up in me. If I worship an uncaring God, then He wouldn't give a passing thought to the fact that He had created a difficult, unmovable man. My heart is drying up inside of me, and I can barely stand it. What can a man do when he decides to fold up his God as though He were a handkerchief and place Him in a bottom drawer, and even forget where he put Him? Though I am entering the outer ring of despair, I have not named it as such and need time to put all the movable parts together and make some kind of sense out of the life I am either living or refusing to live. As I stand there over the coffin, there is a transformation of the God of my childhood, who I could adore with such thoughtless, devotional ease, to someone who has turned His back on me with such sightless indifference. In the black-rooted withering of my faith, I take note of the workings of my annoyed heart and mark the sense of desolation I feel when I demote God to a lowercase g as I kiss Starla's casket before they lower it into the earth.

I throw the first shovelful of dirt into her grave and the second. Niles throws the third and the fourth. Mother, the next two. Then Molly, Fraser, Ike, Betty, then Chad and their children. Then Niles and I finish it off. I step back and survey the crowd; I try to speak but lose the shape of words as they cleave to the roof of my mouth. All sense of direction abandons me and I stumble. Niles and Ike grab my elbows and hold me up, then lead me back to the funeral home limo.

The spring shows early signs of being otherworldly. Mother spent long hours putting my garden into shape after Hugo, and her wizardry can be seen in the texture and spacing of palmettos and leather leaf ferns with morning glories and purple salvia. As a dedicated rosarian, she has dedicated a secret corner of the garden to Peace roses and Joseph's Coat roses and Lady Banks roses, which eventually will curl over the koi pond. Since Mother has come to live with me and Trevor after the storm, she has transfigured my garden from a wasteland to a wonderland in a short space of time. In the great tradition of Charleston gardeners, she can stare at a square foot of mud and urge the shoots of buried lantanas and impatiens to fight for the sunlight.

Back at the house, my friends feed more than two hundred people while Coach Jefferson handles the bartending, as usual. It is a cool night, and our guests walk out in the garden to smell what spring will bring tiptoeing into Charleston in a scant two months. My walk toward the Cooper River seems narcotic and zombielike, but as I make a steady promenade along the seawall, I can feel Charleston beginning to perform the sacred rites of healing my withdrawn heart. To my right, I pass a row of dazzling mansions, and the perfect architecture pulls me tightly to the center of the city's roselike beauty. It is a city of ten thousand secrets and just a couple of answers. Since the day I was born, I have been worried that heaven would never be half as beautiful as Charleston, the city formed where two rivers meet in ecstasy to place a harbor and a bay and an exit to the world.

My mother followed me. Mother and I stand at the point where the rivers meet, and look across to James Island and Sullivan's Island. The sky, pearled with stars, throws a slash of moonlight on the water that lights up both of us. The tenderness of Charleston enfolds me in its solemn vows of palms and waterworks. The bells of St. Michael's ring out for me, and it is surprising that they call out my name, and my name alone.

Walking down Broad Street, the city's soft hands continue to heal the lesions and distempers of my inflamed psyche. As we pass the first floors of houses we peek into the private lives of our neighbors and can study their nighttime activities as though they are anchovies or pilot fish in an aquarium. One family is eating a late-night supper; one solitary woman listens to *Così Fan Tutte* by Mozart. Most families sit in joyless clusters watching television.

Before we make the turn at Tradd Street, Mother stops me. "There's something I need to tell you, Leo. You're not going to like it."

"Hey, it's the day I buried my wife," I say. "A day like any other day."

"It's not perfect timing, I will admit," she says, "but there's never a good time. I'm going back to my convent. My order has accepted me back."

"*Una problema, piccola,*" I tell her in my pidgin Italian. "What about me? Most nuns don't have children."

"You're no problem," she says. "They have a program for former nuns who've married and lost their husbands. Monsignor Max and I have been praying about this for a long time."

"Can I visit you? Hey, Sister, I'd like to visit Mother. She's a nun."

"You'll get used to it," Mother says. "I've been floating on air since I made the decision."

"Did I hear an evil cliché enter your conversation?" I ask in mock consternation.

"Well, that's how I feel, like I'm floating on air. I'd like you to do the honor of driving me up to North Carolina, just as your father did all those long years ago."

The next month I drive Mother to the hospital, and I remain outside the monsignor's room out of respect for the privacy and devotion they had brought to their extraordinary friendship. Mother stays for an hour and is crying softly as I lead her back to the car. I drive her to the house that Father built, and she goes inside the freshly restored home and admires the improvements the construction crew has made. While she inspects the house, I spot a lone magnolia blossom high in one of her trees and scramble up to retrieve it, feeling older with every branch I climb. I break off the flower, the first of the season, inhale its sweetness, and decide it was worth the climb. I hand it to Mother and am delighted when she pins it to her hair.

We drive leisurely on the back roads of the Carolinas; the magnolia's aroma makes the car smell like a broken perfume bottle. We note the exact moment we depart the Low Country and begin to climb the continent with a nearly imperceptible gradualness. Mother names every tree, shrub, and flower we pass, and she applauds when I stop the car and help a snapping turtle across the highway near a black-water creek. We eat lunch in Camden and reach the convent before five o'clock. The mother superior is waiting for us. She embraces Mother and says: "Welcome back, Sister Norberta."

"It's where I want to be, Sister Mary Urban," she replies.

Mother and I take each other in and try to make it easy. But there is nothing on earth that can make this departure anything less than trying. I don't remember when I started loving Mother, but it had happened. Nor do I have any idea when she started loving me, but the knowledge that her love is available in a boundless source had presented itself to me. I can use it as a sword on a pillow or a hermitage; a warm bath, a butterfly garden, or a flow of molten lava. Her love is thorned and complex and it can sometimes hurt me in the most tender places. But who said either love or life would be a cakewalk? Mother and I have fought our way screaming and clawing and lashing out as we rolled in the bloody dust, testing the brute, tensile strength of that armory where the sheet lightning of our love was stored. Our love ties us together forever.

"Thanks for letting me do this, Leo," she says. "It's generous of you."

"My mother's a tough old bird. She's her own woman."

"Will you take care of the monsignor?"

"I'll read him a story every night," I promise.

"I know you're hurting now, Leo, but don't give up on the Church."

"I'm on a sabbatical," I say. "Maybe it'll be a brief one."

"I wasn't meant to be a mother," she confesses. "I'm sorry I was such a poor one."

"Best I ever had," I assured her, and in an instant, she is in my arms.

"Try to meet a nice girl," she whispers. "I'd love for you to become a father."

I look over Mother's shoulder toward Sister Mary Urban and ask, "Can a nun become a grandmother?"

"This one can," the mother superior says with a smile.

Two sisters come down the steps to escort Mother into her once and future life. We kiss good-bye, and I watch as Mother disappears behind those dark, oaken doors. I think of Father making this same trip so many years before. I consider both the congruities and the dangers that circles represent in a human life. Delivering Mother to the convent steps represents a circle in the fate of two men named King. But it seems like a revoking and a starting over. Mother needs a place of refuge now, a place to escape the storms. I let her go. I set her free to drift into the sea-lanes of prayer and simplicity in the frankincensed glooms of a convent working out the dilemmas of darkness itself.

"Mother Superior?" I ask as she turns to go back to her convent.

"Yes, Leo?"

"Does the convent need anything? A year's supply of anything?"

"We need everything," she says. "Let me think. Lightbulbs. Yes, that's our most pressing need at the moment."

The next day I deliver a thousand lightbulbs to the convent's back door, and mark off one more circle as I continue to monitor the navigational quadrants of my own life. Now that I've been alerted, I develop an eye for circles and the strange power they exert over human connections.

CHAPTER 31

Film Studies

As Trevor's strength grows, he begins walking the streets of Charleston with me in the evening. At first, we walk up to Broad Street and back, and Trevor is winded and exhausted when we return to the house. But each day we go farther. By the end of the summer, we are walking the full length of the Battery, turning north, and once reaching the Citadel gates. Often, we walk past the street where we met, and he checks his mother's mailbox and I check the mail for Sister Norberta. I suffer an inner pang when I see the FOR SALE sign in front of Trevor's house, and the phone number of his Realtor, Bitsy Turner.

"I'm absolutely certain that if Bitsy had been born a man, she would've chosen to be gay," he says. "That's a certainty, and not mere speculation. She's a living doll."

"Don't share that with Bitsy," I suggest.

"I would think she'd be honored," Trevor replies. "What's the idle gossip around the Holy City? The juiciest, dirtiest, basest, most disgusting filth you've got?"

"Judge Lawson was caught screwing his poodle," I say. "That's the kind of stuff I hear but can't use in my columns."

"It must've been a miniature poodle," Trevor drawls in reply. "I've caught a peek at his private parts."

"Where on earth did you see his private parts?" I ask as we turn west down Calhoun Street, passing the hospital.

"In the shower room at the yacht club."

"I didn't know they even had a shower room."

"Oh, I've done a lot of things in that shower room. Seldom showered."

"I don't want to hear it," I say.

"So uptight, so repressed, so Catholic." Trevor shakes his head sadly.

"I like it that way."

"I'm starting to miss San Francisco." There is wistfulness in his voice, a lost, dreamy quality that I have not heard in him for a long time. "I remember Saturday nights when I'd walk down Union Street about the time the sun was setting. I was young and beautiful and desirable, the king of any bar I'd choose. I made magic in that city. I made that city magic for a thousand boys."

"How's that AIDS thing going?" I ask.

"Do hush up," he says, "and let me dream my perverted dreams of a young invert on the prowl."

"They put Monsignor Max back in the hospital today," I say. "He may not last much longer. Wanna go up with me to visit him?"

"Naw, I'll see you back at the house."

"You got something against the monsignor?"

"Not my cup of semen," Trevor says with a hitch of his shoulder as he continues on Calhoun Street.

I go up to Monsignor Max's room in the cancer ward and nod to several young priests as they complete their visitation. The room is dark and meditative and I think Max is asleep when I lay a pile of letters from Mother on his nightstand.

"I just received extreme unction," Max says, his voice labored and scratchy.

"Then your soul is pure white."

"One can only hope."

"You're worn-out," I tell him. "Please bless me and I'll be on my way. I'll come back to see you tomorrow."

I kneel by his bed and feel his thumb make the sign of the cross; I'm surprised when he blesses me in Latin. When I kiss him on the forehead, he is already asleep, so I tiptoe out of his room.

I return home and Trevor fixes me a drink. We sit facing each other, as easy in each other's presence as an old married couple. We sit like this most nights and talk of many things: San Francisco, high school, my mother's return to the convent. When we are drunk, we speak of Sheba and Starla, but it is too early in the evening for that.

"I walked past that high school you got kicked out of," Trevor says.

"Bishop Ireland?"

He nods. "It looked very Catholic to me. It even smelled Catholic."

"It's a Catholic school. That's the way it's supposed to look and smell."

"So you still believe all that Catholic bullshit?"

"Yes, I believe in all that Catholic bullshit," I reply.

"And you think you're getting into heaven? Or something like that? That all of you do?"

"Something like that," I say.

"Poor brainwashed Toad." After a long pause, he emits a deep exhalation of breath. "Well, I've got something to tell you, Toad. I know I have to, but I keep putting it off."

"Do it."

"I can't," Trevor says in a small voice. "It's too horrible."

"Horrible?" I echo. "That's a strong word."

"Horrible doesn't begin to do it justice."

For a moment I freeze. Then I repeat, "Do it."

He takes another drink, then he tells me how a few days ago, after he'd begun to regain his strength, he'd started going through his things, including the steamer trunk and the boxes Anna Cole had forwarded to him from San Francisco. He'd come upon a cache of gay pornography I'd sent him many years ago when it was found in storage in my parents' house, presumably left by one of my father's boarders before he married. Having nothing but time on his hands, he had given it a closer look.

"I love gay porn and always have. When you sent the steamer trunk out to me, I was especially curious about the collection from so long ago—those were the dark ages, with production values about zero. All the films are scratchy, older, grainy. A lot of them are homemade, though you have to forgive that. They were pioneers in very dangerous times."

"Glad you enjoyed them," I tell him drily. "Why are you telling me this?"

Trevor takes a breath before he answers. "Well, I delved into the trunk deeper this time and brought out a black box—an old toolbox, very strong. I couldn't get it open in San Francisco, and never bothered with it much. But when I was culling my earthly possessions"—he pauses to take a sip of drink—"I got curious, and shot off the lock with your pistol. By the way, I think it's absurd to own a handgun. I am so antigun."

"I bought that gun because of your lunatic father," I remind him.

"Oh, that old chestnut," Trevor says. "Then it's absurd you didn't buy me one too. Well"—he sighs again—"here goes. I shot off the lock, and there was a private collection in the box. Homemade. You know, the old home movies. I couldn't wait to watch them, and—I made a discovery. An awful discovery, I'm afraid."

"What did you find?"

"Maybe we need to stiffen these drinks," he suggests. "You're going to need it when you see this film. Here's how bad it is—I had to force myself to watch it to be absolutely certain before showing it to you. I had to be sure it was who I thought it was. All week I've been debating destroying the film, and never telling you. I even prayed to God about it—the one I don't believe in."

"What did God say?"

"Well, the cat had His tongue, as usual, but I finally decided it was something you need to know."

"Run it," I tell him.

At three in the morning, I slip past nurses and night watchmen and enter into the stillness of Monsignor Max's room, carrying my old Citadel backpack on my arm. By the dim glow of a nightlight, I remove an old-fashioned movie projector, plug it into the outlet, and turn it on. It hums like a jar filled with wasps, then a badly done home movie comes on, cast in shaking, flickering images against the stark white wall across from the monsignor's bed. The eye of the camera is focused on a bed in an empty, unknown room. The camera is like a staring, motionless eye. Trevor explained that in homemade porn, the camera is often propped near a bed to catch the action. In the grainy film, a priest appears in the room with his arm around the throat of a struggling, naked boy. The boy is beautiful and blond; the priest is handsome, virile, and strong. The boy tries to scream, but the priest stops him with a hand around his mouth. The boy struggles, but he is overpowered and raped by the priest, and raped brutally, as if there were any other way.

The priest is a younger, stronger Max Sadler, and the boy my brother, Steve. Stephen Dedalus King, the brother I found floating in a bloody bathtub the year I fell apart, the year I began my soul treks through mental hospitals and Thorazine hazes, struggling to find the boy I was before I pulled my brother as wreckage from that tub. As I sit there, I remember how I once entertained the horrible thought that my father was somehow complicit in Steve's death, because I'd heard him scream out in a nightmare: "No, Father. No, please." I thought he was calling out in fear of our own gentle father and not the beast who lies dying in the hospital bed beside me.

I let the film run out, the frames turning to a scratched, noisy white, when I realize the monsignor has awakened and is watching the film with me. "I should have destroyed that film," he says finally.

"I wish you had," I tell him, and my mildness draws him out.

"A man's demons are a man's demons," he explains in a chilling, credible voice.

"Must be," I say.

"He was too beautiful not to have," he adds in an almost querulous tone, as if I would have argued. "I couldn't keep my eyes off him. You, on the other hand, were ugly."

"Lucky me," I say. "What was it like to officiate at his funeral?"

"More difficult than you'll ever know. But it didn't stop me, Leo. Even then."

"I know. I've spent the evening viewing your handiwork. How did it come to be stored in my father's house?"

For a moment, he hesitates. When he has gathered strength, he continues in an instructive voice, devoid of conscience: "A silly error. I stored my belongings with your father once, when I moved back to the rectory. I knew I'd lost some of my early collection. But I could hardly ask."

"Your collection seems limited to the very young. Have you ever made love to a man?"

"No. Why would I want to do that?" he asks, as though I am insulting his intelligence. I look at him levelly in the dim light, and he stares back, guiltless.

"That film should be destroyed," he says. "I have confessed my sins and received the last rites. According to the laws of our church, my soul will soar to heaven without blemish."

"You need to pray that God likes child molesters," I tell him coldly. "That he likes to see his nice little altar boys raped by psycho priests."

"You can't touch me, Leo," he says in a dead voice. "My place in the history of the South Carolina diocese is untouchable. My reputation in the religious community is impeccable. You can do nothing to smear it."

I look down at him and think of my brother's agonized, humiliated face. He would rather die than tell my parents that their beloved mentor had raped him. Steve would not have known what kind of language to use to express such a thing, or that such a world even existed.

"If the God I pray to is real," I say, "then you will burn forever in the lake of fire. And because of this film, I'll be swimming in that lake with you. You're a fine Roman Catholic, aren't you, Max?"

"And what about you?" he spits out.

I lean close to the bed to tell him, "On the worst day of my life, I am a better Catholic than you were on your best day."

"I'll be with my Father in heaven, very soon," Max says smugly.

I unplug the projector and whip the cord around my arm. "If you are, then my father will be there. And he will beat the living shit out of you."

He seems unfazed. "But my reputation will be intact. You can't touch it."

"Oh, I don't know," I tell him grimly as I pick up the projector. "I might be able to fog it up a little."

I pack up the projector and walk out of the room. "Leo!" he calls to my retreating back. "Don't leave without my blessing! Let me give you my blessing!"

• • •

The monsignor dies in his sleep later in the morning. His obituary is front-page news, above the fold, in both Charleston newspapers. There are editorials all across the state praising his distinguished life, his ambassadorial skills among the leaders of other religions, the aura of saintliness he brought to his ministry, and his heroic role in the civil rights movement, which was highlighted by his march on the Selma Bridge. HOLY MAN DIES IN HOLY CITY one headline reads. I attend his elaborate funeral and take Communion at the end of the solemn High Mass, attended by Cardinal Bernardin and three other bishops. After the service, I hear parishioners say they wish that Monsignor Max could be canonized as an American saint.

I go to my office immediately afterward and write a dutiful column describing the ceremony in every detail. There is only one detail I leave out: after his burial, I slip back to the graveyard at twilight and spit on his grave. The following day, I go to work on his legacy. For my next column, I take his solid and well-earned reputation, and cut it up for bait.

A Final Prayer

S o.
I had a story to tell, and I told it. After I publish my inflammatory column that makes the name of Monsignor Max anathema in
every house in the city, I begin the process of falling apart in the main-
streams of my own life. When I begin a column with the words "Family
is a contact sport," a sadness overwhelms me in the office, and my editors
send me home for the day. I enter a season of depression and melancholy.
I take account of my life and find that I have lived a lot, but learned very
little.

In a journal, I write this sentence: "Real life is impossible for someone
born with a gift for acting." I think I am writing about Sheba, and continue, "An actor can't experience a real life unless imitating a life made
up by someone else," and I am brought up short when I realize that I'm
not writing about Sheba after all. I'm writing about myself. I find myself
in a black hole of despair, and I have to let it take me down to the darkest places before I can engineer my escape. The film of my brother's rape
plays itself over and over in my head. Valium cannot touch it, nor can
bourbon dim its malignity. Even receiving Communion every day cannot daunt its repellant powers. I can feel my body caving in on itself.

In despair, I find my way back to the office of the psychiatrist who rescued me from the coma of my failed childhood. Dr. Criddle is in her late sixties now, still practicing. After a three-hour session, she informs me with infinite gentleness that I am the most suicidal client who has ever walked into her office. I surprise myself with my response: "I can't wait to die."

She takes me at my word and signs me into the psychiatric ward of the Medical University Hospital of South Carolina. In the morbid pathology of my thinking I note with pleasure that the hospital is on the same street as the J. Henry Stuhr funeral home. I find it a happy coincidence and am soon cave-diving into my consciousness, a lost continent where all the jungles have impenetrable canopies, all the mountains are alpine, and all the rivers contain strange currents of desire and intrigue.

All the king's horses and all the king's shrinks work hard at returning the jigsaw puzzle of my life to order, with help from unexpected sources. In a deep, drug-induced sleep, my body takes me soaring into a world of dreams that help cure the steady ache that has turned my soul into such a lost and ruined place. My father, Jasper King, dives into the chlorinated water at the deep end of a pool to pull me to safety and pound my small back until I vomit and cough up pool water, while my brother, Steve, shouts for me to breathe. I come back from drowning with an indrawn rush of air that feels like deliverance into a brand-new life. I find myself standing beside my father, and we are making cookies for the family that has just moved into a house across the street. Father is struggling to read a recipe from our worn copy of *Charleston Receipts.* We make benne wafers and chocolate chip cookies and give them to everyone on our street and the next one.

Between every house, my father stops to show me how to dance.

A door of one of the houses opens and a pretty nun comes out to join the dance. I don't know it's my mother till she begins dancing with my father, who rewards her with a smile that could light up the known world. Over several dream nights, he returns to me. We fish in Charleston Harbor or look for salamanders and butterflies in the Congaree Swamp. He comes back to teach me how to live with the exuberant gifts he brought to the art of loving a son, of loving anyone. I realize afresh how lucky I am to have been born to such a man. I learned everything I needed to know about the softness of fathers from him. He brought me news from my own interior.

Time becomes a lost country for me, and I don't remember the night when Steve does a surprise encore in those dramatic, multicolored precincts of sleep. We are tossing a football, running through the neighborhood, pretending we are star quarterbacks for a Rose Bowl team, or a Sugar Bowl team, or The Citadel, or even Bishop Ireland. We throw and catch and run through those peerless, queenlike Charleston streets with their houses made of rainbows and lace. I remember what a fine thing it is to have a brother who loves you and protects you and cherishes everything about you. When I wake from the long nightmare of my days, I need to know that.

Another night, a shadow pays a visit and does not identify himself for half the dream. I toss in my sleep, but when the shadow orders me to remain as still as a yard jockey, I recognize the voice of Harrington Canon, who is sitting at his English desk in his antique store. He is grousing that it is now my antique store, and that every night I park my fanny in his house on Tradd Street. He asks why in God's name I do not give more dinner parties and show off the fine china and silverware he left for me.

"You must appreciate beauty for it to endure," he tells me. "That goes for inanimate objects as well as living things, even though I far prefer inanimate objects."

Mr. Canon speaks in his most gossipy, effete manner, complaining about all the shortcomings of the younger generation and its appalling lack of manners and civility. He tells me that we are so boneheaded and slack that he welcomed his death as a liberation from a world he could no longer tolerate.

I hear myself laughing at Mr. Canon. I have not heard myself laughing for a long time.

I begin to look forward to the nighttime ritual when the night nurse brings me a little cupful of pills and I can close my eyes and watch the gold-leaf ceiling paintings fall into their thousand shapes on my closed eyelids. My sleep turns into a pleasure palace, a carnival with tigers leaping through burning hoops, elephants marching in strict formation, and fireworks bursting overhead. I discover that you can dream to waken yourself. I never knew that.

Starla walks out of a cave hidden behind a waterfall. She takes my hand and leads me down a mountain path to a vineyard where she feeds me scuppernong grapes, then dips her hand into a hive of bees and comes out dripping with mountain laurel–scented honey. When I try to apologize to her for my failures as a husband and as a man, she seals my lips with her hand, still dripping with honey. She leads me to a deep pool beneath a waterfall that is as white as a bridal dress above us, as dark as a moonless night below us. We hold each other in a nakedness and silence and make subtle amendments in our drifting away from each other in the swirling currents until we reach a level of comfort and peace we never achieved in waking life.

But the night visitor I welcome most is the radiant and breathtaking Sheba Poe, the eighteen-year-old Sheba, who makes a grand entrance into my dream life. She comes like a ball of fire, all fanfare and glitz, with no trace of a whimper anywhere in earshot. When I last saw her, she was a butchered corpse lying near her blood-soaked mother. Now she approaches me shouting: "Five minutes!" No one knows the art of performance better than Sheba Poe.

"I've come to teach you how to act, Leo," she says. "It's going to be the role of a lifetime. I'm going to teach you all the steps. You're going to hit all your marks, and memorize all the words to perfection. We're starting *now*. No excuses, no doubts, no bullshit. Here is your part, Leo: you're going to act like a happy man. I know, I know—it's the hardest role in the world. Tragedy's easy. But you and I have spent our lifetimes doing tragedy, right? We can do that in our sleep. Buck up. Shut up. Listen to me. Smile. You call that a smile? It's a grimace. Get rid of it. Smile like this," she says, and offers a brilliant demonstration. "Make it come up from the inside like a blush. Will it into your life. Throw yourself into it. Try again. That's better, but still not enough. Put some sunshine into it, Leo! A smile starts in the toes. Plant your feet firmly; let it rise through your legs. Put your groin into it, then let it ride up your spine like a train. Let it shine like fox-fire in your mouth and teeth. Flash it, son—you're on my stage now, and I'll kick your ass if you fake anything. Now, there's a smile! Now let's put some words into that smile. Tell me a story, Leo. Feel it. Show it. Mean it. Oh, the words will come. I'm not asking, sugar—that's an order. You want to be in the nuthouse the rest of your life? I didn't think so. Have you met the guy down the hall, the one who cut off the fingers of his left hand and ate them? Hey, we can use that. Write it, get it to me for a weekend read. Can I act? You're asking *me*? No wonder you're locked up! I'll let you babysit my Academy Award. The smile, Leo. You lost it. Get it right, like this. Yes, my smile, a pretty girl's smile. No, I was never happy. But Leo—I could act my ass off."

The next morning I awake early, and am writing in my journal when the nurse arrives with my breakfast. My smile catches her by surprise, and she mentions it. I have started writing about a boy nicknamed the Toad, whose life unexpectedly begins on Bloomsday in the summer of 1969 when a moving van parks in the driveway across the street, I find two orphans handcuffed to their chairs, and I learn that my mother had been a nun. In all the rules of circuitry and the orbit of planets in their fixed, unbreakable transits, my fate begins to show itself, and I meet the main characters who will take a leading part in the dance, the great arching motion of my life.

In the final week of my hospital stay, a young nurse surprises me by visiting me from her post in the endocrinology department. She is not only lovely and likeable, she possesses that uncommon centeredness that all nurses seem to share. As we talk, I realize with a shock that she has come up here specifically to visit me. When I ask her about it, she explains that I went to high school with her oldest sister, Mary Ellen Driscoll.

"She said that you wouldn't remember her." She holds out her hand for a shake. "I'm Catherine."

"Mary Ellen Driscoll wore pigtails," I say. "You were a Catholic family, and I always wondered why you didn't go to Bishop Ireland."

"No money," Catherine explains. "Dad was a bum, Mom an angel. Same old story. The Irish psycho play."

"I know it well," I say.

"Your wife died, didn't she, Leo?"

"She committed suicide."

She blushes prettily. "I'm so sorry to hear that. I had no idea." She makes an endearingly clumsy attempt to divert me. "So, when are you going to start your column again? I'm a big fan."

"You are?" I say, flattered.

"You always make me laugh," she says with a smile.

"I sure haven't done that for anyone lately."

"You've had a tough patch," she says. "I've had a few of them myself. I'm a single mom. Got a cute kid named Sam, but things have been tough since my divorce," she says. "Ah—if you ever want to call me or anything—I mean—oh, God, shut up, Catherine! I must sound like an idiot to you."

"Are you asking me for a date, Catherine?" I say in surprise.

"No, of course not. Well, yeah. Maybe. Do you like kids?"

"I love kids. Do you make a habit of asking out all the visiting lunatics?"

Her laugh is unaffected and charming. "See? I knew you'd make me laugh. And, no, I don't hit on all the lunatics. But I heard you were leaving and knew it'd be my only chance to meet you. You're Mr. Big in this town, Leo King."

"And what are you, Catherine?"

"I'm Nurse Small."

"Hello, Nurse Small," I say.

"Hello, Mr. Big," she says shyly as she hands me her card. "Here's my phone number."

"You'll be hearing from me, Nurse Small."

She flashes me a brilliant smile. "You're going to like me, Mr. Big."

Upon my release from the hospital, I walk from Calhoun to King Street. I feel like a canary freed from its cage. When I pass the J. Henry Stuhr funeral home, I shoot it the bird and say, "Not yet, pal."

I walk to my office at the *News and Courier,* kiss Kitty Mahoney, and take the good-natured razzing of my colleagues, laughing aloud when Ken Burger asks how I liked the cuckoo's nest. "Better than this place," I shout as I walk into my office. I remove the sign I had placed on the door before I left: GONE CRAZY—BE BACK SOON. LEO KING. I write a column for the next day's morning edition. The kid is back in the saddle.

But there is one more ritual I have to perform before I can be whole again. At five the next morning, I ride my bicycle to the delivery point where Eugene Haverford used to sit in the darkness talking about the news of the day as I folded newspapers with skill and swiftness. Mr. Haverford died nine years ago, and I delivered his eulogy. I needed his help one last time.

"What's our job, son?" he asks in my head.

"To deliver the news of the world, sir," I answer aloud.

"And do it right. Every day of the year, we do it the right way. Now get going. Your customers are waiting for you. They need you."

"They can trust me, sir."

"That's why I hired your little ass."

"Thanks for being so nice to me, Mr. Haverford," I say.

He lights his cigar. "Shut up, kid," he says, but he smiles. "You've got a job to do."

Once more I take off in the darkness. I reach for an imaginary newspaper and hurl it onto the front porch of the first house on Rutledge Avenue. The moon lights up Colonial Lake as the next paper leaves my hand, and the next and the next; my body retains a perfect memory of every house on my long-ago route. I turn left on Tradd, flinging papers with my left and right hands, admiring their arching trajectories. I shout out the names of my customers, many of whom have been dead for years. "Hey, Miss Pickney! Hey, Mr. Trask! How's it going, Mrs. Grimball? Top of the day to you, Mrs. Hamill. Hello, General Grimsley!"

I am riding hard through the most beautiful streets in America, my native city. I know I have to cure myself with Charleston. There is nothing that the Holy City cannot right. I turn south on Legare Street and papers fly out of my hands as I pass the Sword Gate House. I hurl an invisible paper at Mrs. Gervais's house and another at the Seignious house and another at the Maybanks'. I serve the great families of my ethereal city as I ride past concealed gardens flush with morning glories, ligustrum, white oleanders, and lavender azaleas galore. The morning birds sing a concerto for me in my swift flight beneath them. The forgotten music of a city awakening comes back to me as I turn on Meeting Street and hear dogs barking, my papers landing on front piazzas with the same sound that fish make when they leap for joy in brackish lagoons. Ah, the smell of coffee brewing, that secret pleasure I had forgotten! Lawyers, the early risers, are walking to their Broad Street offices like their fathers and grandfathers did before them. It is Charleston. I hear the bells of St. Michael's ring out on the four corners of the law. It is Charleston, and it is mine. I am lucky enough a man that I can sing hymns of praise to it for the rest of my life.

On Bloomsday, Chad and Molly Rutledge give Trevor Poe a going-away party at their mansion on East Bay Street. The night before, Ike, Niles, Chad, and I stay up all night roasting a pig on a spit and telling the stories of our lives. Memories overwhelm us and hold us prisoners of time. The tide is going out in the harbor and will be at its peak when we toast farewell to Trevor on his last evening here. There is good luck in the high tide, a rightness about it that every man and woman in the Low Country knows in their bones, a completion, a summing up, and a good place for an ending. Chad teases us about wearing our Citadel rings, and we make fun of him for not wearing his Princeton one. A wind rises up, and the ties among us are strong and now time-tested, river-tested, and storm-hardened. When I was in the hospital, Chad had surprised me by visiting every day.

After the party, we gather on the third-story piazza and watch the sun light up the harbor with a deep shade of gold that makes it look like a Communion cup. The waters are calm, almost motionless. A great blue heron flies the length of the Battery with classical majesty. Ike holds on to Betty, Molly moves close to Chad, and Niles draws Fraser to him.

Trevor is flying out in the morning for San Francisco, his future uncertain. But so is mine, and so are the fates of the children who play in the yard below. We have been touched by the fury of storms and the wrath of an angry, implacable God. But that is what it means to be human, born to nakedness and tenderness and nightmare in the eggshell fragility of mortality and flesh. The immensity of the Milky Way settles over the city, and the earthworms rule beneath the teeming gardens in their eyeless world. I am standing with my best friends in the world in complete awe at the loveliness of the South.

Late in the afternoon, just before sunset, Trevor lets out a cry and points toward the Cooper River. A school of porpoises is following in a container ship's wake. The sun catches them and turns their bodies into studies in bronze. The porpoise has always been a sign of renewal and of the charged, magical life of the Low Country. As the porpoises pass in review, we let out a cheer. They navigate the deep channel before turning out toward the Atlantic and the Gulf Stream. One of them breaks free and swims toward us, so close to the seawall that we can hear her breathe.

Trevor thinks of it first. He says it aloud, and ends his visit in Charleston with the perfect valedictory word: "Sheba."

But the longer the word hangs in the air, the faster it decomposes, and the great humor that has always provided the granite base of our friendship begins to assert itself. Trevor himself breaks through the bell jar of piety he has glass-blown in our midst. "Did anyone bring a puke bag?" he asks drily. "I can't believe I said something so mawkish. I've been in the South too long."

"I thought what you said was sweet," Niles says. "I like to think that both Starla and Sheba have turned into something water-born and pretty."

"My mountain man," Fraser says with a smile.

Trevor clears his throat. "I was carried away by a rare moment of piffle and nostalgia and even, God forbid, religious sentimentality at its most grotesque. I promise I'll never allow my shallowest, most bourgeois instinct to overcome me again."

Walking up to Trevor, I put my arms around him, and Ike moves to the other side of him. We follow the porpoises as they swim away from us, moving out toward the Atlantic.

"It wasn't sentiment, Trevor," I tell him, my eyes on the departing porpoises. "It was the urge toward art." After a pause, I say, "It's June 16, 1990. What has this group learned more than any other group?"

"Tell it, Toad," Trevor says with a smile.

It is simple, I tell my gathering of friends. We understand the power of accident and magic in human affairs. All of us who are here tonight at the farewell party for Trevor Poe had randomly come together on Bloomsday in the summer of 1969. We know better than anyone the immense, unanswerable powers of fate, and how one day can shift the course of ten thousand lives. Fate can catapult them into lives they were never meant to lead until they stumbled into that one immortal day. What Trevor has tried to do by invoking the memory of Sheba is a powerful attempt at prayer. But it is all right, because today is Bloomsday, and all of us can serve as witnesses that anything can happen during a Bloomsday Summer. Yes, that is it: anything can happen. Yes.

ACKNOWLEDGMENTS

My gratitude to the wonderful Florida novelist Janis Owens, one of the first readers of this book, who was both a great critic and a cheerleader. I came to love her husband, Wendel; her three beautiful daughters, Emily, Abigail, Isabel; and her granddaughter, Lily Pickle.

Great love to Bernie Schein, friend for more than forty years, who has read every manuscript I have written since *The Boo* in 1970. I could wish for no better reader or friend.

A bow to Nan A. Talese, my editor and the first recipient of the Maxwell Perkins Award for Excellence in Editing. This is our fifth book together, Nan, and I owe you a debt I cannot repay.

Great devotion to my agent, Marly Rusoff, and her husband, Mihai Radulescu, who have enriched the writing process with their faith and loyalty.

In memory of my great irreplaceable friend Doug Marlette, whom I talked to every day of my life, who made me laugh and brought me great comfort in a troubled world.

In memory of Jane Lefco, whose loss was one of the most traumatic of my life. Jane, who handled every aspect of my business life, was a rare and fabulous woman. My heart goes out to Stan, Leah, and Michael Lefco.

To Anne Rivers Siddons and her husband, Heyward, lifelong friends, who have opened their homes to us in Charleston and Maine. Very conveniently, they live South of Broad.

To Tim Belk, my piano man in San Francisco, who has been a mentor and inspiration since the day we met in 1967. I owe much of this book to him.

To my cousin Ed Conroy, who thrilled me by becoming The Citadel's head basketball coach, continuing the Conroy basketball tradition since 1963.

To my family, immediate and extended, beloved yet innumerable as a school of herring: I send you my undying love and gratitude for the stories you've provided over the years. Even more love and gratitude to my lovely daughters and adorable grandchildren.

A note of thanks to Cassandra's family, especially her father, Elton King, still on the farm in Alabama; her sisters and nephews; and her rowdy sons.

And to the other special ones: Martha, Aaron and Nancy Schein; Dot, Walt, and Milbrey Gnann; Melinda and Jackson Marlette; Julia Randel; Michael O'Shea; Ann Torrago; Carolyn Krupp; Chris Pavone; Phyllis Grann; Steve Rubin; Leslie Wells; Jay and Anne Harbeck; Zoe and Alex Sanders; Cliff and Cynthia Graubart; Terry and Tommye Kay; Mike Jones; Beverly Howell; John Jeffers; Jim Landon; Scott and Susan Graber; John and Barbara Warley; Kathy Folds; Andrew and Shea St. John; Sean Scappaleto; the late Mike Sargent. In memory of Kate Bockman.

Pat Conroy is the author of eight previous books: *The Boo, The Water Is Wide, The Great Santini, The Lords of Discipline, The Prince of Tides, Beach Music, My Losing Season,* and *The Pat Conroy Cookbook: Recipes of My Life.* He lives on Fripp Island, South Carolina.

A NOTE ABOUT THE TYPE

The text of this book is set in Minion, a font created in 1990 for Adobe Systems. Type designer Robert Slimbach drew his inspiration from the elegant, readable types of the late Renaissance, combining beauty with functionality to create a font that is suitable for many uses.

3 2005 0265549 8